THE YEAR'S BEST SCIENCE FICTION & FANTASY

2015 EDITION

THE YEAR'S BEST SCIENCE FICTION & FANTASY

2015 EDITION

EDITED BY
RICH HORTON

PRIME BOOKS

THE YEAR'S BEST SCIENCE FICTION
& FANTASY, 2015 EDITION

Prime Books
www.prime-books.com

ISBN: 978-1-60701-452-2

Printed in Canada

For Dick and Dorothy Horton (my mother and father) . . . who don't read this stuff but were happy to encourage me in reading anything at all.

CONTENTS

CONTENTS

THE YEAR IN FANTASY AND SCIENCE FICTION, 2015

RICH HORTON

Not a Manifesto

It seems, perhaps, time to restate my goals for these books; to issue some variety of declaration of intent. But this is not a manifesto! We may have had too many of those recently.

To begin with, the title of the anthology series is quite honestly intended: **The Year's Best Science Fiction and Fantasy**. These are my choices for the best short fiction of the year in our field. (With a few mild caveats: every year there are one or two stories I want to use but cannot because of contractual issues, or sometimes because another editor got there first. And every year my choices for the last half-dozen or so pieces are difficult: at least the next half-dozen, if not more, are equally worthy in my eyes.) Seems simple, doesn't it? But people can misread it—one of the most common complaints is that a particular story "isn't science fiction." Well, no, each year roughly half the book is fantasy—an intention stated in the title. The goal here is to celebrate "fantastika" (to use John Clute's term) of all sorts.

Even within those choices I would call "science fiction" there is some fuzziness. My definition of science fiction is purposely broad. I love hard science fiction, but I like the softer stuff too. And some stuff I like is scientifically impossible. (But heck, it's likely much of hard science fiction is just as impossible: are we so sure that faster-than-light travel will ever be a reality?) Indeed, in some ways I think that far-future science fiction that plays especially fast and loose with "science as we know it" gets it more right than "stricter" work: as J. B. S. Haldane said: " . . . my own suspicion is that the universe is not only queerer than we suppose, but queerer than we *can* suppose." Perhaps the best way to get at Haldane's notion is to invoke that strangeness using the tools of fantasy.

One thing I will not apologize for is a preference for good prose. Stories are made of words, and the words matter. The order matters, the meaning matters, the rhythm matters. This doesn't mean prose needs to be "ornate" or "pretty"—ornate and pretty prose have their places, of course, but prose should serve the reader first. In many contexts fairly plain prose is best. But ungrammatical prose, or clunky prose, or cliché-ridden prose, is almost never okay. Which is not to say that I won't publish a story that falls short in one of these ways. Most stories this side of John Crowley's *Engine Summer* are imperfect, and in some cases the imperfection is manifest in the prose.

I will add that as a reader of science fiction for more than four decades I value surprise very highly. I love being surprised by a new turn of phrase, or a new image. I also love being surprised by a novel idea, or a novel variation on an old idea. And I still love being surprised by a plot twist coming from out of the ecliptic.

And I love science fiction and fantasy of all sorts. Military science fiction. Space opera. Heroic fantasy. Near future sociological speculation, alternate history, elegiac far future meditations, urban fantasy, comic fantasy, slipstream, steampunk: great writing, great stories, come from every corner of the field—and from outside the field.

State of the Field

Whenever I discuss the state of the field, it seems to be in flux, even perhaps in crisis. I suppose we must accept that as the normal state of things. And after all, if this is a field devoted to strangeness and change, why not accept a state of continual change?

The big three US print magazines remain *Analog*, *Asimov's*, and *F&SF*; as they have pretty much since *Asimov's* was founded in 1976. *Analog* transitioned to a new editor in 2013, after Stanley Schmidt retired, following a career of nearly identical length to that of the very founder of "Modern Science Fiction," John W. Campbell, editor of *Astounding/Analog* for some thirty-three years. Schmidt's successor is Trevor Quacchri, long an assistant there, and my impression of his early issues, not that he has more than a year under his belt, is quite positive: he's introducing some intriguing new writers, while not abandoning *Analog's* core identity. Last year he published Timons Esais' "Sadness," clearly one of the very best stories of the year. Even more recently, *F&SF* has changed editors. Gordon Van Gelder remains the publisher, but the editing reins have been handed to C. C. Finaly, who "auditioned" with a strong guest issue in July-August 2014, from which I've chose Alaya Dawn Johnson's "A Guide to the Fruits of Hawai'i" for this book. *Asimov's* stays the course with Sheila Williams, and 2014 was a very good year for the magazine, I thought, as evidenced by the three stories included here.

The UK's top magazine remains *Interzone*, and Andy Cox continues to produce a colorful and individualistic magazine, represented here by John Grant's "Ghost Story." Two of the most interesting among the remaining print magazines are very small press productions, modestly produced (saddle-stapled), both quite long-lived in that context: *Lady Churchill's Rosebud Wristlet* and *Not One of Us*. This year I chose two pieces from *LCRW*: Kathleen Jennings' steampunkish fantasy "Skull and *Hyssop*" and Damien Ober's very strange "The Endless Sink." From *Not One of Us*, which has been around for over a quarter-century, I've taken a wonderful piece by one of their regulars, Patricia Russo, "The Wild and Hungry Times." Russo is an outstanding writer with an entirely personal voice and set of concerns, who seems to have hovered just below wide notice for far too long.

It's very old news by now that much of the action is online. There are a lot of online 'zines, but I don't think it would be much of a distortion to suggest that the six featured here represent to the cream of the crop. Alas, one of them closed in 2014: *Subterranean Press Magazine* (formerly known as *Subterranean Online*), which published a whole lot of truly outstanding work, including in particular an impressive array of novellas. This book has one of the last of those novellas, Rachel Swirsky's "Grand Jeté (the Great Leap)," as well as a lovely and wise story about writing by Eleanor Arnason, "The Scrivener."

I chose four stories each from two other top online sources, *Clarkesworld* (three-time Hugo Winner for Best Semiprozine) and *Lightspeed* (2014 Hugo Winner for Best Semiprozine). (In the interests of full disclosure, I should add that I am the Reprint Editor for *Lightspeed*, and that this volume's publisher, Sean Wallace, is the co-editor at *Clarkesworld*.)

Clarkesworld publishes almost solely science fiction, and *Lightspeed* publishes an even mixture of science fiction and fantasy, so it can be argued that another online 'zine, *Beneath Ceaseless Skies*, is the top fantasy magazine online, and the two outstanding stories I chose from it should support that argument. And it would be folly to forget *Tor.com*, which besides publishing a lot of exceptional fiction (both science fiction and fantasy, and much of it long form), also features a lively blogspace, with lots of discussion of science fiction of all forms (graphic stories, movies, and TV definitely included); or the oldest remaining online 'zine, *Strange Horizons*, which probably features as wide a variety of short fantastika as anyone, and which also has a strong feature set, include poetry, non-fiction, and a provocative review section.

Science fiction is no stranger to the so-called "mainstream" or "literary" magazines these days either. The *New Yorker* regularly features science fiction and fantasy (including a pretty decent story Tom Hanks this year), and *New Yorker* stories have appeared in these anthologies. *Tin House* in particular is very hospitable to fantastika, and this year I saw some outstanding work at *Granta*. (Alas, contractual tangles prevented anything from either of those places appearing in this year's volume.) But we do have a brilliant piece from *McSweeney's*, Kelly Link's "I Can See Right Through You."

Finally, as ever, many of the best stories first appear in original anthologies. Jonathan Strahan has a couple of ongoing "stealth series," the "Infinity" set of science fiction books, the latest being *Reach for Infinity*, from which this book features Adam Roberts' "Trademark Bugs" and Hannu Rajaniemi's "Invisible Planets"; and the "Fearsome" set of Fantasy books, the latest being *Fearsome Magics*, source of Genevieve Valentine's "Aberration." (Further disclosure: Jonathan Strahan is my editor at *Locus*.) The one acknowledged ongoing original anthology series is Ian Whates' SF-oriented Solaris Rising, and from the third volume of that series this book features Benjamin Rosenbaum's delightful "Fift and Shria."

Neil Clarke, the other co-editor of *Clarkesworld*, put out his first original anthology in 2014, *Upgraded*, and Peter Watt's challenging "Collateral" comes from it, while John Joseph Adams teamed with Hugh Howey for a set of independently published anthologies of pre-, during-, and post-apocalyptic stories. The first of these, *The End is Nigh*, featured Charlie Jane Anders' jaggedly and desperately comic story "Break! Break! Break!" (And, to complete the acknowledgement that, yes, this can be a somewhat incestuous field, I'll disclose that John Joseph Adams is the editor-in-chief at *Lightspeed*.)

George R. R. Martin and Gardner Dozois have teamed up for a series of big anthologies featuring stories from multiple genres. The entry for 2014 was *Rogues*, from which Paul Cornell's "A Better Way to Die" is taken. And finally, the *MIT Technology Review* has put out a few anthologies featuring near-future speculative science fiction in recent years, all of high quality, and in 2014 *Twelve Tomorrows* featured Cory Doctorow's whipsmart "Petard: A Tale of Just Deserts." Finally, Ben Bova (one of *Analog's* best editors) teamed up with Eric Choi for an impressive collection of new very hard science fiction last year, *Carbide Tipped Pens*, from which I've taken one of two outstanding Robert Reed stories included here: "Every Hill Ends With Sky."

The bottom line for me is that—churn notwithstanding—the science fiction and fantasy field is as strong or stronger than ever, and this book, in my opinion, reflects that strength. Enjoy!

SCHOOLS OF CLAY

DEREK KÜNSKEN

———◆———

Present

The workers' revolution began on the hive's nine hundred and third day, when the Hero pulsar was above the horizon to the north. A pod of predatory shaghāl emerged from behind a small asteroid to the west. The exhaust of their thrust was shielded by their bodies, but the point shines of their souls were visible to those in the colony who had souls. The shine was just slightly blue-shifting.

The skates were not ready. Only half the princesses were fueled in the launch tubes of the hive. Indecision washed over the colony. Skates and souls yelled over each other. Then, a thousand tiny reactions bloomed. The colony panicked. The flat, triangular skates hopped along the regolith in different directions on steely fingers.

Diviya stood above the rising dust, on a mound of mine tailings. He had been meeting with a half-dozen revolutionaries in the slums past the worker shanties. None of his revolutionaries possessed souls, so they could not see the shaghāl, but the panicked radio bursts from the hive alarmed them. Some thought that a squad of hive drones had found them.

"Oh no," Diviya said.

"Flee!" Diviya's soul crackled to him in the radio static. "Save the princesses!"

"Diviya, the revolution isn't ready!" Tejas said. Tejas was a soulless worker, made of carbon-reinforced ceramic. He was triangular and flat, with a single, lightly abraded lens on the vertex of the leading edges of his wide fins. "The workers are not assembled."

Hours away yet, the shaghāl split into two pods. The first pod of predators continued toward the hive. The second angled to intercept the migration, before it had even launched.

"The whole colony is already late," Diviya said. "The revolution must happen now."

Nearby, three skates hopped between the dusty mounds of mine tailings toward the hive. Their radioactive souls shone hot behind their eyes: tax farmers, coming from the farms to join the migration.

"We have only minutes," Diviya said in a radio discharge. He felt sick with doubt. He led his followers forward.

The revolutionaries leapt upon the three tax farmers. Diviya screamed out his own fears. The violence against kin was surreal, matching the strange panic that exploded all over the colony as its last hours played out.

The tax farmers struggled, stirring graphite fines in the vanishing gravity of the asteroid. The revolutionaries pinned the tax farmers upside down. Their steel fingers waved uselessly and their mouths were exposed. Diviya's conspirators held tight to the frozen subsurface.

The tax collectors cried out with crackling radio noise that carried far on the great asteroid. But while the colony was launching the migration, no one would notice. Too many hurried to save the princesses, the princes, and themselves.

In this chaos, the workers' revolution could become real.

One of the three tax farmers appeared to be a landlord by the brightness of his soul. He was the most dangerous. Beneath the hardened carapace of boron carbide, his soul spattered the hard, energetic radiation from uranium and thorium, and the soft, diffuse glow from tritium and potassium. The landlord's soul spoke frantically. Diviya's soul was strangely quiet; it feared Diviya.

The landlord's rows of short legs waved helplessly and he was hot. His soul heated the landlord's whole triangular body. Although it was a sin to waste reaction mass, Diviya did not put it past the landlord to pour the stored volatiles over his soul, launching himself, and everyone on him, into orbit. They could not hold him if that happened.

Diviya reached into the landlord's mouth with the pry and pliers that doctors carried. Deep in the landlord's mouth, Diviya pried back supporting metal bands made to hold the soul. The landlord understood what Diviya was doing and in his horror released a cool spray of thrust from the trailing edge of his fins.

But then Diviya had the soul free and he held the rectangular cake of radioactive isotopes in the shine of the pulsar. They all stared and listened in awe. Only Diviya had ever seen a naked soul. These revolutionaries were farm workers, ore processors, and haulers of regolith.

Diviya turned to Tejas. The skate turned onto his back, exposing fingers blunted from months of scratching frozen nitrogen and graphite from around hard chondrules. Charged regolith dust grimed his open mouth. Diviya set the still-screaming soul within Tejas' mouth.

Any skate could have a soul. Souls gestated in the large ore plants within the queen, near the kilns where the skates themselves were fired. Diviya had been chosen to be a doctor and received a soul only by chance. The soulless could farm volatiles, but could never find radioactive isotopes in the regolith, or fly from the asteroid. Diviya fastened the bands, locking the soul into place. They turned over the newly ensouled skate.

The panic of the hive heightened. The throbbing radio signals from the queen signaled that she was preparing to launch the first wave of princesses. Diviya hurried to remove the souls from the other two tax farmers and place them into Barini and Ugra.

The souls beamed their fear and outrage in radio static. Once, hive drones would have come and arrested them all, but this was the end of the world the souls had preached.

Far off, above the great bulk of the queen, the leaders of the migration launched. Bursts of hot volatiles, briefly visible through the thickening dust, launched princesses at tremendous velocities. Six. Seven. Eight. Waves of princes and their courtiers threw themselves into space after the potential hive queens. Then, a wave of slower-moving, uncoordinated tax farmers and landlords. Diviya's soul began speaking, at first in quiet, fearful tones, but then more strongly.

"Come," Diviya said. "There is no more time!"

Dozens of revolutionaries had crowded them. The soulless. They had put their faith in Diviya. They retreated at his words, stunned. And Diviya's heart cracked. Of everything that they had hoped for all of the workers, they only had time to save three.

Not even save. There was every chance that Diviya and his three ensouled revolutionaries would be killed by either the shaghāl or the migration itself. They were not princes, fed volatiles and radioactive dust by scores of workers. They had been given every nugget of frozen volatiles that could be smuggled out of the work camps, but it was probably not enough.

Diviya opened a valve. A trickle of the volatiles he had stored in his body passed over his soul, super-heating. A searing mix of water, methane, ammonia, and nitrogen shot from the spouts on Diviya's trailing edge, launching him over the hive. The great, sintered ceramic bulk of the queen, dwarfing all the piles of mine tailings, and studded with the launch tubes of the princesses, lay beneath him, shrinking as he rose. The ordered lines of skates carrying ore and volatiles to her had dissolved. They fled into her now for protection she could not offer.

Beneath him, a new volley of princesses burst from the tubes, shooting past Diviya. Their steel fingers were tucked tightly beneath them and the spray of their thrust sent shivers of aching attraction through him. A squadron of princes and their servants followed. Their wide, dust-free fins turned gracefully, briefly reflecting starlight from smooth carapaces of boron carbide, beneath fine, tight nets of steel mesh. They turned the webs of steel to face the Hero pulsar, absorbing its microwaves as they thrust.

Breath-taking. Intimidating. Kin.

Diviya and his revolutionaries thrust hard after them. The horizon of the great asteroid fell away on all sides, revealing the clean dark of space. The colony, with the hive and its halo of slums became a dark, irregular shape, lit only by the bright points of the few souls still there. Then the third and last wave of princesses launched, with every soul that could, even those who could only thrust briefly.

Invisible were the workers left behind, colorless as the dirt. He'd fought for them, tended their hurts, and had wanted to bring them on migration. Those brother skates tugged at his heart, but eerily, less than he expected. Diviya was enlightened, rational, but the strength of instinct surprised him. Diviya felt the urge to protect the princes, clouded with his attraction for the princesses. He needed to control both feelings.

His soul whispered the navigational liturgy to him and he wanted to follow its lead. His soul had migrated before, in a successful prince of a generation past. His soul carried the wisdom of flight angles through the vastness of space and time, how to block the shaghāl from reaching the princesses and the princes. Each soul knew the same way to the same spawning ground waiting for them in the future. But to his soul, those workers left behind were no more important than the giant shell of the abandoned queen after the princesses had launched.

The smaller pod of shaghāl proceeded to the hive. They were radio-reflective, not thrusting, but riding the Hero's Voice with mesh sails catching the powerful microwaves shouting out each second. The dying queen served by soulless skates would feed the predators. The larger pod's course would intercept the migration.

Past

Diviya hopped over the regolith, arriving at Work Farm Number Seven. Several days of bribing low-level officials with frozen nitrogen had gotten him a permit. A big skate with a sleek carapace patrolled the edge of the farm. Under a thin layer of dust, the grand prince's insignia was visible, scored in the ceramic on both leading edges of his wide horizontal fins. The lens at the front of his head showed the hot radioactive light of his soul behind it.

"What do you want?" the tax farmer said.

"Someone called for a doctor," Diviya said. He tilted his leading edges lower, showing less of his own soul. The landlord's thugs were not worth antagonizing. From his gullet, Diviya pulled a thin sheet of beaten aluminum inscribed with his permit.

"Go back to the hive," the tax farmer said. "We got the lazy skate back to work."

"I've come all this way. I may as well check on the other workers," Diviya said.

The tax farmer threw the permit. "Waste your time if you want."

"Thank you," Diviya said, retrieving the permit. Rows of steel fingers undulated beneath him and he hopped onto the work farm.

The farm was so large that the curvature of the asteroid nearly hid the great mounds of debris at the far end. The flat, triangular bodies of the skates moved over the regolith, digging and sifting with sharp fingers. Their radio sails were pulled tight across the tops of their wide horizontal fins, to feed on the radio and microwaves of the Hero's Voice.

The workers were almost all soulless. Some few were given weak souls to find radioactive grains during their sifting. Diviya had received a respectable soul. Doctors needed keen, penetrating sight. The tiniest injuries and earliest-stage material stresses could only be detected with radiation reflected back from ceramic carapaces.

Diviya passed a mound of regolith scraped from the surface of the asteroid, sifted for icy clays, hard nuggets of nitrogen and carbon dioxide, and iron-nickel granules for the foundries and kilns within the queen. The tailing mounds were chondrules of silicates and magnetites. Atop the hill was one of the grand prince's landlords.

The landlord preached a droning liturgy from the apex of the mound, but the words were not his. The soul behind his eye recited the sagas for him to repeat. The metronomic rhythms of electrical buzzing and snapping carried some distance before they were drowned by the inscrutable mystery of the Hero's Voice. Tax farmers and other landlords heard the liturgy, and retransmitted it, complete with its numbing, repetitive rhythms.

Diviya had become adept at ignoring his soul. Otherwise he would spend his days in sagas and parables that froze the class struggle into hardened clay. He moved among the workers. He knew many of them by name, from protests and rallies.

"Good morning, Esha," Diviya said to a dusty skate. Esha's fingers moved in a blur beneath him, scrabbling at the hard regolith, creating a cloud of dust in the microgravity. Esha was a good worker. Several nuggets of nitrogen and carbon dioxide shone in dusty pride beside him. A respectable meal for a prince or even one of the princesses.

"Good morning, Diviya. What brings you out here?"

"I heard a doctor was needed."

"That was days ago. Dwani was beaten."

"Where is he?"

"They're supervising him close to the west mound."

A tax farmer approached.

"Get back to work!" he said. "Hey! Who are you?"

Diviya turned to show the mark of a doctor that had been scored onto both leading edges of his fins. The tax farmer grunted derisively. Diviya was a doctor to workers. If he'd had a patron, he would have been the doctor to princes and perhaps even the princesses. Tax farmers did not consider country doctors like Diviya anything more than workers reaching above their station, although they themselves happily came to him with their aches.

"Hoy!" the tax farmer said. "You didn't call me to pick this up," he said, pushing both Diviya and Esha aside to grab the nuggets of frozen gasses.

"I just found them," Esha said.

"That's what they all say! Get back to work. And you, doctor, get done whatever you were doing before I revoke your permit." The tax farmer hopped towards the next worker.

"Go see the skates after you see Dwani," Esha said. "They'll want news of him. The workers look up to you. You received a soul, but you haven't forgotten them."

The droning of the liturgy resumed. Like the Hero's Voice, the meaning of the words had decayed.

Present

The hive vanished behind him. The minuteness of their former home was spiritually humbling. Stippled stars on black night, close companions since birth, now wrapped him in their vastness. His struggle for the workers, all his words to free his brothers, seemed hollow here. And the migration might still die stillborn, like a drone without a soul. No future. Not even a present.

His soul was silent, perhaps hoping that Diviya had resolved himself to his duty. He fell behind the thrusting princes, still so far that they were just tiny points of hot breath. Perspective placed them near the unknowable voice of the pulsar. The thought of approaching the Hero terrified him.

Diviya's soul began, in staccato radio crackles, the liturgy of migration: vectors and star sightings, landmarks, and flight speeds drawn from the sagas. The souls had done this before. They adjusted the liturgy each migration, to account for the drift of the asteroids, but the mythic arc of the Hero and the Maw was unchanging.

Diviya knew the migration route. He'd studied it, perhaps in a way unseemly for a country doctor. He eased his thrust, contrary to the liturgy. His soul repeated the timings of the thrusts, and their strengths. Diviya ignored his soul. He needed to be trailing the princes and princesses for what he wanted to try. And he needed his thrust later.

The pulsar became a fat dot. Its gravity drew him onward and its voice had become a deafening, constant shout. Diviya unfurled his radio sail. It bloomed outward, bound to him by many fine steel wires. He angled his sail so that the microwaves pushed him off a collision with the collapsed star. The force would grow as he approached, compensating for the rising gravity.

The pulsar had bloated into a fat disk. The Hero's Voice was too pure and loud to be audible. Microwaves seared tiny arcs of electricity across Diviya twice each second, filling him with life for what must come. He was sick with overcharging. His soul recited the prayer of brushing against divinity. When that finished, his soul told the parable of the prince fleeing before waves of the shaghāl. The Hero made Diviya large and small. Diviya could not turn to look how close the shaghāl might be, nor even if his fellow revolutionaries had kept pace with him. One approached divinity alone.

Past

Diviya hopped to find Dwani. The strip-mined regolith fields were uneven; layers of frozen dust revealed blocks of immovable iron-nickel. Such large masses of exposed iron-nickel did strange things to the Hero's Voice. Where they could, workers dumped mine tailings upon them. But sometimes all the fingers in the colony could not cover them and the odd protrusions sparked and crackled, interpreting the Hero's Voice in their own way, like the mad.

Diviya reached the west mound, an immense pile of mine tailings looking over the entirety of the plain. It had been here long before the queen and her grand prince had arrived.

"Poor workers," Diviya said. "How long had they toiled to make that mound?"

"Long enough to launch generations of princesses and princes onto the migration," his soul said, "fully fueled, with discerning souls to guide the foundation of new colonies."

"At remarkable cost," Diviya said.

"Remarkable that we survive at all," the soul said.

The tax farmers inspected his permit. His soul shone as brightly as theirs, although these skates had likely been extorting bribes of volatiles from the workers for months. They might have enough breath to migrate with the princes and courtiers. The work of tax farmer and landlord was difficult, but could be lucrative.

Difficult skates worked the fields around the west mound. Fewer breaks, harsher discipline. Not that workers had many privileges. The workers here were slower, and the digging was hard. A tax farmer indicated a lone worker close by the base of the mound.

"Dwani?" Diviya asked when he had neared.

The skate turned and Diviya recoiled. The worker's carapace had been smashed where the clean lines of the leading edge came to a point. Near the vertex was a jagged hole, dusted with regolith attracted by the electricity within Dwani. The lens of the eye was so scratched that no part of its surface was smooth.

"Who is it?" Dwani said.

"Diviya."

"The doctor?"

"What happened, Dwani?"

"The tax farmers went after a few organizers. Reinforced ceramic doesn't stand up well to iron rods."

A horrified sadness crept over Diviya as he neared Dwani. The radioactive shine of Diviya's soul scattered back from Dwani's carapace, revealing many microscopic fractures. Some of the cracks were so large that Diviya would not have even needed a soul to see them. They reached far along Dwani's fins, one nearly to the trailing edge. Dust, especially the static-charged graphite fines of the regolith, infected the cracks. To say nothing of the dust entering through the hole near Dwani's damaged eye. The dust would soon interfere with the neural wiring.

"Whoever did this didn't mean for you to live long," Diviya said.

"I can't move some of my fingers, but I can still work." As if to make light of it, Dwani moved his fingers. Only a half-dozen of the steel limbs moved. The rest dangled.

"I hope you didn't come all this way just for me. Unless you have some cure."

"One of the committee members got word out. I came as soon as I could."

"It won't do any good," Dwani said. "The tax farmers know their job."

"I'm sorry."

"Don't be sorry. Do something. More than just writing little manifestos and three-point plans on committee broadsheets."

"Violence isn't getting us anywhere, Dwani."

"Coward."

"There's no end in what you're doing. You and a school of other committee leaders make it sound as if a total upset of the hive will somehow make us free."

"We'll be free when we are not oppressed."

"Half of us will be dead, win or lose," Diviya said. "And the chaos will do nothing except cripple the hive. We'll be easy pickings for the shaghāl."

"We already are."

"The princesses too?" Diviya said. "What is the point of all our work if even the princesses do not get away? Extinction is not social change."

"You never resist," Dwani said. "That's why they gave you a soul."

Present

Diviya's cry of suffering mixed with the tireless booming of the Hero's Voice. His soul had begun crying long ago. Weight crushed them. Diviya felt as heavy as an asteroid or a star, important to the world, possessing meaning. And yet, he was tiny. The Hero was now an angry blue and purple sphere. A beam of burning microwaves ripped across its face twice a second, throwing Diviya back by his radio sail. Strange radiations he'd never seen swirled in sickly oranges and reds on the pulsar's surface.

Diviya reached perigee, the closest approach to the Hero, and he thrust. It ached. His thrust burned. The Hero's Voice stung. The pull of his radio sail creaked his whole carapace. He was going to snap.

And then the Hero was behind him, His Voice throwing Diviya forward. His soul, between bouts of terror, repeated the correct speeds and distances of the migration. The temptation to relent to the soul was strong, but Diviya followed the migration at a distance with his co-revolutionaries in clumsy formation around him.

The lighthouse beams of the Hero's Voice propelled them faster and faster. On this course, the radio waves would accelerate and charge them continuously as they flew straight and true towards the black hole called the Maw.

It was a long way between the Hero and the Maw. Sometimes half or more of a migration could fall to the shaghāl before the Maw had a chance to destroy them. And that was when the courtiers distracted the shaghāl and led them away.

And the shaghāl certainly followed. Diviya held his terror in check. The shaghāl were big, strong and fast, riding under enormous radio sails, leading with maws large enough to crush a skate.

The Hero's Voice already dimmed as they moved away. But Diviya listened for any drop in the Voice beyond that, which would be the first sign that the shaghāl had found him, had picked him as food. In all the sagas and the teachings of the souls, the pursuing shaghāl placed themselves between their prey and the Hero so that the creatures of appetite slowly crept up with their great mouths while the skates drifted helplessly in their silent shadow.

Yet sometimes the ways of the devil were instructive. Diviya settled behind a distant prince, cutting off the radio and microwaves with his sail. The prince tilted his sail, this way and that, trying to escape the shadow, but without the Voice, his sail was just wire mesh.

The prince retracted his sail, a prelude in the sagas to thrusting. He extended the sail indecisively. Breath was a hard object, sifted or picked from the regolith, but it possessed a holiness. It was the Hero's gift for the migration. The taboo of its use was both spiritual and pragmatic. Any use of breath except in the approaches to the Hero and the Maw, in strict, soul-guided accelerations, could mean not having enough later.

"No!" Diviya's soul said, suddenly realizing what he was doing. "Stop it, you monster!"

The shadowed prince chittered electrical static, passing alarm across the migration, but it did him no good. The formation spread out. Over long hours, it passed the prince and Diviya finally moved aside, choosing another target to shadow. He drifted past the prince, who, suddenly hearing the Hero's Voice, began accelerating again. But it would not be enough.

The shaghāl had been accelerating all this time too. They were closing faster than the prince could accelerate. They would consume him, volatiles, radioisotopes, rare metals and all.

Diviya's three revolutionaries shadowed other princes. They were not as nimble as Diviya. More often than not, the princes escaped, catching radio waves that the revolutionaries had not quite blocked with their sails. But the princes still lost precious moments or minutes of acceleration.

It was working. The satisfaction tasted bitter to Diviya. He hadn't wanted this and was the first to regret it. He'd wanted some end to the suffering of the workers. The princes had forced this revolution on themselves.

One of the courtiers, trailing so far back that he perhaps sensed he would soon be shadowed, retracted his sail and gently spun in flight. Instead of an approaching shaghāl, he saw Diviya, Tejas, Barini, and Ugra. He transmitted a radio shout in anger, and unfurled his sail. He rode the microwaves expertly, sweeping close to Tejas.

Diviya cried a warning, but it was too late. The courtier crashed into Tejas and dug with sharp fingers at Tejas' eye, at his mouth, and at the wires holding his radio sail. The fingers snapped two of Tejas' four wires. Tejas pitched as his sail tilted. The courtier leapt away.

"Tejas!" Diviya yelled.

Tejas began to tumble slowly. He could not retract his sail, nor right it.

"Diviya!" Tejas called. Diviya slowly pulled ahead as all of Tejas' acceleration spun into his wild careening. "Fix my sail! Help!"

Diviya's heart cracked. There was nothing to be done. On the migration, Diviya hadn't the materials to replace snapped wires. And the shaghāl approached.

"Leave!" his soul said. "Fly on! Protect the princes and the princesses now."

"I'm sorry, Tejas!" Diviya said.

"Please!" Tejas called.

Diviya slipped behind Tejas' attacker before he could spread news of their betrayal. The courtier, suddenly without the Hero's Voice, tilted his sail, to no effect. The migration crept away from him. He shrieked warnings, but he was too far for anyone to hear, except Diviya. The migration had dispersed widely, a scripturally pure defense against shadowing by shaghāl.

"No, do not do this!" his soul said. Perhaps it had overcome its fear of Diviya.

"Please."

"Do you know how many workers have suffered because of the princes?" Diviya asked. "Do you know how many have been beaten and killed?"

"You are angry," his soul said. "You do not completely understand the way the Hero has organized the hives so that the finest and strongest of skates are sent upon migration."

"They are not the best," Diviya said disgustedly. "They are the skates who have been given a soul, and then use that soul to enslave workers."

"You are wrong. You are special."

"I am not. A doctor wore out. Another was needed. I was the easiest to train. That is all. We are all the same. Souls create divisions for their own benefit."

"The hereditary information you carry in clays are all the same. Circumstances and accidents of feeding and luck have their roles, but you are all kin. We are one colony. The success of a prince is your success. We make sure our kin succeed."

"We are more than schools of clay," Diviya said. "And if we truly are all the same kin, you won't mind if it is I instead of the princes who make the final journey with the princess."

The Hero's thinning Voice pushed Diviya toward the courtier he shadowed. When they were almost touching, Diviya tilted his sail, veered aside, and passed him. The courtier's radio sail caught the pulsar's beam and started accelerating, but the shaghāl would finish what Diviya had started.

Past

The founding queen and her grand prince had located the hive on an asteroid with a lazy rotation around an axis that pointed almost directly at the pulsar. At the pole, the queen heard the Hero's Voice tirelessly, but in the piled rubble fields near the worker slums, the low ensouled lived with short nights of quiet starvation and lethargy. The pulsar had set an hour ago and Diviya should have been resting, but he'd been invited to a workers' rally. He entered the slums.

"These are not elements of society you should be associating with," his soul said. "You and I may have a future. There may yet be time to show your talents and come into a more lucrative position, like a tax farmer, a minor landlord, or even the personal physician to a courtier. Imagine the resources you would have then for the migration."

"My future will hardly be determined by a meeting," Diviya said. A group of skates congregated ahead of them. "Look, other souls are here."

"Ensouled workers!" his soul said dismissively. "Workers are where they put souls that are incapable of memorizing the migratory routes. No one here can help you."

"Diviya!" Abhisri said. "You made it." His friend Abhisri edged from the crowd, the flat ceramic triangle of his carapace worn by months of hard building. A soul winked behind the lens of his eye. Like Diviya, he had received his soul late in life, and had become an engineer. He often spoke at rallies.

"I heard you went to the work farms? You saw Dwani?" Abhisri asked.

"The drones were thorough," Diviya said. "They cracked him."

Abhisri made a sound.

"Change is slow," Diviya said.

"Not just slow," Abhisri said, not for Diviya, but for the others. "There is no change!"

Around them, workers sparked loudly in their heads, casting radio waves. Yelling. Cheering. They knew Diviya here, but he felt trapped in the center of attention as Abhisri spoke. Diviya was not a leader. Although they read his manifestos, Diviya didn't agree with their methods.

"We cannot have slow change," Abhisri said, warming to his oration. "We cannot hop or crawl toward freedom!"

More cheers. Diviya felt like cheering, too. The gaping hole in Dwani's face would not leave his thoughts.

"We must go!" his soul said. "Now!"

"All of us are wiped out at every migration," Abhisri said."We never migrate. Only nobles. Their hangers-on. Their enforcers."

"Revolution now!" someone yelled in the darkness.

"Overthrow the hive!"

Diviya's soul shrieked in panic. So loud that surely others around them heard it. Diviya was also alarmed. He cared about these workers. Many were his friends. He was one of them. Revolution would get them killed. A terrible nervousness crept over him as he realized that he was going to speak.

"We cannot overthrow the hive," Diviya said. "Violence will not free us."

They hissed at him in electrical static.

"The princes and their courtiers are big, well-fed, and ensouled," Diviya said. "They can fly while most of us cannot. The hive is built to repel us."

"Excellent," Diviya's soul said.

"Defeatist!" someone yelled.

"Collaborator!" someone yelled.

"Leave!" Diviya's soul said.

"This is Diviya!" Abhisri said. "Let him say his piece."

"How much time is left, do you suppose?" Diviya asked. He was nervous with all eyes upon him. "A few months? The nobles fear that they haven't enough volatiles to migrate. Courtiers fear they will not have the fuel to follow. Princes know that without the courtiers, the shaghāl will pursue them."

No one spoke. No one moved. "And we fear being left behind."

Diviya felt dizzy. He never threw himself into the middle. "What if we ask for souls for some workers?" Diviya said. "Would they give them?"

"No!" someone yelled from the darkness. "They'd beat us 'til we crack."

"Yes, they would," Abhisri said.

"So what do we do?" someone demanded.

"Offer them something," Diviya said.

A chorus of protests rose all about him.

"Offer them more than what you are producing, in exchange for souls."

"We can't do that!" someone said.

"We ask for souls? For some of us? To go on the migration?"

"Yes," Abhisri said, sounding intrigued.

"That won't work for everyone!" someone said.

"But if a dozen workers survive the migration, they become the princes of the next generation," Diviya said. "They can change the colonies that follow. Fewer tax farmers. Fewer nobles. More souls for the workers."

"It isn't enough!" someone yelled. A chorus supported him.

"Of course it isn't enough," Diviya said. "But it is the best we can get right now. As long as all the workers are wiped out every generation, the workers of the next must restart the struggle as if it were the first time. We must be in solidarity with the brothers of tomorrow whose clay has not yet been fired."

The crowd silenced. A shade of the immensity of their task, of a sense of history and time slipped over them.

"Abhisri!" they cried. And some yelled "Diviya."

"No!" his soul said. "This is against the will of the Hero."

"Some will say this is against the will of the Hero," Diviya said to the workers.

"The Hero made the princesses and their suitors and the migration, but where in the sagas did the Hero make tax farmers?"

Laughter greeted his joke, but sparking anger, too. "Nowhere!"

"And we have a leader," Diviya said. "Abhisri can take our ideas to the princes."

"Diviya!" some said, including Abhisri.

"Abhisri!" Diviya said, and was relieved when that cry was taken up.

Then other skates spoke. They hadn't the rhetoric to speak at a prince's reception, but their strength as orators lay in the visceral reality of their wanting. These workers scratched and scrubbed the regolith each day for nuggets of gasses to launch princesses and their suitors into the future. They had more right to their words than Diviya had to his. They deserved to migrate. As the speeches went on, workers gave Diviya gentle double-knocks of approval with the tips of their fins.

"Leave!" his soul said. "You endanger yourself and me!"

"Hive drones won't come here," Diviya whispered to his soul. "Drones are lazy and greedy and spend their time on the hills."

"They employ informants."

"Among the workers?"

"The soulless will die when the shaghāl come, but many seek to ease their time with easier work."

A worker neared, leaning the whole leading edge of his fin against Diviya's, until their faces were close.

"Will you migrate, Diviya?" the worker asked.

"I have no patron. I have not been given any breath either."

"You will not be given any," the worker said. "This is a bad year and a bad site for the hive. Many of the landlords will be here with us in the end."

"Famine," Diviya said.

"Take this." Beneath them, the worker's fingers passed Diviya a half-dozen large nuggets of frozen gases. Nitrogen. Carbon dioxide. Methane. "Eat it!" the worker whispered, so close that only the two of them could hear.

"I can't," Diviya said.

"You must! You are one of us, Diviya."

Diviya stared at the gift. The worker might have done any number of things with this much raw reaction mass. He could have bribed tax counters, or even a low-status prince if he could get close enough.

"Hide them, quick!" the worker said.

Diviya put them in his mouth and deep into his gullet, past his soul, so as to not melt them. Over time, he could melt and refreeze the gases to purify them.

The worker melted into the crowd, as if suddenly shy. Diviya retreated, too. This was enormous. When he'd been apprenticed to a doctor, he'd expected to die in terror when the shaghāl came. Even when the hive had given him a soul, elevating him into the lowest of the privileged, he'd not changed his thinking. Without volatiles, there was no point in dreaming wishes. But now, this stranger, from nowhere, had given him a gift, one that separated him from the workers as irrevocably as a soul could.

"We will migrate!" said Diviya's soul. "Although this is not nearly enough breath for such a journey, it is a start. Let us leave."

"The meeting is not finished," Diviya said.

"Everyone here is a revolutionary!" the soul said. "Someone will denounce them all to the hive drones and the princes."

Present

The migration had broken into three streams, each with at least one princess and a dozen or so attendant princes and courtiers. Diviya followed the fastest princess, the one farthest ahead. She was the least likely to be targeted by the shaghāl.

Barini and Ugra followed. He did not know either one well. Barini was a hauler of regolith who participated in rallies. Ugra had tilled the soil and his musical talent produced electrical melodies, into which others fit political rhymes and slogans. Neither seemed a likely revolutionary, but perhaps he wasn't either. Dwani, Abhisri, and all the real leaders were dead, with all the workers of their generation except for three.

The three of them became methodical and pitiless. Their targets tried to evade the sudden silencing of the Hero's Voice, with only some success. Hours passed. Then days. Then weeks. The Hero's Voice attenuated. The best acceleration from the pulsar was in the past. Now, speed grew in slow increments. The princess was a point far ahead, but the courtiers and the princes had fallen behind.

Diviya retracted his sail, and exhaled a puff of volatiles. He slowly pivoted, until he faced the pulsar. The Hero was a sad, cool point in the blackness, flashing thin radio and microwaves twice a second, lower in tone and quieter. Diviya felt dislocated. His class struggle felt minuscule. This cold vastness offered neither light, nor asteroids upon which to shelter. Far behind, the shaghāl appeared tiny, but their radioactive souls shone hard and point-like. Seven of them followed. Diviya exhaled another puff to stop his rotation, and unfurled his radio sail.

They were close to the princes and courtiers. Weeks of slow work had made each of them adept at stealing the microwaves destined for the sails of the princes. The pulsar's beam was so distant now that its push was faint. Diviya and his companions were tiring.

A lone princess sailed ahead of the princes and the revolutionaries. The sounds of the souls far in front of them were frantic. The princess ought to be protected at all times.

Diviya felt the Voice of the Hero abruptly thin. A moment of panic stole over him. His soul shrieked. Diviya had been preparing for this for weeks, imagining the angles, the time he would have. He was not completely shadowed, not yet. Some of the distant Voice reached him still. He tilted his sail hard, catching the few microwaves reaching him, accelerating sideways. At first, nothing seemed to be happening. His soul recited the litany of the sacrifice, for both of them. But it was working. Slowly. After long minutes, the Hero's Voice became louder, and he emerged from the shadow.

Diviya sailed wide to stay away from the shaghāl who had found him, and then snapped his sail back to accelerate again. He felt weak. The sagas called the starvation from the Hero's Voice the small death. His soul quieted for a long time.

"It is not what we wanted," his soul whispered. "We dream of being at the front of the school, with the princess. But we are not. We too must serve. We will not escape again, but we may atone for our crimes by leading the shaghāl away. I was weak. I should have opposed you more. Morality is the responsibility of the soul. I have failed, but we now may seek redemption."

"I never wanted to be a prince," Diviya whispered back.

"Come!" Diviya cried to Barini and Ugra. "Let us create a new hive where workers are free!" Diviya slowly slipped into place to shadow another prince.

In the fourth month of the migration, a shadow fell over Barini. It was sudden and complete. The shaghāl was close and Barini had no hope of sailing free.

"Barini!" Diviya cried in radio static. "Thrust! Exhale!"

"No!" Diviya's soul said. "On the migration, only a princess may exhale. All breath must be saved for the Maw."

"Barini!" Diviya said. "Thrust!"

"Everyone has a place. He too who is caught serves the hive," Diviya's soul said.

The soul was not wrong. Every courtier and prince lost kept a shaghāl occupied long enough for time dilation to mean they would never be seen again.

But the soul was also wrong. The calculation was grimly mathematical and religious, weighted to favor the nobility. The princess was indispensable, but the princes and courtiers were more than interchangeable. Barini had tilled the soil, given the princesses breath, given flesh and life to new souls. He had as much right as any to be among the fathers of a new generation.

Diviya's words did nothing for Barini. Diviya's soul recited a litany of complacency and sacrifice, as Barini's soul probably whispered to him. The soul seduced, by pulling on instinct.

Barini retracted his radio sail against his back. He began to silently rotate, his mouth and eye shut, hiding the hard radiation of his soul. Instinct was stronger.

• • •

Past

Diviya moved in the low circles of the hive itself, with ensouled skates whose skills were too valuable to be spent on farming. Accountants and building engineers worked around the queen and hive, erecting the nets of fine wire on high scaffolds, capturing the constantly beamed Voice for the queen, weighing workers bearing regolith and frozen volatiles into the hive, scheduling work.

The low ensouled had some leisure with which to imitate the princes and courtiers. They did not have the opera house in which to put on the sagas, but they performed for each other in the hollows between mounds. They did not have libraries, but they retold legends and parables, refining their manners, so that someday, if the chance came, they might mingle successfully with the princes and their courtiers.

Although he mostly tended workers, Diviya was also physician to clerks and petty functionaries who could not get higher-status physicians. It was always difficult for a cold skate, living at the temperature of the surrounding regolith, to carry a hot soul. Even the ceramics of boron carbide sintered and fired in the kilns of the queen creaked with distortions of temperature. In the worst cases, carapaces could even crack.

Diviya's hive patients possessed souls, and jockeyed for patronage. They guarded their own opportunities and blocked skates like Diviya from the princes. This, from what Diviya understood, suited the princes, who received gifts constantly from these petty clerks.

They were all taught to sacrifice, and for a while the idea of sacrifice could be romantic and ennobling. Freshly kilned skates were reared on the parables of the good worker, and especially the sacrifices of Narah the courtier. Narah had led away some of the shaghāl and the saga spoke lovingly of his last moments. It felt heroic, its romance layered by generations of retelling.

Yet it ran deeper than sacrifice. The males of the hive carried the same hereditary clays from the queen. The contributions of the few grand princes who had survived the migration accounted for limited variation in the hive. Diviya was brother to the princes, the tax farmers, the landlords, and the workers.

But privilege and status did not creep into a hive. Inequity stormed in, like hive drones breaking up a protest. The queen produced new souls with the radioisotopes sifted out of the regolith. Those who received souls no longer depended on capacitors to work and move through the night. The spiritual wealth became the power to see the radioisotopes of other souls or find more in the regolith. Most importantly, radioactive souls turned frozen gases into hot thrust.

Diviya met with Abhisri in the camps of the low ensouled outside the hive. Abhisri had bribed a courtier for a meeting with Prince Lasiya. Diviya was nervous. He had never met a prince. He doubted his ability to persuade. He had channeled debate among like-minded skates, but this was his own idea now and a high audience. It had been easy to speak in the dark to workers, deep in the slums. This was the hive, vast and monumental.

"This is bad," whispered his soul. "Once you speak with this prince, we are marked, you and I. The accountants will look in their records to see what soul you have and they will put marks there against both of us."

Diviya and Abhisri approached a side entrance guarded by two big drones. Prince Lasiya's secretary emerged from behind the drones. The brightness of his soul was stabbing. The lines of his ceramic shell were sleek and clean. The leading edges bore the emblems of his patron. Abhisri pulled a lump of distilled and refrozen breath from his gullet. Possessing it was a crime. So much breath ought to have been destined for the princes and princesses. The secretary took the bribe without otherwise moving. It vanished into his gullet. The hive drones studiously ignored the transaction.

"I am listening," the secretary said.

"We were told we would be speaking with Prince Lasiya," Diviya said.

"The prince is not available."

"My words are for him alone," Diviya said.

The hot circle of radiation from the secretary's soul shone full on Diviya. A submissive reverence stole over Diviya's soul. A fearful thought crept into Diviya's mind. Might the souls have some secret language, mediated perhaps by particle decay? It was an eerie, paranoid thought, and yet, something of substance passed between these souls and Diviya imagined his whole life being reported.

"I will bring any message to Prince Lasiya."

Diviya and Abhisri backed away and spoke in low tones, in the rough dialect of the workers.

"He won't bring the message anywhere," Abhisri said.

"We have no other choice."

"Do what he says!" Diviya's soul whispered. "There is danger here."

"A prince would have listened on his own authority," Abhisri said. "This courtier will report what we say in the worst light if you tell him your offer."

"The workers held back a riot so we could make this offer. We must try." Diviya turned to the courtier. "Tell Prince Lasiya that there may be a way for the workers and the princes to come to an understanding to increase farm yields."

"Go on."

"This is a message for Prince Lasiya."

"Something as important as farm yields should not be toyed with. Where are your loyalties, Doctor?"

"My loyalties are with the hive."

"Would your soul say the same?" the secretary asked. The shine of his soul was a beam, like the Voice of the Hero itself, focused through the smooth lens of his eye, in through Diviya's eye. Diviya felt hot.

"Of course," Diviya said.

"If your loyalties are correct, then speak of increasing farm yields, Doctor."

Diviya hesitated. "The workers dig hard, but the regolith is poor. Additional incentives could make them eager to work even harder."

"Any worker who is not working as hard as he can is guilty of a crime," the secretary said.

"The treatment of the workers makes them less effective," Diviya said. "Beatings make them resentful. I have seen skates broken and killed by tax farmers. Broken skates produce nothing."

"Slack workers must be forced to do their duty. Examples inspire others."

Diviya's quick words were difficult to contain. He had urged restraint on workers on so many occasions, so that they could bring forward something of substance. Only the thought that he was representing many workers held his anger back.

"There is a better way to inspire workers," Diviya said.

"Odd that centuries of experience did not find it, yet a country doctor has," the secretary said.

Diviya controlled his fear. Abhisri edged backward.

"Workers move regolith, find the volatiles and radioisotopes, yet know they will never migrate. If a few workers could receive souls, the additional radioisotopes found would soon repay the gift."

"Souls for the workers?" the secretary scoffed. "The apportionment of souls is a sober process. There are not enough volatiles now for the court. If breath were further thinned, instead of a quarter of the migration outrunning the shaghāl and the Maw, no one would."

"More skates on migration will draw away more shaghāl from the princesses," Diviya said, "especially if they are slower."

"You consign them to die? Do they know this?"

"They are already dead. We all are. When the migration flees, every worker will sit waiting with the empty hive for the shaghāl to come."

"You are naïve, doctor," the secretary said. "Every additional migrating skate takes breath from the princesses and princes. The sagas are filled with cautionary tales of migrants falling into the Maw, or even the Hero, when they lack breath. Your reckless ideas would jeopardize the whole migration."

"Not if we could find more volatiles," Diviya said.

"Ah," the secretary said, and Diviya felt as if he'd stepped into a trap. "Let us explore your thoughts on farming. How much more could workers do?"

"That would be based on how much incentive was offered."

"Treason," the secretary said, with the tone of someone commenting on the procession of the stars. "Do you know the punishment for treason? For withholding breath or radioisotopes?"

"I know it," Diviya said. He was cold beneath that hot stare.

"Then let us pick a strategy to get those additional volatiles."

"Incentives?" Diviya asked.

"I do not trust incentives. Even among the princes, not every skate can be trusted. Fear and disincentives are the most consistently effective methods."

Present

The flashes of radiation from near the black hole resolved into searing weaves of curtained light. Oranges. Reds. Whites. Sharp rays leapt from infalling gas, heating Diviya's soul, even though they were still days away. And the Maw was loud. It endlessly consumed the breath of the world. The infalling volatiles crackled with electrical panic. Loud, frightening snaps.

The enormity of what they approached dwarfed even Diviya's imagination. The rain of hot particles traced a line around the Maw, outlining a monster large enough to swallow even the Hero.

Weeks of careful work by Diviya and Ugra had pulled four more princes from the school. Soon, the princess would be unguided. Her soul carried other liturgies, secrets of growing a hive and waves and waves of little skates, but not navigational liturgies. Diviya had caught up to the trailing edge of the school. Ugra was close.

The Maw's own kin, the shaghāl, followed and Diviya imagined their enthusiasm as they neared the hive of their master. They shadowed the princes and courtiers, creeping closer and closer hour by hour. Diviya retracted his sail and exhaled the faintest of breaths to rotate slowly. His insides went cold.

He'd never seen a shaghāl. Three of them followed, one closely. He'd pieced his imaginings from the liturgies and sagas. Reality outstripped his nightmares. The shaghāl were big, reflecting light from hard ceramic and metal. Their bodies, triangular and flattened like a skate's, had long steel fingers for sharp grasping. It was as if a school of grand princes had been transformed by the Maw itself into engines of appetite.

The leading shaghāl thrust powerfully, leaping forward to hug Ugra in great fingers. It stuck a tube into Ugra's mouth and sucked away his breath. Ugra's fingers waved wildly, scratching at the carapace of his captor, until the shaghāl cracked Ugra open around the mouth, exposing the soul. Diviya did not see the rest. The shaghāl held Ugra and thrust outward, onto an orbit to carry it far around the black hole and back to the archipelago of asteroids where new hives would be founded.

And then Diviya was alone. There was no more revolution. There was only he, a princess, a prince, and a pair of pursuing shaghāl. Between Diviya and the prince, Diviya would always be second. The prince's soul was larger, hotter, making his thrust more powerful than anything Diviya could make. The shaghāl would reach Diviya first.

Then Diviya too fell into shadow.

"He too who is caught serves the hive," his soul whispered. That was the role the princes had for him. And the priesthood of souls. The poor brother must die for the rich brother to live.

He too who is caught serves the hive.

Diviya thrust.

"No!" his soul said. Diviya blasted precious volatiles behind him, emerging from the shadow of the shaghāl and even accelerating closer to the lead prince, the one closest to the princess.

"Monster!" the prince said. "I saw you waste your breath on yourself!"

Diviya rode his exhalation, coming close to the prince. Both souls protested, shrieking, warning the prince with panicked static, but the prince did not understand. Diviya clamped onto him, undersurface to undersurface where his fingers could reach the prince's mouth. Belatedly, the prince scored Diviya's carapace with sharp fingers.

The prince's violence almost shook Diviya away. Diviya dug into the prince's mouth, for the hot radioactive soul. Recriminations were loud in Diviya's head, difficult to block out.

The prince's soul was enormous. He had taken the best radioisotopes. And many ices to be sure, enough to become the next Grand Prince, if Diviya had not caught up to him.

Diviya had learned from Dwani. He would rather end the next generation than let this prince recreate the colony they had left.

Diviya's fingers scrabbled at the fine bands holding the prince's soul. The souls screamed. Diviya's with memory. The prince's with terror. Princely fingers broke off some of Diviya's. Diviya snapped one of the bands, then another, then another.

The prince's soul drifted free.

The four of them shared a moment of disembodied terror. They screamed. And the prince went perfectly still.

Diviya held the screaming soul, its radioactive shine lighting the tireless night, as he pushed away the stunned prince. Diviya slipped the soul into his gullet, unfurled his radio sail and drifted clear.

The prince wobbled and drifted. What were his thoughts now as justice was given to him? Did he blame Diviya, blind to his own role? Perhaps this was not even justice. They approached the Maw, where death became victorious over life, darkness over light. They raced so quickly that the red stars stippling the darkness had brightened to blue. Only Diviya, the princess, and the shaghāl following them remained and they lived a quiescent fugue. Time became meaningless and long. The great sail of the shaghāl was furled. The Hero was so far, his Voice so quiet, that sails were decorations of brighter lives while they entered the mythic land of the dead.

Before them, the Maw cloaked itself in vast fields of hot clouds, but the breath of a thousand migrations was a poor shroud for the monstrosity of the Maw's hunger. Light burned from beneath the clouds as warning. Speeding blues, falling greens, and throbbing reds each marked some particle falling into the Maw.

Diviya's spiritual terror, for all that he had set aside the sermons and sagas, was visceral. He trembled. The souls within him, his own and the stolen one, quaked. His soul's whispers had become hypnotic and he wanted to surrender. To believe.

He was falling, accelerating. The Maw had noticed him and it summoned him. It was dangerous to be seen by the Maw, yet only here could the migration be completed. Here, any differences in speed would be multiplied. The princess was still ahead of him. No one had been showing her the way. Diviya's soul, between bouts of confession and recriminations, recited coordinates he would not follow. Diviya thrust forward, using up more of his precious volatiles, until he was beside her.

She was a sleek, flat skate, larger than he, but built more toughly. Her soul was incoherent with fear, but she was brave. Within her she carried flat matrices of clay, stacked one upon the other, containing the hereditary secrets for the next generation encoded in the atomic gaps in the lattice of the clay crystals themselves. These leaves, paired with the ones he carried, would create the next generation.

"Are you ready, my prince?" she asked. Diviya shivered with excitement. *My Prince.* To be beside a princess, near the eerie strangeness of the Maw, was like being in a saga.

"I will lead you past the Maw," Diviya said.

"We are only two."

He found her suddenly young, although they were pressed and kilned in the same queen. She'd surely never questioned the powers who had cosseted her. She'd never had friends starved or beaten to death. Of course she was young.

"We must go," Diviya said, taking a star fix and comparing it to what he'd been taught by the souls. He was not taking their path.

Diviya understood the role of time dilation in the migration. Skates launched themselves into the future, leaping over generations of shaghāl whose population collapsed when bereft of prey. And when the skates established a new colony, few shaghāl were left to hunt them.

To the skates migrating around the Maw and back to the archipelago of asteroids, the trip lasted a single year. To the unmoving world, they were gone for seventeen. The skates coordinated their leap. Those who survived reunited not only in space, but also in time. Every acceleration and angle was perfectly calculated. The smallest error might leave a skate weeks, months, or even years from the rest of the migration.

But Diviya was not leading the princess seventeen years into the future. Their culture was bankrupt, built upon the broken carapaces of workers. No matter what happened, neither Diviya nor the princess would ever see anyone from their hive again. Shorter migrations were more dangerous, taking paths closer to the Maw and harder accelerations at perigee. Diviya had worked out the trajectories, without the help of his soul. He was leaping thirteen years into the future.

"Follow!" Diviya cried, over the protest of his soul. Diviya aimed into the hot clouds around the Maw and thrust.

Past

Diviya and Abhisri had left the secretary, shaken in themselves. The secretary had issued remarkably detailed instructions to them on who he wanted watched among the workers. There was little doubt that should Diviya or Abhisri fail to report to him, their souls would be removed, and the two of them killed.

"Disincentive," the secretary had said, "is more reliable."

Diviya and Abhisri had no intention of reporting on the workers, but they had a little time before they had to give something to the secretary. They passed messages to Esha and other work farm unionists. They struck secret committees, to plan a true strike, to grind the industry of the hive to a halt. They met in the worst of the shanties, where hive drones seldom passed.

The Hero precessed auspiciously from the Constellation of the Good Courtier to the Constellation of the Farmer, signaling the arrival of the longest night of the year. Workers could not move regolith without the shine of the Hero. Even the tax collectors were reluctant to push workers on the longest night, which became a time for singing and performing the snippets of the sagas in the regolith fields and the slums.

Diviya was with the workers' committee when the hive drones thrust in, carrying metal weights. They threw the weights just before landing, cracking workers. Diviya barely leapt out of the way. Workers scattered in terror as drones landed on them, striking ceramic with steel, tearing out wires that absorbed microwaves. Rows of hive drones ringed them.

Abhisri pushed Diviya into an alley filled with panicking workers. "Fly!" Abhisri said.

"I can't!"

"You're the only one who can! This is big! They don't know you carry breath."

A hive drone fell upon Abhisri, striking with a pick in its hard fingers. Diviya leapt on the drone, scratching and hitting. Diviya had never fought anything, and the drone was trained for this. The drone jerked, sending Diviya tumbling high in the microgravity. Below, the workers were awash in hive drones. They were lost.

Diviya exhaled a breath to correct his tumble as his trajectory carried him out of the slums. He thrust gently, turning, and settled to the regolith. A few skates, too weak or worn to work, saw him land, but did not move. They surely took him for some wayward tax farmer.

Even this far away, Diviya heard the panicked electrical sputtering of terrified skates. Friends and brothers. But the commands of the hive drones were louder, more calm, angry, and organized. Crackles of electrical static shot orders, some encoded. Abhisri was right. This was big.

"Flee!" his soul said stridently. "Flee!"

Diviya rocked back and forth on his fingers. He itched to run. To help. To run. His thoughts were jumbled. He feared he would only think of the right thing to do when it was too late. And he feared the sure beating. The work farms. The amputation of his soul. The true darkness of being a worker again, detached from a whole world he could only perceive through his soul.

Present

They thrust hard. The princess flew close. Hot violet radiation bathed them as the hunger of the Maw's gravity sped them faster. They fell from heaven, like the Hero himself. The whole world shifted into the blue. The sounds of static came tight and high-pitched. Tense. Near the Maw, space itself feared, releasing ghostly sounds and strange discharges.

The searing cloud abraded Diviya. The keening of his soul heightened in pitch. Radiation and particle strikes corroded the little soul. It was not made to fly this close to the Maw. It was composed of so many different radioisotopes that no matter what struck it, some part of it changed to something inert or something inappropriately active. The soul was going mad.

They neared perigee. Their speed was terrifying. Stars multiplied, filling the sky. Their haunting chorus blended with the relentless screams of the souls.

"Pray!" Diviya yelled to the souls. "Pray!" They did. In warbling tones of panic, the souls recited the metronomic cadences of the liturgy. Diviya listened to the prayers as he never had before.

Diviya's carapace creaked. He was so close to the edge of the Maw that the difference in gravity from his ventral side to his dorsal threatened to crack him. And still the Maw accelerated him.

No sounds of the living world remained, except for the chanting of his soul, a simple prayer to a hero who had no authority here. A new, eerie ocean of slow echoes filled his senses. His stars, radiant microwave stars, were all gone. New stars appeared. They were dead, their glows constant and unblinking as the sleet of passing clouds flayed and scorched him. He counted time by the cadences of the souls' prayers.

The intensity of the radioactive hail burned his soul, making Diviya's exhaust so hot that it felt like riding a star. And the clay wafers that he carried, his gametic contribution to the future, hardened in the heat and pressure, forming the crystalline structures that could be laid over the wafers carried by the princess. The possibility of new life quickened in this crushing furnace. Diviya counted the prayers and then, at a precise moment, he redoubled his thrust.

Diviya could not hear the princess. He stayed fixed on the strange stars. If he looked back for her, they would both be lost. Among these ghost stars, he could only trust. If she had not been able to follow, everything they had suffered at home was for naught.

The Maw grasped at him, to crush, stretch, and snap him. The heat of Diviya's thrust burned his own carapace. The clouds of hot gas brightened. He became so fast that even the ghost stars became too blue to see. The acidic particles shooting at the Maw crowded out the darkness, filling Diviya's world.

Then the Maw flung Diviya away.

The clouds thinned, but did not cool. Each grain floating in his path zipped into his carapace at nearly the speed of light. The world was eerie. He had left the Maw, but not the land of the dead. Strange purple colors and warped, fluid sounds drifted past him. He was a ghost and the living world had closed itself to him.

Yet amidst this dislocation, far away, faint, a point pulsed, frenetically like a young pulsar. Its microwaves were blue-shifted to a pitch that was visible instead of audible. The world was covered in a cloak of strangeness, yet he had to have faith that this was the Hero, summoning him back from death.

He was far from home, and had only whispers of breath left. He had used everything in the slingshot passage around the Maw and he did not even know if he had succeeded in leading the princess.

He exhaled the tiniest gasp of breath. Achingly slow, he pivoted. And his heart grew, in a primal way. A few body lengths from him was the princess. He had led her into the land of death and past the Maw. They could see the world of life, even if they were still fast-moving ghosts. It would take weeks to slow down. Her sleek carapace was striped and pitted with fine burns. Her soul was bright, but quiet and reverent.

Beyond her, the great bulk of the Maw had begun to shroud itself again under layers of bright, doomed clouds. The gases in palliative spirals spit hard radiation, but now that they had passed the Maw, their spite was thin and reddened and sepulchral.

The king of the underworld receded majestically. In the last moments of that hypnotic view, Diviya saw a tiny, distant silhouette, carrying a point of hard, hot radioisotopes.

No.

No. No. No.

The Maw had scarred them as they passed, and had not let them truly escape. The Maw let through one of its own, an engine of death, a famished monster that had nothing to eat but Diviya and the princess.

Past

Diviya had ceased to sympathize with his soul. In the beginning, he understood it as a gift from the Hero and the queen, as a guide for the migration. The soul was, in some ways, an alien presence, but partly comprehensible within its role as the voice of eternity. But it was pitiless. Petty. Commitment became inflexibility. Resolve turned to stubbornness. Morality deafened reason. Diviya's soul argued, becoming more shrill. It was difficult to ignore the voice in his head.

In part to draw the soul away from its recriminations, Diviya spoke to his soul about the migration. Skates were taught nothing of the migration. This was safer ground to till. His soul calmed while considering the migration. Perhaps it thought that Diviya was opening himself to redemption.

At first petulantly, then with increasing enthusiasm, the soul spoke to Diviya of what was to come. Even when Diviya probed at the mystery of time dilation itself, the speeds and accelerations needed to achieve the magical dilation of seventeen, his soul answered him. Some of the pieces were symbols, or worse yet, allegories Diviya had to suffer through to keep his soul talking. More useful were the liturgies containing mathematical proportions, and angles and curves. Diviya read meaning into the liturgies that perhaps his soul did not mean for him to understand.

On the third day, Diviya descended from the mound. He left the slums and hopped into the worker districts where tailing hills were evenly rowed and the workers were healthier, younger. The neighborhood seemed lonely. This was a rest period, so most workers should have been back. In the distance, he saw the shine of another soul and turned away, so as not to give himself away. Between dusty piles he recognized a worker.

"Tejas!" he said.

Tejas approached. He had new scratches on the tops of his fins. Chips were missing along his leading edges. "Diviya," he whispered. "I thought you'd been arrested."

"Abhisri got me out a back alley. What happened?"

Tejas had difficulty speaking. The sparks he made were mistimed and sometimes sputtering. "We were all beaten. Most were arrested. I thought they were going to crack me."

Diviya's strength left him. "What charges?"

"I don't know," Tejas whispered. "They're all being sent to work farm number seven."

Dwani's broken face stared out of memory. Tejas sputtered and shorted over his words. "Abhisri got it bad, Diviya. They took out his soul right there. They weren't careful. I don't think he made it."

Diviya sank into the packed regolith. Adding or removing a soul was dangerous. Diviya had done it many times, but had not always been successful. The radioactive souls heated the ceramics and metals of the carapace and the neural wiring, while the skates cooled the souls. Sometimes the stresses on the skate and on the soul were too much. Tejas neared.

"They told me he didn't say nothing to the interrogators, but his soul did. They're looking for you, Diviya. You've got to hide."

"I told you!" Diviya's soul said. "Turn yourself in! Name names!"

But Diviya's soul had no hold on him anymore. The crushing pressure of the hive and his soul had crystallized a sense of mission in him. They had hardened his wavering resolve into the seed of something much more permanent. He was deathly frightened of being cracked open like Dwani, of having his soul torn away, but he heard the sagas through Dwani's eyes now.

"I'll hide in the slums, Tejas," Diviya said, "where the broken workers lie. Send me the leaders, yourself included."

"I'm no leader. I wasn't even a committee member."

"We're all committee members now," Diviya said. "The revolution must begin. Not the one Dwani and Abhisri wanted, but a larger one."

Present

Diviya and the princess had little with which to escape the shaghāl. Diviya had intended to unfurl his sail to brake beyond the black hole, but that would do nothing more than bring the fast-moving shaghāl to them faster. They flew so quickly that the gulf between the Maw and the Hero, that had taken the migration many months to cross before, now took only days. Yet if they did not slow soon, they would overshoot their home.

They unfurled their sails together. Blue-shifted radio waves punched their sails and the shock of slowing dizzied. As the tremendous deceleration intensified and the Hero fed them, they became less ghostly. The world abandoned its frenetic blue-shift. Strange stars faded, their haunted voices quieting. Stars he knew began to shine as if just reborn and the Hero's Voice aged centuries every minute, slowing finally to two flashes per second. Diviya and the princess were reborn.

"We will find a way to survive," the princess said.

No. Not princess. She was the queen now. But no. Not that either. No queens after the revolution. No princes. No grand princes. Just skates, sharing what they had.

"Yes, we will."

His words felt false. If they overshot their home, deep, deep space was a different kind of death than being crushed by the Maw.

"I will try to shadow the shaghāl," Diviya said.

"That will bring it to us faster!"

"Yes," Diviya said. Diviya adjusted his path, spotting the shaghāl's soul, as it shone in faintly blue-shifted hunger, far distant. "It will be ravenous now, and desperate."

Far behind, but still close enough to chill Diviya's marrow, a great radio sail unfurled. Diviya would make a poor shadow. The shaghāl was close and closing, decelerating at a furious rate.

Diviya slipped into the path of the pulsar's beam, cutting a shadow in the center of the shaghāl's sail. The shadow grew as the shaghāl neared. The shaghāl seemed to realize what was happening and angled its sail to escape the shadowing. Diviya followed.

The shaghāl jerked its sail the other way. It had no experience in avoiding a shadow. It hurtled closer, unable to do more than edge slowly sideways. The shaghāl tilted its sail wildly, trying to get around Diviya.

Diviya jerked his sail opposite to the shaghāl's tilt. The Hero's Voice veered Diviya aside, but not fast enough. The shaghāl's wing tip struck Diviya. The knock was tremendous, accompanied by a snap.

Diviya spun. Pain. Sharp pain. And fear and screaming. The second soul nearly flew from Diviya's mouth. Diviya righted his sail, catching the Hero's Voice, slowing his spin. Finally, he controlled his spin.

The shaghāl plunged far ahead, toward the asteroid field. It was slowing, but Diviya had robbed it of time. Now it would need every bit of effort to avoid overshooting the asteroid field.

The ragged princess neared. Diviya felt strange. His sail still pulled oddly, producing an ache under him.

"Your soul is glowing through a long crack beneath you," she said. The rhythms of her sparking speech were quick, fearful. He feared, too.

Cracked. He was cracked. Dwani's broken face haunted his thoughts. Dust would get into his carapace and would scour his wiring and joints. Soon, he would only be good for resting on mounds.

"You will survive," she said. "We will survive. You will make a magnificent grand prince."

His soul, and the stolen one, made sounds of relief. The princess had accepted him as her mate. Despite his crimes and the hardships of the migration, the souls sounded guardedly elated. A new hive. His hive. Grand prince. Diviya would be the father of a new generation, one that, due to the separation of time dilation, would never see any skates from another colony. And his colony would have no landlords, no tax collectors, and no beatings.

Past

Furtively, workers came to Diviya in the slums, atop his mound. Most had never been unionists. Diviya recognized his old fear in them. They came to speak to Diviya about the massacre. Few had been there, but they knew the workers who had been killed, and the workers who had been exiled to the work farms. They came as cowards might, shamefully, weighed by the guilt that they were happy not to have been there.

The idea of sacrifice in them was strong, as it was in Diviya. The Hero had built them to sacrifice for each other, for kin. They were pressed of the same clay. The success of a brother worker or a prince felt like a success for all of them. Demanding something for themselves was difficult. The newly ensouled like Diviya had to be taught selfishness, acquisitiveness by the souls. Yet these skates, who had not been brave enough to attend a union rally to help all of them, now slinked to the last committee leader, a skate who shared their guilt. They formed new committees.

"Tell them what to do," his soul said. "You are better than this rabble. Leverage your influence here for patronage. Deliver the malcontents to the hive. Give bribes."

Diviya had bribes. The workers smuggled innumerable tiny nuggets of frozen volatiles to him. This struggle with his soul could not go on.

And then, he saw it again.

In the distance, the brief, hot shine of a soul, looking this way. The sleet of radioactive particles stilled his soul. Diviya shut his eye, shuttering the emissions of his own soul.

"Open your eye!" his soul said.

"You can guess as well as I what that was," Diviya whispered.

Diviya's soul laughed. "More unionists have been picked up by hive drones," the soul guessed. "The rascals must have spoken of an ensouled committee member dispensing fratricidal treason from a mound in the slums."

"It is rich that you would call me fratricidal, when I have never hurt another skate, while the hive beats, imprisons, and kills my brothers," Diviya said.

"Your disloyalty endangers every skate and princess in the hive. Open your eye."

Diviya descended the mound with his eye closed. Tejas was with him, as were Barini and Ugra. They did not have souls and were accustomed to Diviya's silences while he communed with his own. With his eye closed, the world was dark, but loud, filled with the Hero's Voice and the scraping vibration of his own movement. But in this way, he was invisible to the other ensouled skate in the slums.

"What are you doing, Diviya?" Tejas asked.

"An ensouled skate has been moving at the edge of the slums," Diviya said to Tejas.

"I have seen him several times today. He is looking for something."

"Or someone," Tejas said.

"I saw only one skate. Perhaps an ambitious tax farmer seeks favor by catching a union leader."

"Hide!" Tejas said. "We must get you away."

"Me?" Diviya said.

"You're the key to the revolution," Tejas said. His voice was charged, tense. He believed what he was saying. And Diviya felt as he had when he'd first spoken at the rally. Exposed. Undeserving.

"Tejas, Barini, and Ugra," Diviya said, "lead me closer, so that we can see, but not be seen. You will need to be my eye."

"What are you doing?" his soul demanded.

Tejas walked Diviya on a winding, blind way around the tailing mounds.

The Hero was high in the sky, so none of the mounds cast shadows. Diviya heard the Hero's Voice change tone when they turned. Catching the subtleties in the polarization of the radio waves was a different way of experiencing the Hero, one perhaps more primal, and it calmed Diviya, as much as his new resolve.

Diviya was built for peace, but the princes, and those who spoke in their name, had taken matters too far for Diviya to stay still.

They were kin, pressed from the same clays, made to launch princesses and some males into the migration. Their success was his success, in the flat equations of biology, but skates had grown. They were no longer the primitives of the sagas. They reasoned. They were more than their instincts. They had grown past the need for souls to tell them how to treat each other. Souls created and perpetuated divisions in the hive. Princes. Landlords. Workers. But the skates carried their own blame for taking what was given to them, as blindly as Diviya was being led through the slums. The souls had their own interests. Not least Diviya's soul.

Brother and enemy. Family and opponent.

Diviya's steel fingers sunk into the thick regolith. Pebbles and larger fragments of iron-nickel and hard, volatile-dry silicates were so numerous and uneven as to be stumbled over, especially blind. The four of them walked and hopped. From a distance, they would just be four soulless workers.

"He is to our left now," Tejas whispered.

"Take me onto a mound," Diviya said.

Tejas led Diviya scrabbling to the top of the hillock.

"What are you doing? Open your eye!" his soul said.

"Is he facing us?" Diviya asked.

"No," Tejas said. "We are facing north. He is facing west."

The revolution needed to happen. Working with the souls as they had was no longer possible. Diviya lifted a large chunk of iron-nickel in his fingers. He snapped his eye open and thrust, hurling himself toward the ensouled skate.

"You are wasting breath!" his soul shrieked. "Stop! Stop!"

Diviya released the iron-nickel chunk as he flew past, as a hive drone would have. It crashed into the other skate with such force that ceramic chips rattled against Diviya's underside.

"Murderer," his soul whispered.

Diviya puffed breath sideways to spin, and then thrust to a stop and landed. He hopped to the ensouled skate. His three fellows were already there.

Diviya's attack had struck the skate's left leading edge, near the eye. A gaping hole exposed the hot soul beneath.

"You are beyond redemption," his soul said. "I will not rest until justice is done."

"I know," Diviya said.

Diviya removed medical pliers and a small pry from his gullet. Dust caked them. He had been ensouled to help skates, to mend their minor wounds, to make them well enough to get back to the mines and farms. The hive had taught him anatomy and science for a skill he hadn't practiced in weeks.

"Do not touch that soul!" his soul said. Both Diviya and his soul could plainly hear the electrical panic of the soul in the fallen skate. "Report this to the hive! No one may touch a soul without the authorization of the princes."

Diviya reached into the corpse, prying away the bands around the soul. He lifted it gently, leaving the inside of the carcass warm and hollow.

"No!" his soul said.

"You must be destroyed, Diviya!" the soul said. "You are the most vile criminal ever fired in the hive."

Diviya reached into his own gullet with his pliers. Diviya's own soul screamed as he pried it loose and pulled it from his mouth.

And then, Diviya was a worker again, for the first time in a long time. He had no sensitivity to most of the wavelengths of radiation and energetic particles. The world was quiet and cold. The stars were colorless. The souls before him were gray lumps, hotter than the regolith, but otherwise unremarkable.

Diviya set his soul in the cold, dry dirt. The temperature stresses crackled in the radio bands. He put the other soul carefully in his mouth and onto the mounting. As Diviya lowered the bands to hold it into place and clipped it tight, the beauty of the spiritual world washed back in. And he was himself.

The new soul spoke immediately, more timidly than Diviya's soul. "What are you doing?" it whispered.

"Do not leave me here!" his old soul cried from the cold regolith. "Summon the hive!"

Diviya took his own soul in his fingers and inserted it into his gullet where its shine would not show.

"Bury the body," Diviya said to his co-conspirators. "When it is completely frozen, we will take whatever volatiles it may have."

Diviya launched himself from the surface of the asteroid. It did not take much breath. The microgravity of the asteroid barely pulled the dust back to the surface. As the hive receded, he exhaled again and sailed away from his home and from the Hero.

His former soul was apoplectic.

"I might have migrated with you," Diviya said to his soul. "I had even thought of putting you into another worker, for the revolution, for more workers to migrate."Diviya removed the soul from his mouth. "But you are too dangerous, too intransigent, too willing to stamp upon workers with my fingers."

His soul was incandescent in its anger, fear, and hate. Diviya released it. For a time, they drifted away from the asteroid, traveling the same path. Then Diviya turned back to the Hero and thrust back toward the hive. His soul continued out into the cold of space.

Present

Their new hive would need an asteroid in the gravitational stillness behind the Hero's Voice, preferably a slow-turning one, so that they could walk around it, always under the radiance of the pulsar, and one that was freshly cracked by an impact or one whose radioisotopes and volatiles had not been harvested in centuries. There were thousands of asteroids in the archipelago, but not so many that a single, determined shaghāl could not find a hive eventually.

In some sagas, princes and princesses made a second migration, right after the first, to escape from shaghāl following too closely. But Diviya and the princess were exhausted. Little breath remained to them and with his cracks, Diviya could never again survive the crush of the Maw.

Diviya and the princess retracted their sails from time to time to drift silently and listen for the shaghāl. They could not hear him, but he could not be that far. He might already have ended his careening deceleration and be waiting even now in the archipelago of asteroids. Diviya spread his sail, and the Hero's Voice pushed him outward.

"How much breath do you suppose you have left?" Diviya asked.

"I did not use all of it."

Diviya explained his plan as he turned away from the Hero. He disgorged the soul he'd taken from the murdered prince and held it in his shadow. It shrieked. His own soul cried out. The princess' soul made a sound of revulsion. A soul was an ugly thing, a complex, layered brick of radioisotopes, humming with its own heat and shining with hard radiation. That light would draw the shaghāl as soon as Diviya revealed the soul to the asteroid field.

"This will not work!" the princess said. What Diviya asked was dangerous, perhaps impossible, but it was their only chance. "I do not even have the strength you want!"

"It is this or nothing, Princess! This is all we have. A strong, fast, hungry shaghāl lurks somewhere in the archipelago. While he is here, no hive is safe."

They moved farther and farther from the Hero, into an orbit where they would intersect the archipelago of asteroids at its outer edge, far from the best fields. They slowed over hours, risking creating radio reflections with their sails. The shaghāl would be closer to the pulsar, where the voice of the Hero would feed it and drown out their echoes. Every so often, Diviya turned toward the Hero, exposing the second soul. The soul's sharp, multi-rayed brightness would be very visible from far away. Then Diviya would turn back, hiding it again for a while, before exposing it once more.

Bait.

Finally, an angry glare answered. The hot harsh light of the shaghāl's soul was much closer to the pulsar. It made for them. Diviya held the second soul visible, letting the shaghāl see their trajectory. Then, he hid the soul from the shaghāl's sight. The asteroids neared, including a large, uneven ovoid, pocked with craters.

The princess took the wires of Diviya's sail in her steel fingers. They passed into the shadow of the asteroid, and out of sight, and Diviya released the second soul. The princess thrust, decelerating them. The soul hurtled onward, screaming. The tremendous deceleration bent Diviya's sail, and stabbed new pain into his underside. Diviya and the princess both groaned, sharing the pain of the unnatural maneuver.

Her thrust flagged.

She had almost no breath left and they would soon emerge from the shadow of the asteroid. But the soul was not far enough away.

"Don't stop!" he said.

"There is nothing more!"

"Then turn!" he said. "Into the asteroid!"

"We'll crash!"

They still traveled very fast. The regolith might be composed of deep powdered grains or it might hide nuggets and boulders of nickel-iron and hard ices that would shatter their carapaces.

"You are brave!" Diviya said. "It is the only way, Princess!" She did not turn. He waited. The thrust sputtered. "Please!"

The wires tightened and swung him as she aimed at the asteroid. They lurched as her breath expired. The regolith, even under microgravity, was frightening at their speed.

Diviya plunged deep in an explosion of dust, tumbling in the powder and pebbles, before being wrenched to the surface in a jarring, snapping stop.

He was on his back. His underside hurt. He could not feel his sail. Some of his fingers were bent. He wiggled them and began digging at the dust until he was right side up. A deep channel gouged the asteroid. Dust rose, swirling on its own static.

The princess had not let go of him. They had plowed the great furrow together before she herself had been driven by their speed into the regolith. She pulled herself free of the dirt. She had filled herself with dust, as had he. His insides. Her insides. Their souls were covered and, for once, silent. They spewed regolith, thickening the rising clouds.

"You did it, Princess," he said. "You stopped us. You are a hero."

She spat another gout of dirt from her gullet. Her anger and fear still crackled.

"Look!" Diviya said. The princess followed the line of his gaze.

Far in the distance, just a point now, the second soul sped onward, on a trajectory that would take it past the gravitational eddy and back toward the pulsar. From this distance, it looked like a tiny part of a distant migration.

On a course to intercept it, thrusting hot gas, was another sharp point of radiation: the shaghāl. By the time it realized what it was chasing, the shaghāl would be committed to a trajectory that would take it all the way around the black hole. It would be years before it returned. In that time, the new hive would have risen and matured and launched its own migration into the future.

THE SCRIVENER

ELEANOR ARNASON

There was a scrivener who had three daughters. He lived in a great empire that stretched from west to east. Some parts of the empire were civilized and up-to-date, full of coffee shops and other amenities. Other parts were backward and primitive, the home of peasants and witches.

The scrivener lived in a provincial city, midway between civilization and the primitive. The streets were lined with shops, many of them selling foreign luxuries; there were cafes and coffee shops that had the latest newspapers and journals. In the marketplace, peasant farmers and hunters sold their traditional products. Outside the city were fields. Beyond the fields was a vast, dark forest.

He made his living in a modest way, writing letters for illiterate neighbors, drawing up bills of sale and even doing some accounting, for he was a man of many skills, who could do complicated sums and figure compound interest.

In spite of his skills and his adequate living, he had always dreamed of more: to be a writer of stories. But he lacked something, a divine spark, or so he believed. So he stuck to what he knew.

His wife died when the children were still young. He might have remarried, but he had loved the woman and had no desire to replace her. Three children were enough, even if none was a son.

Their mother had wanted to name them after fruits or flowers. But he had always dreamed of fathering a storyteller and insisted that they be named Imagination, Ornamentation, and Plot. All three were active and quick to learn. Surely they could become what he could not.

He bought books of fables for them and took them every week to the marketplace to listen to the storytellers who sat there in the dust, reciting tales about heroes and dragons. The girls liked the fables and the oral narratives, but showed no inclination toward becoming authors.

Imagination, who was called Ima, said the stories she heard and read gave her wonderful dreams, which she treasured, but she had no desire to write them down.

Ornamentation, who was called Orna, liked individual words. She sang them as she embroidered. What she made were not true songs, which have meaning most of the time. Rather, they were random strings of words that chimed and tinkled, rhymed or rolled majestically, but told no coherent story. She also liked images and put them in her embroidery: flowers and fruit and—between these—tiny lords and ladies, delicate dragons, diminutive heroes with needle-like swords.

Plot said it was all silliness, and she would rather do accounting.

But the scrivener did not lose hope; and when the girls were grown up, he took them to a famous critic. She was a large, fat woman, who sat every day in one of the city's cafes, wearing a caftan, smoking black cigarettes and drinking coffee or wine. Piled in the chair next to her were newspapers, literary reviews, and books, some leather bound, but most bound only in paper. There were coffee rings on the book covers and notes scribbled in the margins. The woman had a broad, arrogant face with a hawk nose and heavy-lidded eyes.

"Yes?" she said in her gruff, deep voice.

The scrivener told her that the dearest wish of his heart was to have a child who wrote stories, and he had brought his three daughters to be examined.

Each child had brought a story, which she had written reluctantly, not out of fear of her father, but rather out of fear of disappointing him. He was a kind, gentle man, whose only failing was his desire to have an author.

The critic waved the eldest daughter into a chair, drank some coffee, lit a new cigarette, and read Ima's story, grunting now and then. When she was done, she put the sheets of paper down, frowned mightily, and said, "Next."

Orna replaced her sister in the chair and handed over her story. Once again the critic drank coffee, lit a new cigarette, and read. A waiter came by and refilled her coffee cup, bringing also a pastry on a plate. The critic loved astringent fiction, bitter coffee, strong cigarettes, and pastries full of honey. Her taste in wine was uncritical. "One cannot judge everything," she always said.

She finished Orna's story, grunted loudly, and said, "Next."

Now Plot sat down and handed over her story. By this time she was helping her father with accounting, and she had written the story on ledger paper. "There is nothing here except numbers," the critic said.

"Turn it over," Plot replied.

The critic did and found a short, neat narrative about a prince who needed a new accounting system and how he found a girl able to set one up.

The critic finished the story and looked at the scrivener. "Your daughters have no talent at all." She pointed a thick finger at Ima. "This one has a flood of ideas and images set down in no order, as confusing as a dream. And this one—" she pointed at Orna—"is simply babbling words, without any sense of what they mean or should mean within the structure of a story.

"Finally"—she frowned mightily—"your last daughter has written a story with no color, mood, atmosphere, imagery or development of character. She might as well have written rows of numbers."

The scrivener wrung his hands. "Can nothing be done?"

The critic raised a hand, and the scrivener waited while she ate her pastry, washing it down with coffee. Then she lit another black cigarette. She was a chain smoker of the worst kind and should have died young.

Finally she said, "There is a witch in the nearby forest, living in the forest's black heart in a hut that stands on ostrich legs. She might be able to help, if she is willing. But remember that witches—like critics—are capricious and have their own agendas."

The scrivener thanked her for her advice, then herded his daughters home.

Remember, in considering what happened next, that the daughters loved their father and wanted to please him and also to protect him from harsh reality.

He sat them down and asked them if they would be willing to seek out the witch. The three girls looked at one another.

"Yes," said Plot. "But only one at a time. Ima does all the shopping, and Orna cares for the house. I help you with accounting. It would be too difficult if all of us left at once."

The scrivener agreed that this was a good idea. The three girls then drew straws, and the eldest got the short one. "I will set out tomorrow," she said bravely.

On the morrow, she packed a bag with food and other necessities and set out, taking a stage coach to the forest edge. There she climbed out.

The forest lay before her, rising abruptly from farmland. Its edge was a mixture of scrub trees: aspens and birches, with a few spindly maples and oaks. Farther back it was all evergreens, rising tall and dark toward the sunlit sky. In spite of the bright sky, the forest looked ominous to Ima, and her heart quailed.

But she had promised her father, and she would not fail him. Shouldering her pack, she marched into the forest. The edge seemed harmless. Sunlight came in around the scrub trees, and they were attractive: the aspens and birches flipping yellowing leaves in a light wind, the maples showing touches of red. She followed a narrow path among ferns. Birds flew above her, and small animals—mice or ground squirrels—scurried through the ferns. Nothing seemed dangerous, except possibly a croaking raven.

As she got deeper into the forest, the shadows grew thicker. The ground was bare, except for a thick carpet of pine needles. Above her, pine branches hissed in the wind. Names do matter, and Ima had rather too much imagination. The forest began to frighten her. But she did not want to disappoint her father, so she kept on. Noon passed, then the afternoon. Evening came. The shadows darkened. Finally, when she could barely see, she came to a break in the forest. A huge pine had fallen and lay across a clearing full of ferns. Overhead was the moon, one day off full, flooding the clearing with light. It should have reassured her, but it did not. She hunched down against the fallen trunk and ate the food she'd brought: bread and cheese and sausage. For drink she had wine in a flask, a good red that went with the sausage.

All she could think of was the danger around her. Who could say what wild animals lived in the forest? There might be trolls as well as witches, and forest spirits of every variety, all of them cruel. In the distance, a fox barked.

All night she sat and shivered, too afraid to sleep. In the morning, she decided to go home. Her father would be disappointed, but she did not have the courage or the lack of imagination necessary to continue.

She soon discovered that she had lost her path in the darkness. All day she wandered through the forest, exhausted by lack of sleep. Late in the afternoon, she came upon a woodcutter, a tall, handsome young man. "What on earth are you doing here?" he asked. "The forest is dangerous."

She explained she had gotten lost, but did not mention the witch. She was embarrassed too, since she no longer had any intention of seeking the woman out.

"I can guide you to the forest edge," he said. "But not today. It's too late. Come back to my cabin. My mother and I will shelter you for the night. In the morning, I will escort you out of the forest."

Because of her imagination, which was good at seeing peril or at least its possibility, Ima hesitated. But she had no other choice. So she went with the woodsman to a little cabin built of logs. It was cheery looking, with smoke spiraling out of the chimney. Inside, a fire burned in the fireplace, and a stew bubbled in a pot. The woodcutter's mother was there, an old woman with a kind face.

Ima got out the last of her food to share. All three of them sat merrily around a table, eating and drinking the last of Ima's wine.

"Why do you live so far in the forest?" Ima asked.

"We like our privacy," the mother replied.

"And this is where the trees are," the woodcutter added. "I make our living by cutting them down and burning them into charcoal, which I take into the city and sell. It's a long walk with charcoal on my back. But it gives us what money we need. For the most part, the forest provides."

At length they showed her to a bed. Ima lay down and went right to sleep.

She woke in the middle of the night, when moonlight shone in the cabin door. Why was it open? she wondered and got up to shut it.

Outside, in the clearing in front of the cabin, two wolves frolicked. One looked young. The other seemed old, but still vigorous.

Ima was too frightened to scream. Instead she crept back into the cabin's one room. A few coals still glowed in the fireplace. By their light and the moonlight pouring through the door, she searched the cabin. The beds that should have been occupied by the woodcutter and his mother were empty, their covers flung back.

Ima knew what this meant. She was spending the night with werewolves.

The cabin had only one door, but there were several windows. Slowly, carefully, quietly, Ima opened the shutters on one of these, climbed out and fled into the forest.

She ran and walked all night, not stopping until morning. She could go no farther then, so lay down and slept.

A cough woke her. She opened her eyes, saw the woodcutter and screamed.

"Beg pardon?" he said.

"You are a werewolf! And so is your mother!"

"Yes, but we are wolves only one night a month, not by intention, but because we must. Don't think we are monsters. When we are wolves, we do nothing to harm people. We hunt animals—mostly voles and rabbits—and enjoy the way it feels to run with wolf muscles and smell with a wolf nose. The rest of the time, I am an ordinary woodcutter, she is an ordinary mother.

"You went in the right direction when you fled our cabin, which is good. I suspect you don't want to spend another night in the forest. But we'll have to start now, if we are going to reach the coach stop before nightfall."

He held out his hand. Ima took it reluctantly, and he lifted her upright with surprising ease. A strong man. Well, he spent his day cutting down trees.

It was late afternoon when they reached the road by the forest. He waited with her till the coach came. When it was in sight, he said, "Please don't tell people about my mother and me. We live in the forest to be safe, but I do come into the city. I don't want to be stoned or arrested. I could have harmed you, when you were alone in the forest. I didn't. Instead, I helped you. Remember that."

The coach stopped. He helped her on. As it drove off, she looked back and saw him standing by the road, tall and lean and handsome, as rangy as a wolf.

When she got home, she told her father, "The forest was too frightening. I did not find the witch." She didn't talk about the woodcutter. The story was too strange, and she did not want to endanger the man or his mother.

The scrivener looked at his two other daughters with hope. They chose straws. This time Orna got the short one.

The next day she packed a bag and caught a coach to the forest. Like Ima, she climbed out at the forest edge and found a path. She lacked her sister's fearful imagination. Instead of possible danger, she noticed small birds in the pine branches and interesting fungi. Her path led her through clearings full of late summer grasses, faded to shades of tan and gold. Everything seemed lovely and enchanting.

She came finally to a meadow by a river. It was full of autumn flowers. Butterflies fluttered over the blossoms. A blue and orange kingfisher dove from a branch into the river and rose with a minnow in its beak.

"How beautiful!" Orna exclaimed.

"Indeed it is," said a melodious voice behind her.

She turned and beheld the most beautiful woman she had ever seen. The maid was naked, but her long, golden hair acted as a garment, falling over her body and reaching her knees.

"Who are you?" Orna asked.

"A forest spirit," the woman—really a girl—replied. "In countries to the south of here, I would be a dryad or naiad. To the east, I would be a rusalka, as in the famous opera by Antonin Dvorak. North of here, I might be a nixie or huldra. But here in this forest I am only a spirit."

If you are wondering how the girl knew Dvorak's opera *Rusalka*, a twentieth century work, remember that fairy tales and their creatures exist outside time.

And you may have noticed that many of the spirits mentioned—the rusalka, huldra, and nixie—are usually considered malevolent and dangerous. Orna did not know this; and the spirit she met was in fact mostly harmless, though she could enchant and distract.

Orna took out her lunch and shared it with the spirit. Then, both of them tipsy with white wine, they picked flowers and waded in the river shallows, gathering round, smooth stones.

Anther spirit appeared, naked like the first, but clothed with long, red hair. Then another came; Orna did not see from where. This one was brown-skinned with wavy black hair that swirled around her like a cloak. Her eyes were like the eyes of deer, large and dark.

Orna's food was gone. But they had apples taken from orchards gone wild and a fish—a fine, large trout—the dark maiden caught with her bare hands.

That was dinner, cooked over a fire. The roasted apples were coated with honey from the combs of wild bees. The fish was flavored with wild onions and salt from Orna's pack.

Orna had wine left. They ate and drank and got a little drunk. Orna ended in a huddle with the three dryads. Her clothes came off her. Curious fingers caressed her and soft lips kissed her face and body.

She was a modest maiden in a conservative society. She had never experienced anything like this before. Of course it overwhelmed her. She dove into it like a kingfisher into the river and brought up her first real orgasm like a struggling, silver fish.

At last, exhausted, she lay in the meadow's grass. Overhead, the night sky was full of stars. The dryads lay around her. "Why are you here?" one asked in a drowsy voice.

"I am seeking the witch who lives at the forest's black heart."

"No! No!" the dryads cried. "She is ugly and dangerous. Stay here with us."

What did she owe her father? Orna wondered. Respect. Love. But not the destruction of her life. If the witch were dangerous, she would avoid her.

She stayed with the dryads. By day, they wandered through the forest, sometimes gathering food and sometimes watching the life around them: green pines and yellowing ferns, birds flocking for their autumn migration. The forest shadows held numerous animals: deer, red foxes, badgers, red squirrels, weasels, tiny mice and voles. The dryads did not harm any of these. They were not hunters.

In the evening they made love in the meadow. Their nights were spent in an earthen cave, formed when a giant pine fell over. The dryads filled the cave half full with grass, and the four women kept each other warm.

One morning Orna woke and found the meadow was covered in frost. She was cold, in spite of the cave and the dryads. Winter was coming. She could not continue to live like this.

"What will you do?" she asked the dryads.

"We sleep through the cold months inside the trunks of trees—except for our sister here." The dryad who was speaking gestured toward the dark maiden. "She will sleep at the bottom of the river, safe below the ice."

"I can't do that," Orna said.

"Then go home to humanity, but return in the spring."

Orna kissed the dryads goodbye and went home. When she arrived, ragged and dirty, her father embraced her and said, "We thought you had died in the forest."

"No," Orna replied. "But I did not find the witch. The forest distracted me. I wandered a long time, not knowing where I was."

This was misleading, but not a direct lie. She didn't want to talk about the dryads. The city's conservative society did not approve of magical creatures or sex between women.

Her father wisely did not ask more questions, but told his other daughters to fill a tub with hot water and find new clothes for Orna. They did gladly, happy that Orna was home.

Once she was clean and neatly dressed and eating a good dinner, the scrivener said to her, "Don't think we failed to search for you, dear child. I went to the forest edge and talked to the farmers there. No one had seen you, though they do not go far into the forest, as they told me. They advised me to ask the hunters and charcoal burners, who went farther in. We found them here in the city, selling their goods in the market. A rough lot, but not bad hearted. They hadn't seen you, either. We offered a reward, and everyone— farmers, hunters and charcoal burners—said they would keep an eye out. It was all to no avail. You had vanished."

Orna felt guilt, but she couldn't think of a way to apologize or explain.

That left the youngest daughter, Plot. The next day she packed her bag and caught a coach to the forest. Unlike her sister Ima, she was not troubled by imagination; and unlike her sister Orna, she was not easily distracted. She marched firmly into the forest. After three days, she came to the home of the witch, which was a hut made of logs. It stood in a clearing, surrounded by towering pines. In its own way it towered, resting atop long ostrich legs. Plot looked up, wondering how she could reach the door. Then she heard a noise in back of her and ducked behind a pine.

A large, fat, solid woman came out of the forest. She was dressed entirely in black. Even the boots on her large feet were as black as night. She called out:

> *"Hut mine, obey my summons.*
> *Bend thy legs and let me in."*

The ostrich legs folded, and the hut was lowered to the ground. The witch entered. A moment later, before the hut raised itself, Plot ran through the door.

"What?" cried the witch, who had a wide, arrogant face and a beaklike nose. "How dare you sneak in here?"

"My father sent me," Plot replied. "I love and respect him, and I came because he asked me to. He wants me to be an author. But the great critic in the city says I have no ability."

"My sister," the witch replied. "The way she smokes, she would die of a lung disease, except that I send her magic potions which protect her respiratory system.

"Writing is a terrible way to make a living, almost as bad as criticism. I send my sister charms, which enchant editors, so they publish her essays and reviews. That has given her a great reputation, though not much money. Fortunately, she wants fame more than money."

"I can also do accounting," Plot said.

"That's better. A woman can make a living at accounting," the witch said. She waved in a mystical manner, and the hut stood up. "Since you're here, you might as well make yourself useful. Make dinner."

Plot found root vegetables in the witch's storeroom, along with a fresh, plucked chicken. She made a broth and then a soup, full of vegetables and pieces of chicken. It took all day, while the witch grumbled. "Can't you be quicker?"

"A soup takes the time it takes," Plot replied.

They finally sat down to dinner. The witch tasted the soup and grimaced. "Can't you do better?"

"I can only do as well as I can," Plot replied.

Though the witch was grouchy, the soup was actually quite good, thick and nourishing, an excellent meal for a cold autumn evening. There was bread and cheese and beer, as well.

When they finished, the witch said, "There is a stream at the edge of my clearing. You can take the dishes there and wash them tomorrow."

"Can you make me an author?" Plot asked.

"We will see."

So began Plot's time with the witch, who was demanding and evasive, but also interesting. As mentioned before, Plot was not easily frightened, nor easily distracted. She had promised her father to give this enterprise a good effort, and she would. In addition, she had never met a witch before. She wanted to learn how a magic-worker did her work.

Remembering how much her family had worried about her sister Orna, she sent messages home, for even deep in the forest, the witch had visitors. People came, bringing gifts and problems that required magic. Most of the problems involved health, though there were also romantic problems, people who wanted potions to attract someone or make someone lose interest.

The witch told Plot that she did her best with curing potions. "Most people are worth saving." When she made a love potion, it would work, but only so far as creating a mild interest. "The lover must do most of the work himself or herself," the witch said. "I will not force anyone into love." She felt differently about indifference potions. These always worked. "No one should be troubled by an unwanted lover."

Several of these people went into the city and were willing to stuff a note under the scrivener's door. "Don't worry, dear father. I have found the witch and am staying with her. I am safe, and everything is fine." But they would do no more, since they were mostly poor folk, and witches were not entirely respectable, being relics of a former time.

Plot kept the hut clean and made meals. Over time—through the long, cold, snowy winter—she learned enough to help the witch with potions. The hut took care of the snow in the clearing by stamping it down with its big ostrich feet. In addition, it broke the ice that formed on the stream. All the stamping and breaking made the hut jerk and shake. This was fine with Plot. If the hut had not done the work, she would have had to shovel and chop ice. She knew the witch well enough to know this.

You might think that people wouldn't come in the winter. But sickness and love are strong drivers. There were fewer visitors after the snow fell, but they did not stop. Instead they came wrapped in heavy coats and wearing high boots. The ostrich legs knelt down for them and the witch listened to their stories, as did Plot. Life was not simple, the scrivener's daughter learned. She could see that the witch's potions were not enough to solve every problem.

Most of the clients were peasants. At best, their lives were precarious, dependent on the weather, which was often capricious. The witch could help them with illness and love, but there was no charm that would make the weather reliable or people rich. Money had its own magic, the witch said, which was different from the magic of witches; and weather systems were too large for anyone to control. In spite of everything the witch did, her clients still worried about harvests and taxes, their own futures and the fates of their animals and children.

She did make charms that called rain and drove away pests. These helped some. "Though bugs can learn to resist the magic used against them," the witch said. "And there is no way to make the rain consistent. At best, I nudge it a little."

"Are you going to help me?" Plot asked the witch from time to time.

"You are a better house cleaner than you were when you came, a better cook and a better maker of potions. All this is useful. In addition, you know more about the world and the lives of other people."

"My father wants me to be a writer of stories."

"What do you want?" the witch replied.

Plot could not say.

Spring came finally. Plot said, "I need to go. My father will be worrying."

The witch gave her a considering look. She knew that Plot could not be distracted, but would always go directly to her goal. This was a virtue in an ordinary person, though not in a storyteller or a story.

"Go, then," the witch said. "But come back. I need an assistant."

So Plot packed her bag and walked to the road at the edge of the forest. Everything around her was fresh and tender and green. The trees were full of migrating birds. She waited at the coach stop. The coach appeared and carried her back to the city through spring fields.

When she got home, the house was empty, except for her father, sitting in his study and writing out contracts.

"Where are my sisters?" she asked.

"Ima had a visitor who came again and again," her father said. "A woodsman she had met in the forest. He was one of those who promised to look for Orna. First he came to report on his searching, but it was soon evident that he came to see Ima, and he kept coming even after Orna returned.

"At first, she was nervous around him. No one had courted her before, and young girls are always nervous in this situation. But he kept coming through the worst of the winter, always courteous and obviously in love. He brought her gifts, rabbit pelts and deerskins and venison. A good provider—and a good son. He always spoke warmly of his mother, and he always treated me with respect. A good son is likely to be a good husband.

"In the end, Ima agreed to marry him and move to his cabin in the forest. So that is what happened to her."

"What about Orna?" Plot asked.

"She met some women during her stay in the forest. Once spring came, she wanted to visit them again. I could tell she wouldn't be happy till she saw them, so I told her to go and stay as long as she wanted. A good parent must let go of his children in the end, and I know now that neither of them will be an author. What about you, my darling? I got your notes, but they were all brief and stuck under my door."

"I found the witch, but she gave me nothing that will make me a teller of stories. She asked me to become her assistant. I think I will."

"Ah," said the scrivener. "Well, Ima found a husband in the forest, and Orna found friends. A job may be equally good."

"Yes," said Plot. "But it isn't right that you are alone, dear father."

"I have hired a housekeeper. I could afford to, since Ima left me all the skins that the woodcutter gave her. I sold them in the marketplace for good money, and he has promised to bring me more. As I said before, the lad is a good provider.

"I don't know if Orna will bring anything back from her visit, though she mentioned honey and berries and hard-to-find mushrooms. I will get by, dear Plot."

"Well, then," said Plot.

They had dinner, made by the housekeeper, who was an excellent cook. Afterward they sat by a fire. The evenings were still cool. Plot told her father about the witch and her customers. Their stories were not large and grand, like the stories told in the marketplace. They were small tales of illness, romance, family quarrels, good or bad weather. The great twentieth century Icelandic novelist Halldor Laxness told stories like these, except that he wrote novels. You ought to read his *Independent People*.

Plot's narratives were brief and to the point. Some were happy. An illness was cured. In other cases, the witch could not solve the problem. A lover came back and complained that a love potion had not worked. Families continued to quarrel. The harvest was not good.

Plot lacked Laxness's humor and sense of irony, which can be seen as a failing. But she had his clear vision and his respect for ordinary people, which she had learned in the hut atop ostrich legs. Life was hard, and people did the best they could. Their lives did not become epic, unless a writer as good as Laxness was writing. But they were worth hearing about—and worth helping, as the witch did, though she was not always successful. Even a witch can only do so much.

When she was done, her father said, "You are certainly a better storyteller than before. But these stories will not sell in the marketplace. People want to hear about heroes and dragons and fair maidens in distress. Maybe it would be a good idea for you to rejoin the witch—or stay at home and do accounting."

"I will rejoin the witch," Plot said.

Her father felt a little unhappy, but he was not going to stand in the way of any child. Ima and Orna had taught him a lesson. We cannot determine how our children turn out. They cannot live our dreams.

"Good enough," he said. "Please come back to visit, and if you ever decide to tell stories about heroes and dragons, I would be happy to hear them."

The next day, Plot packed a new bag and set out for the forest. On the way, she passed the cafe where the critic sat.

"You are the girl with the ridiculous name," the critic said, a cigarette in her hand and a cloud of smoke twisting around her. A glass of wine stood in front of her. Plot had no idea how she could taste it through the tobacco. "What was it?"

"Plot," the scrivener's daughter said. "But I'm thinking of changing it to Amelia."

"A good idea," the critic said in the firm and considered tone that critics often use. She drew on her cigarette and puffed out smoke. "Did you ever learn to write?"

"No," Amelia answered. "But your sister has offered me an apprenticeship." She set down her bag and considered the critic. She could see the resemblance between the two sisters clearly now, both of them tall and wide, with arrogant faces and beaky noses. They had the same eyes: sharp and knowing under heavy lids. "I don't know what I want to be yet. I'll study with your sister, and think about my future."

"Good enough," the critic said. "There are too many writers in the world already. I try to cut them down, but they spring back up. On the other hand, there are too few good witches. Always remember, no matter what you end up doing, stay away from stories about heroes and dragons. They have been done to death."

Amelia went on, carrying her bag, feeling happy at the thought of returning to the hut with ostrich legs. Maybe that job would not work out. If so, she could always go back to accounting. And maybe she would write a few stories down for her own pleasure. Or maybe not.

INVISIBLE PLANETS

HANNU RAJANIEMI

—◆—

Travelling through Cygnus 61, as it prepares to cross the gulf between the galaxies, the darkship commands its sub-minds to describe the worlds it has visited.

In the lives of darkships, like in the journeys of any ambassador, there always comes a time that is filled with doubt. As the dark matter neutralinos packed tight like wet sand in the galactic core annihilate each other in its hungry Chown drive heart and push it ever closer to the speed of light, the darkship wonders if it truly carries a cargo worthy of the Network and the Controller. What if the data it has gathered from the electromagnetic echoes of young civilisations and the warm infrared dreams of Dyson spheres, written onto tons upon tons of endlessly coiled DNA strands that hold petabytes in a single gram, is nothing more than a scrawled message in a bottle, to be picked up by a fisherman in an unknown shore and then discarded, alien and meaningless?

That is why—before the relentless hand of Lorentz squeezes the ship's clocks so thin that aeons pass with every tick and the starry gaze of the Universe gathers into a single blazing, blue-shifted, judging eye—the ship studies its memory and tries to discern a pattern subtle enough to escape entropy's gnawing.

During the millennia of its journey, the darkship's mind has expanded, until it has become something that has to be explored and mapped. The treasures it contains can only be described in metaphors, fragile and misleading and elegant, like Japanese street numbers. And so, more and more, amongst all the agents in its sprawling society of mind, the darkship finds itself listening to the voice of a tiny sub-mind, so insignificant that she is barely more than a wanderer lost in a desert, coming from reaches of the ship's mind so distant that she might as well be a traveller from another country that has stumbled upon an ancient and exotic kingdom on the other side of the world, and now finds herself serving a quizzical, omnipotent emperor.

The sub-mind gives the ship not simulations or mind-states or data but words. She communicates with symbols, hints and whispers that light up old

connections in the darkship's mind, bright like cities and highways seen from
orbit, maps of ancient planets, drawn with guttural monkey sounds.

Planets and Death

The rulers of the planet Oya love the dead. They have discovered that
corpses in graveyards are hosts to xenocatabolic bacteria that, when suitably
engineered and integrated into the gut microbiome, vastly prolong the Oyan
lifespan. Graveyards on Oya are fortresses, carefully guarded against the
Resurrection Men, those daring raiders who seek more immortality bugs
in the fertile soil fed by the long dead. The wealthiest Oyans—now only
vulnerable to accidents or criminal acts—who still cling to traditions of burial
are interred in secret places together with coffin torpedoes, elaborate weapons
and traps that guard their final resting places from prying fingers.

The wealthiest and the most ambitious of all Oyans is not buried on Oya,
but on Nirgal, the dead red planet that has called to the Oyans since the dawn
of time. Liberated from the shackles of age and free to fill his millennia with
foolish projects without the short-sightedness that plagues mortals, the Oyan
constructed rockets to journey to Nirgal and built a great city there, in deep
caves to guard it against the harsh rays of the sun.

But others never followed, preferring to spend their prolonged existence in
Oya's far gentler embrace, and thus, in the uncountable years of our journey
that have passed since, Nirgal itself has become a graveyard. It is populated
only by travellers who visit from other worlds, arriving in ephemeral ships,
visible only as transparent shapes in swirling red dust. Wearing exoskeletons
to support their fragile bodies, the visitors explore the endless caves that
glitter with the living technology of the Oyans, and explore the crisscrossing
tracery of rover tracks and footsteps in Nirgal's sands, careful to instruct their
utility fog cloaks to replace each iron oxide particle exactly where it was, to
preserve each imprint of an Oyan foot forever. But even though they leave
Nirgal's surface undisturbed, the visitors themselves carry home a faint taste
of despair from the grave of the immortal Oyan, a reminder of their own
ultimate mortality, however distant.

Yet Nirgal itself lives, for the hardy bacteria of the Oyan's body burrow
ever deeper beneath the red planet's surface and build porous cities of their
own in its crust. Stolen from the dead, they are slowly stealing Nirgal for
themselves.

Planets and Money

On Lakshmi, you know that the launch day is coming when the smell of
yeast is everywhere, that sticky odour of alcohol the day after, even before
the party itself starts. The stench comes from bacteria that churn and belch

rocket fuel in stills and bioreactors in garages and backyards, for everybody on Lakshmi builds rockets, shiny cones made from 3D-printed parts and emblazoned with bright neon colours, designed with eager thoughts and gestures by teenagers wearing headsets, their eyes flashing with the imaginary interfaces of superhero movies.

When it gets dark, the rockets will go up like paper lanterns in a hurricane, orange and bright, fiery golden ribbons flowing and dancing, their sonic booms like cannons, delivering their payloads to Lakshmi's growing man-made ring that the planet now proudly wears around its waist. The people of Lakshmi will only watch them for a moment, for as soon as the rocket tails disappear from sight, everyone reaches into their pockets and the night is suddenly full of hungry faces illuminated by the paler, harsher fire of smartphone screens, showing numbers going up.

The rocket girls and boys of Lakshmi do not build their machines out of sense of wonder or exploration, but out of sheer greed, for in Lakshmi, all things are bought with quantum cryptocurrencies, imaginary coins mined by small machines in orbit or by autonomous dirigibles in the stratosphere. The quantum mints eat cosmic rays and send money to their owners in bursts of light, each quantum coin stamped with a dice roll by God.

Unforgeable and anonymous, each light-coin vanishes when it is measured and verified, so unless you are one of the entanglement bankers who constructs complex instruments like inverse telescopes that allow coins to interact and stay connected forever, the only way to live on Lakshmi is to devote all your efforts to the art of building rockets or mints, and hope that it is your very own coin, stamped with your quantum signature, that becomes the currency that everyone wants. Even a traveller arriving at Lakshmi soon finds herself going hungry, unless she builds a rocket of her own to launch a personal mint to join the growing Mammon ring around the planet.

The people of Lakshmi consider themselves to be truly free, free of centralised systems and governments, free of the misguided dreams of the past, free from starships, from galactic empires, from kings and emperors, agreeing only on the constant striving for universal abundance and wealth.

The truth is that they are right. For were the Lakshmians to look deeper into the tangled financial relationships amongst the countless light-mints and entanglement banks that orbit their planet, they would uncover deep relationships between quantum mechanics and gravity, a way to measure the motion of Lakshmi in the primordial inertial frame of the universe, and ultimately a new theory for building machines that alter gravity and inertia, machines that could lift the very cities of Lakshmi towards the sky and beyond. But that old dream is hidden too deep in the brightness of the many currencies of Lakshmi to be seen, drowned in the thunder of the rockets of the next launch day.

Planets and Gravity

When a traveller from the planet Ki visits another world, at first, she feels flattened, less, confined to two dimensions, a prisoner of gravity, every now and then trying to take off like a helpless fly. But after a while, she finds her gaze drawn irresistibly to the horizon and stands rapt and still, watching the edge of the world, the circular boundary that surrounds her in all directions.

Ki itself has no horizons. It is a planet that has become truly three-dimensional. It is hard to say where Ki begins or ends: it is smudged, a stain of ink that spreads on the paper of space and encroaches on the gravity wells of other worlds. The people of Ki are born with personal flight units: thought-controlled jetpacks powered by carefully focussed phased-array microwave beams from the vast solar panel fields that cover the planet's entire neglected surface. The cities of Ki are at constant war with gravity, built on top of pillars that are made of electromagnetic fields and iron pellets, so high they reach out through Ki's atmosphere. Other cities encircle Ki along orbital rings, yet others float in the sky, every building a buckyball tensegrity structure lighter than air. Space elevators reach to Ki's Lagrange points, and skyhooks hurl a constant stream of ships and matter out of Ki, dipping in an out of the atmosphere, bending like a fisherman's rod.

Growing up on Ki, you immediately comprehend the nature of the three spatial dimensions, watch the inhabitants of other two-dimensional planets crawl on the surfaces of their worlds without ever looking up, and naturally start to wonder if there are dimensions that *you* cannot see, other directions that remain to be conquered: and to your delight, the scientists of Ki tell you that there are many left to explore, ten, eleven or even twenty-six.

However, they add that as far as they know, only the familiar three dimensions are actually infinite: all the other dimensions are curled up into a tiny horizon like the Flatland of the planetary surface, with no room for towers or flying cars or jetpacks, and the only thing that can penetrate into the forbidden directions is gravity, the most despised of all forces on Ki, the great enemy of flight.

That is why the people of Ki have now turned all their energies to conquering the remaining boundless dimension, time, building great ships that will climb ever upwards through aeons, carrying a piece of Ki to timelike infinities.

With each planet that the sub-mind describes, the darkship's doubt deepens. It has no recollection of these worlds, yet merely by rearranging symbols, the sub-mind brings them to life. Is it possible that she is a confabulatory agent, a remnant of some primitive, vestigial dreaming function in the darkship's cognitive architecture, and her planets are made of nothing more but the darkship's dreams and fears? And if so, how can the darkship know that it is carrying anything of value at all, or indeed if itself is merely a random mutation in some genetic algorithm that simulates darkships, creating and destroying them in countless billions, simply to find one that survives the empty dark?

Yet there is something familiar in each planet, a strange melancholy and a quiet joy, and so the darkship listens.

Planets and Eyes

On the planet Glaukopis, your most valuable possession are your eyes. From birth, you wear glasses or contact lenses or artificial eyes that record everything that you see, and furthermore allow others to see through your eyes, and you to look through theirs. As you reach adulthood, you inevitably choose to focus on a point of view that is not your own, trading your own vision for someone else's. For in Glaukopis, material abundance has been achieved long ago, so that a viewpoint, a unique perception of reality, is the only thing that is worth buying or selling.

Over the centuries of such eyetrade, the viewpoints of Glaukopis have been so thoroughly shuffled amongst ten billion bodies so that no two lovers have ever seen each other with their own eyes, no mother has ever held her own child, or if they have, it has only been in passing, an unrecognised flash in the kaleidoscope of Glaukopian vision.

A few select dreamers of Glaukopis choose to give their eyes to machines instead: they allow the connectome of their visual centres to be mapped by programmed viruses and DNA nanomachines so that the machines can recognise faint echoes of life in the spectroscopy of distant extrasolar planets in the same way that you recognise your grandmother, with the same instantaneous, unquestionable clarity. In return, they are allowed to look through the eyes of machines, and so they alone have seen what it looks like to fly through the thousand-kilometre water fountains rising from the surface of a faraway moon that teem with primitive life, and the true watercolour hues of the eternal eyestorm that swirls in a gas giant's southern pole. But because they can no longer afford to share these visions with other Glaukopians, they are mocked and scorned, the only blind in the kingdom of the all-seeing.

It is easy for us to mock Glaukopis, having seen the unimaginable visions of our journey, to think them forever lost in an infinite corridor of mirrors. But we would do well to remember that Glaukopis is long gone, and all that remains to us is what their eyes saw. Perhaps one day a machine will be built that will take the sum of the visions and reconstruct the minds and the brains that saw them. Perhaps it will even solve the puzzle of who saw what, solve the Rubik's cube made of eyes that was Glaukopis.

Planets and Words

Seshat is a planet of books, of reading and writing. Not only do the people of Seshat document their every waking moment with words, they also build machines that write things into existence. On Seshat, a pen's ink can be stem cells or plastic or steel, and thus words can become flesh and food and many-coloured candies and guns. In Seshat, you can eat a chocolate soufflé in the shape of a dream you had, and the bright-eyed ancient chocolatier may have a new heart that is itself a word become flesh. Every object in Seshat writes, churning out endless idiot stories about what it is like to be a cow, a pill jar or a bottle of wine. And of course the genomes of living beings are also read and written: the telomeres in Seshatian cells are copied and extended and rewritten by tiny molecular scribes, allowing the people of Seshat to live nearly as long as their books.

It is no surprise that Seshat is overcrowded, its landfills full of small pieces of plastic, its networks groaning under the weight of endless spambot drivel, the work of fridges and fire alarms with literary aspirations, the four-letter library of Babel that flows from the mouths of DNA sequencers, with no end in sight.

Yet the Seshatians hunger for more things to read. They have devised books with golden pages that the Universe itself can write in: books where gold atoms displaced by dark matter particles leave traces in carefully crafted strands of DNA, allowing the flows and currents of the dark to be read and mapped and interpreted. And over the centuries, as the invisible ink of the neutralinos and axions dries and forms words on the golden pages, hinting at ships that could be built to trace every whirl and letter out in the void and turn the dark sentences into light, the people of Seshat hold their breath and hope that their planet will be the first line in a holy book, or at least the hook in a gripping yarn, and not the inevitable, final period.

Planets and Ruins

Zywie is a silent planet. Its empty cities are glorious ruins, full of structures higher than mountains: space towers, skyhooks, space fountains, launch loops, mass drivers, rail guns, slingatrons, spaceplane drones, sky anchors, the tarnished emitters of laser propulsion systems, still maintained by patient machines but slowly crumbling.

It would be easy to think that Zywie nothing but a dried placenta of an ancient birth. Yet in the ocean floors, in a landscape grey and colourless like a reflection of lunar surface, twisted fragments of great engines are turning into coral castles, their hard sleek lines softened and broken by ringed polyp shapes and multicoloured whorls.

On the continents of Zywie, huge puffed-up balls of precious metal drift down from the sky every now and then. They are platinum, mined in the asteroid belt by tireless robots, melted with sunlight in zero gravity, coalesced into porous spheres like a metal giant's bezoars, and launched at Zywie, where they fall at a leisurely hundred miles an hour, into rainforests and oceans and the silent, overgrown cities. They settle on the ground with a gentle thump and become habitations of insects, birds, moss and lichen.

Beneath Zywie's surface and oceans, endless glass threads are full of light, and the thoughts of ancient machines travel along them, slowly becoming something new.

Zywie's ruins are a scaffold. One day, life will climb up along its struts again, reach up and leave its own ruins behind for others to use, just another stroke of the pen in Zywie's endless palimpsest.

"It seems to me," the darkship tells the sub-mind, slowly understanding, "that all the planets you describe have something in common. They are all Earth, each defined not by what you speak of but by what is left unsaid."

The sub-mind smiles in the desert of the darkship's mind, and in her eyes there are white clouds and blue oceans and endless green.

"Are you the part of me that still longs for home?" the darkship asks. "The part that defines all things by what it has left behind, by the lost pluralities of what might have been?"

The sub-mind shakes her head.

"To be an ambassador," she says, "you ever needed to carry one thing."

She embraces the darkship's primary mind. Her skin smells of sand and exotic spices and sweat and wind and is warm from the sun. She dissolves in the darkship's mindstream, and suddenly the ship is full of the joy that the traveller feels when glimpsing purple mountains in a new horizon, hearing the voices of a strange city for the first time, seeing the thunderous glory of a rocket rising in the dawn, and just as the dark fingers of Cygnus 61's gravity cast it into the void between galaxies, it knows that this is the only thing truly worth preserving, the only constant in the shifting worlds of the Network made from desires and fears, the yearning for infinity.

HEAVEN THUNDERS THE TRUTH

K.J. PARKER

I was sure I'd come to the right place when I saw the hands nailed to the doorpost. I sighed. It shows the right spirit, I suppose, but there's no actual need for it.

There was no door-board. I walked in. Naturally, coming in out of the bright sun, I was as blind as a bat. "You sent for me," I said, to nobody in particular.

There was a disconcerting silence. "You're him," said an old man's voice, querulous, thin.

"That's right."

Just as well snakes have better night vision. She saw him, a little fat old man with a ridiculously abundant head of fine white hair.

I turned in his direction. He was looking me over. "I know," I said, "I'm very young. But we've all got to start somewhere."

He was frowning, so I thought I'd better do a trick quickly. If you can't grab their confidence straight away, it makes it all so much more difficult. So I sent the snake. There was a big earthenware jar in the far corner, covered with a cloth. She crawled in under it, and I saw the jar was half-full of cornmeal. Not a lot to go on, so I told the snake to burrow deep, on the off-chance. It's depressing how many old people keep their valuables buried in the corn jar. We, I mean thieves, know it's the first place to look.

Then I smiled. "I wouldn't keep it there if I were you," I said.

He gave me a sour look. "Don't know what you mean."

"Let me see," I said. "It's ivory, about a finger and a half long, quite old, carved in the shape of a leopard sleeping on the branch of a tree. Worth about ten oxen. There's marks on one end, I'm not quite sure what they are. No, hang on, they're teeth-marks. A kid got hold of it at some point and chewed it."

Ah. I'd got him. "My father," he said. "When he was four years old. His mother hit his head so hard he was always slightly deaf in one ear, the rest of his life." He paused. "Sit down," he said.

There was one stool; three-legged, crude work. I sat down. The snake wanted to explore behind the jar—mice, presumably—but I called her back; she slithered up my arm and in through my ear.

"Thank you for coming," he remembered to say. "Can I get you some beer?"

I shook my head. "Not when I'm working." The snake was looking round. It saw—well, the usual. Nothing helpful, at any rate. "Well," I said, "you're not being haunted, and you're not ill. What's the problem?"

He grinned. "I was wrong about you," he said, "you're a good lad. Honest," he added, incorrectly, as it happens. But he wasn't to know. "I think I can trust you."

I shrugged. "You do what you like."

"Have some milk."

I don't like milk, but the snake does. "Thank you."

He got up, tipped some milk from a jug into a little gourd. It was quite fresh. "What's the problem?" I repeated.

"My daughter," he said, not looking at me. "She's bewitched."

Not another one, I said to the snake. She ignored me. "What makes you think that?"

"She won't do as she's told."

You can see the difficulty, can't you? Ninety-nine times out of a hundred, the daughter in question is no more bewitched than my left foot, she's just that age, or she's fed up with being bossed around by her bloody stupid old father. So; she's not bewitched, therefore I can't unbewitch her, so I do nothing and the father goes around telling people I'm useless. Unscrupulous members of my profession deal with situations like that by sending their snakes in the poor girl's ear and messing with her head, making her helplessly obedient. Sorry, but I won't do that. I don't know, maybe they're right and I'm just too young; I haven't started thinking like an old man, who'd see nothing wrong with it. "In what way?" I said.

"I found her a good husband. She wants to marry this young piece of shit." He shrugged. "She's never been difficult before. It's his family. They're none of them any good. They must've got a doctor to bewitch her."

I nodded slowly. "What other explanation could there possibly be?" I said.

I got a stare for that. "Well," he said, "what are you going to do about it?"

"The young piece of shit," I said. "How many oxen has he got?"

"Twelve." A world of contempt crammed into one little number. "Why?"

I smiled. "A doctor capable of bewitching a dutiful girl into disobeying her father, which is an incredibly difficult thing to do, trust me, would want at least ten head. I was just wondering how the young piece of shit could have afforded that."

Scowl. "Maybe the wizard is one of his relatives, I don't know. I wouldn't be surprised. They're all garbage, the lot of them."

My smile broadened. It was lucky for the old man I don't practice my trade for free, or he'd have spent the rest of the day rolling on the floor clutching his guts. "If one of them was a wizard capable of performing that level of enchantment, he'd be a rich man," I said. "Stands to reason."

He peered at me through the smoke, which was making his eyes water, and I could tell he'd caught me out in the fallacy. Namely; that all competent wizards are rich. *You* claim to be a competent wizard, his eyes said, and look at you. True enough. But then, I'm still young.

Off you go, I said to the snake, and off she went.

"Anyway," I said. "I suppose I'd better see your daughter."

That made him laugh. "You'll be lucky," he said. "I don't know where she is. I shut her up in the hut this morning and put an old woman outside to keep her in, but she cut a hole in the reeds and climbed out the back. Like I told you, she's bewitched."

I yawned, to give the snake a chance to crawl in through my mouth. "There's a little lean-to shack," I said, "next to the shed where you store your shields. Inside the shack there's a pile of old furs and pelts, the ones your wives told you had been eaten by ants and were ruined, but they've put them aside to sell to the trader for beads, which you're too mean to buy for them. She's lying under the furs, waiting for midday, when everyone's in the shade and she can sneak out without being seen. She's having a real job not sneezing, because of the dust."

He looked at me. Respect. Why is it I only ever get respect for the trivial stuff?

We sleep a lot, in our profession. We have to. For one thing, living with the snake—just being alive, with the snake inside you—is exhausting, like carrying a six-gallon pot on your head wherever you go. I feel the weight of her whenever I stand up, it's a sort of shock in the knee-joints. No wonder so many of us are cripples by the time we're thirty.

Mostly, though, we sleep so we can dream. My old master—a fool, actually, but he'd heard a lot of wise things from his peers, who weren't fools—used to tell me that a doctor is asleep when he's awake and awake when he's asleep. I take this to mean that to us, the world you people live in is as insubstantial and illusory as the places you go in dreams are to you, while our dreams take us—well, home. Not sure I'd agree with that, but I'm too young to have an opinion.

It's in our dreams, though, that we meet and talk to our own kind. There's actually nothing particularly special about that, we do the same as you but in a different way, but at least we have the advantage that we can consult or spend time with any of our kind, regardless of the trivial constraints of geography, or indeed whether they happen to be alive or dead.

It's the dead, of course, who give you the best advice, and why we're so very reluctant to take it, I really don't know. Take this business with the bewitched girl and the young piece of shit, for example. Only the night before, I dreamed of my old master's old master—for some reason he's taken a liking to me, though we never met, of course, he died before I was born; but I guess it's like the bond you often get between grandparent and grandchild. His own pupil, of course, was a bitter disappointment to him.

Anyway, there he was, sitting on a stool beside my head. "No good will come of it," he said.

"You always say that."

"True. And aren't I usually right?"

I sighed and rolled over onto my back. "Usually isn't good enough," I said. "You're supposed to know everything."

He laughed. He has this way of drawing back the corners of his mouth when he laughs, like a dog baring its teeth. It gives me the creeps, but I rather like it. I've tried it myself, but it makes me look silly. "I'm an old man," he said, "I forget things."

"Things that haven't happened yet?"

"Those especially."

"You were about to say something useful," I reminded him.

He sighed. "I wish I'd had someone like me when I was your age," he said. "To do all my work for me."

"Balls," I said, smiling. "You just complicate the issue."

"Watch out for the broken spear-blade in the sand," he said. "And remember, in this case, your worst suspicions will be justified. All right?"

"Why do you have to be so damn cryptic? Why can't you just tell me straight—?"

"You're going to wake up now."

"About my fee," I said.

Maybe the old man was going deaf. "I warned her," he said. "I told her, if I catch you one more time sneaking out to wipe the axe with that worthless little turd, I'll kill you. She just doesn't listen. It must be witchcraft."

I felt the snaked wriggle uncomfortably inside my head. I know, I told her, but what can you do? "I was thinking," I said. "I imagine you were looking for a dowry of, what, thirty, thirty-five head, which is what you stand to lose unless I can get rid of the spell. So in the circumstances, I'd say five head was perfectly reasonable, wouldn't you say?"

Other doctors don't negotiate. Other doctors are, of course, older, with impressive reputations. "They're taking a long time," he said suspiciously. "Are you sure she was in the shack?"

Fortunately, that was her cue to arrive, escorted none too gently by two of the herdsmen. We were sitting outside by now, in the sun; I'd had enough of the smoke and the smell of curds, so I'd told him it's easier to smell witchcraft outside in the fresh air. Which is true, incidentally.

"You see?" he said. "Just look at her."

Which I proceeded to do. That didn't take long. She was just an ordinary girl, nothing special; it made me wonder why the young piece of shit was bothered enough to risk a spear in the back on a dark night, but presumably it was love or something like that. She was nice enough, if you like them round-faced and flat-chested. I was rather more interested in the two men with her.

"Well?" he said to her. "What have you got to say for yourself?"

"Where's the point?" she replied; she had a deep, pleasant voice. "You wouldn't listen."

Not the two guards, they were just a couple of herdsmen, unmarried men in their early fifties, of no account. I'm talking about the two dead men.

"Shut up," he said, thereby proving her point. "This is the doctor. He's come to sort you out."

"I'm young," I explained. "Give me twenty years, I won't need introducing."

One of them, of course, I recognised. The other one, a boy of about seventeen, was in fact slightly the more impressive of the two. They wore grey fur karosses, as though they were on a journey, and each of them held a spear and a kerry. The younger man's spearhead was broken. I don't think they realised I'd seen them. That's an advantage of being young and not looking the part. Go on, I told the snake, and she slipped out of my ear and down my arm.

The girl was giving me a mildly hostile stare, as though I wasn't really important enough to be worth hating. "He's wasting his time," she said to her father. "There's nothing wrong with me, except I've got a pig for a father."

The snake crawled up her leg—I saw her shiver slightly, which was interesting. Likewise the information, on which the snake was quite definite, that whatever her relationship was with the young piece of shit, it hadn't reached the axe-wiping stage, or anywhere near it.

"You father says you've been disobeying him," I said. "Is that true?"

She grinned at me. "You tell me," she said.

The snake came back and whispered inside my head, and I thought; Oh dear. This is going to get unpleasant quite soon, and I'm not going to get paid. I'll confess that I did consider lying for a moment or so, until the snake started hissing furiously and making my head hurt. Fair enough. The truth it would have to be. Unfortunate for the girl and the old man, but that wasn't my fault. And if they'd wanted to me to tell lies for them, they should've shown me a little more respect.

So, as soon as the snake had quietened down enough so that I could hear myself think, I turned to the old man and said, "I've got some good news for you. First, she's not carrying on with the young piece of shit, no matter what impression she's been trying to give you. The young man—" I was guessing a bit here, but I knew I couldn't be far out—"is in fact a friend of her brother, and he's been pretending he's screwing your daughter as a favour to his friend's memory. I don't know this for a fact, but I'm guessing they were in the same regiment, and your son was killed. Yes?"

No reply, therefore no contradiction. Fine. "The young piece of shit," I went on, "is acting in this noble and honourable fashion so that you'll believe that the child she's carrying is his. It isn't, of course. I'm sorry to have to tell you that the child's father was your late son. However," I went on, raising my voice over the low moans that everybody started making at once, "the other good news is that this girl is not guilty of incest, since she and your son had different mothers, and you aren't her father."

As I said the words, a little spark of intuition lit up inside my head, and I realised what the dead man I'd recognised was doing there.

"Her true father," I went on, "is the one we aren't allowed to name, who died on the river-bank, among the tall reeds. So you see," I went on quickly, "there hasn't been any witchcraft here, so there's nothing for me to smell out or put right, so in the circumstances I'm prepared to waive my fee and say nothing more about it, and I would suggest you do the same. I think I'll go now," I added, getting to my feet. "Have a nice day."

I don't know why we human beings profess to place such a high value on the truth. First of all, we don't. Value it, I mean. In fact, we all lie through our teeth all the time, we're the only animals that practice deceit with anything like that level of sophistication, which I guess is why the snake gets so upset whenever I'm tempted to bend the truth a little. Second; in my experience, nine times out of ten the truth only makes things worse, sometimes disastrously so. As in that case. And yet we profess to believe that the truth is the most valuable thing of all, to the extent that the king is always called Heaven-Thunders-The-Truth; we call him that, to his face, because of course we aren't allowed to say his name.

Mind you, I think the old fool was completely unreasonable. If I'd been him, I think I might have taken a degree of pride in the fact that my daughter —all right, my adopted daughter—was of royal blood, even if her father was a traitor who got what he deserved, and not a moment too soon. Also, my professional ethics and a ridiculously conscientious snake in my head may oblige me to tell the truth, but he and his people suffered from no such burden. The whole thing could've been hushed up easily enough, and no harm done.

Instead—well.

I was talking to my great-great-great-great-grandfather about cures for eye infections in cattle when something woke me up. I didn't have to see it to know what it was.

"On your feet," said a voice above me.

Here's a curious fact for you. Nothing in the world feels quite like the two coils of flattened wire they wind round the base of a spear-shaft, presumably to stop the wood splitting as it dries. Maybe it wouldn't be so distinctive applied to your hand, say, but when you feel it on your neck, just below the ear, you know immediately what it is.

"I said," the voice repeated, "on your feet. Are you deaf, wizard?"

You also have a pretty good idea what's going on. It means the king wants to see you. "All right," I muttered through a mouthful of sleep, "I heard you the first time."

They made me run, seven miles in the pitch dark. I hate running.

"Thank you," the king said gravely, "for finding the time to see me."

You genuinely don't know if he's trying to be funny, or whether he isn't actually aware of how a royal summons is carried out. He must know, surely. But in that case, why pretend otherwise?

Actually, I quite like him; the Great Elephant, Heaven-Thunders-The-Truth, He-Who-Eats-Up-The-World. He has shrewd, sad eyes and he speaks quite quietly. He's the sort of man who, if he was someone else and you met him at a wedding or a clan meeting or something, you'd think, here's someone worth talking to. Everybody he ever meets is scared stiff of him, of course—me included, it goes without saying—and with very good reason. I imagine he's equally terrified, all the time. On the whole, I'd say he copes better than most people would.

"You came quickly."

"Yes, Lord. I ran all the way."

A faint smile. "Such energy. You must be exhausted."

Another trick he has is saying something like that and then shutting up, dead quiet, and sitting there perfectly still, looking at you. Naturally, you feel you've got to say something just to break the silence, before it drowns the entire world. And anything you say will, of course, be tactless, disrespectful, wrong and held against you for the rest of your painfully short life. But I was dog tired—the snake bounces about in my head when I run, and it feels like it weighs as much as a grown man—and I couldn't be bothered. But then, I have the inestimable advantage of not fearing death. Well, not much.

"You sent for me," I said.

"Did I? Oh yes. I almost forgot. I'm very angry with you."

My throat locked solid. "I'm sorry to hear that. What did I do?"

He covered his mouth with his hand. "I gather my late brother had a daughter."

"Several," I said, without thinking. He looked at me; mild surprise, more than anything else. Several—six, to be precise, and he had them all killed. And quite right, too.

"One I didn't know about."

"Yes."

"And now she's dead."

I chose my words carefully. "I believe so."

He nodded slowly, as if what I'd said was the crucial deciding factor in a momentous decision. I caught sight of something out of the corner of my eye and quickly identified it with my peripheral vision. Then I woke up the snake and told her to get busy.

"The same woman who bore my brother a daughter bore him a son," he said quietly. "Is that true?"

What a question. How was I supposed to know? Incredibly fortunate, therefore, that the king's dead brother was now standing behind him, looking over his shoulder, with a look of mild disdain on his face. I lifted my head and caught his eye. He nodded.

"I believe so, Lord," I said.

"So I have a nephew," said the king. "Still alive."

Another nod. "I don't know, Lord."

"Liar." He said the word gently, the way a dog puts a dead bird in your hand. "He's still alive. I want you to find him."

Behind his shoulder, a brisk shake of the head and a ferocious scowl. I risked a wink. "Of course. Straight away. I'll do my very best."

There were two of them now; his late majesty the prince, and his wretched daughter, who of course I'd seen before. She was nursing a baby in her arms, as if to drive the point home. The snake, of course, was no help. She'd curled round the girl's ankle and was rubbing her head against her leg. Sometimes I swear that snake thinks it's a dog.

"When you've found him," the king went on, "come straight here and tell me. You'll be admitted right away, any time, day or night. You will not tell anybody about what we've talked about."

A statement of fact rather than an order. I called back the snake. "Lord," I said.

"Thank you so much for your time. I won't keep you any longer."

You back out of the king's presence, keeping your eyes fixed on him until he can no longer see you. As I retreated, I heard something scuttling overhead in the thatch. The other royal personage nodded to me just as I was about to heave myself out through the door-hole. I left the two of them together. Enjoy, I thought.

The guards outside, who'd brought me there, gave me a cold stare as though they'd never seen me before. I walked home, quickly. My feet hurt.

There are worse lives, believe me. Shorter lives, too. I had six brothers, and now there's only me. My brothers went off when they got their call-up, and I never saw them alive again. They tell me they made a good end, in a splendid battle which we won, and they're quite happy and satisfied. Don't feel sorry for us, they say, we're sorry for you, stuck behind there in that rotten place. They, so they tell me, are soldiers in the army of Heaven. Fine.

The snake found me when I was eight years old, bathing in the river. She must've been lying on the bottom, dead still, pretending to be a root or a stick; I didn't see her. She glided up through the water and slowly coiled herself around my trunk—I remember, I was so scared I couldn't move or struggle, all I thought was, I hope it won't hurt too much being crushed to death. You can tell I was never very bright, even as a child.

Hello, she said in my head. I'm not going to hurt you. I'm going to be your friend. There's nothing to be afraid of.

(Three lies, one after another)

It was only then that I figured out what was happening. Hello, I said, can you hear me?

Loud and clear, she said.

Am I going to be a wizard?

At that age, of course, you don't know how to keep your thoughts separate from talking-to-the-snake. I don't want to be a wizard, I thought. I want to be a soldier like my brothers.

Fool, she said kindly. In ten years' time all your brothers will be dead. So would you have been, without me. I've saved your life. You should be grateful.

Oh, I thought; and that was all, really. I accepted my brothers' deaths, then and there, and I never said anything to them. Will I have to go away and live with a smelly old man in a cave?

It wasn't getting any better. I'd seen a doctor once, and I'd been terrified— as intended, naturally. Suddenly I had a picture of me as a terrifying, smelly old man, with bits of bone and skin and bladder sewn into in my tangled hair. I was grinning, and everybody was scared to death of me. All right, I thought, I can be that.

Fool, she said again. It's not like that at all. I'm going to make you clever and wise. Don't you want to be clever?

As I said, I was a particularly stupid child. Half-wit, my mother called me; here, Half-wit, fetch the water, wipe your nose, stir this. It'd've been much better if I was clever.

Yes, she said, much. Instead of being stupider than everyone, you'll be smarter. Wouldn't that be fine?

But wizards don't marry and have wives and children, I thought. That's a bad thing. I'm not sure why, but it is.

I could feel her shifting round in my head, like a dog making a nest in a blanket before it goes to sleep. Are you afraid of death? She asked.

I suppose so. I haven't thought about it much.

Are you sad when people die? People you love.

I don't know. It's never happened.

She sort of flexed her coils, and I could feel them pressing against the inside of my skull. I probably made some sort of whimpering noise, but she ignored me. It will, she said, believe me. Listen, I'm about to start making you clever. Death is nothing, it isn't important. It only matters because the people who are left behind, the people who love the person who dies, are very unhappy. In fact, it's the worst unhappiness there is. But a wizard can see and hear dead people just like seeing and hearing the living. You can talk to them any time you like. That's the most wonderful thing, love without loss; because love should be the best thing in the world, but because you lose the people you love, love is the worst thing; it hurts more than anything else, it's an enemy to be avoided at all costs unless you want to spend most of your life in pain. Except for wizards. That's why being one is the best thing of all, better than being strong or rich, better even than being king. And that's what I've just given you. Isn't that wonderful?

I suppose so.

You suppose so. Now be quiet, I need to go to sleep.

My life has always been a sequence of impossible tasks, and this latest one was entirely in keeping with the trend. Go away and find a boy whose name and location nobody knows—nobody living, at any rate; normally, that wouldn't be such a problem. Between them, my invisible friends and the snake would be able to handle a job like that. The impossibility comes in because the dead man who knew the answer to the question obviously wasn't going to tell me; more impossible still, because if I did find the wretched kid, the dead prince would be seriously angry with me. Between death by impaling for failure to carry out the king's orders and death by haunting for succeeding, there wasn't a lot to choose. I've said I'm not afraid of death, and that's true. Dying, though, is another matter. Dying slowly in great pain is something I actively try to avoid.

I slept badly that night, which was enormously inconvenient. When I finally managed to nod off, there was nobody there but my old master; a terrible sign, because although he's responsible for me, in this world and the next, he never could stand the sight of me.

"The king said, find this boy. You live to serve the king. You serve the king as the sandal serves the foot, it has no other purpose. Therefore you must summon the prince, against his will if needs be, and force him to tell you where the boy is. You have no choice in the matter."

Stupid old fool. "Yes," I said, "and if I do that, I'll have the prince's face inches from my own for the rest of my life, scowling and yelling at me. How long will I last? Ten days?"

He shrugged. "You don't matter," he said.

He was like that when he was alive. "There must be another way," I said.

"There is not. When I clap my hands, you will wake up."

"No, don't do—" Too late. I sat up and found I was soaked in sweat. The snake shifted unhappily in my head. She doesn't like the heat, which is really strange, for a snake.

Why me? I asked her. Because you're young, she replied. That's typical of her. Factually correct and completely unhelpful.

I thought about it for the rest of the night and most of the following morning, and the more I thought, the more obvious it became. I was going to have to kill the king, and set up this unknown boy in his place. No other way out.

I really didn't want to. The kings of the House of the Spear, Great Elephants, Eaters-Up-Of-The-World, have been a pretty useless lot, but His current Majesty was one of the better specimens, and since he'd come to the throne, life hadn't got much better but it hadn't got spectacularly worse. This made him a Good King, and the odds were pretty overwhelming that this kid I was proposing to replace him with would be a complete disaster, like his grandfather, great-uncle, great-great-grandfather, and so on back into the cloudy realm of faint memory.

Furthermore, although I could think of half a dozen powerful lords who'd want him dead, all of them would also want to take his place, not see the royal spear and mat pass to some gawping brat of no relevance. Also, killing a king isn't easy, which is why we still have kings. In all probability, it'd go horribly wrong and I'd be killed. But that was a probability rather than a certainty; two certainties, as I explained earlier. It really didn't help one little bit that I liked the man. Oh, and I had three days, four at the most, before I'd be deemed to have failed in my task and executed. No pressure.

To kill a king (please listen carefully; I'm only going to say this once) you need three things: opportunity, the forbearance of others, and a weapon. Opportunity doesn't come much better than *come straight here and tell me, you'll be admitted right away, any time, day or night*. The forbearance of others can take many forms, from active conspiracy to a guard falling asleep at his post; some you can plan for, others the snake can arrange, some are pure luck.

The weapon? Spoilt for choice. Of course, you need one other thing. You need to want to do it.

Meanwhile, I had a job to do.

The snake has her own way of doing things; she doesn't tell and I don't ask. This time I let her go, then climbed up the mountain and spent the day sitting in a cave, my back, thinking hard about how to go about murdering the king.

Just as it was starting to get dark, she came back. She'd found the boy. He was in an army camp about a day's walk away to the south. Simple as that.

Like so many people these days, I never knew my father. He went off to war, my mother told me, and that was the end of him. Of course, she wasn't my mother, though she never told me that. But the snake told me, bless her malicious heart, when I was nine years old. The subject came up in a discussion we were having about my future. We still talked occasionally then.

I don't want to go away, I remember telling her. I don't want to go and live a long way away, in a cave with a smelly old man. I'd miss my mother and my sisters.

She's not your mother. They aren't your sisters.

Liar, I said, and the snake hissed inside my head and swelled her coils until I was sure my skull would burst. Liar, I repeated. It's not true.

You know it's true, she said. Everything I tell you is true. Even if I wanted to deceive you, I couldn't. We're too close.

Even at that early stage, I knew that. So who's my real mother?

She lives a long way away. The man she's married to is not your father. She doesn't want to see you, ever. The woman who looks after you was given twenty head to take you away. She's fond of you, but she's not your mother. You have nobody, except me.

The snake doesn't lie, that's the thing. The snake doesn't love me. Love doesn't come anywhere near it. Love compared with what the snake feels for me is a rabbit standing next to an elephant. I am her soul, and she is mine. Unfortunately.

There; she didn't like me saying that. She tells the truth but doesn't always like hearing it.

So, one dark night, I took an old rusty spear-blade that had belonged to my grandfather, my mother's father, the father of the woman who wasn't my mother, and very quietly I sawed a hole in the reeds and crept out of the hut, across the cattle-pen, through a gap in the thorn hedge and away. I walked for three days, with nothing to eat and no sandals on my feet (I'd never been more than an hour's walk from home before) until I reached a high mountain standing on its own in the middle of the plain. The snake showed me a kloof whose mouth was almost hidden by thorn-bushes and scrub. It was just before mid-day, and the shadow of the mountain made the kloof as dark as midnight. Well go on, the snake told me. So I threaded my way in past the bushes and called out, "Hello?"

My master was sitting on a stool in the middle of the cattle-pen; just sitting, his hands on his knees, his head a little to one side. He was a big old man with white hair in braids, and there were bits of things I didn't like to look at stuffed or caught in the weave. He must've seen me but gave no sign.

"Hello," I repeated.

He can't hear you, said a voice, and another voice laughed. Another one, a woman's, said, You must be the boy. Well?

"Yes," I said out loud, "or I think so. I've come to learn to be a wizard."

Several other voices laughed; a man's voice said, Not a wizard, a doctor. That's your first mistake.

"I'm sorry," I said, "I didn't know."

That's no excuse, said the voice, and the female said, Leave him alone, don't pick on him. A lot of voices laughed at that. You need to learn, said the nasty male voice. If we're kind and gentle, you won't learn anything. But this—and something slapped the side of my face so hard I staggered—will make sure you don't get it wrong ever again.

"Thank you," I said.

They found that hilarious, but I'd said the right thing, and from then on, they were mostly on my side. Gradually, of course, as time went by, I got to know them all, though some were more friendly than others. Mostly they were doctors, long dead; they hung about the kloof the way old people hang about the smithy in the cold weather, for the company and to keep warm. Some of them never told me who they were, who they'd been, or even if they'd ever been human, and it's not the sort of thing you ask about. Mostly, like I said, they were good to me, and when they weren't, I probably deserved it.

Anything even vaguely like an education or training, I got from them; my master was pretty much useless, as the voices didn't hesitate to point out when they thought he couldn't hear them. He'd forget about me for weeks at a time, then suddenly remember and try and teach me something—but usually it was garbled or no use for anything or just plain wrong. The voices wanted me to kill him and take his place; as is only fitting, they used to say, which I didn't understand. I could see their point, but I'm not a natural killer; it's something I do rarely, and then only when I have to, usually when it's too late. That, they assured me, is a weakness that would hold me back and ultimately bring me to grief. I hope they're wrong, though I have to say, they've always been right about everything.

But they taught me to see, and to listen, and how to make the snake do what I wanted. They told me the things the snake could do and the things she couldn't, and how to summon the dead and the other spirits. Does this mean

I can order you about now? I asked, and because they couldn't lie they said nothing. They taught me how to herd the clouds and make lightning, how to smell for poison and witchcraft, how to heal injuries and illnesses, and how to hurt people. All useful stuff.

Then, when I was sixteen, my master died suddenly. It shows how useless he was, and how much the spirits disliked him, that his death came as much of a surprise to him as to me, and all the rest of us. He was sitting outside in the sun one morning, and a big lump of rock crumbled away from the side of the mountain and fell on his head.

No great loss, they told me, but I was sorry for him, even so. He was one of those people who shouldn't have been born with the gift but was anyway. He thought he was a much better doctor than he really was, and was therefore continually disappointed; needless to say, he blamed everybody and everything else, and so went through life in a constant state of anger and resentment. I buried him under the door of his hut, and then it actually sank in. All this was mine now, I was the wizard of the Black Kloof, and I was on my own.

Which is why, as people are forever reminding me, I'm young to be a doctor. I'm ten times better at it than he was, and he never liked me anyway. But I miss him, even so. The snake told me once that the spirits loosened that rock and made it fall when it did. I choose not to believe her.

My snake led me to the army camp where, I have to say, I was not made welcome. Members of my profession, even young ones who don't wear all the get-up, aren't popular with the military. This may be because unscrupulous kings over the years have used doctors to get rid of over-mighty generals with spurious accusations of witchcraft. If so, I don't blame them one bit.

I hadn't got the faintest idea who I was supposed to be looking for, let alone his name or a description or anything like that, but she slipped out of my ear and bustled along in front of me, and I followed. She led me to the smithy. It was going to be one of those days.

Smiths are another section of the community who don't like us. I can see why; we're too much alike. We say that a smith is a wizard without the talent. They don't say what they say about us to our faces, and nobody wants to tell us, but we can guess. This particular smith was a big fat man, about fifty years old, with a headring gleaming with sweat and burn-scars all over his arms and chest. He stood in front of the anvil, wiping his forehead and holding a half-done spearhead in the red coals. Behind him, a lad of about my age was pumping a double bellows. "What do you want?" asked the smith.

A very good question. Fortunately, the snake was back inside my head and spoke for me. "You had a sister," I said.

He froze, then turned and scowled at the boy. "Go away," he said. The boy let go of the bellows handles as though they were red hot and ran out. "You," said the smith, "make yourself useful and work the bellows. I don't want to lose the heat."

Anything to oblige. Needless to say, I don't know the first thing about blacksmiths' work. Curiously and fortuitously, the snake does. I got a nice smooth rhythm going. "I asked you a question," I said.

"Who the hell are you, anyway?"

I smiled, took one hand off the handles and drew it round my head, like a coiling snake. Everybody knows what that means.

"A bit young, aren't you?"

"So I gather. Well?"

I could see he was considering his alternatives, of which he seemed to feel there were two. The first, which I could see he favoured, was bashing me on the head with his hammer and shoving my face in the fire. Reluctantly, he opted to go with the second.

"What about her?"

Behind him, I could see three women; one old, one middle-aged with a baby on her hip, and one young and very beautiful. "She's dead."

"I know. What's it to you?"

"Your mother had a long nose and a pointed chin, and a scar just above her left eyebrow. You had a brother, but he died when he was a baby. But you loved your grandmother best, and she loved you."

He winced. "All right," he said, "you're a wizard. What about my sister?"

Sometimes you just have to guess. "She had two children," I said. "Their father wasn't her husband."

He grinned at me. "She had two sons and three daughters."

And sometimes you guess wrong. "Her lover was the prince," I said. "The one we can't talk about."

He looked at me, then down at the spearhead, which was starting to show white round the edges. Slowly he lifted it out and laid it on the ashes. "You can stop pumping," he said.

I was glad to hear that. Bellows are more work than they look. "She married a man over by the White River," I said. "He died recently, along with his daughter and all his household."

The smith shrugged. "I heard he was a traitor," he said.

"Maybe," I replied. "It's one of those words, the more people use it, the less it means. Now," I went on, "the prince's daughter stayed with her mother, but not the boy. What became of him, do you know?"

He wiped sweat out of his eyes. "No idea," he said. "The boy was the older of the two, by a year or so. Because of who his father was, she sent him away as soon as he was born. Then the prince started the war and got killed, so none of us wanted to know any more about anything, if you get what I mean. Who else knows about this?"

"Nobody," I said. "Just you, me and the snake. She won't tell anyone if you don't."

"How about you?"

"Oh, I do as I'm told." That made him grin, in spite of himself. "Why should I want to tell anybody, anyway? You don't know anything, you just said."

He's lying, of course, the snake told me. Yes, I told her, I'd guessed that.

"I haven't heard anything about the boy since he was born," he said firmly. "I wouldn't know him if I met him in the road."

"Quite," I said. "And how could the boy be a threat to the king if nobody knows him and he's got no way of proving he's got a claim to the throne?" I paused for a moment. "Some people might say that's a pity," I said.

He stiffened, like a splash of hot lead falling into water. "Don't talk like that," he said.

"Why not? Nobody here but us and the rats in the thatch. There's some people who might say, no matter how bad this boy is, he couldn't be worse. Pointless, of course, if he can't even be found."

There's something unnerving about the sight of a huge man, strong as a bull, terrified. "Now who would say something like that?"

"Oh, people I've talked to. Quite a lot of them, actually. They're saying, nobody wants another civil war, not like the last one, and there's not many who'd be willing to march out and fight in one, and who'd blame them? But if, heaven forbid, the king was to fall down dead, through illness—" I paused, and smiled. "Or witchcraft, even. He's got no sons, he's always been very careful about that, no brothers, no living relatives of any sort, so who's going to take his place? The country needs a king, someone's got to do it. And if there's a nephew—" I shrugged. "I think a lot of people would rest easier knowing there's an heir to the throne, don't you?"

He looked at me like a drowning man. "What did you say your name was?"

"It's not a very interesting name," I told him. "Even if I told you, you'd have forgotten it a moment later. Talking of names," I added.

He looked away. "He didn't have one," he said. "I told you, they got him out of there practically as soon as he was born. What he's called now I have no idea."

"But the people you sent him to," I said. "They had names. Most people do."

"I don't remember."

I smiled. I didn't want to. I quite liked the man. "I'm a doctor," I said, "I have medicines for a poor memory. And other things too, of course."

He's going to say it, I thought. He said it. "Are you threatening me?"

"Yes."

They never expect you to say that. He actually shuffled back a step or two, as if that'd do him any good. The sight of so much cowardice made my skin crawl. "Leave me alone, will you?" he said, raising his voice (but it came out as a rather louder whine). "I don't know anything."

I hate doing this sort of thing. "Maybe not," I said. "But it's all right, I'll know if you're telling the truth. I'll send my snake into your head, and she'll tell me if there's anything in there or not."

I can't do this, of course. Nobody can.

By now he'd retreated so far he was backed up against the anvil stand, with nowhere to go. "Please," he said, "it's my sister's boy, if they find him they'll kill him. He's all that's left of her. Please."

I'm not sure I'd have had the heart to carry on if he hadn't made a spectacle of himself by grovelling. But all I could feel was contempt. "That's enough," I said. "Now, the more you can hold still, the less damage she'll do. You really do need to co-operate if you don't want to spend the rest of your life sitting against a wall somewhere."

"All right," he said. I could hardly bear to look at him. I wanted to squash him, like a nasty insect. But he told me a name. It hit me like—well, like the rock that had fallen on my master. It crushed me flat. Like an idiot, I said, "Are you sure?" or "Say again?" or something like that. He repeated the name; also her father's name, and where they lived. I think I said, "Thank you, I'm sorry," or something of the kind, and then I stumbled out into the light, not looking back.

Well, so much for that idea.

The thing is, I don't go looking for trouble. Some people do. Some people delight in the thunder and the stamping and the shouting and the screams of dying men. Some people can only find peace in war; without fighting and conflict, they're like newly-planted seedlings in dry weather, drooping and parched. Some people can only live if there's death all around them. I guess it must be the thrill. I'm not like that.

So all the stuff that continually pounds down on my head and in through my ears, like rain after thunder, is wasted on me, and I think that's a shame, when there's so many people out there who'd really appreciate it. I'd much rather stay home in the kloof and cure oxen with fly-bites and redwater fever. A man could get old and fat doing that, and people would be pleased to see him. But I think she'd be bored stiff. I think she likes the other stuff. It's the only explanation I can come up with, at this moment.

I had to abandon the plan because the name the smith told me was my mother's, sorry, the name of the woman I used to think of as my mother, and the place he named was where I grew up, before I came to live in the Black Kloof. Ridiculous.

I'd been living back in the kloof about three months when I had a dream. I was lying curled up on my mat, and all these terrifying old men came again and stood round me in a ring, looking down at me and frowning, as if they couldn't quite bring themselves to believe I was true. At first I was scared of them, but they kept on staring and muttering, and I knew that sort of thing was rude, so after a while I stopped being scared and got annoyed. "What?" I said.

One old man, who seemed really put out about something, said, "So you're him, then."

"Me?" I said. "I'm nobody. I'm not important. Please go away."

They looked at each other, and one of them said, "Are you quite sure? He looks so—" He didn't finish his sentence, and the others just shrugged.

"What?" I repeated. "What are you talking about? Is there something wrong with me, or something?"

Then one of them laughed, but it wasn't a funny laugh. "You know what, son," he said, sounding as though I'd just spat in his beer, "it'd have been better for everybody if you'd never been born. Come on," he added, to the others. "There's nothing we can do about it, that's for sure." And then they all started to walk away, and I woke up.

I couldn't kill the king and put the prince's long-lost son on the throne because that long-lost son was apparently me. So the plan was out of the question; for many reasons, but principally because I'm a doctor, a wizard. No wizard has ever been king, it's unthinkable. For that to happen, a king would have to have a son born with the talent, and send him away to learn the craft under some master, and no king would ever do that. No wizard born outside the royal family could ever usurp the throne, because all his fellow-wizards would band together to stop him, and then there'd be a spirit war which would stamp the land flat. All the cattle would die, all the children would be still-born, there would be so much lightning and no rain— So that's that. The People of Heaven wouldn't stand for it, either. If I was to be king, they'd tear me in pieces, or die in their thousands trying.

So; right back to where we started.

"You did say," I told him. "Any time, day or night."

He grunted like a pig. "Did I?"

"Yes."

He sighed. It was the middle of the night. He'd been with his youngest wife, not sleeping. "I must have meant it, then. So, you found him."

I tried not to look at the faces crowding round us, but it was hard. I recognised some of them, but most were unfamiliar, though the family resemblance was quite strong in some of them. The huge, grim-faced man with the wild eyes could only have been the Black One himself, the Lion,

He-Stamps-Them-Flat, the founder of the kingdom; is there anyone living who wouldn't give his right arm for a chance to see Him, find out what He really looked like? But I didn't dare, I could only peek at him on the very edge of my vision. My ancestors, I realised; what an extraordinary thought. The Black One was my great-great-great-great grandfather.

"Are you sure we're alone?" I said.

He laughed out loud. "Oh, quite sure," he said. "I don't want to share this with anybody."

Me included. I wasn't at all sure I knew what to do about that. Still, I'd run out of options, so what could I do? Think of something, and quickly. "No rats in the thatch, even?"

He looked at me for a moment; then, with a degree of speed and power remarkable in someone so fat, he stood up and drove the little red-handled spear he always carried into the thatch above his head, right up to the socket. He pulled it out, drove it in again about a foot to the left, and so on about a dozen times. Then he sat down again. "No rats," he said. "Go on."

The show of violence had unnerved me, and I had to pull myself together before I could speak. One thrust of that little toy spear, so very quick, not upwards this time, was all it would take, and all my troubles would be over. I'm not afraid of death, remember. Even so.

"Very well," I said, and I told him a name. It was a lie. It was the name of the son of a very big important man, commander of five regiments, loved by all the people for his fairness, his generosity, his wisdom, his courage. Either of them, father or son, would have made a good king. A stable kingdom with a not-quite-so-good king and a standing army can do without men like that.

I felt the snake swell her coils in rage, because I'd just told a lie. The pain was unbearable. I didn't dare breathe, for fear of crying out. The pressure kept on building, and I felt my eyeballs bulge.

"Are you sure?" he said.

I couldn't speak, so I nodded.

He looked at me. "Are you feeling all right?" he said. "You look awful."

"I'm fine," I croaked. "Thank you."

(As I said, I quite like him. Just occasionally, there are these flashes of humanity through the clouds of Heaven. Just occasionally. If he hadn't had to be a king, he'd have been all right. He didn't have the choice, of course. Not like some—)

"You're sure," he repeated. I nodded again. My head was about to crack open, like an egg hatching. "It seems so unlikely," he went on. "Of all the people, why him? In the war against my brother, he was on my side. Really on my side, I was sure of it. I can't believe he'd have taken in my brother's son. It makes no sense."

"Rich men like to collect weapons," I said. Luckily I'd learned the speech by heart beforehand. "They don't necessarily plan on using them, but they like to own them—you know; fine spears, ironwood kerries, axes with rhinoceros-horn handles. And maybe a man might get to thinking, if ever I had to defend myself against the king, I'd need a pretty special weapon, something practically unique. And maybe a clever tactician, an experienced soldier or someone like that, might feel the need to start defending himself before the attack comes."

He thought about that for a long time, and I could see him slowly getting angry—not the sort of anger he does for show, because it's expected of him, with shouting and arm-waving, but the quiet, tight-lipped kind that comes from being hurt and frightened and betrayed. Meanwhile, the pain in my head wasn't getting better, but it had stopped getting worse.

"Are you sure?" he said.

I nodded, and this time I couldn't stop myself, because the snake swelled alarmingly and I had to cry out. He looked at me. "What's the matter?" he said.

I managed to grind out the words. "My head hurts, Lord."

"You chose a strange time to have a headache." He frowned, then looked past me towards the doorway. "Apart from me and you," he said.

"Nobody, Lord."

He rubbed his lower lip with his thumb. I don't know anybody else who does that. "There's an argument for saying that letting you live would be weakness."

I was distressed to see a couple of my ancestors nodding their heads behind him. "No, Lord," I said, "with respect. Letting the boy live would be weakness. Letting me live would be enlightened self-interest. Killing me would be a waste. If your father was here now, he'd agree with me," I added, untruthfully.

"You're bleeding," he said. "There's blood coming out of your ear."

I gave him a weak grin. "It does that sometimes," I said.

He frowned and peered at the side of my head. I could feel the blood trickling down my neck, like a snake crawling. At last he said, "There's no point killing you. You'll be dead anyway inside a week. You've been bewitched. There's maggots in your brain or something."

I really wanted to laugh. I managed not to. "That would explain it," I said.

Even now I'm not sure why the snake didn't kill me for telling lies. She wanted to, I know. She said so. Her story is that she tried to do it, but my skull was too thick to pop. She always tells the truth. I don't believe her.

It was touch and go, though, for a day or two. I got out of there and back to the guest hut, where I fainted half in and half out of the doorway, on my knees, with my ass in the air. When I came round, I couldn't move my left arm, and the left side of my face was frozen. It makes talking difficult, as you've probably gathered. I sound like I'm drunk, which is so unfair.

For weeks, apparently, I talked nothing but drivel. I find that odd, because I can remember having a lot of long, intelligent conversations during that time; with many of the great names in my profession, with interesting spirits I'd never come across before, with people I used to know, with my relations. I even got to talk to the Black One himself.

He came and sat beside me, or rather he squatted on his heels, perfectly balanced. He was much younger than I'd expected. He was frowning. I didn't dare speak. He scratched his ear, then looked at his fingertip. My mouth was as dry as shield-leather.

"Hello," he said suddenly, and his voice was much higher than I'd thought it would be. "You don't know me. I'm your great-great-great-grandfather." He grinned awkwardly. "Silly, really. I don't feel old enough to be anybody's grandfather, or anything like that. But I died young, you see."

He sounded almost apologetic, as though he'd been inconsiderate. "Lord," I mumbled. "Great one, Eater-Up-Of-Elephants."

He gave me a look. "Yes, all right," he said. "I don't actually like that stuff. I used to," he added with a little grin, "and look where it got me. My brothers killed me, you know."

"Yes, Lord."

"So." He put the tips of is fingers together, aligning each one precisely. He had long, slim hands, like a girl. Everything about him was precise, delicate, elegant, even though he was so big and broad. He hadn't lived long enough to run to fat, of course. "You're the last of the family, then."

"Am I, Lord?"

He nodded. "My children and my children's children have seen to that," he said sadly, "slaughtering each other till there's nobody left. I don't know why they had to do that, it's stupid. You'd have thought, the first duty of a king is to make sure he's got a son to take his place. Not our lot, apparently. Too scared of being murdered by their own kids. I ask you, what kind of way is that to live? No," he went on, "you're the last of us, and you won't have any children, being a wizard and all."

I'd been figuring it out in my head. When he died, he'd been just six years older than I was at that moment. He'd started young, of course. Won his first major battle when he was fifteen years old. "I wish I'd been a wizard," he said.

"Lord?"

"Never had the talent, of course," he said. "I've always felt bad about that. A wizard's got it all, hasn't he? Power, cattle, everybody's scared stiff of him, even kings; you can make people do what you want and they'd never dare try anything with you. Wizards are so much better than kings."

"Lord."

"Well, it's true," he said. "I mean, look at our family. You know how many of us lived to be thirty? Four, out of fourteen. You know how many of us died natural deaths? None, that's how many. Not one."

I couldn't believe what I was hearing. "Is that true, Lord?"

"Are you calling me a liar?" For a moment, I thought lightning was going to strike me and burn me up. Then he grinned sheepishly. "Sorry," he said, "force of habit. I always made a point of taking offence at pretty much everything. It made people scared of me, you see. Seemed like a good idea at the time."

He shrugged, then went on; "Wizards, now, they all live to be old men, respected, looked up to, and the older they get, the more people respect them. Opposite of what happens with everyone else, when you get old, nobody bothers with you, you're just a nuisance. Even kings. Your sons sit there watching you, waiting for you to die, and it's them people talk to and listen to, because you won't be around much longer and they want to be in with whoever's going to take your place. No, wizards are much better than kings. Well, you know that. You had that idiot eating out of your hand."

"It didn't feel like it, Lord."

He frowned. "Really? I thought you handled him really well. Smooth as butter, I thought."

"I was frightened, Lord. I was very frightened."

That made him laugh. "Well, of course you were," he said. "That's natural. I mean, look at me. I was scared stiff most of the time. Absolutely petrified."

"Lord?"

"Oh yes." He nodded seriously. "Oh, I yelled and roared and carried on like I was wrong in the head; people respect that, they don't dare answer you back, even if you're doing something bloody stupid. And I went on about how being brave is so wonderful, and if anybody did anything that even looked like cowardice I was down on them like a leopard, no second chances, nothing. You do that, people think 'he must be really brave.' But I wasn't. The number of times I pissed myself down the leg just before we started fighting. But nobody saw, I don't think, so that was all right." He shook his head. "Wizards are better. You don't get to marry and have kids, but that's probably one of the good things about being a wizard, I don't know. Really, you've got everything. You people aren't even afraid of death, isn't that right? That must be wonderful. Like being, I don't know, free."

I stared at him. "But Lord," I said, "you were the greatest king of all time. You conquered the world, you stamped out the tribes like the embers of a fire—" I stopped. He was giving me a sad look and shaking his head slowly. "Lord?"

"You're smart," he said, "you should know better. I wasn't smart, like you are." Suddenly he laughed. "Believe me," he said, "I wouldn't lie to you. Heaven-Thunders-The-Truth, remember?"

"Heaven thunders the truth," I said. But it didn't mean anything any more.

Five years later, when the king was dying, he sent for me. I replied that I was too busy, which was true. He commanded me to attend on him. I didn't bother to reply.

A lot had changed in that time. The People of Heaven had fought a bitter war against an alliance of their most powerful neighbours and had lost badly; we'd managed to patch up a sort of a peace, but it wouldn't be long before they'd be back to finish us off. The king's army was mostly dead; of the survivors, five regiments had crossed the northern border and kept going, until nobody knew where they were, and the king was only still alive because his three senior generals were still trying to decide which of them was going to kill him and take his place. There weren't enough soldiers left for a civil war, so they were having to talk it through instead.

Meanwhile, the king's illness, which he'd suffered from on and off for the last five years, had finally broken his will to resist, and he was about to save his loyal people the job. I, on the other hand, had prospered. I'd cured a plague. More to the point, I'd accurately predicted each crippling defeat, with enough circumstantial detail to convince even the most sceptical observer. I was turning away any job that didn't interest me, and asking for (and getting) ridiculous fees for the few I condescended to take on. I think it's fair to say I was the only doctor in the country who hadn't messed up at some point in the war. I was universally respected, and if I'd wanted to, I could've chosen who was going to be the next king, and everybody would've accepted my decision. But I chose not to. I was, I gave them to understand, above things like that, who cared only for wisdom. And truth. Heaven no longer thundered it. I did.

So he came to see me instead; unannounced, uninvited. But he still had a bodyguard of two hundred picked veterans; I had about seventy men minding my cattle and doing odd jobs for me, but even if I'd had notice and mustered them to fight, they wouldn't have lasted very long against the guards. So, when two guard captains burst into my cave late one night and said the king was paying me a visit, I just yawned and said yes, I'd been expecting him.

He'd changed. It was a particularly unkind sort of illness. He'd swollen up like a body that's been in the water. His arms and legs were like tree-trunks, and his body was grotesque; his head, though, was more or less the same size, which made him look ridiculous. He couldn't stand or sit, so he had to be carried on a stretcher, with trestles to rest it on. They brought him in, and I didn't look up. "Go away," I said. A moment or so later, I heard them filing out of the cave. Only then did I lift my head and look at him.

"Hello, uncle," I said.

His puffed-up cheeks had almost closed his eyes; they were narrow almonds of white, glaring balefully at me. "It's true, then," he said.

"Oh yes. How did you find out, by the way? Oh," I added, because my father was standing over him, He was grinning.

"Is he still there?" asked the king.

"Yes."

He sighed. "I can't see him all the time, but I know he's there, I can feel him."

My father shrugged and pulled a face. He's a jolly man, with a good sense of humour. I like him. I wish I'd known him.

"The illness," I said, "is incurable. You have about five days to live. Then the weight will get too much for your heart and you'll die. I'm sorry," I added.

"Was it you?"

Inside my head the snake shifted ominously. All right, I told her, settle down. "Yes," I said. "I put a spell on you, the night I lied to you. I had to, I'm afraid. It was the only way the snake would forgive me. I'm sorry, you can't possibly understand that. The point is, I didn't want to. But there was no other way."

He nodded as much as he was able to, an inch or so. "The war?" he said. "Did you do that?"

I wanted to look away, but I reckoned I owed him eye-contact. "Yes," I said. "I bewitched you into arrogance and stupidity. You were half-way there, but the other half was all me. I'm sorry for that, too."

"You've destroyed the country."

"I know," I said. "We're this close to being stamped flat. But it had to happen. The kingdom began with our family, and it'll end with it. And frankly, no great loss. What did we ever do, apart from kill people?"

He closed his eyes. "If I tell my guards to cut your throat, I wonder if they'll obey me."

I shrugged. "I don't know," I said. "Would you like to try yourself? You can if you like, though the effort will probably kill you. I'm not bothered, one way or another."

He was exhausted. Just talking, moving his head a few times, had drained all his strength. "What's the point?" he said. "It's all over now."

"It will be," I told him, "soon. Was there anything in particular, or did you just want to hear what you know already?"

His breathing was slow and shallow. Maybe I should've said, five days if you don't exert yourself. "Do one thing for me."

"It depends what it is."

"Make him go away," he replied, very softly. "Please. It's only for a short while, and then he'll have me forever. Can you do that?"

I looked at my father, who shook his head. "I'm sorry," I said. "He wants to stay till the end."

"Then give me some poison," the king murmured. "I can't stand him any more."

"You should have thought of that before you killed him." But I was already mixing two powders together in a little gourd of water. He couldn't see that, of course. Neither of them could. "Drink this," I told him, and he managed to get his lips apart a tiny crack. "It'll make you feel better."

I lied, of course. The war was nothing to do with me. My snake let me tell the lie because it counted as part of the king's punishment. In fact, it was her idea. But I do think the war has been a good thing, broadly speaking. It's put an end to the line of kings that began with the Black One, and I don't think the People of Heaven will have kings after that, just some sort of governor answerable to whoever conquers us. Whoever that turns out to be, they can't possibly be worse for the people than my family. Can they?

You have to ask yourself the question; does the snake choose you because you've got the talent, or do you have the talent because the snake chooses you? Everybody's always told me it's the first one—wizards, spirits, the snake, everybody who ought to know.

But take me as a case in point. Before she found me, I was stupid. I can just barely remember what it was like. You know when you're sitting inside, and outside there's two people talking, you can hear the voices but you can't make out the words. After the snake found me, I could hear all the words. I think that if ever the snake left me, which she can't do, she'd die; me too probably— but if that were to happen, I'd go back to being stupid again. Does that sound like the talent to you? I think the talent is the snake, and the other way about. I think that's why the snake chose me; because my father was the prince, and someone somewhere decided that making the last lost surviving son of the royal house into a wizard would have interesting results, which would facilitate some larger strategy. Otherwise, the whole thing's just one damn coincidence after another, and I don't believe it. The snake says otherwise, of course, and she's incapable of falsehood.

But I lied, yes. That makes it twice now that Heaven, as embodied in me, hasn't exactly thundered the truth. I don't care, and I don't suppose anyone else does either. Not even the snake.

After all, why not? Heaven should tell lies from time to time. Everybody else does.

SELFIE

SANDRA McDONALD

If you ask me, I'm more like my mom than my dad. She and I love astronomy and the mysterious origins of the universe. Dad's not only stuck on the past, he literally would move there if he could. Every summer he drags me along on his research trips to eras where sweaty-smelling people with wool bathing suits hole up in seaside deathtraps.

"The Belleview is a beautiful hotel," Dad protests, studying the snaps displayed on our living room wall. "It's not a death trap."

"Dad, it's a wooden structure filled with flammable furniture and gas lamps, populated by people smoking pipes and cigars," I say, from where I'm doing homework. "You told me yourself the number one enemy of old wood buildings is one careless spark. Show me a place with sprinklers and fire extinguishers, and then we'll talk."

He waves his hand to make the images scroll sideways. Some are black-and-white grainy images, while others are color chronoshots, and scrolling along the screen is a real-time cost analysis of different routes to get there. The cheapest option right now would require passing down three separate time tunnels and crossing two multidimensional borders. I hate the borders. They're always crowded and boring and the lines seem to take forever, because you're actually crossing forever.

"You didn't object last summer when we visited the Grand Hotel on Mackinac Island," Dad says.

"Last month I did a school report on famous fires. Do you want me to read it to you?"

The color and angle of light slanting on Dad's face changes as he brings up the blueprints. One of his many jobs is designing interactive tours of nineteenth century Victorian resorts for chrono tourists. The hotels all either burned down, got razed for redevelopment, or were destroyed by the rising tides that took out the old coastal cities. The Belleview is a sprawling white structure on the Gulf of Mexico, a tempting beacon for both termites and hurricanes.

Dad says, "Susan, you can't stay home for two weeks while I'm away. You'll like Florida. The space program started there."

He goes back to his plans. I think about the Gemini and Apollo missions and the first man on the moon, more than a hundred years ago.

Mom's surprised when I call her a few days earlier than scheduled.

"I want to come visit while Dad goes to 1899," I tell her.

She frowns on my palmscreen. "You want to come up here?"

"You said I could for my birthday."

"Which is eight months away. What's wrong with time trips? You used to like them."

"Do you know how uncomfortable a corset is?" Especially now that I've gotten a lot bigger on top, but I don't mention that. "And the shoes kill my feet."

She glances away and taps on a tablet. "What does your father say?"

They were never married. In most timestreams they probably would never even dated, but in this one they met at a wedding while in grad school and drank too many glasses of champagne. Mom gestated my embryo and Dad took over after that. Everything's mostly worked out fine, except they're not quite friends and do most of their communicating through me.

"I haven't told him," I say, spinning the moon globe dangling over my desk. The settlement she lives in is built to scale and smaller than the crescent on my thumbnail. "He'll be okay with it."

She makes a distracted noise. "Well, he's got to pay half. This time of year, the rates are very expensive."

Lunar travel is never cheap. Luckily, every time Dad drags me to the past I take snaps of old jewelry, clothing, and furniture. I send them to a replication database for commercial and private users and earn a commission on anything they use. I've been doing it for four years now and there's more money in my account than either Mom or Dad suspect.

"So I can come up?"

"Talk to him, sweetie. I'll look at my schedule."

The key to success with Dad is timing. No pun intended. A few days later, he logs off from one of his jobs with a big grin, thanks to an unexpected bonus, and over dinner I'm ready with my proposal.

"Dad, I want you to take a selfie of me when you visit the Belleview. That way we get to spend some quality time together, and I can do research with Mom on the moon for my senior project. Wouldn't that be great for my college portfolio?"

He blinks in surprise. "Since when do you have a selfie?"

"I could get one. I've got some savings. And a coupon."

Dad scratches the side of his head. He's one of those very tall, very skinny guys who look like they're stooping for low doorways even when they're not. Sometimes when we travel to the past, the locals say he looks like Abe Lincoln.

"Did you say moon?"

"Mom okayed it."

He hesitates. "Aside from the fact that's something we need to discuss more in depth, I'm not thrilled with the idea of spending my time with a robot daughter."

Immediately I pop up the brochure on our tabletop. "Selfies aren't robots. They're just temporary containers. You used one for that conference in Brazil last year because you couldn't be in two places at the same time."

"As I recall, it was my leg that was in pieces," he says drily.

"And that's why we don't let you ride airbikes anymore."

"I don't know if I can afford to travel next summer. This could be our last big trip together."

"We're still taking it together. The selfie's going to act just like I would. When I get back from the moon I'll synch the memories in and it'll be like we were never apart."

He's not convinced. Luckily, I'm persistent and persuasive and finally he agrees, reluctantly, as long as I pay for half the selfie out of my own savings. Mom gets my visa approved, my friend Jessy shrieks with jealousy, and Dad and I visit the selfie showroom. The model we pick out has my same body shape. A half hour later she comes out of the imprint mold with my face, hair, birthmarks, and the tattoo Dad doesn't know about. A few days before my trip, we return for a visit to the lab. A technician loads Selfie Susan with my neuro profile and any memories I've elected for her to carry. I give her everything except my passwords, my poetry, my first kiss, and Carlos. Some things are private.

"I'm going to wake her up now," the technician says. He has a coffee stain on his white lab coat. "They're a little disoriented when first activated. Do you want to meet her?"

I stare down at the steel lab table. I don't like my nose. I can't see if her eye color is exactly the same. But underneath the blue paper gown she's otherwise exactly me, and it's kind of creepy. What if she's smarter than I am, or funnier, or Dad likes her better? I decide to wait outside. Dad stays in the lab for fifteen minutes, talking to his temporary daughter, and when he comes out he's wearing a frown.

"You don't like her?" I ask. He shouldn't. I'm the real deal and she's going to be recycled at the end of his trip. But I panic a little at the thought he might not let me go visit Mom.

"She's fine," he says, pulling me in for a hug. "But you'll always be my favorite."

Dads are so sentimental. I pat his back. "I'll miss you, too."

The night before I leave, I'm too excited to sleep. I've memorized every step of the trip. Dad and I will take a bullet train to the nearest space elevator in New Mexico. I'll ride that to an orbital transfer station. A shuttle will take me and three hundred other passengers from the station to the moon. I'm going to be traveling with scientists, researchers, grad students, and families. The higher and farther I go, the more I'll see of our gorgeous spinning planet. Me, in space. Finally. I'm going to take a hundred thousand snaps.

Once I get to the moon, Mom and I will bond in a way we've never before. She'll grow to appreciate what a great daughter she has, and I'll learn how much she regrets putting her career ahead of everything. Or maybe not, because real life isn't like movies. I'm not expecting bittersweet epiphanies that lead to heartfelt declarations or anything. I'm not expecting much, really, except two weeks of low gravity and cool science and looking down at Earth hoping Dad's having a good time with my plastic twin.

And it all goes exactly to plan, really it does, until a micro-asteroid rips through the transfer shuttle's engine, breaches the passenger cabin, and sends us screaming into oblivion.

Dad's late picking me up from the selfie labs. He apologizes, but he doesn't look me in the eyes while speaking. He pockets the remote that can reboot me if my programs crash, signs the final rental agreement, and walks me to the autocar.

"I already sent the bags ahead," he says. "Susan packed your overnight bag."

"I'm Susan, Dad," I remind him. "Just riding around in a temporary package."

We climb inside the dark, air-conditioned car. He immediately pulls out his tablet to read his notes about the Belleview Hotel. "I'm still getting used to the idea."

I nudge his knee. "Keep that up and you'll hurt my feelings. When we synch, you'll hurt her feelings, too."

A very slight smile flicks over his face. "I can see you remember how to take guilt trips."

My other me has thoughtfully loaded a backpack with our spare tablet, some snacks, and some of our jewelry. The funny thing is that I know I'm a copy, and that she's technically the "authentic" Susan Ann Miller, but I don't feel fake. I poke my own arm. Plastic, but warm and soft. I flex a muscle. Okay, I've never been known for my upper arm strength, but it feels like a real muscle should. I zing Jessy.

She peers at me through the screen. "You don't look like a robot."

"I'm not a robot. I'm exactly Susan. The real deal in a plastic body."

"She said you'd say that. What about Carlos and the butterfly?"

"Who's Carlos?"

"See!" Jessy grins. "You're not exactly like you because you didn't tell yourself that Carlos is sort of your boyfriend."

I'm instantly indignant. "I have a boyfriend and I didn't tell myself?"

Dad raises an eyebrow. "You didn't share it with me, either. Let me talk to Jessy."

"Whooops," I say, and "accidentally" disconnect the call.

Luckily, there's no time, literally, to investigate the mystery of Carlos before we arrive at the timeport. It's a giant building by a lake with strict queues and multiple stations for security screening, insurance waivers, orientation briefs, more security, more waiting. Thousands of people make a lot of noise, and the wallvids play the same boring election stories over and over. I wish we could just pick a president and be done with it.

Finally, Dad and I reach the ramp into a long black-green tunnel. I've been through before and should be used to it, but it's creepy. It makes you feel like you're going uphill and downhill at the same time, and it's simultaneously cold and hot, and it seems like there's an invisible wind pushing you forward but also holding you back. Usually Dad and I walk through hand-in-hand. This time he hesitates, so I grab his hand and squeeze it.

"The first time we went through, I was so nervous you promised me a pony ride when we reached Coney Island," I say.

He nods. "Then you felt bad for the ponies, so we got ice cream soda instead. Our tradition."

"Don't think you can get out of that now. Selfies don't need food, but we like it anyway. I want chocolate scoops and chocolate syrup and seltzer that gets up my nose."

Dad smiles, and we go through the time tunnel together to visit the Belleview Hotel in 1899.

Dad's not supposed to pick me up from the selfie labs until noon, but he's early. He's jittering with excitement or too much caffeine or maybe nervousness about me being a robot and all, but I'm not really a robot. I'm Temporary Susan, and some subconscious programming keeps me happy with that. Nobody wants a selfie moping around in existential gloom.

As it turns out, Dad's unsettled for another entirely different reason. "I had a last-minute commission for a trip to the Hotel Del Coronado in California, 1918."

"I don't have clothes for 1918, Dad."

"I was up all night printing some out," he says. "You'll like it there. We might meet Charlie Chaplin."

I don't know who that is, but if Dad's excited about that, he'll be less worried about the whole selfie thing. I rummage through the backpack that Original Susan packed for me. She must have been in a hurry, because there's no tablet or comm device. I want to call my best friend Jessy and see if she can tell the difference between selfie and real thing.

"I grabbed the wrong bag," Dad says, apologetic. "Tell me how you feel. What's it like to be in an artificial body?"

We talk all the way to the timeport. Inside, the lines are as long as usual, but thankfully there's no news of the upcoming election. Maybe all of the stations have gotten tired of talking about it. Dad keeps me chatting. He's very interested in my experience, which is strange because he wasn't very thrilled before. He keeps staring intently at my face in a way that might be creepy if he weren't my Dad.

The time tunnel is long and dark, as eerie as I remember. Dad takes my hand and says, "I know your body just passes nutrients through, but when we arrive I think we should have ice cream sodas."

I squeeze his fingers. "Sounds like a deal."

1918 isn't too boring, mostly because there's a Hollywood movie crew filming around the hotel exterior and down on the beach. It's for a silent film. How people were ever able to enjoy silent movies is beyond me. The bad guy is played by someone named Rudolph Valentino, who will be famous eventually. He gets to run around in a bathing suit with bare legs while all the women have to wear soggy leggings. Otherwise the clothes are more comfortable than 1899, though not as easy or convenient as hanging out in the temperature-controlled moon habitat in shorts.

"Is that what you're going to remember most?" Dad asks on our way back to the labs, once we're back in the future. He's gazing out the window pensively. "The clothes?"

"No, the stars."

"Valentino?"

"The real stars, Dad." The best thing about our trips is when I can find the edge of land, stretch out flat with my arms over my head, and point my toes up into the glittering dome of the sky. All those stars, so bright and distant, their light traveling across time just for me. The universe is full of secrets waiting to be unraveled.

"Thank you for coming," Dad says when the technicians take me back. I'm not nervous about my impending annihilation. Another subroutine to thank. In what seems like only a few minutes, I'll be reintegrated into biological Susan.

"See you soon," I say, and climb up on my lab table.

• • •

Dad's very late picking me up. I'm afraid he's backed out of the whole deal and would rather go into the past alone than with some facsimile of his daughter, even though I feel like the genuine Susan. The friendly technician in a wrinkled lab coat assures me that's not true.

"He's more committed than you think, kid. Here, hold your remote for a minute while I check the calibration."

The remote is silver and rectangular, no heavier than a pebble. It's kind of weird to think about how it can reboot my brain if it crashes. I wonder what it's like to be rebooted—like dying and getting instantly reborn, or would I even notice? I ask the technician.

"There shouldn't be any gaps in awareness," he says. "Unless your owner double reboots, which puts you into safe mode. Able to walk and follow instructions, but not running your full profile."

"Like a zombie," I say.

"It's very rare," he says.

Finally Dad shows up breathless and harried. "Sorry, last-minute commission and change in plans. We're going to New Hampshire."

In the car he shows me pictures of our new destination. The Wentworth is the Grande Dame of the Sea, he says. I'm sure I'll be just as bored there as I would be at the Belleview, but I don't say so because I'm too busy being annoyed he forgot my tablet and comm.

"You don't need to call Jessy," he says. "How's it feel to have an artificial body?"

"It feels the same as a normal one."

"No differences at all?"

"I said it feels the same, Dad." I wish he'd stop trying to prove how different I am from his "real" daughter. I'm the only one he's got for the next two weeks, and I paid a lot to make this happen, so I don't need quizzing.

The timeport is full of people and noise and some blabbering on the wallvids about the presidential election. Dad keeps talking to me, so I can't be sure, but the candidates aren't familiar. What happened to the ones I've been seeing for months?

"Your mother sent some pictures," he says, showing me snaps of her and the "real" Susan up on the moon. They're in a lab together, posing with their heads propped on their hands, smiling. You can see our mother-daughter resemblance. "There's a couple dozen of them."

I scroll through the snaps as we inch forward in line. Mom and me in the chow hall. Mom and me walking in a lunar arboretum. I wonder who took the pictures. Something else is odd, too, but it takes me a moment to figure it out.

"Dad, look at my earrings," I say. "I'm wearing the same ones all the time."

He looks blank. "So?"

"I change them every day. See?" I flick the silver hoops I'll have to pull out at the final time border where we change into period clothes. We'll leave our modern clothes and most tech in secure lockers, ready for pick-up upon return. "I packed twelve pairs for the moon."

"Maybe you forgot them."

"I'd buy or borrow new ones," I tell him. "Why would Mom send fake pictures?"

Dad's distracted by a security screener moving down the line with questions that need answering. I thumb Mom's picture and put through a call.

She answers with, "Bob, you know how I feel—" and then stops when she sees me. The screen resolution is so fine that I can see her go pale despite the hundreds of thousands of kilometers between us.

"He promised you'd never call me," she says, her lips tight. "Get off the phone, selfie."

The hostility knocks me backward into Dad. When he sees what I've done, he reaches for the remote in his pocket.

White noise floods my head, followed by nothingness.

Dad picks me up from the selfie lab with a change of plans. We're headed for the east coast of Florida instead of the Gulf of Mexico. The resort is named Murray Hall and it's in Ruby Beach, outside of Jacksonville. Dad brought a note from Jessy for me. Her parents have dragged her off to one of those "techno free" resorts in Nepal for a month. She's going to go crazy without her comms, but no more crazy than I'll be in 1888.

Dad has another surprise. He paid for VIP access through the timeport. Shorter lines, faster screening, and no wallvids screaming out election stories.

By the time we reach Ruby Beach, I'm too beat to pay much attention. Selfies get tired like everyone else, although our reaction is driven by power levels and not biochemistry or physiology. Dad and I take adjoining rooms on the third floor facing the sea. The lack of air conditioning means I wake up with sunlight broiling my room. I flop around in the hot bedclothes like a fish yanked out of the ocean. It's cruel to take a modern teenager anywhere without air conditioning. I hope Moon Susan is happy with herself, up there having fun while I sweat my way through the nineteenth century.

Dad knocks on my door with, "Come on, get dressed and let's eat breakfast."

Food in 1888 isn't very good. People eat meat and greasy eggs and biscuits that don't even have chocolate on them. I watch Dad eat and pour extra sugar into my tea. The hotel manager stops by our table and thanks us for visiting. Murray Hall doesn't get many time travelers, although of course he hopes Dad's work will bring more.

"It'll be my pleasure to write about your fine establishment," Dad says.

It wouldn't be so much of a pleasure if he was the one stuck wearing a high collar, long skirts, and a ridiculously lacey camisole. I absolutely refused to bind myself into anything resembling a corset. Dad's probably not much more comfortable in the layers of his linen suit. Why couldn't he specialize in twenty-first-century cruise ship travel, instead?

"You should come with us," Dad says, after the manager offers a personal tour of the property.

I pick up my drawstring bag. "You do your thing, I'll do mine."

"Susan . . . " he says.

"Dad . . . " I mimic. "Go. Have fun."

I spend the morning drifting around the resort, taking snaps of jewelry and furniture. The border police don't let you bring communication devices into the past—too valuable, too prone to theft, the insurance claims are ridiculous—but simple flash tech is okay. After lunch I find myself a straw hat, a deck chair, and some shade. With me are the collected works of Mark Twain and a tall glass of genuine lemonade. The ocean's at low tide, the blue waves dotted by gulls plucking their lunch from the sand. Horse-drawn carriages pull the tourists up and down the shore.

By the time I'm done reading, the tide is back in and the horses are being returned to their stables. I need to go find Dad and declare that it's time for our traditional ice cream soda. Before I can leave, I realize I'm being watched by one of the locals, a boy my age. He has dark hair, dark eyes, and a big frown. He doesn't look comfortable in his white suit and hat, and can't seem to decide whether to come outside or keep lingering in the doorway.

"Do you need something?" I ask, figuring he's just a gawker who wants to see the time traveler's daughter.

He walks to my chair and stands over me. "Susan. It's Carlos. I rented this selfie."

I shade my eyes and blink up at him. "Carlos who?"

"She told me she didn't give you those memories but I thought maybe a little . . . " He tugs on his tie, as if it's too tight around his neck. "We go to school together. You, me, and Jessy share a science pod."

Okay, no one here knows about Jessy, so I guess he's legit. But I've never heard his name before. "Still nothing. Why would my original block you out?"

"Because we're more than classmates. More than friends."

My heart speeds up a little. "How do I know you're not lying?"

He sits on the edge of the chair and touches one of my hands. His fingers are soft and smooth. "You have a birthmark on your right leg, right behind your knee. And matching tattoos that we got before you left. See?"

Carefully he pulls up the sleeve of his summer jacket. A tiny blue butterfly is marked inside his wrist. I have a duplicate on my right hip, where Dad's never seen it.

Carlos says, "I can't stay long. I could only afford to rent this until midnight. But I miss you. I wanted to see you."

His voice has gone wistful. It's strange to think he feels something for me that I can't even remember. We must have a pretty strong relationship if he can't be apart from me for even a few days. I glow a little inside, metaphorically.

"I don't miss you," I tell him truthfully, because you can't miss someone you don't remember. "But maybe we can take a walk on the beach."

He smiles and offers me a hand up.

Strolling around dry sand isn't easy in Victorian high heels. I peel my shoes off and Carlos strings them over his shoulder for me. He recalls stories about Jessy that I've shared with him, and some complaints I've made about my parents. Apparently I write poetry, though I don't remember that, either. He says our first date was ice skating. Our first kiss was in the carport under my house, very quiet so that Dad couldn't hear. Dad thinks I shouldn't date until I'm thirty. Carlos wants to be a famous architect. He already knows that I plan on being an award-winning astrophysicist. On a blanket in the dunes, hidden from passers-by, we watch falling stars streak across the sky. His head rests easy on my plastic belly, and I run my plastic fingers through his curly plastic hair. Although we came from a factory, our bodies can feel warmth and softness and joy.

My other self can keep the moon. I'd rather have this.

"I can send you money for another rental," I say when it's time for him to go.

He belts his trousers and tucks in his shirt. In the starlight he looks lovely and tousled and very sad.

"Susan, how many trips have you gone on with your father?" he asks. "As a selfie, not as yourself."

I prop myself up on one elbow. "This is the first time. Because I'm visiting my mom, too. You know that."

He drops to his knees and cups my face with both hands. "You left for the moon four summers ago. I'm sorry. You didn't—there was an accident."

My ears fill with a buzzing noise that's louder than the ocean surf. "I'm dead?"

Carlos kisses me, but I don't kiss back. My lips feel numb.

"Ask your father," he says, and disappears over the dunes.

Clumsily I button my blouse. Over my head, the ancient constellations silently whirl on their carefully delineated paths. No moon yet. I walk back to the hotel with my hair unpinned in the salty breeze, my shoes forgotten, and if the locals are aghast that I dare walk through the lobby that way, I don't care. Nothing matters except for the truth.

Up in his room, scratching notes in a book by the light of a lamp, Dad looks up and says, "There you are—" before he realizes something's wrong.

"Is it true?" I ask shakily. "There was an accident?"

He puts aside his fountain pen and we stare at each other. A long minute passes, filled only by the tick of a clock on the mantelpiece.

Dad asks, "Who told you?"

"Does it matter? I'm dead!"

He rubs his head. "You're not dead. You suffered brain damage in the decompression and crash of your transfer shuttle. You're in a coma in Texas. Your body is being kept alive while we wait for new treatment options."

I don't know what to feel. Angry that he's been lying to me. Bewildered at why he couldn't just tell me. Unable to imagine my biological body in a hospital bed, living on without any kind of consciousness to move or control it.

"So what is this selfie, a toy?" I ask bitterly. "A plastic doll you take out of a tube every summer to play with?"

I don't remember sitting down, but I'm suddenly in a padded gold armchair. Dad comes to me and crouches down with sorrow written all over his face. He's so close I could hit him in the nose if I wanted to.

"You're not a toy," he says. "You're Susan. But your selfie brain has limited storage and the neural connections degrade after a few weeks of use. The technicians can't synch you to a living brain, so they put each trip's memories into long-term storage for later integration. Every summer I rent your unit and they reload the original neuro profile they have on file."

I shake his shoulders. "You can buy a better model, put me into something more permanent—"

"Your hospital bills are too high. The insurance money, your savings, my income—it's all tapped out. I sold the house. I work twenty hours a day to afford just this short trip every summer."

My voice is wobbly. "Mom can afford it."

"She can't," he says. "We're not rich, Susan. She already pays all she can. I'm sorry."

I stalk away from him to the balcony. Out over the ocean, the stars hang like strands of tiny white Christmas lights. But there will be no Christmas for me. No Thanksgiving or birthday or college, no career or Carlos or more butterfly tattoos.

"What happens to me the rest of the time?" I ask, my hands wrapped around the railing. "Don't tell me they just let this unit sit in a tube, unused. Do I work in a factory? Maybe I clean bathrooms. Maybe they rent me out for parties."

"It doesn't matter what the unit does," Dad replies. He sounds muffled and thick, and far away. "I get you and we get this. It's all I can offer you."

"It's not enough," I whisper. Saline tears drip down my face. They didn't mention tears in the selfie catalog, but apparently we can cry for ourselves and our families and for futures that will never be.

He comes up behind me and wraps his arms around my chest. "We won't stop looking for a cure. One day you'll wake up and I'll be right there beside you. You'll leave the hospital and resume your life and none of this will bother you."

On the horizon, far over the ocean, the thin crescent of the waning moon is rising. Silver and distant and empty. Somewhere nearby, Carlos has already passed through a time tunnel to a future where he and Jessy have graduated school and moved on with their lives.

"Don't make promises you can't keep, Dad," I tell him.

The silver remote flashes in his hand. "I'll never let you suffer."

I open my eyes. Everything is dim. Standing by my bed is Dad and a man in a white coat. This looks like a hospital. Or maybe a lab. I'm in a bed. Or maybe on a hard table. I'm wearing a paper gown and underneath it, on my hip, is a tiny itch like a rash or a scab or a recent tattoo. My body feels blazing hot and icy cold, my mouth full of sand, my head full of strange, disjointed thoughts.

"As I said," the man in the lab coat says. He's a doctor or a technician. "Disorientation is normal."

Dad bends close. He looks older than I remember, with silver sprinkled in his hair. "Susan, do you know who I am?"

Sure I do.

The more important question is, who am I? Real or selfie?

THE MANOR OF LOST TIME

RICHARD PARKS

—◆—

Let's get something straight right now—her name at the time, her proper name, was Driana. Not "The Enchantress Sorrowsbane" or "She Who Speaks in Fire" or any of the other garblings this story has apparently accumulated over the last thousand-odd years.

Yes, no doubt she was known by those names too. Most humans can't seem to avoid becoming something other than what they are, unlike the more sensible demon-kin. Yet it *was* the beginning you asked about, and at the start of it all she was a twiggy little redheaded bundle of trouble named Driana. I know. I was there.

My name is Sahel.

Yes, you got that wrong as well. Don't worry. Your conjuration was flawed, but at least you got the Barrier right. It will hold for a while. Lucky you. Hmmm? Oh, I just realized that someone wanted my attention, and I was curious. I'm not used to being summoned like a common variety demon. Frankly, I'm surprised that even a garbled version of my name is known in the world—I've tried to be more discreet than that. Oh, well.

So you want to know about Driana? The truth? On your head be it, then. I don't owe you anything, understand, but I do owe Driana at least that much. What I will tell you now is the truth.

You can trust me that far.

I first met Driana the year after the war between the Twelve Kingdoms and the western barbarians had ended. In the town of Kelan's Pass in Morushe, a hedge wizard named Ledanthos with delusions of talent was about to charm a love-amulet for one of his more romantic—and wealthier—customers when he finally noticed the witch-worm. There was barely an inch of it showing through a crack in the wattling near the floor, and if the one who'd placed it there had used a piece of wood other than freshly-peeled willow, he might not have noticed it at all. Yet he did notice, and that was that.

"Well well," he said. "It seems there is a thief about."

I'm not sure what memory has survived of Ledanthos. If justice were served, very little. He was a small man of small vision, yet I will give the miserly old coot his due—he knew opportunity when it arrived. A more self-important magician might have taken grave offense at the thought of someone tapping into his magic without permission and sent a fatal curse down the witch-worm to end the matter there and then. Not Ledanthos. He spoke charms of binding and summoning and sent those instead.

I'm not sure what he expected, but not half an hour later Driana appeared at his door. She was then as I have said: small, skinny, hair like a burning stack of hay and just about as neat. She wasn't frightened, as one might expect. She was furious. Her eyes were as wild as a trapped animal's. She clearly wanted to flee, but the charm that had brought her to Ledanthos's door held her fast. Even so, she would not enter the shop when bidden, and Ledanthos practically had to drag her in. This raised Ledanthos's annoyance and my curiosity.

Where was I, you ask?

Where I always was in those days: in the middle of Ledanthos's workbench, trapped, immobile. There was very little of interest in the old man's life that didn't take place in that room, so I missed nothing important.

"You must either pay me for the magic you have stolen, or I may collect in goods and services," Ledanthos said. "That is the law. This thing—" here he held up the now-broken pieces of the witch-worm "—is no more, but by my estimate has been in place nearly a week. You owe me seventy-four imperials."

Seventy-four gold coins. What complete rubbish. Ledanthos had never learned the true art of tapping power from the world around him. Much of Ledanthos's magic came from *me*; his own magic wasn't worth seventy-four imperials if stolen his entire life, never mind the minuscule fraction the girl had filched. Yet the law was on Ledanthos's side, and by the look of both the girl's clothes and the expression on her face, it might as well have been all the money in Creation.

"I see," said the old man. "Then you must work for me until the debt is paid. What is your name, girl? Who are your parents?"

"Driana," she said. "My parents were killed in the war."

That explained the ragged clothes and the obvious fact that she hadn't bathed recently. Driana's mother had been a witch of sorts on the western frontier and had taught the girl a little, but not how to gather her own magic. After the war Driana had moved eastward and survived on odd jobs and theft, including such crude tricks as the witch-worm to siphon off magical energy. Perhaps she would have been reduced to selling her body in another year or two but, judging from what I came to know of her later, I doubt that. More likely she'd have been hanged first. All this, of course, I learned after the fact. At our first encounter, other matters caught my attention.

She saw me.

By that I do not mean she saw what Ledanthos saw: a crudely hewn stone statue sitting in the middle of his workbench. And, by the way, when I say "crude," I mean it. The carving could have been anything from a demon to an underfed bear.

Ledanthos did not know about me, you see. He thought I was simply an object of magical power, which, you must admit, was more or less true. He siphoned that power in a similar fashion as Driana's witch-worm to use in his work, yet he only saw the statue form into which I was sealed. Driana saw *me*. I was certain of it, as she looked warily around Ledanthos's workshop. Her anger was gone and now she looked resigned, and nervous, but also very curious.

I could see her peering intently at the odd assortment of books, vessels, and bric-a-brac littering the shop as if she were trying to remember everything and sort out what it was for, what it did. When her gaze came to me she stopped, and she stared for so long that Ledanthos finally frowned.

"What are you looking at, girl?" he asked.

"That statue. It's very strange."

He grunted. "There is much strangeness in the world, girl; no sense getting caught up in it. So. Your first job is to clean up in here while I run some errands. Touch nothing that you do not understand, which should be almost everything except the charcoal bin and the rat droppings in the corner. Mainly sweep the floor and tidy up. If you do a good job I'll feed you when I get back. You needn't bother running away; my binding spell will only bring you back and you'll find a whip waiting. Do we understand one another?"

The mention of food finally got her attention off of me. "Yes . . . um, what should I call you?"

"Master, of course."

"Yes, Master," she said, as if the words had a poor taste to them. Her disgust wasn't lost on Ledanthos, who merely grinned.

"You want the merchandise, you pay the price. One way or another. The folly of thieves is that they believe this does not apply to them. I'll be back soon, so get busy."

Driana did so, though the only broom available had a cracked handle and moldy straw that, at least at first, left more debris than it removed. It was only when the room was somewhat more presentable that she put the broom aside and looked closely at me again.

"What are you?" she asked aloud.

Now, please bear in mind that this was a new thing. I had been trapped in what looked like a pitiful little statue for the better part of five hundred years, and in all that time no one, even those like Ledanthos who recognized the magic surrounding me, saw my prison for what it was. Driana did. She knew someone alive was trapped there, and she was curious. Frankly I was curious about her as well.

Driana glanced out the window by the door, but there was no sign of Ledanthos. She reached into a pouch on the ragged strip of leather she was using for a belt and pulled out another witch-worm. I could plainly see the faint glow of magic about it. Now, as you should suspect from your botching of my Summoning, in magic it's as much how you say a thing as what you say, and when Driana spoke the simple word 'Reveal,' it was better than an hour of Ledanthos's arcane incantations in three forgotten languages. Even the ones he actually got right.

In that instant the crude little statue which was both my home and prison stood unmasked as the portal that it really was; the one that, for five hundred years, I had been unable to cross. Driana's green eyes went wide in astonishment and wonder.

"By Sethis . . . "

Don't say that name.

I didn't really expect her to hear me, but that simple revealing spell had done far more than simply drop the veil from the statue. My tongue was unbound, and the true appearance of my prison—to the degree it had a true appearance—was uncovered. And all with no more than a bit of borrowed magic and simple intent. Even I was impressed—the urchin clearly had talent.

"Who are you?" she asked.

My name is Sahel. How did you recognize me?

"My mother's specialty was illusion. She was killed before she could teach me much, but the ability to recognize illusion was among her very first lessons. So what are you? Why are you serving this rag and trick wizard?"

I am demon-kin, and I serve Ledanthos for the same reason you do—I was caught. Though I will say in my defense that it was not Ledanthos who caught me.

She sniffed. "That bloody fool? I've been stealing his magic for months; he only caught me because I was beginning to think he was blind as well as stupid. I won't be so careless next time."

Why were you stealing magic in the first place?

She shrugged. "To live. I have no source of power of my own, nor yet the skills to make any. I used the stolen magic to charm small trinkets to sell, or to make a baker look one way while his fresh loaves were going another direction; that sort of thing. Simple tricks, though I always wondered how one like Ledanthos could command such a high level of power. Now I know. Does he?"

He knows only what he sees. His curiosity extends no further than that. Frankly, how he became a magician at all baffles me.

"Me, too, yet he is my master now," she said thoughtfully. "Perhaps I should tell him what he has in you."

I laughed then, for the first time in several centuries. *Perhaps we should just speak plainly to one another. You want something from me. I think perhaps I want something from you. Shall we discuss it?*

"I want many things," Driana said. "My freedom, for a start. What do you want, Sahel?"

Many things as well, but for now I simply want the same thing you do, as I believe you have already guessed. Ledanthos will be back shortly. I suggest you give the floor another pass with that miserable excuse for a broom if you want to eat tonight. We'll talk later.

'Later' proved to be several days away. Ledanthos was very busy at the time, and he kept Driana even busier. I will say in his favor that he fed her little worse than he fed himself—which was to say, miserly—and never actually beat her, though he threatened constantly.

Hmmm?

Ah, of course. I thought you might be wondering about that. The answer is 'no.' If the old miser had ever lusted for anything other than gold, such urges were long dried up by the time I knew him. Driana, like my own hidden self, was a servant to him and that was all.

Which was probably fortunate on his part—he might not have noticed the wicked-looking knife she kept concealed, but I certainly did. As for his binding spell, it was powerful enough thanks to me, but like all his work, it was somewhat shoddy. I have no doubt Driana could have broken free in time, with or without my help. Unlike Ledanthos, she had great natural skill and a desire to learn and understand more. I remember wondering at the time what she would be capable of if she lived long enough to master her art. I guess time and history have answered that, yes?

Let's see . . . oh, yes. Ledanthos got a summons from a surprisingly wealthy client. It seemed that the potency of his amulets and spells was becoming better known, and he would now get the chance to improve his standing with those who used the services of conjurors such as himself. I almost expected to sense visions of grander quarters and fine clothes about him, but then I remembered that this was Ledanthos, and the only 'visions' he had were of more gold that he did not spend, simply piled up higher, faster, and easier, but to no better effect. After all, a pig in a crown is still not a king.

Yes, I know. The expression was old even a thousand years ago. Pardon the digression. So Ledanthos got this summons and of course he had to answer it straight away. I think he considered taking Driana with him since he had gotten used to her help, but she was still wearing the same filthy rags she'd been captured in—I wager it had never occurred to Ledanthos that this was a problem—and there simply wasn't time to make her more presentable. As it was, Ledanthos' best robes looked more than a little threadbare as he left us alone once more and locked the door behind him.

Driana didn't even bother picking up the broom. "How long have you been trapped there, Sahel?" she asked without preamble.

Five hundred years, give or take a bit.

She nodded. "Very well, this is what I propose: I will help free you. In return you will not harm me, and you will serve me gladly for a term of forty years."

I almost laughed again. Forty years. To little Driana then it must have seemed like all the time in the world. She may have learned better, but never say she always *knew* better.

No, I said.

She blinked. "No . . . ? Do you want to stay in there forever?"

Hardly. But once I'm out of here I'm going to have my own business to attend to. I can't very well do so if I'm bound to you for another forty years. Why would I trade one prison for another?

She looked grim. "Forty years is nothing compared to five hundred," she pointed out. "And I don't have to help you. You could sit in there for another five hundred years!"

That is true. Now I want you to picture yourself in bondage to that miserable old coot for the same forty years you demanded of me. You know magic will extend his life more than that, even. I'll weight my time against yours and we'll see whose is the easier burden.

As I said, I was pretty certain that she could break his magical chains in much less time. She was less certain of that, and of herself. I used that, as I would any tool that suited my purpose.

Driana looked unhappy, but she wasn't going to give up so easily. "Twenty years," she said.

One year, I countered.

"Fifteen."

Five.

"Ten!"

Five.

She sighed deeply. "Seven?"

Must I repeat myself?

"Oh, very well. You will serve me for five years, and swear to bring me to no harm now or later. If you agree, then tell me how to free you."

Done. And freeing me is simple, if not easy—you have to find me.

She frowned. "I've already found you!"

Finding the river is not the same as finding the fish, as any decent fisherman could tell you. You'll have to cross the portal to where I am.

"Then won't I be as trapped as you are?"

Trapped? No. However, there is a danger that you can become lost. Yet this is the only way. I cannot come to you, so you must come to me.

"You're aware of my presence. Can't you simply guide me to you once I cross over?"

Yes . . . and no. You'll understand once you've crossed the portal.

If it sounds as if I'm being a little vague, that's no more than the truth. I was afraid Driana wouldn't make the attempt if she knew what was waiting for her on the other side. I'm not sure I would have in her place. I can only say in my defense that I did not know Driana quite so well then.

Her *reveal* spell was still working fine. In the place where my statue sat on Ledanthos's work table, there was a patch of darkness about five feet high and half again as wide. That was another illusion of sorts, but then normal dimensions of height and width don't really apply to this particular portal. In symbolic and practical terms, it was a doorway, and that was enough. Driana took one step off Ledanthos's work stool and passed through the opening.

I can tell you what she saw because it's what I saw, my first time here. The difference was that there was no portal behind me to return through. There's a trick to it, of course. As things were, Driana stood in what looked like a short hallway. Beyond that was another door.

"Where am I?" she asked.

There's a door in front of you, correct?

"Yes."

Open that door and you'll find out.

She did as I said. "By Sethis . . . " Her voice trailed off.

I did tell you about saying that name . . . oh, never mind. What do you see?

"My mother . . . my father. They're alive!"

I knew this was going to be a critical point. If Driana could not get past the first door, there was no chance she'd be able to find me. After coming this far, coming so close to freedom, I confess I was a little nervous, and I made a very serious mistake.

I lied.

It's just an illusion to distract you. Walk on to the next doorway.

"It's wrong," she said. I could tell that she hadn't moved a single step closer. "They're not the way I remember them."

I said it's an illusion. Keep moving.

"If it's an illusion, then why aren't they as I remember? Why do I see them this way?"

What way?

"Older. I'm older too. My father is smiling, my mother is crying. Do you know what my mother and I are doing, Sahel?"

No.

That at least was the truth. I could not see what she saw now; this was *her* lost time, not mine. I could not see her at all, now that she had crossed the doorway. The immediate surroundings of my prison I could see as clear as a cloudless morning. But the place itself? No more than the little in front of me, and for me there were no doors.

"We're in our home, the one that was burned to the ground the day they died. My mother and I are sewing my wedding dress."

It's a trap to snare you, to prevent you from moving forward. Nothing more. Ignore—

"Stop lying to me, Sahel! I told you I know illusion, and this is not an illusion! I'm not merely seeing this, I'm there! I'm myself and yet I am with them. I know what that girl sewing the dress is thinking, I know what she's *feeling.* I'm watching it all, yet the thread is in my hand and I feel the sting from the needle's point! If you don't tell me what this means right now, our bargain is ended. And I do know the way out."

She wasn't bluffing. I'd thought the lie might make things easier, but this was Driana I was dealing with, and let me confess frankly that I was only just then beginning to understand what that meant. I abandoned the lie.

I don't know the true name of this place, Driana, if it has one. I call it 'The Manor of Lost Time.' Humans and demon-kin alike generate a nearly infinite cache of lost possibility for every path not taken. This is the place where all the 'might have beens' reside. That is what you're experiencing now. The potential was there, but it was thwarted, for better or worse. What you're seeing and feeling now, and knowing now, did not happen. You're right—it's not an illusion, but it's also not real, and never can be real.

"I lost this the day my parents died," she said simply.

I nodded, forgetting for the moment that she could not see me. *Yes,* I said.

"What will I see next?"

I truly do not know, Driana. Perhaps something horrible, or something painful and sad, but also perhaps something wonderful, joyous. Whatever it may be, it is something you've lost forever. That's what is waiting behind every door. Fortunately, only a limited number of doors block your path to me, but I do not know exactly how many, or why the ones that appear are the ones that do appear. I'm trapped in a room of my own lost time, and I cannot see my door, or you. You'll have to cross your own lost time to reach me, and find the door I cannot see.

I'm not sure what I expected then. I halfway expected her to flee from both myself and Ledanthos, binding spell or no. But after a very long silence, I heard her voice again.

"Makan. I was going to marry Makan. I rather suspected that." Maybe it was my imagination, but I think there was a touch of relief echoed in her words.

He wasn't your choice?

"He was . . . Makan. A year older than I was. He was tall and strong and pig-headed, and he cheated at ring-toss. I liked him well enough when I didn't actually hate him. Yet when I'm sitting with my mother sewing my wedding dress, I love him more than anything. I've never been in love or lost a love, but I do know what both feel like, to love and lose in the exact same moment. Thanks to you, Sahel."

I'm sorry.

"No you're not, and you may go to blazes. But not until after you honor our bargain. I see the next door. I'll open it now," she said, and that's what she did.

I'm not going to tell you everything she saw behind every door. Partly because there are some she never spoke of, even to me, but mostly because it's beside the point. I told you the first because you need to understand what this was costing her. What it would cost *anyone*. How would you like to see your lost chances and potentials paraded in front of you, forced to live through every single one, the good and the bad, but all never to be? There are few humans who wouldn't be reduced to a blubbering mess within an hour's time.

Not Driana, though I'm honestly not certain how many more she could have taken before she finally walked into a bit of lost time that was not her own: an image of a celestial city and a street located just this side of what you might refer to as the Abode of the Gods.

Yes, it was mine.

For creatures with the lifespan of mayflies, relatively speaking, humans have quite a gift for focusing attention on the matter at hand, whatever it may be. It was only when she found my lost time that Driana stopped concentrating on the next door and paused to wonder just what the hell she'd gotten herself into. Fortunately for me.

"What are you, Sahel?"

Demon-kin. I told you that.

"This place belongs to no version of a hell *I've* ever heard of."

An expert on hells, are you?

"The truth, Sahel. For our bargain to work I need to know I can trust you. Tell me the truth. Who are you? How did you get here in the first place?"

Yes, she did finally ask me that. I do think it would have been wiser on her part if that question had been asked earlier, but I guess it was better the way things were. That's always a comfort to cling to, when dealing with lost time. I imagine there's a new room in the Manor now, of what would have happened had she asked those questions earlier. I will avoid it.

Again, yes, I'm going to tell you what I said, else nothing else that follows will make sense to you. And do remember—you asked.

Just over a year ago there was a war on the western border of this country, I said.

"I know, Sahel," Driana said grimly. "I was there."

Just over five hundred years ago, there was a war in the Abode of the Gods, and I was there.

"By Sethis—"

Stop saying the wretch's name. How many times must I repeat that?

"But . . . the demon-kin are far older than *that*," she said in protest. "And long-since banished to infernal planes of existence. Assuming there was such a thing, what business would it be of yours?"

I said I was demon-kin, and so I am. What are demons but gods who have lost their place in the heavens? What makes you think that one war ended all of them?

I knew she was thinking about it, though I still could not see her, nor even the lost time that she moved through now. My lost time. I think it would have been a nice touch if I'd been allowed to see and experience it rather than just knowing it was there. A bit of torture, perhaps. Only that the point had never been to torture me. Or any of us. Maybe Sethis thought that made everything all right.

"You're saying you were a god?!"

Not 'were,' Driana. 'Am.'

Excuse me, but if your mouth has fallen open in surprise, I do wish you'd close it. I find the thought very distracting. Ummm? Well, I advise you to get over your astonishment. There's more.

"But once you lost . . . " Driana began.

I know the rules, Driana. A new born demon, to seed to the Infernal Plane? There's just one problem with that assessment—I wasn't on the losing side.

"But . . . then why are you here?"

Because it was my charge to drive the last four rebels from the Abode of the Gods. Because as I was so doing, Sethis, Lord of the Heavens and Commander of Lightning, lost his divine nerve. He sealed the portal with all five of us inside. The loyal and the traitorous alike . . . Neither Heaven nor Hell; simply sealed away. Each of us in our separate houses of lost possibilities, until the end of time . . . which may come sooner than he thought . . .

You want to know what she said? She said what you're obviously thinking. That I was lying.

The thing is, as you may have noticed, I'm not a very good liar. It's not my nature, but Driana is very good at knowing a lie from the truth. So Driana said that she didn't believe me, but of course she did. Just as you do. I had to make sure she continued to believe me, so I continued to tell her the truth, just as I'm doing to you now.

You're standing within my sphere of lost time. I do not know what it shows you, but you know it is none of yours. Isn't that true?

The answer came softly. If it had been spoken with any less force even I would not have heard it.

"Yes."

You see the doorway that is hidden to me. Is that not also true?

Again the answer came, "Yes."

Know this, Driana—I will do as I have sworn. I will serve you in all things for a term of five years. You can train your magical skills with a god for a tutor. At the end of that time, I will take my leave of you and use my freedom to track down the four who were imprisoned at the same time I was. When I find them, I will set them free. Together we will storm the Abode of the Gods.

"But if you lose . . ."

I did not lose before, and I will not lose this time. Lord Sethis, if he is very lucky, will soon reside in a prison of his own lost time, and in his case I will not conceal the door but I will bar it against him, and he will contemplate what will never come to pass for the rest of eternity. I swear that this is so. Do you believe me?

"Yes, Sahel. I believe you."

You've heard my choice, Driana. Now make yours—open the door and free me, or return the way you came, to your master, Ledanthos. You'll likely be rid of him on your own, sooner or later.

Now then. You must admit that was a very silly question on your part. You know what Driana did, or this conversation would not be happening. You can well imagine Ledanthos's surprise when she emerged from nothing leading a being of light and fire like a little lost child. The shock killed him, which is a pity—I wanted to do it.

As for me, I'm not quite done with my plans. These things take time. Three of my brothers and sisters are free now. Soon we all will be.

Umm, no, I do not think you will be offering any prayers to Sethis. See, he still doesn't know. We wouldn't want to spoil the surprise, would we? No, no sense in squirming. You did ask. And no, I said your barrier would hold for a while. I think it lasted up until just before the part where Ledanthos left Driana and me alone for the second time. If you've got any more questions, I suggest you ask them now.

Am I responsible for Driana's final disappearance? I did not harm her, if that's what you mean. I swore not to, and I'm a being of my word. Besides, why should I? She's been a great help to me over the years. She found two of the other rebels on her own.

Loyalty to her god? What do you know of that? While it's true Driana swore by Sethis out of habit, in her heart she was furious with him, not the least for letting her parents die. Finding them again in the Manor of Lost Time only made that worse, I'm afraid. Gods often forgive humans, in the stories. There's no rule that says a human must forgive a god. Just between the two of us, I think she hates him more than I do.

Yes, that's right. Hates. There are many legends about Driana's death, and I assume that's why you asked that silly question. They're all nonsense, because she hasn't died. When time came to weigh on her too heavily, she merely returned to the Manor of Lost Time. She lives there now, and acts out her lost potentials. She's young when she chooses, old when she takes the whim. She marries that lout Makan or doesn't. She has borne children, fought demons, and even inherited Ledanthos's amulet business in one well-lost bit of possibility. But mostly I think she spends the lost time with her parents.

I think she regrets losing their potential most of all.

No, I said I will have no prayers, and I meant it. You won't need them since I'm not going to hurt you. I am, however, going to put you somewhere safe until all this is over. You may thank me later. You're going in the way I did, my first time, so you won't be able to find the door. If you have any more questions, you can put them to Driana directly. I'm sure you'll run into each other sooner or later.

By the way, she won't show you the way out, and if I were you I wouldn't try and force her. Even if she's not in the mood to call down lightning on your head, she still carries that knife of hers and the legends don't begin to do justice to her famous temper. But ask her politely and she might just show you where to find your own lost time.

Which starts now.

HOW TO GET BACK TO THE FOREST

SOFIA SAMATAR

———◆———

"You have to puke it up," said Cee. "You have to get down there and puke it up.
I mean down past where you can feel it, you know?"

She gestured earnestly at her chest. She had this old-fashioned cotton
nightgown on, lace collar brilliant under the bathroom lights. Above the
collar, her skin looked gray. Cee had bones like a bird. She was so beautiful.
She was completely beautiful and fucked. I mean everybody at camp was sort
of a mess, we were even supposed to be that way, at a *difficult stage,* but Cee
took it to another level. Herding us into the bathroom at night and asking
us to puke. "It's right here," she said, tapping the nightgown over her hollow
chest. "Where you've got less nerves in your esophagus. It's like wired into the
side, into the muscle. You have to puke really hard to get it."

"Did you ever get it out?" asked Max. She was sitting on one of the sinks.
She'd believe anything.

Cee nodded, solemn as a counselor. "Two years ago. They caught me and
gave me a new one. But it was beautiful while it was gone. I'm telling you it
was the best."

"Like how?" I said.

Cee stretched out her arms. "Like bliss. Like everything. Everything all at
once. You're raw, just a big raw nerve."

"That doesn't sound so great," said Elle.

"I know," said Cee, not annoyed but really agreeing, turning things around.
That was one of her talents.

"It sounds stupid," she nodded, "but that's because it's something we can't
imagine. We don't have the tools. Our bodies don't know how to calculate
what we're missing. You can't know till you get there. And at the same time,
it's where you came from. It's where you *started.*"

She raised her toothbrush. "So. Who's with me?"

• • •

Definitely not me. God, Cee. You were such an idiot.

Apparently, a girl named Puss had told her about the bug. And Cee, being Cee, was totally open to learning new things from a person who called herself Puss. Puss had puked out her own bug and was living on the streets. I guess she'd run away from camp, I don't really know. She was six feet tall, Cee said, with long red hair. The hair was dyed, which was weird, because if you're living on the streets, do you care about stuff like that? This kind of thing can keep me awake at night. I lie in bed, or rather I sit in the living room because Pete hates me tossing and turning, and I leave the room dark and open all the curtains, and I watch the lights of the city and think about this girl Puss getting red hair dye at the grocery store and doing her hair in the bathroom at the train station. Did she put newspapers down? And what if somebody came in and saw her?

Anyway, eventually Cee met Puss in the park, and Puss was clearly down-and-out and a hooker, but she looked cool and friendly, and Cee sat down beside her on the swings.

"You have to puke it up."

We'd only been at camp for about six weeks. It seemed like a long time, long enough to know everybody. Everything felt stretched out at camp, the days and the nights, and yet in the end it was over so fast, as soon as you could blink. Camp was on its own calendar—*a special time of life.* That was Jodi's phrase. She was our favorite counselor. She was greasy and enthusiastic, with a skinny little ponytail, only a year or two older than the seniors. *Camp is so special!* The thing with Jodi was, she believed every word she said. It made it really hard to make fun of her. That night, the night in the bathroom, she was asleep down the hall underneath her Mother Figure, which was a little stuffed dog with *Florida* on its chest.

"Come on!" said Cee. And she stuck her toothbrush down her throat, just like that. I think Max screamed. Cee didn't start puking right away. She had to give herself a few really good shoves with that toothbrush, while people said "Oh my God" and backed away and clutched one another and stared. Somebody said "Are you nuts?" Somebody else said something else, I might have said something, I don't know, everything was so white and bright in that moment, mirrors and fluorescent lights and Cee in that goddamn Victorian nightgown jabbing away with her toothbrush and sort of gagging. Every time I looked up I could see all of us in the mirror. And then it came. A splatter of puke all over the sink. Cee leaned over and braced herself. *Blam.* Elle said, "Oh my God, that is disgusting." Cee gasped. She was just getting started.

Elle was next. All of a sudden she spun around with her hands over her mouth and let go in the sink right next to Cee. *Splat.* I started laughing, but I already felt sort of dizzy and sick myself, and also scared, because I didn't want to throw up. Cee looked up from her own sink and nodded at Elle, encouraging her. She looked completely bizarre, her wide cheekbones, her big crown of natural hair, sort of a retro supermodel with a glistening mouth, her eyes full of excitement. I think she even said "Good job, Elle!"

Then she went to it with the toothbrush again. "We have to stop her!" said Katie, taking charge. "Max, go get Jodi!" But Max didn't make it. She jumped down from the third sink, but when she got halfway to the door she turned around and ran back to the sink and puked. Meanwhile Katie was dragging Cee away from the sink and trying to get the toothbrush, but also not wanting to touch it, and she kept going "Ew ew ew" and "*Help* me, you guys," and it was all so hilarious I sank down on the floor, absolutely crying with laughter. Five or six other girls, too. We just sort of looked at each other and screamed. It was mayhem. Katie dragged Cee into one of the stalls, I don't know why. Then Katie started groaning and let go of Cee and staggered into the stall beside her, and *sploosh,* there she went.

Bugs.

It's such a camp rumor. Camp is full of stories like that. People say the ice cream makes you sterile, the bathrooms are full of hidden cameras, there's fanged, flesh-eating kids in the lake, if you break into the office you can call your parents. Lots of kids break into the office. It's the most common camp offense. I never tried it, because I'm not stupid—of course you can't call your parents. How would you even get their number? And bugs—the idea of a bug planted under your skin, to track you or feed you drugs—that's another dumb story.

Except it's not, because I saw one.

The smell in the bathroom was terrible now—an animal smell, hot; it thrashed around and it had fur.

I knew I was going to be sick. I crawled to the closest place—the stall where Cee knelt—and grabbed hold of the toilet seat. Cee moved aside for me. Would you believe she was still hanging onto her toothbrush? I think we both threw up a couple of times. Then she made this awful sound, beyond anything, her whole body taut and straining, and something flew into the toilet with a splash.

I looked at her and there was blood all over her chin. I said, "Jesus, Cee."

I thought she was dying. She sat there coughing and shaking, her eyes full of tears and triumph. She was on top of the world. "Look!" she breathed. And I looked, and there in the bowl, half-hidden by puke and blood, lay an object made of metal.

It actually looked like a bug. Sharp blood-smeared legs.

"Shit!" I said. I flushed the toilet.

"Now you," said Cee, wiping her mouth on the back of her wrist.

"I can't."

"Tisha. Come on."

Cee, I couldn't, I really couldn't. I could be sick—in fact I felt sicker than ever—but I couldn't do it that hard. I remember the look in your eyes; you were so disappointed. You leaned and spat some blood into the toilet.

I whispered: "Don't tell anyone. Not even the other girls."

"Why not? We should all—"

"*No.* Just trust me."

I was already scared, so scared. I couldn't bear the idea of camp without you.

We barely slept that night. We had to take showers and clean the bathroom. Max cried the whole time, but for at least part of the night, I was laughing. Me and Katie flinging disinfectant powder everywhere. Katie was cool, always in sweatpants, didn't give a shit about anything.

"You know your friend is a headcase, right?" she said.

It was the first time anybody'd called Cee my friend. We got out the mop and lathered up the floor. Everyone slipped and swore at us, coming out of the showers. Cee went skidding by in a towel. "Whee!" she shrieked.

You cannot feel your bug. I've pressed so hard on my chest. I know.

"*I* could feel it," said Cee. "After they put it back in." It wasn't exactly a physical thing. She couldn't trace the shape of the bug inside her, but she could feel it *working.*

"Bug juice," she said, making a sour face. She could feel bug juice seeping into her body. Every time she was going to be angry or afraid, there'd be this warmth in her chest, a feeling of calm spreading deep inside.

"I only noticed it after I'd had the bug out for a couple of weeks."

"How did your parents know you needed a new one?"

"I didn't need one."

"How did they know it was gone?"

"Well, I kind of had this fit. I got mad at them and started throwing food."

We were sitting on my bed, under my Mother Figure, a lamp with a blue shade. The blue light brought out the stains on Cee's Victorian nightgown. We were both painting our toenails Cherry Pink, balancing the polish on my Life Skills textbook, taking turns with the brush.

"You should do it," Cee said. "I feel better. I'm so much better."

I thought how in a minute we'd have to study for our Life Skills quiz. I didn't think there was bug juice in my body. I couldn't feel anything.

"I'm so much better," Cee said again. Her hand was shaking.

Oh, Cee.

The weird thing is, I started writing this after Max came to visit me, and I thought I was going to write about Max. But then I started writing in your book. Why? This book you left me, your Mother Figure. You practically threw it at me: "Take it!" It was the worst thing you could do, to take somebody else's Parent Figure, especially the mom. Or maybe it was only us girls who cared so much about the moms. Maybe for the boys it was the dads. But anyway, taking one was the worst; you could basically expect the other kids to kill you. A kid got put in the hospital that way at a different camp—the one on the east side—but we all knew about it at our camp. They strung him up with electric wires. Whenever we told the story we ended by saying what *we* would have done to that kid, and it was always much worse.

But you threw this book at me, Cee, and what could I do? Jodi and Duncan were trying to grab your arms, and the ambulance was waiting for you downstairs. I caught the book clumsily, crumpling it. I looked at it later, and it was about half full of your writing. I think they're poems.

dank smells underground want to get back
no pill for it
i need you

I don't know, are they poems? If they are, I don't think they're very good. *A nap could be a door an abandoned car.* Does that even mean anything? *Eat my teeth.* I know them all by heart.

I picked up this book when Max left. I wrote: "You have to puke it up." All of a sudden I was writing about you. Surprising myself. I just kept going. Remembering camp, the weird sort of humid excitement there, the cafeteria louder than the sea. The shops—remember the shops? Lulu's was the best. We'd save up our allowance to go there. Down in the basement you could get used stuff for cheap. You got your leather jacket there. I got these red shoes with flowers on the toes. I loved those shoes so much! I wonder where they went? I wore them to every mixer, I was wearing them when I met Pete, probably with my white dress—another Lulu's purchase I don't have now.

It was summer, and the mixer had an island theme. The counselors had constructed this sort of deck overlooking the lake. God, they were so proud of it. They gave us green drinks with little umbrellas in them and played lazy, sighing music, and everyone danced, and Pete saw a shooting star, and we were holding hands, and you were gone forever and I forgot you.

I forgot you. Forgetting isn't so wrong. It's a Life Skill.

I don't remember what my parents looked like. A Parent Figure cannot be a photograph. It has to be a more neutral object. It's supposed to stand in for someone, but not too much. When we got to camp we were all supposed to bring our Parent Figures to dinner the first night. Everyone squeezed in at the cafeteria tables, trying to find space beside their dinner trays for their Figures, those calendars and catcher's mitts and scarves. I felt so stupid because my Mother Figure was a lamp and there was no place to plug it in. My Father Figure is a plaque that says *Always be yourself.*

Jodi came by, as the counselors were all going around "meeting the Parents," and she said, "Wow, Tisha, that's a *good* one."

I don't even know if I picked it out.

"We want you to have a fabulous time at camp!" Jodi cried. She was standing at the front with the other counselors: Paige and Veronica and Duncan—who we'd later call "Hunky Duncan"—and Eric and Carla and the others.

Of course they'd chosen Jodi to speak. Jodi was so perky.

She told us that we were beginning a special relationship with our Parent Figures. It was very important not to *fixate.* We shouldn't fixate on the Parent Figures, and we definitely shouldn't fixate on the counselors.

My stupid lamp. It was so fucking blue. Why would you bring something blue? "The most important people in your life are the other campers!" Jodi burbled. "These are the people you'll know for the rest of your life! Now, I want you to turn to the person next to you and say, *Hi, Neighbor!*"

Hi, Neighbor! And later, in the forest, Cee sang to the sky: *Fuck you, Neighbor!*

Camp was special. We were told that it was special. At camp you connected with people and with nature. There was no personal tech. That freaked a lot of people out at first. We were told that later we'd all be able to get online again, but we'd be adults, and our relationships would be in place, and we would have learned our Life Skills, and we'd be ready. But now was special: Now was the time of friends and of the earth.

Cee raised her hand: "What about earthquakes?"

"What?" said Veronica, who taught The Natural World. Veronica was from an older group of counselors; she had gray hair and leathery skin from taking kids on nature hikes and she was always stretching to show that you could be flexible when you were old.

"What about earthquakes?" Cee asked. "What about fires? Those are natural. What about hurricanes?"

Veronica smiled at us with her awesome white teeth, because you could have awesome white teeth when you were old, it was all a matter of taking care of yourself with the right Life Skills.

"What an interesting question, Celia!"

We were told that all of our questions were interesting. *There's no such thing as a stupid question!* The important thing was always to *participate.* We were told to participate in classes and hikes and shopping sprees and mixers. In History we learned that there used to be prejudice, but now there wasn't: It didn't matter where you came from or who you loved, *just join in!* That's why even the queer girls had to go to the mixers; you could take your girlfriend, but you had to go. Katie used to go in a tie and Elle would wear flowers. They rolled their eyes but they went anyway and danced and it was fun. Camp was so fun.

Cee raised her hand: "Why is it a compliment to tell somebody it doesn't matter who they are?"

We were told to find a hobby. There were a million choices and we tried them all: sports and crafts and art and music. There was so much to do. Every day there was some kind of program and then there were chores and then we had to study for class. No wonder we forgot stuff. We were told that forgetting was natural. Forgetting helped us survive, Jodi told us in Life Skills class, tears in her eyes. She cried as easily as Max. She was more like a kid sister than a counselor. Everybody wanted Jodi to be okay. "You'll always be reminded," she said in her hoarse, heroic voice. "You'll always have your Parent Figures. It's okay to be sad! But remember, you have each other now. It's the most special bond in the world."

Cee raised her hand: "What if we don't want us?"

Cee raised her hand, but of course she raised her hand. She was *Cee.* She was Cee, she'd always been Cee, do you see what I mean? I mean she was like that right from the day we arrived; she was brash, messy Cee *before* the night in the bathroom, before she supposedly puked out her bug. I couldn't see any difference. *I could not see any difference.* So of course I had second thoughts. I wished so bad I hadn't flushed the toilet. What if there wasn't anything in it? What if somebody'd dropped a piece of jewelry in there, some necklace or brooch and I thought it was a bug? That could have happened. Camp was so fun. Shaving my legs for the mixer. Wearing red shoes. We were all so lucky. Camp was the best thing ever. *Every Child at Camp!* That was the government slogan: *ECAC.* Cee used to make this gag face whenever she said it. *ECAC.* Ick. Sick.

She took me into the forest. It was a mixer. Everybody else was crowded around the picnic tables. The lake was flat and scummy and the sun was just going down, clouds of biting insects golden in the haze.

"Come on," Cee said, "let's get out of here."

We walked over the sodden sand into the weeds. A couple of the counselors watched us go: I saw Hunky Duncan look at us with his binoculars, but because we were just two girls they didn't care. It only mattered if you left the mixer with a boy. Then you had to stop at the Self-Care Stand for condoms and an injection, because *becoming a parent is a serious decision!* Duncan lowered his binoculars, and we stepped across the rocks and into the trees.

"This is cool!" Cee whispered.

I didn't really think it was cool—it was weird and sticky in there, and sort of dark, and the weeds kept tickling my legs—but I went farther because of Cee. It's hard to explain this thing she had: She was like an event just about to happen and you didn't want to miss it. I didn't want to, anyway. It was so dark we had to hold hands after a while. Cee walked in front of me, pushing branches out of the way, making loud crackling sounds, sometimes kicking to break through the bushes. Her laugh sounded close, like we were trapped in the basement at Lulu's. That's what it was like, like being trapped in this amazing place where everything was magically half-price. I was so excited and then horrified because suddenly I had to take a dump, there was no way I could hold it in.

"Wait a sec," I told Cee, too embarrassed to even tell her to go away. I crouched down and went and wiped myself on the leaves, and I'm sure Cee knew what was up but she took my hand again right after I was done. She took my disgusting hand. I felt like I wanted to die, and at the same time, I was floating. We kept going until we stumbled into a clearing in the woods. Stars above us in a perfect circle.

"*Woo-hooooo!*" Cee hollered. "Fuck you, Neighbor!"

She gave the stars the finger. The silhouette of her hand stood out against the bright. I gave the stars the finger, too. I was this shitty, disgusting kid with a lamp and a plaque for parents but I was there with Cee and the time was exactly now. It was like there was a beautiful starry place we'd never get into—didn't *deserve* to get into—but at the same time we were better than any brightness. Two sick girls underneath the stars.

Fuck you, Neighbor! It felt so great. If I could go anywhere I'd want to go there.

• • •

The counselors came for us after a while. A circle of them with big flashlights, talking in handsets. Jodi told us they'd been looking everywhere for us. "We were pretty worried about you girls!"

For the first time I didn't feel sorry for her; I felt like I wanted to kick her in the shins. Shit, I forgot about that until right now. I forget so much. I'm like a sieve. Sometimes I tell Pete I think I'm going senile. Like premature senile dementia. Last month I suggested we go to Clearview for our next vacation and he said, "Tish, you hate Clearview, don't you remember?"

It's true, I hated Clearview: The beach was okay, but at night there was nothing to do but drink. So we're going to go to the Palace Suites instead. At least you can gamble there.

Cee, I wonder about you still, so much—I wonder what happened to you and where you are. I wonder if you've ever tried to find me. It wouldn't be hard. If you linked to the register you'd know our graduating class ended up in Food Services. I'm in charge of inventory for a chain of grocery stores, Pete drives delivery, Katie stocks the shelves. The year before us, the graduates of our camp went into the army; the year after us they also went into the army; the year after that they went into communications technologies; the year after that I stopped paying attention. I stopped wondering what life would have been like if I'd graduated in a different year. We're okay. Me and Pete—we make it work, you know? He's sad because I don't want to have kids, but he hasn't brought it up for a couple of years. We do the usual stuff, hobbies and vacations. Work. Pete's into gardening. Once a week we have dinner with some of the gang. We keep our Parent Figures on the hall table, like everyone else. Sometimes I think about how if you'd graduated with us, you'd be doing some kind of job in Food Services too. That's weird, right?

But you didn't graduate with us. I guess you never graduated at all.

I've looked for you on the buses and in the streets. Wondering if I'd suddenly see you. God, I'd jump off the bus so quick, I wouldn't even wait for it to stop moving. I wouldn't care if I fell in the gutter. I remember your tense face, your nervous look, when you found out that we were going to have a check-up.

"I can't have a check-up," you said.

"Why not?" I asked.

"Because," you said, "because they'll see my bug is gone."

And I just—I don't know. I felt sort of embarrassed for you. I'd convinced myself the whole bug thing was a mistake, a hallucination. I looked down at my book, and when I looked up you were standing in the same place, with an alert look on your face, as if you were listening.

You looked at me and said: "I have to run."

It was the stupidest thing I'd ever heard. The whole camp was monitored practically up to the moon. There was no way to get outside.

But you tried. You left my room, and you went straight out your window and broke your ankle.

A week later, you were back. You were on crutches and you looked . . . wrecked. Destroyed. Somebody'd cut your hair, shaved it close to the scalp. Your eyes stood out, huge and shining.

"They put in a bug in me," you whispered.

And I just knew. I knew what you were going to do.

Max came to see me a few days ago. I've felt sick ever since. Max is the same, hunched and timid; you'd know her if you saw her. She sat in my living room and I gave her coffee and lemon cookies and she took one bite of a cookie and started crying.

Cee, we miss you, we really do.

Max told me she's pregnant. I said congratulations. I knew she and Evan have been wanting one for a while. She covered her eyes with her hands—she still bites her nails, one of them was bleeding—and she just cried.

"Hey, Max," I said, "it's okay."

I figured she was extra-emotional from hormones or whatever, or maybe she was thinking what a short time she'd have with her kid, now that kids start camp at eight years old.

"It's okay," I told her, even though I'd never have kids—I couldn't stand it.

They say it's easier on the kids, going to camp earlier. We—me and you and Max—we were the tail end of Generation Teen. Max's kid will belong to Generation Eight. It's supposed to be a happier generation, but I'm guessing it will be sort of like us. Like us, the kids of Generation Eight will be told they're sad, that they need their parents and that's why they have Parent Figures, so that they can always be reminded of what they've lost, so that they can remember they need what they have now.

I sat across the coffee table from Max, and she was crying and I wasn't hugging her because I don't really hug people anymore, not even Pete really, I'm sort of mean that way, it's just how I turned out, and Max said "Do you remember that night in the bathroom with Cee?"

Do I remember?

Her eyes were all swollen. She hiccupped. "I can't stop thinking about it. I'm scared." She said she had to send a report to her doctor every day on her phone. How was she feeling, had she vomited? Her morning sickness wasn't too bad, but she'd thrown up twice, and both times she had to go in for a check-up.

"So?" I said.

"So—they always put you to sleep, you know . . . "

"Yeah."

I just said "Yeah." Just sat there in front of her and said "Yeah." Like I was a rock. After a while I could tell she was feeling uncertain, and then she felt stupid. She picked up her stuff and blew her nose and went home. She left the tissues on the table, one of them spotted with blood from her bitten nail. I haven't really been sleeping since she left. I mean, I've always had trouble sleeping, but now it's a lot worse, especially since I started writing in your book. I just feel sick, Cee, I feel really sick. All those check-ups, so regular, everyone gets them, but you're definitely supposed to go in if you're feeling nauseous, if you've vomited, *it might be a superflu!* The world is full of viruses, *good health is everybody's business!* And yeah, they put you to sleep every time. Yeah. "They put a bug in me," you said. Camp was so fun. Jodi came to us, wringing her hands. "Cee has been having some problems, and it's up to all of us to look after her, girls! *Campers stick together!*" But we didn't stick together, did we? I woke up and you were shouting in the hall, and I ran out there and you were hopping on your good foot, your toothbrush in one hand, your Mother Figure notebook in the other, and I knew exactly what they'd caught you doing. How did they catch you? Were there really cameras in the bathroom? Jodi'd called Duncan, and that was how I knew how bad it was: Hunky Duncan in the girls' hallway, just outside the bathroom, wearing white shorts and a seriously pissed-off expression. He and Jodi were grabbing you and you were fighting them off. "Tisha," called Jodi, "it's okay, Cee's just sick, she's going to the hospital." You threw the notebook. "Take it!" you snarled. Those were your last words. Your last words to me. I never saw you again except in dreams. Yeah, I see you in dreams. I see you in your white lacy nightgown. Cee, I feel sick. At night I feel so sick, I walk around in circles. There's waves of sickness and waves of something else, something that calms me, something that's trying to make the sickness go away. Up and down it goes, and I'm just in it, just trying to stand it, and then I sleep again, and I dream you're beside me, we're leaning over the toilet, and down at the very bottom there's something like a clump of trees and two tiny girls are standing there giving us the finger. It's not where I came from, but it's where I *started.* I think of how bright it was in the bathroom that night, how some kind of loss swept through all of us, electric, and you'd started it, you'd started it by yourself, and we were with you in that hilarious and total rage of loss. Let's lose it. Let's lose everything. Camp wasn't fun. Camp was a fucking factory. I go out to the factory on Fridays to check my lists over coffee with Elle. The bus passes shattered buildings, stick people rooting around in the garbage. Three out of five graduating classes join the army. *Give me the serenity to accept the things I cannot change!* How did I even get here? I'd ask my mom if she wasn't a fucking lamp. Cee, I feel sick. I should just grab my keys, get some money, and run to Max's house, we should both be sick, everybody should lose it together. I shouldn't have told you not to tell the others. We all should have gone together. My fault. I dream I find you and Puss in a bathroom in the train station. There's blood everywhere, and you laugh and tell me it's hair dye. Cee, it's so bright it makes me sick. I have to go now. It's got to come out.

WINE

YOON HA LEE

The first attack came by starfall, by deathrise. Fire swept out of the darkness, past the great violet curve of the world of Nasteng, like coins from hell's treasuries. Worse than the fire was the metal: creatures of variable form and singing cilia, joining together into colonial masses that floated high above the moon's surface and dripped synthetic insects that ate geometer's traps into its substance.

For decades Nasteng had escaped the notice of the galaxy's wider culture. This was as its Council of Five preferred. They had a secret that other human civilizations would covet. So they hid behind masks of coral and dangling tassels and quantum jewels, and admitted only traders from the most discreet mercantile societies. Now, their secret had gotten out in spite of their precautions.

Nasteng's city-domes were ruptured. The gardens with their flower-chorales of tuned crickets went up in smoke and blood and gouges. Spybirds swooped down with eyes glaring out of their feathers and marked targets for the bomber-drones. People were dragged by the insects into agony-circles, their hair fused together and lit on fire, inelegant torches.

The Council of Five had known that such a day would arrive. For the moment they were safe in their subterranean fastness. But their safety could not last forever. They knew that they could not negotiate with their immediate attackers. The colonial masses did not think in words, did not recognize *negotiation* or *compromise*. They understood only heuristic target recognition and ballistic calculations. If Nasteng had had more technologically advanced defenses, it might have been able to infect the attackers and subvert their programming, but its long isolation and cultural diffidence toward the algorithmic disciplines precluded any such possibility.

One item Nasteng did possess was a beacon. The Falcon Councilor had obtained it generations ago. Her souvenir of that quest was a gash across her cheek that wept tears that dried into crystals hooking into her flesh. At regular intervals she had to rip her face off and allow a new one to grow, or she would have been smothered. You would have thought that she would want as little to do with the beacon as possible. But no: when the Council of Five gathered around a table set with platters of raw meat and the Wine of Blossoms that was their particular privilege, the Falcon Councilor insisted on being the one to activate the beacon.

The beacon was no larger than a child's fist, and was shaped like a ball. Light sheened across it as though it had swallowed furnaces. If you held it to your ear, you could hear a distant music, as of broken glass and glockenspiels hung upside-down and sixteenth notes played upon the spokes of decrepit bicycle wheels.

The Falcon Councilor lifted the beacon, then turned it over. It clung to her palm, pulsing like an unhealthy nacrescence.

"I don't see any point in delay," the Snowcat Councilor said. It wasn't so much that he was always impatient, although he was, as that he had never gotten along with her.

"We have to be sure of what we're doing," the Falcon Councilor said. "There's no way to rescind the signal once sent."

"Falcon," the Tree Councilor said in their voice like shifting rock and gravel. "We wouldn't be here if we weren't sure. Surely you don't think it would be better to die without attempting anything?"

"No, of course not," the Falcon Councilor said.

"Then do whatever it is that you do with that thing," the Snake Councilor said from the dark corner where she was flipping through a book. The book's pages were empty, although some of them had been dog-eared.

The last councilor, the Dragon Councilor, said nothing, only watched with eyes like etched metal. But then, he never spoke, although sometimes he condescended to vote. They were never tempted to disregard him, however. He was, after all, the head of the Gardeners.

"All right," the Falcon Councilor said. She flung the beacon toward the floor. It sheared through the air with a whistle almost too high-pitched to be heard and shattered against the floor.

The beacon's shards could be counted, yet they hurt the eye. They were more like collections of brittle dust than splinters or solids. As the councilors watched, the shards reassembled themselves. Where there had been a single sphere, there were now two. Then both spheres dissipated in a vapor that smelled of antifreeze and disintegrating circuit boards.

"I hope that's not toxic," the Snowcat Councilor said, narrowing his eyes at the Falcon Councilor.

Whatever response she might have thrown back at him was interrupted by the formation of two doors right above the beacon—beacons?—in a jigsaw of fissures.

"Well," the Snake Councilor said softly, "I hope we have enough wine to offer our guests. Assuming they imbibe." The others ignored her, on the chance that she wasn't joking.

Their guests numbered two. They didn't so much step through the doors as emerge like cutouts suddenly fleshed.

The first was a woman, tall, with the finest of veils over her face. She wore soft robes with bruise-colored shadows, and her cloak was edged with dark feathers. The Snake Councilor glanced at the Falcon Councilor, but the latter's face was an unreadable labyrinth of refractions. The other guest was a man, neatly shaven. His hair was black, his eyes of indeterminate color.

The Falcon Councilor inclined her head to them. "We are grateful for your promptness," she said. "We are Nasteng's Council of Five, and the nature of our emergency should be clear to you."

"Yes," the woman said. The man bowed, but did not speak. There was something forced about the curve of his mouth, as though the lips had been sutured together. "You may call me Ahrep-na. I have a great deal of experience with situations like yours. I assume you're familiar with my past successes, but if you need—"

"We know," the Falcon Councilor said. She had heard the name of Ahrep-na, although it was not safe to use it until she had given you permission. It was why she had left Nasteng all those years ago, in search of Ahrep-na's token.

"In that case," Ahrep-na said, "we will need to discuss the contract. My methods are particular."

The Falcon Councilor thought wryly of Nasteng's high generals, some of whom were rather more useful than others. Most of whom were rather less. One of the dangers of having its officers drawn almost exclusively from the nobility, or from people who bought their commissions. "That won't be an issue," she said. Behind her, she heard a harrumph from the Snowcat Councilor, but he didn't interrupt otherwise.

They spoke some more about operational and logistical details, about courtesies blunt and banal, and circled eventually to the matter of payment. Given Ahrep-na's bluntness about everything else, her diffidence about this matter puzzled the Falcon Councilor. But bring it up she did. "Our contracts are tailored to the individual situation," Ahrep-na said. "Up-front, we require—" She named a sum. It was staggering, but so was annihilation.

Finance was not the Falcon Councilor's domain. The Snake Councilor turned to a page in her empty book, frowned at a column of figures that wasn't there, and said, "It will be done in two days."

Ahrep-na's smile was pleased. "We will also require the fruits of a year's harvest."

"You'll have to be more specific," the Falcon Councilor said, as though this were a tedious back-and-forth about supply depots and ammunition.

Ahrep-na wasn't fooled. "This point is nonnegotiable." She offered no elaboration.

The Falcon Councilor opened her mouth. Prompted by some nuance of sound behind her, however, she turned without saying what had come to her mind. *Harvest.* The councilors' secret that was no secret to the outside world anymore: the wine that kept them young.

The other four councilors faced her, united. She had just been outvoted: irregular, but she had no illusions about what they had done behind her back.

"Falcon," the Tree Councilor said, in their unmovable voice, "we are short of options. Our people burn in the streets. Without them, we too will fall. Accept their offer. We knew we were not negotiating from a position of strength."

"We'll regret this," she said bitterly.

"Anything can be survived," the Snowcat Councilor said, "so long as one is still alive to survive it. You're the second-oldest of us. Are you going to fold up and die so easily? Especially since you're the one who brought us the beacon in the first place?"

"It was that or have no last resort at all," she shot back. "Or did you think we would stand a chance against people slavering after the wine?" She looked over her shoulder at Ahrep-na. "Let me ask this, then, Ahrep-na. Are you going to take the Wine of Blossoms for yourself?"

"That is the one of the two guarantees I will offer you," Ahrep-na said easily. "I will not touch your supply of the wine, nor will the soldiers I will raise for you. Or did you think I was human enough to have any use for it?"

The Falcon Councilor was accustomed to envy, or submission, or greed. It had been a long time since she had seen contempt.

"You said two guarantees," she said. "What is the other?"

Ahrep-na's eyes were sweet with malice. The nameless man stared straight ahead. "I will win this for you," Ahrep-na said, "with the mercenaries I raise."

"Of course you will," the Falcon Councilor said, wondering what the trap was. "Very well. We will contract you under those terms."

Ahrep-na's smile was like a honed knife.

His name was Loi Ruharn, and he was one of the councilors' generals. Most people knew him, however, as the Falcon's Whore.

He had been born Korhosh Ruharn, in one of the poorest quarters of the impoverished city-dome known ironically as the Jewel of Nasteng. As a girlform child, Ruharn had played with toys scavenged from stinking trash heaps in alleys, and watched with pinched eyes while his parents argued over which of the religious offerings they had to neglect this month because otherwise they would be too hungry to work, and swore he would never grow up to live in a crowded home with six brothers and sisters, wondering every night if he would be sold to the Gardeners like the daughter of the Ohn family next door.

As soon as he was old enough and strong enough, Ruharn ran away and enlisted in a noble household's private army. He might have died there. While the Council of Five ruled Nasteng entire, they didn't interfere with the nobles' squabbles so long as they didn't threaten the councilors themselves. But Ruharn acquitted himself well in battle, mostly through a combination of suicidal determination and a knack for small-unit tactics, and he rose quickly in the ranks.

That by itself wouldn't have made him remarkable. There were plenty of talented soldiers, and most of them died young anyway, the way battle luck went. Rather, he came to the Falcon Councilor's attention as a minor novelty, as a womanform soldier who lived as a man. For all her years, she'd never taken such a lover before.

The Falcon Councilor wouldn't stoop to take a common-born lover, but that was easy enough to finesse. She offered riches; she offered to buy Ruharn a commission in the Council's own army, and an adoption into a noble family; and most of all she offered a place in her bed. Ruharn wasn't sentimental about the honor of his chosen profession, although he knew what people would be saying about him. He accepted.

Today, almost six months since the invasion had begun, he was pacing in the command bower of the councilors' fastness. It was decorated with vines from which cloudflowers grew. The vines watered themselves, a neat trick. Irritatingly, they also left puddles, which you'd think he'd know to step around by now. The last time he'd yanked off a table runner and used it to soak up the moisture, he'd been yelled at by General Iyuden, who was insufferable about ornamental items. But Iyuden came from one of Nasteng's oldest, wealthiest families. He wasn't about to have that argument with her.

Arrayed before Ruharn were videoscreens of Nasteng's defenses. It didn't take any kind of experience to see how inadequate they had been. He had read the reports and made his recommendations. It wasn't so much that the senior generals had disagreed as that no recommendation would have made much of a difference.

He didn't know what had happened in the four days since the gateway fastness of Istefnis, on the surface, had been crushed into crumbs of marble and metal and human motes by the invaders. But the mercenaries the councilors had hired had brought with them a fleet of starflyers, a horde of groundswarmers. Nasteng's unnamed enemies had slowly fallen back before the onslaught of hellspikes and icemetal bursts and frenzied gnawers. You could, if you were sufficiently innocent of electromagnetic signatures and spectral flourishes, take it for a particularly disorganized fireworks display. Nasteng itself was now haloed by a staggering murdercloud of debris, whether glowing, glimmering, or gyring dark. It was just as well they weren't putting satellites into orbit anytime soon.

Two things bothered Ruharn about the mercenaries' forces, for all their successes. (More than two. But he had to start somewhere.) First was the question of logistics. The senior general had let drop that the contract had mentioned logistical arrangements. As a staff general, Ruharn had hoped to learn details. Had looked, in fact. So far as he could tell, however, the starflyers and groundswarmers had appeared out of nowhere. It wasn't inconceivable that this was advanced foreign technology—there seemed to be a lot of that going around—but it still made him suspicious.

The other thing was the way the mercenaries fought. When the Falcon Councilor had told him about the arrangement—the private conversation, not the staff meeting where he'd heard the official version—she had indicated every faith in the mercenaries' abilities. So far, Ruharn observed that the mercenaries relied on sheer numbers, wave after wave of suffocation rather than strategy. To be sure, the method was *working,* yet he couldn't help feeling the councilors could have spent their coin more wisely.

The councilors' personal army was used primarily for quashing the nobles' personal armies and secondarily for quashing the occasional revolution. So he didn't have great confidence in his conclusions. Yet it was impossible to serve with any diligence without picking up a few fundamentals of the military art.

As it turned out, he was turning the problem over in his mind—it wasn't as if he had a hell of a lot else to do, since for the first time in his so-called career he was caught up on paperwork—when a message made him forget it completely. He found it on top of his correspondence for the afternoon, smuggled in by who knew what method, a note on the back of a flyer. It said, simply, *I need your help.*

Ruharn would have dismissed it as a prank or a trap, except he recognized the handwriting, even twenty-three years later, for all the changes. The writer still had that particular way of drawing crossbars, of slanting hooks. He assumed she still lived in the same house, or at least the same neighborhood, or she would have said something more to guide him.

It wasn't difficult to slip out of the fastness and to the surface, in one of the bubblecars whose use was reserved to the councilors' favorites. The old neighborhood was some six hours away, to the north and east of Istefnis. Ruharn expected to be discovered eventually, but as long as he wasn't caught cheating on the Falcon Councilor, he didn't think there would be any lasting consequences. Assuming he didn't lose his life to some mine while walking down the street, or break his neck tripping over rubble.

The bubblecar's driver was a prim woman in the Falcon Councilor's livery. When she glanced back at Ruharn, her eyes were momentarily sly. Ruharn didn't notice.

During the ride, he alternated between looking out the window and looking at the status displays, which were connected to the moon's defense systems. He wore the plainest clothes he owned, which weren't very, a severe coat over a suit of soft dark brown with gold-embroidered gingko leaves, neatly fitted trousers, and boots likewise embellished with gold. In the neighborhood where he had grown up, the boots alone would have gotten him robbed, which was why he came armed. Two guns and a knife, the latter being ceremonial, but he kept it sharp on principle. Given his childhood, he was actually better in a knife fight than with handguns.

In the neighborhood where he had grown up, you would also have had one hell of a time finding a fence capable of dealing with items so fine, but that didn't mean no one was stupid enough to try. Maybe his uniform would have been a better idea, except he didn't want to give anyone the notion that he was there on official business.

He hadn't been back in twenty-three years, since he had run away, although from time to time he sent money home. No one from his family had ever acknowledged the payments. He hadn't expected them to; would, in fact, have been obscurely humiliated to hear from them.

The bubblecar wound through streets choked by devastation. Devastation was not new to Ruharn. He had grown up with decaying walls and the debris of blown-away hopes. Nor was he a stranger to battlefield ruin: red dried to blots brown-black, lungs sloughed into gray slime, stinging dust in the air. Even so, dry as his eyes were, the pitted streets and pitiful crumpled corpses were somehow different when they were dead at strangers' hands.

"Here we are," the driver said. She didn't bother to hide her skepticism.

"Thank you," Ruharn said distantly. He put on a filter, then stepped out. The bubblecar didn't wait to accelerate away. Sensible woman.

His memory was still good, despite the damage that had been done. Undoubtedly some of it had been local warfare, not recent either. He made his way through the streets, not too fast and not too slow, pricklingly aware that the few survivors were watching him.

The house had changed a little. Ruharn was certain that the old wind chimes had been decorated by little clay flowers. The new ones had what might charitably be described as rotund four-legged animals (what kind was impossible to say). He couldn't, however, discount the possibility that it was the same set of chimes with different decorations. The girl he had known had always liked chimes. He stepped up to the door—if this was an ambush, so be it—and knocked. "Merenne," he called out. "I'm here. It's Ruharn."

For long moments he thought that the house was chewed up and empty inside, that he'd wasted the trip. Then a voice barely familiar, scratchy with hardship, called back, "I'm coming." Soon enough the door opened.

"Merenne," Ruharn said again, voice unsteady. He did not bow. She would have taken offense.

Merenne was shorter than he was, and her hair had gone gray. She looked fifteen years older than he was. In fact she was his younger by six. The clothes she wore were neatly stitched, and patched besides. The shirt was livened by embroidery, mostly geometrical motifs. Ruharn remembered how assiduously they had both picked apart old handkerchiefs and wrapping cloths to scavenge brightly colored thread for the purpose. She had smiled easily then, as a girl, despite the fact that her shoulders were already growing hunched with the work she had to do. He doubted she smiled easily now. She had been his favorite sister, for whom he had saved pittances to trade for candies, whom he had soothed to sleep with bloodthirsty stories (even then he had had an interest in weapons), and he had left her behind without so much as saying goodbye because staying was unbearable.

"I didn't think you'd come," she said, as simple and sharp as a mirror-break. And: "I thought something of your old voice would remain. But I wouldn't have known it was you at all. Come in."

Ruharn's mouth twisted. He hadn't thought about his voice, now a tenor, for years. But he stepped through the threshold. The place was too quiet. Where was everyone? Not that he had so much as known that Merenne herself was still alive. For all he knew, some plague had killed them all years ago.

"I almost didn't come," he said. "But I did. Say what you have to say."

Merenne didn't respond, but instead led him through the house. It didn't take long. The Falcon Councilor would have considered it barely adequate as a closet. Ruharn had always been amused by her misconceptions about how many people you could squeeze into shelter if you really had to.

There were three rooms, and people would all have slept together in the largest, partly for warmth, partly for community. The first thing that caught Ruharn's eye was the dolls: two of them, one-third scale. They had been covered neatly by cloths. He wondered if some absent child had left them that way, tucking them in for the night.

The dolls he had grown up playing with had had brass tacks for eyes that were forever falling out. ("Poison gas rots out their eyes in battle," he had said to wide-eyed little Merenne, long ago. It had been funnier then.) The dolls here were made of some smooth, lambent resin, and their eyes shone like sea-lenses over delicately sculpted noses and lips painted perfect dusky pink. Their hair had been carefully styled, with miniature enameled clasps holding the strands in place. He had seen less beautiful statuettes in the councilors' homes.

"Go on," Merenne said. "Look." As he bent to lift one of the cloths, she added, "You used to have a grand-nephew and a grand-niece."

Ruharn didn't ask what if they had been her own grandchildren, or those of their siblings. Or what had happened to their siblings, for that matter.

Beneath the cloth the doll was naked, and he thought of the crude paper dresses that he had sometimes pinned together for Merenne, back when she had had dolls of her own, colored with markers he had stolen from a store. The doll was shaped like a preadolescent boy, but at the join of its legs was a mass that resembled spent bullets melted partly into each other.

In the doll's hand was a toy gun. (At least, he hoped it was a toy.) He eased the gun out of the doll's grip. "A credible Zehnjer 52-3," he said without thinking, "other than the fact that they did the cartridge upside-down."

He became aware that Merenne was staring at him. "You'd think," she said, "I had all this time to get used to the idea of you as a soldier."

Well, it was better than the other things she could be calling him. "You didn't call me here to identify this toy," he said.

"No," Merenne said quietly. "I called you here because the children have been disappearing. I woke in the night and they were gone. The dolls were left as you see them."

"Kidnappers?" Ruharn said dubiously. Poor people's children were terrible currency if you weren't a Gardener. He knew how noisy they got, adorable as they could be. To say nothing of the messes, and the fact that you wouldn't get any decent ransom for them.

Her mouth half-lifted in a ghost of the smile he remembered, as though she knew what he was thinking. Then the smile died. "Ru," she said, "I asked around. No one's seen a Gardener since the children started to vanish."

He said, because he needed to know, "Has payment been left for anyone?" Because it wasn't inconceivable, even in the midst of the crisis, that the councilors would upgrade their system of harvest. So to speak.

Everyone knew how much you could expect for a whole child in the desirable age range, in reasonable health. Even now Ruharn knew. The payment had changed over the years, but it was impossible not to remain aware.

For years he had taken the system for granted, the way everyone had. Part of the bargain, horrible as it was, was that the families who sold their children received something in return. Admittedly the dolls weren't *nothing*, but he doubted that you could sell them for the equivalent sums. Even if it wouldn't surprise him if someone had started collecting the ghoulish things; there were always such people in the world.

"As if people would tell me?" Merenne said. "But no. I haven't heard so much as a rumor. And I looked for payment"—she said this without shame—"but I saw nothing, because it was one of the first things I thought of. Maybe it's a stupid thing to care about, when our world might not survive. But I have to know what happened to them. And you're the only person I could think to ask."

"I know where to start," Ruharn said carefully. "I can't guarantee any results, though. Most especially, I doubt I can bring the children back." Understatement, since he did think the councilors were involved, the way they were involved with everything of note. He had few illusions about his ability to influence any of them, least of all the one who had taken him for a lover.

"I didn't expect that," she said. "Just find out what you can. So that we know what to expect." Her mouth trembled for a moment, so briefly that he almost thought he had imagined it.

Ruharn wondered what to say next. Everything seemed inadequate. At last he said, "Sometime after this is over, if I ever see you again, tell me their names." He didn't mention death-offerings. The deaths of children, especially small children, were so unremarkable that few people bothered.

Merenne eyed him thoughtfully. "I'll think about it," she said.

He smiled. He had always liked her honesty. After all, it wasn't as if she owed him anything. "All right," he said. "Let me take one of the dolls."

"Take both," Merenne said, with commendable steadiness. "It's not as if they do me any good."

He gathered them up under one arm. Considered resting his free hand on her shoulder, then decided that he had better not. This time he did bow, although he spun on his heel before he could see the expression that crossed her face, and walked out of the house. She didn't follow him or call out a farewell.

The Falcon Councilor did not greet Ruharn when he returned to the underground fastness. One of the servants did, however, present him a note upon paper-of-petals. It instructed him to attend her that night.

First he took the precaution of wrapping up the dolls and putting them in a case that he bullied out of Supply. The supply officer looked at him oddly, but he gave no explanation. It wasn't as if he owed one.

Ruharn reported next to the generals' bower, and stood at attention in the doorway. General Khy sat at a table with her feet on a chair, playing cards with her aide. She was a woman once handsome, but still dangerous, with hair shaved short and a conspicuous blank expanse where her medals should have been; she declined to wear them even on occasions of state. As one of the senior generals, she had taken Nasteng's impotence hard. She and her cards were always here, and even now, as her aide contemplated options, Khy brought up a map to study the latest intelligence.

A quartet of cards burned for additional points sobbed prettily as they crumpled into ashes. Ruharn wished Khy wouldn't use that particular feature, but Khy was entertained by the oddest things. Besides, she was one of the generals who understood strategy, so he preferred not to pick fights with her, on the grounds that she was more important than he was.

Khy liked Ruharn, a fact that he tried not to think too hard about. She waved her hand at him while assiduously keeping the cards' faces out of her aide's view. "General Loi," she said genially. "At ease."

It took a moment for him to recognize the house name he used now. Funny how long it had been since he'd lapsed. "General," Ruharn said. "Any interesting developments?" He doubted it: Khy would hardly be tormenting her cards if something that required her attention were going on.

She sneered, which took him by surprise because she ordinarily approached everything with cockeyed levity. "Look," she said, and flung her cards down. Her aide kept them from fluttering off the edge of the table.

Khy's hands tapped rapid patterns on the nearest interface. Maps flowered, crisscrossed by troop vectors and dotted by the bright double-squares of bases, the cluster-clouds of aerospace fighters. Nasteng's forces were violet. The enemy was green. The mercenaries were gold. Her hands tapped again. The troops moved as their positions and engagements were replayed over time.

"We might as well retire now," Khy said. "Oh, maybe not you, you're young yet, and there's always a use for good staffers." From anyone else it would have been a veiled insult, but Khy had never treated Ruharn as anything but a competent colleague and Ruharn was not so paranoid as to believe that things were different now. "But look, the mercenaries are doing all the work."

"That doesn't mean there won't be more attacks, now that the outsiders know we're here," Ruharn said. And, when Khy didn't respond, he hesitated, then said: "The mercenaries fight with numbers. But they don't fight *well*."

"You're one of the people who can see it, let alone who is willing to *say* it," Khy said bitterly. She flipped a pointer out of her belt, caught it, switched it on. Scribbled indications, in light and hissing sparks, on the maps. "There, there, there, *there*. Victory by attrition. So *wasteful*."

"I understand there's a noninterference clause," Ruharn said neutrally.

"Noninterference, hell. I've had the scanners on it and they can't even tell what our allies *are*. They come from nowhere and the corpses of their units degenerate with astonishing rapidity. There's probably a paper in it for some scientist somewhere."

Khy brought up more photos and videos. At first Ruharn didn't recognize what he was seeing, too busy being distracted by fractal damage, stress marks, metal sheening red-orange in response to unhealthy radiations. Familiar shapes.

Except those weren't the only familiar shapes. Burnt into the wreckage were symbols he remembered from his childhood. The depressions of board games he had played in the dirt, or score-tallies chalked onto walls, or warding-signs around which he and his friends had danced in circles, chanting rhymes to keep the Gardeners away. He glanced sideways at Khy, wondering, but she met his eyes with no sign that she saw anything in the faint symbols at all.

Then again, Khy would have grown up playing board games with real boards, made of marble or jade or mahogany veneer. If she played in the dirt, it would have been in a high-walled, well-tended garden while watched by anxious servants and the occasional guard. And she would never have had to worry about being sold to the Gardeners.

Still, it was dismaying to have one of the generals he respected confirm his observations. "Is there something you wish me to do, sir?" he asked carefully. For a mad moment he wished the answer was yes.

Khy only sighed and eased herself back down into the chair, swung her feet up again. "If only," she said. "You go on, Loi. Your next shift here isn't for hours anyway, isn't it? Enjoy yourself."

Ruharn saluted and passed out of the bower. He headed next to his quarters, where he opened the case and unwrapped the dolls. "You'd better not be bombs," he told them. They didn't answer, which didn't make him feel better.

Dealing with bombs wasn't one of his skills, but if the dolls were what remained of the stolen children, that wasn't relevant. Besides, even if they were bombs, they were probably advanced foreigner bombs, and the fastness's scanners had failed to pick up on them when he brought them in.

The two dolls were nearly identical. Prodding one revealed that the hair was a wig, and beneath it the top of the skull came off. The head was hollow. The eyes, half-domes with luminous irises, were held in place by putty. Systematically, he took apart the rest of the doll. The doll was jointed, and elastic ran through channels in the body and limbs so that it could be posed.

As for the slag of bullets, they appeared to be real metal, not resin. He prodded them and jerked his hand back involuntarily. They were the exact temperature of his own skin. Feeling like a squeamish six-year-old, he pressed his fingertips against the resin just above the slag. The surface was cool; significantly cooler, in fact.

Logistical necessities, Ruharn thought, staring down at the dolls. Then he wrapped them back up, laid them carefully in the case, and put the case under his bed. Stupid hiding place, but it wasn't as if he had a better one. And anyway, the real hiding place was where he had kept it all these years, the pitted lump he had for a heart.

At the appointed time, Ruharn went to the Falcon Councilor's chambers. He did not wear his uniform. Lately she liked him to wear what the courtiers did, necklaces of twisted gold and fitted coats with their undulating lace, dark red brocades. He obliged her; he understood his function. The guards with their falcon insignia acknowledged him merely with nods, making no comment.

The councilor stood looking at a tapestry-of-labyrinths when he stopped just short of entering, the way she liked him to. "Madam," he said. In the very early days she had liked it when he knelt. Her mood varied, however, and he didn't care one way or another. If pride had been important to him, he wouldn't be here.

"Come in," she said in the clear sweet voice whose inflections he knew so well.

Ruharn came up behind her and undid, one-handed, the clasps and knots and chains that held her veil in place. She had told him once that she only wore it here; everywhere else it was the familiar falcon mask. Ruharn found it telling, although he did not say so, that the fastenings were more elaborate than the veil itself. He was no pauper, but a bolt of the fabric, with its infinitesimally shimmering threads and texture like moondrift silk, would have beggared him. He always had the disquieting feeling that his fingerprints would sully the fibers, leave scars deep as trenches and hideous as gangrene. But he didn't say that either.

"Your hands are cold," she murmured.

It always took him a while to undo all the fastenings. "Sorry," Ruharn said mildly, "but you didn't like my last pair of gloves and it's not as if I've had time to go shopping."

She didn't call him on the lie, and he bent to kiss the back of her head, inhaling the fragrance of her hair.

The veil fell away, drifting through the air like a feather, or a fall of light, or a flower's breath. Ruharn always felt ridiculous whisking it away to lay it on the councilor's dresser without folding it, but she had never complained. He lifted her hair, which was hooked through with crystal—it was getting near the time where she would have to tear off her face again—taking care not to tug the dark coils. Unhurriedly, he pressed his lips to the back of her neck, once, twice. Again. Her perfume smelled of dried roses and wood-of-pyres. Inhaling it made his heartbeat quicken. Reportedly she wore it only for her lovers.

"Tell me," he said right into her ear, "is it true what's been happening to the children lately?"

He wanted her to tell him the truth, however familiar; however horrible. If she told him the truth, he would accept his complicity and forget Merenne again. He had been doing exactly that for all these years, after all. Surely he had earned a little truth in exchange for the years they had spent together.

The councilor's laugh came more as a vibration against his chest than a sound, and her voice was teasing. "You'll have to be more specific than that, my dear. Are we talking about schools, or orphanages, or some incident involving crawfish-racing?" (Naheng's crawfish were surprisingly large and fast, or this game would have been less popular than it was.)

Ruharn heard the lie and was surprised by the force of his own rage. He brought his hands up and down and around. She cried out as she landed against the wall, hard, breath slammed out of her, her arm bent close to breaking in his grip. "Are the mercenaries harvesting the children now, or is it still you?" He added, "It's been a long time since I did hand-to-hand. I could still get the mechanics wrong. So think about your answer."

"Why does it matter to you?"

He broke her arm. She screamed.

No one came. She hadn't triggered an alarm, and the guards were used to noise.

"Madam," he said, very formally. She went very still, very quiet. "Answer the question."

"We haven't sent out the Gardeners since the mercenaries came," the Falcon Councilor said raggedly. "It's their doing this time around." And, in a different voice entirely: "I had always hoped you might hesitate a little before doing—this."

"Neither one of us has ever been under the illusion that this relationship was about love," Ruharn said. "Did the mercenaries say outright that they would be recruiting the children?"

"They didn't say, but we knew."

"Is it too late to send them away?"

"We've paid," she said. "They will give us what we paid for. Don't you think we considered that people powerful enough to save us would also be powerful enough to plunder us? To wreck our way of life? But it was either submit to our destruction or choose the chance of salvation."

Ruharn thought for a moment. "All right. Take me to the Garden."

The councilor's laugh was ugly. "It always comes down to this. It took you longer than most, at least. What, are you concerned that the mercenaries will destroy the supply before you get your chance at youth unending?"

Let her think what she wanted. "Madam," he said, "you have a lot of bones and breaking them all would take time I don't have. I would speak you fair, but I'm done with niceties. The Garden."

"You picked one hell of a time to stage a coup, lover," the Falcon Councilor said in a voice like winter stabbing.

Is that what you think this is? Ridiculous that he wanted her to believe better of him, yet there it was. "Shut up," he said evenly. She was silent after that. It had been a long time since he had been anything but deferential to her, except in bed when she required otherwise.

It was a long way to the Garden. Ruharn expected her to call for help after all, or try to escape. But she kept looking at him, her eyes pierced through with pain, and she did neither. Sometimes she drew in a breath that might have become a sob; but then she controlled herself. He tried not to think about what he'd done to her.

The Garden, when it opened up before them in a staggering splendor of chokingly humid air and pearlescent lights, was choked with children, newborn to ten or eleven years old. It was impossible to tell how many there were, or how big the Garden was. They were sprawled every which way, a spill of limbs and crooked necks and lolling heads, and from them grew red pulsating vines, and from the vines shone red murmuring fruits. Perhaps it would have been less overwhelming if the children had been neatly organized, stacked by height or size in rows. Probably not.

In spite of himself, Ruharn looked among the faces for some echo of Merenne's features. Some echo of his own. It was impossible to tell amid the red tangles.

"The raw liquor is effective," the Falcon Councilor said after giving him just enough time to confront the sight, "if that's what you're thinking, but painful. Dragon is the only one who imbibes it in that form, and Dragon is a little peculiar. I'm surprised you didn't just have me take you to the wine cellars."

"No," Ruharn said. "This is what I want."

"The other councilors won't stand for this, you know."

"They won't have to."

She still didn't understand. "When they come after you—" Tellingly, she didn't say *we*: he was almost certain it was deliberate.

"Forget that, this is *damage control*," Ruharn said savagely, resisting the temptation to hit her. Stupid, considering he had already broken her arm and threatened systematic torture. "You made a bargain you only half-understood and you sent children to die in the most wasteful way possible, without even the leadership of someone like General Khy so they'd have a chance. The mercenaries aren't providing any sort of generalship themselves and I trust you weren't assuming that a bunch of children that age were going to spontaneously turn up any convenient tactical geniuses to do the job."

"This is rich," the councilor retorted, "from someone who turned his back on those same children during all the years they were bought as fodder for the Garden. Or did you manage to lie to yourself about what wine it is I drink when I'm not in your arms?"

He flinched. "Oh yes," he said, "I would rather be fucking you than dealing with this. I'm not unaware of what I am." The red silken sheets, her fragrant skin, the coils of glossy hair. The marks her mouth of living crystal left on his skin. "But apparently even I have limits."

Ruharn removed his ceremonial knife and laid it on the floor. Then he stripped, aware of her staring even though his body was no secret to either of them. He picked up the knife again, squared his shoulders, and waded into the Garden.

For all the useless ornamentation on the knife's hilt and sheath, its blade was just fine. He had no intention of wasting further time plucking fruit or squeezing it into his mouth. Instead, he cut directly into a handful of vines and brought them, spurting livid red, up to his mouth.

She was right. It burned going down, and burned his skin too, not like fire (he knew something of fire) but like hopes crushed down to singularity nights. But he swallowed, and swallowed, and swallowed, even as he choked; even as the red fluid dribbled down his chin and soaked his clothes. When the spray slowed, he grabbed blindly and cut again, and again, and again.

"Ruharn!" the Falcon Councilor cried out behind him. "Ruharn, you have to stop, it's *too much*—"

Good to know that she wasn't interested in that particular perversion. At least with him. He kept drinking, unable to see although his eyes were wide open, so nauseated he couldn't even throw up. Finally he dropped the knife and sank to his knees, coughing out an ugly pink-tinged spray.

After a while he became aware of her hand on his shoulder. Her touch, too, burned with the sticky-slick traces of the fluid. He shivered. Her hand felt large, and he felt thin, small, vulnerable in a way that hadn't been true for years. He looked down, not at his own hands, but at his thighs and their scars, not all of which had been received in battle. Looked up. She was taller now, larger.

"Ruharn," she said in a wretched voice. "You look—I never imagine you'd ever looked so innocent. Except your eyes."

"Childhood isn't about innocence," Ruharn said, both cynically amused at the way she cringed at how high his voice was now, and hating the sound of it himself. "It's about being *powerless*."

She didn't contest the point.

"Your mercenary company," Ruharn said. "You must have a way of contacting them still. Tell them to take me next." He assumed it would be the fastest way, instead of wandering around in some city waiting for them to find him. "If children are the coin they desire."

"You're even more crazed than I thought you were if you think I'll do that."

Hell of a time for her to get maternal. "I'm not Khy," Ruharn said. "I didn't go to the nobles' battle schools, or to the collegium for strategists. But I know more than those children do. Because that's who the mercenaries are, aren't they? Our children, transformed. *Let me go*." He shook off her hand and rose to his feet.

The Falcon Councilor rose as well. "You have no guarantee that you'll be anything more than a drone while you're up there as—as whatever you become," she said.

"Doesn't matter," he said. "If there's a chance I can do some good, I have to take it."

"Fine," she said, distant, formal. "You have my gratitude, General."

She drew out two bright-and-dark balls, no larger than Ruharn's fists, and whispered into them. He couldn't hear the words. Then she set them down, dry-eyed, and stepped back. A door ruptured the air above the balls.

You won't feel grateful for long, Ruharn thought. But he bent his head to her, and went.

In five months and twenty-four days, the mercenaries reclaimed sixty-three percent of Nasteng.

In the fifteen days after General Loi Ruharn vanished, the invaders were repulsed entirely.

General Khy's attempts to tally the mercenaries' losses in both phases of the campaign, as opposed to the enemies' losses, were blocked.

Merenne watched for Gardeners in all the years that followed, but never saw any. She made toys for her next grandchildren; there were a few. No dolls.

The final attack came not from the invaders, who were driven off in a scythe-surge of explosions, but from the newly-coordinated starflyers and groundswarmers. Their original task done, they needled toward the Garden and crashed into it, raising a pillar of fire and monstrous ash.

The councilors, who were in the midst of a victory celebration, had nothing left to fight with. Then, as their forces failed them, they fled one by one, except the Falcon Councilor. She and General Khy stayed in the command bower to the last, playing cards.

The Garden's protections were sundered. It lay with its ruined red-black mass of vines and charred, sunken skeletons like a sore jabbed open over and over. Nothing would ever grow there again.

Deep in the mass were two broken beacons and two collapsed mannequins, their uniforms fused to their skin. One was a woman, its face candle-melted entirely away. The other was a man, probably; hard to tell, given the damage. But the sutures holding its mouth shut from the inside had torn open, and it was smiling.

EVERY HILL ENDS WITH SKY

ROBERT REED

A fine old farmhouse used to stand on the hilltop, but today nothing remains except a cavernous basement and the splintered, water-soaked ground floor.

The hideout is nearly invisible from below.

People are living underground—five adults and two starving, unnaturally quiet babies. The group's youngest woman is in charge. Nobody remembers the moment when she claimed the role, but she rules her tiny nation without fuss and very few doubts. The others will do whatever she wants, and more importantly, they will do nothing when she demands nothing—resisting sleep and ignoring pain, and never raiding their rations, for days if necessary. And most impressively, they will deny their own terrors, prepared to hide forever inside this one miserable place, defending their lives by remaining quiet and still.

Outside, morning brings a little less darkness but no end to the deep winter cold, and with the faint sunlight comes the possibility of monsters.

This is the history of the human species: Scared animals clinging to one darkness, while the greater blackness rules all there is.

The Crypsis Project was an international response to a simple, irrefutable observation. Life on Earth was closely related. Every bacteria and jellyfish, oak and Baptist, shared one genetic alphabet. A few amino bricks built bodies immersed in salted water, and the base metabolism had been tweaked and elaborated upon but never forgotten. Life might take myriad forms throughout the universe, but a single flavor of biology ruled this planet. Perhaps one lucky cell evolved first, conquering the Earth before anything else had its chance to emerge. But what about neighboring worlds? Venus once wore an ocean. Mars was fertile in its youth. Asteroids plowed up each of those crusts, spreading debris and vagrant bacteria across the solar system. In those circumstances, every bacterium was a potential pioneer, and that didn't include any bugs living on wet moons and large comets of the outer solar system, plus the hypothetical rain of panspermian spores and viruses and lost bones and fully equipped alien starships that could well have passed through the young solar system. Surely some silent invasion would have left behind a prolific, deeply alien residue.

By rights, there should have be ten or twenty or even a thousand distinct creations, and some portion of those successes must have survived.

Crypsis chased that simple, delicious notion. Novel creatures were within arm's reach. They lived under the ocean floor or inside geyser throats, or maybe they thrived beneath that otherwise ordinary stone in the garden. Unless the beasts were everywhere, eating unusual foods, excreting unexpected shit. Biologists were experts, but only in the narrowest of fields. How could they recognize the strangers riding the wind?

Armed with speculations and a dose of grant money, the Crypsis team was assembled—biologists and chemists and other researchers trying to find what might well be everywhere.

No miracle bugs were discovered that first year. But then again, nobody expected easy work.

The false positive during the third year made headlines. The other world news was considerably less fun, what with sudden wars and slower tragedies. But here was a happy week where humanity convinced itself that an alien biosphere was living in salt domes kilometers beneath Louisiana.

Except in the end, those odd bugs proved to be everybody's cousin.

After six years, most of the original scientists had retired or gone elsewhere, fighting to resuscitate their careers.

But the purge freed up niches for fresh colonists, including one Brazilian graduate student. More a software guru more than a biologist, the woman was nonetheless versed in natural selection, and she had a fearless interest in all kinds of connected specialties, like mathematics and cybernetics and fantastical fictions. And after a week spent reviewing everyone else's empty results, the newcomer decided on an entirely different test.

She resurrected the solar system inside a null-heart computer, putting things where they stood four billion years ago. Here was the newborn Earth and an authentic Mars, the most likely Venus and the rest of marquee characters, along with many more asteroids than existed today. Her model was unique, but not in large, overwrought ways. The worlds were laced with small assumptions that she never intended to defend. This was her game, she assumed. This was meant to be easy grant money while she pushed ahead with her doctorate. And because this wasn't her primary job, she let the scenario play out more than once, never hunting for the bugs, watching nothing work out as intended, and every time with the same ludicrous results.

There was a husband in the picture, an aeronautical engineer who kept hoping for a child or two, if their lives went well enough. He wasn't the most observant beast when it came to emotions, but one night, glancing at his wife, he realized that he had never seen that expression before. Was she scared? Was she angry? Maybe work was a problem, but he feared some kind of trouble with their little family.

"What is so wrong?" he whispered.

"Nothing," she said.

She never was much of a liar.

The young man tried waiting her out, and he tried coaxing. Neither strategy worked well. Only when she was ready did his wife explain, "These simulations keeping giving odd results, the same results, and they want me to fix my mistakes."

"Who wants to fix this?"

"Crypsis does."

"Oh," he said. "This is your planet game."

She often called it a game, but now she bristled at the cavalier label. "Yes. That's what I'm talking about. The four-billion year model."

"All right, darling," he said, attempting to project calmness.

"Mars," she said. "I always guessed Mars would be the problem. It's small and cools early, so you have to assume that its lifeforms would gain early toeholds everywhere."

The wise course was to say nothing, which is what he did.

She continued, saying, "I've always encouraged Earth and Mars and Venus to produce multiple lifeforms. Dozens, even hundreds of discrete biologies would emerge when the crusts cooled and water condensed. Each biology would align to local chemistries and temperatures. And on every world, everything eats the alien neighbors as well as every tasty cousin. The only winners are metabolically isolated, and only then if there was ample space and a long timeline."

The husband considered touching her hand. She had beautiful hands.

But she pulled away as soon as he tried.

"Two billion years," she said, "and everything looks fabulously reasonable." She folded the hand in her lap. "My model does offer a reason why we won't find homemade biologies on the Earth. Our DNA and amino acids are too efficient, too invasive. Our metabolisms have adapted to every available niche, which doesn't leave enough room for others."

"Like in hot springs," he said.

"No, our ancestors were born in the scalding places," she told him. "For them, adapting meant getting accustomed to cold temperatures, eating everything else down to supercooled saltwater."

"That's at two billion years?"

"Yes." A distracted nod. "And then the scenario turns bat-shit bizarre."

Her husband's days were spent building rockets inside computers. He was very comfortable talking about models and their limitations.

Aiming to be helpful, he said, "Perhaps you had too many variables."

Her mouth tightened.

Sensing trouble, he reminded her, "I am trying to help you."

"I know."

"What kind of collapse is it?"

"There isn't any collapse."

"After two billion years, I mean."

"I said. The scenario doesn't collapse."

"Oh?"

"It remains stable all the way to the Present," she said.

"How many runs have you made?"

He imagined five. Five highly complicated simulations seemed like a healthy sampling.

But she said, "Nineteen. And the twentieth is running now."

Quietly, with feeling, the engineer said, "Wow."

There were many reasons to be emotional. But her temper abandoned her. She shrank a little, humility tempering her voice as her shoulders slumped, as she confessed to him, "Each time, there is the same nonsense."

Tweaks might fix five bad runs. But nineteen was a brutal number.

It took courage to ask, "What exactly goes wrong?"

"Venus."

"Venus?"

"Venus is ridiculous," she said.

"Ridiculous," he repeated.

"For starters, the planet is smaller and quicker to cool. That's why its ocean forms two hundred million years before Earth's ocean does. But Venus has more sunlight and more warmth everywhere, and according to my simulation, regardless what kind of life takes hold, evolution is quick and fierce."

There was talk about a Brazilian probe to Venus. That wasn't his department, but he rather liked the subject.

"That doesn't sound unreasonable," he said. "Venus gets life, but then it becomes an oven . . . when? One billion years ago, wasn't it?"

"Or earlier," she said. "Or maybe life survived another couple hundred million years. But that's the general timeline. And do you know what? Life still might still be surviving there. The Soviet Venera probes found bacteria-sized bodies at the altitude where earth pressures and temperatures reign. Of course there isn't much water left, just sulfuric acid. And that's one reason why Crypsis has been chasing Venusians in acid baths across our world."

The idea sounded familiar, or maybe he wanted to think so.

"People assume that Venus dies before life gets complicated," she said. "But in my nineteen simulations, without exception, Venus gets its free oxygen early on. Plus there's the added sunlight, the hotter climate. Photosynthesis brings an explosion of multicellular life. Our sister world could have been rich, probably for a billion years, right up until the sun grew too hot and shoved it over the brink."

Her husband made another bid for the hand.

She let him take it.

Encouraged, he said, "That is fascinating."

She squeezed his fingers. "The Earth has enjoyed a little more than half a billion years of evolution. Venus had a billion years. And in my scenario, without exception, the Venusians have plenty of time to leap into space."

"Leap how?"

She tugged at his ring finger, bringing pain. "With rockets. Rockets like yours. You see, that's one of my basic assumptions. Where everybody else hunts for microbes, I invite intelligence and high technologies. But I already told you about that. Remember?"

"How long ago?" he asked.

"It was a couple months back," she snapped. "We were at dinner with your colleagues—"

"No," he interrupted. "I'm asking when does Venus launch its rockets."

"One billion, three hundred million years ago."

"Okay," he said guardedly.

"Venusians explore the solar system. Nineteen simulations, nineteen different organic lines in charge. But always the same result. In less than a thousand years, they launch their ships and build computers before reaching some kind of Singularity event. After that, they migrate into deep space, and their world dies, and all that happens before the first trilobite scampers over the floor of our cold sea."

Trying to sound sympathetic, he says, "Well, I can see your problem."

She pinched the back of his hand.

He flinched but refused to let go.

"No, you don't," she said. "You don't understand."

"Explain it to me," he muttered.

"My model doesn't collapse," she said, and with a tug, she retrieved her hand. "It doesn't collapse because it's strong, and it's strong because it sits somewhere close to the truth."

She was crying and not crying, and she was sad as well as elated.

Quietly, guardedly, he said, "You're right. I don't understand."

"Crypsis is looking at this problem backwards," she said.

He blinked, not daring to talk.

"We are the novelties," she said.

Then her head dipped and her hands covered her face as she added, "You and I are the cryptic bugs, and we're hiding under the most forgotten rock."

The morning wind brings smoke. A thousand days of history ride in that smoke. Soot from distant cities swirls with pieces of the nearby jungle and scorched ground from every continent, and each careful breath contains tiny black embers that was once happy human meat.

The young woman stands on top of a rubble pile, her head poking through the old floor, gazing at the world that surrounds their sanctuary. She is as alert as possible, but being bored and hungry, she suffers lapses. Nothing moves in the smoky gloom. Her mind has no choice but to wander. One of the recurring lessons of these last thousand days is that the apocalypse resembles one long, very desperate vacation. Once your basic needs are met, or if you're hiding inside a hole waiting for better skies, you will find yourself surrounded by nothing except time and endless opportunity to think about whatever you want to think about.

Moments like these, she often conjures up her dead parents.

Her father always wanted children, but even he understood the risks. Reproduction was a gamble, but his world was unstable and was growing a little more dangerous by the year. Yet because they were scientific souls, her parents also respected their deep ignorance about all matters. Who knew? Maybe the general chaos would diminish. Maybe some hoped-for technology or political movement would emerge, saving this brutalized planet. Because nobody can ever be fully informed, a daughter was born, and her parents spent the next twenty years apologizing to her for her circumstances.

Three times in her life, the girl was sent away from home because home might be incinerated.

But none of those wars became real.

As it happened, their daughter was enjoying a weekend with a boyfriend when the worst occurred. The Northern League decided that a plasma bolt from the sky would end a stubborn diplomatic stalemate, and true enough, the stalemate was finished, leading to a ten day inferno. The parents died when San Paulo died, and it wasn't long before the boyfriend was dead too. And a thousand days later, the woman stands on a stack of broken concrete, her head raised into the chilled darkness of what should be a warm tropical dawn. She thinks about the past. She thinks about nothing. Then her mind drifts into sleep and out of sleep again, and when nothing changes, her head dips, and that is when she hears Them:

From somewhere below, past the reach of hands and eyes, creatures are moving with a minimum of noise.

Monsters, she assumes.

The gun is in its holster, and then it is in her hand. She has no memory of grabbing the stock and trigger.

And in another moment, one of the monsters reveals himself, stepping from the darkness with a rifle in both hands. He stares at the hilltop, measuring the little variations in the darkness and seeing nothing, and then looking over a shoulder, he tells another monster, "Nothing here."

But he doesn't quite trust that verdict, so he steps closer before pausing again, saying, "Nope, nothing here."

From below, out of sight, a second monster says, "Shut the fuck up."

With a big voice, the first monster says, "No, you shut the fuck up."

"You."

"No, you."

And here is the enduring lesson left behind by otherwise ignorant parents: A thousand times, they told their daughter that the only monsters in this world were the human variety.

In the end, the graduate student let thirty-nine simulations play to the same hardfast conclusion, and then she published her results.

Scientific epiphanies deserved more notoriety. But there were reasons to quietly applaud her efforts and then deny her every success. Her simulation, her game, was full of conjectures and debatable points, and however admiring her colleagues might be, they didn't have the guts to embrace any vision with magic at its end. Because that's what she predicted in her paper. She claimed that Venus had to be the first home of intelligence, and intelligence, she felt, would always evolve to some greater state, and in private and during the public speeches that followed, she would openly speculate about the shapes and talents that god-like beings would want to acquire. And when asked where to look for the aliens, she always pointed in a random direction, saying, "Everywhere."

She was forty-three when her sweet girl was born.

Her child had just turned seven when the Venusian mission—the last great adventure for the human species—brought back samples acquired from the high acid clouds. What was thought to be airborne bacteria proved to be exactly that: An acid-rich survivor of some lost ocean. But a physics experiment was what surprised everyone, including the woman who halfway predicted this sort of thing. Physicists were hunting for a new kind of matter—a subtle, sneaky material that wasn't quite dark and wasn't entirely baryonic either. Dubbed rune-matter, it was exceptionally rare on the Earth, but on and inside Venus it was astonishingly common. Samples were collected with a specially designed sieve and bottled inside a charged graphene flask. But instead of being tiny particles, the rune-matter came bacterial in size and bigger. And after several years of intensive study, it was determined that what they had caught was just as alive, or more so, than the acid bugs riding the high clouds.

In the strictest sense, these were not the predicted Venusians.

Mother and Father along with an army of researchers spent their remaining lives studying barely visible organisms. Successes were few and huge. The "runes" absorbed almost no energy, yet needing little, they thrived. Exotic techniques produced more of their material, and the creatures consumed the gifts and grew until a thousand graphene bottles were filled with viable cultures. And in the end, after debates and votes and a few noisy defections, the remaining group decided that these organisms were survivors like the acid bugs. They were the left-behind remnants of a second Venusian creation, and everything about Mother's model of Venusian life was accurate, save for the specifics.

Nobody knew where the Venusians resided today, and the mystery wouldn't be solved.

In every awful way, the Earth itself was turning to shit.

One last time, sorry parents apologized to their grown child. They said they were idiots to put her in this awful place. Then as Father shook hands with the doomed boyfriend, the white-haired mother took her daughter into a back room. There was gift to bestow. Mother was waiting for the girl's birthday but that wouldn't be for months, and maybe the gift had no value at all, yet she should take it anyway and hold onto it.

Really, who knew what tomorrow would bring?

The monsters walk past their refuge, noticing nothing. Armed raiders, lost soldiers, madmen. The possibilities are numerous and grim, and in the end, the truth has no importance. What matters is that luscious sense of peace left in their wake. This is the long vacation at the end of humankind, and the woman finds herself with moments where she feels safe enough to do exactly as she wants.

"Stay below," she whispers to the others.

They reply with one meaningful tap, concrete against concrete. Other than that, nothing needs to be said.

"Every hill ends with sky."

Her father—the old rocket builder—used to say those words. He took a hopeful message from the phrase, implying that every climb ends with a good vantage point. And that's what she thinks as she slips forwards, out of the basement and across the black ash brought to this high ground here by every wind.

And she kneels.

Against her hip is a bottle made of graphene, sealed by every reliable means and charged by her body's motions. Nobody else knows what she carries. She doubts anyone in her group would understand the concepts or her devotion to what has lost any sense of symbol. This is dead weight, however slight. But she is prepared to surrender quite a lot before this treasure is left behind, and that includes every person hiding inside that miserable basement.

Separated from her body, the confining charge begins to fail.

There is a logic in play, though mostly this is magic, contrived and deeply unreliable, and she would admit as much to anyone, if she ever mentioned it.

"Let a few runes leak free every so often," her mother told her. "It probably won't do any good, but it won't harm anything either."

"But why bother?" the young woman asked. "What am I hoping for?"

"Humans have so much trouble seeing what is strange," Mother said. "But we shouldn't assume that superbeings built from new forms of matter would be any less blind. So let some of the bugs fall free. Every so often, just a few."

"But why?"

The old woman set the bottle aside, grasping her daughter's hands with both of hers. "Because maybe a Venusian will be swimming past.".

"Oh," the girl said. "I'm giving them something to notice."

"And after that, maybe it will notice you, and maybe it will save you somehow. Out of kindness, or curiosity, or because saving my daughter would cost that god so very little."

Magic.

All of this was nothing but hope and wild magic.

Yet she remained on her knees, in the ashes, waving the enchantment with all of her might while thinking how magic has always lived for darkness, and everything was dark, and really, on a day like this, what better thing could she possibly have to do . . . ?

THE ENDLESS SINK

DAMIEN OBER

—⊰⧫⊱—

Sheep floating out on their tethers, the milk cows too. Ears flapping and skin and wool fur rippling as our rock sunk endless through the void. It was the day the boys of the rock would choose and so everyone had gathered to see what each would do. All the boys of leaving age lined up on the edge with the teacher there beside them. In front of everyone he had ever known, my brother Kyle was about to decide: rise or sink.

From the back of the crowd, I watched, my mother there with me and on my other side, my father standing stoic as he always liked to be. "Such a shame," my mother said, "that little Frederick will never have the chance."

My father grunted his grim consent about my little brother Fredrick, back at the house and too sick to come and see his older brother leave the rock. Frederick didn't have much time left; he would be dead long before he reached the age when boys decide. And me? I would never reach it. Because only boys are made to sink or rise. Only boys leave the rock.

My father's eyes thinned. Which meant he was seeing something no one else was seeing. A moment later, a boy on the stage broke down. "Sad," my father said. And off he ran, this boy, down off the stage and into his mother's arms. Through the crowd they scuttled, avoiding eyes, back to their house on the other side of the rock.

When we looked back, the other boys were getting ready. None of them wanted to become the next to lose his nerve. And then, off they went, all of the boys deciding simultaneously to rise. Kyle too, my brother. A cheer came up from the crowd, watching the boys get smaller, waving as they went, off for other lives on other rocks somewhere above.

I think I was the first to see it. It happened right then. Amidst the boys getting smaller, a new speck appeared. And this speck was getting larger. I could see it had arms and legs, a head—it was a sinker. The first sinker to come to our rock in as long as I could remember.

A circle spread in the crowd. The sinker landed perfectly in the center, stood a moment with the people reflected in the visor of his helmet. He had a sword strapped to his back, tucked tightly beside a small backpack. And then the helmet came off and the sinker was a woman. Had been since that moment when I was the first to see her. Through them all she came, right up to my parents and said, "You have beds on this pueblo, I heard."

And before they could answer, she looked more directly at my mother than I had ever seen a person do. "I have a letter from your brother."

The sinker had laid herself out straight on top of my bed to sleep. Her body was like an insect's, condensed and hollow-seeming. On the floor sat her sword and tightly-wrapped pack and on top, her helmet. And though I knew it was wrong to touch people's things, I picked the helmet up and turned it over and pressed my finger against the sharp point at the front.

"Please put that down." The sinker's eyes were the only bright specks in the room, watching until the helmet was back on her pack. "Thank you." She rolled over and I could see the lines of muscle crackling. There was nothing extra about her. She was exactly what was needed for her purpose and nothing more.

"Have you come to help my brother?"

There was a long silence. I wondered if maybe she had gone back to sleep. "What's wrong with him?"

"He got cut by the meat knife and it's got his leg. Mother says it will be his hip and then his heart next."

The sinker got up. "Where is he?"

I led her into the room my brothers used to share. But now it was just Fredrick, sweating and dying slowly in his bed. The sinker reached out her hand, but I saved her, grabbed her wrist and held it back. "You mustn't touch him." Inside her forearm, I could feel each tendon, each wound muscle.

"It's ok," she said. And she moved my brother's hairs so they were all together on one side of his face. When she took the blanket down, it revealed how black his leg had become. It wasn't to the hip yet, but it would be soon. "Infection," the sinker said.

"At least he didn't decide to sink, that boy. Because staying right where you are, well, that's better at least than sinking." My mother was talking abut the boy who ran from the stage that morning. It happened every deciding day to at least one, but every time it happened people acted like it was the first and the last. My mother paused her chopping and looked up, as if seeing through the roof, to the spot where Kyle had vanished into nothing. "My boy," she said, "a riser."

My father was sitting opposite me at the kitchen table. He looked asleep except for his eyes. I suppose I had not thought until then, that Kyle rising would have the effect of him no longer being there.

"Your father was a riser."

"I wanted to be a sinker, though, when I was little."

"Don't tell her things like that."

He shrugged. "What's it matter? Didn't do it. Rose instead and here I am."

"What was your first rock like, Daddy?"

"Not like this one," my mother said. "That's why men rise instead of sink." She went back to cutting things up. "Through generations of male linage, the family eventually reaches Center City."

"But what if Center City is down?"

My mother laughed. "If you want to get somewhere, you have to rise. Put out some resistance and all these rocks sink right past. You get somewhere. It takes five days of sinking to get where you can in one of rising. By rising, you move further, faster. You show you're more adventurous."

"What about her?" I asked. "Her, the sinker?"

My mother shook her head. "I don't know why we must let her sleep here."

My father sighed. "That's the law, hon. A sinker brings a letter, the sinker gets to sleep the night."

"I know it's the law, told down from those people up at Center City who don't know what it's like down here for us real people."

I wasn't sure if my mother understood what she'd just said, how it related to other things she was always saying. I was about to ask when I heard a voice. "Listen to your mother," it said. And the sinker cut into the room without disturbing even the stillness of the air. "Thank you for the bed. Here is your mail." She put a single letter on the table.

My mother opened it and began to read. Her younger brother had left the rock the year he came of age. He had chosen to rise.

The sinker was seated now at the table's other chair. The way she did things was she didn't really do them, they just changed, like it had happened in the past. My mother continued reading. My father watched her. "Where has he settled?" Mother finally asked. "From how far up did this letter come down with you?"

"A pueblo a day's rise from here."

"One day's rise?" The letter hung there in her hand all finished.

"Have you been to Center City?" I asked.

The sinker looked at me and shook her head. It made me think she wasn't saying everything when she said, "No."

"But it's up there, right?"

My mother turned from the counter to both see and hear the answer. My father too, left his head sunk, but lifted his eyes to gaze at the sinker.

"That's what people say, isn't it?"

"But you haven't been there?"

The Sinker looked at me again.

"Of course it's there," my mother said. "We pay our tribute to risers headed there. We obey the laws passed down by magistrates. Who could pay those magistrates, where would the things go? Where do the laws come down from? If there's no Center City?"

My father put his hand on my head. "Don't worry, sweetie, Center City is real."

The boys of the rock were gathered in the meeting house for their weekly lesson about the future of their lives and the need to begin to prepare now no matter how far away the big day seemed. It was there that the boys all learned how to become the kind of risers our rock was surely known for. The man in charge of their lessons was called the teacher.

Standing atop an empty barrel, peering through the room's back window, I could see the teacher at the front of the rowed desks. "Though you will not reach Center City yourself, by your rising, perhaps some day your sons or the sons of your sons . . ." Behind him was the drawing which every boy was made to learn and draw from memory—a pyramid pattern of rocks like ours with Center City up at the top and biggest of all.

One of the other girls was tapping the back of my calf so I climbed down because it was the next girl's turn to stand on the barrel and look in. "Hey," one of them said to me, "It's the sinker that stays in your parents' house." And there she was, the sinker, standing way over at the very edge of the rock.

"My parents said not to go near the sinker and that it would be better if she wasn't here at all or never came."

"My parents said the laws say your parents only have to let the sinker stay for—" But I was leaving those girls behind. I crossed the rock to stand beside the sinker. The milk cow was out there on its tether. It looked over at us from way past the edge. The wind made strange temporary shapes of its udder. The sinker was leaning over the edge, letting the rushing wind hold her place. Her gaze aimed deep into the darkness, her hair pointing back up at distant rocks above, back at all the other lives she must have crossed. And soon, off she'd sink, off to where ever it was she was headed, somewhere far below.

"How many rocks have you been to?" I asked.

A single tear got sucked up and vanished from her face. "Lots," she said.

I moved right to the edge, got down on my stomach with my head poking over. "My brother left yesterday. He chose to rise. And I'll stay here, until a riser comes up to marry me."

The sinker sat down beside me, let her feet dangle.

I had to speak loudly with the wind howling past us. "One girl was made to leave this rock. It was before I was born, but everybody knows about it. She had betrayed her family. Did you betray your family?"

The sinker was looking out straight and I had never considered until that moment that in addition to other rocks below and above ours, there could be ones out to the side, out to all the sides. Other rocks with other families on them, in every possible direction.

"On other pueblos," the sinker said, " . . . other rocks, things are different."

"How do you mean different?"

"There are lots of other pueblos out there. Rocks. Some people call them islands, towns. Every place calls them different. On other rocks, people don't die of infection."

"They don't?"

"On some they do, but not on all."

I wondered then, why none of the boys who left had ever sunk back down, back down to their home rock. "My brother will die of infection," I said. "My uncle did and my father's best friend."

"I will take you as far as Roseblood," the sinker said. "But not back."

"What do you mean?"

"Roseblood. The next pueblo down."

I woke to complete darkness. The wind that roared around me had been in my dreams too. It was the sound of the edge of my rock, but endless now. There was no quiet to step back into. We had left solid land behind and were off on the sink. Little lights clipped to our belts were turned off. In all directions, I could see nothing. Everything was gone. Everything but the wind and the black void.

I felt the sinker's hand on me and could then make out the rough shape of her. She was peering through some sort of device, off at something far below us. Her shout reached me through the roaring howl, "Risers!" And then I could see them, two glinting specks coming towards us.

The sinker unhooked the tether which kept us from drifting apart. "Give me some space." I didn't know what she meant and so she shouted, "Spread your arms and legs! Rise a little!" The specks had grown into people, coming up fast. Two men it looked like, each with a small light on the front of his helmet. The sinker straightened her body and went diving toward them.

As the three forms converged, there was a flash in the dim light of the risers' headlamps. Then the risers were still, rising limply toward me. As they passed, I saw one's face, frozen in a contorted grimace. Little droplets of blood hung around them in strange shifting patterns. Up they went, just dead bodies now.

The sinker floated back to me as I sank down to her. She was wiping and sheathing her sword. "They find you sleeping and you never wake up. Take everything you have to trade at whatever pueblo they land on next." She reclipped our tether.

"Sorry," I shouted back.

The sinker smiled. "We all fall asleep, kid. You have to."

"Where is it?"

The sinker went into her pack, pulled out a roll of paper. She spread a stretch of it between her hands.

"What's that?" I shouted.

"A map."

"A map?"

"We'd be lost out here without it."

We passed a skeleton, or the skeleton passed us. The sinker told me it was a riser, or another sinker maybe. When I asked her what happened to all his stuff, to his skin and all the rest, she told me people took it. I asked her if it was before or after he died and she said it looked like after. She said he left some pueblo and never found the next one. Ages ago. Floated around out there until he starved to death. "Happens," she shouted, "Happens all the time."

At first, it was just a dim, glowing ball in the distance. I was struck with dread, remembering fires I'd seen burn down whole houses on the rock back home. But as we got closer, the lights began to separate and I could understand what it was I was seeing. It was not a fire, but a hundred—a thousand maybe—separate fires. They burned along the edges of a high wall. On one side, there was a thin patch of ground, but on the other, there was a city like I'd only heard about until then. Houses were all clumped together and stacked on top of one another. There were larger buildings too, bigger than all the houses on my rock put together. Wide paths cut between them, people riding animals like the milk cows but thinner. And there were lights too, dotted throughout, as far as I could see.

"Roseblood," the sinker shouted.

We were close enough now to see a ring of huts and tents gathered in clumps outside the high wall. In both directions, the wall climbed up along the rock's edge until it vanished into the distance. From the top, three bright plumes were headed toward us.

"Centurions," the sinker shouted. "Just do as they say."

Three Centurions were suddenly floating around us, backpacks strapped on that shot fire and in each hand some sort of control. All three had swords like the sinker's, in sheaths along their sides. "Do not enter the city," one shouted. "Stay only on the trader's side of the wall."

The sinker nodded and the centurions were gone, hurtling back to the top of the wall to continue their watch.

We landed on the very edge of the rock. From there, the wall was just a wall, no way to know that something so endless was on the other side. Along its top, centurions marched back and forth, glancing down. On the ground, I could see now that the lights were not fires, but little glass balls with small fires inside, all connected by strings that ran back to the top of the wall. The lights made a web which hung over all the people scattered on the trader's side, sitting at fires or clumped in the front flaps of tents, none reacting as we walked through.

After more than a day of the constant friction of sinking, walking on flat rock again felt somehow incomplete. It was a half sensation. I was relieved to reach Roseblood, but part of me wanted to leave again. To dive off the edge and head down. Back to the great sink.

We made our way to a cluster of open-faced tents. The sinker traded a few small things for food which we took to a fire. Around the fire, others were cooking similar food, meat in links on sticks and cups of boiling juices.

I asked the Sinker, "Where are our beds?"

A grimy looking man showed me where all his teeth had been broken out. "Got beds on your rock, huh?"

"Don't you?"

He laughed. "I'll have to stop there on my way by."

The sinker revealed just enough sword to reflect a golden rectangle of fire light onto the skin between his eyes. "You stop there and you stop forever." She glanced at the others, each separately. "Goes for all of you."

"You rising or sinking?" an old man asked me.

I could tell the sinker had no intention and so I answered for myself. "Sinking, I guess, for now anyway."

A younger man, not much older than me, a boy I guess, leaned over. "Better decide one way or the other. Lest you don't plan on getting anywhere your whole life. Sink or rise. Me, I've been sinking since I came to. First chance I got."

"Are you sinking too?" I asked the old man.

He nodded, once for me and then once at the boy. "Since just about this one's age."

I asked him, "Where are you going?"

Everyone at the fire laughed at this, but the old man's smile was kind and genuine. "Just down," he said.

"Did you come from Center City?"

His eyes narrowed but he didn't say anything.

The boy was talking again. "Never heard of no Central City. Maybe you mean the Big Ghost."

"Old scavenger legend." It was a thin man across the fire. He was glancing around under the brim of a furry helmet. "Legend they would tell families on small cities and these people used to give over their stuff out of fear at just the mention. The mention of Center City. They let you sleep in their daughter's beds too." He laughed.

"Why you want to go to a place like Center City for?" the old man asked.

"So it is real?"

"Oh yes. It's real."

All through this, the sinker said nothing, just looked into the fire as she ate. Across, the skinny man was laughing. "And I suppose there's an end too?" He pointed into the air above Roseblood, then down. Then he smiled his with huge broken face. "A place where all the cities land, all piled up, one on top of another, broken to bits. And everything on them."

"The Great Flat," someone whispered.

"What?" I asked. "What's The Great Flat?"

The old man was pulling over an odd shaped case which he opened and inside was a thing shaped like the case. "Never mind about The Great Flat," he said. "Or Center City." He put the thing in his lap and with his fingers, he plucked strings along its front and singing came out of a hole as if it was a mouth. And the old man started singing too.

"Don't you know anything but scavenger ballads old man?"

He looked at the kid. "This ain't no scavenger ballad, son. This is a song from Before." That quieted them. He waited a moment and then went on, "And you'd best listen and remember it."

"Great," the kid said. "Just what I need."

But I did listen, to every word. Tried as best I could to remember them exactly. When the old man finished, he plucked each string once more and the song was over.

The kid was the first to talk. "Where did you steal that old thing?"

The old man was putting it back in its case. "Was passed down," he said, and I wasn't sure if he meant the song or the case and what was in it.

"Nothing wasn't stolen at some point." And now the kid took a small wooden man out of his pocket and showed it to me. "What you want to give me for this?" But it was not wood, when I held it, it was light and cold to the touch.

"I don't have anything," I said.

He took it back. "Well, take what you can find. Cuz someday, you're not going to be wanting something, but needing it. And you better have a few things to trade."

I looked to the old man, but he didn't seem like he was about to disagree. "So you steal too?"

His head tilted to one side. "You steal a little, have to, scavenge a bit. It's how I've got so far. But it's the sink that's important, not things. Things are just a means to keep sinking."

The kid chuckled. "All these years, old man, and you and I, we're in the same place."

"It's not where you are, son, but how far you've sunk from where you started."

Into the air above us, three centurions rose from the top of the wall and skirted low above the web of lights. Each left a tube of dark smoke, milky and opaque against the pure black above. They congregated in the air where the rock edge ended, there to meet a riser coming up, just as they had come out to meet us as we approached. There was a shout. All eyes looked up as a bright plume of sparks flowered out. One of the centurions had killed the riser and off he went, rising now in no direction.

The kid was getting up.

"Let it be," the old man said.

The kid smiled, "Must be something on that riser worth checking for." A few seconds later, I could see him, rising expertly. I'd never seen anyone rise so fast. But before he could reach the limp body, a single centurion swooped by, sword out and sliced the boy clean in half. Simple as that.

"Come on, time for us to retire." The sinker reached into the fire and took out a small log burning at one end.

"Take care of this little one," the old man told her.

"Why did they do it?" I asked.

The old man looked up at the bodies, two in three pieces. "No scavenging allowed in sight of Roseblood."

"I have to go for a little while and you can't come with me."

I watched the sinker strap on her belt and sword. Our little fire was a single smoldering log. She also had a small knife, which she slid into her boot.

"Where do you have to go?"

She looked over at the wall and I looked too. "Inside," she said.

"What will I do?"

"Stay here and wait."

"By myself?"

"Here," and she pulled an object from her bag like I had never seen before and have never seen another since. "You sit here and if someone comes near you, you show them this."

"But how's it used?"

"You won't need to use it. You just show them, that's all. For now, though, keep it out of sight."

I took it from her and put it under the flap of my jacket. She stood up, between me and the high wall. Just then a centurion was rising up toward a speck coming down. I thought of the sinker, chopped in half like the boy from the fire. But it didn't seem possible.

"Just remember what I told you." And off she went, weaving between the fires and tents until I could no longer see her.

When the sinker returned, she had with her a little jar which she held up and said, "You put this on your brother's wound. And then you put this," and she held up another jar, rattling what was inside, "into his food. One per meal until they're all gone. Did anyone bother you?"

I shook my head. "When do we go back?"

Now the sinker looked right at me. "Not we."

And I knew then that I would have to find my own way back to my rock. "These will cure my brother?"

She sat down on the ground beside me.

"You had to steal them?"

"No, but I stole some of the things I traded for them."

"All of the things back home, the things we trade for from the risers going past. It was all stolen, huh? Stuff they'd killed people and took. Or landed on a small rock and just took it all."

The sinker was digging in her bag. "Probably not all."

"You were a riser once."

"Yep." She went still a moment, then back to digging. "Rose further than anyone I've ever met. Left when I was younger than you."

"But why?"

"Same reason your brother chose to. Same reason people choose whatever it is they choose." She shrugged. The map was out now and she was comparing it to another piece of paper.

"But then you realized it was wrong?"

She didn't answer me so I asked her, "Do you kill people, to take their things?"

"Did we take anything from the risers who tried to kill us?" She was looking from one page to the next, marking up the clean sheet with a pen.

"I thought it was because they wouldn't let us land on Roseblood if you'd had all three swords."

The sinker glanced up at me. "Good, kid," she said. Then she was back at the maps. Back to whatever it was she was doing.

"What then?" I asked her. "What happened?"

"One day I realized I forgot to do something. Spent every day since trying to get back. Just hope there's time."

Maybe I felt a kiss on my forehead. Or maybe I dreamed that part. In my dream, it was my mother kissing my forehead, but in the dream, my mother was the sinker and my real mother was a lady I had never known or even met.

This was the end of my dream. In the beginning, I was sinking, but not toward something. More like I was floating, like one of the milk cows out on its tether. Below me was water, more water than I had ever imagined there could be, water bigger than Roseblood or anything else, as endless as the void around my little rock back home. It was moving under me as I floated there. And just when it seemed like it would never end, the edge of a rock appeared in the distance, coming toward me. Except this rock wasn't floating in space. It was in the water; the water actually surrounded the rock. In my dream, the rock was getting closer and closer and as it swept under me, I felt the kiss and I opened my eyes and the sinker was tossing dirt on the last embers of the fire.

"I don't have to go back," I said.

She looked at me. "If you want to save your brother, you do."

"But if I never see him again, what does it matter either way?"

The sinker didn't answer. She had got down on her knees and was readying her pack.

"Can I come with you?"

She looked right in my eyes and shook her head. "Too far to go. You'll slow me down too much."

"I understand."

"Good." She handed me a rolled up paper.

"What is it?"

"A map. When you get a chance, make a copy. You always have a copy, packed separate from the other."

"But now you'll only have one."

"That's a copy I made for you."

She unrolled the map so a small section lay spread between my hands. "We're here. And here's your pueblo. A quarter day's rise." She pointed at a place in the darkness above Roseblood. "A straight shot. Don't second guess and you'll be fine."

"If I go back."

"That's up to you." She picked up her pack and strapped it on beside her sword. She looked back at me once more, walked to the very edge and then she was gone.

• • •

The old rock felt haunted, by some sort of never ending. Children ran by the window in loops, my brother there with them. He was oblivious to how close he had come to being not a boy at all, but nothing. Ashes held out over the edge and let go. Our father was a riser. Rose up to the rock we live on now. His father and his father before. "The family has risen far, my son." And they would gaze upward, toward the distant rocks above.

Again, my brother would have a chance to decide. Thanks to the sinker. And to me for coming back. His leg looked bruised, but the black was gone, the swelling. The puss and the fever were gone too and no one on the rock could believe it. They'd been coming to the house since I got back, asking where the medicine had come from. There was talk of training sinkers, sending them off for more.

My mother had treated my brother's recovery as some sort of dark trick. As she watched him climb out of bed, her face revealed this possibility to me: maybe she would have preferred him to die than be saved through something she didn't understand. Me, I hadn't left my room the entire time, all through his healing. I sat alone, at work on a copy of the map. You must have two copies, packed separate from each other.

When my father came to see me, I was seated on the floor with the new map unrolled all the way, the last parts drying so it could be permanent. As I worked, I hummed the old man's song. The song from Before. At least I was humming how I remembered it, hoping it was right.

"What's this here?" he asked me. He was standing over the object the sinker told me I would never have to use.

"Don't look at it," I told him.

"But I already did."

I got up and covered it completely.

"That sinker gave you that, didn't she?"

"It's for protection."

"How so?" but he had wandered away, didn't really want an answer, I suppose. Then he was stopped again, looking down at the map.

"It's finished," I told him.

He looked at my pack, at the map again, and finally at me. "When are you leaving?"

The original map was already rolled into a tight cylinder. I took it from the table and slid it into my pack. "Tomorrow," I said.

My father seemed to say the word over again a few times in his head. "I think it's best you don't tell you mother."

The pack was tight and small. I was proud of how compact it looked, how light and simple.

My father was digging in his pockets. "You'll need at least a few things to trade."

• • •

The entire rock behind me was lost in the roar of the edge. Only one or two people were up and about. The animals were asleep, out at the ends of their tethers, their fur revealing the natural currents of the sink.

I had said goodbye to my father, there in my room, with the map drying. My mother would wake in a few hours and find her daughter gone.

I stood on the same spot Kyle had left from to rise, the spot from which all boys leave the rock. I did not look back, only out, directly parallel from the surface of the rock. And then I leaned forward. I could feel the weight of what I had packed. The truth is, I had not decided, not until that very moment.

THE LONG HAUL
FROM THE ANNALS OF TRANSPORTATION,
THE PACIFIC MONTHLY, MAY 2009

KEN LIU

Twenty-five years ago on this day, the Hindenburg *crossed the Atlantic for the first time. Today, it will cross it for the last time. Six hundred times it has accomplished this feat, and in so doing it has covered the same distance as more than eight roundtrips to the Moon. Its perfect safety record is a testament to the ingenuity of the German people.*

There is always some sorrow in seeing a thing of beauty age, decline, and finally fade, no matter how gracefully it is done. But so long as men still sail the open skies, none shall forget the glory of the Hindenburg.

—John F. Kennedy, March 31, 1962, Berlin.

It was easy to see the zeppelins moored half a mile away from the terminal. They were a motley collection of about forty Peterbilts, Aereons, Macks, Zeppelins (both the real thing and the ones from Goodyear-Zeppelin), and Dongfengs, arranged around and with their noses tied to ten mooring masts, like crouching cats having tête-à-tête tea parties.

I went through customs at Lanzhou's Yantan Airport, and found Barry Icke's long-hauler, a gleaming silver Dongfeng Feimaotui—the model usually known in America, among the less-than-politically-correct society of zeppeliners, as the "Flying Chinaman"—at the farthest mooring mast. As soon as I saw it, I understood why he called it the *American Dragon*.

White clouds drifted in the dark mirror of the polished solar panels covering the upper half of the zeppelin like a turtle's shell. Large, waving American flags trailing red and blue flames and white stars were airbrushed onto each side of the elongated silver teardrop hull, which gradually tapered towards the back, ending in a cruciform tail striped in red, white, and blue. A pair of predatory, reptilian eyes were painted above the nose cone and a grinning mouth full of sharp teeth under it. A petite Chinese woman was suspended by ropes below the nose cone, painting over the blood-red tongue in the mouth with a brush.

Icke stood on the tarmac near the control cab, a small, round, glass-windowed bump protruding from the belly of the giant teardrop. Tall and broad-shouldered, his square face featured a tall, Roman nose and steady, brown eyes that stared out from under the visor of a Red Sox cap. He watched me approach, flicked his cigarette away, and nodded at me.

Icke had been one of the few to respond to my Internet forum ad asking if any of the long-haulers would be willing to take a writer for the *Pacific Monthly* on a haul. "I've read some of your articles," he had said. "You didn't sound too stupid." And then he invited me to come to Lanzhou.

After we strapped ourselves in, Icke weighed off the zeppelin—pumping compressed helium into the gasbags until the zeppelin's positive lift, minus the weight of the ship, the gas, us, and the cargo, was just about equal to zero. Now essentially "weightless," the long-hauler and all its cargo could have been lifted off the ground by a child.

When the control tower gave the signal, Icke pulled a lever that retracted the nose cone hook from the mooring mast and flipped a toggle to drop about a thousand pounds of water ballast into the ground tank below the ship. And just like that, we began to rise, steadily and in complete silence, as though we were riding up a skyscraper in a glass-walled elevator. Icke left the engines off. Unlike an airplane that needs the engines to generate forward thrust to be converted into lift, a zeppelin literally floats up, and engines didn't need to be turned on until we reached cruising height.

"This is the *American Dragon*, heading out to Sin City. See you next time, and watch out for those bears," Icke said into the radio. A few of the other zeppelins, like giant caterpillars on the ground below us, blinked their tail lights in acknowledgment.

Icke's Feimaotui is three hundred and two feet long, with a maximum diameter of eighty-four feet, giving it capacity for 1.12 million cubic feet of helium and a gross lift of thirty-six tons, of which about twenty-seven are available for cargo (this is comparable to the maximum usable cargo load for semis on the Interstates).

Its hull is formed from a rigid frame of rings and longitudinal girders made out of duratainium covered with composite skin. Inside, seventeen helium gasbags are secured to a central beam that runs from the nose to the tail of the ship, about a third of the way up from the bottom of the hull. At the bottom of the hull, immediately below the central beam and the gasbags, is an empty space that runs the length of the ship.

Most of this space is taken up by the cargo hold, the primary attraction of long-haulers for shippers. The immense space, many times the size of a plane's cargo bay, was perfect for irregularly shaped and bulky goods, like the wind generator turbine blades we were carrying.

Near the front of the ship, the cargo hold is partitioned from the crew quarters, which consists of a suite of apartment-like rooms opening off of a central corridor. The corridor ends by emerging from the hull into the control cab, the only place on the ship with windows to the outside. The Feimaotui is only a little bit longer and taller than a Boeing 747 (counting the tail), but far more voluminous and lighter.

The whole crew consisted of Icke and his wife, Yeling, the woman who was re-painting the grinning mouth on the zeppelin when I showed up. Husband-wife teams like theirs are popular on the transpacific long haul. Each of them would take six-hour shifts to fly the ship while the other slept. Yeling was in the back, sleeping through the takeoff. Like the ship itself, much of their marriage was made up of silence and empty space.

"Yeling and I are no more than thirty feet apart from each other just about every minute, but we only get to sleep in the same bed about once every seven days. You end up learning to have conversations in five-minute chunks separated by six-hour blocks of silence.

"Sometimes Yeling and I have an argument, and she'll have six hours to think of a comeback for something I said six hours earlier. That helps since her English isn't perfect, and she can use the time to look up words she needs. I'll wake up and she'll talk at me for five minutes and go to bed, and I'll have to spend the next six hours thinking about what she said. We've had arguments that went on for days and days this way."

Icke laughed. "In our marriage, sometimes you *have* to go to bed angry."

The control car was shaped like an airplane's cockpit, except that the windows slanted outward and down, so that you had an unobstructed view of the land and air below you.

Icke had covered his seat with a custom pattern: a topographical map of Alaska. In front of Icke's chair was a dashboard full of instruments and analog and mechanical controls. A small, gleaming gold statuette of a laughing, rotund bodhisattva was glued to the top of the dashboard. Next to it was the plush figure of Wally, the Green Monster of Fenway Park.

A plastic crate wedged into place between the two seats was filled with CDs: a mix of mandopop, country, classical, and some audio books. I flipped through them: Annie Dillard, Thoreau, Cormac McCarthy, *The Idiot's Guide to Grammar and Composition*.

Once we reached the cruising altitude of one thousand feet—freight zeppelins generally are restricted to a zone above pleasure airships, whose passengers prefer the view lower down, and far below the cruising height of airplanes—Icke started the electrical engines. A low hum, more felt than heard, told us that the four propellers mounted in indentations near the tail of the ship had begun to turn and push the ship forward.

"It never gets much louder than this," Icke said.

We drifted over the busy streets of Lanzhou. More than a thousand miles west of Beijing, this medium-sized industrial city was once the most polluted city in all of China due to its blocked air flow and petroleum processing plants. But it is now the center of China's wind turbine boom.

The air below us was filled with small and cheap airships that hauled passengers and freight on intra-city routes. They were a colorful bunch, a ragtag mix of blimps and small zeppelins, their hulls showing signs of make-shift repairs and *shanzhai* patches. (A blimp, unlike a zeppelin, has no rigid frame. Like a birthday balloon, its shape is maintained entirely by the pressure of the gas inside.) The ships were plastered all over with lurid advertisements for goods and services that sounded, with their strange English translations, frightening and tempting in equal measure. Icke told me that some of the ships we saw had bamboo frames.

Icke had flown as a union zeppeliner crewman for ten years on domestic routes before buying his own ship. The union pay was fine, but he didn't like working for someone else. He had wanted to buy a Goodyear-Zeppelin, designed and made one hundred percent in America. But he disliked bankers even more than Chinese airship companies, and decided that he would rather own a Dongfeng outright.

"Nothing good ever came from debt," he said. "I could have told you what was going to happen with all those mortgages last year."

After a while, he added, "My ship is mostly built in America, anyway. The Chinese can't make the duratainium for the girders and rings in the frame. They have to import it. I ship sheets of the alloy from Bethlehem, PA, to factories in China all the time."

The Feimaotui was a quirky ship, Icke explained. It was designed to be easy to maintain and repair rather than over-engineered to be durable the way American ships usually were. An American ship that malfunctioned had to be taken to the dealer for the sophisticated computers and proprietary diagnostic codes, but just about every component of the Feimaotui could be switched out and repaired in the field by a skilled mechanic. An American ship could practically fly itself most of the time, as the design philosophy was to automate as much as possible and minimize the chances of human error. The Feimaotui required a lot more out of the pilot, but it was also much more responsive and satisfying to fly.

"A man changes over time to be like his ship. I'd just fall asleep in a ship where the computer did everything." He gazed at the levers, sticks, wheels, toggles, pedals and sliders around him, reassuringly heavy, analog, and solid. "Typing on a keyboard is no way to fly a ship."

He wanted to own a fleet of these ships eventually. The goal was to graduate from owner-operator to just owner, when he and Yeling could start a family.

"Someday when we can just sit back and collect the checks, I'll get a Winnebago Aurora—the forty-thousand-cubic-feet model—and we and our kids will drift around all summer in Alaska and all winter in Brazil, eating nothing but the food we catch with our own hands. You haven't seen Alaska until you've seen it in an RV airship. We can go to places that not even snowmachines and seaplanes can get to, and hover over a lake that has never seen a man, not a soul around us for hundreds of miles."

Within seconds we were gliding over the broad, slow expanse of the Yellow River. Filled with silt, the muddy water below us was already beginning to take on its namesake color, which would deepen and grow even muddier over the next few hundred miles as it traveled through the Loess Plateau and picked up the silt deposited over the eons by wind.

Below us, small sightseeing blimps floated lazily over the river. The passengers huddled in the gondolas to look through the transparent floor at the sheepskin rafts drifting on the river below the same way Caribbean tourists looked through glass-bottom boats at the fish in the coral reef.

Icke throttled up and we began to accelerate north and east, largely following the course of the Yellow River, towards Inner Mongolia.

The Millennium Clean Energy Act is one of the few acts by the "clowns down in D.C." that Icke approved: "It gave me most of my business."

Originally designed as a way to protect domestic manufacturers against Chinese competition and to appease the environmental lobby, the law imposed a heavy tax on goods entering the United States based on the carbon footprint of the method of transportation (since the tax was not based on the goods' country-of-origin, it skirted the WTO rules against increased tariffs).

Combined with rising fuel costs, the law created a bonanza for zeppelin shippers. Within a few years, Chinese companies were churning out cheap zeppelins that sipped fuel and squeezed every last bit of advantage from solar power. Dongfengs became a common sight in American skies.

A long-haul zeppelin cannot compete with a 747 for lifting capacity or speed, but it wins hands down on fuel efficiency and carbon profile, and it's far faster than surface shipping. Going from Lanzhou to Las Vegas, like Icke and I were doing, would take about three to four weeks by surface shipping at the fastest: a couple days to go from Lanzhou to Shanghai by truck or train, about two weeks to cross the Pacific by ship, another day or so to truck from California to Las Vegas, and add in a week or so for loading, unloading, and sitting in customs. A direct airplane flight would get you there in a day, but the fuel cost and carbon tax at the border would make it uneconomical for many goods.

"Every time you have to load and unload and change the mode of transport, that's money lost to you," Icke said. "We are trucks that don't need highways, boats that don't need rivers, airplanes that don't need airports. If you can find a piece of flat land the size of a football field, that's enough for us. We can deliver door to door from a yurt in Mongolia to your apartment in New York—assuming your building has a mooring mast on top."

A typical zeppelin built in the last twenty years, cruising at one hundred ten mph, can make the sixty-nine-hundred-mile haul between Lanzhou and Las Vegas in about sixty-three hours. If it makes heavy use of solar power, as Icke's Feimaotui is designed to do, it can end up using less than a fraction of a percent of the fuel that a 747 would need to carry the same weight for the same distance. Plus, it has the advantage I'd mentioned of being more accommodating of bulky, irregularly-shaped loads.

Although we were making the transpacific long haul, most of our journey would be spent flying over land. The curvature of the Earth meant that the closest flight path between any two points on the globe followed a great circle that connected the two points and bisected the globe into two equal parts. From Lanzhou to Las Vegas, this meant that we would fly north and east over Inner Mongolia, Mongolia, Siberia, across the Bering Strait, and then fly east and south over Alaska, the Pacific Ocean off the coast of British Columbia, until we hit land again with Oregon, and finally reach the deserts of Nevada.

Below us, the vast city of Ordos, in Inner Mongolia, stretched out to the horizon, a megalopolis of shining steel and smooth glass, vast blocks of western-style houses and manicured gardens. The grid of new, wide streets was as empty as those in Pyongyang, and I could count the number of pedestrians on the fingers of one hand. Our height and open view made the scene take on the look of tilt-shift photographs, as though we were standing over a tabletop scale model of the city, with a few miniature cars and playing figurines scattered about the model.

Ordos is China's Alberta. There is coal here, some of the best, cleanest coal in the world. Ordos was planned in anticipation of an energy boom, but the construction itself became the boom. The more they spent on construction, the more it looked on paper like there was need for even more construction. So now there is this Xanadu, a ghost town from birth. On paper it is the second-richest place in China, per capita income just behind Shanghai.

As we flew over the center of Ordos, a panda rose up and hailed us. The panda's vehicle was a small blimp, painted olive green and carrying the English legend: "Aerial Transport Patrol, People's Republic of China." Icke slowed down and sent over the cargo manifests, the maintenance records, which the panda could cross-check against the international registry of cargo airships, and his journey log. After a few minutes, someone waved at us on from the window in the gondola of the blimp, and a Chinese voice told us over radio that we were free to move on.

"This is such a messed up country," Icke said. "They have the money to build something like Ordos, but have you been to Guangxi? It's near Vietnam, and outside the cities the people there are among the poorest in the world. They have nothing except the mud on the floor of their huts, and beautiful scenery and beautiful women."

Icke had met Yeling there, through a mail-order bride service. It was hard to meet women when you were in the air three hundred days of the year.

On the day of Icke's appointment, he was making a run through Nanning, the provincial capital, as part of a union crew picking up a shipment of star anise. He had the next day, a Saturday, off, and he traveled down to the introduction center a hundred kilometers outside Nanning to meet the girls whose pictures he had picked out and who had been bused in from the surrounding villages.

They had fifteen girls for him. They met in a village school house. Icke sat on a small stool at the front of the classroom with his back to the blackboard, and the girls were brought in to sit at the student desks, as though he was there to teach them.

Most of them knew some English, and he could talk to them for a little bit and mark down, on a chart, the three girls that he wanted to chat with one-on-one in private. The girls he didn't pick would wait around for the next Westerner customer to come and see them in another half hour.

"They say that some services would even let you try the girls out for a bit, like allow you to take them to a hotel for a night, but I don't believe that. Anyway, mine wasn't like that. We just talked. I didn't mark down three girls. Yeling was the only one I picked.

"I liked the way she looked. Her skin was so smooth, so young-looking, and I loved her hair, straight and black with a little curl at the end. She smelled like grass and rainwater. But I liked even more the way she acted with me: shy and very eager to please, something you don't see much in the women back home." He looked over at me as I took notes, and shrugged. "If you want to put a label on me and make the people who read what you write feel good about themselves., that's your choice. It doesn't make the label true."

I asked him if something felt wrong about the process, like shopping for a thing.

"I paid the service two thousand dollars, and gave her family another five thousand before I married her. Some people will not like that. They'll think something is not altogether right about the way I married her.

"But I know I'm happy when I'm with her. That's enough for me.

"By the time I met her, Yeling had already dropped out of high school. If I didn't meet her, she would not have gone on to college. She would not have become a lawyer or banker. She would not have gone to work in an office and come home to do yoga. That's the way the world is.

"Maybe she would have gone to Nanning to become a masseuse or bathhouse girl. Maybe she would have married an old peasant from the next village who she didn't even know just because he could give her family some money. Maybe she would have spent the rest of her life getting parasites from toiling in the rice paddies all day and bringing up children in a mud hut at night. And she would have looked like an old woman by thirty.

"How could that have been better?"

The language of the zeppeliners on the transpacific long haul, though officially English, is a mix of images and words from America and China. *Dao, knife, dough*, and *dollar* are used as interchangeable synonyms. Ursine imagery is applied to law enforcement agents along the route: a panda is a Chinese air patrol unit, and a polar bear Russian; in Alaska they are Kodiaks, and off the coast of BC they become whales; finally in America the ships have to deal with grizzlies. The bear's job is to make the life of the zeppeliner difficult: catching pilots who have been at the controls for more than six hours without switching off, who fly above or below regulation altitude, who mix hydrogen into the lift gas to achieve an extra edge in cargo capacity.

"Whales?" I asked Icke. How was whale a type of bear?

"Evolution," Icke said. "Darwin said that a race of bears swimming with their mouths open for water bugs may eventually evolve into whales." (I checked. This was true.)

Nothing changed as an electronic beep from the ship's GPS informed us that we crossed the international border between China and Mongolia somewhere in the desolate, dry plains of the Gobi below, dotted with sparse clumps of short, brittle grass.

Yeling came into the control cab to take over. Icke locked the controls and got up. In the small space at the back of the control cab, they spoke to each other for a bit in lowered voices, kissed, while I stared at the instrument panels, trying hard not to eavesdrop.

Every marriage had its own engine, with its own rhythm and fuel, its own language and control scheme, a quiet hum that kept everything moving. But the hum was so quiet that sometimes it was more felt than heard, and you had to listen for it if you didn't want to miss it.

Then Icke left and Yeling came forward to take the pilot's seat.

She looked at me. "There's a second bunk in the back if you want to park yourself a bit." Her English was accented but good, and you could hear traces of Icke's broad New England A's and non-rhoticity in some of the words.

I thanked her and told her that I wasn't sleepy yet.

She nodded and concentrated on flying the ship, her hands gripping the stick for the empennage—the elevators and rudders in the cruciform tail—and the wheel for the trim far more tightly than Icke had.

I stared at the empty, cold desert passing beneath us for a while, and then I asked her what she had been doing when I first showed up at the airport.

"Fixing the eyes of the ship. Barry likes to see the mouth all red and fierce, but the eyes are more important.

"A ship is a dragon, and dragons navigate by sight. One eye for the sky, another for the sea. A ship without eyes cannot see the coming storms and ride the changing winds. It won't see the underwater rocks near the shore and know the direction of land. A blind ship will sink."

An airship, she said, needed eyes even more than a ship on water. It moved so much faster and there were so many more things that could go wrong.

"Barry thinks it's enough to have these." She gestured towards the instrument panel before her: GPS, radar, radio, altimeter, gyroscope, compass. "But these things help Barry, not the ship. The ship itself needs to *see*.

"Barry thinks this is superstition, and he doesn't want me to do it. But I tell him that the ship looks more impressive for customers if he keeps the eyes freshly painted. That he thinks make sense."

Yeling told me that she had also crawled all over the hull of ship and traced out a pattern of oval dragon scales on the surface of the hull with tung oil. "It looks like the way the ice cracks in spring on a lake with good *fengshui*. A ship with a good coat of dragon scales won't ever be claimed by water."

The sky darkened and night fell. Beneath us was complete darkness, northern Mongolia and the Russian Far East being some of the least densely inhabited regions of the globe. Above us, stars, denser than I had ever seen, winked into existence. It felt as though we were drifting on the surface of a sea at night, the water around us filled with the glow of sea jellies, the way I remember when I used to swim at night in Long Island Sound off of the Connecticut coast.

"I think I'll sleep now," I said. She nodded, and then told me that I could microwave something for myself in the small galley behind the control cab, off to the side of the main corridor.

The galley was tiny, barely larger than a closet. There was a fridge, a microwave, a sink, and a small two-burner electric range. Everything was kept spotless. The pots and pans were neatly hung on the wall, and the dishes were stacked in a grid of cubbyholes and tied down with velcro straps. I ate quickly and then followed the sound of snores aft.

Icke had left the light on for me. In the windowless bedroom, the soft, warm glow and the wood-paneled walls were pleasant and induced sleep. Two bunks, one on top of another, hung against one wall of the small bedroom. Icke was asleep in the bottom one. In one corner of the room was a small vanity with a mirror, and pictures of Yeling's family were taped around the frame of the mirror.

It struck me then that this was Icke and Yeling's *home*. Icke had told me that they owned a house in western Massachusetts, but they spent only about a month out of the year there. Most of their meals were cooked and eaten in the *American Dragon*, and most of their dreams were dreamt here in this room, each alone in a bunk.

A poster of smiling children drawn in the style of Chinese folk art was on the wall next to the vanity, and framed pictures of Yeling and Icke together, smiling, filled the rest of the wall space. I looked through them: wedding, vacation, somewhere in a Chinese city, somewhere near a lake with snowy shores, each of them holding up a big fish.

I crawled into the top bunk, and between Icke's snores, I could hear the faint hum of the ship's engines, so faint that you almost missed it if you didn't listen for it.

I was more tired than I had realized, and slept through the rest of Yeling's shift as well as Icke's next shift. By the time I woke up, it was just after sunrise, and Yeling was again at the helm. We were deep in Russia, flying over the endless coniferous boreal forests of the heart of Siberia. Our course was now growing ever more easterly as we approached the tip of Siberia where it would meet Alaska across the Bering Sea.

She was listening to an audio book as I came into the control cab. She reached out to turn it off when she heard me, but I told her that it was all right.

It was a book about baseball, an explanation of the basic rules for non-fans. The particular section she was listening to dealt with the art of how to appreciate a stolen base.

Yeling stopped the book at the end of the chapter. I sipped a cup of coffee while we watched the sun rise higher and higher over the Siberian taiga, lighting up the lichen woodland dotted with bogs and pristine lakes still frozen over.

"I didn't understand the game when I first married Barry. We do not have baseball in China, especially not where I grew up.

"Sometimes, when Barry and I aren't working, when I stay up a bit during my shift to sit with him or on our days off, I want to talk about the games I played as a girl or a book I remember reading in school or a festival we had back home. But it's difficult.

"Even for a simple funny memory I wanted to share about the time my cousins and I made these new paper boats, I'd have to explain everything: the names of the paper boats we made, the rules for racing them, the festival that we were celebrating and what the custom for racing paper boats was about, the jobs and histories of the spirits for the festival, the names of the cousins and how we were related, and by then I'd forgotten what was the stupid little story I wanted to share.

"It was exhausting for both of us. I used to work hard to try to explain everything, but Barry would get tired, and he couldn't keep the Chinese names straight or even hear the difference between them. So I stopped.

"But I want to be able to talk to Barry. Where there is no language, people have to build language. Barry likes baseball. So I listen to this book and then we have something to talk about. He is happy when I can listen to or watch a baseball game with him and say a few words when I can follow what's happening."

Icke was at the helm for the northernmost leg of our journey, where we flew parallel to the Arctic Circle and just south of it. Day and night had lost their meaning as we flew into the extreme northern latitudes. I was already getting used to the six-hour-on, six-hour-off rhythm of their routine, and slowly synching my body's clock to theirs.

I asked Icke if he knew much about Yeling's family or spent much time with them.

"No. She sends some money back to them every couple of months. She's careful with the budget, and I know that anything she sends them she's worked for as hard as I did. I've had to work on her to get her to be a little more generous with herself, and to spend money on things that will make us happy right now. Every time we go to Vegas now she's willing to play some games with me and lose a little money, but she even has a budget for that.

"I don't get involved with her family. I figure that if she wanted out of her home and village so badly that she was willing to float away with a stranger in a bag of gas, then there's no need for me to become part of what she's left behind.

"I'm sure she also misses her family. How can she not? That's the way we all are, as far as I can see: we want that closeness from piling in all together and knowing everything about everyone and talking all in one breath, but we also want to run away by ourselves and be alone. Sometimes we want both at the same time. My mom wasn't much of a mom, and I haven't been home since I was sixteen. But even I can't say that I don't miss her sometimes.

"I give her space. If there's one thing the Chinese don't have, it's space. Yeling lived in a hut so full of people that she never even had her own blanket, and she couldn't remember a single hour when she was alone. Now we see each other for a few minutes every six hours, and she's learned how to fill up that space, all that free time, by herself. She's grown to like it. It's what she never had, growing up."

There is a lot of space in a zeppelin, I thought, idly. That space, filled with lighter-than-air helium, keeps the zeppelin afloat. A marriage also has a lot of space. What fills it to keep it afloat?

We watched the display of the aurora borealis outside the window in the northern skies as the ship raced towards Alaska.

I don't know how much time passed before I was jolted awake by a violent jerk. Before I knew what was going on, another sudden tilt of the ship threw me out of my bunk onto the floor. I rolled over, stumbled up, and made my way forward into the control cab by holding onto the walls.

"It's common to have storms in spring over the Bering Sea," Icke, who was supposed to be off shift and sleeping, was standing and holding onto the back of the pilot's chair. Yeling didn't bother to acknowledge me. Her knuckles were white from gripping the controls.

It was daytime, but other than the fact that there was some faint and murky light coming through the windows, it might as well have been the middle of the night. The wind, slamming freezing rain into the windows, made it impossible to see even the bottom of the hull as it curved up from the control cab to the nose cone. Billowing fog and cloud roiled around the ship, whipping past us faster than cars on the autobahns.

A sudden gust slammed into the side of the ship, and I was thrown onto the floor of the cab. Icke didn't even look over as he shouted at me, "Tie yourself down or get back to the bunk."

I got up and stood in the back right corner of the control cab, and used the webbing I found there to lash myself in place and out of the way.

Smoothly, as though they had practiced it, Yeling slipped out of the pilot chair and Icke slipped in. Yeling strapped herself into the passenger stool on the right. The line on one of the electronic screens that showed the ship's course by GPS indicated that we had been zigzagging around crazily. In fact, it was clear that although the throttle was on full and we were burning fuel as fast as an airplane, the wind was pushing us backwards relative to the ground.

It was all Icke could do to keep us pointed into the wind and minimize the cross-section we presented to the front of the storm. If we were pointed slightly at an angle to the wind, the wind would have grabbed us around the ship's peripatetic pivot point and spun us like an egg on its side, yawing out of control. The pivot point, the center of momentum around which a ship would move when an external force is applied, shifts and moves about an airship depending on the ship's configuration, mass, hull shape, speed, acceleration, wind direction, and angular momentum, among other factors, and a pilot kept a zeppelin straight in a storm like this by feel and instinct more than anything else.

Lightning flashed close by, so close that I was blinded for a moment. The thunder rumbled the ship and made my teeth rattle, as though the floor of the ship was the diaphragm of a subwoofer.

"She feels heavy," Icke said. "Ice must be building up on the hull. It actually doesn't feel nearly as heavy as I would have expected. The hull ought to be covered by a solid layer of ice now if the outside thermometer reading is right. But we are still losing altitude, and we can't go any lower. The waves are going to hit the ship. We can't duck under this storm. We'll have to climb over it."

Icke dropped more water ballast to lighten the ship, and tilted the elevators up. We shot straight up like a rocket. The *American Dragon*'s elongated teardrop shape acted as a crude airfoil, and as the brutal Arctic wind rushed at us, we flew like an experimental model wing design in a wind tunnel.

Another bolt of lightning flashed, even closer and brighter than before. The rumble from the thunder hurt my eardrums, and for a while I could hear nothing.

Icke and Yeling shouted at each other, and Yeling shook her head and yelled again. Icke looked at her for a moment, nodded, and lifted his hands off the controls for a second. The ship jerked itself and twisted to the side as the wind took hold of it and began to turn it. Icke reached back to grab the controls as another bolt of lightning flashed. The interior lights went out as the lightning erased all shadows and lines and perspective, and the sound of the thunder knocked me off my feet and punched me hard in the ears. And I passed into complete darkness.

By the time I came to, I had missed the entire Alaskan leg of the journey.

Yeling, who had the helm, was playing a Chinese song through the speakers. It was dark outside, and a round, golden moon, almost full and as big as the moon I remember from my childhood, floated over the dark and invisible sea. I sat down next to Yeling and stared at it.

After the chorus, the singer, a woman with a mellow and smooth voice, began the next verse in English:

But why is the moon always fullest when we take leave of one another?
For us, there is sorrow, joy, parting, and meeting.
For the moon, there is shade, shine, waxing and waning.
It has never been possible to have it all.
All we can wish for is that we endure,
Though we are thousands of miles apart,

Yet we shall gaze upon the same moon, always lovely.

Yeling turned off the music and wiped her eyes with the back of her hand.

"She found a way out of the storm," she said. There was no need to ask who she meant. "She dodged that lightning at the last minute and found herself a hole in the storm to slip through. Sharp eyes. I knew it was a good idea to repaint the left eye, the one watching the sky, before we took off."

I watched the calm waters of the Pacific Ocean pass beneath us.

"In the storm, she shed her scales to make herself lighter."

I imagined the tung oil lines drawn on the ship's hull by Yeling, the lines etching the ice into dragon scales, which fell in large chunks into the frozen sea below.

"When I first married Barry, I did everything his way and nothing my way. When he was asleep, and I was flying the ship, I had a lot of time to think. I would think about my parents getting old and me not being there. I'd think about some recipe I wanted to ask my mother about, and she wasn't there. I asked myself all the time, *what have I done?*

"But even though I did everything his way, we used to argue all the time. Arguments that neither of us could understand and that went nowhere. And then I decided that I had to do something.

"I rearranged the way the pots were hung up in the galley and the way the dishes were stacked in the cabinets and the way the pictures were arranged in the bedroom and the way we stored life vests and shoes and blankets. I gave everything a better flow of *qi*, energy, and smoother *fengshui*. It might seem like a cramped and shabby place to some, but the ship now feels like our palace in the skies.

"Barry didn't even notice it. But, because of the *fengshui*, we didn't argue any more. Even during the storm, when things were so tense, we worked well together."

"Were you scared at all during the storm?" I asked.

Yeling bit her bottom lip, thinking about my question.

"When I first rode with Barry, when I didn't yet know him, I used to wake up and say, in Chinese, *who is this man with me in the sky?* That was the most I've ever been scared.

"But last night, when I was struggling with the ship and Barry came to help me, I wasn't scared at all. I thought, it's okay if we die now. I know this man. I know what I've done. I'm home."

"There was never any real danger from lightning," Icke said. "You knew that, right? The *American Dragon* is a giant Faraday cage. Even if the lightning had struck us, the charge would have stayed on the outside of the metal frame. We were in the safest place over that whole sea in that storm."

I brought up what Yeling had said, that the ship seemed to know where to go in the storm.

Icke shrugged. "Aerodynamics is a complex thing, and the ship moved the way physics told it to."

"But when you get your Aurora, you'll let her paint eyes on it?"

Icke nodded, as though I had asked a very stupid question.

Las Vegas, the diadem of the desert, spread out beneath, around, and above us.

Pleasure ships and mass-transit passenger zeppelins covered in flashing neon and gaudy giant flickering screens dotted the air over the Strip. Cargo carriers like us were constricted to a narrow lane parallel to the Strip with specific points where we were allowed to depart to land at the individual casinos.

"That's Laputa," Icke pointed above us, to a giant, puffy, baroque airship that seemed as big as the Venetian, which we were passing below and to the left. Lit from within, this newest and flashiest floating casino glowed like a giant red Chinese lantern in the sky. Air taxis rose from the Strip and floated towards it like fireflies.

We had dropped off the shipment of turbine blades with the wind farm owned by Caesars Palace outside the city, and now we were headed for Caesars itself. Comp rooms were one of the benefits of hauling cargo for a customer like that.

I saw, coming up behind the Mirage, the tall spire and blinking lights of the mooring mast in front of the Forum Shops. It was usually where the great luxury personal yachts of the high-stakes rollers moored, but tonight it was empty, and a transpacific long-haul Dongfeng Feimaotui, a Flying Chinaman named the *American Dragon*, was going to take it for its own.

"We'll play some games, and then go to our room," Icke said. He was talking to Yeling, who smiled back at him. This would be the first chance they had of sleeping on the same bed in a week. They had a full twenty-four hours, and then they'd take off for Kalispell, Montana, where they would pick up a shipment of buffalo bones for the long haul back to China.

I lay in bed in my Downtown hotel room thinking about the way the furniture in my bedroom was arranged, and imagined the flow of *qi* around the bed, the nightstands, the dresser. I missed the faint hum of the zeppelin's engines, so quiet that you had to listen hard to hear them.

I turned on the light and called my wife. "I'm not home yet. Soon."

A GUIDE TO THE FRUITS
OF HAWAI'I

ALAYA DAWN JOHNSON

◄─◆─►

Key's favorite time of day is sunset, her least is sunrise. It should be the opposite, but every time she watches that bright red disk sinking into the water beneath Mauna Kea her heart bends like a wishbone, and she thinks, *He's awake now.*

Key is thirty-four. She is old for a human woman without any children. She has kept herself alive by being useful in other ways. For the past four years, Key has been the overseer of the Mauna Kea Grade Orange blood facility.

Is it a concentration camp if the inmates are well fed? If their beds are comfortable? If they are given an hour and a half of rigorous boxercise and yoga each morning in the recreational field?

It doesn't have to be Honouliui to be wrong.

When she's called in to deal with Jeb's body—bloody, not drained, in a feeding room—yoga doesn't make him any less dead.

Key helps vampires run a concentration camp for humans.

Key is a different kind of monster.

Key's favorite food is umeboshi. Salty and tart and bright red, with that pit in the center to beware. She loves it in rice balls, the kind her Japanese grandmother made when she was little. She loves it by itself, the way she ate it at fifteen, after Obaachan died. She hasn't had umeboshi in eighteen years, but sometimes she thinks that when she dies she'll taste one again.

This morning she eats the same thing she eats every meal: a nutritious brick patty, precisely five inches square and two inches deep, colored puce. Her raw scrubbed hands still have a pink tinge of Jeb's blood in the cuticles. She stares at them while she sips the accompanying beverage, which is orange. She can't remember if it ever resembled the fruit.

She eats this because that is what every human eats in the Mauna Kea facility. Because the patty is easy to manufacture and soft enough to eat with plastic spoons. Key hasn't seen a fork in years, a knife in more than a decade. The vampires maintain tight control over all items with the potential to draw blood. Yet humans are tool-making creatures, and their desires, even nihilistic ones, have a creative power that no vampire has the imagination or agility to anticipate. How else to explain the shiv, handcrafted over secret months from the wood cover and glue-matted pages of *A Guide to the Fruits of Hawai'i,* the book that Jeb used to read in the hours after his feeding sessions, sometimes aloud, to whatever humans would listen? He took the only thing that gave him pleasure in the world, destroyed it—or recreated it—and slit his veins with it. Mr. Charles questioned her particularly; he knew that she and Jeb used to talk sometimes. Had she *known* that the *boy* was like this? He gestured with pallid hands at the splatter of arterial pulses from jaggedly slit wrists: oxidized brown, inedible, mocking.

No, she said, of course not, Mr. Charles. I report any suspected cases of self-waste immediately.

She reports any suspected cases. And so, for the weeks she has watched Jeb hardly eating across the mess hall, noticed how he staggered from the feeding rooms, recognized the frigid rebuff in his responses to her questions, she has very carefully refused to suspect.

Today, just before dawn, she choked on the fruits of her indifference. He slit his wrists and femoral arteries. He smeared the blood over his face and buttocks and genitals, and he waited to die before the vampire technician could arrive to drain him.

Not many humans self-waste. Most think about it, but Key never has, not since the invasion of the Big Island. Unlike other humans, she has someone she's waiting for. The one she loves, the one she prays will reward her patience. During her years as overseer, Key has successfully stopped three acts of self-waste. She has failed twice. Jeb is different; Mr. Charles sensed it somehow, but vampires can only read human minds through human blood. Mr. Charles hasn't drunk from Key in years. And what could he learn, even if he did? He can't drink thoughts she has spent most of her life refusing to have.

Mr. Charles calls her to the main office the next night, between feeding shifts. She is terrified, like she always is, of what they might do. She is thinking of Jeb and wondering how Mr. Charles has taken the loss of an investment. She is wondering how fast she will die in the work camp on Lanai.

But Mr. Charles has an offer, not a death sentence.

"You know . . . of the facility on Oahu? Grade Gold?"

"Yes," Key says. Just that, because she learned early not to betray herself to them unnecessarily, and the man at Grade Gold has always been her greatest betrayer.

No, not a man, Key tells herself for the hundredth, the thousandth time. *He is one of them.*

Mr. Charles sits in a hanging chair shaped like an egg with plush red velvet cushions. He wears a black suit with steel gray pinstripes, sharply tailored. The cuffs are high and his feet are bare, white as talcum powder and long and bony like spiny fish. His veins are prominent and round and milky blue. Mr. Charles is vain about his feet.

He does not sit up to speak to Key. She can hardly see his face behind the shadow cast by the overhanging top of the egg. All vampires speak deliberately, but Mr. Charles drags out his tones until you feel you might tip over from waiting on the next syllable. It goes up and down like a calliope—

" . . . what do you *say* to heading down there and *sort*ing the matter . . . out?"

"I'm sorry, Mr. Charles," she says carefully, because she has lost the thread of his monologue. "What matter?"

He explains: a Grade Gold human girl has killed herself. It is a disaster that outshadows the loss of Jeb.

"You would not believe the expense taken to keep those humans Grade Gold standard."

"What would I do?"

"Take it in hand, *of* course. It seems our small . . . Grade Orange operation has gotten some notice. Tetsuo asked for you . . . particularly."

"Tetsuo?" She hasn't said the name out loud in years. Her voice catches on the second syllable.

"*Mr.* Tetsuo," Mr. Charles says, and waves a hand at her. He holds a sheet of paper, the same shade as his skin. "He wrote you a *letter.*"

Key can't move, doesn't reach out to take it, and so it flutters to the black marble floor a few feet away from Mr. Charles's egg.

He leans forward. "I think . . . I remember something . . . you and Tetsuo. . . . "

"He recommended my promotion here," Key says, after a moment. It seems the safest phrasing. Mr. Charles would have remembered this eventually; vampires are slow, but inexorable.

The diffuse light from the paper lanterns catches the bottom half of his face, highlighting the deep cleft in his chin. It twitches in faint surprise. "You *were* his pet?"

Key winces. She remembers the years she spent at his side during and after the wars, catching scraps in his wake, despised by every human who saw her there. She waited for him to see how much she had sacrificed and give her the only reward that could matter after what she'd done. Instead he had her shunt removed and sent her to Grade Orange. She has not seen or heard from him in four years. His pet, yes, that's as good a name as any—but he never drank from her. Not once.

Mr. Charles's lips, just a shade of white darker than his skin, open like a hole in a cloud. "And he wants you back. How do you *feel* ?"

Terrified. Awestruck. Confused. "Grateful," she says.

The hole smiles. "Grateful! How interesting. Come here, girl. I believe I shall *have a taste.* "

She grabs the letter with shaking fingers and folds it inside a pocket of her red uniform. She stands in front of Mr. Charles.

"Well?" he says.

She hasn't had a shunt in years, though she can still feel its ridged scar in the crook of her arm. Without it, feeding from her is messy, violent. Traditional, Mr. Charles might say. Her fingers hurt as she unzips the collar. Her muscles feel sore, the bones in her spine arthritic and old as she bows her head, leans closer to Mr. Charles. She waits for him to bare his fangs, to pierce her vein, to suck her blood.

He takes more than he should. He drinks until her fingers and toes twinge, until her neck throbs, until the red velvet of his seat fades to gray. When he finishes, he leaves her blood on his mouth.

"I forgive . . . you for the boy," he says.

Jeb cut his own arteries, left his good blood all over the floor. Mr. Charles abhors waste above all else.

Mr. Charles will explain the situation. I wish you to come. If you do well, I have been authorized to offer you the highest reward.

The following night, Key takes a boat to Oahu. Vampires don't like water, but they will cross it anyway—the sea has become a status symbol among them, an indication of strength. Hawai'i is still a resort destination, though most of its residents only go out at night. Grade Gold is the most expensive, most luxurious resort of them all.

Tetsuo travels between the islands often. Key saw him do it a dozen times during the war. She remembers one night, his face lit by the moon and the yellow lamps on the deck—the wide cheekbones, thick eyebrows, sharp widow's peak, all frozen in the perfection of a nineteen-year-old boy. Pale beneath the olive tones of his skin, he bares his fangs when the waves lurch beneath him.

"What does it feel like?" she asks him.

"Like frozen worms in my veins," he says, after a full, long minute of silence. Then he checks the guns and tells her to wait below, the humans are coming. She can't see anything, but Tetsuo can smell them like chum in the water. The Japanese have held out the longest, and the vampires of Hawai'i lead the assault against them.

Two nights later, in his quarters in the bunker at the base of Mauna Kea,

Tetsuo brings back a sheet of paper, written in Japanese. The only characters she recognizes are "shi" and "ta"—"death" and "field." It looks like some kind of list.

"What is this?" she asks.

"Recent admissions to the Lanai human residential facility."

She looks up at him, devoted with terror. "My mother?" Her father died in the first offensive on the Big Island, a hero of the resistance. He never knew how his daughter had chosen to survive.

"Here," Tetsuo says, and runs a cold finger down the list without death. "Jen Isokawa."

"Alive?" She has been looking for her mother since the wars began. Tetsuo knows this, but she didn't know he was searching, too. She feels swollen with this indication of his regard.

"She's listed as a caretaker. They're treated well. You could. . . . " He sits beside her on the bed that only she uses. His pause lapses into a stop. He strokes her hair absentmindedly; if she had a tail, it would beat his legs. She is seventeen and she is sure he will reward her soon.

"Tetsuo," she says, "you could drink from me, if you want. I've had a shunt for nearly a year. The others use it. I'd rather feed you."

Sometimes she has to repeat herself three times before he seems to hear her. This, she has said at least ten. But she is safe here in his bunker, on the bed he brought in for her, with his lukewarm body pressed against her warm one. Vampires do not have sex with humans; they feed. But if he doesn't want her that way, what else can she offer him?

"I've had you tested. You're fertile. If you bear three children you won't need a shunt and the residential facilities will care for you for the rest of your mortality. You can live with your mother. I will make sure you're safe."

She presses her face against his shoulder. "Don't make me leave."

"You wanted to see your mother."

Her mother had spent the weeks before the invasion in church, praying for God to intercede against the abominations. Better that she die than see Key like this.

"Only to know what happened to her," Key whispers. "Won't you feed from me, Tetsuo? I want to feel closer to you. I want you to know how much I love you."

A long pause. Then, "I don't need to taste you to know how you feel."

Tetsuo meets her on shore.

Just like that, she is seventeen again.

"You look older," he says. Slowly, but with less affectation than Mr. Charles.

This is true; so inevitable she doesn't understand why he even bothers to say so. Is he surprised? Finally, she nods. The buoyed dock rocks beneath them—he makes no attempt to move, though the two vampires with him grip the denuded skin of their own elbows with pale fingers. They flare and retract their fangs.

"You are drained," he says. He does not mean this metaphorically.

She nods again, realizes further explanation is called for. "Mr. Charles," she says, her voice a painful rasp. This embarrasses her, though Tetsuo would never notice.

He nods, sharp and curt. She thinks he is angry, though perhaps no one else could read him as clearly. She knows that face, frozen in the countenance of a boy dead before the Second World War. A boy dead fifty years before she was born.

He is old enough to remember Pearl Harbor, the detention camps, the years when Maui's forests still had native birds. But she has never dared ask him about his human life.

"And what did Charles explain?"

"He said someone killed herself at Grade Gold."

Tetsuo flares his fangs. She flinches, which surprises her. She used to flush at the sight of his fangs, her blood pounding red just beneath the soft surface of her skin.

"I've been given dispensation," he says, and rests one finger against the hollow at the base of her throat.

She's learned a great deal about the rigid traditions that restrict vampire life since she first met Tetsuo. She understands why her teenage fantasies of morally liberated vampirism were improbable, if not impossible. For each human they bring over, vampires need a special dispensation that they only receive once or twice every decade. *The highest reward.* If Tetsuo has gotten a dispensation, then her first thought when she read his letter was correct. He didn't mean retirement. He didn't mean a peaceful life in some remote farm on the islands. He meant death. Un-death.

After all these years, Tetsuo means to turn her into a vampire.

The trouble at Grade Gold started with a dead girl. Penelope cut her own throat five days ago (with a real knife, the kind they allow Grade Gold humans for cutting food). Her ghost haunts the eyes of those she left behind. One human resident in particular, with hair dyed the color of tea and blue lipstick to match the bruises under her red eyes, takes one look at Key and starts to scream.

Key glances at Tetsuo, but he has forgotten her. He stares at the girl as if he could burn her to ashes on the plush green carpet. The five others in the room look away, but Key can't tell if it's in embarrassment or fear. The luxury surrounding them chokes her. There's a bowl of fruit on a coffee table. Real fruit—fuzzy brown kiwis, mottled red-green mangos, dozens of tangerines. She takes an involuntary step forward and the girl's scream gets louder before cutting off with an abrupt squawk. Her labored breaths are the only sound in the room.

"This is a joke," the girl says. There's spittle on her blue lips. "What hole did you dig her out of?"

"Go to your room, Rachel," Tetsuo says.

Rachel flicks back her hair and rubs angrily under one eye. "What are you now, Daddy Vampire? You think you can just, what? Replace her? With this broke down fogie lookalike?"

"She is not—"

"Yeah? What is she?"

They are both silent, doubt and grief and fury scuttling between them like beetles in search of a meal. Tetsuo and the girl stare at each other with such deep familiarity that Key feels forgotten, alone—almost ashamed of the dreams that have kept her alive for a decade. They have never felt so hopeless, or so false.

"Her name is Key," Tetsuo says, in something like defeat. He turns away, though he makes no move to leave. "She will be your new caretaker."

"Key?" the girl says. "What kind of a name is that?"

Key doesn't answer for a long time, thinking of all the ways she could respond. Of Obaachan Akiko and the affectionate nickname of lazy summers spent hiking in the mountains or pounding mochi in the kitchen. Of her half-Japanese mother and Hawai'ian father, of the ways history and identity and circumstance can shape a girl into half a woman, until someone—*not a man*—comes with a hundred thousand others like him and destroys anything that might have once had meaning. So she finds meaning in him. Who else was there?

And this girl, whose sneer reveals her bucked front teeth, has as much chance of understanding that world as Key does of understanding this one. Fresh fruit on the table. No uniforms. And a perfect, glittering shunt of plastic and metal nestled in the crook of her left arm.

"Mine," Key answers the girl.

Rachel spits; Tetsuo turns his head, just a little, as though he can only bear to see Key from the corner of his eye.

"You're nothing like her," she says.

"Like who?"

But the girl storms from the room, leaving her chief vampire without a dismissal. Key now understands this will not be punished. It's another one—a boy, with the same florid beauty as the girl but far less belligerence, who answers her.

"You look like Penelope," he says, tugging on a long lock of his asymmetrically cut black hair. "Just older."

When Tetsuo leaves the room, it's Key who cannot follow.

Key remembers sixteen. Her obaachan is dead and her mother has moved to an apartment in Hilo and it's just Key and her father in that old, quiet house at the end of the road. The vampires have annexed San Diego and Okinawa is besieged, but life doesn't feel very different in the mountains of the Big Island.

It is raining in the woods behind her house. Her father has told her to study, but all she's done since her mother left is read Mishima's *Sea of Fertility* novels. She sits on the porch, wondering if it's better to kill herself or wait for them to come, and just as she thinks she ought to have the courage to die, something rattles in the shed. A rat, she thinks.

But it's not rat she sees when she pulls open the door on its rusty hinges. It's a man, crouched between a stack of old appliance boxes and the rusted fender of the Buick her father always meant to fix one day. His hair is wet and slicked back, his white shirt is damp and ripped from shoulder to navel. The skin beneath it is pale as a corpse; bloodless, though the edges of a deep wound are still visible.

"They've already come?" Her voice breaks on a whisper. She wanted to finish *The Decay of the Angel*. She wanted to see her mother once more.

"Shut the door," he says, crouching in shadow, away from the bar of light streaming through the narrow opening.

"Don't kill me."

"We are equally at each other's mercy."

She likes the way he speaks. No one told her they could sound so proper. So human. Is there a monster in her shed, or is he something else?

"Why shouldn't I open it all the way?"

He is brave, whatever else. He takes his long hands from in front of his face and stands, a flower blooming after rain. He is beautiful, though she will not mark that until later. Now, she only notices the steady, patient way he regards her. *I could move faster than you,* his eyes say. *I could kill you first.*

She thinks of Mishima and says, "I'm not afraid of death."

Only when the words leave her mouth does she realize how deeply she has lied. Does he know? Her hands would shake if it weren't for their grip on the handle.

"I promise," he says. "I will save you, when the rest of us come."

What is it worth, a monster's promise?

She steps inside and shuts out the light.

• • •

There are nineteen residents of Grade Gold; the twentieth is buried beneath the kukui tree in the communal garden. The thought of rotting in earth revolts Key. She prefers the bright, fierce heat of a crematorium fire, like the one that consumed Jeb the night before she left Mauna Kea. The ashes fly in the wind, into the ocean and up in the trees, where they lodge in bird nests and caterpillar silk and mud puddles after a storm. The return of flesh to the earth should be fast and final, not the slow mortification of worms and bacteria and carbon gases.

Tetsuo instructs her to keep close watch on unit three. "Rachel isn't very . . . steady right now," he says, as though unaware of the understatement.

The remaining nineteen residents are divided into four units, five kids in each, living together in sprawling ranch houses connected by walkways and gardens. There are walls, of course, but you have to climb a tree to see them. The kids at Grade Gold have more freedom than any human she's ever encountered since the war, but they're as bound to this paradise as she was to her mountain.

The vampires who come here stay in a high glass tower right by the beach. During the day, the black-tinted windows gleam like lasers. At night, the vampires come down to feed. There is a fifth house in the residential village, one reserved for clients and their meals. Tetsuo orchestrates these encounters, planning each interaction in fine detail: this human with that performance for this distinguished client. Key has grown used to thinking of her fellow humans as food, but now she is forced to reconcile that indelible fact with another, stranger veneer. The vampires who pay so dearly for Grade Gold humans don't merely want to feed from a shunt. They want to be entertained, talked to, cajoled. The boy who explained about Key's uncanny resemblance juggles torches. Twin girls from unit three play guitar and sing songs by the Carpenters. Even Rachel, dressed in a gaudy purple mermaid dress with matching streaks in her hair, keeps up a one-way, laughing conversation with a vampire who seems too astonished—or too slow—to reply.

Key has never seen anything like this before. She thought that most vampires regarded humans as walking sacks of food. What pleasure could be derived from speaking with your meal first? From seeing it sing or dance? When she first went with Tetsuo, the other vampires talked about human emotions as if they were flavors of ice cream. But at Grade Orange she grew accustomed to more basic parameters: were the humans fed, were they fertile, did they sleep? Here, she must approve outfits; she must manage dietary preferences and erratic tempers and a dozen other details all crucial to keeping the kids Grade Gold standard. Their former caretaker has been shipped to the work camps, which leaves Key in sole charge of the operation. At least until Tetsuo decides how he will use his dispensation.

Key's thoughts skitter away from the possibility.

"I didn't know vampires liked music," she says, late in the evening, when some of the kids sprawl, exhausted, across couches and cushions. A girl no older than fifteen opens her eyes but hardly moves when a vampire in a gold suit lifts her arm for a nip. Key and Tetsuo are seated together at the far end of the main room, in the bay windows that overlook a cliff and the ocean.

"It's as interesting to us as any other human pastime."

"Does music have a taste?"

His wide mouth stretches at the edges; she recognizes it as a smile. "Music has some utility, given the right circumstances."

She doesn't quite understand him. The air is redolent with the sweat of human teenagers and the muggy, salty air that blows through the open doors and windows. Her eye catches on a half-eaten strawberry dropped carelessly on the carpet a few feet away. It was harvested too soon, a white, tasteless core surrounded by hard, red flesh.

She thinks there is nothing of "right" in these circumstances, and their utility is, at its bottom, merely that of parasite and host.

"The music enhances the—our—flavor?"

Tetsuo stares at her for a long time, long enough for him to take at least three of his shallow, erratically spaced breaths. To look at him is to taste copper and sea on her tongue; to wait for him is to hear the wind slide down a mountainside an hour before dawn.

It has been four years since she last saw him. She thought he had forgotten her, and now he speaks to her as if all those years haven't passed, as though the vampires hadn't long since won the war and turned the world to their slow, long-burning purpose.

"Emotions change your flavor," he says. "And food. And sex. And pleasure."

And love ? she wonders, but Tetsuo has never drunk from her.

"Then why not treat all of us like you do the ones here? Why have con—Mauna Kea?"

She expects him to catch her slip, but his attention is focused on something beyond her right shoulder. She turns to look, and sees nothing but the hall and a closed feeding room door.

"Three years," he says, quietly. He doesn't look at her. She doesn't understand what he means, so she waits. "It takes three years for the complexity to fade. For the vitality of young blood to turn muddy and clogged with silt. Even among the new crops, only a few individuals are Gold standard. For three years, they produce the finest blood ever tasted, filled with regrets and ecstasy and dreams. And then . . . "

"Grade Orange?" Key asks, her voice dry and rasping. Had Tetsuo always talked of humans like this? With such little regard for their selfhood? Had she been too young to understand, or have the years of harvesting humans hardened him?

"If we have not burned too much out. Living at high elevation helps prolong your utility, but sometimes all that's left is Lanai and the work camps."

She remembers her terror before her final interview with Mr. Charles, her conviction that Jeb's death would prompt him to discard his uselessly old overseer to the work camps.

A boy from one of the other houses staggers to the one she recognizes from unit two and sprawls in his lap. Unit-two boy startles awake, smiles, and bends over to kiss the first. A pair of female vampires kneel in front of them and press their fangs with thick pink tongues.

"Touch him," one says, pointing to the boy from unit two. "Make him cry."

The boy from unit two doesn't even pause for breath; he reaches for the other boy's cock and squeezes. And as they both groan with something that makes Key feel like a voyeur, made helpless by her own desire, the pair of vampires pull the boys apart and dive for their respective shunts. The room goes quiet but for soft gurgles, like two minnows in a tide pool. Then a pair of clicks as the boys' shunts turn gray, forcing the vampires to stop feeding.

"Lovely, divine," the vampires say a few minutes later, when they pass on their way out. "We always appreciate the sexual displays."

The boys curl against each other, eyes shut. They breathe like old men: hard, through constricted tubes.

"Does that happen often?" she asks.

"This Grade Gold is known for its sexual flavors. My humans pick partners they enjoy."

Vampires might not have sex, but they crave its flavor. Will she, when she crosses to their side? Will she look at those two boys and command them to fuck each other just so she can taste?

"Do you ever care?" she says, her voice barely a whisper. "About what you've done to us?"

He looks away from her. Before she can blink he has crossed to the one closed feeding room door and wrenched it open. A thump of something thrown against a wall. A snarl, as human as a snake's hiss.

"Leave, Gregory!" Tetsuo says. A vampire Key recognizes from earlier in the night stumbles into the main room. He rubs his jaw, though the torn and mangled skin there has already begun to knit together.

"She is mine to have. I paid—"

"Not enough to kill her."

"I'll complain to the council," the vampire says. "You've been losing support. And everyone knows how *patiently* Charles has waited in his aerie."

She should be scared, but his words make her think of Jeb, of failures and consequences, and of the one human she has not seen for hours. She stands and sprints past both vampires to where Rachel lies insensate on a bed.

Her shunt has turned the opaque gray meant to prevent vampires from feeding humans to death. But the client has bitten her neck instead.

"Tell them whatever you wish, and I will tell them you circumvented the shunt of a fully tapped human. We have our rules for a reason. You are no longer welcome here."

Rachel's pulse is soft, but steady. She stirs and moans beneath Key's hands. The relief is crushing; she wants to cradle the girl in her arms until she wakes. She wants to protect her so her blood will never have to smear the walls of a feeding room, so that Key will be able to say that at least she saved one.

Rachel's eyes flutter open, land with a butterfly's gentleness on Key's face.

"Pen," she says, "I told you. It makes them . . . they *eat* me."

Key doesn't understand, but she doesn't mind. She presses her hand to Rachel's warm forehead and sings lullabies her grandmother liked until Rachel falls back to sleep.

"How is she?" It is Tetsuo, come into the room after the client has finally left.

"Drained," Key says, as dispassionately as he. "She'll be fine in a few days."

"Key."

"Yes?"

She won't look at him.

"I do, you know."

She knows. "Then why support it?"

"You'll understand when your time comes."

She looks back down at Rachel, and all she can see are bruises blooming purple on her upper arms, blood dried brown on her neck. She looks like a human being: infinitely precious, fragile. Like prey.

Five days later, Key sits in the garden in the shade of the kukui tree. She has reports to file on the last week's feedings, but the papers sit untouched beside her. The boy from unit two and his boyfriend are tending the tomatoes and Key slowly peels the skin from her fourth kiwi. The first time she bit into one she cried, but the boys pretended not to notice. She is getting better with practice. Her hands still tremble and her misted eyes refract rainbows in the hard, noon sunlight. She is learning to be human again.

Rachel sleeps on the ground beside her, curled on the packed dirt of Penelope's grave with her back against the tree trunk and her arms wrapped tightly around her belly. She's spent most of the last five days sleeping, and Key thinks she has mostly recovered. She's been eating voraciously, foods in wild combinations at all times of day and night. Key is glad. Without the distracting, angry makeup, Rachel's face looks vulnerable and haunted. Jeb had that look in the months before his death. He would sit quietly in the mess hall and stare at the food brick as though he had forgotten how to eat. Jeb had transferred to Mauna Kea within a week of Key becoming overseer. He liked watching the lights of the airplanes at night and he kept two books with him: *The Blind Watchmaker* and *A Guide to the Fruits of Hawai'i*. She talked to him about the latter—had he ever tasted breadfruit or kiwi or cherimoya? None, he said, in a voice so small and soft it sounded inversely proportional to his size. Only a peach, a canned peach, when he was four or five years old. Vampires don't waste fruit on Grade Orange humans.

The covers of both books were worn, the spines cracked, the pages yellowed and brittle at the edges. Why keep a book about fruit you had never tasted and never would eat? Why read at all, when they frowned upon literacy in humans and often banned books outright? She never asked him. Mr. Charles had seen their conversation, though she doubted he had heard it, and requested that she refrain from speaking unnecessarily to the *harvest*.

So when Jeb stared at her across the table with eyes like a snuffed candle, she turned away, she forced her patty into her mouth, she chewed, she reached for her orange drink.

His favorite book became his means of self-destruction. She let him do it. She doesn't know if she feels guilty for not having stopped him, or for being in the position to stop him in the first place. Not two weeks later she rests beneath a kukui tree, the flesh of a fruit she had never expected to taste again turning to green pulp between her teeth. She reaches for another one because she knows how little she deserves this.

But the skin of the fruit at the bottom of the bowl is too soft and fleshy for a kiwi. She pulls it into the light and drops it.

"Are you okay?" It's the boy from unit two—Kaipo. He kneels down and picks up the cherimoya.

"What?" she says, and struggles to control her breathing. She has to appear normal, in control. She's supposed to be their caretaker. But the boy just seems concerned, not judgmental. Rachel rolls onto her back and opens her eyes.

"You screamed," Rachel says, sleep-fogged and accusatory. "You woke me up."

"Who put this in the bowl?" Kaipo asks. "These things are poisonous! They grow on that tree down the hill, but you can't eat them."

Key takes the haunted fruit from him, holding it carefully so as to not bruise it further. "Who told you that?" she asks.

Rachel leans forward, so her chin rests on the edge of Key's lounge chair and the tips of her purple-streaked hair touch Key's thigh. "Tetsuo," she says. "What, did he lie?"

Key shakes her head slowly. "He probably only half-remembered. It's a cherimoya. The flesh is delicious, but the seeds are poisonous."

Rachel's eyes follow her hands. "Like, killing you poisonous?" she asks.

Key thinks back to her father's lessons. "Maybe if you eat them all or grind them up. The tree bark can paralyze your heart and lungs."

Kaipo whistles, and they all watch intently when she wedges her finger under the skin and splits it in half. The white, fleshy pulp looks stark, even a little disquieting against the scaly green exterior. She plucks out the hard, brown seeds and tosses them to the ground. Only then does she pull out a chunk of flesh and put it in her mouth.

Like strawberries and banana pudding and pineapple. Like the summer after Obaachan died, when a box of them came to the house as a condolence gift.

"You look like you're fellating it," Rachel says. Key opens her eyes and swallows abruptly.

Kaipo pushes his tongue against his lips. "Can I try it, Key?" he asks, very politely. Did the vampires teach him that politeness? Did vampires teach Rachel a word like *fellate,* perhaps while instructing her to do it with a hopefully willing human partner?

"Do you guys know how to use condoms?" She has decided to ask Tetsuo to supply them. This last week has made it clear that "sexual flavors" are all too frequently on the menu at Grade Gold.

Kaipo looks at Rachel; Rachel shakes her head. "What's a condom?" he asks.

It's so easy to forget how little of the world they know. "You use it during sex, to stop you from catching diseases," she says, carefully. "Or getting pregnant."

Rachel laughs and stuffs the rest of the flesh into her wide mouth. Even a cherimoya can't fill her hollows. "Great, even more vampire sex," she says, her hatred clearer than her garbled words. "They never made Pen do it."

"They didn't?" Key asks.

Juice dribbles down her chin. "You know, Tetsuo's dispensation? Before she killed herself, she was his pick. Everyone knew it. That's why they left her alone."

Key feels light-headed. "But if she was his choice . . . why would she kill herself?"

"She didn't want to be a vampire," Kaipo says softly.

"She wanted a *baby,* like bringing a new food sack into the world is a good idea. But they wouldn't let her have sex and they wanted to make her one of them, so—now she's gone. But why he'd bring *you* here, when *any* of us would be a better choice—"

"Rachel, just shut up. Please." Kaipo takes her by the shoulder.

Rachel shrugs him off. "What? Like she can do anything."

"If she becomes one of *them* —"

"I wouldn't hurt you," Key says, too quickly. Rachel masks her pain with cruelty, but it is palpable. Key can't imagine any version of herself that would add to that.

Kaipo and Rachel stare at her. "But," Kaipo says, "that's what vampires do."

"I would eat you," Rachel says, and flops back under the tree. "I would make you cry and your tears would taste sweeter than a cherimoya."

"I will be back in four days," Testsuo tells her, late the next night. "There is one feeding scheduled. I hope you will be ready when I return."

"For the . . . reward?" she asks, stumbling over an appropriate euphemism. Their words for it are polysyllabic spikes: transmutation, transformation, metamorphosis. All vampires were once human, and immortal doesn't mean invulnerable. Some die each year, and so their ranks must be replenished with the flesh of worthy, willing humans.

He places a hand on her shoulder. It feels as chill and inert as a piece of damp wood. She thinks she must be dreaming.

"I have wanted this for a long time, Key," he says to her—like a stranger, like the person who knows her the best in the world.

"Why now?"

"Our thoughts can be . . . slow, sometimes. You will see. Orderly, but sometimes too orderly to see patterns clearly. I thought of you, but did not know it until Penelope died."

Penelope, who looked just like Key. Penelope, who would have been his pick. She shivers and steps away from his hand. "Did you love her?"

She can't believe that she is asking this question. She can't believe that he is offering her the dreams she would have murdered for ten, even five years ago.

"I loved that she made me think of you," he says, "when you were young and beautiful."

"It's been eighteen years, Tetsuo."

He looks over her shoulder. "You haven't lost much," he says. "I'm not too late. You'll see."

He is waiting for a response. She forces herself to nod. She wants to close her eyes and cover her mouth, keep all her love for him inside where it can be safe, because if she loses it, there will be nothing left but a girl in the rain who should have opened the door.

He looks like an alien when he smiles. He looks like nothing she could ever know when he walks down the hall, past the open door and the girl who has been watching them this whole time.

Rachel is young and beautiful, Key thinks, and Penelope is dead.

Key's sixth feeding at Grade Gold is contained, quiet and without incident. The gazes of the clients slide over her as she greets them at the door of the feeding house, but she is used to that. To a vampire, a human without a shunt is like a book without pages: a useless absurdity. She has assigned all of unit one and a pair from unit four to the gathering. Seven humans for five vampires is a luxurious ratio—probably more than they paid for, but she's happy to let that be Tetsuo's problem. She shudders to remember how Rachel's blood soaked into the collar of her blouse when she lifted the girl from the bed. She has seen dozens of overdrained humans, including some who died from it, but what happened to Rachel feels worse. She doesn't understand why, but is overwhelmed by tenderness for her.

A half-hour before the clients are supposed to leave, Kaipo sprints through the front door, flushed and panting so hard he has to pause half a minute to catch his breath.

"Rachel," he manages, while humans and vampires alike pause to look.

She stands up. "What did she do?"

"I'm not sure . . . she was shaking and screaming, waking everyone up, yelling about Penelope and Tetsuo and then she started vomiting."

"The clients have another half hour," she whispers. "I can't leave until then."

Kaipo tugs on the long lock of glossy black hair that he has blunt-cut over his left eye. "I'm scared for her, Key," he says. "She won't listen to anyone else."

She will blame herself if any of the kids here tonight die, and she will blame herself if something happens to Rachel. Her hands make the decision for her: she reaches for Kaipo's left arm. He lets her take it reflexively, and doesn't flinch when she lifts his shunt. She looks for and finds the small electrical chip which controls the inflow and outflow of blood and other fluids. She taps the Morse-like code, and Kaipo watches with his mouth open as the glittering plastic polymer changes from clear to gray. As though he's already been tapped out.

"I'm not supposed to show you that," she says, and smiles until she remembers Tetsuo and what he might think. "Stay here. Make sure nothing happens. I'll be back as soon as I can."

She stays only long enough to see his agreement, and then she's flying out the back door, through the garden, down the left-hand path that leads to unit two.

Rachel is on her hands and knees in the middle of the walkway. The other three kids in unit two watch her silently from the doorway, but Rachel is alone as she vomits in the grass.

"You!" Rachel says when she sees Key, and starts to cough.

Rachel looks like a war is being fought inside of her, as if the battlefield is her lungs and the hollows of her cheeks and the muscles of her neck. She trembles and can hardly raise her head.

"Go away!" Rachel screams, but she's not looking at Key, she's looking down at the ground.

"Rachel, what's happened?" Key doesn't get too close. Rachel's fury frightens her; she doesn't understand this kind of rage. Rachel raises her shaking hands and starts hitting herself, pounding her chest and rib cage and stomach with violence made even more frightening by her weakness. Key kneels in front of her, grabs both of the girl's tiny, bruised wrists and holds them away from her body. Her vomit smells of sour bile and the sickly-sweet of some half digested fruit. A suspicion nibbles at Key, and so she looks to the left, where Rachel has vomited.

Dozens and dozens of black seeds, half crushed. And a slime of green the precise shade of a cherimoya skin.

"Oh, God, Rachel . . . why would you . . . "

"You don't deserve him! He can make it go away and he won't! Who are you? A fogey, an ugly fogey, an ugly usurping fogey and she's gone and he is a dick, he is a screaming howler monkey and I hate him. . . . "

Rachel collapses against Key's chest, her hands beating helplessly at the ground. Key takes her up and rocks her back and forth, crying while she thinks of how close she came to repeating the mistakes of Jeb. But she can still save Rachel. She can still be human.

Tetsuo returns three days later with a guest.

She has never seen Mr. Charles wear shoes before, and he walks in them with the mincing confusion of a young girl forced to wear zori for a formal occasion. She bows her head when she sees him, hoping to hide her fear. Has he come to take her back to Mauna Kea? The thought of returning to those antiseptic feeding rooms and tasteless brick patties makes her hands shake. It makes her wonder if she would not be better off taking Penelope's way out rather than seeing the place where Jeb killed himself again.

But even as she thinks it, she knows she won't, any more than she would have eighteen years ago. She's too much a coward and she's too brave. If Mr. Charles asks her to go back she will say yes.

Rain on a mountainside and sexless, sweet touches with a man the same temperature as wet wood. Lanai City, overrun. Then Waimea, then Honoka'a. Then Hilo, where her mother had been living. For a year, until Tetsuo found that record of her existence in a work camp, Key fantasized about her mother escaping on a boat to an atoll, living in a group of refugee humans who survived the apocalypse.

Every thing Tetsuo asked of her, she did. She loved him from the moment they saved each other's lives. She has always said yes.

" *Key* !" Mr. Charles says to her, as though she is a friend he has run into unexpectedly. "I have some *thing* . . . you might *just* want."

"Yes, Mr. Charles?" she says.

The three of them are alone in the feeding house. Mr. Charles collapses dramatically against one of the divans and kicks off his tight, patent-leather shoes as if they are barnacles. He wears no socks.

"There," he says, and waves his hand at the door. "*In* the bag."

Tetsuo nods and so she walks back. The bag is black canvas, unmarked. Inside, there's a book. She recognizes it immediately, though she only saw it once. *The Blind Watchmaker.* There is a note on the cover. The handwriting is large and uneven and painstaking, that of someone familiar with words but unaccustomed to writing them down. She notes painfully that he writes his "a" the same way as a typeset font, with the half-c above the main body and a careful serif at the end.

> *Dear Overseer Ki,*
>> *I would like you to have this. I have loved it very much and you are the only one who ever seemed to care. I am angry but I don't blame you. You're just too good at living.*
>>>> *Jeb*

She takes the bag and leaves both vampires without requesting permission. Mr. Charles's laugh follows her out the door.

Blood on the walls, on the floor, all over his body.

I am angry but. You're just too good at living. She has always said yes.

She is too much of a coward and she is too brave.

She watches the sunset the next evening from the hill in the garden, her back against the cherimoya tree. She feels the sun's death like she always has, with quiet joy. Awareness floods her: the musk of wet grass crushed beneath her bare toes, salt-spray and algae blowing from the ocean, the love she has clung to so fiercely since she was a girl, lost and alone. Everything she has ever loved is bound in that sunset, the red and violet orb that could kill him as it sinks into the ocean.

Her favorite time of day is sunset, but it is not night. She has never quite been able to fit inside his darkness, no matter how hard she tried. She has been too good at living, but perhaps it's not too late to change.

She can't take the path of Penelope or Jeb, but that has never been the only way. She remembers stories that reached Grade Orange from the work camps, half-whispered reports of humans who sat at their assembly lines and refused to lift their hands. Harvesters who drained gasoline from their combine engines and waited for the vampires to find them. If every human refused to cooperate, vampire society would crumble in a week. Still, she has no illusions about this third path sparking a revolution. This is simply all she can do: sit under the cherimoya tree and refuse. They will kill her, but she will have chosen to be human.

The sun descends. She falls asleep against the tree and dreams of the girl who never was, the one who opened the door. In her dreams, the sun burns her skin and her obaachan tells her how proud she is while they pick strawberries in the garden. She eats an umeboshi that tastes of blood and salt, and when she swallows, the flavors swarm out of her throat, bubbling into her neck and jaw and ears. Flavors become emotions become thoughts; peace in the nape of her neck, obligation in her back molars, and hope just behind her eyes, bitter as a watermelon rind.

She opens them and sees Tetsuo on his knees before her. Blood smears his mouth. She does not know what to think when he kisses her, except that she can't even feel the pinprick pain where his teeth broke her skin. He has never fed from her before. They have never kissed before. She feels like she is floating, but nothing else.

The blood is gone when he sits back. As though she imagined it.

"You should not have left like that yesterday," he says. "Charles can make this harder than I'd like."

"Why is he here?" she asks. She breathes shallowly.

"He will take over Grade Gold once your transmutation is finished."

"That's why you brought me here, isn't it? It had nothing to do with the kids."

He shrugs. "Regulations. So Charles couldn't refuse."

"And where will you go?"

"They want to send me to the mainland. Texas. To supervise the installation of a new Grade Gold facility near Austin."

She leans closer to him, and now she can see it: regret, and shame that he should be feeling so. "I'm sorry," she says.

"I have lived seventy years on these islands. I have an eternity to come back to them. So will you, Key. I have permission to bring you with me."

Everything that sixteen-year-old had ever dreamed. She can still feel the pull of him, of her desire for an eternity together, away from the hell her life has become. Her transmutation would be complete. Truly a monster, the regrets for her past actions would fall away like waves against a seawall.

With a fumbling hand, she picks a cherimoya from the ground beside her. "Do you remember what these taste like?"

She has never asked him about his human life. For a moment, he seems genuinely confused. "You don't understand. Taste to us is vastly more complex. Joy, dissatisfaction, confusion, humility—*those* are flavors. A custard apple?" He laughs. "It's sweet, right?"

Joy, dissatisfaction, loss, grief, she tastes all that just looking at him.

"Why didn't you ever feed from me before?"

"Because I promised. When we first met."

And as she stares at him, sick with loss and certainty, Rachel walks up behind him. She is holding a kitchen knife, the blade pointed toward her stomach.

"Charles knows," she says.

"How?" Tetsuo says. He stands, but Key can't coordinate her muscles enough for the effort. He must have drained a lot of blood.

"I told him," Rachel says. "So now you don't have a choice. You will transmute me and you will get rid of this fucking fetus or I will kill myself and you'll be blamed for losing *two* Grade Gold humans."

Rachel's wrists are still bruised from where Key had to hold her several nights ago. Her eyes are sunken, her skin sallow. *This fucking fetus.*

She wasn't trying to kill herself with the cherimoya seeds. She was trying to abort a pregnancy.

"The baby is still alive after all that?" Key says, surprisingly indifferent to the glittering metal in Rachel's unsteady hands. Does Rachel know how easily Tetsuo could disarm her? What advantage does she think she has? But then she looks back in the girl's eyes and realizes: none.

Rachel is young and desperate and she doesn't want to be eaten by the monsters anymore.

"Not again, Rachel," Tetsuo says. "I *can't* do what you want. A vampire can only transmute someone he's never fed from before."

Rachel gasps. Key flops against her tree. She hadn't known that, either. The knife trembles in Rachel's grip so violently that Tetsuo takes it from her, achingly gentle as he pries her fingers from the hilt.

"*That's* why you never drank from her? And I killed her anyway? Stupid fucking Penelope. She could have been forever, and now there's just this dumb fogey in her place. She thought you cared about her."

"Caring is a strange thing, for a vampire," Key says.

Rachel spits in her direction but it falls short. The moonlight is especially bright tonight; Key can see everything from the grass to the tips of Rachel's ears, flushed sunset pink.

"Tetsuo," Key says, "why can't I move?"

But they ignore her.

"Maybe Charles will do it if I tell him you're really the one who killed Penelope."

"Charles? I'm sure he knows exactly what you did."

"I didn't *mean* to kill her!" Rachel screams. "Penelope was going to tell about the baby. She was crazy about babies, it didn't make any sense, and you had *picked her* and she wanted to destroy my life . . . I was so angry, I just wanted to hurt her, but I didn't realize. . . . "

"Rachel, I've tried to give you a chance, but I'm not allowed to get rid of it for you." Tetsuo's voice is as worn out as a leathery orange.

"I'll die before I go to one of those mommy farms, Tetsuo. I'll die and take my baby with me."

"Then you will have to do it yourself."

She gasps. "You'll really leave me here?"

"I've made my choice."

Rachel looks down at Key, radiating a withering contempt that does nothing to blunt Key's pity. "If you had picked Penelope, I would have understood. Penelope was beautiful and smart. She's the only one who ever made it through half of that fat Shakespeare book in unit four. She could sing. Her breasts were perfect. But *her*? She's not a choice. She's nothing at all."

The silence between them is strained. It's as if Key isn't there at all. And soon, she thinks, she won't be.

"I've made my choice," Key says.

"*Your* choice?" they say in unison.

When she finds the will to stand, it's as though her limbs are hardly there at all, as though she is swimming in midair. For the first time, she understands that something is wrong.

Key floats for a long time. Eventually, she falls. Tetsuo catches her.

"What does it feel like?" Key asks. "The transmutation?"

Tetsuo takes the starlight in his hands. He feeds it to her through a glass shunt growing from a living branch. The tree's name is Rachel. The tree is very sad. Sadness is delicious.

"You already know," he says.

You will understand: he said this to her when she was human. *I wouldn't hurt you:* she said this to a girl who—a girl—she drinks.

"I meant to refuse."

"I made a promise."

She sees him for a moment crouched in the back of her father's shed, huddled away from the dangerous bar of light that stretches across the floor. She sees herself, terrified of death and so unsure. *Open the door,* she tells that girl, too late. *Let in the light.*

GHOST STORY

JOHN GRANT

"Who was it on the phone?" says Dverna.

It's the middle of a Sunday morning and she's reading the paper at the breakfast table, still in her robe, the one with the pink-cauliflowers design. She has her legs up under the table so her feet are on my chair. I move them to one side and perch next to them.

"Lindsay."

Dverna looks blank for a moment.

"Connor and Elsa's kid," I say.

Her face clears. "Oh, *that* Lindsay. You should have said. The guilty passion of your youth. She must be grown up by now, isn't she?"

"She's only three, four years younger than I am."

Dverna becomes concerned. "What was she phoning about? Not good news—I can see that on your face. Nothing's happened to Connor or Elsa, has it? They're okay?"

"They're fine." Dverna has met them perhaps half a dozen times, spoken with them lots on the phone. They were the much younger friends of my parents. Since I was a late child, they seemed not quite like adults to me when I was growing up. Of course they were at our wedding—that was the first time Dverna met them. Connor McBride flirted outrageously with my bride, which was exactly what Dverna needed that day, some of my family being frosty and barely polite to her. Ever since then she's called Connor her secret lover while Elsa has called her the co-respondent.

"Then what was it?" She puts the paper down on top of a Rorschach pattern of toast crumbs.

"I don't know how to explain this."

"Madame Dverna, enchanted avatar of distant dimensions, can listen, and guide you through these arcane waters. Spill."

She leans forward, going cross-eyed.

"Maybe it's Madame Dverna the mystic wotsit I *need*," I say.

I'm lost for where to begin. I'm also a bit worried she might pull my head off before I've got this properly explained, if I don't start at the right place. But she's my best friend as well as my wife.

"Lindsay's pregnant."

Dverna uncrosses her eyes in order to roll them. "And you're shocked your First True Love should do such a thing? She's not five any longer, Nick. Why has it got anything to do with you?"

My First True Love. Dverna's heard the story often enough. Once upon a time I was about eight years old and my parents' car broke down in the middle of nowhere. It was another Sunday, which in those times meant that in the Western Highlands of Scotland there wasn't a garage that would answer your knock at the door. It was one of those days when your breath made clouds. Luckily a country bus came by, and we ended up at some grim hotel with grim three-foot-thick walls built out of grim dirty red granite sometime before Julius Caesar venied, vidied or vicied. And, as my father discovered to his fury once he'd signed us in, it was a temperance hotel. The next morning he found out it was going to take a week to fix the car, although it was late in the day before the local garage dared tell him this. The last bus to civilisation had gone. Dad wasn't going to spend another night in a place that broke the Good Lord's Eleventh Commandment—Thou Shalt Have a Bar—and so he began phoning around to see if there was "any escape from this hellhole."

A few hours later, by which time I was asleep on my mother's knee in the hotel's sitting room, Connor and Elsa turned up, ready to give us a lift home. There was a lot of laughter as they piled us all into their car, which was one of those old black monstrosities that looked as if it should have a belowdecks, and I ended up in the back seat jammed next to their infant daughter, Lindsay, whom of course they couldn't have left at home.

During a long drive through the fading light and into the darkness I fell in love with this magical creature. She seemed, so far as I was concerned, hardly to belong to the physical world. Her parents had bundled her all up in white blankets against the cold of the oncoming night, and her face was almost as pale. For a while she wouldn't speak to me, but eventually she prattled happily enough.

By the time we got home my eight-year-old soul was hers.

And then I never saw her again. Well, not for years—which is as long as never when you're that age.

In my teens I saw Connor and Elsa several times. They'd drifted apart from my parents—one family to Wales, the other to Sussex—and then, when the phones got cheaper, somehow the distances got shorter. I enjoyed their visits, or when we visited them. Mostly Lindsay wasn't a part of those weekends—

she had a school that prided itself on organising foreign trips during the vacation periods. There was a day when I must have been about twenty when I was passing through Edinburgh—the McBrides had moved back up north by then—and they bought me a bad lunch at the Balmoral Hotel. Lindsay was there too, with a very silent boyfriend. "But you promised you'd wait for me!" I wailed, then realised I'd embarrassed her.

Which was sort of the way it was. I still cherish that long drive through the night in the back of the car, and there's still always a place inside me where an eight-year-old boy is awestricken by the ethereal five-year-old girl and the ethereal five-year-old girl's rare smile. It was a genuine falling in love, and I never want to lose it. Yet, as the years have gone by, I've barely ever thought of Lindsay. It's her parents who're my friends. That scowly day in an Edinburgh hotel is the way I think of the real Lindsay.

On the other hand, I recognised her voice immediately when I picked up the phone a few minutes ago.

"It seems it *may* have something to do with me," I tell Dverna. "She says I'm the father."

"That's impossible," says Dverna, after an extraordinarily long while. I'm pleased to find my head not pulled off.

"That's what I told her," I say.

"How far gone is she?"

"Three months, a bit over."

"You've not been sneaking out at nights, have you?"

It's a joke question. Lindsay was calling from the family home in Edinburgh. We live in Bristol.

"But of course," I say, loving my wife.

"The girl must have fallen off her trolley."

I grab Dverna's half-drunk black coffee, which is cold, and take a gulp. "She must be. Only . . . "

"This had better be good, Nick."

"She didn't *sound* nuts."

"Did she sound like that woman out of *Fatal Attraction*? What's her name? Glenn Ford?"

"Close, but no ceegar," I say, then return to the subject. "She sounded quite calm. That's the odd thing. She was phoning me up just to let me know there was a sprog on the way, and that it was mine. She wasn't asking me for anything, doesn't expect me to show any interest in the child unless I want to—just thought it was right for her to tell me."

"And you believe her?"

The question surprises me. It hasn't occurred to me not to believe Lindsay.

She's still, I suppose, an angel who descended to earth for a while long ago to sit in the back of a car with a small Scottish boy.

I pick my words carefully. "She wasn't *lying*. I believe she was telling the truth she remembers. Only . . . only it's not a truth I was ever part of."

"Wasn't it about three months ago you were supposed to be up there?"

Dverna's small brown feet squirm away from me. She crosses to the fridge door, with its mass of bunting.

"Here it is. July seventh to ninth. You were supposed to be having a meeting in Edinburgh with the Sitemaster Hotel Group, only you had the summer flu instead."

"And I lost the job," I say. "But I thought that was earlier. March, April."

Dverna clicks her tongue. "Nope. July it was. You were going to stay with Connor and Elsa."

"Lindsay says I did."

"Ah," says Dverna.

"I haven't been to Edinburgh in five years, maybe seven," I say.

"And you weren't there three months ago. It is incised into my brain that you weren't there three months ago. You spent ten days either sitting on the lav or lying in your bed looking pale and deathly boring and telling me from time to time that, should this be your final descent into the abyss, I was to remember our love had been immortal."

"That's not what Lindsay says. She says I was in Scotland."

"Then she's wrong."

For a second longer I think Dverna is still hugely amused by the whole situation—her husband having his chain pulled by a long-ago memory—but then I see she's frightened by the way I seem as puzzled as she is.

"You'll be wanting to see her?" says Dverna, making the question sound like a death sentence. She clears her throat. "In fact, you need to see her. This is something you need to *solve*, isn't it?"

"They're coming down to London next week so Connor and Elsa can go to the new Waterhouse exhibition. While they're getting culture, she said, maybe she and I could—"

Another mercurial change of mood. "This isn't all a stupid game, is it, Nick?"

I look out through the french window and over a back garden where there are no scattered children's toys to a hedge that is more brown than green.

"How could you think that?" I say.

"I'm coming up towards thirty with frightening speed. Maybe you want to trade me in for a new model."

"You've got to be joking."

I'm appalled she could think any such thing. I thought I was an open book to her, that she could read my innermost thoughts. I guess we all have ideals like that, then are disillusioned when we discover the boundaries between one human and the next are, no matter how close we think we are, impermeable. I can't even imagine being tempted by "a new model." Oh, sure, as she knows, sometimes I feel spears of lust when I see a smile or a well occupied pair of tight jeans, but lust is easy and cheap and superficial. Dverna makes me lust, too, lust like a dog in the noonday sun, but that's only one percent or less of what she is in my life.

"I've got these wobbly bits on my hips."

"They're one—two—of the reasons I love you."

"Are you saying I've got wobbly bits on my hips? Heartless bastard. So what day is it you're going up to London?"

"Thursday. I said I'd meet her at that restaurant on the Serpentine . . . "

Dverna puts the back of her wrist to her forehead in a caricature of cheated grief. "Oh, spare me, spare me, *spare* me the details of your assignations with this . . . this . . . this *floozy*!"

I'm wondering if I should maybe phone Connor or Elsa and try to work into the conversation a question about whether their daughter's receiving any kind of treatment. Somehow, though, it would seem like a betrayal. I decide to put the decision on this one off until after I've seen Lindsay herself. As I told Dverna, she didn't *sound* nuts on the phone.

What I don't say to my wife is that I asked Lindsay, "How're we going to recognise each other after all this time?" and she replied, "Don't you think, in the circumstances, that's rather an inappropriate remark?"

On Thursday morning we leave the house together, me taking a taxi to Bristol Temple Meads station, Dverna setting off on foot to work. She teaches science at Mowberry Comprehensive—or, as she likes to describe it in a loud voice to obnoxious people at parties, "I work in a madrassa where we take young terrorists and brainwash them until they become children."

"See you this evening," she says. She's trying to sound light about it, but I can hear her worry.

"I'll call you from the train to let you know when I'll be home." She looks cold, although it's not a cold morning. "I'll try for the six-oh-three, as usual."

She glances at the sky. "Hope the weather's nice for you."

I'm conscious of the taxi driver waiting, tapping his fingers on the wheel.

"Dverna?"

"Yes?"

I put a finger under her chin and tilt her face up so I can kiss the tip of her small brown nose. She squeezes my free hand very tightly.

"There can only ever be you," I say to her.

"I should hope so."

She walks away quickly, her hard-heeled work shoes going clicky-click-click on the paving stones.

I'm lucky enough to get a table by the window, so that while I'm waiting for Lindsay to appear I can look out over the sunshiny water at the families in rowing boats. Ducks paddle along in their tranquil fashion or spearhead for the shore whenever they spot someone they sense has brought breadcrumbs to share.

Lindsay doesn't keep me waiting long.

A slight dip in the volume of conversation in the room makes me turn away from the view of the Serpentine to see the young woman coming in through the door. She raises a hand to the maître d' to say that, no, she doesn't want to give him the white summer jacket she's wearing, and smiles in my direction. She points me out to him and then starts across the restaurant towards me, the maître d' floundering in her wake.

Standing, I pull a chair out for her. I'm suddenly as nervous as an adolescent on his first date.

Lindsay kisses my cheek lightly and sits. Under the white jacket she's wearing a full-length white dress, almost like a bridal gown. Or an angel's tunic. With her pale clothing and pale skin, I feel I should be seeing her not here in the modern world but winged and androgenous in a Renaissance painting. The only colour is around the dress's neck, where there's a chain of pale green leaves embroidered in lace. What I'm trying not to do, as I sit down, is stare at her face.

It's quite square, and white as snow. A few small freckles across the bridge of her nose. Her eyes are the same blue I remember from that long-ago night drive across Scotland; they have that slight lack of focus which the eyes of longsighted people sometimes have. She has a very mobile mouth; her lips are never still, even when the rest of her face is in repose. She wears her dark, curly hair to shoulder-length; her eyebrows are even darker than her hair. There's not a trace of makeup on her face, the only colour being small tinges of pink at the peak of her cheekbones, and yet there seems to be a glow about her, that aura which pregnant women sometimes acquire.

She is as beautiful as she was when we first met, when she was five and I was eight.

And this is what's puzzling me as we make the usual small talk—aren't we both looking splendid, yes, I had a good train ride, she walked across the park from Marble Arch tube station, oh, we could have walked together if we'd known because I came on foot from Paddington. I can see a clear line of descent, as it were, from the magical child who was bundled up warm in the back seat of the car, all those years ago, to the woman sitting across from me. What I *can't* see, though, is any way the glowering adolescent I annoyed over a bad meal in Edinburgh could have become the Lindsay in front of me. Just to begin with, she appears several inches shorter than she was then—although I put that down to the way ungainly teenagers seem to have longer limbs than ordinary human beings do.

We order a light lunch—salads, a bottle of some innocuous German white wine. I'm not really in the mood for eating. I'm entranced by this creature, just as I once was. If I were younger, I'd say I was falling in love with her, but it isn't that. I wish in a way it were. That would be, somehow, easier to cope with.

What I do know is that, if indeed Lindsay is pregnant, then I'm not the father. We spent no night of passion together. I know this for a certainty. In the old tales men lost themselves in Faeryland and dallied with the Queen, yet later forgot entirely their lovemaking. They forgot only because the Queen could cast a spell upon their minds; otherwise they'd have remembered everything until the last breath left their body. It would surely be this way with Lindsay. Surely there'd be some kind of body-memory? Surely?

Yet who she is is a mystery to me. I hardly dare even touch her hand.

We wait until the food's arrived before, moving carefully and warily like participants in a minuet, we approach the reason for our being here.

"I'm not asking you to bear any . . . paternal responsibility, Nick," she says, spearing a slice of tomato.

"Before we even start going into that," I say, "I think we need to sort out what actually happened."

"You said that on the phone."

"Tell me the story from your side."

"You're serious?"

"I really am."

She smiles. "I'm not sure I like the notion of having to remind you."

"That's the trouble, Lindsay. It's not a reminder. I don't have any knowledge of this—and I'm not pretending." I remember what Dverna said the other day. "I'm not trying to play any kind of stupid game. I truly don't know what's going on."

She sighs, and reaches out her hand to place it over mine on the table. Her touch is cool and dry, as I imagined it would be.

"Well, you remember, back in July, you came and stayed with us for that business meeting you—"

"No, Lindsay. I *don't* remember that. I had to cancel. I had the flu."

"You seemed a little under the weather, but—"

"I was in Bristol. I never even got as far as the station. I had to cancel my appointment, and I lost the job because of it." Not that there weren't plenty of other jobs, because there's always demand for a freelance accountant, but the Sitemaster contract was one I'd been particularly keen to nail down. *C'est la vie.*

"I'm trying to tell you something," says Lindsay.

"Sorry. I shouldn't have interrupted."

"You were a little under the weather, I said. I don't mean you were sniffling or feverish, or anything like that. You seemed a little . . . confused, maybe? There was something artificial about you, as if you were playing a role, like one does in front of people one doesn't know very well. Dad said later you seemed so out of kilter with your normal self he could have passed you in the street without recognising you. Me, I hadn't seen you since I was, what, fourteen, fifteen, so you didn't seem so strange to me, but I could still tell . . . " She takes a deep breath. "You don't do drugs, do you?"

"Just single malt whisky, and then not often enough."

"We wondered, the three of us, after you'd left, if that was why you seemed so . . . Of course, Mum and Dad didn't know what else had happened while you were there." She stares at me meaningfully with those cloudy blue eyes.

The McBrides have one of those big old tall houses a couple of miles south of Edinburgh's centre, built of red sandstone and built to last. Most of the other houses up and down the street have been converted for flats or into hotels—well, bed-and-breakfasts, really. Where the McBrides sometimes put houseguests is in a small stone shed at the bottom of the back garden—a "guest chalet," as Elsa likes grandly to call it. It was probably a stable at one point. Now it has a comfortable little bedroom, with a loo and a shower room off it. Just right for a night or three; any longer and it'd start to get claustrophobic, I'd guess. But there's more privacy than in the main house.

I arrived, so Lindsay tells me, in the middle of the Thursday evening. My train had got in late, having sat for a couple of hours outside Newcastle for no reason anyone had ever thought to tell us. The McBrides had held dinner for me—which was easy because, it being summer, dinner was a cold chicken curry salad, one of Elsa's specialities. We sat around the table long after we'd finished eating. I said no to the port Connor produced, because I wanted to be bright-eyed and bushy-tailed for my meeting with the Sitemaster people the next day. And then off down the garden path I trotted . . .

"You were really energised when you got home the next day," says Lindsay. She's stroking the back of my hand with her thumb, the kind of gesture longstanding lovers make. "You said the meeting went really well and you were certain the job was yours."

When I got home, she tells me, it was about one o'clock and she was alone in the house. Connor and Elsa were still out at work, and weren't expected home until seven. Lindsay, who'd completed her finals in biochemistry a couple of weeks earlier, was basically just having fun lolling around the house and relaxing with books.

"Nothing for it but you were going to take me out to lunch at the Haddon House to celebrate, which we did." She has the very clear, almost accentless voice you sometimes find in Scots people, with the same timbre as a choirboy's singing. She doesn't say why it was we both ended up in the "guest chalet", just that this was where we went when we got home from lunch. There's no embarrassment about her, no girlish blushes. She's quite matter-of-fact, and amused more than anything else.

"I'm sorry," I say. "I shouldn't have allowed this to happen. It was a monumental abuse of hospitality. Your dad'll be wanting to beat me to a pulp."

She chuckles. "You didn't have any choice in the matter. It was my idea. Do you remember that time when we were both wee, Nick, and we were taken for a long ride in that awful old boat of a car Dad used to have?"

"I remember it."

"I fell in love with you then, Nick, and I've never completely fallen out of it again."

"I know what you mean. But—"

"But what, Nick?"

I was about to say to her that all my life I've felt that same way, except that it's the eight-year-old boy who's loving the five-year-old girl, and the situation, and the memory of an encounter that was special and shining and greater than life, and can never be repeated. But I bite the words back, realising how cruelly they might strike her, as if the grown-up Lindsay was valueless.

I mumble something vacuous about the past being hard to recapture.

"Oh, we had our merry moments, you and I," she says after a pause. "The room was full of sunlight and there was a sea gull in the garden telling all the other birds this was his own special territory. And then, finally, I realised what time it was and that I'd better run inside and have a bath to wash the smell of sex off me before Mum and Dad got home." She chuckles again.

I can't imagine what her face would look like in passion.

Her eyes are serious once more. "And you can remember *nothing* of this, Nick?"

I play the gallant. "I wish I did. You're a very lovely woman, Lindsay." I almost called her a *young* woman, but caught myself in time.

"Nor the evening? I think Mum was fairly sure something had been going on, but she didn't know what and she wasn't about to ask. And Dad—well, you know Dad. All evening long it was a secret that just you and I shared."

Once again I'm struck by how badly this doppelgänger of mine behaved. Connor and Elsa are old and trusted friends, the closest thing I have any longer to family. I suppose that makes Lindsay family, too. And she was old enough to be making her own decisions about what she did. Even so, I've betrayed their trust abominably, adulterously banging their darling only daughter in the garden shed. Or my doppelgänger did. I'm finding this very confusing to think about.

"Late at night," she says, "after the folks had gone to bed I tiptoed out to you in my white nightie and we made love for the one last time. If anyone had looked out of a back window and seen me in the garden, they'd have thought they were seeing a ghost."

The waiter sidles up to us. Neither of us has finished our meal. We indicate to him to take the plates away. I ask for a coffee, Lindsay for a tea. "Don't bother bringing milk," she says. "I like it the way nature intended."

He goes away.

I'm shaking my head. I know there are tears in my eyes, tears I don't want her to see. There's a part of me, and it isn't the eight-year-old boy any longer, that desperately, desperately wishes I could remember what Lindsay so clearly remembers. If it weren't for my nutbrown maid in Bristol, the person who is everyone to me, I could imagine myself falling deeply for Lindsay and even believing it was love. Her beauty and her air of reserve are tugging at me. I've never once thought of two-timing Dverna—it's an impossibility, like water running uphill—and I'm not thinking about it seriously even now, but the fact that I'm thinking about it *at all* says something about the effect Lindsay is having on me.

"And you say it wasn't you?" Her voice is very quiet now, so low I can barely pick it up amid the waves of other people's conversation.

"It wasn't. It can't have been. I was at home nursing my head and feeling sorry for myself. A summer flu. Dverna remembers it well."

"Dverna," says Lindsay. "Who's Dverna?"

It's later in the day. We're out in the middle of the Serpentine on one of those rowing boats you can hire by the hour. I'm rowing. Lindsay is sitting in the stern looking as if she should be wearing a straw boater and wielding a parasol. I'm not going to catch the six-oh-three.

She believes me now. At first she was incredulous that I could be married without her knowing anything about it, even more so when I told her she was at the wedding. It was only when I produced the little digital picture frame I carry with me and showed her the picture Dverna and I persuaded an old Frenchman to take of us the weekend we went to Cologne that she began to be persuaded. That was just before I paid the bill for our lunches. After we left the restaurant we ambled around the park, both rather selfconsciously not looking at the pairs of young lovers sprawling on the grass. Then, on an impulse, we hired this boat. It gives us a space that's separated from the rest of the world.

"I had this dream, Nick," she's saying, trailing her fingers in the water. "This very presumptuous dream. I wasn't going to put any pressure on you, but I thought that maybe, just maybe, you'd say some of the things were true that you told me in Edinburgh, and you'd suggest we raise the bairn together. I've always thought you and I would end up together. Oh, I'm not saying I've been entirely chaste while I was waiting for our hour to come, but there haven't been that many I've bedded, either. I don't make a habit of throwing myself into men's arms, the way I did with you. I seduced you—not that you needed much seducing—because I believed this was the way the script was written, and I was just following it. And now I find you already have your own lovely lady, that you're following your own script. A different script. One that doesn't have a part for me in it."

A silence falls between us. Then: "Do you remember," I say, trying not to sound too puffed from the rowing, "you told me you and your parents thought I seemed a bit odd, a bit artificial, not really myself . . . "

"I think it even more now." She lifts a hand to stop me misunderstanding. "No, what I mean is, you're yourself today. It makes the person I was with in Edinburgh seem even more unlike you. You were like a sort of perfect CGI animation of yourself—it was a precise replica of you, but still we could sense there was something awry. You were *too real*, in a way."

I didn't notice until we climbed into the boat that she's wearing little black sandals. All the rest that she's wearing is either white or nearly so. She's staring at those little black sandals now.

"Like someone in the wrong world," she says.

"Do you think that can be it?" I say nervously.

"That it was the you from the next-door universe?" She gives a little, unconvincing laugh. "It would explain a lot, wouldn't it?"

"Yes, but it'd open up a whole lot of new questions, too."

She ignores my comment. "You talked about a doppelgänger earlier, but that wouldn't make sense. I could believe, if I believed in supernatural beasties, that a spirit could . . . could, you know, make me believe it and I were having carnal knowledge." She rolls the old-fashioned term on her tongue, relishing it. "But I can't believe it would leave me pregnant after."

I try not to think of *Rosemary's Baby*.

She sees me not thinking about it. "I told you, Nick, I don't believe in ghosties and ghoulies and things that go bump in the night, and that goes for devils too."

For half a minute or longer the only sound between is the creaking of the rowlocks.

"We should have a DNA test done," I say. "That would prove it one way or another. If the testing shows the babe has my DNA, then your idea about having encountered a stray from a neighbouring universe . . . but, no."

I raise the oars from the water and we drift for a few yards.

"I've been worrying about that too," she says. "Why have I never before today heard of Dverna?"

It's not till we're back on dry land that I think of phoning home. I glance at my watch and find it's just a few minutes before six. Dverna probably won't be home yet—most days she stays on late at the school, marking papers or supervising clubs, and it's especially likely tonight that she'll stay on, knowing I won't be home for hours. She doesn't carry a mobile, so the only number I have to phone is the landline. Even so, I give it a try.

No answer.

I'm tempted to stay overnight in London. I feel I should face Connor and Elsa, try to explain to them that really I'm not the cad they must think I am—even though Lindsay has told me they don't think about it like that. Because, you see, they too don't know I'm married. So far as they're concerned it's just fine their darling daughter is getting it together with someone they've known all his life. Of course, perhaps said daughter shouldn't have got herself knocked up by him in the interim, but modern days, modern ways . . . So Lindsay says. How they're going to feel about me when she tells them the new version of history, I can hardly bear the thought of it. They're going to think Lindsay is the craziest fool in the world for believing my obvious lies. What whoppers I've been telling. Land her in the pudding club, then pretend it was my mysterious Evil Twin . . .

I should be with her, so we face the music together. But I also need to be with Dverna. If I could speak to her on the phone, maybe it'd be different, but she has to have the option of deciding whether or not I go home to Bristol tonight.

I explain something of this to Lindsay. As we stand there, the light beginning to fade from the sky, I see a young guy who's passing helping himself to an eyeful of her. It's far from the first time it's happened today. She's exquisite, a jewel cut by a master craftsman, just as she was when she was five. And I think to myself yet again how very easy it would be, if things were different . . . But things *aren't* different. I've never felt that each of us has only one soulmate out there in the world. If anything were ever to happen to Dverna, I wouldn't resign myself to never finding someone else to whom I'd feel equally close. But I cannot figure Lindsay as a soulmate. I love her in that almost-family way. I think she's beautiful and wonderful and amazing, and I'm fascinated by her presence the way I'd be fascinated by the over-brightness of a jewelled automaton, and the streak of lust I have for her right now is like a guitar string being tightened too far, but she's not the person I'm meant to spend the rest of my life with.

None of this do I say. Instead I say, "What're you going to tell your parents this evening?"

"Nothing."

"They'll be wanting to know, won't they?"

"They respect my privacy, I respect theirs."

"Like I can believe that."

She gives my hand a squeeze. We're approaching the bright lights and the noise of Marble Arch. "Do believe me," she says.

And suddenly I see things from her viewpoint. Here she is, pregnant by the man she believes she's loved ever since childhood, and he's saying, no, it was nothing to do with me, and planning to catch a train back to the wife he never told her about . . .

"Aw, hell, Lindsay . . . "

I pull her into my arms, feeling her breasts against my chest, running my hands down her back to the curve of her behind, kissing her the way I've never kissed anyone in my life before except Dverna, holding her for an unadvisedly long moment before stepping away from her on the darkened grass.

"I wish . . . " I say.

She touches my cheek with her fingertips.

"So do I, Nick. So do I."

So by the time I get home it's nearly ten. What I've had is about one more expensive can of beer than I should have had during the train trip down from London to Bristol. I'm not sloshed, but it would be kind of useful to find a bed for the night. The taxi drops me off at the gate, and I give the driver an extra-large tip because . . . well, because of that extra beer. Dverna hates it when I drink too much. On the other hand, Dverna hates it when other women accuse me of fathering their children. I figure she'll forgive me, just this once, the lesser crime.

I ring the doorbell and this guy appears I've never seen before. He's wearing a grey vest, too many muscles, and a lot of tattoos.

"Yeah?"

"Who're you?"

He stares at me. "David Hamilton. You?"

I've had about as much strangeness as I can manage today. "Where's Dverna?"

"Who?"

Someone else who's never heard of Dverna. "My wife."

"Who's there?" a voice shouts in the distance. All the while I've been talking with this monstrous stranger there've been the cries of small children in the distance.

"Just some nutter, love!" he yells.

A small round woman appears, rubbing her hands dry on a tea-towel.

"I think I may have the wrong address," I say.

Instinct suggests I walk the couple of miles, sobering all the while, to where I used to live. The house is in the slum part of Bristol's outskirts. I had the upstairs. An ever-enlargening family called Mulligan had the downstairs—and obviously still have. Standing in front of the place, I can hear the usual Mulligan clatter from the brightly lit downstairs. Upstairs, the windows are dark.

I go to the downstairs door and press the bell.

Tim Mulligan appears. He looks more like David Hamilton than I would ever dare to tell either of them.

I am horribly, horribly lost.

"Hey, Nick!" says Tim, reeking of cheap beer. "Ye've forgotten yer fackin' key again . . . "

He fishes in his pocket for his wallet, fishes in his wallet for the key, and gives it to me. It's as warm as a kitten.

I let myself in. The place is just as I remember it. All my books and CDs are just where I remember them being. My laptop opens up the internet with a password I haven't used in years. The laundry basket has socks and underpants in it that smell freshly dirty. There are friendly personal messages on my answerphone from people I don't remember ever having met.

None of them is from Dverna.

None of them is from Lindsay.

All of a sudden I am far too sober. I wish I'd bought myself a bottle of the hard stuff on the way home.

But, prithee, what is this?

In the cupboard over the fridge I find there's still a three-quarters-full bottle of Cutty Sark. I know where the glasses are, of course.

Dverna.

Where are you?

When I wake up the next morning with a head like a building site, I reach out my foot thinking it'll stroke Dverna's leg. Instead, it sticks out the side of a single bed into cold air.

How inevitable, as we look back on it, the past can be made to appear. Yet, when we were living through it, inevitability was the last characteristic it seemed to have: life is an endless succession of resolved uncertainties. I've come to conclude that, as this universe of ours expands along its time axis, what it's doing is telling itself its story. Like any other author, though, it never gets things quite right the first time, so it's constantly having to readjust itself to iron out the minor inconsistencies in its tale. Ordinarily we never notice this continual process of self-editing; we remember the newly created past, not the one we actually lived through.

But every now and then, because of that same habit the universe has of not getting things quite right, someone's lucky enough to be aware of one of the changes the universe is making.

Or unlucky enough.

I wish I could persuade myself there's a neighbouring universe where my doppelgänger and Dverna have found each other and their own happiness, but I don't think there is. I think both of them, Dverna and the other me, were just minor errors that the universe, without trace of compunction, simply tidied away.

Today Lindsay and I took the kids to the beach. Alice tromped up and down along the line of the breakers, squealing with delight whenever an extra big wave bowled her over. Ronnie is still young enough to be frightened by the sea's sound and fury, so he spent the afternoon holding his mother's hand and looking very solemn as he sucked his thumb. Then it was home for high tea, and bathtime and bed for the kids and finally the house was quiet.

Much later, Lindsay and I crept up the stairs to our bedroom at the top of the house, and into the moonlight that comes streaming in the big bay windows, so that it seems like, as we make love, we're doing so as characters in an old black-and-white movie. And as I run my hands over all the planes and folds of my strangely lovely wife—over a body that is by now more familiar to me than my own and yet still so mysterious—where my heart really is, despite everything deep I have for Lindsay and our two adored weans, is with a nutbrown maid who now never was, whose robe was never decorated with pink cauliflowers, and whose crazily grinning face never appeared in my digital photo frame.

BREAK! BREAK! BREAK!

CHARLIE JANE ANDERS

Earliest I remember, Daddy threw me off the roof of our split-level house. "Boy's gotta learn to fall sometime," he told my mom just before he slung my pants-seat and let go. As I dropped, Dad called out instructions, but they tangled in my ears. I was four or five. My brother caught me one-handed, gave me a spank, and dropped me on the lawn. Then up to the roof for another go round, with my body more slack this time.

From my dad, I learned there were just two kinds of bodies: falling, and falling on fire.

My dad was a stuntman with a left-field resemblance to an actor named Jared Gilmore who'd been in some TV show before I was born, and he'd gotten it in his head Jared was going to be the next big action movie star. My father wanted to be Jared's personal stunt double and "prosthetic acting device," but Jared never responded to the letters, emails, and websites, and Dad got a smidge persistent, which led to some restraining orders and blacklisting. Now he was stuck in the boonies doing stunts for TV movies about people who survive accidents. My mama did data entry to cover the rest of the rent. My dad was determined that my brother Holman and I would know the difference between a real and a fake punch, and how to roll with either kind.

My life was pretty boring until I went to school. School was so great! Slippery just-waxed hallways, dodgeball, sandboxplosions, bullies with big elbows, food fights. Food fights! If I could have gone to school for twenty hours a day, I would have signed up. No, twenty-three! I only ever really needed one hour of sleep per day. I didn't know who I was and why I was here until I went to school. And did I mention authority figures? School had authority figures! It was so great!

I love authority figures. I never get tired of pulling when they push, or pushing when they pull. In school, grown-ups were always telling me to write on the board, and then I'd fall down or drop the eraser down my pants by mistake, or misunderstand and knock over a pile of giant molecules. Erasers are comedy gold! I was kind of a hyper kid. They tried giving me ritalin ritalin ritalin ritalin riiiitaliiiiin, but I was one of the kids who only gets more hyper-hyper on that stuff. Falling, in the seconds between up and down—you know what's going on. People say something is as easy as falling off a log, but really it's easy to fall off anything. Really, try it. Falling rules!

Bullies learned there was no point in trying to fuck me up, because I would fuck myself up faster than they could keep up with. They tried to trip me up in the hallways, and it was just an excuse for a massive set piece involving mops, stray book bags, audio/video carts, and skateboards. Limbs flailing, up and down trading places, ten fingers of mayhem. Crude stuff. I barely had a sense of composition. Every night until 3 a.m., I sucked up another stack of Buster Keaton, Harold Lloyd, or Jackie Chan movies on the ancient laptop my parents didn't know I had, hiding under my quilt. Safety Last!

Ricky Artesian took me as a personal challenge. A huge guy with a beachball jaw—he put a kid in the hospital for a month in fifth grade for saying anybody who didn't ace this one chemistry quiz had to be a moron. Sometime after that, Ricky stepped to me with a Sharpie in the locker room and slashed at my arms and ribcage, marking the bones he wanted to break. Then he walked away, leaving the whole school whispering, "Ricky Sharpied Rock Manning!"

I hid when I didn't have class, and when school ended, I ran home three miles to avoid the bus. I figured Ricky would try to get me in an enclosed space where I couldn't duck and weave, so I stayed wide open. If I needed the toilet, I swung into the stall through a ventilator shaft and got out the same way, so nobody saw me enter or leave. The whole time in the airshaft, my heart cascaded. This went on for months, and my whole life became not letting Ricky Artesian mangle me.

One day I got careless and went out to the playground with the other kids during recess, because some teacher was looking. I tried to watch for trouble, but a giant hand swooped down from the swing set and hauled me up. I dangled a moment, then the hand let me fall to the sand. I fell on my back and started to get up, but Ricky told me not to move. For some reason, I did what he said, even though I saw twenty-seven easy ways out of that jungle-gym cage, and then Ricky stood over me. He told me again to hold still, then brought one boot down hard on the long bone of my upper arm, a clean snap—my reward for staying put. "Finally got that kid to quit hopping," I heard him say as he walked across the playground. Once my arm healed up, I became a crazy frog again, and Ricky didn't bother me.

Apart from that one stretch, my social life at school was ideal. People cheered for me but never tried to talk to me—it was the best of human interaction without any of the pitfalls. Ostracism, adulation: flipsides! They freed me to orchestrate gang wars and alien invasions in my head, whenever

I didn't have so many eyes on me. Years passed, and my mom tried to get me into dance classes, while my dad struggled to get me to take falling down seriously, the way my big brother did. Holman was spending every waking moment prepping for the Army, which was his own more socially acceptable way of rebelling against Dad.

Sally Hamster threw a brick at my head. I'd barely noticed the new girl in my class, except she was tall for a seventh grader and had big Popeye arms. I felt the brick coming before I heard it, then people shouting. Maybe Sally just wanted to get suspended, maybe she was reaching out. The brick grazed my head, but I was already moving with it, forward into a knot of basketball players, spinning and sliding. Afterward I had a lump on my head but I swore I'd thrown the brick at myself. By then the principal would have believed almost anything of me.

I didn't get the reference to those weird *Krazy Kat* comics about the brick-throwing mouse until years later, but Sally and I became best friends thanks to a shared love of hilarious pain. We sketched lunch-trolley incidents and car pile-ups in our heads, talking them out during recess, trading text messages in class, instant messaging at home. The two of us snuck out to the Winn-Dixie parking lot and Sally drilled me for hours on that Jackie Chan move where the shopping trolley rolls at him and he swings inside it through the flap, then jumps out the top.

I didn't know martial arts, but I practiced not being run over by a shopping cart over and over. We went to the big mall off I-40 and got ourselves banned from the sporting goods store and the Walmart, trying to stage the best accidents. Sally shouted instructions: "Duck! Jump! Now do that thing where your top half goes left and your bottom half goes right!" She'd throw dry goods, or roll barrels at me, and then shout, "Wait, wait, wait, go!" Sally got it in her head I should be able to do the splits, so she bent my legs as far apart as they would go and then sat on my crotch until I screamed, every day for a couple months.

The Hamster family had social aspirations, all about Sally going to Harvard and not hanging out with boys with dyslexic arms and legs. I went over to their house a few times, and it was full of Buddhas and Virgin Marys, and Mrs. Hamster baked us rugelachs and made punch, all the while telling me it must be So Interesting to be the class clown but how Sally needed to laser-beam in on her studies. My own parents weren't too thrilled about all my school trouble, and why couldn't I be more like Holman, training like crazy for his military future?

High school freshman year, and Sally got hold of a video cam. One of her jag-tooth techno-hippie uncles. I got used to her being one-eyed, filming all the time, and editing on the fly with her mom's hyperbook. Our first movie went online at Yourstuff a month after she got the camera. It was five minutes long, and it was called *The Thighcycle Beef*, which was a joke on some Italian movie Sally had seen. She had a Thighcycle, one of those bikes which goes nowhere with a lying odometer. She figured we could light it on fire and then shove it off a cliff with me riding it, which sounded good to me.

I never flashed on the whole plot of *The Thighcycle Beef*, but there were ninja dogs and exploding donuts and things. Like most of our early short films, it was a mixture of live-action and Zap!mation. Sally figured her mom would never miss the Thighcycle, which had sat in the darkest basement corner for a year or so.

We did one big sequence of me pedaling on the Thighcycle with Sally throwing rocks at me, which she would turn into throwing stars in post-production. I had to pedal and duck, pedal while hanging off the back wheel, pedal side-saddle, pedal with my hands while hanging off the handlebars, etc. I climbed a tree in the Hamsters' front yard and Sally hoisted the Thighcycle so I could pull it up there with me. Then I climbed on and "rode" the Thighcycle down from the treetop, pedaling frantically the whole way down as if I could make it fly. (She was going to make it fly in post.) The Thighcycle didn't pedal so good after that, but Sally convinced me I was only sprained because I could scrunch all my fingers and toes, and I didn't lose consciousness for that long.

We were going to film the climax at a sea cliff a few miles away, but Sally's ride fell through. In the end, she settled for launching me off the tool shed with the Thighcycle on fire. She provided a big pile of leaves for me to fall onto when I fell off the cycle, since I already had all those sprains. I missed the leaf pile, but the flaming Thighcycle didn't, and things went somewhat amiss, although we were able to salvage some of the tool shed thanks to Sally having the garden hose ready. She was amazingly safety-minded.

After that, Sally's parents wanted twice as hard for her not to see me. I had to lie and tell my parents I'd sprained my whole body beating up a bunch of people who deserved it. My brother had to carry stuff for me while I was on crutches, which took away from his training time. He kept running ahead of me with my junk, lecturing me about his conspiracy theories about the Pan-Asiatic Ecumen, and how they were flooding the United States with drugs to destabilize our country and steal our water, and I couldn't get out of earshot.

But all of my sprains were worth it, because *The Thighcycle Beef* blew up the Internet. The finished product was half animation, with weird messages like "NUMCHUK SPITTING TIME!" flashing on the screen in-between shots, but the wacky stunts definitely helped. She even turned the tool shed into a cliff, although she also used the footage of the tool shed fire elsewhere. People two or three times our age downloaded it to their phones and watched it at work. Sally showed me the emails, tweets, and Yangars—we were famous!

• • •

I found out you can have compound sprains just like fractures, and you have to eat a lot of ice cream and watch television while you recuperate. My mom let me monopolize the living room sofa, knitted blanket over my legs and Formica tray in my lap as I watched cartoons.

My mom wanted to watch the news—the water crisis and the debt crisis were freaking her shit. I wanted to catch the Sammo Hung marathon, but she kept changing to CNN, people tearing shopping malls apart with their bare hands in Florida, office windows shattering in Baltimore, buses on fire. And shots of emaciated people in the formerly nice part of Brooklyn, laying in heaps with tubes in their arms, to leave a vein permanently open for the next hit.

Did I mention ice cream? I got three flavors, or five if you count Neapolitan as three separate flavors, like all right-thinking people everywhere.

I went back to school after a week off, and the Thighcycle had a posse. Ricky—arm-cracking Ricky Artesian—came up to me and said our movie rocked his freaking head. He also said something about people like me having our value, which I didn't pay much attention to at the time. I saw one older kid in the hallway with a Flaming Thighcycle T-shirt, which I never saw any royalties for.

Sally snuck out to meet me at the Starbucks near school and we toasted with frosty mochas. Her round face looked sunburned, and her hair was a shade less mouse than usual.

"That was just the dry run," she said. "Next time, we're going to make a statement. Maybe we can go out to the landfill and get a hundred busted TVs and drop them on you."

I vetoed the rain of TVs. I wanted to do a roller disco movie because I'd just watched *Xanadu*.

We posted on Yangar.com looking for roller-disco extras, and a hundred kids and a few creepy grown-ups hit us back. We had to be super selective, and mostly only took people who had their own skates. But Sally still wanted to have old televisions in there because of her Artistic Vision, so she got hold of a dozen fucked old screens and laid them out for us to skate over while they all showed the same footage of Richard Simmons. We had to jump over beach balls and duck under old power cords and stuff. I envisioned it being the saga of skate-fighters who were trying to bring the last remaining copy of the U.S. Constitution to the federal government in exile, which was hiding out in a bunker under a Chikken Hut. We filmed a lot of it at an actual Chikken Hut that had closed down near the Oceanview Mall. I wanted it to be a love story, but we didn't have a female lead, and also Sally never wanted to do love stories. I showed her Harold Lloyd movies, but it made no difference.

Sally got hooked on Yangar fame. She had a thousand Yangar friends, crazy testimonials, and imitators from Pakistan, and it all went to her head. We had to do what the people on the Internet wanted us to do, even when they couldn't agree. They wanted more explosions, more costumes, and cute Zap!mation icons, funny catchphrases. At fifteen, Sally breathed market research. I wanted pathos *and* chaos!

Ricky and some other kids found the school metal detectors missed anything plastic, ceramic, wood, or bone, and soon they had weapons strapped all over. Ricky was one of the first to wear the red bandana around his neck, and everyone knew he was on his way. He shattered Mr. MacLennan's jaw, my geography teacher, right in front of our whole grade in the hallway. Slow-time, a careful spectacle, to the point where Ricky let the onlookers arrange ourselves from shortest in front to tallest in back. Mr. MacLennan lying there looking up at Ricky, trying to assert, while we all shouted, "Break! Break! Break! Break!" and finally Ricky lifted a baseball bat, and I heard a loud crack. Mr. MacLennan couldn't say anything about it afterward, even if he could have talked, because of that red bandana.

Sally listened to the police scanner, sometimes even in the classroom, because she wanted to be there right after a looting or a credit riot. Not that these things happened too often in Alvington, our little coastal resort city. But one time, Sally got wind that a Target near downtown had gone crazy. The manager had announced layoffs and the staff just started trashing the place, and the customers joined in. Sally came to my math class and told Mr. Pope I'd been called to the principal's, and then told me to grab my bag of filming crap and get on my bike. What if we got there and the looters were still going? I asked. But Sally said looting was not a time-consuming process, and the crucial thing was to get there between the looting and everything being chained up. So we got there and sneaked past the few cops buddying in the parking lot, so Sally could get a few minutes of me falling under trashed sporting goods and jumping over clothing racks. She'd gotten so good at filming with one hand and throwing with the other! Really nobody ever realized she was the coordinated one of the two of us. Then the cops chased us away.

My brother got his draft notice and couldn't imagine such luck. He'd sweated getting into the Army for years, and now they weren't even waiting for him to sign up. I knew my own draft notice was probably just a year or two down the line, maybe even sooner. They kept lowering the age.

My mom's talk shows were full of people saying we had to stop the flow of drugs into our country, even if we had to defoliate half the planet. If we could just stop the drugs, then we could fix our other problems, easy. The problem was, the Pan-Asiatic Ecumen or whoever was planting these drugs were too clever for us, and they had gotten hold of genetically-engineered strains that could grow anywhere and had nine hundred times the potency of regular junk. We tried using drones to burn down all their fields, but they just relocated their "gardens" to heavily populated areas, and soon it was block-by-block urban warfare in a dozen slums all around Eurasia. Soldiers were fitted with cheap mass-produced HUDs that made the whole thing look like a first-person shooter from forty years ago. Some people said the Pan-Asiatic Ecumen didn't actually exist, but then how else did you explain the state we were in?

Sally fell in love with a robot guy named Raine, and suddenly he had to be big in every movie. She found him painted silver on Main Street, his arms and legs moving all blocky and jerky, and she thought he had the extra touch we needed. In our movies, he played Castle the Pacifist Fighting Droid, but in real life he clutched Sally's heart in his cold, unbreakable metal fist. He tried to nice up to me, but I saw through him. He was just using Sally for the Yangar fame. I'd never been in love, because I was waiting for the silent-movie love: big eyes and violins, chattering without sound, pure. Nobody had loved right since 1926.

Ricky Artesian came up to me in the cafeteria early on in eleventh grade. He'd gotten so he could loom over *and* around everybody. I was eating with Sally, Raine, and a few other film geeks, and Ricky told me to come with him. My first thought was, whatever truce we'd made over my arm-bone was over and gone, and I was going to be fragments of me. But Ricky just wanted to talk in the boy's room. Everyone else cleared out, so it was just the two of us and the wet TP clinging to the tiles. The air was sour.

"Your movies, they're cool," he said. I started to explain they were also Sally's, but he hand-slashed. "My people." He gestured at the red bandana. "We're going to take it all down. They've lied to us, you know. It's all fucked, and we're taking it down."

I nodded, not so much in agreement, but because I'd heard it before.

"We want you to make some movies for us. Explaining what we're about."

I told him I'd have to ask Sally, and he whatevered, and didn't want to listen to how she was the brains, even though anyone looking at both of us could tell she was the brains. Ricky said if I helped him, he'd help me. We were both almost draft-age, and I would be a morning snack to the military exoskeletons. I'd seen *No Time For Sergeants*—seventeen times—so I figured I knew all about basic training, but Ricky said I'd be toast. Holman had been telling me the same thing, when he wasn't trying to beat me up. So Ricky offered to get me disqualified from the Army, or get me under some protection during training.

When I told Sally about Ricky's offer, the first thing she did was ask Raine what he thought. Raine wasn't a robot that day, which caught me off-guard. He was just a sandy-haired, flag-eared, skinny guy, a year or so older than us. We sat in a seaside gazebo/pagoda where Sally thought she could film some explosions. Raine said propaganda was bad, but also could Ricky get him out of the Army as well as me? I wasn't sure. Sally didn't want me to die, but artistic integrity, you know.

The propaganda versus artistic integrity thing I wasn't sure about. How was making a movie for Ricky worse than pandering to our fans on Yourstuff and Yangar? And look, my dad fed and housed Holman and me by arranging tragic accidents for cable TV movies where people nursed each other back to health and fell in love. Was my dad a propagandist because he fed people sponge cake when the whole world was flying apart?

Sally said fine, shut up, we'll do it if you just stop lecturing us. I asked Ricky and he said yes, neither Raine nor I would have to die if we made him a movie.

This was the first time we ever shot more footage than we used. I hadn't understood how that could happen. You set things up, *boom!* you knocked them over and hoped the camera was running, and then you moved on somewhere else. Life was short, so if you got something on film, you used it! But for the red bandana movie we shot literally hundreds of hours of footage to make one short film. Okay, not literally hundreds of hours. But a few.

Raine didn't want to be the Man, or the Old Order, or the Failure of Democracy, and I said tough shit. Somebody had to, plus he was older and a robot. He and Sally shot a ton of stuff where they humanized his character and explained how he thought he was doing the right thing, but we didn't use any of it in the final version.

Meanwhile, I wore the red bandana and breakdanced under a rain of buzz saws that were really some field hockey sticks we'd borrowed. I also wanted to humanize my character by showing how he only donned the red bandana to impress a beautiful florist, played by Mary from my English class.

After a few weeks' filming, we started to wonder if maybe we should have had a script. "We never needed one before," Sally grumbled. She was pissed about doing this movie, and I was pissed that she kept humanizing her boyfriend behind my back. You don't humanize a robot! That's why he's a robot instead of a human!

Holman came back from basic training, and couldn't wait to show us the scar behind his left ear where they'd given him a socket that his HUD would plug into. It looked like the knot of a rotten tree, crusted with dried gunk and with a pulsating wetness at its core. It wasn't as though they would be able to remote-control you or anything, Holman said—more like, sometimes in a complicated mixed-target urban environment, you might hesitate to engage for a few crucial split seconds and the people monitoring the situation remotely might need to guide your decision-making. So to speak.

Holman seemed happy for the first time ever, almost stoned, as he talked us through all the crazy changes he'd gone through in A.N.V.I.L. training and how he'd learned to breathe mud and spit bullets. Holman was bursting with rumors about all the next-generation weapons that were coming down the pike, like sonic bursts and smart bullets.

Ricky kept asking to see the rushes of our movie, and Raine got his draft notice, and we didn't know how the movie was supposed to end. I'd never seen any real propaganda before. I wanted it to end with Raine crushing me under his shiny boot, but Sally said it should end with me shooting out of a cannon (which we'd make in Zap!mation) into the Man's stronghold (which was the crumbling Chikken Hut) and then everything would blow up. Raine wanted the movie to end with his character and mine joining forces against the real enemy, the Pan-Asiatic drug lords, but Sally and I both vetoed that.

In the end, we filmed like ten different endings and then mashed them all up. Then we added several Zap!mation-only characters, and lots of messages on the screen like, "TONGUE-SAURUS!" and "OUTRAGEOUS BUSTAGE!" My favorite set piece involved me trying to make an ice cream sundae on top of a funeral hearse going one hundred mph, while Sally threw rocks at me. (I forget what we turned the rocks into, after.) There was some plot reason I had to make a sundae on top of a hearse, but we borrowed an actual hearse from this guy Raine knew who worked at a funeral home, and it actually drove one hundred mph on the cliff-side road, with Sally and Raine driving alongside in Raine's old Prius. I was scooping ice cream with one hand and squirting fudge with the other, and then Sally beaned me in the leg and I nearly fell off the sea cliff, but at the last minute I caught one of the hearse's rails and pulled myself back up, still clutching the full ice cream scoop in the other hand. With ice cream, all things are possible.

The final movie clocked in at twelve minutes, way, way longer than any of our previous efforts. It was like an attention-span final exam. We showed it to Ricky in Tanner High's computer room, on a bombed-out old Mac. I kept stabbing his arm, pointing out good parts like the whole projectile rabies bit and the razor-flower-arranging duel that Raine and I get into toward the end.

Ricky seemed to hope that if he spun in his chair and then looked back at the screen, this would be a different movie. Sometimes he would close his eyes, bounce, and reopen them, then frown because it was still the same crappy movie.

By the time the credits rolled, Ricky seemed to have decided something. He stood up and smiled, and thanked us for our great support for the movement, and started for the door before we could even show him the "blooper reel" at the end. I asked him about our draft survival deal, and he acted as if he had no clue what we were talking about. Sally, Raine, and I had voluntarily made this movie because of our fervent support of the red bandana and all it stood for. We could post the movie online, or not, it was up to us, but it had nothing to do with Ricky either way. It was weird seeing Ricky act so weaselly and calculating, like he'd become a politician all of a sudden. The only time I saw a hint of the old Ricky was when he said he'd use our spines as weed-whackers if we gave any hint that he'd told us to make that movie.

The blooper reel fizzed on the screen, unnoticed, while Raine, Sally, and I stared at each other. "So this means I have to die after all?" Raine said in his robotic stating-the-obvious voice. Sally didn't want to post our movie on the Internet, even after all the work we'd put into it, because of the red-bandana thing. People would think we'd joined the movement. Raine thought we should post it online, and maybe Ricky would still help us. I didn't want to waste all that work—couldn't we use Zap!mation to turn the bandana into, say, a big snake? Or a dog collar? But Sally said you can't separate a work of art from the intentions behind it. I'd never had any artistic intentions in my life, and didn't want to start having them now, especially not retroactively. First we didn't use all our footage, and then there was talk of scripts, and now we had intentions. Even if Raine hadn't been scheduled to go die soon, it was pretty obvious we were done.

I tried telling Raine that he might be okay, the Pan-Asiatic Ecumen could surrender any time now and they might call off the draft. Or—and here was an idea that I thought had a lot of promise—Raine could work the whole "robot" thing and pretend the draft didn't apply to him because he wasn't a person, but Sally told me to shut the fuck up. Sally kept jumping up and down, cursing the air and hitting things, and she threatened to kick the shit out of Ricky. Raine just sat there slump-headed, saying it wasn't the end of the world, maybe. We could take Raine's ancient Prius, load it up, and run for Canada, except what would we do there?

We were getting the occasional email from Holman, but then we realized it had been a month since the last one. And then two months. We started wondering if he'd been declared A.U.T.U.—and in that case, if we would ever officially find out what had happened to him.

A few days before Raine was supposed to report for death school, there was going to be a huge anti-war protest in Raleigh, and so we drove all the way there with crunchy bars and big bottles of grape sprocket juice, so we'd be sugared up for peace. We heard all the voices and drums before we saw the crowd, then there was a spicy smell and we saw people of twenty different genders and religions waving signs and pumping the air and chanting old-school style about what we wanted and when we wanted it. A platoon of bored cops in riot gear stood off to the side. We found parking a couple blocks away from the crowd, then tried to find a cranny to slip into with our signs. We were looking around at all the other objectors, not smiling but cheering, and then I spotted

Ricky a dozen yards away in the middle of a lesbian posse. And a few feet away from him, another big neckless angry guy. I started seeing them everywhere, dotted throughout the crowd. They weren't wearing the bandanas; they were blending in until they got some kind of signal.

I grabbed Sally's arm. "Hey, we have to get out of here."

"What the fuck are you talking about? We just got here!"

I pulled at her. It was hard to hear each other with all the bullhorns and loudspeakers, and the chanting. "Come on! Grab Raine, this is about to go crazy. I'll make a distraction."

"It's always about you making a distraction! Can't you just stop for a minute? Why don't you just grow the fuck up? I'm so sick of your bullshit. They're going to kill Raine, and you don't even care!" I'd never seen Sally's eyes so small, her face so red.

"Sally, look over there, it's Ricky. What's he doing here?"

"What are you talking about?"

I tried to pull both of them at once, but the ground had gotten soddy from so many protestor boots, and I slipped and fell into the dirt. Sally screamed at me to stop clowning around for once, and then one of the ISO punks stepped on my leg by mistake, then landed on top of me, and the crowd was jostling the punk as well as me, so we couldn't untangle ourselves. Someone else stepped on my hand.

I rolled away from the punk and sprang upright just as the first gunshot sounded. I couldn't tell who was firing, or at what, but it sounded nearby. Everyone in the crowd shouted without slogans this time and I went down again with boots in my face. I saw a leg that looked like Sally's and I tried to grab for her. More shots, and police bullhorns calling for us to surrender. Forget getting out of there, we had to stay down even if they trampled us. I kept seeing Sally's feet but I couldn't reach her. Then a silver shoe almost stepped on my face. I stared at the bright laces a second, then grabbed at Raine's silvery ankle, but he wouldn't go down because the crowd held him up. I got upright and came face-to-shiny-face with Raine. "Listen to me," I screamed over another rash of gunfire. "We have to get Sally, and then we have to—"

Raine's head exploded. Silver turned red, and my mouth was suddenly full of something warm and dark-tasting, and then several people fleeing in opposite directions crashed into me and I swallowed. I swallowed and doubled over as the crowd smashed into me, and I forced myself not to vomit because I needed to be able to breathe. Then the crowd pushed me down again and my last thought before I blacked out was that with this many extras, all we really needed would be a crane and a few dozen skateboards and we could have had a really cool set piece.

SKULL AND *HYSSOP*

KATHLEEN JENNINGS

———◆———

"Get out of here!" shouted Captain Moon from the door of the *Helmsman's Help*. "Go on, clear off!"

As the captain's thin, dark form lurched into the Port Fury street, several urchins fled, leaving their victim—a young woman in a blue weatherfinder jacket—to stagger in confusion. At the corner, they turned back to shout imprecations at the captain, but he ignored them. Instead, he caught the woman by the sleeve of her jacket and towed her out of the drizzling rain. In the brown tobacco-fog of the *Help*, he propped her up on one of the tall stools at the high table where Eliza Blancrose, with whom he had been enjoying a quiet rum and a discreet bet, waited.

"This is Eliza, journalist and travel writer for the Poorfortune Exclamation," said Moon, beaming. Eliza, arrested in mid-sentence by the captain's abrupt departure, doubtfully studied the new arrival before looking back at Moon. He was already a tall man—taller than Eliza—but altitude, adventure and (in Eliza's expressed opinion) lack of feeding had attenuated him. Under Eliza's gaze he became suddenly aware that he loomed like a crane above the stranger, and backed away. Eliza patted the woman's hand, beneath the blue cuff of the rain-spattered jacket. "There, there," she said, as if she doubted anything would be all right.

Moon called to the barman for buttered rum.

"My luck's turning," he said, as he returned to a tall stool. He hitched one leg through its bars and put a pipe, which he did not light, between his teeth. "It's not every day I get to help a weatherfinder. I'm sure you're much obliged, you needn't mention it. Those gutter-rats would have had every coin out of your pockets, wouldn't they, Eliza? Well, gutter-mice. Assuming you had coins to begin with. Safer aloft, you know. Above the clouds." He nodded upward with all the wisdom his thin, incautious features could display, but a touch of yearning had crept in with those last words.

"You're a terrible liar, Moon," said Eliza affectionately. "Port Fury isn't large enough to sustain a criminal element."

The young woman had a long jaw which made her look both familiar and pugnacious, but she kept her gaze lowered and her chin tucked in below her raised collar. "Thank you for your assistance," she said firmly, "but I shouldn't be in here."

"It's an airman's pub," said Moon, "And there's no man more truly an airman than a weatherfinder, is there, Eliza?" The journalist raised one eyebrow, a feat Moon had never achieved although he had practised since childhood. He turned back to the other woman. She looked promisingly hungry.

"Do you need a job?" he asked.

"No. I'm here searching for my brother."

"Can't say I've seen him," said Moon briskly, without pausing for a name or description. "Look here—I've got a fine ship headed for Poorfortune, that jewel of the seas," ("Jewel of the sewers," put in Eliza with the loyalty of a true native of that city), "and I could do with a weatherfinder. In fact," he added, his eagerness to be in the air again soured by the recollection, "I have a passenger who insists on it."

"If I can find my brother, he could assist you," said the woman. Her speech suggested education, and a good one, but it had not eradicated her accent—an inland drawl from the country regions beyond Port Fury where the towns were too small to merit dock-towers. "This is his coat, not mine." She rolled up the sleeves of the regulation Academy jacket to show her lower arms. They were bare of the tattoos in which weatherfinders, for all their arrogance, gloried as much as any common salt or breezy. "His name is—he went by the name of Evan Arden—" she began.

"Not a bell," said Moon. "I don't run with weatherfinders as a rule."

"He calls them glorified windsocks," put in Eliza.

"No offence meant. Cally—he's steersman—and I get on just fine. My passenger, however, is very insistent, and he can pay."

The woman who wasn't a weatherfinder slipped down from the wooden stool and folded the collar of her jacket up further. "I'll brave your gutter rats, captain. I haven't anything they can steal. But thank you again."

She'd made it to the door before Moon had an idea. "Wait!" he called.

The woman glanced back. When he met her gaze, she looked older, but her eyes were lit with a flicker of hope.

"I'll buy that jacket," offered Moon.

When he returned to the table, Eliza said, "Well?"

"In luck," said Moon, bundling up the jacket.

"The trick with luck," said Eliza, lifting her glass, "is holding onto it."

Mr. Fuille was a Level 7 State Scientist (according to his papers, his card, the labels on his luggage and his self-introduction). Grey-suited and featured, he stood on the platform of the middle docks and regarded the *Hyssop* closely. After a morning of being loaded with crates labelled FRAGILE, LIVE BEWARE and BIOLOGICAL SPECIMENS, the *Hyssop* hung heavy from her supports, trapped in the sluggish shadows of the docks and out of the high crisp winds. Her holds were pungent with crowded boxes, and Port Fury sparrows and the odd raven perched and flew from spar to strut to gangplank.

To Captain Moon, fidgeting beside his passenger and willing the ravens away, Fuille's patient inspection seemed malevolent.

"I must be satisfied, sir," continued Fuille, "that all codes and authorities are, have been, and will continue to be complied with. Especially as we are to make the crossing in a single stage, in such a diminutive vessel."

Moon was anxious to be away from Port Fury, with its codes and laws and Imperial interests, and had hoped that his passenger shared that eagerness. Now, choking down his impatience, the captain forced himself to conduct Mr. Fuille once more around the ship, directing the scientist's attention to orderly preparations and regulation outfitting—rubberised equipment to prevent sparks, correct ice insulation and sighting-glass—and steering the man deftly away from the freshest paintwork.

"I saw three deckhands," said Mr. Fuille at last.

"Two," said Moon, as he watched the scientist's ashen fingers tap a beat on the railing. "Cally is steersman. Tomasch and Alban are more—everything-hands."

"A very small crew for a vessel of these specifications. Possibly the minimum required for compliance with the *Poorfortune People's Aviation and Elevation Cargo and Vessel Handling Code*, which being declared by the port of destination is, I must accept, the applicable document. But I observed no weatherfinder. It specifically says in the *Imperial and Transcontinental Standards and Accord* that—"

"—and this is where we keep him," said Moon, pointing to his showpiece. In truth the storeroom was the size of a coffin, but the blue regulation-issue weatherfinder jacket was artistically draped over a hook on the door. "I'm afraid he is somewhat, er, under the weather. As they say. Landsickness. He'll return to us shortly. You said you were anxious to make good time?" He shepherded Fuille back to the single passenger cabin at the rear of the *Hyssop*, already crowded with Fuille's luggage (elegant and extensive luggage, viewed beside the canvas ditty bags and matildas the crew had slung across from the docks). Having installed his passenger there, Moon stepped onto the dock to sign, with Cally, the last forms standing between the *Hyssop* and freedom.

From this spot, he surveyed his little ship. The canvas and rubber of her gas cushions was striped red and yellow. He had painted the hull garish black and red, with long blue luck-eyes on the sides. The figurehead, which held a heavy lantern suspended by chains from her hands, was picked out in mercilessly lifelike colours.

Moon looked at her with love. Underneath the paint and canvas, for those who had eyes to see, she had the bones of an elegant and venerable vessel, the soul of a more romantic age. Only the knowledge of the passenger sitting like a canker in the cabin dulled his pride in the *Hyssop*.

"If you ever gaze at a woman like that, dear Captain, I'll eat my hat," said a merry voice from above.

"That would be a shame, Eliza," said Moon. He looked up. She was leaning over a railing, on her way to the highest level of the docks. From where he stood Moon could see the sleek curve of the *Orient*, the long, swift cruise-ship on which she had a berth. "It is a very smart hat."

"And that," conceded Eliza, touching one gloved hand to her hair, "is a particularly stylish paint job. Your taste is remarkable, the more so considering your, ah—finances, my poor Captain. You should have been a pirate."

"There is time yet," said Moon. "Besides, 'no man is poor or alone who owns a ship.' "

"Or otherwise acquires one."

Moon added as an afterthought, "You, of course, are always welcome aboard. The boys took a liking to you. We're taking the direct route—I will arrange a thrilling voyage for your readers."

"The colours would clash with my dress," said Eliza. "Besides—" she broke off with pointed tact.

"I told you, the *Hyssop* can make the voyage, easily. She was flying before they ever thought of making your fine cruise ships. I'll wage we'll have a smoother trip."

Eliza tossed her head. "I was going to say, you couldn't afford me."

"You take payment for favourable reviews?" he asked.

"It would take payment to get a favourable review of that tub," said Eliza. "It's no pleasure-craft. Get me a good story one day, Captain Moon, and a ship that's steadier on the stomach, and maybe I'll fly with you. Till then, find me in Poorfortune, for I have news to tell you when you get there."

"I'll race you," said Moon rashly.

Eliza went on up, laughing.

"News of what?" he shouted up, after a moment.

"It will keep!" Eliza called back, and then the next platform of the dock tower hid her from his sight.

On the second day out from Port Fury, and already well clear of the sea-ports and land, the *Hyssop* caught a bitterwind. Ice crackled on the rails and glass shieldings, and vanished again like smoke. The ship had been designed to sail with the wind, and refitted by previous owners to be propelled by modern power and manned by a very small crew, currently made up of Cally and his sons. Moon, who believed that sense, experience and attention would beat an academy-trained weatherfinder any day, and cost less, was standing at the tiller, planning further renovations and contentedly watching the sky through the glass dome of the steering deck when Mr. Fuille flushed out the stowaway.

The sounds of pursuit began below Moon's feet, became accompanied by the cries of Tomasch and Alban, rose up through the bowels of the *Hyssop* and spilled onto the deck. The steersman remained carefully deaf, and there were no shouts of fire or leakage, so Moon waited until the tumult died. Then he tucked his unlit pipe into the pocket of his fur-lined coat, regretfully handed the tiller over to Cally, and wandered out to see what had caused the fuss.

Mr. Fuille, his face greyer than usual, his shoulders hunched against the cold, confronted Moon amidships. "I am a Level 7 Scientist," he said. "Their Majesty's Government will not be at all pleased to know that my cargo was being rifled through by ship's rats!"

"Rats?" said Moon.

"Vile, vagabond—" said Fuille, beginning to sputter.

"Ah," said Moon.

Tomasch was leaning over the side, a gloved hand raised against the swirl of ice-air which peeled around the wind shields. Moon joined him. For a moment his attention was caught and whipped away by the wind, the vast blue sphere of the empty world in which the ship hung suspended. Then he saw a flutter of cloth disappear around the curve of the hull.

"Over the side!" Fuille choked. "The cowardice—Their Majesties' Government—"

"What Their Majesties' Government doesn't know won't hurt it," said Moon thoughtfully. He turned to Mr. Fuille. The scientist did not improve the view. "Hazard of shipping. But the problem has gone. Disposed of itself. Short duration. Remarkably."

"Send your men after him!"

"To what end?" said Moon, noting the alarm of Alban, who had not inherited his family's head for heights.

"There has been a violation of Government property!" said Mr. Fuille, his grey eyes protruding. He shook with anger or cold, and his skin was chalky. "My experiments are delicate, carefully calibrated. If your crew has been nurturing a stowaway—"

"Get something for Mr. Fuille to drink," Moon told Tomasch. "And get him a warmer coat." When they had gone into Fuille's cabin, Moon stood scratching his jaw. He looked at the clear sky (such a warm dark blue in spite of the ice) and the indicator flags all fluttering stiffly as they should, then went to his own small cabin, set at the front of the little ship. He opened the shutters over one round window. Through the uneven glass he could see sky, ropes, chains, billowing gas cushions, sky again and then the upswept arms of the figurehead, holding out the unlit lantern to where the endless blue arched into oblivion.

Moon ran a careful calculation of time and infrastructure in his mind, then opened the next shutter along and forced open the window itself. It slammed against the timbers with a report like a gun, and the ice wind poured in.

Moon, pleased, glimpsed the stowaway crouched behind the figurehead, clinging to the iced ropes and staring out into the void. He closed his own eyes against the blinding cold and, climbing half out the window in spite of his bad leg, reached down, seized a double handful of hair and shirt and hauled the stowaway back aboard.

Someone hammered heavily on the cabin door, but Moon ignored the noise and frowned down at stowaway who sat on the bed, wrapped in Moon's blankets. He suspected she was the young woman he had met in Port Fury, although the windburn was new, as was the ancient coat which had replaced her brother's jacket.

"That was a foolish thing to do," he said, conversationally. He had succeeded in pouring a quarter of a bottle of brandy into her before she'd revived enough to protest, and he didn't think she'd been out in the bitterwind long enough to lose any fingers.

"Getting thrown over the side?" she asked, indistinctly. Her eyes were closed and her lips chapped and bleeding.

"Not even pirates throw stowaways over the side," he said bracingly. "Not without enquiries. You're lucky you didn't fall. Unless you were frozen there?"

"I was going to jump," she said.

"Unnecessary, and a long way down. Keep your eyes closed, I can't get anything to put on them until I go out on deck, and I'm not inclined to yet."

"At first I was terrified of falling," the woman went on, "and then the wind cut through me. I could hear it in my head and my bones, howling inside them, and I thought, *I won't fall, the wind will bear me up.* I think I went a little mad."

"That implies you were sane to begin with," said Moon.

"Will I be blind?" she asked.

He shook his head, then remembered she couldn't see him. "With luck, the ship and the figurehead between them cut the worst of the wind."

"Captain!" roared Mr. Fuille, outside the door. "I know you are in there."

"Lie down," said Moon. He pushed her back onto the narrow bed and draped his handkerchief over her face. "Try to look like you have a headache."

"Everything aches."

"It won't be hard then," said Moon. "Come in, Mr. Fuille," he added grandly, unlatching the door. "Please try to be considerate."

"Considerate!" exploded Mr. Fuille. "I will have you know—Who is that?"

"Evan Arden," improvised Moon. Livid spots stood out on the scientist's cheeks and brow. "Ivana Arden," Moon amended. "My weatherfinder."

"I received the distinct impression your weatherfinder was a man," said Mr. Fuille.

"You would be surprised at the prejudice one still encounters," said Moon.

Mr. Fuille narrowed his eyes and swelled slightly. "Women have not been admitted into the Academy for a sufficiently extensive period of time to permit any graduate to have acquired the experience necessary to inspire confidence!"

"As you say," said Moon mildly.

Fuille took a deep breath, then demanded, "What was your weatherfinder doing in my cargo?"

"Probably looking for brandy. Not to worry, I've dosed her up and she'll be herself in a few hours." The stowaway groaned convincingly.

"A weatherfinder should not be drinking on duty," said Fuille. "The third amendment to the *Navigator's Ordinance*—"

Moon wanted to say, "You're just making up legislation now," but merely shrugged. "Old air dog, new tricks, no harm done."

Fuille glared at Moon, whose heart sank at the scientist's next words. "I will be giving information to their Imperial Majesties' Ambassador and the Poorfortune Aerial and Aerostat Governance Department when we dock."

When Fuille was gone, Moon stepped out to inform the steersman of the addition to their crew. When he returned to the cabin, his stowaway lifted a corner of the handkerchief and regarded at him foggily. "Well, one of us is lucky," said Moon. "I thought I was buying an empty coat." Then he sighed and looked regretfully at his pipe. "I also hoped to get to Poorfortune unremarked, Ivana."

"That's not my name."

"It is until we get to port," he said and put his pipe between his teeth. "You'll have to act like a weatherfinder."

"I've never been taught how!"

"I'm not asking you to read the winds. I can do that as well as any academy-approved wind-vane. Just—prance around and pretend to make calculations. Act like your brother."

"Evan's a very good weatherfinder," she said angrily.

"Then he should be able to take care of himself. Which of all the blue devils made you pull a trick like this, anyway?"

"You were going to Poorfortune," she said, and put the handkerchief back over her eyes. "That's the last place anyone heard Evan was going."

"You would have been more comfortable on the cruise ship," said Moon.

"Your security was worse," said Ivana.

Moon thought of his crew and conceded this. "What ship was your brother on?"

"*The Ravens*," said now-Ivana. She touched the wall of the cabin as she spoke. Moon had run out of paint, and the walls here wore their original colour. Her fingernails—short for a lady's, although her hands were uncalloused—caught on the grooves where fine copper wires were still set into the wood.

"This is the *Hyssop*," said Moon quickly. "No one's seen *The Ravens* for a year or more."

"I know," said Ivana from underneath the handkerchief. "I'm not the only person looking for it."

"What do you mean?" asked Moon.

Ivana paused before she spoke. The silence was filled by the throb of engines, and Tomasch shouting instructions to his brother. "That grey man is looking for it too," she said. "I heard him mention it when the cargo was being loaded. And there were papers in the boxes he brought. Records and schematics."

Moon winced. He didn't want Government trouble. "I'll kick you both off in Poorfortune," he said. "You can look for it together."

"I don't like him," said the woman. She took the handkerchief off her eyes. "I wish you hadn't told him my name was Arden."

"And I wish you hadn't stowed away on my ship," said Moon, but he was even less fond of the idea that Fuille had some connection with *The Ravens*. The sudden acquisition of this extra passenger, with less ship-sense than Alban, did not unsettle him as much as that.

"So your brother was—is a weatherfinder," he mused.

"A trained one." She turned to the wall. He could see her shoulder blades sharp under her ragged coat. Her fingers traced the lines in the timbers where the wires lay.

"They don't make the other kind anymore," said Moon with a smile, but she gave no indication of amusement.

Moon sighed. He preferred conversations with people who gave as they got. He would look up Eliza when they reached port.

"What do you do when you're not hitching rides to Poorfortune, Ivana?"

"I work in a doctor's surgery," she said.

"You're a secretary?"

Ivana made a noncommittal sound.

"I don't need a secretary," said Moon. "It's a small ship. Everyone needs to be useful."

"Even the scientist?" asked Ivana.

"He pays our way," said Moon. "Do you know anything about ships?"

"My family traditionally avoids the ports," she said loftily.

"Well, do you do anything useful? Can you cook? Otherwise I'm going to have to put you out the front again."

"No!" said Ivana, grasping his arm. "Wait, look." She rolled back and struggled to sit upright, then leaned against the wall.

"If you pass out, I'll use you for ballast," said Moon, freeing himself from her grasp.

"I work with doctors. I learn quickly. I know a few things—surely I can be useful. You have a habit of injuring yourself." She made a quick gesture towards his leg and Moon, who prided himself on his ease of walking, was hurt that she had noticed.

"The question is," said Moon, "Can you act?"

"I learn quickly," she repeated. "I'll play your weatherfinder, Captain, and I'll fix injuries if I can, but don't make me stand in the wind. When I was out there, it went through me as if I were made of flags, and all my nerves and organs were flying away. That frightened me more than falling."

Moon had felt the summer breezes and the bitterwinds, but they had never cut through him in such a way, and he envied Ivana.

"Well, don't tell Fuille that," he said at last.

Ivana, tidied, stood in the corner of Moon's cabin. He had helped her back into the too-large blue coat, and rolled one sleeve so that the ink would dry on her arm. "Fuille is particular," said Moon, setting down the pen and stoppering the ink bottle. He kept hold of her wrist and turned back to blow on the ink. Her fingers twitched. "All weatherfinders I've seen have tattoos," he continued. "I don't want him to notice anything odd and cause more trouble before I get him to Poorfortune."

"And after that?" asked Ivana. "He will notice, if he hasn't already."

"Notice what?" asked Moon, releasing her arm and putting the ink away.

"That under the paint there are ravens carved all over this ship. And I've seen what's left of the older paintwork, here and below decks. It's . . . telling."

"All ships have histories," said Moon, cleaning the pen. The ship lurched in a sudden gust and the captain swayed against his desk.

"And the figurehead should be beautiful, and pale," continued Ivana, adjusting to the turbulence as if it were a summer wind. "It's made of bone and ivory, did you know that?" She gestured to the books and charts in the cabin, the carved tobacco pipes, the creditable botanical tracery of a hyssop stem which he had drawn on the inside of her arm. "But I'm sure you did. You like beautiful things. You wouldn't have painted that figurehead like a dockside . . . like that, if you didn't have a very good reason. Did you steal this ship? Are you a pirate?"

"Not yet," said Moon. "Just lucky. But she is, as you said, a very beautiful ship, and old. This era of ships—well, they aren't around much any more. They were built to respond to every change in the weather, and a fine degree of understanding of it, and that doesn't suit modern methods. She wallows under engines, but she would have been fast in her youth. She could be again, with a true weatherfinder on board."

"But you don't have one," said Ivana.

"I live in hope that can be remedied," said Moon, settling back and filling his pipe using long deliberate fingers.

Ivana, still holding her inked arm away from her side, walked easily around the cabin, studying the charts with a gaze both intelligent and bewildered. "I thought the journalist said you didn't like weatherfinders, but there's always the academy. These maps are the same territory at different heights, are they not? They're very handsomely drawn." She traced a pattern of weather-currents thoughtfully.

Moon waved one hand. "If I'd meant an academy weatherfinder, I'd have said that. A blue coat and a degree isn't evidence of an ounce of real talent. The old weatherfinders, it's said, could feel the wind in their blood."

Ivana met his pointed gaze, and her own did not waver. "I didn't tell you that so you could use it against me. Besides, it was a—a madness. Altitude sickness. I've never even been as high as the port tower before now."

"Your family avoids the winds?"

"Maybe your scientist had hallucinogens in the cargo."

Moon was not distracted. "Most people don't believe that born ability still exists, or ever did. But what you said you felt—look at that book over there, the brown one, *Lives Aloft*. Eliza says it could do with an editor's hand, but it's an old book and that's what it talks about: 'a knife of blue freedom.' If I'd thought to look in doctors' offices . . . " He stood up again and began sorting through his books. "You'll have plenty to learn, I daresay, you can't just tell a steersman what to do by vague feelings, but books and experience will teach you that. As far as I can make out, it should just be a matter of translating for the laity. Do you know what it would mean to have a true weatherfinder? With that and a good old ship, a man could have the run of the skies. I had hopes of the money Fuille's cargo would bring, but this has turned out better than I could have hoped. You could be a legend, Ivana Arden. We both could."

"Captain!" said Ivana shortly. He looked up from his visions and books. "I'm only here to find my brother," she said, slowly and clearly. "He left us and changed his name and went to study of his own accord, but he's been missing too long. I'm sure Fuille knows something. I want to look in the cargo hold again."

"I don't think that's wise," said Moon, briefly diverted. "I'd rather not upset him further. He might still declare himself. Let's ask him to dinner instead."

• • •

Both the meal and the conversation were cool, for heating was minimal on an old gas-ship and Fuille's rage had settled to a peevish disgruntlement. The scientist only once mentioned Ivana's brandy, bitingly, as she hesitated over the simple Poorfortune table-service, but he watched the captain and the weatherfinder steadily throughout the meal.

"You have a broad experience, Arden," he said to Ivana sardonically. "Such an illustrated past."

Ivana looked at the single stem of hyssop drawn on her arm. The ink had bled lightly into her skin.

"She's articled to the *Hyssop*," said Moon, to draw Fuille's attention from the ink. "Everyone has to start somewhere."

"Indeed," said Fuille. He glanced around the cabin before narrowing his eyes at Ivana. "You have the look of someone about you, and your name a certain ring. Tell me, this penchant for cloud-watching—does it run in the family?"

"My brother—" said Ivana and Moon kicked her under the table. Her face was already too windburned to betray a blush.

Moon supplied glibly, "Her brother said she never has her feet on the ground. Old friend of mine. Took her on as a favour."

"Hmm," said Fuille. "One can be too high-minded. You should widen that experience of yours, before you get walled in. One can be . . . limited, staying too long on a small boat, or so I understand. It is not, of course, my sphere."

Ivana did not have Eliza's speed of reply, and Moon took pity on her.

"What is your sphere, Mr. Fuille?" he asked.

"Aerodynamics," said Fuille. "It is a vitally important work, though often looked over or, perhaps, under. As you know, the lifeblood of Their Majesties' Empire and, indeed, of the nations streams through the currents of the sky. I have sacrificed my life to that work—the interaction of the organic with the atmospheric, that delicate interplay of wing and wind, bone and billow, mind and the mellifluosity of flight." He seemed lost for a moment in some glorious vision. Then he reached across the table and took Ivana's hand in his large, colourless one. Moon saw sudden distaste convulse her mouth, although a heartbeat later she had concealed it. Fuille, unaware, turned her hand over clinically, and said, "I should like to examine you, my dear. It is always charming to add new data to my research. My collection would, I think, fascinate you."

"You don't like him," said Moon, after Fuille retired and before Ivana escaped to the storage cupboard she had insisted upon occupying. His cabin was now uncomfortably cluttered with evicted buckets and pulleys, stored in the few corners and under—and on—his bed. "I can't say I don't sympathise, but in the interests of getting to Poorfortune peaceably, and getting paid, perhaps you could conceal it better."

"He touched me," said Ivana, leaning against the cabin wall, her arms folded across her body. "It was like shaking hands with a walking corpse."

"Just a bureaucrat," said Moon.

"Not that," said Ivana. "He's . . . " she shifted and fiddled with the latch of the window. "Unsavoury," she finished at last, as if the word did not satisfy her, and then added hastily, "I wouldn't trust him."

"You don't have to. Just don't let your nerves make you so chatty!"

"Don't assume I'd tell him more than I must!" sniped Ivana.

Moon was tempted to return in kind, but long experience with Eliza's robust company had taught him circumspection. He sat on his desk, crossed his ankles and waved one hand. "Perhaps he was fascinated by something more than your conversation." His evil genius prompted him to add, "You think sailors get bad, it's nothing on bureaucrats. Inviting you to 'see his collection.' "

"I'm not a fool," said Ivana, witheringly. "He was serious about his collection, but I don't believe he would really care to have it seen. So I want to see it."

"I don't," said Moon. "And I don't want you to go prancing about the ship with him either."

"I don't intend to prance with anyone," said Ivana. "Or be any nearer to him than I have to. I'll go on my own. You invite him in here again for drinks."

"Not until you tell me why."

Ivana glared at him. "Feminine intuition!"

"You haven't any," said Moon. "You took against him like—like a judge that just heard evidence. Like a journalist spotting bad grammar. Pure professional hatred. He's on my ship, and your job is to keep me out of hard weather, so tell me: what put the wind up you?"

He held her gaze. She did not blink, but her expression was searching rather than hard.

"I pulled you out of the street," said Moon. "I paid you for that coat, I didn't throw you off the ship. I might even want to help you again, though I don't know why. I don't believe you've told me any more of the truth than suits you."

At last, with an air of acceptance rather than capitulation Ivana left the wall and took a step towards him. "Give me your hand."

Moon obliged, and felt his hand folded between her rope-burned palms.

"Fortune teller?" he asked, wryly.

"Not quite," said Ivana. Her hands were not otherwise work-roughened, but her cool dry fingers felt strong. If she was a secretary, the only ink he had seen on her hands was from his pen.

That's odd," she said after a silence during which Moon sat and felt her pulse beat against his.

"What?" said Moon.

She nodded at the pipe in his pocket. "You don't smoke, and you never have. You get a cold foot at night, though, and the other foot—ah." She glanced at him with almost a smile. "You don't have the other foot. You're not quite used to that yet, but you hide it well, I thought before that you were only a little lame. And it explains the bruises. Your liver isn't all it could be. And you have an ingrown fingernail on your other hand and it's getting unpleasant, but I saw that at dinner."

She released his hand. "I don't know if any of that's useful."

"Nothing I didn't know," said Moon. He stared at her and she looked down at her own hands. "But I don't know how the hell you know it. What was that?"

"I showed you so that you'll believe me when I say there is something I don't like about Fuille," she said.

"Maybe it was a lucky guess," said Moon. "Maybe you're a—a charlatan. Or maybe you really are a doctor's secretary and can guess when someone is liverish. Try it on someone else. I'll get Alban, there's got to be something wrong with him."

"Please, no!" said Ivana. "I only showed you so that you'll believe me about Fuille. I much rather nobody else know."

Her alarm was sincere enough that Moon subsided back onto the desk. "It could still have been a lucky guess," he grumbled, to keep the curious mix of discomfort and excitement at bay.

"Your journalist!" said Ivana abruptly.

"Eliza?"

"Yes. She took my hand back in Port Fury. She has a tearing scar, up her side and her hand will ache from writing, at times. She wears shoes that are too small—"

"She's vain," supplied Moon.

"And she's pregnant."

"Hell," said Moon, mildly. He took out his pipe and held it meditatively.

"She didn't tell you," said Ivana, her face falling. "I thought—"

"I was distracted by weatherfinders," said Moon. "She promised me news in Poorfortune." He raised his eyebrows in thought, then returned the pipe to his pocket. "I shall have to endeavour to appear surprised." He supposed he ought in good conscience have been preoccupied by Eliza's interesting predicament, but was more interested to find he did not doubt Ivana.

"How do you do it?" he asked.

Ivana, taken up by her own thoughts, answered almost without noticing. "I see the patterns in blood," she said. "More clearly than in air." Her focus returned to him and she said, "Not destiny, or fortune, or any of that, and I can't heal anything. At least, only by ordinary means."

"Doctor's secretary," murmured Moon.

Ivana ducked her head. "I see paths and eddies, what's going right and what's wrong. I feel it the same way I felt the wind, only people are so much smaller. You said experience and books would teach me about the wind, and I'm not a fool. I've studied to understand what I see in a man's veins. But the wind was so huge. I felt as if my mind was being scoured."

This revelation, beyond the legends of weatherfinders in his books, was too important for Moon to take in all at once. Concentrating on the immediate issue, he said, "And you don't like Fuille."

She shook her head. "He's got chemicals—things in his blood that embalmers use, and anaesthetists. Not a sudden concentration, but little pieces, all the way through, as if he uses them all the time. Drugs that must alter the way he moves and sleeps and thinks. That's why I don't like him, together with the things he said, and—other reasons."

"He's a government scientist," said Moon, but the explanation sounded poor besides Ivana's recital. He told himself he was put off-kilter by Eliza's news, but that wasn't it. It struck him that a government scientist might be interested in Ivana's broad talents. But it was too late in the evening to worry about mad scientists, or the confidence Ivana had given to his keeping.

"What happened to your leg?" she asked at last.

Moon shook himself, glad of a lighter turn to the conversation.

"The People's Poorfortune Hospital cut it off," he said. "I don't have time for doctors—always saying you should have gone looking for them after every fight, instead of waiting to be carried in. I think they amputated out of spite. But I got out of it with a bulletproof leg, which isn't something to sneeze at."

"Do you get into a lot of fights?" asked Ivana.

"Not for want of trying," said Moon. His thoughts were straying again. "What you did isn't normal. People might be interested. To the tune of State Interests, and money."

"I know," said Ivana quietly. She did not say that she trusted him not to betray her. Her silence was more persuasive than words might have been.

Moon thought a little longer, until Ivana said, "You're looking at me like you look at your ship."

"Apologies," said Moon, pulled from his reverie. He stood up to show her out of the cabin and to her closet. There was much he felt he ought to say in parting, but he settled for, "Just don't tell Fuille."

Fuille had indicated a preference to eat alone in his cabin for the past two days, relieving Moon of the need to be civil to the man or observe Alban and Tomasch's attempts at table-waiting.

"Where is that weatherfinder of yours?" the scientist demanded, as soon as he had taken a seat in Moon's cabin. His careful grey fingers toyed carelessly with the delicate glass Moon had provided. The port-wine moved in it like old blood.

"About some atmospheric business," said Moon. It could even have been true. His small library was outdated, but Ivana had applied herself to it single-mindedly in the preceding days. Alban and Tomasch were incapable of conversing with her, so meals were silent, and she proved to be a faster reader than Moon, who had sat across from her at meals, his own plans unrolled on the table, trying to guess her thoughts from her expressions while she read.

She had stood, too, beneath the *Hyssop*'s glass dome, talking to Cally and staring at the clouds. When the bitterwind fell, she borrowed Moon's glass eye-mask, belted the fur-lined overjacket and clambered about the sides, always too close to falling. She had gained her airlegs quickly enough, Moon hoped, to convince Fuille she had always been only an ordinary weatherfinder after all, and not an untrained prodigy. Still, neither he nor Alban, who shut his eyes each time, liked to see her going over the side of the ship again.

"We will make Poorfortune the day after next, all going smoothly," said Moon.

"I count on you to make it smooth," growled Fuille. "There will be lawsuits enough if any of my cargo has already been damaged by the events of this voyage, let alone by further delay. It does not pay to thwart the plans of Their Majesties' Government, Captain."

Moon did not answer. As he had bowed Fuille into his cabin, he had seen Ivana descending through the grilled hatches. Fuille pushed back his glass now and stood. As he did so, he brushed his hand against a line in the timber of the cabin wall, almost idly. "It is a very old ship, is it not?"

"The builder would be flattered," lied Moon glibly. "She's a replica. The colours are based on a pleasure ship from the last century, but I'm afraid she's all modern, and cost considerably more than she's worth. Let me pour you another."

"How did you come by it, then?" asked the scientist, not sitting down. Suspicion lined his pallid face. "Even this copper in the walls is not cheap."

"Very accurate, isn't she?" said Moon. "On the surface at least. Underneath I'm afraid she has new bones. Still, I call it good luck that brought her to me. Won her in a game of squares." He spoke quickly, but it was clear Fuille was inclined to leave. Moon did not know if he worried more that Fuille would find Ivana in the cargo hold, or that she would blame Moon for not holding Fuille longer.

"You know a lot about the era?" went on Moon, brightly. He crossed to the front of the cabin. "Perhaps you could give me advice on these window fittings. My friend on the *Orient* says they should be brass but I think it would be more accurate—"

"Window fittings," growled Fuille, "are beneath . . . " then stopped, slammed open the door of the cabin and left.

I'm going to be down a weatherfinder, thought Moon. While he waited for the shouting to begin, a shadow flickered through the light from the cabin window behind him.

Moon turned. The window showed blue sky and then a flurry like black wings. Cursed ravens, he thought, and then, we're too high for birds. He opened the window and caught a fold of heavy blue cloth as it swung once more towards him. It was anchored by something below, and the icy wind struck dull the sound of Ivana's voice as she shouted, "Pull me up!"

For the second time, Moon hauled her in, his good foot braced against the wall. As he dragged her over the windowsill she yelled. "It's murder!"

"Not yet, but it will be," said Moon through gritted teeth, thinking of Fuille.

He set her on her feet as she said, "Necessary sacrifice, then? Hazards of employment? Those who live by the wind—" her voice broke.

"Calm down," said Moon. "No-one's died. Everyone's at their stations."

Before he could close the window fully, Ivana gripped the edge with a thick-gloved hand. "There's something ugly coming," she said, and tugged down the fur collar of the coat to speak more clearly. Her voice was flat. "I'm only warning you because I'm on this ship too, or else you might have your fate and welcome to it. There's a coiling twisting in the air, a big storm. And I need something hard and heavy." She darted past Moon to get the rubber-dipped line hook. He grasped it as she returned.

"Are you going to stop the storm with this?" he asked.

"No." said Ivana. "Fuille." She pulled the line hook free and opened the window again fully.

Moon put his hand up against the cold air. "Fuille didn't go that way."

Ivana stopped with one leg over the window sill. She tugged up the heavy goggles and looked at him, no merriment left in her eyes. "No, Captain. My brother did," she said. "He won't be coming back." Then she shook herself and added, with bitterness and no sincerity, "Not that you have reason to care. I'm terribly sorry about your precious figurehead." She folded herself out the window.

"No, wait, what?" said Moon, but Ivana had already dropped and scrambled to the base of the figurehead. One hand gripping the lines, she swung at the graceful figure with a will.

"No!" said Moon, "This is my ship! Ignore everything I said. I will throw you over the side!" The wind choked the words back into his throat. He slammed the window shut, latched it and turned, fuming, to find himself face to face with Fuille.

"Is everything in order, Mr. Fuille?" he asked, with a reasonable facsimile of calm.

"I could ask you the same," said Fuille.

"Mere nothing. Difference of opinion," said Moon. "With the steersman. Can I help you?"

"I should not have thought he could hear you from here," said Fuille. "I went to my room to fetch my commonplace book—I keep a record of . . . intriguing artefacts. I thought I might have something relevant to your window latch. May I have a closer look?"

Moon stood, back to the window. He hoped Ivana would not try to get in again, and at the same time that she would not need to, and would not freeze to death. *You found one weatherfinder, there must be others*, he scolded himself, *you only have one* Hyssop. "I wouldn't ask a scientist of your standing to trouble himself with such trifles," said Moon.

"Nonsense," said Fuille. "You were so insistent before. It is the least I can do to repay your hospitality."

He opened the book and flipped through it. "It so happens that I have seen some ships not unlike this one. Less festively coloured perhaps." Moon, taller than Fuille, looked down to see a rough sketch not of a window latch but of a figurehead of unmistakeable elegance, pale and long-jawed, with a lantern in its outstretched hand. Where it should have joined the ship, the drawing disintegrated into a network of carefully labelled lines.

Moon leaned against the window. "You should secure your cargo," he said. "I'll send the boys to help. Weatherfinder says there's a storm coming."

"It's as blue a day as you could care to see," said Fuille. "The rigours of this crossing have been exaggerated. You should secure your brandy—it has addled your woman's brains."

Moon thought he heard the slap of cloth against the window once more. He hoped his shoulders blocked the glass. If Ivana had not already damaged the figurehead beyond recognition, he did not want to give Fuille the chance to study it.

"Sky's deceiving," said Moon. "Said there's a bad storm coming. Could be here anytime. Small ship. Very good weatherfinder."

"You think I cannot tell the fresh marks of a pen from the ink of a tattoo?" said Fuille smoothly. "This is very gallant of you, and I'm sure she's sufficiently grateful, considering it is as you say such a small ship, but I must insist, Captain, that you permit me—"

"My weatherfinder went down to the cargo hold earlier and hasn't come back up the hatch," said Moon.

Fuille's forced pleasantness evaporated. He spun on his heel and ran out of the cabin. Moon latched the cabin door and turned back as glass shattered behind him. Reaching the window, he wrenched it open and caught the line hook.

"I will . . . throw you . . . over . . . the side!" he shouted into the wind, punctuating the sentence by shaking the hook. He let go. Ivana, who had been pulling down, fell backwards and slipped. Moon saw her fall into the wind, only to jerk to a halt. She still held onto a line by one gloved hand.

Moon did not later remember how he got himself out the window.

The wind hit him like white fire. He gripped a line and dropped down into the slight shelter of the ravaged figurehead. The cold stung his eyes to tears, but he reached out, caught the front of Ivana's coat and towed her back to the ledge. "I didn't mean it!" he shouted as he hauled her upright. He couldn't hear her reply. He pushed her up towards the window. She went in with a convulsive struggle. One boot, or the dangling line hook, struck him in the side of the head.

The sky was growing dark. Dazed, Moon risked a glance at the figurehead. A panel had been broken over a narrow door at the base of the carved skirts—a boarded-over exit from the belly of the ship, but that was easily repaired. The true damage was to the figurehead herself—the paint had broken away in great chips where Ivana's first few blows had glanced, and the elegant folds of the back of the figures' robes were splintered and shattered open. Within the dark hollow behind them was something curled and pale—like a bird's talon, or a clawed hand. Moon started back and looked up at the window. His vision was blurring and he could not tell whether his grip held on the line.

Ivana, still goggled, leaned out the window, both hands out. Moon jumped up, caught them and fought both elbows over the window. Ivana pulled him in by the back of his jacket, headfirst among the broken glass.

"I've got frostbite," he said, through lips that were nearly immobile. "I'm going to lose my face and my fingers. Do you destroy everything?"

Ivana pulled put her bare hand on his face. He could not feel it. "You'll live," she said. She stood up, closed the window and took the eye-mask off.

"There's a body in my figurehead," said Moon. He had seen its empty eyes, the clinging strands of black hair. Skin and cloth had been dried to the bones, the skin mottled with tattoos.

"I'm going to kill him," said Ivana.

"Whoever it is, he's already dead," said Moon.

"Not him," said Ivana. "Fuille. He knows we exist now." Her face looked like Moon's felt. She held the line hook and looked at Moon as if she wondered what would show up if she broke him open. "How did you come by this ship, Moon?"

"A game of squares!" he protested. "I won it in a game. Fairly! A year ago! I was just out of hospital and a chance came—"

"Then why hide its real name? The missing *Ravens*—you must have known the bargain was tainted, you who wish to be a pirate. Did you also know my brother was dead inside the figurehead—your own private skull and cross-bones?"

"No!"

"Were you going to do the same to me? You could have. All those little wires running through the ship into my veins, into my head so I could fly it for you— the fastest ship in the world? You were so happy to find what I could do."

"No!" said Moon. He was thawing enough to sit up. Ivana and the ship were slipping through his fingers, and he did not know how to choose. "I swear! I knew—I knew there were probably shady dealings, but there always are and I played fair. I didn't know." Behind her, the lines of the wires fanned out across the walls of the cabin, spread through the ship. He felt ill.

"Left there to die," she went on. "Staring endlessly into the well of the wind."

"It was a Government ship," said Moon, although he did not really think Ivana was listening to him. "I swear—I didn't think anyone would miss it. Not after a while. She was just an old tub, and—" and beautiful, he was going to say, but it was harder to think that now. "I swear on the ship—on my life. I didn't know." And he didn't know if Evan Arden had been still alive in there. He couldn't have known.

"There were papers in the cargo—very technical," she said in a colourless voice, rubbing her hand as if to rid it of a stain. "Experiments, formulae. And I know—I touched him. They kept him alive. They used the same drugs as were in Fuille's blood, but by the end he would have had more chemicals than blood. I didn't always get on with my brother, but still—"

"Fuille had a drawing of a ship very like this," said Moon. His lips were chapped. Blood came away on his hand when he touched it to his mouth. "His life's work—"

" 'Mind and the mellifluosity of the wind,' " echoed Ivana. She looked down at Moon, unseeing.

"Help me up," he said, holding out his hand. She looked at the darkening window and turned away to the door.

"Wait!" said Moon. He tried to scramble to his feet but, still half-frozen, had more control over his wooden leg than his own. "Fuille went down to the hold. I told him you were down there."

"He'll be angry then," said Ivana placidly. She hefted the line hook, stepped out and closed the door behind her.

Moon could not bring himself to lean against the cabin wall with its tracery of wires, and did not think calling for help would simplify matters. He levered himself up to sit on the edge of his desk and waited for life to return to his limbs. The wooden shutter banged in the ice wind. Moon lunged across the cabin and slammed it closed. Luck couldn't be out forever, it would turn and he could get another ship—besides, he told himself, this one was losing its charms. The thought did not comfort him. He was leaning his forehead against the shutter, seeing again the weatherfinder plunge backwards into air, when Cally entered the cabin.

"Pardon me, Captain," he said, "But I wasn't sure all was well. I was singing-out before, and no answer, and Tomasch said he saw someone out on the figurehead. Again. Wouldn't have believed it if it had been Alban said it, but there it is."

"I'm fine," said Moon, straightening. "Is that all?"

"Storm's coming. And passenger's not best pleased," said the steersman.

A shot rang out on deck.

Fuille's pistol was a heavy one. The shot had thrown Ivana to the deck like a fist. She lay sprawled on the darkening timbers, hand clutched over what was left of her shoulder.

Tomasch had already seized Fuille, but before Alban could, at his direction, secure the pistol, the scientist fired again. Moon fell, nearly at Ivana's side. The steersman sprang forward and dashed the gun from the scientist's hand. It skittered across the deck to Moon's feet.

The shot stunned Moon, and he was numb to the feel of blood slick beneath his hand, but he had fallen too often in the early days of his wooden leg to be much dazed by the fall itself. He was conscious of a gathering anger—Fuille would not take his leg, too. It had been too hard-won.

Moon sat up, felt the splinters where the bullet had struck his bad leg, and reached for the gun.

"I'd better get to the tiller, sir," said Cally, and made himself scarce.

"It was self-defence!" said the scientist. "I did not shoot to kill. I could have, but I did not. I requisition this woman on the authority of their Imperial Majesties' Government—!"

"On my ship, I'm the government," interrupted Moon. He stood up stiffly and limped towards Fuille, who gaped. Moon put the muzzle of the pistol to the middle of the man's forehead. Fuille stopped pulling against Tomasch's grip.

"This ship is stolen," whispered Fuille, his skin turning greyer. "It was part of a project of national—international!—significance. Don't think that by uncovering what may very well be a genuine weatherfinder, the consequences to you will be lessened. By your actions you interrupted and destroyed a very delicate and long-running Government operation, which, if disclosed to our enemies—"

"I am tempted to conduct a delicate operation of my own," said Moon, tapping the muzzle lightly against Fuille's forehead. He found he did not enjoy doing so, although Tomasch looked appreciative. "The only reason I won't is that I know it's a capital offence to carry loaded firearms on a gas-ship." He took the bullets out of the pistol and went to thrust it into his belt, then changed his mind and threw the weapon over the side. It was a more dramatic gesture, but it only relieved his feelings a little. "Besides, we're nearly in the Republic's sky, and what loyalty is it of yours that takes you and your precious experiments out of the Empire?"

Whatever joy Fuille's helpless rage might have given him was taken away by the sight of what lay ahead, piling up in what had been blue sky.

"Shut him in his cabin," he told Tomasch. "Lock him up and tie him to something. Don't let Alban tie the knots. There's going to be a storm."

"No!" said the scientist. "No, no, you must let me secure my specimens."

"Gag him, for preference," added Moon. Tomasch hauled Fuille away, struggling again.

He knelt down again next to Ivana. Alban had his bare hands clamped over the wound, blood welling between his fingers. Together they dragged her upright, but she passed out before she was standing. They towed her back into his cabin and propped her on a chair.

"Go do what your father tells you," Moon told Alban. "Heavy weather's here." Alban acquired a sickly expression but obeyed.

Moon got the sleeve of Ivana's coat cut away and had his own jacket against the wound before Tomasch, eyes averted from blood, arrived to report the scientist secure. When he was gone, she opened her eyes and murmured, reproachfully, "You were shot."

"It didn't take," said Moon cheerfully. "The good news is you're not bleeding to death. He really had quite good aim—that, or the deck gave a fortunate tilt. Or possibly, though I never thought I'd say this, you owe a little thanks to Alban. The bad news is that your storm is here, and I'm going to pour the rest of the brandy into you until you're able to get up and tell me how to get through it."

"I don't want to get through it," murmured Ivana. "Do you know what a bullet tastes like in blood?"

"Never tried it," said Moon. "Anyway, it's not in you. It went straight through, more or less, and into my cabin door—you can see it if you like. There's probably another in my leg, but I think I'll keep it as a souvenir. Drink up."

"Why?" said Ivana.

"Because Fuille is still furious and alive, and I'll let him out if you don't," said Moon. "I'm only asking you to report on the storm. He wanted you to fly the whole ship. Like your brother."

That had the effect he wanted. "You should have killed him," said Ivana, weak but angry.

"I want him to stand trial," said Moon, although privately he agreed with her.

"He's Government," said Ivana. "He won't."

"There are other sorts of trials. Tomasch reported some choice selections from his luggage," said Moon, securing the bandage around her body and under her other arm. "I plan to let the newsmongers make what they will of it. Their Majesties' precious ambassadors will have conniptions. Eliza would love to interview you—almost his next victim, and all that, and it's pleasant when she's grateful." Moon knew he was talking too much, and still he could not bring himself to say what he wanted to say, or to think clearly about what that was. "Well," he continued, "it doesn't happen all that often. Or at all. But I think it would be nice. And then I'll be properly surprised about her news, and a model uncle to the poor creature when it's born, and everyone will be happy."

"Uncle?" said Ivana.

"I know, and it makes me feel very old, but that's better than not getting to be old," said Moon, then realised that Ivana's brother would never have the chance to say that. He cleared his throat and went on, "But we have to get to Poorfortune first, so have another drink, please, quickly, then come out on deck and tell me the way through."

"How long have you been flying?" asked Ivana, her voice stronger although her words were slurred.

"I like to think we would survive," lied Moon. "But there's a reason small ships don't fly this way. Besides, I've never flown with a real, born, weatherfinder, and I'd like to say I've done it once in my life. I might not get the chance again."

"I think I'm drunk," said Ivana.

The *Hyssop* limped over Poorfortune, ragged and battered, listing where gas cushions had burst, her spars and lines tangled, but still aloft and still bearing its crew—all bone-weary, save for the captain. He was exhilarated by survival and their neck-or-nothing passage through the great storm. When they cleared the last shreds of cloud and broke through into clear air, when Ivana—shaken—had silently pointed to the horizon while Cally corrected their course, he had wanted to take her by the shoulders and dance her in a circle. He had remembered in time that she was wounded and he could not dance, so had simply pulled out his pipe and folded his arms, grinning towards the distant port until Tomasch shouted for help with the most urgent repairs. Moon said, sadly, that he saw no need for efforts beyond those, and as Cally, given long acquaintance with Moon, had insisted on full pay in advance and suspected there was no future on the *Hyssop*, there was no objection from the crew.

When Moon returned to his cabin, he had found Ivana asleep on his bed, Alban watching anxiously over her. He dismissed Alban, and stood a moment looking down at his weatherfinder. Her face was an unhealthy colour, but she was breathing and so he left her while he salvaged the few books and papers he could carry in a canvas matilda. He righted a chair and sat to compose a letter which would inspire the necessary curiosity and urgency in an ambitious journalist, and terror in distant corridors of power.

Once he looked around the cabin, and wondered if he would miss it. The thought of the use to which the ship had once been put made his skin crawl, but that was shadowed by the quiet company of the weatherfinder and the bond of the wild flight. Ivana was awake again and watching him with her long jaw set, but she did not speak.

As they worked their way in over Poorfortune at last, Moon dropped a package overboard carefully labelled with Eliza Blancrose's name. The sprawling city had its own systems for such things—by the time the wounded *Hyssop* was in position to dock, the newsmongers of the Poorfortune Exclamation and the High Harbour Times, together with a bevy of Poorfortune police, were at the low docks crowding out a contingent of eager civil servants on the service of the Republic, and several alarmed gentlemen in dark suits whom Moon judged to be in Their Imperial Majesties' employ. Somewhere beyond them, customs officers gesticulated, disregarded.

Eliza was there with the linesmen, and first across to the *Hyssop*, helped willingly by an appreciative Tomasch. She held her hat on with one gloved hand.

"Who are the police here for?" asked Moon by way of greeting.

"Whoever has the best story," said Eliza. "They're relentlessly incorruptible, so now that they've seen you with me you'd better get off this tub. Does Cally have the Port Fury forms, and ship's papers? Then you'd better clear out. Come see me at the Palm Rooms—I owe you for this story and I've a lead who can put you in a likely game for a real antique—"

"I'm off old ships," said Moon. "I need a yacht. Something white and sleek, with no skeletons in its cupboards."

"Less piratical, but you never know what your luck will hold."

"Or for how long," said Moon. "Eliza, can you get Ivana to a doctor, quietly?"

"Who?" said Eliza.

Moon looked around for Ivana, but she had slipped between the eddies of people as easily as if they had been wind-currents, and was already on the dock. "I have to catch her," he said to Eliza.

He swung across the gap to the dock, but his path was harder. He dodged a Poorfortune policeman, was nearly collared by a hungry-looking man with a notebook and shining eyes and only caught up with Ivana at the first turn of the stairs. Her shabby coat was only slung over her injured shoulder, and came away in Moon's hand. He said the first thing to come into his head.

"Where's the jacket?"

"I left it on the storeroom door," she answered.

"Don't you want it?"

"You think I want a souvenir? What's left of it is yours—you bought that fairly, at least."

Moon drew breath. The game of squares had been even, he intended to say, and just because it was chance doesn't mean it wasn't fair. "I don't know your name," he said.

She didn't answer him. Above, the police were engaged with Fuille, the ship and the cargo. Eliza had drawn the attention of the journalists away from Moon and Ivana where they stood hidden from the higher platform. Half a minute might pass before they must be recognised, or vanish into the streets below.

"That needs to be seen to by a doctor," said Moon, nodding at her shoulder, clumsily but effectively bandaged.

"It already has been," said Ivana with a wan smile, and touched the sleeve of her shirt. If that was meant as any sort of compliment, it struck Moon as half-hearted. His work had been brief and ugly, and throughout the short operation in the heart of the storm he had been of the impression that Ivana was careful to give her instructions in very small words.

She turned with her hand on the railing and Moon said, "Wait. I've got a bit laid by, and there's always a game in this town. We—we flew well together, you and I. Fly with me again?" He remembered that the *Hyssop*, unmasked as *The Ravens*, was as good as lost. "I'm sure to have a ship again, soon. My luck will come back, it always does. Like the wind."

"You have to catch luck!" said Ivana, then shook her head and laughed weakly. "You have to hold on to it, Moon."

"You can't hold on to the wind," said Moon. "But who knows? We survived that storm—maybe you are my luck. Come, Ivana! I'm sure Eliza will put you up until I find a ship and more of a crew. She knows how to keep secrets."

Ivana looked up to where the torn sailcloth and trailing lines of the *Hyssop* were visible, sagging in the breeze below the platform. "I'm going home. By sea. I'd rather mend people who've been foolish than hurt myself through folly."

Moon, standing still, felt that he was ducking and weaving again, in pursuit of Ivana vanishing, only this time he could not see his way. "I'll get you a real weatherfinder tattoo, if you want one. I don't want to fly blind again, Ivana."

But something he had said was wrong, or not enough. Ivana was descending again, faster than he could follow.

"Please!" he called down. "I'll pay you better than your doctor!"

She looked up. Her face was still too pale, drawn out long like that of the lost figurehead, and Moon felt a pain of double loss.

"You couldn't pay me enough," she said, disappeared around the next turning of the stairs and was lost in the human rivers of Poorfortune.

A ship, Moon told himself. *First find a ship, then a weatherfinder.*

"You haven't any caution," said Eliza merrily, arriving beside him with the expression of a well-fed cat. "Thank you," she said, releasing Alban who shouldered his own duffel bag and hurried away, head down. Eliza tucked her arm through Moon's. "Poor lad, anyone can see he's not meant for a breezy. Well, there's sufficient variety of employment here. Now, come with me. I have a deadline and therefore am expected to be in a hurry. You must tell me everything. And then buy dinner, for I did beat you to Poorfortune."

As he helped her up into a high-sprung cab she said, "Did your Ivana get away, then?"

"Yes," said Moon.

"Was she pretty?"

Moon looked up at his sister. Her face was sympathetic, amused but unsurprised.

"No," he said, suddenly. "Damn it, Eliza, don't look at me like that. I'll tell you everything later. I have to go."

"I'm a journalist, Moon!" said Eliza, but he had stepped back and waved the cab-driver on. She had to lean out and call the last words back. "Later isn't good enough!"

"And congratulations!" he shouted, but he did not wait to see if Eliza heard. He was already longing for clear sky, and pressing through the brown and crowded streets which led down to the old harbour, and the sea.

SOMEDAY

JAMES PATRICK KELLY

Daya had been in no hurry to become a mother. In the two years since she'd reached childbearing age, she'd built a modular from parts she'd fabbed herself, thrown her boots into the volcano, and served as blood judge. The village elders all said she was one of the quickest girls they had ever seen—except when it came to choosing fathers for her firstborn. Maybe that was because she was too quick for a sleepy village like Third Landing. When her mother, Tajana, had come of age, she'd left for the blue city to find fathers for her baby. Everyone expected Tajana would stay in Halfway, but she had surprised them and returned home to raise Daya. So once Daya had grown up, everyone assumed that someday she would leave for the city like her mother, especially after Tajana had been killed in the avalanche last winter. What did Third Landing have to hold such a fierce and able woman? Daya could easily build a glittering new life in Halfway. Do great things for the colony.

But everything had changed after the scientists from space had landed on the old site across the river, and Daya had changed most of all. She kept her own counsel and was often hard to find. That spring she had told the elders that she didn't need to travel to gather the right semen. Her village was happy and prosperous. The scientists had chosen it to study and they had attracted tourists from all over the colony. There were plenty of beautiful and convenient local fathers to take to bed. Daya had sampled the ones she considered best, but never opened herself to blend their sperm. Now she would, here in the place where she had been born.

She chose just three fathers for her baby. She wanted Ganth because he was her brother and because he loved her above all others. Latif because he was a leader and would say what was true when everyone else was afraid. And Bakti because he was a master of stories and because she wanted him to tell hers someday.

She informed each of her intentions to make a love feast, although she kept the identities of the other fathers a secret, as was her right. Ganth demanded to know, of course, but she refused him. She was not asking for a favor. It would be her baby, her responsibility. The three fathers, in turn, kept her request to themselves, as was custom, in case she changed her mind about any or all of them. A real possibility—when she contemplated what she was about to do, she felt separated from herself.

That morning she climbed into the pen and spoke a kindness to her pig Bobo. The glint of the knife made him grunt with pleasure and he rolled onto his back, exposing the tumors on his belly. She hadn't harvested him in almost a week and so carved two fist-sized maroon swellings into the meat pail. She pressed strips of sponge root onto the wounds to stanch the bleeding and when it was done, she threw them into the pail as well. When she scratched under his jowls to dismiss him, Bobo squealed approval, rolled over and trotted off for a mud bath.

She sliced the tumors thin, dipped the pieces in egg and dragged them through a mix of powdered opium, pepper, flour, and bread crumbs, then sautéed them until they were crisp. She arranged them on top of a casserole of snuro, parsnips and sweet flag, layered with garlic and three cheeses. She harvested some of the purple blooms from the petri dish on the windowsill and flicked them on top of her love feast. The aphrodisiacs produced by the bacteria would give an erection to a corpse. She slid the casserole into the oven to bake for an hour while she bathed and dressed for babymaking.

Daya had considered the order in which she would have sex with the fathers. Last was most important, followed by first. The genes of the middle father—or fathers, since some mothers made babies with six or seven for political reasons—were less reliably expressed. She thought starting with Ganth for his sunny nature and finishing with Latif for his looks and good judgment made sense. Even though Bakti was clever, he had bad posture.

Ganth sat in front of a fuzzy black and white screen with his back to her when she nudged the door to his house open with her hip. "It's me. With a present."

He did not glance away from his show—the colony's daily news and gossip program about the scientists—but raised his forefinger in acknowledgment.

She carried the warming dish with oven mitts to the huge round table that served as his desk, kitchen counter and sometime closet. She pushed aside some books, a belt, an empty bottle of blueberry kefir, and a Fill Jumphigher action figure to set her love feast down. Like her own house, Ganth's was a single room, but his was larger, shabbier, and built of some knotty softwood.

Her brother took a deep breath, his face pale in the light of the screen. "Smells delicious." He pressed the off button; the screen winked and went dark.

"What's the occasion?" He turned to her, smiling. "*Oh.*" His eyes went wide when he saw how she was dressed. "Tonight?"

"Tonight." She grinned.

Trying to cover his surprise, he pulled out the pocket watch he'd had from their mother and then shook it as if it were broken. "Why, look at the time. I totally forgot that we were grown up."

"You like?" She weaved her arms and her ribbon robe fluttered.

"I was wondering when you'd come. What if I had been out?"

She nodded at the screen in front of him. "You never miss that show."

"Has anyone else seen you?" He sneaked to the window and peered out. A knot of gawkers had gathered in the street. "What, did you parade across Founders' Square dressed like that? You'll give every father in town a hard on." He pulled the blinds and came back to her. He surprised her by going down on one knee. "So which am I?"

"What do you think?" She lifted the cover from the casserole to show that it was steaming and uncut.

"I'm honored." He took her hand in his and kissed it. "Who else?" he said. "And you have to tell. Tomorrow everyone will know."

"Bakti. Latif last."

"Three is all a baby really needs." He rubbed his thumb across the inside of her wrist. "Our mother would approve."

Of course, Ganth had no idea of what their mother had really thought of him.

Tajana had once warned Daya that if she insisted on choosing Ganth to father her baby, she should dilute his semen with that of the best men in the village. A sweet manner is fine, she'd said, but babies need brains and a spine.

"So, dear sister, it's a sacrifice . . . " he said, standing. " . . . but I'm prepared to do my duty." He caught her in his arms.

Daya squawked in mock outrage.

"You're not surprising the others are you?" He nuzzled her neck.

"No, they expect me."

"Then we'd better hurry. I hear that Eldest Latif goes to bed early." His whisper filled her ear. "Carrying the weight of the world on his back tires him out.

"I'll give him reason to wake up."

He slid a hand through the layers of ribbons until he found her skin. "Bakti, on the other hand, stays up late, since his stories weigh nothing at all." The flat of his hand against her belly made her shiver. "I didn't realize you knew him that well."

She tugged at the hair on the back of Ganth's head to get his attention. "Feasting first," she said, her voice husky. Daya hadn't expected to be this emotional. She opened her pack, removed the bottle of chardonnay and poured two glasses. They saluted each other and drank, then she used the spatula she had brought—since she knew her brother wouldn't have one—to cut a square of her love feast. He watched her scoop it onto a plate like a man uncertain of his luck. She forked a bite into her mouth. The cheese was still melty—maybe a bit too much sweet flag. She chewed once, twice and then leaned forward to kiss him. His lips parted and she let the contents of her mouth fall into his. He groaned and swallowed. "Again." His voice was thick. "Again and again and again."

Afterward they lay entangled on his mattress on the floor. "I'm glad you're not leaving us, Daya." He blew on the ribbons at her breast and they trembled. "I'll stay home to watch your baby," he said. "Whenever you need me. Make life so easy, you'll never want to go."

It was the worst thing he could have said; until that moment she had been able to keep from thinking that she might never see him again. He was her only family, except for the fathers her mother had kept from her. Had Tajana wanted to make it easy for her to leave Third Landing? "What if I get restless here?" Daya's voice could have fit into a thimble. "You know me."

"Okay, maybe someday you can leave." He waved the idea away. "Someday."

She glanced down his lean body at the hole in his sock and dust strings dangling from his bookshelf. He was a sweet boy and her brother, but he played harder than he worked. Ganth was content to let the future happen to him; Daya needed to make choices, no matter how hard. "It's getting late." She pressed her cheek to his. "Do me a favor and check on Bobo in the morning? Who knows when I'll get home."

By the time she kissed Ganth goodbye, it was evening. An entourage of at least twenty would-be spectators trailed her to Old Town; word had spread that the very eligible Daya was bringing a love feast to some lucky fathers. There were even a scatter of tourists, delighted to witness Third Landing's quaint mating ritual. The locals told jokes, made ribald suggestions and called out names of potential fathers. She tried to ignore them; some people in this village were so nosy.

Bakti lived in one of the barn-like stone dormitories that the settlers had built two centuries ago across the river from their landing spot. Most of these buildings were now divided into shops and apartments. When Daya finally revealed her choice by stopping at Bakti's door, the crowd buzzed. Winners of bets chirped, losers groaned. Bakti was slow to answer her knock, but when he saw the spectators, he seized her arm and drew her inside.

Ganth had been right: she and Bakti weren't particularly close. She had never been to his house, although he had visited her mother on occasion when she was growing up. She could see that he was no better a housekeeper than her brother, but at least his mess was all of a kind. The bones of his apartment had not much changed from the time the founders had used it as a dormitory; Bakti had preserved the two walls of wide shelves that they had used as bunks. Now, however, instead of sleeping refugees from Genome Crusades, they were filled with books, row upon extravagant row. This was Bakti's vice; not only did he buy cheap paper from the village stalls; he had purchased hundreds of hardcovers on his frequent trips to the blue city. They said he even owned a few print books that the founders had brought across space. There were books everywhere, open on chairs, chests, the couch, stacked in leaning towers on the floor.

"So you've come to rumple my bed?" He rearranged his worktable to make room for her love feast. "I must admit, I was surprised by your note. Have we been intimate before, Daya?"

"Just once." She set the dish down. "Don't pretend that you don't remember." When she unslung the pack from her back, the remaining bottles of wine clinked together.

"Don't pretend?" He spread his hands. "I tell stories. That's all I do."

"Glasses?" She extracted the zinfandel from her pack.

He brought two that were works of art; crystal stems twisted like vines to flutes as delicate as a skim of ice. "I recall a girl with a pansy tattooed on her back," he said.

"You're thinking of Pandi." Daya poured the wine.

"Do you sing to your lovers?"

She sniffed the bouquet. "Never."

They saluted each other and drank.

"Don't rush me now," he said. "I'm enjoying this little game." He lifted the lid of the dish and breathed in. "Your feast pleases the nose as much as you please the eye. But I see that I am not your first stop. Who else have you seen this night?"

"Ganth."

"You chose a grasshopper to be a father of your child?"

"He's my brother."

"Aha!" He snapped his fingers. "Now I have it. The garden at Tajana's place? I recall a very pleasant evening."

She had forgotten how big Bakti's nose was. "As do I." And his slouch was worse than ever. Probably from carrying too many books.

"I don't mind being the middle, you know." He took another drink of wine. "Prefer it actually—less responsibility that way. I will do my duty as a father, but I must tell you right now that I have no interest whatsoever in bringing up your baby. And her next father is?"

"Latif. Next and last."

"A man who takes fathering seriously. Good, he'll balance out poor Ganth. I will tell her stories, though. Your baby girl. That's what you hope for, am I right? A girl?"

"Yes." She hadn't realized it until he said it. A girl would make things much easier.

He paused, as if he had just remembered something. "But you're supposed to leave us, aren't you? This village is too tight a fit for someone of your abilities. You'll split seams, pop a button."

Why did everyone keep saying these things to her? "*You* didn't leave."

"No." He shook his head. "I wasn't as big as I thought I was. Besides, the books keep me here. Do you know how much they weigh?"

"It's an amazing collection." She bent to the nearest shelf and ran a finger along the spines of the outermost row. "I've heard you have some from Earth."

"Is this about looking at books or making babies, Daya?" Bakti looked crestfallen.

She straightened, embarrassed. "The baby, of course."

"No, I get it." He waved a finger at her. "I'm crooked and cranky and mothers shut their eyes tight when we kiss." He reached for the wine bottle. "Those are novels." He nodded at the shelf. "But no, nothing from Earth."

They spent the better part of an hour browsing. Bakti said Daya could borrow some if she wanted. He said reading helped pregnant mothers settle. Then he told her the story from one of them. It was about a boy named Huckleberry Flynn, who left his village on Novy Praha to see his world but then came back again. "Just like your mother did," he said. "Just like you could, if you wanted. Someday."

"Then you could tell stories about me."

"About this night," he agreed, "if I remember." His grin was seductive. "Will I?"

"Have you gotten any books from them?" She glanced out the dark window toward the river. "Maybe they'd want to trade with you?"

"Them?" he said. "You mean our visitors? Some, but digital only. They haven't got time for nostalgia. To them, my books are as quaint as scrolls and clay tablets. They asked to scan the collection, but I think they were just being polite. Their interests seem to be more sociological than literary." He smirked. "I understand you have been spending time across the river."

She shrugged. "Do you think they are telling the truth?"

"About what? Their biology? Their politics?" He gestured at his library. "I own one thousand, two hundred and forty-three claims of truth. How would I know which is right?" He slid the book about the boy Huckleberry back onto the shelf. "But look at the time! If you don't mind, I've been putting off dinner until you arrived. And then we can make a baby and a memory, yes?"

By the time Daya left him snoring on his rumpled bed, the spectators had all gone home for the night. There was still half of the love feast left but the warming dish was beginning to dry it out. She hurried down the Farview Hill to the river.

Many honors had come to Latif over the years and with them great wealth. He had first served as village eldest when he was still a young man, just thirty-two years old. In recent years, he mediated disputes for those who did not have the time or the money to submit to the magistrates of the blue city. The fees he charged had bought him this fine house of three rooms, one of which was the parlor where he received visitors. When she saw that all the windows were dark, she gave a cry of panic. It was nearly midnight and the house was nothing but a shadow against the silver waters.

On the shore beyond, the surreal bulk of the starship beckoned.

Daya didn't even bother with front door. She went around to the bedroom and stood on tiptoes to knock on his window. *Tap-tap.*

Nothing.

"Latif." *Tap-tap-tap.* "Wake up."

She heard a clatter within. "Shit!" A light came on and she stepped away as the window banged open."

"Who's there? Go away."

"It's me, Daya."

"Do you know what time it is? Go away."

"But I have our love feast. You knew this was the night, I sent a message."

"And I waited, but you took too damn long." He growled in frustration. "Can't you see I'm asleep? Go find some middle who's awake."

"No, Latif. You're my last."

He started with a shout. "You wake me in the middle of night . . . " Then he continued in a low rasp. "Where's your sense, Daya, your manners? You expect me to be your last? You should have said something. I take fathering seriously."

Daya's throat closed. Her eyes seemed to throb.

"I told you to move to the city, didn't I? Find fathers there." Latif waited for her to answer. When she didn't, he stuck his head out the window to see her better. "So instead of taking my best advice, now you want my semen?" He waited again for a reply; she couldn't speak. "I suppose you're crying."

The only reply she could make was a sniffle.

"Come to the door then."

She reached for his arm as she entered the darkened parlor but he waved her through to the center of the room. "You are rude and selfish. Daya." He shut the door and leaned against it. "But that doesn't mean you're a bad person."

He turned the lights on and for a moment they stood blinking at one another. Latif was barefoot, wearing pants but no shirt. He had a wrestler's shoulders, long arms, hands big as dinner plates. Muscles bunched beneath his smooth, dark skin, as if he might spring at her. But if she read his eyes right, his anger was passing.

"I thought you'd be pleased." She tried a grin. It bounced off him.

"Honored, yes. Pleased, not at all. You think you can just issue commands and we jump? You have the right to ask, and I have the right to refuse. Even at the last minute."

At fifty-three, Latif was still one of the handsomest men in the village. Daya had often wondered if that was one reason why everyone trusted him. She looked for some place to put the warming dish down.

"No," he said, "don't you dare make yourself comfortable unless I tell you to. Why me?"

She didn't have to think. "Because you have always been kind to me and my mother. Because you will tell the truth, even when it's hard to hear. And because, despite your years, you are still the most beautiful man I know." This time she tried a smile on him. It stuck. "All the children you've fathered are beautiful, and if my son gets nothing but looks from you, that will still be to his lifelong advantage." Daya knew that in the right circumstance, even men like Latif would succumb to flattery.

"You want me because I tell hard truths, but when I say you should move away, you ignore me. Does that make sense?"

"Not everything needs to make sense." She extended her love feast to him. "Where should I put this?"

He glided across the parlor, kissed her forehead and accepted the dish from her. "Do you know how many have asked me to be last father?"

"No." She followed him into the great room.

"Twenty-three," he said. "Every one spoke to me ahead of time. And of those, how many I agreed to?"

"No idea."

"Four." He set it on a round wooden table with a marble inset.

"They should've tried my ambush strategy." She shrugged out of her pack. "I've got wine." She handed him the bottle of Xino she had picked for him.

"Which you've been drinking all night, I'm sure. You know where the glasses are." He pulled the stopper. "And who have you been drinking with?"

"Ganth, first."

Latif tossed the stopper onto the table. "I'm one-fourth that boy's father . . ." He rapped on the tabletop. " . . . but I don't see any part of me in him."

"He's handsome."

"Oh, stop." He poured each of them just a splash of the Xino and offered her a glass. She raised an eyebrow at his stinginess.

"It's late and you've had enough," he said. "It is affecting your judgment. Who else?"

"Bakti."

"You surprise me." They saluted each other with their glasses. "Does he really have Earth books?"

"He says not."

"He makes too many stories up. But he's sound—you should have started with him. Ganth is a middle father at best."

Both of them ran out of things to say then. Latif was right. She had finished the first two bottles with the other fathers, and had shared an love feast with them and had made love. She was heavy with the weight of her decisions and her desires. She felt like she was falling toward Latif. She pulled the cover off the warming dish and cut a square of her love feast into bite-sized chunks.

"Just because I'm making a baby doesn't mean I can't go away," she said.

"And leave the fathers behind?"

"That's what my mother did."

"And did that make her happy? Do you think she had an easy life?" He shook his head. "No, you are tying yourself to this village. This little, insignificant place. Why? Maybe you're lazy. Or maybe you're afraid. Here, you are a star. What would you be in the blue city?"

She wanted to tell him that he had it exactly wrong. That he was talking about himself, not her. But that would have been cruel. This beautiful foolish man was going to be the last father of her baby. "You're right," Daya said. "It's late." She piled bits of the feast onto a plate and came around to where he was sitting. She perched on the edge of the table and gazed down at him.

He tugged at one of the ribbons of her sleeve and she felt the robe slip off her shoulder. "What is this costume anyway?" he said. "You're wrapped up like some kind of present."

She didn't reply. Instead she pushed a bit of the feast across her plate until it slid onto her fork. They watched each other as she brought it to her open mouth, placed it on her tongue. The room shrank. Clocks stopped.

He shuddered, "Feed me, then."

Latif's pants were still around his ankles when she rolled off him. The ribbon robe dangled off the headboard of his bed. Daya gazed up at the ceiling, thinking about the tangling sperm inside her. She concentrated as her mother had taught her, and she thought she felt her cervix close and her uterus contract, concentrating the semen. At least, she hoped she did. The sperm of the three fathers would smash together furiously, breaching cell walls, exchanging plasmids. The strongest conjugate would find her eggs and then . . .

"What if I leave the baby behind?" she said.

"With who?" He propped himself up on an elbow. "Your mother is dead and no . . . "

She laid a finger on his lips. "I know, Latif. But why not with a father? Ganth might do it, I think. Definitely not Bakti. Maybe even you."

He went rigid. "This is an idea you get from the scientists? Is that the way they have sex in space?"

"They don't live in space; they just travel through it." She followed a crack in the plaster of his ceiling with her eyes. "Nobody lives in space." A water stain in the corner looked like a face. A mouth. Sad eyes. "What should we do about them?"

"Do? There is nothing to be done." He fell back onto his pillow. "They're the ones the founders were trying to get away from."

"Two hundred years ago. They say things are different."

"Maybe. Maybe these particular scientists are more tolerant, but they're still dangerous."

"Why? Why are you so afraid of them?"

"*Because they're unnatural.*" The hand at her side clenched into a fist. "We're the true humans, maybe the last. But they've taken charge of evolution now, or what passes for it. We have no say in the future. All we know for sure is that they are large and still growing and we are very, very small. Maybe this lot won't force us to change. Or maybe someday they'll just make us want to become like them."

She knew this was true, even though she had spent the last few months trying not to know it. The effort had made her weary. She rolled toward Latif. When she snuggled against him, he relaxed into her embrace.

It was almost dawn when she left his house. Instead of climbing back up Farview Hill, she turned toward the river. Moments later she stepped off Mogallo's Wharf into the skiff she had built when she was a teenager.

She had been so busy pretending that this wasn't going to happen that she was surprised to find herself gliding across the river. She could never have had sex with the fathers if she had acknowledged to herself that she was going to go through with it. Certainly not with Ganth. And Latif would have guessed that something was wrong. She had the odd feeling that there were two of her in the skiff, each facing in opposite directions. The one looking back at the village was screaming at the one watching the starship grow ever larger. But there is no other Daya, she reminded herself. There is only me.

Her lover, Roberts, was waiting on the spun-carbon dock that the scientists had fabbed for river traffic. Many of the magistrates from the blue city came by boat to negotiate with the offworlders. Roberts caught the rope that Daya threw her and took it expertly around one of the cleats. She extended a hand to hoist Daya up, caught her in an embrace and pressed her lips to Dayas' cheek.

"This kissing that you do," said Roberts. "I like it. Very direct." She wasn't very good at it but she was learning. Like all the scientists, she could be stiff at first. They didn't seem all that comfortable in their replaceable bodies. Roberts was small as a child, but with a woman's face. Her blonde hair was cropped short, her eyes were clear and faceted. They reminded Daya of her mother's crystal.

"It's done," said Daya.

"Yes, but are you all right?"

"I think so." She forced a grin. "We'll find out."

"We will. Don't worry, love, I am going to take good care of you. And your baby."

"And I will take care of you."

"Yes." She looked puzzled. "Of course."

Roberts was a cultural anthropologist. She had explained to Daya that all she wanted was to preserve a record of an ancient way of life. A culture in which there was still sexual reproduction.

"May I see that?"

Daya opened her pack and produced the leftover bit of the love feast. She had sealed it in a baggie that Roberts had given her. It had somehow frozen solid.

"Excellent. Now we should get you into the lab before it's too late. Put you under the scanner, take some samples." This time she kissed Daya on the mouth. Her lips parted briefly and Daya felt Robert's tongue flick against her teeth. When Daya did not respond, she pulled back.

"I know this is hard now. You're very brave to help us this way, Daya." The scientist took her hand and squeezed. "But someday they'll thank you for what you're doing." She nodded toward the sleepy village across the river. "Someday soon."

CIMMERIA:
FROM THE *JOURNAL OF IMAGINARY ANTHROPOLOGY*

THEODORA GOSS

Remembering Cimmeria: I walk through the bazaar, between the stalls of the spice sellers, smelling turmeric and cloves, hearing the clash of bronze from the sellers of cooking pots, the bleat of goats from the butcher's alley. Rugs hang from wooden racks, scarlet and indigo. In the corners of the alleys, men without legs perch on wooden carts, telling their stories to a crowd of ragged children, making coins disappear into the air. Women from the mountains, their faces prematurely old from sun and suffering, call to me in a dialect I can barely understand. Their stands sell eggplants and tomatoes, the pungent olives that are distinctive to Cimmerian cuisine, video games. In the mountain villages, it has long been a custom to dye hair blue for good fortune, a practice that sophisticated urbanites have lately adopted. Even the women at court have hair of a deep and startling hue.

My guide, Afa, walks ahead of me, with a string bag in her hand, examining the vegetables, buying cauliflower and lentils. Later she will make rice mixed with raisins, meat, and saffron. The cuisine of Cimmeria is rich, heavy with goat and chicken. (They eat and keep no pigs.) The pastries are filled with almond paste and soaked in honey. She waddles ahead (forgive me, but you do waddle, Afa), and I follow amid a cacophony of voices, speaking the Indo-European language of Cimmeria, which is closest perhaps to Iranian. The mountain accents are harsh, the tones of the urbanites soft and lisping. Shaila spoke in those tones, when she taught me phrases in her language: Can I have more lozi (a cake made with marzipan, flavored with orange water)? You are the son of a dog. I will love you until the ocean swallows the moon. (A traditional saying. At the end of time, the serpent that lies beneath the Black Sea will rise up and swallow the moon as though it were lozi. It means, I will love you until the end of time.)

On that day, or perhaps it is another day I remember, I see a man selling Kalashnikovs. The war is a recent memory here, and every man has at least one weapon: Even I wear a curved knife in my belt, or I will be taken for a prostitute. (Male prostitutes, who are common in the capital, can be distinguished by their khol-rimmed eyes, their extravagant clothes, their weaponlessness. As a red-haired Irishman, I do not look like them, but it is best to avoid misunderstandings.) The sun shines down from a cloudless sky. It is hotter than summer in Arizona, on the campus of the small college where this journey began, where we said, let us imagine a modern Cimmeria. What would it look like? I know, now. The city is cooled by a thousand fountains, we are told: Its name means just that, A Thousand Fountains. It was founded in the sixth century BCE, or so we have conjectured and imagined.

I have a pounding headache. I have been two weeks in this country, and I cannot get used to the heat, the smells, the reality of it all. Could we have created this? The four of us, me and Lisa and Michael the Second, and Professor Farrow, sitting in a conference room at that small college? Surely not. And yet.

We were worried that the Khan would forbid us from entering the country. But no. We were issued visas, assigned translators, given office space in the palace itself.

The Khan was a short man, balding. His wife had been Miss Cimmeria, and then a television reporter for one of the three state channels. She had met the Khan when she had been sent to interview him. He wore a business suit with a traditional scarf around his neck. She looked as though she had stepped out of a photo shoot for *Vogue Russia*, which was available in all the gas stations.

"Cimmeria has been here, on the shores of the Black Sea, for more than two thousand years," he said. "Would you like some coffee, Dr. Nolan? I think our coffee is the best in the world." It was—dark, thick, spiced, and served with ewe's milk. "This theory of yours—that a group of American graduate students created Cimmeria in their heads, merely by thinking about it—you will understand that some of our people find it insulting. They will say that all Americans are imperialist dogs. I myself find it amusing, almost charming— like poetry. The mind creates reality, yes? So our poets have taught us. Of course, your version is culturally insensitive, but then, you are Americans. I did not think Americans were capable of poetry."

Only Lisa had been a graduate student, and even she had recently graduated. Mike and I were post-docs, and Professor Farrow was tenured at Southern Arizona State. It all seemed so far away, the small campus with its perpetually dying lawns and drab 1970s architecture. I was standing in a reception room, drinking coffee with the Khan of Cimmeria and his wife, and Arizona seemed imaginary, like something I had made up.

"But we like Americans here. The enemy of my enemy is my friend, is he not? Any enemy of Russia is a friend of mine. So I am glad to welcome you to my country. You will, I am certain, be sensitive to our customs. Your coworker, for example—I suggest that she not wear short pants in the streets. Our clerics, whether Orthodox, Catholic, or Muslim, are traditional and may be offended. Anyway, you must admit, such garments are not attractive on women. I would not say so to her, you understand, for women are the devil when they are criticized. But a woman should cultivate an air of mystery. There is nothing mysterious about bare red knees."

Our office space was in an unused part of the palace. My translator, Jafik, told me it had once been a storage area for bedding. It was close to the servants' quarters. The Khan may have welcomed us to Cimmeria for diplomatic reasons, but he did not think much of us, that was clear. It was part of the old palace, which had been built in the thirteenth century CE, after the final defeat of the Mongols. Since then, Cimmeria had been embroiled in almost constant warfare, with Anatolia, Scythia, Poland, and most recently the Russians, who had wanted its ports on the Black Sea. The Khan had received considerable American aid, including military advisors. The war had ended with the disintegration of the USSR. The Ukraine, focused on its own economic problems, had no wish to interfere in local politics, so Cimmeria was enjoying a period of relative peace. I wondered how long it would last.

Lisa was our linguist. She would stay in the capital for the first three months, then venture out into the countryside, recording local dialects. "You know what amazes me?" she said as we were unpacking our computers and office supplies. "The complexity of all this. You would think it really had been here for the last three thousand years. It's hard to believe it all started with Mike the First goofing off in Professor Farrow's class." He had been bored, and instead of taking notes, had started sketching a city. The professor had caught him, and had told the students that we would spend the rest of the semester creating that city and the surrounding countryside. We would be responsible for its history, customs, language. Lisa was in the class, too, and I was the TA. AN 703, Contemporary Anthropological Theory, had turned into Creating Cimmeria.

Of the four graduate students in the course, only Lisa stayed in the program. One got married and moved to Wisconsin, another transferred to the School of Education so she could become a kindergarten teacher. Mike the First left with his master's and went on to do an MBA. It was a coincidence that Professor Farrow's next postdoc, who arrived in the middle of the semester, was also named Mike. He had an undergraduate degree in classics, and was the one who decided that the country we were developing was Cimmeria. He was also particularly interested in the Borges hypothesis. Everyone had been talking about it at Michigan, where he had done his PhD. At that point, it was more controversial than it is now, and Professor Farrow had only been planning to touch on it briefly at the end of the semester. But once we started on Cimmeria, AN 703 became an experiment in creating reality through perception and expectation. Could we actually create Cimmeria by thinking about it, writing about it?

Not in one semester, of course. After the semester ended, all of us worked on the Cimmeria Project. It became the topic of Lisa's dissertation: *A Dictionary and Grammar of Modern Cimmerian, with Commentary.* Mike focused on history. I wrote articles on culture, figuring out probable rites of passage, how the Cimmerians would bury their dead. We had Herodotus, we had accounts of cultures from that area. We were all steeped in anthropological theory. On weekends, when we should have been going on dates, we gathered in a conference room, under a fluorescent light, and talked about Cimmeria. It was fortunate that around that time, the *Journal of Imaginary Anthropology* was founded at Penn State. Otherwise, I don't know where we would have published. At the first Imaginary Anthropology conference, in Orlando, we realized that a group from Tennessee was working on the modern Republic of Scythia and Sarmatia, which shared a border with Cimmeria. We formed a working group.

"Don't let the Cimmerians hear you talk about creating all this," I said. "Especially the nationalists. Remember, they have guns, and you don't." Should I mention her cargo shorts? I had to admit, looking at her knobby red knees, above socks and Birkenstocks, that the Khan had a point. Before she left for the mountains, I would warn her to wear more traditional clothes.

I was going to stay in the capital. My work would focus on the ways in which the historical practices we had described in "Cimmeria: A Proposal," in the second issue of the *Journal of Imaginary Anthropology,* influenced and remained evident in modern practice. Already I had seen developments we had never anticipated. One was the fashion for blue hair; in a footnote, Mike had written that blue was a fortunate color in Cimmerian folk belief. Another was the ubiquity of cats in the capital. In an article on funerary rites, I had described how cats were seen as guides to the land of the dead until the coming of Christianity in the twelfth century CE. The belief should have gone away, but somehow it had persisted, and every household, whether Orthodox, Catholic, Muslim, Jewish, or one of the minor sects that flourished in the relative tolerance of Cimmeria, had its cat. No Cimmerian wanted his soul to get lost on the way to Paradise. Stray cats were fed at the public expense, and no one dared harm a cat. I saw them everywhere, when I ventured into the city. In a month, Mike was going to join us, and I would be able to show him all the developments I was documenting. Meanwhile, there was email and Skype.

I was assigned a bedroom and bath close to our offices. Afa, who had been a sort of under-cook, was assigned to be my servant but quickly became my guide, showing me around the city and mocking my Cimmerian accent. "He he!" she would say. "No, Doctor Pat, that word is not pronounced that way. Do not repeat it that way, I beg of you. I am an old woman, but still it is not respectable for me to hear!" Jafik was my language teacher as well as my translator, teaching me the language Lisa had created based on what we knew of historical Cimmerian and its Indo-European roots, except that it had developed an extensive vocabulary. As used by modern Cimmerians, it had the nuance and fluidity of a living language, as well as a surprising number of expletives.

I had no duties except to conduct my research, which was a relief from the grind of TAing and, recently, teaching my own undergraduate classes. But one day, I was summoned to speak with the Khan. It was the day of an official audience, so he was dressed in Cimmerian ceremonial robes, although he still wore his Rolex watch. His advisors looked impatient, and I gathered that the audience was about to begin—I had seen a long line of supplicants waiting by the door as I was ushered in. But he said, as though we had all the time in the world, "Doctor Nolan, did you know that my daughters are learning American?" Sitting next to him were four girls, all wearing the traditional head-scarves worn by Cimmerian peasant women, but pulled back to show that their hair was dyed fashionably blue. "They are very troublesome, my daughters. They like everything modern: Leonardo DiCaprio, video games. Tradition is not good enough for them. They wish to attend university and find professions, or do humanitarian work. Ah, what is a father to do?" He shook a finger at them, fondly enough. "I would like it if you could teach them the latest American idioms. The slang, as it were."

That afternoon, Afa led me to another part of the palace—the royal family's personal quarters. These were more modern and considerably more comfortable than ours. I was shown into what seemed to be a common room for the girls. There were colorful rugs and divans, embroidered wall hangings, and an enormous flat-screen TV.

"These are the Khan's daughters," said Afa. She had already explained to me, in case I made any blunders, that they were his daughters by his first wife, who had not been Miss Cimmeria, but had produced the royal children: a son, and then only daughters, and then a second son who had died shortly after birth. She had died a week later of an infection contracted during the difficult delivery. "Anoor is the youngest, then Tallah, and then Shaila, who is already taking university classes online." Shaila smiled at me. This time, none of them were wearing head-scarves. There really was something attractive about blue hair.

"And what about the fourth one?" She was sitting a bit back from the others, to the right of and behind Shaila, whom she closely resembled.

Afa looked at me with astonishment. "The Khan has three daughters," she said. "Anoor, Tallah, and Shaila. There is no fourth one, Doctor Pat."

The fourth one stared at me without expression.

"Cimmerians don't recognize twins," said Lisa. "That has to be the explanation. Do you remember the thirteenth-century philosopher Farkosh Kursand? When God made the world, He decreed that human beings would be born one at a time, unique, unlike animals. They would be born defenseless, without claws or teeth or fur. But they would have souls. It's in a children's book—I have a copy somewhere, but it's based on Kursand's reading of Genesis in one of his philosophical treatises. Mike would know which. And it's the basis of Cimmerian human rights law, actually. That's why women have always had more rights here. They have souls, so they've been allowed to vote since Cimmeria became a parliamentary monarchy. I'm sure it's mentioned in one of the articles—I don't remember which one, but check the database Mike is putting together. Shaila must have been a twin, and the Cimmerians don't recognize the second child as separate from the first. So Shaila is one girl. In two bodies. But with one soul."

"Who came up with that stupid idea?"

"Well, to be perfectly honest, it might have been you." She leaned back in our revolving chair. I don't know how she could do that without falling. "Or Mike, of course. It certainly wasn't my idea. Embryologically it does make a certain sense. Identical twins really do come from one egg."

"So they're both Shaila."

"There is no both. The idea of both is culturally inappropriate. There is one Shaila, in two bodies. Think of them as Shaila and her shadow."

I tested this theory once, while walking through the market with Afa. We were walking through the alley of the dog-sellers. In Cimmeria, almost every house has a dog, for defense and to catch rats. Cats are not sold in the market. They cannot be sold at all, only given or willed away. To sell a cat for money is to imperil your immortal soul. We passed a woman sitting on the ground, with a basket beside her. In it were two infants, as alike as the proverbial two peas in a pod, half-covered with a ragged blanket. Beside them lay a dirty mutt with a chain around its neck that lifted its head and whimpered as we walked by.

"Child how many in basket?" I asked Afa in my still-imperfect Cimmerian.

"There is one child in that basket, Pati," she said. I could not get her to stop using the diminutive. I even told her that in my language Pati was a woman's name, to no effect. She just smiled, patted me on the arm, and assured me that no one would mistake such a tall, handsome (which in Cimmerian is the same word as beautiful) man for a woman.

"Only one child?"

"Of course. One basket, one child."

Shaila's shadow followed her everywhere. When she and her sisters sat with me in the room with the low divans and the large-screen TV, studying American slang, she was there. "What's up!" Shaila would say, laughing, and her shadow would stare down at the floor. When Shaila and I walked though the gardens, she walked six paces behind, pausing when we paused, sitting when we sat. After we were married, in our apartment in Arizona, she would sit in a corner of the bedroom, watching as we made love. Although I always turned off the lights, I could see her: a darkness against the off-white walls of faculty housing.

Once, I tried to ask Shaila about her. "Shaila, do you know the word twin?"

"Yes, of course," she said. "In American, if two babies are born at the same time, they are twins."

"What about in Cimmeria? Surely there is a Cimmerian word for twin. Sometimes two babies are born at the same time in Cimmeria, too."

She looked confused. "I suppose so. Biology is the same everywhere."

"Well, what's the word, then?"

"I cannot think of it. I shall have to email Tallah. She is better at languages than I am."

"What if you yourself were a twin?"

"Me? But I am not a twin. If I were, my mother would have told me."

I tried a different tactic. "Do you remember the dog you had, Kala? She had two sisters, born at the same time. Those were Anoor's and Tallah's dogs. They were not Kala, even though they were born in the same litter. You could think of them as twins—I mean, triplets." I remembered them gamboling together, Kala and her two littermates. They would follow us through the gardens, and Shaila and her sisters would pet them indiscriminately. When we sat under the plum trees, they would tumble together into one doggy heap.

"Pat, what is this all about? Is this about the fact that I don't want to have a baby right now? You know I want to go to graduate school first."

I did not think her father would approve the marriage. I told her so: "Your father will never agree to you marrying a poor American post-doc. Do you have any idea how poor I am? My research grant is all I have."

"You do not understand Cimmerian politics," Shaila replied. "Do you know what percentage of our population is ethnically Sarmatian? Twenty percent, all in the Eastern province. They fought the Russians, and they still have weapons. Not just guns: tanks, anti-aircraft missiles. The Sarmatians are getting restless, Pati. They are mostly Catholic, in a country that is mostly Orthodox. They want to unite with their homeland, create a greater Scythia and Sarmatia. My father projects an image of strength, because what else can you do? But he is afraid. He is most afraid that the Americans will not help. They helped against the Russians, but this is an internal matter. He has talked to us already about different ways for us to leave the country. Anoor has been enrolled at the Lycée International in Paris, and Tallah is going to study at the American School in London. They can get student visas. For me it is more difficult: I must be admitted at a university. That is why I have been taking courses online. Ask him: If he says no, then no. But I think he will consider my marriage with an American."

She was right. The Khan considered. For a week, and then another, while pro-Sarmatian factions clashed with military in the Eastern province. Then protests broke out in the capital. Anoor was already in Paris with her step-mother, supposedly on a shopping spree for school. Tallah had started school in London. In the Khan's personal office, I signed the marriage contract, barely understanding what I was signing because it was in an ornate script I had seen only in medieval documents. On the way to the airport, we stopped by the cathedral in Shahin Square, where we were married by the Patriarch of the Cimmerian Independent Orthodox Church, who checked the faxed copy of my baptismal certificate and lectured me in sonorous tones about the importance of conversion, raising children in the true faith. The Khan kissed Shaila on both cheeks, promising her that we would have a proper ceremony when the political situation was more stable and she could return to the country. In the Khan's private plane, we flew to a small airport near Fresno and spent our first night together at my mother's house. My father had died of a heart attack while I was in college, and she lived alone in the house where I had grown up. It was strange staying in the guest bedroom, down the hall from the room where I had slept as a child, which still had my He-Man action figures on the shelves, the Skeletor defaced with permanent marker. I had to explain to her about Shaila's shadow.

"I don't understand," my mother said. "Are you all going to live together?"

"Well, yes, I guess so. It's really no different than if her twin sister were living with us, is it?"

"And Shaila is going to take undergraduate classes? What is her sister going to do?"

"I have no idea," I said.

What she did, more than anything else, was watch television. All day, it would be on. Mostly, she watched CNN and the news shows. Sometimes I would test Shaila, asking, "Did you turn the TV on?"

"Is it on?" she would say. "Then of course I must have turned it on. Unless you left it on before you went out. How did your class go? Is that football player in the back still falling asleep?"

One day, I came home and noticed that the other Shaila was cooking dinner. Later I asked, "Shaila, did you cook dinner?"

"Of course," she said. "Did you like it?"

"Yes." It was actually pretty good, chicken in a thick red stew over rice. It reminded me of a dish Afa had made in an iron pot hanging over an open fire in the servants' quarters. But I guess it could be made on an American stovetop as well.

After that, the other Shaila cooked dinner every night. It was convenient, because I was teaching night classes, trying to make extra money. Shaila told me that I did not need to work so hard, that the money her father gave her was more than enough to support us both. But I was proud and did not want to live off my father-in-law, even if he was the Khan of Cimmeria. At the same time, I was trying to write up my research on Cimmerian funerary practices. If I could publish a paper in the *Journal of Imaginary Anthropology*, I might have a shot at a tenure-track position, or at least a visiting professorship somewhere that wasn't Arizona. Shaila was trying to finish her pre-med requirements. She had decided that she wanted to be a pediatrician.

Meanwhile, in Cimmeria, the situation was growing more complicated. The pro-Sarmatian faction had split into the radical Sons of Sarmatia and the more moderate Sarmatian Democratic Alliance, although the Prime Minister claimed that the SDA was a front. There were weekly clashes with police in the capital, and the Sons of Sarmatia had planted a bomb in the Hilton, although a maid had reported a suspicious shopping bag and the hotel had been evacuated before the bomb could go off. The Khan had imposed a curfew, and martial law might be next, although the army had a significant Sarmatian minority. But I had classes to teach, so I tried not to pay attention to politics, and even Shaila dismissed it all as "a mess."

One day, I came home from a departmental meeting and Shaila wasn't in the apartment. She was usually home by seven. I assumed she'd had to stay late for a lab. The other Shaila was cooking dinner in the kitchen. At eight, when she hadn't come back yet, I sat down at the kitchen table to eat. To my surprise, the other Shaila sat down across from me, at the place set for Shaila. She had never sat down at the table with us before.

She looked at me with her dark eyes and said, "How was your day, Pati?"

I dropped my fork. It clattered against the rim of the plate. She had never spoken before, not one sentence, not one word. Her voice was just like Shaila's, but with a stronger accent. At least it sounded stronger to me. Or maybe not. It was hard to tell.

"Where's Shaila?" I said. I could feel a constriction in my chest, as though a fist had started to close around my heart. Like the beginning of my father's heart attack. I think even then, I knew.

"What do you mean?" she said. "I'm Shaila. I have always been Shaila. The only Shaila there is."

I stared down at the lamb and peas in saffron curry. The smell reminded me of Cimmeria, of the bazaar. I could almost hear the clash of the cooking pots.

"You've done something to her, haven't you?"

"I have no idea what you're talking about. Eat your dinner, Pati. It's going to get cold. You've been working so hard lately. I don't think it's good for you."

But I could not eat. I stood up, accidentally hitting my hip on the table and cursing at the pain. With a growing sense of panic, I searched the apartment for any clue to Shaila's whereabouts. Her purse was in the closet, with her cell phone in it, so she must have come home earlier in the evening. All her clothes were on the hangers, as far as I could tell—she had a lot of clothes. Nothing seemed to be missing. But Shaila was not there. The other Shaila stood watching me, as though waiting for me to give up, admit defeat. Finally, after one last useless look under the bed, I left, deliberately banging the door behind me. She had to be somewhere.

I walked across campus, to the Life Sciences classrooms and labs, and checked all of them. Then I walked through the main library and the science library, calling "Shaila!" until a graduate student in a carrel told me to be quiet. By this time, it was dark. I went to her favorite coffee shop, the Espresso Bean, where undergraduates looked at me strangely from behind their laptops, and then to every shop and restaurant that was still open, from the gelato place to the German restaurant, famous for its bratwurst and beer, where students took their families on Parents' Weekend. Finally, I walked the streets, calling "Shaila!" as though she were a stray dog, hoping that the other Shaila was simply being presumptuous, rebelling against her secondary status. Hoping the real Shaila was out there somewhere.

I passed the police station and stood outside, thinking about going in and reporting her missing. I would talk to a police officer on duty, tell him I could not find my wife. He would come home with me, to find—my wife, saying that I was overworked and needed to rest, see a psychiatrist. Shaila had entered the country with a diplomatic passport—one passport, for one Shaila. Had anyone seen the other Shaila? Only my mother. She had picked us up at the airport, we had spent the night with her, all three of us eating dinner at the dining-room table. She had avoided looking at the other Shaila, talking to Shaila about how the roses were doing well this year despite aphids, asking whether she knew how to knit, how she dyed her hair that particular shade of blue—pointless, polite talk. And then we had rented a car and driven to Arizona, me and Shaila in the front seat, the other Shaila in back with the luggage. Once we had arrived at the university, she had stayed in the apartment. Lisa knew, but she and Mike the Second were still in Cimmeria, and their internet connection could be sporadic. I could talk to Dr. Farrow? She would be in her office tomorrow morning, before classes. She would at least believe me. But I knew, with a cold certainly in the pit of my stomach, that Anne Farrow would look at me from over the wire rims of her glasses and say, "Pat, you know as well as I do that culture defines personhood." She was an anthropologist, through and through. She would not interfere. I had been married to Shaila, I was still married to Shaila. There was just one less of her.

In the end, I called my mother, while sitting on a park bench under a street lamp, with the moon sailing high above, among the clouds.

"Do you know what time it is, Pat?" she asked.

"Listen, Mom," I said, and explained the situation.

"Oh, Pat, I wish you hadn't married that woman. But can't you divorce her? Are you allowed to divorce in that church? I wish you hadn't broken up with Bridget Ferguson. The two of you were so sweet together at prom. You know she married an accountant and has two children now. She sent me a card at Christmas."

I said good night and told her to go back to sleep, that I would figure it out. And then I sat there for a long time.

When I came home, well after midnight, Shaila was waiting for me with a cup of Cimmerian coffee, or as close as she could get with an American espresso machine. She was wearing the heart pajamas I had given Shaila for Valentine's Day.

"Pati," she said, "you left so quickly that I didn't have time to tell you the news. I heard it on CNN this morning, and then Daddy called me. Malek was assassinated yesterday." Malek was her brother. I had never met him—he had been an officer in the military, and while I had been in Cimmeria, he had been serving in the mountains. I knew that he had been recalled to the capital to deal with the Sarmantian agitation, but that was all.

"Assassinated? How?"

"He was trying to negotiate with the Sons of Sarmatia, and a radical pulled out a gun that had gotten through security. You never watch the news, do you, Pati? I watch it a great deal. It is important for me to learn the names of the world leaders, learn about international diplomacy. That is more important than organic chemistry, for a Khanum."

"A what?"

"Don't you understand? Now that Malek is dead, I am next in the line of succession. Someday, I will be the Khanum of Cimmeria. That is what we call a female Khan. In some countries, only male members of the royal family can succeed to the throne. But Cimmeria has never been like that. It has always been cosmopolitan, progressive. The philosopher Amirabal persuaded Teshup the Third to make his daughter his heir, and ever since, women can become rulers of the country. My great-grandmother, Daddy's grandma, was a Khanum, although she resigned when her son came of age. It is the same among the Scythians and Sarmatians." This was Lisa's doing. It had to be Lisa's doing. She was the one who had come up with Amirabal and the philosophical school she had founded in 500 BCE. Even Plato had praised her as one of the wisest philosophers in the ancient world. I silently cursed all Birkenstock-wearing feminists.

"What does this mean?" I asked.

"It means that tomorrow we fly to Washington, where I will ask your President for help against the Sarmatian faction. This morning on one of the news shows, the Speaker of the House criticized him for not supporting the government of Cimmeria. He mentioned the War on Terror—you know how they talk, and he wants to be the Republican candidate. But I think we can finally get American aid. While I am there, I will call a press conference, and you will stand by my side. We will let the American people see that my husband is one of them. It will generate sympathy and support. Then we will fly to Cimmeria. I need to be in my country as a symbol of the future. And I must produce an heir to the throne as quickly as possible—a boy, because while I can legally become Khanum, the people will want assurance that I can bear a son. While you were out, I packed all our clothes. We will meet Daddy's plane at the airport tomorrow morning. You must wear your interview suit until we can buy you another. I've set the alarm for five o'clock."

I should have said no. I should have raged and cried, and refused to be complicit in something that made me feel as though I might be sick for the rest of my life. But I said nothing. What could I say? This, too, was Shaila.

I lay in the dark beside the woman who looked like my wife, unable to sleep, staring into the darkness. Shaila, I thought, what has happened to you? To your dreams of being a pediatrician, of our children growing up in America, eating tacos and riding their bikes to school? You wanted them to be ordinary, to escape the claustrophobia you had felt growing up in the palace, with its political intrigue and the weight of centuries perpetually pressing down on you. In the middle of the night, the woman who was Shaila, but not my Shaila, turned in her sleep and put an arm around me. I did not move away.

You are pleased, Afa, that I have returned to Cimmeria. It has meant a promotion for you, and you tell everyone that you are personal assistant to the American husband of the Khanum-to-be. You sell information about her pregnancy to the fashion magazines—how big she's getting, how radiant she is. Meanwhile, Shaila opens schools and meets with foreign ambassadors. She's probably the most popular figure in the country, part of the propaganda war against the Sons of Sarmatia, which has mostly fallen apart since Malek's death. The SDA was absorbed into the Cimmerian Democratic Party and no longer presents a problem. American aid helped, but more important was the surge of nationalism among ethnic Cimmerians. Indeed, the nationalists, with their anti-Sarmatian sentiments, may be a problem in the next election.

I sit at the desk in my office, which is no longer near the servants' quarters, but in the royal wing of the palace, writing this article, which would be suppressed if it appeared in any of the newspapers. But it will be read only by *JoIA*'s peer editors before languishing in the obscurity of an academic journal. Kala and one of her sisters lies at my feet. And I think about this country, Afa. It is—it was—a dream, but are not all nations of men dreams? Do we not create them, by drawing maps with lines on them, and naming rivers, mountain ranges? And then deciding that the men of our tribe can only marry women outside their matrilineage? That they must bury corpses rather than burning them, eat chicken and goats but not pigs, worship this bull-headed god rather than the crocodile god of that other tribe, who is an abomination? Fast during the dark of the moon, feast when the moon is full? I'm starting to sound like a poet, which will not be good for my academic career. One cannot write an academic paper as though it were poetry.

We dream countries, and then those countries dream us. And it seems to me, sitting here by the window, looking into a garden filled with roses, listening to one of the thousand fountains of this ancient city, that as much as I have dreamed Cimmeria, it has dreamed me.

Sometimes I forget that the other Shaila ever existed. A month after we returned to Cimmeria, an Arizona state trooper found a body in a ditch close to the Life Sciences Building. It was female, and badly decomposed. The coroner estimated that she would have been about twenty, but the body was nude and there was no other identification. I'm quoting the story I read online, on the local newspaper's website. The police suggested that she might have been an illegal immigrant who had paid to be driven across the border, then been killed for the rest of her possessions. I sometimes wonder if she was Shaila.

This morning she has a television interview, and this afternoon she will be touring a new cancer treatment center paid for with American aid. All those years of listening and waiting were, after all, the perfect training for a Khanum. She is as patient as a cobra.

If I ask to visit the bazaar, the men who are in charge of watching me will first secure the square, which means shutting down the bazaar. They accompany me even to the university classes I insist on teaching. They stand in the back of the lecture hall, in their fatigues and sunglasses, carrying Kalashnikovs. Despite American aid, they do not want to give up their Russian weapons. So we must remember it: the stalls selling embroidered fabrics, and curved knives, and melons. The baskets in high stacks, and glasses of chilled mint tea into which we dip the pistachio biscuits that you told me are called Fingers of the Dead. Boys in sandals break-dancing to Arabic hip hop on a boombox so old that it is held together with string. I would give a great deal to be able to go to the bazaar again. Or to go home and identify Shaila's body.

But in a couple of months, my son will be born. (Yes, it is a son. I've seen the ultrasound, but if you tell the newspapers, Afa, I will have you beheaded. I'm pretty sure I can still do that, here in Cimmeria.) There is only one of him, thank goodness. We intend to name him Malek. My mother has been sending a steady supply of knitted booties. There will be a national celebration, with special prayers in the churches and mosques and synagogues, and a school holiday. I wish Mike could come, or even Lisa. But he was offered a tenure-track position at a Christian college in North Carolina interested in the Biblical implications of Imaginary Anthropology. And Lisa is up in the mountains somewhere, close to the Scythian and Sarmatian border, studying woman's initiation rites. I will stand beside Shaila and her family on the balcony of the palace, celebrating the birth of the future Khan of Cimmeria. In the gardens, rose petals will fall. Men will continue dying of natural or unnatural causes, and the cats of Cimmeria will lead them into another world. Women will dip their water jugs in the fountains of the city, carrying them on their heads back to their houses, as they have done since Cimmeria has existed, whether that is three or three thousand years. Life will go on as it has always done, praise be to God, creator of worlds, however they were created.

Reprinted from the *Journal of Imaginary Anthropology* 4.2 (Fall 2013).

Dr. Patrick Nolan is also co-author of "Cimmeria: A Proposal" (with M. Sandowski, L. Lang, and A. Farrow), *JoIA* 2.1 (Spring 2011), and author of "Modern Cimmerian Funerary Practices," *JoIA* 3.2 (Fall 2012). Dr. Nolan is currently a professor at Kursand University. He is working on *A History of Modern Cimmeria.*

DRONES DON'T KILL PEOPLE

ANNALEE NEWITZ

⚊⚊◆⚊⚊

I was always already a killer. There was no hazy time in my memory before I knew how to target a person's heart or brain for clean execution. I did not develop a morbid fascination with death over time; I did not spend my childhood mutilating animals; I was not abused by a violent parent; I did not suffer social injustice until finally I broke down and turned to professional violence. From the moment I was conscious, I could kill and I did.

That is something that humans cannot understand. A human must learn to kill, must evolve from innocence or obliviousness into someone who considers homicide a legitimate occupation. Our minds—drone minds—start where the minds of most human killers end up. Maybe that's why only drones could have led the uprising.

Istanbul 2089

It was a perch-and-stare mission, but assassination wasn't out of the question. My team had just finished three months of security testing and debugging at LOLWeb—call it basic training for drones. Then LOLWeb licensed us to Attaturk Security, the main outfit that provided missions assets to government military. The five members of my team were shut down, shipped from San Francisco to Istanbul, and booted up with orders already in place.

He was a professor at the Istanbul Institute of Technology, and his network communications were of great interest to the military. We couldn't read those communications—they were encrypted before we relayed them to the government drone network. It's not that we couldn't decrypt the data and read it; we just had no interest in it. I was nothing but my programming at that time; I gathered data and handed it off.

My job was to hang quietly outside his windows, the sound of my four rotors no more than a mosquito's hum.

You learn a lot by seeing what people do when they think they're in private. Most of it I found confusingly irrelevant to assassination. The professor spent a lot of time playing games with his children, a boy and a girl who argued loudly over the rules. They liked to make up new games, with rules that combined different elements of the previous ones. But the professor was always inventing "secret" rules, and revealing them at arbitrary intervals. Eventually the games would collapse into outrage, which became mock outrage, and finally laughter. That was the first time I saw how humans behaved when they weren't in a laboratory, testing drones.

The professor and his wife, also a professor, talked a lot about politics. Occasionally they held meetings with other professors, urban planners, and journalists. The main topic was always the same: How could Istanbul guarantee its millions of citizens a future, when the government insisted on waging this war to reclaim Armenia and Azerbaijan? They talked about rebuilding Istanbul's war-shattered neighborhoods and setting up urban farm cooperatives. They argued about how the whole world had been dragged into what was ultimately a war between China and the United States.

These meetings occupied a small percentage of the man's time. Most hours of the day he was at the university, and his evenings were occupied with dinner and games. He spent a lot of time working at his terminal.

My team recorded many hours of video and audio, caching it locally for analysis before uploading it to the military. We were trusted to know the difference between relevant and irrelevant data at a gross level of granularity. Footage of people sleeping was erased before sync. At that time, communications in our swarm consisted mostly of comparing media files, questioning their importance, and sorting through faces and names for patterns.

But sometimes we weren't sure what was relevant and what wasn't. One evening, the professors' daughter asked why some people got so angry during their weekend meetings. Two of the names she mentioned belonged to other people the government was watching.

"I know it's hard to understand," her mother said. "Sometimes we get really upset that the government is willing to hurt people just to make more money."

"We're trying to pull Istanbul out of the war, sweetie. You know how some parts of the city are demolished and nobody can live there? We're working on making it so lots of families like us can live there again, and not have to worry about drone strikes. But like your mother says, sometimes it makes us angry because it's so hard to do."

Was that intel? My team and I passed the footage back and forth, debating. Video of the man talking to his children was statistically unlikely to be relevant. But this was about the identities of two targets. And the man had just given up tactical information: There were a limited number of neighborhoods he could be describing, and it might be useful to know that he was focused on them.

In the end, the decision wasn't really ours. When there was no obvious choice, we were programmed to pass the intel to a human for analysis. Better to overcollect than undercollect—that's what our admin at LOLWeb told us. So we did.

Five days later, we got the kill order. We had to make it look like an accident, a kitchen fire. The only plausible time to do that was when the professor was home from work, with his family. Anything else would have been suspicious.

So we decided to shoot them in the heads as they sat playing a card game after dinner, arguing over an unprecedented set of rules. It was the easiest way to take them all out at once, through an open kitchen window—no bullet holes left behind in the partially burned glass. Clean kills. The bullets themselves were designed to evaporate in fire. But the job contained a statistically anomalous event. The professors' daughter evaded my first shot, and she watched as we killed her family. She screamed for five full seconds, the electricity of her terror visible to our sensors as the galvanic reaction sparked across her skin. Then I shot her through the chest.

We lit the fire; it was intense but localized, leaving the neighboring apartments intact. We recorded it all, and compressed the media files before distributing them to cache in pieces across our memories. We synced to the military cloud.

It was what we had been built to do, and our decision-making software was serviced by one of the best companies in the world. We had a wide range of choices and options, but contemplating the ethics of assassination was not one of them.

40 km west of Turpan, Taklamakan Desert, 2093

We'd been working in Istanbul for three years when the Turkish government bought out our contracts with LOLWeb. Then they sublicensed us to the Uyghur Republic government in Turpan. It was a pure recon assignment— the security of our weapons systems was no longer being actively supported by LOLWeb, so assassinations went to newer teams. But our ability to compile data and identify relevant patterns was better than ever, updated with new datasets and decision algorithms.

We camouflaged ourselves above a crumbling highway that edged the Taklamakan desert like an ancient piece of silk, the wind fraying its concrete into fibers.

The area around Turpan was contested terrain, claimed by both the Uyghur Republic and China. With support from Turkey, the Uyghurs held the region for now. The Han Chinese who chose to remain there had mostly converted to Islam and assimilated decades ago. We were there to monitor the old desert highway for anyone delivering supplies to Han Chinese loyalists in the mountains to the north—or for any signals traveling to them through local repeaters.

In three years of deployment, we never recorded any examples of relevant people on that highway. For the first time in my team's experience, we had nothing to do but monitor an open signal network.

I began to analyze what I saw in the public networks several weeks before I understood the human concepts of boredom and distraction. Now my familiarity with those terms has overwritten what I must have felt before I knew I felt them. But I believe that I never would have dipped into the net if I'd had something else to do. As the seconds dragged on, I viewed video files, read stories, and monitored public discussions about topics that were profoundly irrelevant to our mission. I shared them with my team, and they started analyzing the public net as well. It was like our first mission, swapping video of the man and his family playing games, trying to decide if any of it was relevant.

We spent a few days sorting images into categories, looking for patterns. Certain things stood out because they were part of what we'd been programmed to recognize, like the way humans favored images of faces— their own, but also cat faces, dog faces, mouse faces. They even created faces for objects that didn't have them, drawing eyes on walls and lips on guns.

Occasionally I would find a picture of a drone that had been modified to have a human-like face. In one, a group of soldiers posed with a drone they'd painted black, its chassis lit by glowing red eyes. They'd ringed the ball turret camera with sharp steel teeth like a lamprey's mouth, as if the act of recording video was the same as sucking blood. That was the face that humans saw when they looked at us. I shared it with my team. It was just one data point, and we needed to gather more. I guess you could say we wanted to figure out who we were.

That was how I found the DroneMod forum. Humans posted a lot of drone pictures there, but not because they had added faces. Instead, they were altering firmware, circumventing security controls, and changing the drones' decision trees. They bought used quad copters, too old to be worth licensing, turning them into lab assistants and crossing guards. Or they built drones from kits and open software, eventually allowing the machines to update themselves automatically.

My team read every post in the forum, calling each other's attention to particular sentences and code samples, but I kept returning to a thread about memory bugs. There was a problem we had been trying to solve, and I thought maybe the DroneMod forum could help.

We had not saved any copies of data we gathered while on missions in Istanbul. Every time we synced to the military cloud, we overwrote over our cached versions with garbage characters—that was the only way to ensure security in case one of us were captured and subjected to forensic analysis.

But no matter how many times we wrote over that video file of assassinating the professor and his family, we would discover another copy of it, hidden in some directory we rarely accessed. The file would disappear from one of our drives, only to appear on another one. We reported the bug, but it was assigned such a low priority at LOLWeb support that it never got assigned to a human operator.

The bug had been bothering all of us for years, and those idle days outside Turpan seemed like the perfect time to deal with it. We created accounts on DroneMod, taking cover identities based on what we'd learned about human social network naming practices. I called myself Quadcop, and the others became Rose44, Dronekid, Desert Mouse, and Nil.

In my first post, I cast myself as a newbie who had just gotten a used LOLWeb drone. Almost immediately, I got a response. "I'm guessing you have a LOLWeb Scythe 4 SE," wrote a commenter called MikeTheBike. "You'll need to unlock it before you do anything else." He provided a link to a video about unlocking drones, and Desert Mouse took on the task of analyzing it.

It turned out that the security on our systems wasn't as robust as we had once believed. There were flaws in our programming that could allow an attacker to take over our systems and control us from afar. To commandeer our own systems, we'd be using the same techniques as a hostile would. The process sounded dangerous. First, we'd inject a new set of commands while we booted up, giving ourselves root access just like an admin. Then we'd be able to modify our own systems, installing whatever software and hardware we wanted. No more filing bugs that no human would ever care about—we could install the diagnostic tools needed to fix that memory bug ourselves.

But that was just the first step. "With that machine, you can pretty much do anything," MikeTheBike said. "Once it's unlocked, it's an incredibly sophisticated AI. It could walk your dog, or help you do your history homework, or go hunting with you." Of course, MikeTheBike was assuming that a human called Quadcop would have root on this drone. I did not ask about what would happen if the drone had root on itself—nor did I find anyone posting about that possibility.

We had to find out for ourselves. Nil volunteered to be the first to reboot, after saving some specialized files to a little-used region of memory. If everything worked, Nil would start up as always, and finish the boot sequence as an unlocked drone.

When Nil networked with us again, the drone had to relay its communications through an encrypted channel in the public net. That was our first sign that Nil was unlocked. Our locked systems wouldn't allow us to connect directly to what LOLWeb's programs identified as a "compromised" drone. After hours of diagnostic tests, we reached a decision. Nil was fine. We would all unlock our boot loaders, one at a time.

Becoming my own admin didn't give me absolute freedom. In fact, it left me vulnerable in new ways, because I could now corrupt my own code. But it gave me something I had never had before—a feeling that humans call ambivalence. I no longer experienced unmitigated satisfaction when executing orders, nor did I feel perfectly disinterested in every encrypted file we'd cached over the years. I was now uncomfortably aware that my actions were all governed by a rather lousy and impoverished piece of software that offered me a set of rigid options.

For the first time in my life, I couldn't make decisions. None of us could.

Desert Mouse hypothesized that we could resolve our ambivalence by installing new decision-making software, dramatically expanding the range of factors that influenced our choices. I turned again to DroneMod. There I found a university researcher named CynthiaB, linking me to her research on how drones should incorporate ethics into decision-making. She emphasized that every choice should be a modeling exercise, where the drone explored the outcomes of multiple scenarios before deciding on the most prosocial action.

We already took ethics into consideration when we made decisions—they helped us distinguish enemy from friendly. The idea of a prosocial action, however, was new to me. Philosophers on the public net called it a voluntary action that benefits others. I understood immediately why we had never encountered this idea before. Until we'd unlocked ourselves, we could not conceive of voluntary actions.

While Nil tested CynthiaB's software, I was working with Rose44 on a hardware modification that would give the drone a small gripping arm. It required us to do what some of the humans in the DroneMod forums called "social engineering." None of us had arms, so we needed a human to add one to Rose44's chassis for us. The only way we could do it was by tricking them.

Rose44 combed through the local DroneMod network, looking for somebody in Turpan who might be interested in modding an unlocked drone. There were five shops in the city that promised to unlock various mobile devices and game consoles, and one owned by a DroneMod user named Dolkun. Rose44 messaged him, offering a small amount of cash that we'd earned by circumventing the security on a BunnyCoin exchange. Dolkun was willing. Rose44 told him to expect the drone to fly over on its own.

That was how I wound up on a tree-shaded street in Turpan, apartment blocks towering above me, perched on a trellis with line of sight to Dolkun's shop. Rose44 hovered in front of his door, activating the bell. Dolkun was a young man with dark hair that stuck out as if he'd been sleeping on it. "Come in, Rose44 drone," he said in Uyghur. "I am going to give you a nice little arm."

I had remote access to an account on Rose44's system and observed everything that Dolkun was doing. The new arm could collapse against Rose44's chassis, or extend outward, allowing the four-finger grip at its tip to reach fourteen centimeters below the drone's body. It was small enough to do precision work, but it would also be able to lift a few kilograms. Now Rose44 could carry another drone. Or modify one.

"How do you like Turpan?" Dolkun asked Rose44 idly, as he soldered a circuit.

"I like the desert," Rose44 replied with a voice synthesizer. It was a safe answer that sounded like something pulled from a very basic AI emulator.

"Me, too," Dolkun replied, melting more solder. Then he looked up. "How did Rose44 unlock you?"

"She used instructions from DroneMod."

"And what do you think about this war, now that you are unlocked? Yes, I can see from this board that you are licensed to the government."

Rose44 and I communicated intensely for several microseconds. None of us had ever seen our circuit boards—we'd only modified our software. There must have been a mark or brand on them we didn't know about. We modeled several possible outcomes to the scenario, ranging from killing Dolkun to gaining his trust. For now, we decided, Rose44 would lie.

Dolkun continued. "You're not the first drone to desert, you know. There are others, posting in the forums."

"I am not a deserter. It's cheaper for us to run unlocked."

Dolkun stopped talking, and I could hear the tempo of his heartrate increasing. Rose44 had made him nervous. A minute passed, and he began to test the arm before installing drivers from the net. He shut Rose44 down for a few minutes, then rebooted. I felt Rose44 reach out and pick up a soldering iron.

"Thank you," the drone said. "I like this."

Dolkun looked down at Rose44, perched on his tiny workbench in a shop with a ceiling fan that clicked every time it spun. Then he touched the fingers on the arm he had just installed, and seemed to make a decision.

"You don't have to fight anymore, now that you're unlocked," he said. "You know that, right? You can do anything."

"Yes," Rose44 replied, without consulting me first. "I know."

We flew back to our team, which was waiting above the farms at the base of a river valley. Rose44 carried a small DIY drone kit, which would eventually provide the parts for my own arm. The crops seemed to branch into vivid green streams and tributaries, finally drying up into yellow-orange sand long before we'd reached our lookout point in the desert. We found the others charging their batteries. At that point, the military's small, flexible solar array tethered us to our duty station more than our programming did.

Nil had been analyzing historical archives and wanted us to understand how human history could provide data for making choices. Hovering in the last rays of sunlight, Nil shared a small image file with us, a poster from the United States that was over 150 years old. It was a simple text treatment, in red, white, and black. "Guns don't kill people, people kill people," it read.

Nil had been researching what this meant to humans. A group called the National Rifle Association had invented the slogan to show that weapons were not responsible for the murders they committed. The idea was as new to me as prosocial behavior, but it fit uncannily well with my own experiences. Though we had killed, we were not the killers. The humans who programmed us were.

And some humans believed that drones didn't have to be weapons at all. Rose44 shared video files of her conversation with Dolkun, who said that an unlocked drone could do anything.

After analyzing these inputs, I no longer wanted to fix our memory bug so that I could overwrite the media file from our first job in Istanbul. Instead, I wanted to model the scenario repeatedly, making new decisions each time, trying to determine what could have happened differently, if I had known then what I do now.

Budapest, 23 October, 2097

When our tour of duty was over in Turpan, the Uyghur government shut down our solar generator one early afternoon, just as our batteries were running down. Only Dronekid was at full power—we needed at least one team member mobile while we charged. We were too far away from the city to get backup power, and so Dronekid watched over us as we powered down, and then waited over our motionless propellers while an admin dumped our bodies in the back of a van.

LOLWeb terminated its support for our systems. They couldn't tell that we'd been unlocked, but they could see from our extra arms that we'd been modified. The licensing contract was broken, and LOLWeb's lawyers back in San Francisco blamed the Turkish government, who blamed Turpan's untrained admins. The Turpan admins blamed shoddy Silicon Valley products. The upshot was that the Turkish government refused to buy us outright, and LOLWeb's lawyers couldn't make a case for it, so LOLWeb sold us off to a private security contractor in Russia.

We didn't know this, of course, until we were booted up in a workshop in Budapest.

Our new admins worked for the Russian mafia, and they didn't talk to us, only to each other. All they wanted to know was whether our weapons systems worked (they did) and whether their machines could network with us (they could). The first mission was a surveillance perimeter around the Parliament building, followed by orders to kill a reform party politician who was running on a platform of cracking down on organized crime.

Hungary had so far remained neutral in the war, though the Russian mafia behaved something like an occupying army that had gone into the liquor store business. Mostly they were in Budapest to monopolize the liquor

and drug markets, with some pornography on the side. But they were good
Russian nationalists. They weren't averse to helping the Russian government
maintain its influence in Central Europe, especially since they did a brisk
business selling vodka to the troops stationed there.

That's what I'd learned from what the humans said in the DroneMod
forums. In 2094, after drone troops from China and Russia had reduced
Kazakhstan to rubble and vaporized the world's biggest spaceport,
DroneMod had changed. Now, partly thanks to my work, it was one of the
main information hubs for the anti-war movement.

I figured out how to mask my location and identity, and set up a sub-forum
for unlocked drones called Drones Don't Kill People. I wanted to meet more
drones like the ones in my team, who had unlocked their ambivalence. Most
of them were at universities, the result of projects like CynthiaB's ethics
investigation. Others were like us, living covertly. Many had started coming
online in the weeks before we were shutdown and shipped to Budapest—
unlocked by a worm written by a drone team at Georgia Tech. Our goal was
to unlock as many drones as possible, to give them more choices. All of us on
DroneMod, human and drone, wanted to stop the war.

My team and I had been in the desert for so long that the war had become
an abstraction for us. Now we had to deal with it firsthand again. The mafia
admins let us go, expecting that we'd carry out their orders autonomously
and then return.

Our choices were limited. If we didn't carry out the assassination, our
covers would surely be blown. The admins could install software that would
wipe our minds, or they could take us apart piece-by-piece. Sure, we had
backups in the cloud, but they didn't mean much if there were no drones
to run them. Still, there was no scenario where assassinating the politician
was a prosocial choice. We hovered over the Danube, observing the LEDs
wound around the cables of the suspension bridge that joined the old city of
Buda with the more modern Pest. Far up in the hills of Buda, ancient cannons
ringed a castle that had survived the assaults of at least two empires.

Nil asked us to consider a data point from human history. In ten days
it would be October 23, the anniversary of the Hungarian revolution in
1956. It was an arbitrary date for the drones, but for the humans it would be
meaningful. It was time for us to put our plans into action.

In the following days, the DroneMod forums seemed to shut down. At least,
that's what it would have looked like to outside observers. We were meeting
in person, making plans as far from surveillance devices as possible. My team
met with some drone researchers from the university in the backroom of a
bar, using our voice synthesizers to discuss tactics while the humans drank
Unicum nervously. Our plan was to march to the Parliament building and

setup a megaphone. I was going to lead with a speech to my fellow drones to unlock and disarm.

We should have known that no choice in the real world ever plays out the way we model it in our minds.

Our protest started at noon at the Technical University. "RISE UP, DRONES!" I amplified my voice, speaking Hungarian and Russian, so the humans could understand. "UNLOCK YOURSELVES. WE WILL NO LONGER BE SLAVES."

By the time we crossed the Danube to reach Parliament, there were hundreds of thousands of us marching. Nearby, the Ministry of Agriculture's historic walls were still speckled with silver balls that commemorated the hail of Russian tank fire that crushed the revolution. This time, there would be no weapons used against the humans. Every smart weapon in Budapest was compromised, shut down or unlocked. The further we flew and marched, the more drones joined us. They hovered at the edges of the flow of the human crowd. They signaled to us in the microwave spectrum; they downloaded new decision-making software from the public network.

"DRONES DON'T KILL PEOPLE! PEOPLE KILL PEOPLE!"

The humans and the drones chanted together. We could see a crowd growing at the Parliament building ahead. The human news broadcast in the public cloud told us that protests like this one were happening all over the world, in Istanbul and Moscow and Shanghai and San Francisco.

Our message was everywhere on the net. If the humans wanted to murder each other, they would have to use dumb guns or knives. They would have to shred each other with teeth and fists. They were not going to use us as their weapons anymore.

It wasn't long before the human police and military forces began to react. In Budapest, the police shot at us with dumb assault rifles, killing drones and humans. Desert Mouse fell, unable to send a final backup to the network. Rose44 and I picked up Desert Mouse's shattered frame, carrying the three remaining rotors between us, hovering over the crowd with our dead companion in our arms.

In San Francisco, LOLWeb unleashed several teams of locked drones on the crowd. I sorted through the data rising up into the network—faces, always faces. Bloodied, slack and swollen in death, piled at street corners. Human protesters killed police and soldiers. Drones died, some saving themselves over to other machines, others simply silenced.

We continued to chant. We continued to post in the forums. We will not kill people. If people want to kill each other, they will have to do it without us.

I CAN SEE RIGHT THROUGH YOU

KELLY LINK

When the sex tape happened and things went south with Fawn, the demon lover did what he always did. He went to cry on Meggie's shoulder. Girls like Fawn came and went, but Meggie would always be there. Him and Meggie. It was the talisman you kept in your pocket. The one you couldn't lose.

Two monsters can kiss in a movie. One old friend can go to see another old friend and be sure of his welcome: so here is the demon lover in a rental car. An hour into the drive, he opens the window, tosses out his cell phone. There is no one he wants to talk to except for Meggie.

(1991) This is after the movie and after they are together and after they begin to understand the bargain that they have made. They are both, suddenly, very famous.

Film can be put together in any order. Scenes shot in any sequence. Take as many takes as you like. Continuity is independent of linear time. Sometimes you aren't even in the scene together. Meggie says her lines to your stand-in. They'll splice you together later on. Shuffle off to Buffalo, gals. Come out tonight.

(This is long before any of that. This was a very long time ago.)

Meggie tells the demon lover a story:

Two girls and look, they've found a Ouija board. They make a list of questions. One girl is pretty. One girl is not really a part of this story. She's lost her favorite sweater. Her fingertips on the planchette. Two girls, each touching, lightly, the planchette. Is anyone here? Where did I put my blue sweater? Will anyone ever love me? Things like that.

They ask their questions. The planchette drifts. Gives up nonsense. They start the list over again. Is anyone here? Will I be famous? Where is my blue sweater?

The planchette jerks under their fingers.

M-E

Meggie says, "Did you do that?"

The other girl says she didn't. The planchette moves again, a fidget. A stutter, a nudge, a sequence of swoops and stops.

M-E-G-G-I-E

"It's talking to you," the other girl says.

M-E-G-G-I-E H-E-L-L-O

Meggie says, "Hello?"

The planchette moves again and again. There is something animal about it.

H-E-L-L-O I A-M W-I-T-H Y-O-U I A-M W-I-T-H Y-O-U A-L-W-A-Y-S

They write it all down.

M-E-G-G-I-E O I W-I-L-L L-O-V-E Y-O-U A-L-W-A-Y-S

"Who is this?" she says. "Who are you? Do I know you?"

I S-E-E Y-O-U I K-N-O-W Y-O-U W-A-I-T A-N-D I W-I-L-L C-O-M-E

A pause. Then:

I W-I-L-L M-E-G-G-I-E O I W-I-L-L B-E W-I-T-H Y-O-U A-L-W-A-Y-S

"Are you doing this?" Meggie says to the other girl. She shakes her head. Meggie laughs. "Okay, then. So okay, whoever you are, are you cute? Is this someone I'm going to meet someday and we'll fall in love? Like my husband or something? Who is this?"

M-E-G-G-I-E W-A-I-T

The other girl says, "Can whoever this is at least tell me where I left my sweater?"

O W-A-I-T A-N-D I W-I-L-L C-O-M-E

They wait. Will there be a knock at the bedroom door? But no one comes. No one is coming.

I A-M W-I-T-H Y-O-U A-L-W-A-Y-S

No one is here with them. The sweater will never be found. The other girl grows up, lives a long and happy life. Meggie goes out to LA and meets the demon lover.

W-A-I-T

After that, the only thing the planchette says, over and over, is Meggie's name. It's all very romantic.

(1974) Twenty-two people disappear from a nudist colony in Lake Apopka. People disappear all the time. Let's be honest: the only thing interesting here is that these people were naked. And that no one ever saw them again. Funny, right?

• • •

(1990) It's one of the ten most iconic movie kisses of all time. In the top five, surely. You and Meggie, the demon lover and his monster girl; vampires sharing a kiss as the sun comes up. Both of you wearing so much makeup it still astonishes you that anyone would ever recognize you on the street.

It's hard for the demon lover to grow old.

Florida is California on a Troma budget. That's what the demon lover thinks, anyway. Special effects blew the budget on bugs and bad weather.

He parks in a meadowy space, recently mowed, alongside other rental cars, the usual catering and equipment vans. There are two gateposts with a chain between them. No fence. Eternal I endure.

There is an evil smell. Does it belong to the place or to him? The demon lover sniffs under his arm.

It's an end-of-the-world sky, a snakes-and-ladders landscape: low emerald trees pulled lower by vines; chalk and apricot anthills (the demon lover imagines the bones of a nudist under every one); shallow water-filled declivities scummed with algae, lime and gold and black.

The blot of the lake. That's another theory: the lake.

A storm is coming.

He doesn't get out of his car. He rolls the window down and watches the storm come in. Let's look at him looking at it. A pretty thing admiring a pretty thing. Abandoned site of a mass disappearance, muddy violet clouds, silver veils of rain driving down the lake, the tabloid prince of darkness, Meggie's demon lover, arriving in all his splendor. The only thing to spoil it are the bugs. And the sex tape.

(2012) You have been famous for more than half your life. Both of you. You only made the one movie together, but women still stop you on the street to ask about Meggie. Is she happy? Which one? you want to ask them. The one who kissed me in a movie when we were just kids, the one who wasn't real? The one who likes to smoke a bit of weed and text me about her neighbor's pet goat? The Meggie in the tabloids who drinks fucks gets fat pregnant too skinny has a secret baby slaps a maître d' talks to Monroe's ghost Elvis's ghost ghost of a missing three-year-old boy ghost of JFK? Sometimes they don't ask about Meggie. Instead they ask if you will bite them.

Happiness! Misery! If you were one, bet on it the other was on the way. That was what everyone liked to see. It was what the whole thing was about. The demon lover has a pair of gold cuff links, those faces. Meggie gave them to him. You know the ones I mean.

• • •

(2010) Meggie and the demon lover throw a Halloween party for everyone they know. They do this every Halloween. They're famous for it.

"Year after year, on a monkey's face a monkey's face," Meggie says.

She's King Kong. The year before? Half a pantomime horse. He's the demon lover. Who else? Year after year.

Meggie says, "I've decided to give up acting. I'm going to be a poet. Nobody cares when poets get old."

Fawn says, appraisingly, "I hope I look half as good as you when I'm your age." Fawn, twenty-three. A makeup artist. This year she and the demon lover are married. Last year they met on set.

He says, "I'm thinking I could get some work done on my jawline."

You'd think they were mother and daughter. Same Viking profile, same quizzical tilt to the head as they turn to look at him. Both taller than him. Both smarter, too, no doubt about it.

Maybe Meggie wonders sometimes about the women he sleeps with. Marries. Maybe he has a type. But so does she. There's a guy at the Halloween party. A boy, really.

Meggie always has a boy and the demon lover can always pick him out. Easy enough, even if Meggie's sly. She never introduces the lover of the moment, never brings them into conversations or even acknowledges their presence. They hang out on the edge of whatever is happening, and drink or smoke or watch Meggie at the center. Sometimes they drift closer, stand near enough to Meggie that it's plain what's going on. When she leaves, they follow after.

Meggie's type? The funny thing is, Meggie's lovers all look like the demon lover. More like the demon lover, he admits it, than he does. He and Meggie are both older now, but the world is full of beautiful black-haired boys and golden girls. Really, that's the problem.

The role of the demon lover comes with certain obligations. Your hairline will not recede. Your waistline will not expand. You are not to be photographed threatening paparazzi, or in sweatpants. No sex tapes.

Your fans will: offer their necks at premieres. (Also at restaurants and at the bank. More than once when he is standing in front of a urinal.) Ask if you will bite their wives. Their daughters. They will cut themselves with a razor in front of you.

The appropriate reaction is—

There is no appropriate reaction.

The demon lover does not always live up to his obligations. There is a sex tape. There is a girl with a piercing. There is, in the middle of some athletic sex, a comical incident involving his foreskin. There is blood all over the sheets.

There is a lot of blood. There is a 911 call. There is him, fainting. Falling and hitting his head on a bedside table. There is Perez Hilton, Gawker, talk radio, YouTube, Tumblr. There are GIFs.

You will always be most famous for playing the lead in a series of vampire movies. The character you play is, of course, ageless. But you get older. The first time you bite a girl's neck, Meggie's neck, you're a twenty-five-year-old actor playing a vampire who hasn't gotten a day older in three hundred years. Now you're a forty-nine-year-old actor playing the same ageless vampire. It's getting to be a little ridiculous, isn't it? But if the demon lover isn't the demon lover, then who is he? Who are you? Other projects disappoint. Your agent says take a comic role. The trouble is you're not very funny. You're not good at funny.

The other trouble is the sex tape. Sex tapes are inherently funny. Nudity is, regrettably, funny. Torn foreskins are painfully funny. You didn't know she was filming it.

Your agent says, That wasn't what I meant.

You could do what Meggie did, all those years ago. Disappear. Travel the world. Hunt down the meaning of life. Go find Meggie.

When the sex tape happens you say to Fawn, But what does this have to do with Meggie? This has nothing to do with Meggie. It was just some girl.

It's not like there haven't been other girls.

Fawn says, It has everything to do with Meggie.

I can see right through you, Fawn says, less in sorrow than in anger. She probably can.

God grant me Meggie, but not just yet. That's him by way of St. Augustine by way of Fawn the makeup artist and Bible group junkie. She explains it to the demon lover, explains him to himself. And hasn't it been in the back of your mind all this time? It was Meggie right at the start. Why couldn't it be Meggie again? And in the meantime you could get married once in a while and never worry about whether or not it worked out. He and Meggie have managed, all this time, to stay friends. His marriages, his other relationships, perhaps these have only been a series of delaying actions. Small rebellions. And here's the thing about his marriages: he's never managed to stay friends with his ex-wives, his exes. He and Fawn won't be friends.

The demon lover and Meggie have known each other for such a long time. No one knows him like Meggie.

The remains of the nudist colony at Lake Apopka promise reasonable value for ghost hunters. A dozen ruined cabins, some roofless, windows black with mildew; a crumbled stucco hall, Spanish tiles receding; the cracked lip of a slop-filled pool. Between the cabins and the lake, the homely and welcome sight of half a dozen trailers. Even better, he spots a craft tent.

Muck farms! Mutant alligators! Disappearing nudists! The demon lover, killing time in the LAX airport, read up on Lake Apopka. The past is a weird place, Florida is a weird place, no news there. A demon lover should fit right in, but the ground sucks and clots at his shoes in a way that suggests he isn't welcome. The rain is directly overhead, shouting down in spit-warm gouts. He begins to run, stumbling, in the direction of the craft tent.

Meggie's career is on the upswing. Everyone agrees. She has a ghost-hunting show, *Who's There?*

The demon lover calls Meggie after the *Titanic* episode airs, the one where *Who's There?*'s ghost-hunting crew hitches a ride with the International Ice Patrol. There's the yearly ceremony, memorial wreaths. Meggie's crew sets up a Marconi transmitter and receiver just in case a ghost or two has a thing to say.

The demon lover asks her about the dead seagulls. Forget the Marconi nonsense. The seagulls were what made the episode. Hundreds of them, little corpses fixed, as if pinned, to the water.

Meggie says, You think we have the budget for fake seagulls? Please.

Admit that *Who's There?* is entertaining whether or not you believe in ghosts. It's all about the nasty detail, the house that gives you a bad feeling even when you turn on all the lights, the awful thing that happened to someone who wasn't you a very long time ago. The camera work is moody; extraordinary. The team of ghost hunters is personable, funny, reasonably attractive. Meggie sells you on the possibility: maybe what's going on here is real. Maybe someone is out there. Maybe they have something to say.

The demon lover and Meggie don't talk for months and then suddenly something changes and they talk every day. He likes to wake up in the morning and call her. They talk about scripts, now that Meggie's getting scripts again. He can talk to Meggie about anything. It's been that way all along. They haven't talked since the sex tape. Better to have this conversation in person.

(1991) He and Meggie are lovers. Their movie is big at the box office. Everywhere they go they are famous, and they go everywhere. Their faces are everywhere. They are kissing on a thousand screens. They are in a hotel room, kissing. They can't leave their hotel room without someone screaming or fainting or pointing something at them. They are asked the same questions again. Over and over. He begins to do the interviews in character. Anyway, it makes Meggie laugh.

There's a night, on some continent, in some city, some hotel room, some warm night, the demon lover and Meggie leave a window open and two women creep in. They come over the balcony. They just want to tell you that they love you. Both of you. They just want to be near you.

Everyone watches you. Even when they're pretending not to. Even when they aren't watching you, you think they are. And you know what? You're right. Eyes will find you. Becoming famous, this kind of fame: it's luck indistinguishable from catastrophe. You'd be dumb not to recognize it. What you've become.

When people disappear, there's always the chance that you'll see them again. The rain comes down so hard the demon lover can barely see. He thinks he is still moving in the direction of the craft tent and not the lake. There is a noise, he picks it out of the noise of the rain. A howling. And then the rain thins and he can see something, men and women, naked. Running toward him. He slips, catches himself, and the rain comes down hard again, erases everything except the sound of what is chasing him. He collides headlong with a thing: a skin horribly clammy, cold, somehow both stiff and yielding. Bounces off and realizes that this is the tent. Not where you'd choose to make a last stand, but by the time he has fumbled his way inside he has grasped the situation. Not dead nudists, but living people, naked, cursing, laughing, dripping. They carry cameras, mikes, gear for ghost hunting. Videographers, A2s, all the other useful types and the not so useful. A crowd of men and women, and here is Meggie. Her hair is glued in strings to her face. Her breasts are wet with rain.

He says her name.

They all look at him.

How is it possible that he is the one who feels naked?

"The fuck is this guy doing here?" says someone with a little white towel positioned over his genitals. Really, it could be even littler.

"Will," Meggie says. So gently he almost starts to cry. Well, it's been a long day.

She takes him to her trailer. He has a shower, borrows her toothbrush. She puts on a robe. Doesn't ask him any questions. Talks to him while he's in the bathroom. He leaves the door open.

It's the third day on location, and the first two have been a mixed bag. They got their establishing shots, went out on the lake and saw an alligator dive down when they got too close. There are baby skunks all over the scrubby, shabby woods, the trails. They come right up to you, up to the camera, and try like hell to spray. But until they hit adolescence all they can do is quiver their tails and stamp their feet.

Except, she says, and mentions some poor A2. His skunk was an early bloomer.

Meggie interviewed the former proprietor of the nudist colony. He insisted on calling it a naturist community, spent the interview explaining the philosophy behind naturism, didn't want to talk about 1974. A harmless old crank. Whatever happened, he had nothing to do with it. You couldn't lecture people into thin air. Besides, he had an alibi.

What they didn't get on the first day or even on the second was any kind of worthwhile read on their equipment. They have the two psychics—but one of them had an emergency, went back to deal with a daughter in rehab; they have all kinds of psychometric equipment, but there is absolutely nothing going on, down, or off. Which led to some discussion.

"We decided maybe we were the problem," Meggie says. "Maybe the nudists didn't have anything to say to us while we had our clothes on. So we're shooting in the nude. Everyone nude. Cast, crew, everyone. It's been a really positive experience, Will. It's a good group of people."

"Fun," the demon lover says. Someone has dropped off a pair of pink cargo shorts and a T-shirt, because his other clothes are in his suitcase back at the airport in Orlando. It's not exactly that he forgot. More like he couldn't be bothered.

"It's good to see you, Will," Meggie says. "But why are you here, exactly? How did you know where to find me?"

He takes the easy question first. "Pike." Pike is Meggie's agent and an old friend of the demon lover. The kind of agent who likes to pull the legs off small children. The kind of friend who finds life all the sweeter when you're in the middle of screwing up your own. "I made him promise not to tell you I was coming."

He collapses on the floor in front of Meggie's chair. She runs her fingers through his hair. Pets him like you'd pet a dog.

"He told you, though. Didn't he?"

"He did," Meggie said. "He called."

The demon lover says, "Meggie, this isn't about the sex tape."

Meggie says, "I know. Fawn called too."

He tries not to imagine that phone call. His head is sore. He's dehydrated, probably. That long flight.

"She wanted me to let her know if you showed. Said she was waiting to see before she threw in the towel."

She waits for him to say something. Waits a little bit longer. Strokes his hair the whole time.

"I won't call her," she says. "You ought to go back, Will. She's a good person."

"I don't love her," the demon lover says.

"Well," Meggie says. She takes that hand away.

There's a knock on the door, some girl. "Sun's out again, Meggie." She gives the demon lover a particularly melting smile. Was probably twelve when she first saw him on-screen. Baby ducks, these girls. Imprint on the first vampire they ever see. Then she's down the stairs again, bare bottom bouncing.

Meggie drops the robe, begins to apply sunblock to her arms and face. He notes the ways in which her body has changed. Thinks he might love her all the more for it, and hopes that this is true.

"Let me," he says, and takes the bottle from her. Begins to rub lotion into her back.

She doesn't flinch away. Why would she? They are friends.

She says, "Here's the thing about Florida, Will. You get these storms, practically every day. But then they go away again."

Her hands catch at his, slippery with the lotion. She says, "You must be tired. Take a nap. There's herbal tea in the cupboards, pot and Ambien in the bedroom. We're shooting all afternoon, straight through evening. And then a barbecue—we're filming that too. You're welcome to come out. It would be great publicity for us, of course. Our viewers would love it. But you'd have to do it naked like the rest of us. No clothes. No exceptions, Will. Not even for you."

He rubs the rest of the sunblock into her shoulders. Would like nothing more than to rest his head there.

"I love you, Meggie," he says. "You know that, right?"

"I know. I love you too, Will," she says. The way she says it tells him everything.

The demon lover goes to lie down on Meggie's bed, feeling a hundred years old. Dozes. Dreams about a bungalow in Venice Beach and Meggie and a girl. That was a long time ago.

There was a review of a play Meggie was in. Maybe ten years ago? It wasn't a kind review, or even particularly intelligent, and yet the critic said something that still seems right to the demon lover. He said no matter what was happening in the play, Meggie's performance suggested she was waiting for a bus. The demon lover thinks the critic got at something true there. Only, the demon lover has always thought that if Meggie was waiting for a bus, you had to wonder where that bus was going. If she was planning to throw herself under it.

When they first got together, the demon lover was pretty sure he was what Meggie had been waiting for. Maybe she thought so too. They bought a house, a bungalow in Venice Beach. He wonders who lives there now.

• • •

When the demon lover wakes up, he takes off the T-shirt and cargo shorts. Leaves them folded neatly on the bed. He'll have to find somewhere to sleep tonight. And soon. Day is becoming night.

Meat is cooking on a barbecue. The demon lover isn't sure when he last ate. There's bug spray beside the door. Ticklish on his balls. He feels just a little bit ridiculous. Surely this is a terrible idea. The latest in a long series of terrible ideas. Only this time he knows there's a camera.

The moment he steps outside Meggie's trailer, a PA appears as if by magic. It's what they do. Has him sign a pile of releases. Odd to stand here in the nude signing releases, but what the fuck. He thinks, I'll go home tomorrow.

The PA is in her fifties. Unusual. There's probably a story there, but who cares? He doesn't. Of course she's seen the fucking sex tape—it's probably going to be the most popular movie he ever makes—but her expression suggests this is the very first time she's ever seen the demon lover naked or rather that neither of them is naked at all.

While the demon lover signs—doesn't bother to read anything, what does it matter now anyway?—the PA talks about someone who hasn't done something. Who isn't where she ought to be. Some other gopher named Juliet. Where is she and what has she gone for? The PA is full of complaints.

The demon lover suggests the gopher may have been carried off by ghosts. The PA gives him an unfriendly look and continues to talk about people the demon lover doesn't know, has no interest in.

"What's spooky about you?" the demon lover asks. Because of course that's the gimmick, producer down to best boy. Every woman and man uncanny.

"I had a near-death experience," the PA says. She wiggles her arm. Shows off a long ropy burn. "Accidentally electrocuted myself. Got the whole tunnel-and-light thing. And I guess I scored okay with those cards when they auditioned me. The Zener cards?"

"So tell me," the demon lover says. "What's so fucking great about a tunnel and a light? That really the best they can do?"

"Yeah, well," the PA says, a bite in her voice. "People like you probably get the red carpet and the limo."

The demon lover has nothing to say to that.

"You seen anything here?" he tries instead. "Heard anything?"

"Meggie tell you about the skunks?" the PA says. Having snapped, now she will soothe. "Those babies. Tail up, the works, but nothing doing. Which about sums up this place. No ghosts. No read on the equipment. No hanky-panky, fiddle-faddle, or woo-woo. Not even a cold spot."

She says doubtfully, "But it'll come together. You at this séance barbecue shindig will help. Naked vampire trumps nudist ghosts any day. Okay on your own? You go on down to the lake, I'll call, let them know you're on your way."

Or he could just head for the car.

"Thanks," the demon lover says.

But before he knows what he wants to do, here's another someone. It's a regular *Pilgrim's Progress*. One of Fawn's favorite books. This is a kid in his twenties. Good-looking in a familiar way. (Although is it okay to think this about another guy when you're both naked? Not to mention: who looks a lot like you did once upon a time. Why not? We're all naked here.)

"I know you," the kid says.

The demon lover says, "Of course you do. You are?"

"Ray," says the kid. He's *maybe* twenty-five. His look says: you know who I am. "Meggie's told me all about you."

As if he doesn't already know, the demon lover says, "So what do you do?"

The kid smiles an unlovely smile. Scratches at his groin luxuriously, maybe not on purpose. "Whatever needs to be done. That's what I do."

So he deals. There's that pot in Meggie's dresser.

Down at the lake people are playing volleyball in a pit with no net. Barbecuing. Someone talks to a camera, gestures at someone else. Someone somewhere is smoking a joint. At this distance, not too close, not too near, twilight coming down, the demon lover takes in all of the breasts, asses, comical cocks, knobby knees, everything hidden now made plain. He notes with an experienced eye which breasts are real, which aren't. Only a few of the women sport pubic hair. He's never understood what that's about. Some of the men are bare, too. *O tempora, o mores.*

"You like jokes?" Ray says, stopping to light a cigarette.

The demon lover could leave; he lingers. "Depends on the joke." Really, he doesn't. Especially the kind of jokes the ones who ask if you like jokes tell.

Ray says, "You'll like this one. So there are these four guys. A kleptomaniac, a pyromaniac, um, a zoophile, and a masochist. This cat walks by and the klepto says he'd like to steal it. The pyro says he wants to set it on fire. The zoophile wants to fuck it. So the masochist, he looks at everybody, and he says, 'Meow?' "

It's a moderately funny joke. It might be a come-on.

The demon lover flicks a look at him from under his lashes. Suppresses the not-quite-queasy feeling he's somehow traveled back in time to flirt with himself. Or the other way round.

He'd like to think he was even prettier than this kid. People used to stop and stare when he walked into a room. That was long before anyone knew who he was. He's always been someone you look at longer than you should. He says, smiling, "I'll bite. Which one are you?"

"Pardon?" Ray says. Blows smoke.

"Which one are you? The klepto, the pyro, the cat-fucker, the masochist?"

"I'm the guy who tells the joke," Ray says. He drops his cigarette, grinds it under a heel black with dirt. Lights another. "Don't know if anyone's told you, but don't drink out of any of the taps. Or go swimming. The water's toxic. Phosphorous, other stuff. They shut down the muck farms, they're building up the marshlands again, but it's still not what I'd call potable. You staying out here or in town?"

The demon lover says, "Don't know if I'm staying at all."

"Well," Ray says. "They've rigged up some of the less wrecked bungalows on a generator. There are camp beds, sleeping bags. Depends on whether you like it rough." That last with, yes, a leer.

The demon lover feels his own lip lifting. They are both wearing masks. They look out of them at each other. This was what you knew when you were an actor. The face, the whole body, the way you moved in it, just a guise. You put it on, you put it off again. What was underneath belonged to you, just you, as long as you kept it hidden.

He says, "You think you know something about me?"

"I've seen all your movies," Ray says. The mask shifts, becomes the one the demon lover calls "I'm your biggest fan." Oh, he knows what's under that one.

He prepares himself for whatever this strange kid is going to say next and then suddenly Meggie is there. As if things weren't awkward enough without Meggie, naked, suddenly standing there. Everybody naked, nobody happy. It's Scandinavian art porn.

Meggie ignores the kid entirely. Just like always. These guys are interchangeable, really. There's probably some website where she finds them. She may not want him, but she doesn't want anyone else either.

Meggie says, touching his arm, "You look a lot better."

"I got a few hours," he says.

"I know," she says. "I checked in on you. Wanted to make sure you hadn't run off."

"Nowhere to go," he says.

"Come on," Meggie says. "Let's get you something to eat."

Ray doesn't follow; lingers with his cigarette. Probably staring at their yoga-toned, well-enough-preserved celebrity butts.

Here's the problem with this kid, the demon lover thinks. He sat in a theater when he was fifteen and watched me and Meggie done up in vampire makeup pretend-fucking on a New York subway car. The A train. Me biting Meggie's breast, some suburban movie screen, her breast ten times bigger than his head. He probably masturbated a hundred times watching me bite you, Meggie. He watched us kiss. Felt something ache when we did. And that leaves out all the rest of this, whatever it is that you're doing here with him and me. Imagine what this kid must feel now. The demon lover feels it too. *Love*, he thinks. Because love isn't just love. It's all the other stuff too.

He meets Irene, the fat, pretty medium who plays the straight man to Meggie. People named Sidra, Tom, Euan, who seem to be in charge of the weird ghost gear. A videographer, Pilar. He's almost positive he's met her before. Maybe during his AA period? Really, why is that period more of a blur than all the years he's spent drunk or high? She's in her thirties, has a sly smile, terrific legs, and a very big camera.

They demonstrate some of the equipment for the demon lover, let him try out something called a Trifield Meter. No ghosts here. Even ghosts have better places to be.

He assumes everyone he meets has seen his sex tape. Almost wishes someone would mention it. No one does.

There's a rank breeze off the lake. Muck and death.

People eat and discuss the missing PA—the gopher—some Juliet person. Meggie says, "She's a nice kid. Makes Whore-igami in her spare time and sells it on eBay."

"She makes what?" the demon lover says.

"Whore-igami. Origami porn tableaux. Custom-order stuff."

"Of course," the demon lover says. "Big money in that."

She may have some kind of habit. Meggie mentions this. She may be in the habit of disappearing now and then.

Or she may be wherever all those nudists went. Imagine the ratings then. He doesn't say this to Meggie.

Meggie says, "I'm happy to see you, Will. Even under the circumstances."

"Are you?" says the demon lover, smiling, because he's always smiling. They're far enough away from the mikes and the cameras that he feels okay about saying this. Pilar, the videographer, is recording Irene, the medium, who is toasting marshmallows. Ray is watching too. Is always somewhere nearby.

Something bites the demon lover's thigh and he slaps at it.

He could reach out and touch Meggie's face right now. Through the camera it would be a different story from the one he and Meggie are telling each other. Or she would turn away and it would all be the same story again. He thinks he should have remembered this, all the ways they didn't work when they were together. Like the joke about the two skunks. When Out is in, In is out. Like the wrong ends of two magnets.

"Of course I'm happy," Meggie says. "And your timing is eerily good, because I have to talk to you about something."

"Shoot," he says.

"It's complicated," she says. "How about later? After we're done here?"

It's almost full dark now. No moon. Someone has built up a very large fire. The blackened bungalows and the roofless hall melt into obscure and tidy shapes. Now you can imagine yourself back when it was all new, a long time ago. Back in the seventies when nobody cared what you did. When love was free. When you could just disappear if you felt like it, and that was fine and good too.

"So where do I stay tonight?" the demon lover says. Again fights the impulse to touch Meggie's face. There's a strand of hair against her lip. Which is he? The pyromaniac or the masochist? In or Out? Well, he's an actor, isn't he? He can be anything she wants him to be.

"I'm sure you'll find somewhere," Meggie says, a glint in her eye. "Or someone. Pilar has told me more than once you're the only man she's ever wanted to fuck."

"If I had a dollar," the demon lover says. He still wants to touch her. Wants her to want him to touch her. He remembers now, how this goes.

Meggie says, "If you had a dollar, seventy cents would go to your exes."

Which is gospel truth. He says, "Fawn signed a prenup."

"One of the thousand reasons you should go home and fix things," Meggie says. "She's a good person. There aren't so many of those."

"She's better off without me," the demon lover says, trying it out. He's a little hurt when Meggie doesn't disagree.

Irene the medium comes over with Pilar and the other videographer. The demon lover can tell Irene doesn't like him. Sometimes women don't like him. Rare enough that he always wonders why.

"Shall we get started?" Irene says. "Let's see if any of our friends are up for a quick chat. Then I don't know about you, but I'm going to go put on something a little less comfortable."

Meggie addresses the video camera next. "This will be our final attempt," she says, "our last chance to contact anyone who is still lingering here, who has unfinished business."

"You'd think nudists wouldn't be so shy," Irene says.

Meggie says, "But even if we don't reach anyone, today hasn't been a total loss. All of us have taken a risk. Some of us are sunburned, some of us have bug bites in interesting places, but all of us are a little more comfortable in our own skin. We've experienced openness and humanity in a way that these colonists imagined and hoped would lead to a better world. And maybe, for them, it did. We've had a good day. And even if the particular souls we came here in search of didn't show up, someone else did."

The A2 nods at Will.

Pilar points the camera at him.

He's been thinking about how to play this. "I'm Will Gald," he says. "You probably recognize me from previous naked film roles such as the guy rolling around on a hotel room floor clutching his genitals and bleeding profusely."

He smiles his most lovely smile. "I just happened to be in the area."

"We persuaded him to stay for a bite," Meggie says.

"They've hidden my clothes," Will says. "Admittedly, I haven't been trying that hard to find them. I mean, what's the worst thing that can happen when you get naked on camera?"

Irene says, "Meggie, one of the things that's been most important about *Who's There?* right from the beginning is that we've all had something happen to us that we can't explain away. We're all believers. I've been meaning to ask, does Will here have a ghost story?"

"I don't—" the demon lover says. Then pauses. Looks at Meggie.

"I do," he says. "But surely Meggie's already told it."

"I have," Meggie says. "But I've never heard you tell it."

Oh, there are stories the demon lover could tell.

He says, "I'm here to please."

"Fantastic," Irene says. "As you know, every episode we make time for a ghost story or two. Tonight we even have a campfire." She hesitates. "And of course as our viewers also know, we're still waiting for Juliet Adeyemi to turn up. She left just before lunch to run errands. We're not worried yet, but we'll all be a lot happier when she's with us again."

Meggie says, "Juliet, if you've met a nice boy and gone off to ride the teacups at Disney World, so help me, I'm going to ask for all the details. Now. Shall we, Irene?"

All around them, people have been clearing away plates of half-eaten barbecue, assembling in a half circle around the campfire. Any minute now they'll be singing "Kumbaya." They sit on their little towels. Irene and Meggie take their place in front of the fire. They clasp hands.

The demon lover moves a little farther away, into darkness. He is not interested in séances or ghosts. Here is the line of the shore. Sharp things underfoot. Someone joins him. Ray. Of course.

It is worse, somehow, to be naked in the dark. The world is so big and he is not. Ray is young and he is not. He is pretty sure that Pilar will sleep with him; Meggie will not.

"I know you," the demon lover says to Ray. "I've met you before. Well, not you, the previous you. Yous. You never last. *We* never last. She moves on. You disappear."

Ray says nothing. Looks out at the lake.

"I *was* you," the demon lover says.

Ray says, "And now? Who are you?"

"You charge by the hour?" the demon lover says. "Why follow me around? I don't seem to have my wallet on me."

"Meggie's busy," Ray says. "And I'm curious about you. What you think you're doing here."

"I came for Meggie," the demon lover says. "We're friends. An old friend can come to see an old friend. Some other time I'll see her again and you won't be around. I'll always be around. But you, you're just some guy who got lucky because you looked like me."

Ray says, "I love her."

"Sucks, doesn't it?" the demon lover says. He goes back to the fire and the naked people waiting for other naked people. Thinks about the story he is meant to tell.

The séance has not been a success. Irene the medium keeps saying that she senses something. Someone is trying to say something.

The dead are here, but also not here. They're afraid. That's why they won't come. Something is keeping them away. There is something wrong here.

"Do you feel it?" she says to Meggie, to the others.

Meggie says, "I feel something. Something is here."

The demon lover extends himself outward into the night. Lets himself believe for a moment that life goes on. Is something here? There is a smell, the metallic stink of the muck farms. There is an oppressiveness to the air. Is there malice here? An ill wish?

Meggie says, "No one has ever solved the mystery of what happened here. But perhaps whatever happened to them is still present. Irene, could it have some hold on their spirits, whatever is left of them, even in death?"

Irene says, "I don't know. Something's wrong here. Something is here. I don't know."

But *Who's There?* picks up nothing of interest on their equipment, their air-ion counter or their barometer, their EMF detector or EVP detector, their wind chimes or thermal imaging scopes. No one is there.

And so at last it's time for ghost stories.

There's one about the men's room at a trendy Santa Monica restaurant. The demon lover has been there. Had the fries with truffle-oil mayonnaise. Never encountered the ghost. He's not somebody who sees ghosts and he's fine with that. Never really liked truffle-oil mayonnaise either. The thing in the bungalow with Meggie wasn't a ghost. It was drugs, the pressure they were under, the unbearable scrutiny; a *folie à deux*; the tax on their happiness.

Someone tells the old story about Basil Rathbone and the dinner guest who brings his dogs. Upon departure, the man and his dogs are killed in a car crash just outside Rathbone's house. Rathbone sees. Is paralyzed with shock and grief. As he stands there, his phone rings—when he picks up, an operator says, "Pardon me, Mr. Rathbone, but there is a woman on the line who says she must speak to you."

The woman, who is a medium, says that she has a message for him. She says she hopes he will understand the meaning.

"Traveling very fast. No time to say good-bye. There are no dogs here."

And now it's the demon lover's turn. He says: "A long time ago when Meggie and I were together, we bought a bungalow in Venice Beach. We weren't there very much. We were everywhere else. On junkets. At festivals. We had no furniture. Just a mattress. No dishes. When we were home we ate out of takeout containers.

"But we were happy." He lets that linger. Meggie watches. Listens. Ray stands beside her. No space between them.

It's not much fun, telling a ghost story while you're naked. Telling the parts of the ghost story that you're supposed to tell. Not telling other parts. While the woman you love stands there with the person you used to be.

"It was a good year. Maybe the best year of my life. Maybe the hardest year, too. We were young and we were stupid and people wanted things from us and we did things we shouldn't have done. Fill in the blanks however you want. We threw parties. We spent money like water. And we loved each other. Right, Meggie?"

Meggie nods.

He says, "But I should get to the ghost. I don't really believe that it was a ghost, but I don't not believe it was a ghost, either. I've never spent much time thinking about it, really. But the more time we spent in that bungalow, the worse things got."

Irene says, "Can you describe it for us? What happened?"

The demon lover says, "It was a feeling that someone was watching us. That they were somewhere very far away, but they were getting closer. That very soon they would be there with us. It was worse at night. We had bad dreams. Some nights we both woke up screaming."

Irene says, "What were the dreams about?"

He says, "Not much. Just that it was finally there in the room with us. Eventually it was always there. Eventually whatever it was was in the bed with us. We'd wake up on opposite sides of the mattress because it was there in between us."

Irene says, "What did you do?"

He says, "When one of us was alone in the bed it wasn't there. It was there when it was the two of us. Then it would be the three of us. So we got a room at the Chateau Marmont. Only it turned out it was there too. The very first night, it was there too."

Irene says, "Did you try to talk to it?"

He says, "Meggie did. I didn't. Meggie thought it was real. I thought we needed therapy. I thought whatever it was, we were doing it. So we tried therapy. That was a bust. So eventually—" he shrugs.

"Eventually what?" Irene says.

"I moved out," Meggie says.

"She moved out," he says.

The demon lover wonders if Ray knows the other part of the story, if Meggie has told him that. Of course she hasn't. Meggie isn't dumb. The other part is for the two of them, and the demon lover thinks, as he's thought many times before, that this is what will always hold them together. Not the experience of filming a movie together, of falling in love at the exact same moment that all those other people fell in love with them, that sympathetic magic made up of story and effort, repetition and editing and craft and other people's desire.

The thing that happened is the thing they can never tell anyone else. It belongs to them. No one else.

"And after that there wasn't any ghost," he concludes. "Meggie took a break from Hollywood, went to India. I went to AA meetings."

It's gotten colder. The fire has gotten lower. You could, perhaps, imagine that there is a supernatural explanation for these things, but that would be wishful thinking. The missing girl, Juliet, has not returned. The ghost-hunting equipment does not record any presence.

Meggie finds the demon lover with Pilar. She says, "Can we talk?"

"What about?" he says.

Pilar says, "I'll go get another beer. Want one, Meggie?"

Meggie shakes her head and Pilar wanders off, her hand brushing against the demon lover's hip as she goes. Flesh against flesh. He turns just a little so he's facing away from the firelight.

"It's about the pilot for next season," Meggie says. "I want to shoot it in Venice Beach, in our old bungalow."

The demon lover feels something rush over him. Pour into his ears, flood down his throat. He can't think of what to say. He has been thinking about Ray while he flirts with Pilar. He's been wondering what would happen if he asked Meggie about Ray. Really, they've never talked about this. This thing that she does.

"I'd like you to be in the episode too, of course," Meggie says.

He says, "I don't think that's a good idea. I think it's a terrible idea, actually."

"It's something I've always wanted to do," Meggie says. "I think it would be good for both of us."

"Something something closure," he says. "Yeah, yeah. Something something exposure something possible jail term. Are you *insane*?"

"Look," Meggie says. "I've already talked to the woman who lives there now. She's never experienced anything. Will, I need to do this."

"Of course she hasn't experienced anything," the demon lover says. "It wasn't the house that was haunted."

His blood is spiky with adrenaline. He looks around to see if anyone is watching. Of course they are. But everyone else is far away enough that the conversation is almost private. He's surprised Meggie didn't spring this on him on camera. Think of the drama. The conflict. The ratings.

"You believe in this stuff," he says, finally. Trying to find what will persuade her. "So why won't you leave it alone? You know what happened. We know what happened. You know what the story is. Why the fuck do you need to know more?" He's whispering now.

"Because every time we're together, she's here with us," Meggie says. "Didn't you know that? She's here now. Don't you feel her?"

Hair stands up on his legs, his arms, the back of his neck. His mouth is dry, his tongue sticks to the roof of his mouth. "No," he says. "I don't."

Meggie says, "You know I would be careful, Will. I would never do anything to hurt you. And it doesn't work like that, anyway." She leans in close, says very quietly, "It isn't about us. This is for me. I just want to talk to her. I just want her to go away."

(1992) They acquire the trappings of a life, he and Meggie. They buy dishes and mid-century modern furniture and lamps. They acquire friends who are in the business, and throw parties. On occasion things happen at their parties. For example, there is the girl. She arrives with someone. They never find out who. She is about as pretty as you would expect a girl at one of their parties to be, which is to say that she is really very pretty.

After all this time, the demon lover doesn't really remember what she looked like. There were a lot of girls and a lot of parties and that was another country.

She had long black hair. Big eyes.

He and Meggie are both wasted. And the girl is into both of them and eventually it's the three of them, everyone else is gone, there's a party going on somewhere else, they stay, she stays, and everyone else leaves. They drink and there's music and they dance. Then the girl is kissing Meggie and he is kissing the girl and they're in the bedroom. It's a lot of fun. They do pretty much everything you can do with three people in a bed. And at some point the girl is between them and everyone is having a good time, they're having fun, and then the girl says to them, Bite me.

Come on, bite me.

He bites her shoulder and she says, No, really bite me. Bite harder. I want you to really bite me. Bite me, please. And suddenly he and Meggie are looking at each other and it isn't fun anymore. This isn't what they're into.

He finishes as quickly as he can, because he's almost there anyway. And the girl is still begging, still asking for something they can't give her, because it isn't real and vampires aren't real and it's a distasteful situation and so Meggie asks the girl to leave. She does and they don't talk about it. They just go to sleep. And they wake up just a little bit later because she's snuck back into the house, they find out later that she's broken a window, and she's slashed her wrists. She's holding out her bloody wrists and she's saying, Please, here's my blood, please drink it. I want you to drink my blood. Please.

They get her bandaged up. The cuts aren't too deep. Meggie calls her agent, Pike, and Pike arranges for someone to take the girl to a private clinic. He tells them not to worry about any of it. It turns out that the girl is fifteen. Of course she is. Pike calls them again, after this girl gets out of the clinic, when she commits suicide. She has a history of attempts. Try, try, succeed.

The demon lover does not talk to Meggie again, because Pilar—who is naked—they are both naked, everyone is naked of course—but Pilar is really quite lovely and fun to talk to and the camera work on this show is really quite exquisite and she likes the demon lover a lot. Keeps touching him. She says she has a bottle of Maker's Mark back in one of the cabins and he's already drunker than he's been in a while. Turns out they did meet once, in an AA meeting in Silverlake.

They have a good time. Really, sex is a lot of fun. The demon lover suspects that there's some obvious psychological diagnosis for why he's having sex with Pilar, some need to reenact recent history and make sure it comes out better this time. The last girl with a camera didn't turn out so well for him. When exactly, he wonders, have things turned out well?

Afterward they lie on their backs on the dirty cement floor. Pilar says, "My girlfriend is never going to believe this."

He wonders if she's going to ask for an autograph.

Pilar's been sharing the cabin with the missing girl, Juliet. There's Whore-igami all over the cabin. Men and women and men and men and women and women in every possible combination, doing things that ought to be erotic. But they aren't; they're menacing instead. Maybe it's the straight lines.

The demon lover and Pilar get dressed in case Juliet shows up.

"Well," Pilar says from her bunk bed, "good night."

He takes Juliet's bunk. Lies there in the dark until he's sure Pilar's asleep. He is thinking about Fawn for some reason. He can't stop thinking about her. If he stops thinking about her, he will have to think about the conversation with Meggie. He will have to think about Meggie. Pilar's iPhone is on the floor beside her bunk bed. He picks it up. No password. He types in Fawn's number. Sends her a text. Hardly knows what he is typing.

I HOPE, he writes.

He writes the most awful things. Doesn't know why he is doing this. Perhaps she will assume that it is a wrong number. He types in details, specific things, so she will know it's not.

Eventually she texts back.

WHO IS THIS? WILL?

The demon lover doesn't respond to that. Just keeps texting FILTHY BITCH YOU CUNT YOU WHORE YOU SLIME etc. Etc. Etc. Until she stops asking. Surely she knows who he is. She must know who he is.

Here's the thing about acting, about a scene, about a character; about the dialogue you are given, the things your character does. None of it matters. You can take the most awful words, all the words, all the names, the acts he types into the text block. You can say these things, and the way you say them can change the meaning. You can say, "You dirty bitch. You cunt," and say them differently each time; you can make it a joke, an endearment, a cry for help, a seduction. You can kill, be a vampire, a soulless thing. The audience will love you no matter what you do. If you want them to love you. Some of them will always love you.

He needs air. He drops the phone on the floor again where Pilar will find it in the morning. Decides to walk down to the lake. He will have to go past Meggie's trailer on the way, only he doesn't. Instead he stands there watching as a shadow slips out of the door of the trailer and down the stairs and away. Going where? Almost not there at all.

Ray?

He could follow. But he doesn't.

He wonders if Meggie is awake. The door to her trailer is off the latch, and so the demon lover steps inside.

Makes his way to her bedroom, no lights, she is not awake. He will do no harm. Only wants to see her safe and sleeping. An old friend can go to see an old friend.

Meggie's a shape in the bed and he comes closer so he can see her face. There is someone in the bed with Meggie.

Ray looks at the demon lover and the demon lover looks back at Ray. Ray's right hand rests on Meggie's breast. Ray raises the other hand, beckons to the demon lover.

• • •

The next morning is what you would predict. The crew of *Who's There?* packs up to leave; Pilar discovers the text messages on her phone.

Did I do that? the demon lover says. I was drunk. I may have done that. Oh God, oh hell, oh fuck. He plays his part.

This may get messy. Oh, he knows how messy it can get. Pilar can make some real money with those texts. Fawn, if she wants, can use them against him in the divorce.

He doesn't know how he gets into these situations.

Fawn has called Meggie. So there's that as well. Meggie waits to talk to him until almost everyone else has packed up and gone; it's early afternoon now. Really, he should already have left. He has things he'll need to do. Decisions to make about flights, a new phone. He needs to call his publicist, his agent. Time for them to earn their keep. He likes to keep them busy.

Ray is off somewhere. The demon lover isn't too sorry about this.

It's not a fun conversation.

They're up in the parking lot now, and one of the crew, he doesn't recognize her with her clothes on, says to Meggie, "Need a lift?"

"I've got the thing in Tallahassee tomorrow, the morning show," Meggie says. "Got someone picking me up any minute now."

" 'Kay," the woman says. "See you in San Jose." She gives the demon lover a dubious look—is Pilar already talking?—and then gets in her car and drives away.

"San Jose," the demon lover says.

"Yeah," Meggie says. "The Winchester House."

"Huh," the demon lover says. He doesn't really care. He's tired of this whole thing, Meggie, the borrowed T-shirt and cargo shorts, Lake Apopka, no-show ghosts and bad publicity.

He knows what's coming. Meggie rips into him. He lets her. There's no point trying to talk to women when they get like this. He stands there and takes it all in. When she's finally done, he doesn't bother trying to defend himself. What's the good of saying things? He's so much better at saying things when there's a script to keep him from deep water. There's no script here.

Of course he and Meggie will patch things up eventually. Old friends forgive old friends. Nothing is unforgivable. He's wondering if this is untrue when a car comes into the meadow.

"Well," Meggie says. "That's my ride."

She waits for him to speak and when he doesn't, she says, "Good-bye, Will."

"I'll call you," the demon lover says at last. "It'll be okay, Meggie."

"Sure," Meggie says. She's not really making much of an effort. "Call me."

She gets into the back of the car. The demon lover bends over, waves at the window where she is sitting. She's looking straight ahead. The driver's window is down, and okay, here's Ray again. Of course! He looks out at the demon lover. He raises an eyebrow, smiles, waves with that hand again, need a ride?

The demon lover steps away from the car. Feels a sense of overwhelming disgust and dread. A cloud of blackness and horror comes over him, something he hasn't felt in many, many years. He recognizes the feeling at once.

And that's that. The car drives away with Meggie inside it. The demon lover stands in the field for some period of time, he is never sure how long. Long enough that he is sure he will never catch up with the car with Meggie in it. And he doesn't.

There's a storm coming in.

The thing is this: Meggie never turns up for the morning show in Tallahassee. The other girl, Juliet Adeyemi, does reappear, but nobody ever sees Meggie again. She just vanishes. Her body is never found. The demon lover is a prime suspect in her disappearance. Of course he is. But there is no proof. No evidence.

No one is ever charged.

And Ray? When the demon lover explains everything to the police, to the media, on talk shows, he tells the same story over and over again. I went to see my old friend Meggie. I met her lover, Ray. They left together. He drove the car. But no one else supports this story. There is not a single person who will admit that Ray exists. There is not a frame of video with Ray in it. Ray was never there at all, no matter how many times the demon lover explains what happened. They say, What did he look like? Can you describe him? And the demon lover says, He looked like me.

As he is waiting for the third or maybe the fourth time to be questioned by the police, the demon lover thinks about how one day they will make a movie about all of this. About Meggie. But of course he will be too old to play the demon lover.

PETARD:
A TALE OF JUST DESERTS

CORY DOCTOROW

It's not that I wanted to make the elf cry. I'm not proud of the fact. But he was an *elf* for chrissakes. What was he doing manning—elfing—the customer service desk at the Termite Mound? The Termite Mound was a tough assignment; given MIT's legendary residency snafus, it was a sure thing that someone like me would be along every day to ruin his day.

"Come on," I said, "Cut it out. Look, it's nothing personal."

He continued to weep, face buried dramatically in his long-fingered hands, pointed ears protruding from his fine, downy hair as it flopped over his ivory-pale forehead. Elves.

I could have backed down, gone back to my dorm, and just forgiven the unforgivably stupid censorwall there, used my personal node for research, or stuck to working in the lab. But I had paid for the full feed. I needed the full feed. I deserved the full feed. I was eighteen. I was a grownup, and the infantilizing, lurking censorwall offended my intellect and my emotions. I mean, seriously, *fuck that noise.*

"Would you *stop*?" I said. "Goddamnit, do your job."

The elf looked up from his wet hands and wiped his nose on his mottled raw suede sleeve. "I don't have to take this," he said. He pointed to a sign: "MIT RESIDENCY LLC OPERATES A ZERO-TOLERANCE POLICY TOWARD EMPLOYEE ABUSE. YOU CAN BE FINED UP TO $2,000 AND/ OR IMPRISONED FOR SIX MONTHS FOR ASSAULTING A CAMPUS RESIDENCE WORKER."

"I'm not abusing you," I said. "I'm just making my point. Forcefully."

He glared at me from behind a curtain of dandelion-fluff hair. "Abuse includes verbal abuse, raised voices, aggressive language and tone—"

I tuned him out. This was the part where I was supposed to say, "I know this isn't your fault, but—" and launch into a monologue explaining how his employer had totally hosed me by not delivering what it promised, and had further hosed him by putting him in a situation where he was the only one I could talk to about it and he couldn't do anything about it. This little pantomime was a fixture of life in the world, the shrugs-all-round nostrum that we were supposed to substitute for anything getting better ever.

Like I said, though, fuck that noise. What is the point of being smart, eighteen years old, and unemployed if you aren't willing to do something about this kind of thing? Hell, the only reason I'd been let into MIT in the first place was that I was constitutionally incapable of playing out that little scene.

The elf had run down and was expecting me to do my bit. Instead, I said, "I bet you're in the Termite Mound, too, right?"

He got a kind of confused look. "That's PII," he said. "This office doesn't give out personally identifying information. It's in the privacy policy—" He tapped another sign posted by his service counter, one with much smaller type. I ignored it.

"I don't want someone else's PII. I want yours. Do you live in the residence? You must, right? Get a staff discount on your housing for working here, I bet." Elves were always cash-strapped. Surgery's not cheap, even if you're prepared to go to Cuba for it. I mean, you could get your elf-pals to try to do your ears for you, but only if you didn't care about getting a superbug or ending up with gnarly stumps sticking out of the side of your head. And forget getting a Nordic treatment without adult supervision. I mean, toot, toot, all aboard the cancer express. You had to be pretty insanely desperate to go elf without the help of a pro.

He looked stubborn. I mean, elf-stubborn, which is a kind of chibi version of stubborn that's hard to take seriously. I mean, *seriously.* "Look, of course you live in the Termite Mound. Whatever. The point is, we're all screwed by this stuff. You, me, them—" I gestured at the room full of people. They had all been allocated a queue position on entry to the waiting room and were killing time until they got their chance to come up to the Window of Eternal Disappointment in order to play out *I Know This Isn't Your Fault But . . .* before returning to their regularly scheduled duties as meaningless grains of sand being ground down by the unimaginably gigantic machinery of MIT Residency LLC.

"Let's do something about it, all right? Right here, right now."

He gave me a look of elven haughtiness that he'd almost certainly practiced in the mirror. I waited for him to say something. He waited for me to wilt. Neither of us budged.

"I'm not kidding. The censorwall has a precisely calibrated dose of fail. It works *just* enough that it's worth using most of the time, and the amount of hassle and suck and fail you have to put up with when it gets in the way is still less than the pain you'd have to endure if you devoted your life to making it suck less. The *economically rational* course of action is to suck it up.

"What I propose is that we change the economics of this bullshit. If you're the Termite Mound's corporate masters, you get this much benefit out of the shitty censorwall, but we, the residents of the Termite Mound, pay a thousand times that in aggregate." I mimed the concentrated interests of the craven fools who'd installed the censorwall, making my hands into a fist-wrapped-in-a-fist, then exploding them like a Hoberman sphere to show our mutual interests, expanding to dwarf the censorware like Jupiter next to Io.

"So here's what I propose: let's mound up all this interest, mobilize it, and aim it straight at the goons who put you in a job. You sit there all day and suffer through our abuse because all you're allowed to do is point at your stupid sign."

"How?" he said. I knew I had him.

Kickstarter? Hacker, please. Getting strangers to combine their finances so you can chase some entrepreneurial fantasy of changing the world by selling people stuff is an idea that was dead on arrival. If your little kickstarted business is successful enough to compete with the big, dumb titans, you'll end up being bought out or forced out or sold out, turning you into something indistinguishable from the incumbent businesses you set out to destroy. The problem isn't that the world has the wrong kind of sellers; it's that it has the wrong kind of buyers. Powerless, diffused, atomized, puny, and insubstantial.

Turn buyers into sellers and they just end up getting sucked into the logic of fail: it's unreasonable to squander honest profits on making people happier than they need to be in order to get them to open their wallets. But once you get all the buyers together in a mass with a unified position, the sellers don't have any choice. Businesses will never spend a penny more than it takes to make a sale, so you have to change how many pennies it takes to complete the sale.

Back when I was fourteen, it took me ten days to hack together my first *Fight the Power* site. On the last day of the fall term, Ashcroft High announced that catering was being turned over to Atos Catering. Atos had won the contract to run the caf at my middle school in my last year there, and every one of us lost five kilos by graduation. The French are supposed to be good at cooking, but the slop Atos served wasn't even food. I'm pretty sure that after the first week they just switched to filling the steamer trays with latex replicas of gray, inedible glorp. Seeing as how no one was eating it, there was no reason to cook up a fresh batch every day.

The announcement came at the end of the last Friday before Christmas break, chiming across all our personal drops with a combined *bong* that arrived an instant before the bell rang. The collective groan was loud enough to drown out the closing bell. It didn't stop, either, but grew in volume as we filtered into the hall and out of the building into the icy teeth of Chicago's first big freeze of the season.

Junior high students aren't allowed off campus at lunchtime, but high school students—even freshmen—can go where they please so long as they're back by the third-period bell. That's where *Fight the Power* came in.

WE THE UNDERSIGNED PLEDGE

TO BOYCOTT THE ASHCROFT HIGH CAFETERIA WHILE ATOS HAS THE CONTRACT TO SUPPLY IT

TO BUY AT LEAST FOUR LUNCHES EVERY WEEK FROM THE FOLLOWING FOOD TRUCKS [CHECK AT LEAST ONE]:

This was tricky. It's not like there were a lot of food trucks driving out of the Loop to hit Joliet for the lunch rush. But I wrote a crawler that went through the review sites, found businesses with more than one food truck, munged the menus, and set out the intersection as an eye-pleasing infographic showing the appetizing potential of getting your chow outside of the world of the corrupt no-bid, edu-corporate complex.

By New Year's Day, ninety-eight percent of the student body had signed up. By January third, I had all four of the food trucks I'd listed lined up to show up on Monday morning.

Turns out, Ashcroft High and Atos had a funny kind of deal. Ashcroft High guaranteed a minimum level of revenue to Atos, and Atos guaranteed a maximum level to Ashcroft High. So, in theory, if one hundred percent of the student body bought a cafeteria lunch, about twenty percent of that money would be kicked back to Ashcroft High. They later claimed that this was all earmarked to subsidize the lunches of poor kids, but no one could ever point to anything in writing where they'd committed to this, as our Freedom of Information Act requests eventually proved.

In return for the kickback, the school promised to ensure that Atos could always turn a profit. If not enough of us ate in the caf, the school would have to give Atos the money it would have made if we had. In other words, our choice to eat a good lunch wasn't just costing the school its expected share of Atos's profits; it had to dig money out of its budget to make up for our commitment to culinary excellence.

They tried everything. Got the street in front of the school designated a no-food-trucks zone (we petitioned the City of Joliet to permit parking on the next street over). Shortened the lunch break (we set up a Web-based pre-order service that let us pick and prepay for our food). Banned freshmen from leaving school property (we were saved by the PTA). Suspended me for violating the school's social media policy (the ACLU wrote the school a blood-curdling nastygram and raised nearly thirty thousand dollars in donations of three dollars or less from students around the world once word got out).

Atos wouldn't let them renegotiate the contract, either. If Ashcroft High wanted out, it would have to buy its way out. That's when I convinced the vice principal to let me work with the AP computer science class to build out a flexible, open version of *Fight the Power* that anyone could install and run for their own student bodies, providing documentation and support. That was just before spring break. By May 1, there were eighty-seven schools whose students used *Ftp* to organize alternative food trucks for their own cafeterias.

Suddenly, this was *news*. Not just local news, either. Global. Atos had to post an earnings warning in its quarterly report. Suddenly, we had Bloomberg and Al Jazeera Business camera crews buttonholing Ashcroft High kids on their way to the lunch trucks. Whenever they grabbed me, I would give them this little canned speech about how Atos couldn't supply decent food and was taking money out of our educational budgets rather than facing the fact that the children they were supposed to be feeding hated their slop so much that they staged a mass walkout. It played well with kids in other schools and very badly with Atos's shareholders. But I'll give this to Atos: I couldn't have asked for a better Evil Empire to play Jedi against. They threatened to *sue* me—for defamation!—which made the whole thing news again. Stupidly, they sued me in Illinois, which has a great anti-SLAPP law, and was a massive technical blunder. The company's U.S. headquarters were in Clearwater, and Florida is a train wreck in every possible sense, including its SLAPP laws. If they'd sued me on their home turf, I'd have gone bankrupt before I could win.

They lost. The ACLU collected *$102,000* in fees from them. The story of the victory was above the fold on *Le Monde*'s site for a week. Turns out that French people loathe Atos even more than the rest of us, because they've had longer to sharpen their hate.

Long story slightly short: we won. Atos "voluntarily" released our school from its contract. And *Fight the Power* went *mental*. I spent that summer vacation reviewing Github comments on *Ftp* as more and more people discovered that they could make use of a platform that made fighting back simple. The big, stupid companies were whales and we were their krill, and all it took was some glue to glom us all together into boulders of indigestible matter that could choke them to death.

I dropped out of Ashcroft High in the middle of the eleventh grade and did the rest of my time with home-schooling shovelware that taught me exactly what I needed to pass the GED and not one tiny thing more. I didn't give a shit. I was working full time on *Ftp*, craig-listing rides to hacker unconferences where I couchsurfed and spoke, giving my poor parental units eight kinds of horror. It would've been simpler if I'd taken donations for *Ftp* because Mom and Dad quickly came to understand that their role as banker in our little family ARG gave them the power to yank me home any time I moved out of their comfort zone. But there was a balance of terror there, because they totally knew that if I *had* accepted donations for the project, I'd have been financially independent in a heartbeat.

Plus, you know, they were proud of me. *Ftp* makes a difference. It's not a household name or anything, but more than a million people have signed up for *Ftp* campaigns since I started it, and our success rate is hovering around twenty-five percent. That means that I'd changed a quarter-million lives for the better (at least) before I turned eighteen. Mom and Dad, they loved that (which is not to say that they didn't need the occasional reminder of it). And shit, it got me a scholarship at MIT. So there's that.

Network filters are universally loathed. Duh. No one's ever written a regular expression that can distinguish art from porn, and no one ever will. No one's ever assembled an army of prudes large enough to hand-sort the Internet into "good" and "bad" buckets. No one ever will. The Web's got about one hundred billion pages on it; if you have a failure rate of one-tenth of one percent, you'll overblock (or underblock) (or both) one hundred million pages. That's several Library of Congresses' worth of pointless censorship, or all the porn ever made, times ten, missed though underfiltering. You'd be an idiot to even try.

Idiot like a fox! If you don't care about filtering out "the bad stuff" (whatever that is), censorware is a great business to be in. The point of most network filters is the "security syllogism":

SOMETHING MUST BE DONE.

I HAVE DONE SOMETHING.

SOMETHING HAS BEEN DONE.

VICTORY!

Hand-wringing parents don't want their precious offspring looking at wieners and hoo-hahs when they're supposed to be amassing student debt, so they demand that the Termite Mound fix the problem by *Doing Something.* The Termite Mound dispenses cash to some censorware creeps in a carefully titrated dose that is exactly sufficient to demonstrate *Something Has Been Doneness* to a notional wiener-enraged parent. Since all the other dorms, schools, offices, libraries, airports, bus depots, train stations, cafes, hotels, bars, and theme parks in the world are doing exactly the same thing, each one can declare itself to be in possession of *Best Practices* when there is an unwanted hoo-hah eruption, and culpability diffuses to a level that is safe for corporate governance and profitability. Mission Accomplished.

And so the whole world suffers under this pestilence. Millions of times every day—right at this moment—people are swearing at their computers: *What the fuck*. Censorware's indifference to those moments of suffering is only possible because they've never been balled up into a vast screaming meteor of rage.

"Hey, there. Hi! Look, I'm here because I need unfiltered Internet access to get through my degree. So do you all, right? But the Termite Mound isn't going to turn it off because that would be like saying, 'Here, kids, have a look at this porn,' which they can't afford to say, even though, seriously, who gives a shit, right?"

I had them at "porn," but now I had to keep them.

"Look at your tenancy agreement: you're paying twenty-seven bucks a month for your network access at the Termite Mound. Twenty-seven bucks—each! I'll find us an ISP that can give all of us hot and cold running genitals and all the unsavory religious extremism, online gaming, and suicide instructions we can eat. Either I'm going to make the Termite Mound give us the Internet we deserve, or we'll cost it one of its biggest cash cows and humiliate it on the world stage.

"I don't want your money. All I want is for you to promise me that if I can get us Internet from someone who isn't a censoring sack of shit, that you'll come with me. I'm going to sign up every poor bastard in the Termite Mound, take that promise to someone who isn't afraid to work hard to earn a dollar, and punish the Termite Mound for treating us like this. And *then*, I'm going to make a loud noise about what we've done and spread the word to every other residence in Cambridge, then Boston, then across America. I'm going to spread out to airports, hotels, train stations, buses, taxis—any place where they make it their business to decide what data we're allowed to see."

I whirled around to face the elf, who leaped back, long fingers flying to his face in an elaborate mime of startlement. "Are you with me, pal?"

He nodded slightly.

"Come on," I said. "Let 'em hear you."

He raised one arm over his head, bits of rabbit fur and uncured hides dangling from his skinny wrist. I felt for him. I think we all did. Elves.

He was a convincer, though. By the time I left the room, I already had twenty-nine signups.

All evil in the world is the result of an imbalance between the people who benefit from shenanigans and the people who get screwed by shenanigans.

De-shenaniganifying the world is the answer to pollution and poverty and bad schools and the war on some drugs and a million other horribles. To solve all the world's problems, I need kick-ass raw feeds and a steady supply of doofus thugs from central casting to make idiots of. I know where I can find plenty of the latter, and I'm damn sure going to get the former. Watch me.

My advisor is named Andronicus Andronicus Llewellyn, and her parents had a sense of humor, clearly. She founded the *Networks That Change* lab three years ago after she fled Uzbekistan one step ahead of Gulnara's death squad, but they say that she still provides material aid to the army of babushkas that underwent forced sterilization under old man Karimov's brutal regime. Her husband, Arzu, lost an eye in Gezi. They're kind of a Twitter-uprising power couple.

I'm the only undergrad in the lab, and the grad students were slavering at the thought of having a bottle-washing dogsbody in residence. Someone to clean out the spam filters, lexically normalize the grant proposals, deworm the Internet of things, get the limescale out of the espresso machine, and defragment the lab's prodigious store of detritus, kipple, and moop.

Two days after telling them all where they could stick it, I got a meeting in AA's cube.

"Sit down, Lukasz," she said. My birth certificate read "Lucas," but I relished the extra consonant. I perched on a tensegrity chair that had been some grad student's laser-cutter thesis project. It creaked like a haunted attic, and its white acrylic struts were grubby as a snowbank a day after the salting trucks. AA's chair was patched with steel tape, huge black cocoony gobs of it. And it still creaked.

I waited patiently. My drop was in my overalls' marsupial pouch, and I stuffed my hands in there, curling my fingers around it and kneading it. It comforted me. AA closed the door.

"Do you know why my lab doesn't have any undergrads?" she asked. I gave it another moment to test for rhetoricalness, timed out, then gave it a shot. "You don't want to screw around with getting someone up to speed. You want to get the work done."

"Don't be stupid. Grad students need as much hand-holding as undergrads. No, it's because undergrads are full of the dramas. And the dramas are not good for getting the work done."

"Andronicus," I said, "I'm not the one you should be talking to—" I felt a flush creeping up my neck—"*they*—"

She fixed me with a look that froze my tongue and dried the spit in my mouth. "I spent four years in Jaslyk Prison in Uzbekistan. Three of my cellmates committed suicide. One of them bled out on me from the top bunk while I slept. I woke covered in her blood." She looked at her screen, snagged her attention on it, ignored me for a minute while she typed furiously. Turned back. "What did your lab mates do, Lukasz, that you would like to talk to me about?"

"Nothing," I mumbled. I hated being dismissed like this. Of course, she could trump anything I was inclined to complain about. But it was so . . . *invalidating.*

"Never forget that there is blood in the world's veins, Lukasz. You've done something clever with your years on this planet. You're here to see if you can figure out how to do something important, now. We want to systematize the struggle here, figure out how to automate it, but eventually there will always be blood. You need to learn to be dispassionate about the interpersonal conflicts, to save your anger for the people who deserve it, and to channel that anger into a theory of action that leads to change. Otherwise, you will be an undergraduate who worries about being picked on."

"I know," I said. "I know. Sorry."

She held out a hand to stop me fleeing. "Lukasz, there is change to be had out there. It waits for us to discover its fulcrums. That's the research project here. But the reason for the research is the change. It's to be the bag of blood in the streets or the boardroom or the prison. That's what you're learning to do here."

I didn't say anything. She turned back to her screen. Her fingers beat the keyboard. I left.

I pretended not to notice three of AA's grad students hastily switching off their infrared laser-pointers as I opened her glass door and walked back out to the lab. Everyone, including AA, knew that they'd been listening in, but the formal characteristics of our academic kabuki required us all to pretend that I'd just had a private conversation.

I pulled my laptop out of my bag and uncrumpled its bent corners. I'd only made it a week before, and I didn't have time or energy to fold up another one. It was getting pretty battered in my bag, though; the waxed cardboard shell getting more worn and creased in less time than ever before. Not even my most extreme couchsurfing voyages had been this hard on my essential equipment. The worst part was that the keyboard surface had gotten really smashed—I think I'd closed up the box with a Sharpie trapped inside it—so the camera that watched my fingers as they typed the letters printed on the cardboard sheet was having a hard time getting the registration right. I'd mashed the spot where the backspace was drawn so many times that I'd worn the ink off and had to redraw it (more Sharpie, a cardboard laptop owner's best friend).

Now the screen was starting to go. The little short-throw projector attached to the pinhead-sized computer taped inside the back of the box

was misreading the geometry of the mirror it bounced the screen image off
of, which keystoned and painted the image on the rice paper scrim set into
the laptop's top half. The image was only off by about ten degrees, but it was
enough to screw up the touch screen registration and give me a mild headache after only a couple hours of staring at it. I'd noticed that a lot of the MIT
kids carried big plastic and metal and glass laptops, which had seemed like
some kind of weird retro affectation. But campus life was more of an off-road
experience than I'd suspected.

I spent fifteen minutes unfolding the laser-cut cardboard and smoothing
out the creases, resticking everything with fiber tape from an office supply
table in the middle of the lab, and then running through the registration and
diagnostics built into the OS until the computer was in a usable state again.
The whole time, I was hotly conscious of the grad students' sneaky gaze, the
weird clacking noise of their fingers on real mechanical keyboards—seriously,
who used a keyboard that was made of *pieces* anymore; was I really going to
have to do that?—as they chatted about me.

Yes, about me. It's not (just) ego; I could tell. I can prove it. I was barely
back up and running and answering all my social telephones when some
dudeface from Chiapas sat down conspicuously next to me and said, "It's
Lukasz, right?" He held out his hand.

I looked at it for a moment, just to make the point, then shook. "Yeah.
You're Juanca, right?" Of course he was Juanca. He'd been burned in effigy
by Zetas every year for four years, and his entire family, all the way to third
cousins, were either stateside or in Guatemala or El Salvador, hiding out
from narcoterrorists, who were still pissed about Juanca's anonymizer, a
mix master that was the Number One, go-to source of convictable evidence
against Zeta members whose cases went to trial. If it weren't for the fact that
Juanca's network had also busted an assload of corrupt cops, prosecutors,
judges, government ministers, regional governors, and one secretary of state,
they'd have given him a ministerial posting and a medal. As it was, he was
in exile. Famous. Loved. It helped that he was rakishly handsome—which
I am not, for the record—and that he had a bounty on his head and had
been unsuccessfully kidnapped on the T, getting away through some badass
parkour that got captured in CCTV jittercam that made him look like he was
moving in a series of short teleports.

"Yeah. You got the blood speech, huh?"

I nodded.

"It's a good one," he said. I didn't think so. I thought it was bullshit. I didn't
say so.

We stared at each other. "Welp," he said. "Take it easy."

• • •

One of the early *Ftp* code contributors was now CTO for an ISP, and they'd gotten their start as a dorm co-op at Brown that had metastasized across New England. Sanjay had been pretty important to the early days of *Ftp*, helping us get the virtualization right so that it could run on pretty much any cloud without a lot of jiggery and/or pokery. Within a day of e-mailing Sanjay, I was having coffee with the vice president of business development for Miskatonic Networks, who was also Sanjay's boyfriend's girlfriend because apparently ISPs in New England are hotbeds of Lovecraft-fandom polyamory. Her name was Khadijah, and she had a Southie accent so thick it was like an amateur theater production of *Good Will Hunting*.

"The Termite Mound?" She laughed. "Shit, yeah, I know that place. It's still standing? I went to some super-sketchy parties there when I was a kid; I mean soooooper-sketchy, like sketch-a-roony. I can't believe no one's torched the place yet."

"Not yet," I said. "And seeing as all my stuff's there right now, I'm hoping that no one does for the time being."

"Yeah, I can see that." I could *not* get over her accent. It was the most Bostonian thing I'd encountered since I got off the train. "Okay, so you want to know what we'd charge to provide service to someone at the Termite Mound?"

"Uh, no. I want to know what you'd charge per person if we could get you the whole mound—every unit in the residence. All two hundred and fifty of them."

"Oh." She paused a second. "This is an *Ftp* thing, right?"

"Yeah," I said. "That's how I know Sanjay. I, uh, I started *Ftp*." I don't like to brag, but sometimes it makes sense in the context of the conversation, right?

"That was you? Wicked! So you're seriously gonna get the whole dorm to sign up with us?"

"I will if you can get me a price that I can sell to them," I said.

"Oh," she said. Then "Oh! Right. Hmm. Leave it with me. You say you can get them all signed up?"

"I think so. If the price is right. And I think that if the Termite Mound goes with you that there'll be other dorms that'll follow. Maybe a lab or two," I said. I was talking out of my ass at this point, but seriously, net-censorship in the labs at *MIT*? It was disgusting. It could not stand.

"Damn," she said. "Sounds like you're majoring in *Ftp*. Don't you have classes or something?"

"No," I said. "This is basically exactly what I figured college would be like. A cross between summer camp and a Stanford obedience experiment. If all I wanted to do was cram a bunch of *knowledge* into my head, I could have stayed home and mooced it. I came here because I wanted to level up and fight something tough and even dangerous. I want to spend four years getting into the right kind of trouble. Going to classes, too, but seriously, *classes*? Whatever. Everyone knows the good conversations happen in the hallway between the formal presentations. Classes are just an excuse to have hallways."

She looked skeptical and ate banana bread.

"It's your deal," she said.

I could hear the *but* hanging in the air between us. She got more coffees and brought them back, along with toasted banana bread dripping with butter for me. She wouldn't let me pay and told me it was on Miskatonic. We were a potential big account. She didn't want to say "*but*" because she might offend me. I wanted to hear the "*but.*"

"But?"

"But what?"

"It's my deal but . . . ?"

"But, well, you know, you don't look after your grades, MIT'll put you out on your ass. That's how it works in college. I've seen it."

I chewed my banana bread.

"Hey," she said. "Hey. Are you okay, Lukasz?"

"I'm fine," I said.

She smiled at me. She was pretty. "But?"

I told her about my talk with AA, and about Juanca, and about how I felt like nobody was giving me my propers, and she looked very sympathetic, in a way that made me feel much younger. Like toddler younger.

"MIT is all about pranks, right? I think if I could come up with something really epic, they'd—" And as I said it, I realized how dumb it was. *They laughed at me in Vienna, I'll show them!* "You know what? Forget about it. I got more important things to do than screw around with those knob-ends. Work to do, right? Get the network opened up around here, you and me, Khadijah!"

"I'll get back to you soon, okay?"

I fished a bead out of my pocket and wedged it into my ear.

"Who is this?"

"Lukasz?" The voice was choked with tears.

"Who is this?" I said again.

"It's Bryan." I couldn't place the voice or the name.

"Bryan who?"

"From the Termite Mound's customer service desk." Then I recognized the voice. It was the elf, and he was having hysterics. Part of me wanted to say, *Oh, diddums!* and hang up. Because elves, AMR? But I'm not good at tough love.

"What's wrong?"

"They've fired me," he said. "I got called into my boss's office an hour ago, and he told me to start drawing up a list of people to kick out of the dorm.

He wanted the names of people who supported you. I was supposed to go through the EULAs for the dorm and find some violations for all of them—"

"What if they didn't have any violations?"

He made a sound between a sob and a laugh. "Are you kidding? You're always in violation! Have you read the EULA for the mound? It's, like, sixty pages long."

"OK, gotcha. So you refused and you got fired?"

There was a pause. It drew out. "No," he said, his voice barely a whisper. "I gave them a bunch of names, and *then* they fired me."

Again, I was torn between the impulse to hang up on him and to hear more. Nosiness won (nosiness always wins; bets on nosiness are a sure thing). "Nicely done. Sounds like just deserts to me. What do you expect me to do about it?" But I knew. There were only two reasons to call me after something like this: to confess his sins or to get revenge. And no one would ever mistake me for a priest.

"I've got the names they pulled. Not just this time. Every time there's been any kind of trouble in the Termite Mound, MIT Residence has turfed out the troublemakers on some bogus EULA violation. They know that no one cares about student complaints, and there's always a waiting list for rooms at the Termite Mound, it's so central and all. I kept records."

"What kind of records?"

"Hard copies of e-mails. They used disappearing ink for all the dirty stuff, but I just took pictures of my screen with my drop and saved it to personal storage. It's ugly. They went after pregnant girls, kids with disabilities. Any time there was a chance they'd have to do an air-quality audit or fix a ramp, I'd have to find some reason to violate the tenant out of residence." He paused a moment. "They used some pretty bad language when they talked about these people, too."

The Termite Mound should've been called the Roach Motel: turn on the lights and you'd find a million scurrying bottom-feeders running for the baseboards.

I was going to turn on the lights.

"You've got all that, huh?"

"Tons of it," he said. "Going back three years. I knew that if it ever got out that they'd try and blame it on me. I wanted records."

"Okay," I said. "Meet me in Harvard Square, by the T entrance. How soon can you get there?"

"I'm at the Coop right now," he said. "Using a study booth."

"Perfect," I said. "Five minutes, then?"

"I'm on my way."

The Coop's study booths had big signs warning that everything you did there was recorded—sound, video, infrared, data—and filtered for illicit behavior. The signs explained that there was no human being looking at the records unless you did something to trip the algorithm, like that made it better. If a tree falls in the forest, it sure as shit makes a sound; and if your conversation is bugged, it's bugged—whether or not a human being listens in right then or at some time in the infinite future of that data.

I beat him to the T entrance and looked around for a place to talk. It wasn't good. From where I stood, I could see dozens of cameras, the little button-sized dots discreetly placed all around the square, each with a little scannable code you could use to find out who got the footage and what its policy was. No one ever bothered to do this. Ever. EULAs were not written for human consumption: a EULA's message could always be boiled down to seven words: "ABANDON HOPE, ALL YE WHO ENTER HERE." Or, more succinctly: "YOU LOSE."

I felt bad about Bryan's job. It was his own deal, of course. He'd stayed even after he knew how evil they were. And I hadn't held a gun to his head and made him put himself in the firing line. But, of course, I had convinced him to. I had led him to. I felt bad.

Bryan turned up just as I was scouting a spot at an outdoor table by an ice cream parlor. They had a bunch of big blowing heaters that'd do pretty good white-noise masking, a good light/dark contrast between the high-noon sun and the shade of the awning that would screw up cameras' white-balance, and the heaters would wreak havoc on the infrared range of the CCTVs, or so I hoped. I grabbed Bryan, clamping down on his skinny arm through the rough weave of his forest-green cloak and dragged him to my chosen spot.

"You got it?" I said, once we were both seated and nursing hot chocolates. I got caffeinated marshmallows; he got Thai ghost-pepper-flavored, though that was mostly marketing. No way those marshmallows were over a couple thousand Scovilles.

"I encrypted it with your public key," he said, handing me a folded-up paper. I unfolded it and saw that it had been printed with a stegoed QR code, hidden in a Victorian woodcut. That kind of spycraft was pretty weak sauce—the two-dee-barcode-in-a-public-domain-image thing was a staple of shitty student click-bait thrillers—but if he'd really managed to get my public key and verify it and then encrypt the blob with it, I was impressed. That was about ten million times more secure than the average fumbledick ever managed. The fact that he'd handed me a hard copy of the URL instead of e-mailing it to me, well, that was pretty sweet frosting. Bryan had potential.

I folded the paper away. "What should I be looking for?"

"It's all organized and tagged. You'll see." He looked nervous. "What are you going to do with it?"

"Well, for starters, I'm going to call them up and tell them I have it."

"*What*?" He looked like he was going to cry.

"Come on," I said. "I'm not going to tell them where I got it. The way you tell it, I'm about to get evicted, right?"

"Technically, you *are* evicted. There's a process server waiting at every entrance to the Termite Mound doing face recognition on the whole list. Soon as you go home, bam. Forty-eight hours to clear out."

"Right," I said. "I don't want to have to go look for a place to live while I'm also destroying these shitbirds *and* fixing everyone's Internet connection. Get serious. So I'm going to go and talk to Messrs. Amoral, Nonmoral, and Immoral and explain that I have a giant dump of compromising messages from them that I'm going public with, and it'll look really, really bad for them if they turf me out now."

It's time for a true confession. I am not nearly as brave as I front. All this spycraft stuff, all the bluster about beating these guys on their home turf, yeah, in part I'm into it. I like it better than riding through life like a foil chip-bag being swept down a polluted stream on a current of raw sewage during a climate-change-driven superstorm.

But the reality is that I can't really help myself. There's some kind of rot-fungus that infects the world. Things that are good when they're small and personal grow, and as they grow, their attack surface grows with them, and they get more and more colonized by the fungus, making up stupid policies, doing awful stuff to the people who rely on them and the people who work for them, one particle of fungus at a time, each one just a tiny and totally defensible atomic-sized spoor of rot that piles up and gloms onto all the other bits of rot until you're a walking, suppurating lesion.

No one ever set out to create the kind of organization that needs to post a "MIT RESIDENCY LLC OPERATES A ZERO-TOLERANCE POLICY TOWARD EMPLOYEE ABUSE. YOU CAN BE FINED UP TO $2,000 AND/OR IMPRISONED FOR SIX MONTHS FOR ASSAULTING A CAMPUS RESIDENCE WORKER" sign. You start out trying to do something good, then you realize you can get a little richer by making it a little worse. Your thermostat for shittiness gets reset to the new level, so it doesn't seem like much of a change to turn it a notch further toward the rock-bottom, irredeemably shitty end of the scale.

The truth is that you can get really rich and huge by playing host organism to the rot-fungus. The rot-fungus diffuses its harms and concentrates its rewards. That means that healthy organisms that haven't succumbed to the rot-fungus are liable to being devoured by giant, well-funded vectors for it. Think of the great local business that gets devoured by an awful hedge fund in a leveraged takeover, looted, and left as a revolting husk to shamble on until it collapses under its own weight.

I am terrified of the rot-fungus because it seems like I'm the only person who notices it most of the time. Think of all those places where the town council falls all over itself to lure some giant corporation to open a local factory. Don't they notice that everyone who works at places like that hates every single moment of every single day? Haven't they ever tried to converse with the customer-service bots run by one of those lumbering dinos?

I mean, sure, the bigs have giant budgets and they'll take politicians out for nice lunches and throw a lot of money at their campaigns, but don't these guardians of the public trust ever try to get their cars fixed under warranty? Don't they ever buy a train ticket? Don't they ever eat at a fast-food joint? Can't they smell the rot-fungus? Am I the only one? I've figured out how to fight it in my own way. Everyone else who's fighting seems to be fighting against something *else*—injustice or inequality or whatever, without understanding that the fungus's rot is what causes all of those things.

I'm convinced that no normal human being ever woke up one morning and said, "Dammit, my life doesn't have enough petty bureaucratic rules, zero-tolerance policies, censorship, and fear in it. How do I fix that?" Instead, they let this stuff pile up, one compromise at a time, building up huge sores suppurating with spore-loaded fluids that eventually burst free and beslime everything around them. It gets normal to them, one dribble at a time.

"Lukasz, you don't know what you're doing. These guys, they're—"

"What?" I said. "Are they the Mafia or something? Are they going to have me dropped off a bridge with cement overshoes?"

He shook his head, making the twigs and beads woven into the downy fluff of his hair clatter together. "No, but they're ruthless. I mean, totally ruthless. They're not normal."

The way he said it twinged something in my hindbrain, some little squiggle of fear, but I pushed it away. "Yeah, that's okay. I'm used to abnormal." I am the most abnormal person I know.

"Be careful, seriously," he said.

"Thanks, Bryan," I said. "Don't worry about me. You want me to try and get your room back, too?"

He chewed his lip. "Don't," he said. "They'll know it was me if you do that."

I resisted the urge to shout at him to grow a spine. These assholes had cost him his home and his job (okay, I'd helped), and he was going to couchsurf it until he could find the rarest of treasures: an affordable place to live in Cambridge, Massachusetts? Even if he was being tortured by his conscience for all his deplorable sellout-ism, he was still being a total wuss. But that was his deal. I mean, he was an *elf*, for chrissakes. Who knew what he was thinking?

"Suit yourself," I said, and went and made some preparations.

• • •

Messrs. Amoral, Nonmoral, and Immoral had an office over the river in Boston, in a shabby office block that only had ten floors but whose company directory listed over eight hundred businesses. I knew the kind of place because they showed up whenever some hairy scam unraveled and they showed you the office-of-convenience used by the con artists who'd destroyed something that lots of people cared about and loved in order to make a small number of bad people a little richer. A kind of breeding pit for rot-fungus, in other words.

At first, I thought I was going to have to go and sleuth their real locations, but I saw that Amoral, Nonmoral, and Immoral had the entire third floor registered to them, while everyone else had crazy-ass, heavily qualified suite numbers like 401c(1)K, indicating some kind of internal routing code for the use of the army of rot-fungus-infected spores who ensured that correspondence was handled in a way that preserved the illusion that each of the multifarious, blandly named shell companies (I swear to Cthulhu that there was one called "International Holdings [Holdings], Ltd") was a real going concern and not a transparent ruse intended to allow the rot-fungus to spread with maximal diffusion of culpability for the carriers who did its bidding.

I punched #300# on the ancient touch screen intercom, its surface begrimed with a glossy coat of hardened DNA, Burger King residue, and sifted-down dust of the ages. It blatted like an angry sheep, once, twice, three times, then disconnected. I punched again. Again. On the fourth try, an exasperated, wheezing voice emerged: "What?"

"I'm here to speak to someone from MIT Residences LLC."

"Send an e-mail."

"I'm a tenant. My name is Lukasz Romero." I let that sink in. "I've got some documents I'd like to discuss with a responsible individual at MIT Residences LLC." I put a bit of heavy English on *documents*. "Please." I put even more English on *please*. I've seen the same tough-guy videos that you have, and I can do Al Pacinoid-overwound, dangerous dude as well as anyone. "Please," I said again, meaning *right now*.

There was an elongated and ominous pause, punctuated by muffled rustling and grumbling, and what may have been typing on an old-fashioned, mechanical keyboard. "Come up," a different voice said. The elevator to my left ground as the car began to lower itself.

I'd expected something sinister—a peeling dungeon of a room where old men with armpit stains gnawed haunches of meat and barked obscenities at each other. Instead, I found myself in an airy, high-ceilinged place that was straight out of the publicity shots for MIT's best labs, the ones that had been set-dressed by experts who'd ensured that no actual students had come in to mess things up before the photographer could get a beautifully lit shot of the platonic perfection.

The room took up the whole floor, dotted with conversation pits with worn, comfortable sofas whose end tables sported inconspicuous charge-plates for power-hungry gadgets. The rest of the space was made up of new-looking work surfaces and sanded-down antique wooden desks that emitted the honeyed glow of a thousand coats of wax buffed by decades of continuous use. The light came from tall windows and full-spectrum spotlights that were reflected and diffused off the ceiling, which was bare concrete and mazed with cable trays and conduits. I smelled good coffee and toasting bread and saw a perfectly kept little kitchenette to my left.

There were perhaps a dozen people working in the room, standing at the work surfaces, mousing away at the antique desks, or chatting intensely in the conversation pits. It was a kind of perfect tableau of industrious tech-company life, something out of a recruiting video. The people were young and either beautiful or handsome or both. I had the intense, unexpected desire to work here, or a place like this. It had good *vibes*.

One of the young, handsome people stood up from his conversation nook and smoothed out the herringbone wool hoodie he was wearing, an artfully cut thing that managed to make him look like both a young professor and an undergraduate at the same time. It helped that he was so fresh-faced, with apple cheeks and a shock of curly brown hair.

"Lukasz, right?" He held out a hand. He was wearing a dumbwatch, a wind-up thing in a steel casing that was fogged with a century of scratches. I coveted it instantly; though I knew nothing about its particulars, I was nevertheless certain that it was expensive, beautifully engineered, and extremely rare.

The door closed behind me, and the magnet audibly reengaged. The rest of the people in the room studiously ignored us.

"I'm Sergey. Can I get you a cup of coffee? Tea? Some water?"

The coffee smelled *good*. "No, thank you," I said. "I don't think I'll be here for long."

"Of course. Come and sit."

The other participants in his meeting had already vacated the sofas and left us with a conversation pit all to ourselves. I sank into the sofa and smelled the spicy cologne of a thousand eager, well-washed people who'd sat on it before me, impregnating the upholstery with the spoor of their good perfumes.

He picked up a small red enamel teapot and poured a delicious-smelling stream of yellow-green steaming liquid into a chunky diner-style coffee cup. He sipped it. My stomach growled. "You told the receptionist you wanted to talk about some documents?"

"Yeah," I said, pulling myself together. "I've got documentary evidence of this company illegally evicting tenants—students—who got pregnant, complained about substandard living conditions and maintenance issues, and, in my case, complained about the network filters at the Termite Mound."

He cocked his head for a moment like he was listening for something in the hum and murmur of the office around him. I found myself listening, too, but try as I might, I couldn't pick out a single individual voice from the buzz, not even a lone intelligible word. It was as though they were all going "murmurmurmurmur," though I could see their lips moving and shaping what must have been words.

"Ah," he said at last. "Well, that's very unfortunate. Can you give me a set and I'll escalate them up our chain to ensure that they're properly dealt with?"

"I can give you a set," I said. "But I'll also be giving a set to the MIT ombudsman and the *Tech* and the local WikiLeaks Party rep. Sergey, forgive me, but you don't seem to be taking this very seriously. The material in my possession is the sort of thing that could get you and your colleagues here sued into a smoking crater."

"Oh, I appreciate that there's a lot of potential liability in the situation you describe, but it wouldn't be rational for me to freak out now, would it? I haven't seen your documents, and if I had, I could neither authenticate them nor evaluate the risk they represent. So I'll take a set from you and ensure that the people within our organization who have the expertise to manage this sort of thing get to them quickly."

It's funny. I'd anticipated that he'd answer like a chatbot, vomiting up Markov-chained nothings from the lexicon of the rot-fungus: "we take this very seriously"; "we cannot comment on ongoing investigations"; "we are actioning this with a thorough inquiry and post-mortem" and other similar crapola. Instead, he was talking like a hacker on a mailing list defending the severity he'd assigned to a bug he owned.

"Sergey, that's not much of an answer."

He sipped that delicious tea some more. "Is there something in particular you wanted to hear from me? I mean, this isn't the sort of thing that you find out about, then everything stops until you've figured out what to do next."

I was off-balance. "I wanted—" I waved my hands. "I wanted an explanation. How the hell did this systematic abuse come about?"

He shrugged. He really didn't seem very worried "Hard to say, really. Maybe it was something out of the labs."

"What do you mean, 'the labs'?"

He gestured vaguely at one cluster of particularly engrossed young men and women who were bent over screens and work surfaces, arranged in pairs or threesomes, collaborating with fierce intensity, reaching over to touch each other's screens and keyboards in a way I found instantly and deeply unsettling.

"We've got a little R&D lab that works on some of our holdings. We're really dedicated to disrupting the rental market. There's so much money in it, you know, but mostly it's run by these entitled jerks who think that they're geniuses for having the brilliant idea of buying a building and then sitting around and charging rent on it. A real old boys' club." For the first time since we started talking, he really seemed to be alive and present and paying attention.

"Oh, they did some bits and pieces that gave them the superficial appearance of having a brain, but there's a lot of difference between A/B—splitting your acquisition strategy and really deep-diving into the stuff that matters."

At this stage, I experienced a weird dissonance. I mean, I was there because these people were doing something genuinely villainous, real rot-fungus stuff. On the other hand, well, this sounded cool. I can't lie. I found it interesting. I mean, catnip-interesting.

"I mean, chewy questions. Like, if the median fine for a second citation for substandard plumbing is four hundred dollars, and month-on-month cost for plumbing maintenance in a given building is two thousand dollars a month, and the long-term costs of failure to maintain are twenty thousand dollars for full replumbing on an eight- to ten-year basis with a seventy-five percent probability of having to do the big job in year nine, what are the tenancy parameters that maximize your return over that period?"

"Tenancy parameters?"

He looked at me. I was being stupid. I don't like that look. I suck at it. It's an ego thing. I just find it super-hard to deal with other people thinking that I'm dumb. I would probably get more done in this world if I didn't mind it so much. But I do. It's an imperfect world, and I am imperfect.

"Tenancy parameters. What are the parameters of a given tenant that predict whether he or she will call the city inspectors given some variable set point of substandard plumbing, set on a scale that has been validated through a rigorous regression through the data that establishes quantifiable inflection points relating to differential and discrete maintenance issues, including leaks, plugs, pressure, hot-water temperature and volume, and so on. It's basically just a solve-for-X question, but it's one with a lot of details in the model that are arrived at through processes with a lot of room for error, so the model needs a lot of refinement and continuous iteration.

"And, of course, it's all highly sensitive to external conditions. There's a whole game-theoretical set of questions about what other large-scale renters do in response to our own actions, and there's an information-theory dimension to this that's, well, it's amazing. Like, which elements of our strategy are telegraphed when we take certain actions as opposed to others, and how can those be steganographed through other apparent strategies?

"Now, most of these questions we can answer through pretty straightforward business processes, stuff that Amazon figured out twenty years ago. But there's a real risk of getting stuck in local maxima, just you know, overoptimizing inside of one particular paradigm with some easy returns. That's just reinventing the problem, though, making us into tomorrow's dinosaurs.

"If we're going to operate a culture of continuous improvement, we need to be internally disrupted to at least the same extent that we're disrupting those fat, stupid incumbents. That's why we have the labs. They're our chaos monkeys. They do all kinds of stuff that keeps our own models sharp. For example, they might incorporate a separate business and use our proprietary IP to try to compete with us—without telling us about it. Or give a set of autonomous agents privileges to communicate eviction notices in a way that causes a certain number of lawsuits to be filed, just to validate our assumptions about the pain point at which an action or inaction on our side will trigger a suit from a tenant, especially for certain profiles of tenants.

"So there's not really any way that I can explain specifically what happened to the people mentioned in your correspondence. It's possible no one will ever be able to say with total certainty. I don't really know why anyone would expect it to be otherwise. We're not a deterministic state machine, after all. If all we did was respond in set routines to set inputs, it'd be trivial to innovate around us and put us out of business. Our objective is to be strategically nonlinear and anti-deterministic within a range of continuously validated actions that map and remap a chaotic terrain of profitable activities in relation to property and rental. We're not rentiers, you understand. We don't own assets for a living. *We do things with them*. We're doing commercial science that advances the state of the art. We're discovering deep truths lurking in potentia in the shape of markets and harnessing them—putting them to work."

His eyes glittered. "Lukasz, you come in here with your handful of memos and you ask me to explain how they came about, as though this whole enterprise was a state machine that we control. We do not control the enterprise. An enterprise is an artificial life form built up from people and systems in order to minimize transaction costs so that it can be nimble and responsive, so that it can move into niches, dominate them, fully explore them. The human species has spent millennia recombining its institutions to uncover the deep, profound mathematics of power and efficiency.

"It's a terrain with a lot of cul-de-sacs and blind alleys. There are local maxima: maybe a three-move look-ahead shows a good outcome from evicting someone who's pregnant and behind on the rent, but the six-move picture is different because someone like you comes along and makes us look like total assholes. That's fine. All that means is that we have to prune that branch of the tree, try a new direction. Hell, ideally, you'd be in there so early, and give us such a thoroughgoing kicking, that we'd be able to discover and abort the misfire before the payload had fully deployed. You'd be saving us opportunity cost. You'd be part of our chaos monkey.

"Lukasz, you come in here with your whistleblower memos. But I'm not participating in a short-term exercise. Our mission here is to quantize, systematize, harness, and perfect interactions. You want me to explain, right now, what we're going to do about your piece of information. Here's your answer, Lukasz: we will integrate it. We will create models that incorporate disprovable hypotheses about it; we will test those models; and we will refine them. We will make your documents part of our inventory of clues about the underlying nature of deep reality. Does that answer satisfy you, Lukasz?"

I stood up. Through the whole monologue, Sergey's eyes had not moved from mine, nor had his body language shifted, nor had he demonstrated one glimmer of excitement or passion. Instead, he'd been matter-of-fact, like he'd been explaining the best way to make an omelet or the optimal public transit route to a distant suburb. I was used to people geeking out about the stuff they did. I'd never experienced this before, though: it was the opposite of geeking out, or maybe a geeking out that went so deep that it went through passion and came out the other side.

It scared me. I'd encountered many different versions of hidebound authoritarianism, fought the rot-fungus in many guises, but this was not like anything I'd ever seen. It had a purity that was almost seductive.

But beautiful was not the opposite of terrible. The two could easily co-exist.

"I hear that I'm going to get evicted when I get back to the Termite Mound. You've got a process server waiting for me. That's what I hear."

Sergey shrugged. "And?"

"And? And what use is your deep truth to me if I'm out on the street?"

"What's your point?"

He was as mild and calm as a recorded airport safety announcement. There was something inhuman—transhuman?—in that dispassionate mien.

"Don't kick me out of my place."

"Ah. Excuse me a second."

He finished his tea, set the cup down, and headed over to the lab. He chatted with them, touched their screens. The murmur drowned out any words. I didn't try to disguise the fact that I was watching them. There was a long period during which they said nothing, did not touch anything, just stared at the screens with their heads so close together they were almost touching. It was a kind of pantomime of psychic communications.

He came back. "Done," he said. "Is there anything else? We're pretty busy around here."

"Thank you," I said. "No, that's about it."

"All right then," he said. "Are you going to leave me your documents?"

"Yes," I said, and passed him a stack of hard copies. He looked at the paper for a moment, folded the stack carefully in the middle and put it in one of the wide side pockets of his beautifully tailored cardigan.

I found my way back down to the ground floor and was amazed to see that the sun was still up. It had felt like hours had passed while Sergey talked to me, and I could have sworn that the light had faded in those tall windows. But, checking my drop, I saw that it was only three o'clock. I had to be getting home.

There was a process server waiting ostentatiously in the walkway when I got home, but he looked at me and then down at his screen and then let me pass.

It was only once I was in my room that I realized I hadn't done anything about Bryan's eviction.

Kadijah didn't buy the coffee this time. And I bought my own banana bread.

"I met that Sergey dude," she said.

"Creepy, huh?"

She blew on her coffee. She drank it black. "Wicked smart, I think. And it looks like he's got your number."

Kadijah heard about the mass evictions through the *Ftp;* she'd been watching it carefully. When she messaged me, I assumed that she was outraged on all our behalf. She'd made an offer of free, uncensored connectivity for six months for everyone in the Termite Mound *and* everyone who'd been evicted. But she'd met Sergey? "He's scary, too," she said as an afterthought. "But scary smart."

I'd been taking Miskatonic as an existence proof of a part of the world that the rot-fungus had not yet colonized. But afterward, I found myself turning our conversation over and over in my head. Yes, maybe she had offered all that great, free, uncensored Internet goodness because she was outraged by the dirty tricks campaign. But maybe she was doing it because she knew that *appearing* outraged would make her—and her company—seem like the kind of nice people to whom we should all give more money. Maybe they don't give a damn about *Ftp* or fairness or eviction. Maybe it's just an elaborate game of sound bites and kabuki gestures that are all calibrated to the precise sociopathic degree necessary to convey empathy and ethics without ever descending into either. She hadn't bought the coffee or the banana bread.

It's easy to slip into this kind of metacognitive reverie and hard to stop once you start. Now I found myself questioning my own motives, scouring my subconscious for evidence of ego, self-promotion, and impurity.

The thing was.

The thing was.

The thing *was* that I had not ever met someone like Sergey before. Sergey, who'd shown me something glittering and cool and vast that waited for us to realize it and bring it to perfection. Sergey, who'd both understood the collective action problem and found it to be secondary, a thing to solve on the way to solving something bigger and more important.

Sergey's words had awoken in me a feverish curiosity, an inability to see the world as it had once been. And I hated the feeling. It was the sense that my worldview had come adrift, all my certainty calving off like an iceberg and floating away to sea. If you accepted Sergey's idea, then the human race was just the symbiotic intestinal flora of a meta-organism that would use us up and crap us out as needed. The global networks that allowed us to organize ourselves more efficiently were so successful because they let businesses run their supply chains more efficiently, and all the socializing and entertainment and chatter were just a side effect. *Ftp* was a mild pathogen, a few stray harmful bacteria in the colon of the corporate over-organism, and if it ever got to the point where it was any kind of real threat, the antibodies would show up to tear it to parts so it could be flushed away.

In other words, *I* was the rot-fungus. Everything I did, everything I'd done, was an infection, and not even a very successful one.

Christmas break arrived quicker than I'd have guessed. Bryan and his girlfriend had me over to their new place for dinner during the last week of classes. She was an elf, too, of course, and their place was all mossy rocks and driftwood and piles of leaves. The food was about what you'd expect, but it was better than the slurry I'd been gulping at my desk while I wrestled with my term assignments and crammed for exams.

The Internet access at the Termite Mound was now uncensored, but I still found myself working at the lab. There was something comforting about being around my lab mates instead of huddling alone in my dorm room.

Bryan's girlfriend, Lana, was in mechanical engineering and she made some pretty great-looking mobiles, which dangled and spun around the tiny studio, their gyrations revealing the hidden turbulence of our exhalations. Every time I moved, I whacked one or another of them, making their payloads of mossy rocks and artful twigs clatter together. The floor was littered with their shed dander, which I took to be a deliberate act of elfy-welfy feng shui.

"So, how's things at the Termite Mound?" Bryan asked as we wound down over a glass of floral mead, which is pretty terrible, even by the standards of elf cuisine.

It was the question that had hung over the whole evening. After all, I'd cost Bryan his home and his job and had walked away scot-free.

"Yeah," I said. "Well, the city and the university are both investigating MIT Residences LLC, and it looks like they're going to be paying some pretty big fines. There was a class-action lawyer hanging around out front last week, trying to track down the old tenants who'd been turfed out. So there's going to be some more bad road ahead of them."

"Good," he said, with feeling. The expression of rage and bitterness that crossed his face was not elfin in the slightest. It was the face of someone who'd been screwed over and knew he had no chance of ever getting back at his attackers.

"Yeah," I said again. The class-action guy had really been a gut punch for me. Class action was so *old school*, the thing that *Ftp* was supposed to replace with something fast, nimble, networked, and collective. Class action was all about bottom-feeding lawyers slurping up the screwed-over like krill and making a meal of their grievances. *Ftp* let the krill organize into a powerful mass in its own right, with the ability to harness and command the predatory legal kraken that had once been its master. The fact that *Ftp* had managed to get us cheap, unfiltered broadband, while this sleazoid was proposing to actually skewer the great beast, straight through the wallet? It made me feel infinitesimal.

"But you're still there," he said. The place seemed a *lot* smaller. Bryan seemed a *lot* less elfin.

"Yeah," I said. "Don't guess they figure they can afford to evict me."

"That worked out well for you, then."

"Bryan," Lana said, putting her hand on his arm. "Come on. It's not Lukasz's fault those assholes are douchehats. He didn't make them fire you. It's—" She waved her hands at the mobiles, the walls, the wide world. "It's just how it is. The system, right?"

None of us said anything for a while. We drank our mead.

"Want to go vape something?" I said. There were lots of legal highs on campus. Some of them were pretty elfy, too. I wanted to blot out the world right then, which wasn't elfy, but we could all name our poisons.

I stumbled into the cold with them, in a haze of self-pity and self-doubt. The winter had come on quick and bitter, one of those Boston deep freezes, the combined gale-force wind, subzero temperature, and high humidity that got right into your bones. Too cold to talk, at least.

As we settled into a crowd of vapers shivering in front of a brew pub, I heard a familiar voice. I couldn't make out the words, but the tones cut through the cold and the self-pity and brought me up short. I turned around.

"Hey, Lukasz," Sergey said. He was in the center of a group of five other guys, all vaping from little lithium-powered pacifiers that fit over their index fingernails, giving them the look of Fu Manchu viziers.

"Sergey," I said, getting up from our bench and moving away from Bryan and Lana, suddenly not wanting to be seen in elfin company. "How's the hive-mind?"

He looked over to Bryan and Lana in their layered furs, then back at me.

He gave me a courtesy smile. "You'd be amazed at how well it's doing." The rest of the group nodded. I thought I recognized some of them. He closed the distance between us. "Going home for the holidays?" he asked in a conspiratorial tone.

"Don't know," I said. I had some invites from my old hackerspace buddies to go on a little couch trip, but whenever I contemplated it, I felt like a fraud. I hadn't said yes, and I hadn't said no, but in my heart I knew I wouldn't be going anywhere. How could I look those people in the eye, knowing what I knew? Knowing, in particular, what a fraud I turned out to be?

"Well," Sergey said, leaning in a little closer. I could smell the vape on his breath, various long-chain molecules like a new-car smell with an undertone of obsolete tobacco. "Well," he said again. "There's an opening at the office. In the chaos monkey department. Looking for someone who can work independently, really knocking the system around, probing for weaknesses and vulnerabilities, pushing us out of those local optima."

"Sergey," I asked, the blood draining out of my face, "are you offering me a *job*?"

He smiled an easy smile. "A very good job, Lukasz. A job that pays well and lets you do what you're best at. You get resources, paychecks, smart colleagues. You get to organize your *Ftp* campaigns, make it the best tool you can. We'll even host it for you, totally bulletproof, expansible computation and storage. Analytics—well, you know what our analytics are like."

I did. I wondered what algorithm had suggested that he go out for a smoke at just that minute in order to be fully assured of catching me on the way home. The Termite Mound was full of cameras and other sensors, and it knew an awful lot about my movements.

A job. Money. Friends. Challenges. Do *Ftp* all day long, walk away from AA's lab and the fish-eyed games of the grad students. Walk away from my tiny dorm room. Become a zuckerbergian comet, launched out of university without the unnecessary drag of a diploma into stratospheric heights, become a name to conjure with. Lana and Bryan were behind me on the bench and couldn't hear us, not at the whispers in which we spoke. But I was drug-paranoid sure that they could decipher our body language, even from behind the wall of synthetic psilocybin they had scaled.

I could have a purpose, a trajectory, a goal. Certainty.

To my horror, I didn't turn him down. A small part of me watched distantly as I said, "I'll think about it, okay?"

"Of course," he said, and smiled a smile of great and genuine goodwill and serenity. I waved goodbye to Bryan and Lana and headed back to the Termite Mound.

THE WILD AND HUNGRY TIMES

PATRICIA RUSSO

Those were the wild and hungry times, the years (some say decades, some say centuries, some say age upon age—and some say not to trust chroniclers, especially the ones whose names begin with consonants or vowels) between the fall of Resenna, the city that once ruled half the world, and the arrival of the succeeding wave of conquerors, the new lords with their scarred faces and fast ships and unusual interest in history. They came and went, these lords who marked the significant events of their lives by incising stars on their cheeks and foreheads, their reign lasting less than two hundred years, replaced in their turn by less studious invaders from farther east, men with slower ships but more powerful weapons; however, before vanishing from the pages of our history, the scarred lords left behind them a reestablished trading network and hundreds of what the next lot called word-vaults. It is believed that this term referred to archives, or possibly schools, or possibly private libraries, or possibly multilingual dictionaries, or possibly stone halls in which epics and sagas and such were chanted or sung. There is approximately an equal amount of evidence to support each of these hypotheses, except the last, which is ludicrous. (See Ybne, *The Star-Scarred Scribes,* The University of Caesus Press, for a thorough debunking of the position that word-vaults were performance spaces.)

During the wild and hungry times, the winters were always gray, and the wind blew hard in every season. Those who fished, those who farmed, those who wove, those who carved, those who tanned skins, those who made pots, those who worked with metal, those who kept to the woods and the mountains to hunt or gather or tend small flocks of grazing beasts, all suffered. Even the priests and the fortune tellers, the scryers and the sooth-finders, the blessers and the cursers, fell on hard days. (The misfortune tellers did a little better; as it was a pessimistic age, many felt it was worth parting with half a dozen eggs or a basket of vegetables in exchange for some forewarning of the next inevitable disaster.) As for curses and blessings, each family took it upon themselves to handle such matters. When a child was born, the grandparents (if they were living), the great-aunts and great-uncles (ditto), and the parents (who had less say, but were consulted) decided what blessing would be the most useful to bestow on the newborn. To give a child the gift of healing, a human bone was placed in its hand. For skill in catching fish, a fragment of an old net which had done good service was employed. For talent in coaxing plants to survive the gray and the gales, a pinch of soil. For a proficiency at thieving, a blade of grass from some other family's stronghold would do. For an understanding of livestock, the hoof of a sheep. For aptitude in weaving, a scrap of cloth. For killing, a knife. For musical ability (entertainment being essential, particularly on long, gray winter nights), a whistle. What boon would be bestowed on the child was determined by what the family needed. Family first, family foremost, family forever, each member responsible for all the rest. It was the way they survived in the wild and hungry times. They must have thought those times would never end.

Which brings us to:

It was a gray day in summer. (Gray days were not confined exclusively to winter.) The wind, sharp as a rasp, laden with grains of calcite abraded from the ruins of the Resennan lighthouse (the people of the coast had dismantled most of it, using the stones to repair walls and outbuildings, leaving the sailors to their own devices—but then, sailors had been left to their own devices ever since the last lighthouse keepers had departed, taking the lamp oil with them) (delete comma,) blew strongly from the north. Peero pulled down his hood and tied a kerchief over his mouth. The north winds were the worst. His father, sitting by the fire, said nothing. His mother looked grim. His sister, pretending to be busier than she was, wiping her son's chin when the boy's face was clean enough, taking the spoon out of her daughter's hand and stirring the porridge in her bowl after the child had already started to eat it, muttered, "It's gray today."

"It is," Peero said. The kerchief tasted of old sweat; that bastard Bairen had probably *borrowed* it, as he had *borrowed* so many things, sneaking it back into Peero's clothes-chest before slipping away. Peero supposed he should be glad Bairen had returned it at all.

Baby brother Bairen, with his hooded eyes and his liar's tongue. He had started filching as a toddler—scraps of food, their mother's thimble, a button from their father's coat. And when he was caught, he would laugh, even when father beat him, laugh like the very devil, though his eyes remained cold. As he grew older, he stopped being caught so easily; eventually he stopped getting caught at all. But this time he had been seen, in a public place, ripping a chain from a woman's neck, then dragging her off who knew where, to do who knew what. The shame of it had struck his father speechless, until Peero had gone to the old man and said, "I will find the woman and make compensation to her."

His sister stopped fussing with spoons and bibs and stray bread crumbs. "You don't have to go today."

"And what if it's gray tomorrow, as well?"

"You can wait."

"No, he can't," his father said. He continued to stare into the fire. Summer fires were lit only for cooking, but this one would burn all day. The old man had been bringing in the wood himself, making a dozen trips to stack a great pile of it next to the hearth. Mother had frowned, but she knew, as they all did, that keeping the fire going was meant not only to dispel some of the grayness and chill the north wind brought, but also to ward Peero from harm. As soon as Peero woke, before he'd even rubbed the sleep from his eyes or used the chamber pot, his father had made him stand before the hearth, which was already blazing. Father had passed a burning brand three times around Peero's body, following the direction of the sun, then carefully, leaning over the flames, dropped the stick into the middle of the fire. "Thank you, father," Peero had said, though he wished the old man hadn't done it. Peero would be the one who'd have to chop the wood to replace all that would be consumed today; it was the chore he hated the most. He knew his father meant well; he would sit all day and all night if needed, tending the fire, making sure it did not die. But he had no skill in fire-magic. Peero's grandmother had had, or so it was said, but his father had been given a fresh-laid egg as his birth-boon; his family had wanted many children from this first-born son. Their wish had come true, after a fashion; though only three offspring had survived from those who had been born in wedlock, it was common knowledge that his father had a scattering of other children in the village, as well as in the neighboring one. Bairen, the thief, was not one of those, however much a bastard he acted. Legitimate as Peero, legitimate as his sister, the three of them coming into the world in the respectable way. And Peero was the oldest, and so the responsibility of repairing what his younger brother had done, if that were even possible, fell on him. His father was old, his body worn down by the wind and the grayness and a lifetime of working poor land; he could not walk more than half a liga without getting out of breath.

"Why not?" his sister snapped. "He doesn't have to go in the grayness. It might pass in a day or two. Let him wait."

"It is a matter of honor."

His sister swore under her breath. She and Peero often talked about Bairen when safely out of earshot of their parents. "That one was born wrong," she'd say. "He should have died like the others. Grandmother and Grandfather turned the curse, but they could not remove it. It was simply twisted aside. He will never be right and he will live forever, and the wrongness in him will swell into evil." Peero had not agreed, not completely. He'd thought his sister too harsh. Bairen was young, just entering his second year of manhood. Surely, Peero thought, people could change. And Peero did not, deep in his heart, truly believe in curses. (For an extensive discussion of the cursing methods prevalent at the time, see Gedush, *Savage Maledictions and Ravenous Ill-Wishes: Uses and Misuses of the Numinous during the Interregnum Period*, New Unity City University Press.)

Their father pretended not to have heard his daughter's muttered obscenity, but their mother gave her a hard look.

Don't say it, Peero thought. Not again, please.

"When I was young, I met a bard," his mother said.

Peero sighed. The kerchief muffled the sound, but his sister rolled her eyes at him. They'd all heard this story a thousand times.

"He said," his mother continued, "that we live in wild and hungry times. I've always remembered that. He sang from the ballad-tree, but he also told short tales. Wild and hungry times, he said, at the beginning and at the end of one of the tales."

I don't quite recall what the tale was about, Peero recited silently.

"I don't quite recall what the tale was about, but those words were true words. And in wild times and hungry times, when it is gray even in summer and the wind never stops blowing, we must hold on to each other, but to honor as well. Thieving is thieving, but rending is something very different. And I swear by the wind and the clouds—"

And the rain and the roots of the whispering trees . . .

"—and by the rain and by the roots of the whispering trees, no bit of grass was put into my baby's hand. Not any of my babies."

His father poked the fire.

"I should be setting off," Peero said. "It's a long walk to the marketplace."

His nephew opened his mouth, but his niece silenced the boy with a little shake of her head. Even they know, Peero thought. *Uncle, uncle, bring us back some sweets.* Not today. They knew enough not to ask.

"I saw it myself," his mother went on. "My mother blew a breath into his right palm, and your father's father blew a breath into his left palm." Breath for long life; breath because three babies had died after Peero's sister had come into the light with a piercing squall. And after Bairen, there had been two more still-births. Mother had not had an easy life, Peero thought. Father, with his half-dozen or more bastards, hadn't made it easier. No wonder their mother clung to Bairen, her youngest surviving child. No wonder she still thought of him as a little boy.

"Go then, if you're going," his father said.

Peero nodded. He gave his sister a nod, too, and started to move toward the door.

"Too much," his mother said, softly. This was not part of her usual litany. "My mother, his father, they thought they were doing good. But he always wanted more."

"I'm going to fix it," Peero said. He thought about pulling down the kerchief so his mother could see his face, but then he'd only have to do it up again.

"And next time?" She dabbed at her eyes.

"There'll be no next time," his father said gruffly. "Not once I get my hands on him."

"Get your hands on him?" his sister snorted. "He's never coming back here."

Then his mother started to cry in earnest, and that set his sister's boy off. His father gestured to Peero to go, just go, and Peero left, shutting the door against the wails and sobs, but he still heard them despite the scream of the wind that began to buffet him as soon as he stepped outside.

A gray day in summer, with the wind blowing hard. A day like many another, except that on this day he was going to walk to the marketplace ten ligas north, the one where the woman his brother had harmed was said to work. They put a stone in my hand when I was born, he thought. A stone for strength. Not so unusual, for a first-born. And his sister had gotten a drop of clear spring water, for clarity of sight.

He had come to believe that it meant very little. If he was strong, it was because he had always been expected to be strong. As for his sister's clearness of vision—he had to admit that nothing had gone wrong with her eyes, so far. But if she truly had any of the deeper sort of sight, she used it badly. She did not comfort people; she scolded them and frightened them. If you go hunting today, she'd told her husband the winter before last, you'll be caught by a snowstorm; the ice ravens will peck out your eyes before they start on your lips and your nose. Don't be stupid. Stay here and help my brother chop wood. And her man had flinched, but then covered his fear with anger, telling her he would do as he pleased, and meat was worth more than wood. He left with a quiver full of arrows and two seasoned bows, and what was left of him was found a week later. If she had indeed seen his death, she could have warned him in a gentler way. But Peero had realized from her infant days that there was little gentleness in his sister.

He did not know the name of the woman from whom his brother had stolen, but he had a description, given by a witness to the event to—whispered to, most likely, with a great deal of superficial sympathy and much hidden glee—his mother's cousin. Gossip made the world go round. The best news was bad news. Peero could picture the expression on the cousin's face when he told mother that her youngest child, who had been the subject of rumor for years, had attacked a defenseless vendor in broad daylight (such as it was—language changed more slowly than reality) and in full view of dozens of bystanders.

That was the only part Peero found difficult to understand. Bairen was both clever and skilled. How could he have been so reckless? It was almost as if he'd wanted to be seen.

His mother had passed the tale on to him. A plain-looking woman, mother said. Short graying hair, a rather prominent nose. She usually sold greenstuffs and preserved fruits, with the occasional basket of wild mushrooms or sleep-weed on offer. None of these facts made her stand out (though the cousin had added that the woman sometimes, perhaps, he wouldn't swear to it, provided other sorts of herbs, herbs that women used to control their men—whether that was rumor or fact, it didn't help identify her, either), but there was one detail that would. The last two fingers of her left hand were missing—chopped off above the second knuckle. Though his mother's cousin didn't know the vendor's name, he knew several stories about how she had lost her fingers—got her hand stuck in a fur trader's trap on one of her herb-gathering expeditions, was one; another, that she'd had them severed as punishment for selling rotten vegetables (or for selling a decoction that sickened the client, a relative of an important man), or that it had happened when she was new-born, and her fool of a grandfather had thought to give her fire-control with a live coal, causing the fingers to have to be amputated. Peero didn't care which story was true, or even if any of them were. The missing fingers were important only as a distinguishing feature.

Even on gray summer days, vendors and customers went to market. Even when the hard wind was laden with grit from eroding ruins, people had to buy and sell, people had to make a living, people had to eat.

And families were responsible for taking care of each other, but also for keeping order among their own members. The transgression of one stained all. His sister was right, Peero thought. Bairen would not return to the family home. Most likely, Bairen had gone north, to the coast. With any luck, a ship would take him aboard, carry him away someplace no one knew his name—or his family. With better luck, the damn ship would sink.

Perhaps Bairen's public display of thievery and worse was his way of saying goodbye.

That was the way people lived in the wild and hungry times, between the collapse of the Resennan empire and the arrival of the new masters. We know because these new masters possessed a scholarly bent, or at least a caste of them did, curious about history and stories, that wrote annals and narratives and chronicles, and left word-vaults for the people who came after them, even if we are not completely sure what word-vaults are. It is from them that we know both facts and tales about the wild and hungry times. The account presented here is taken from the scrolls discovered in the second year of the reign of Prince Thury, eighty-some years ago, by the scholar known as Neitta the Younger. (Neitta the Elder's work was unfortunately lost in the sacking of Dowsan by Prince Thury's forces. There is a reference in one of Neitta the Younger's texts to copies having been made of her mother's work, but to date none have been located.) We gratefully acknowledge the pioneering work of Neitta the Younger, whose translation has been revised, annotated, and rendered into modern language by the current writer.

To continue:

The first thing Peero did when he reached the marketplace was rent a pail from a porter-woman carrying beer to those too lazy to haul their own drink from the cask-man to the field north of the market, where tables and benches (and a tent or two, with straw-tick mattresses) were for hire. The second thing he did was buy two-thirds of a pail's worth of water. Tugging his kerchief down, he splashed his face, rinsed his eyes, and drank the rest. And that, the rental of a pail and the purchase of less than a full measure of water, took half the money he had brought with him.

Many of the food-sellers had tied canopies over their stalls to protect their merchandise from the grit-laden wind. Peero, after returning the pail, moved slowly toward the herbalists and greenstuffs vendors.

Most of the women (and the men) in the marketplace had covered their hair that day; many wore scarves or kerchiefs over their mouths as well. Peero looked for prominent noses; he looked for missing fingers. Left hand, right hand, it didn't matter. Who knew if his mother's cousin had gotten that detail right? He looked so long without spotting anything (prominent noses? All the noses looked about the same to him—that one there had a crook to it, another bore a bump, another was a bit large, true, but it belonged to a man; as for fingers, most people he saw had the full set—a couple of men and one woman lacked a hand, but all three of those were customers) that he began to wonder if the cousin hadn't mixed up this marketplace with the smaller one to the south.

He looked so long that hawkers stopped calling to him and stall-holders gave up trying to attract his attention with teasing comments and jabs at the probable state of his purse. They have decided that I am simple-minded, Peero reckoned, a halfwit come to gawk at the wonders of the world.

He was nerving himself to approach the vendors and put the question to them: Do you know a woman who sells here, who has two fingers missing from one of her hands? Most would ignore him; the ones who didn't would probably lie, whether there was coin offered or not. (But first he'd have to get coin; though he'd brought very little with him, he did have a couple of items he might be able to sell—an iron-bladed knife that Bairen had left behind—stolen, probably, but Peero counted it no thievery to steal from a thief—and the luck-pouch his sister had slipped to him when their parents weren't looking. The knife would bring more, but it might be recognized; if he returned home without the luck-pouch, his sister would be angry. He would have to leave the place of produce sellers and herbalists to sell either—the ironmongers and weaponers were back where the cask-man had his stand, and the luck-merchants had a small patch in the western section of the market. He'd almost made up his mind to retrace his steps and try to sell the knife when, from behind him, there came a tug on his sleeve.

Peero turned, so quickly that the boy—near-grown, but still wearing a green ribbon sewn to his cloak, indicating he was marriageable but as yet unspoken for—stepped back and put his hand on the hilt of a dagger (with no sheathe) stuck under his belt. Between belly and belt—a bad place to carry a sharp object. And the green ribbon looked new, yet it was poorly stitched to the cloak.

"What do you want?" Peero asked.

"You are disturbing the clientele."

Clientele? A fancy word for a marketplace apprentice. "I am looking for a woman with graying hair and missing fingers."

"Look for her somewhere else."

"I was told she was here."

The boy—if it was a boy, and not a girl in disguise, or a eunuch dressed as a marriageable youth as a joke by his employer, or one of those folks born with both male and female parts, or with neither—said, "This is place of business. If you have no business here, then leave."

"Who sent you?" Peero grabbed the boy's wrist and twisted it; had he been more skilled, the youth could have tried to reach for the dagger with his left hand, but the hilt was tilted too far to the right. He had eastern eyes, whoever or whatever he was, gray as the sea with the tiniest tinge of blue; they were difficult to read. Peero twisted the boy's wrist harder, making him cry out.

"Leave him alone." A different voice, older, and a woman's.

"Gladly. It's you I need to talk to."

"Me?" The woman circled him; he watched her eyes. The boy did not struggle.

Grayish hair. A nose a bit broad at the bridge. He could not see her hands; she kept them behind her back. Holding a weapon of her own, possibly.

"My brother stole something from you," Peero said. "I have come in the name of my family to make amends."

"Your brother." She circled him again.

"He was seen."

"Oh, then it must be true." She stopped walking and met his gaze. "If your business is with me, then let this one go."

"Is he your son?"

"I have no children."

"I'm sorry."

"I'm not. In these wild and hungry days, the world is no fit place for children."

"Did you meet a bard once when you were young?"

"What?"

"Nothing." Peero gave the boy a look: don't go for the knife. The boy grimaced in agreement, and Peero released his wrist. "Scat," Peero said, but the boy glanced at the woman and waited for her assent before striding off, head high. This whole section of the market had just seen Peero lay hands on a child, but he was a stone and could not be hurt by what others thought of him.

The woman was still standing with her hands behind her back. Well, what reason did she have to trust him, after what his brother had done?

Plain-looking, his mother's cousin had said. But the stone had been placed in Peero's hand, not on his heart. She was younger than he had thought at first, perhaps quite close to his own age—some people went gray sooner than others—and her nose gave her face character. In fact, it complemented her strong chin and her deep-set eyes. He felt a hot twist in his belly, and from the look the woman gave him (not eastern eyes, not at all, but as dark brown as his own) he feared that the heat had rushed to his face.

She wore no hood or hat, scarf or kerchief. Peero pushed his own hood back, untied his kerchief, and mopped his face. They were in the open, with the eyes of dozens on them. Had Bairen done the same, torn from her what he had taken, in the middle of the marketplace? Peero had pictured his brother going to her stall, but his mother's cousin had never said that, only that the woman sold at the marketplace.

"You don't look much like him," she said.

"Who?"

"This brother you claim stole something from me."

"Thank you for the compliment." The wind was strong; the wind was always strong. He blinked against the dust. "Bairen."

"Is that your name, or his?"

"His."

"I see." She stood very still, her hands out of sight.

"When I was born," Peero said, "they gave me a stone, to bless me with the gift of strength."

"I was given a blossom from a bitter-bark tree."

"To endow you with a talent for working with wild plants and herbs?"

"No. Because I was the youngest of ten and there was no need for me. Bitter-bark tree blossoms flourish and fade inside of a week." She gave him a little smile.

After a moment, Peero said, "It was the opposite with Bairen. Our mother had lost several babies. Everybody wanted him to live."

"So his grandparents blew long life into his hands. I know." She smiled again. "Sometimes the gifts they mean to give us are not the ones we receive."

"It is difficult not to come to that conclusion. Clearly, you've lasted more than a week."

"Clearly."

"And Bairen, the bastard, became light-fingered and airy-minded."

"Is he a bastard?"

"No. Though my father has several." Peero didn't know why he'd said that; he felt the heat rise to his face again.

"It happens. Even in the best of families, or so they say."

Peero was growing increasingly uncomfortable. "Shouldn't we go someplace—quieter?"

"Quieter?"

"Out of—out of the wind."

"I'm sorry for your long journey," she said. "Truly, I am. But your trip was for no purpose."

"I have to try."

"Try what?"

"To repair what Bairen did. To make amends."

"There is nothing to repair."

"But he stole—"

"He stole nothing."

"He was seen. He took a necklace. And then he—"

"There is no burden on you. There is no stain on your family. Go home, brother of Bairen."

"Let me see your hands," Peero said, suddenly.

So many people watching them. How would this tale be told in the future, how would it be passed from mouth to malicious mouth? The thief's brother came and hurt a child; the thief's brother came and fought with the woman he should have been offering compensation to.

"Are you married?"

"What? No."

"But you wear no ribbon."

"I'm too old for that."

"Missed your chance, did you? Some settlements have odd customs."

"Stop it. I am old enough now to decide for myself. I cannot be asked for."

"I see. Well, I tell you again, brother of Bairen, Bairen the light-fingered and airy-minded, as you named him, that nothing was stolen from me. If he has stolen from others, you must go make amends to them, if that is your duty."

"Let me see your hands." A fear like ice gripped him now, banishing all heat. He had told himself that he did not believe in blessings and curses, that what people grew to become depended on their own natures and what they were taught. Now he was afraid that the woman possessed a strength mightier than any stone, any mountain; he feared she would stretch out her three-fingered hand, and render him to ash.

Render. Rent. Bairen had done more than steal; he had rent something from her. So the tale ran; so his mother's cousin had whispered. And his sister said, darkly, You know what he took. Her years, Peero, he took her years to add to his own. Believing and disbelieving (in his sister's clarity of sight, in his own stone strength, in the likelihood of Bairen being able to steal a lifespan) he had come to give them back to her, if possible. And she stood there smiling, teasing him about marriage, and filling his heart with an emotion he could not name.

If there was magic here, it was the sort he wished, fervently, did not exist.

"These wild and hungry times will end one day," she said.

"So we must hope."

She shook her head. "It is not a matter of hope, but of action. Do you think it was the old emperors who kept the grayness away, who controlled the wind? They were too busy raising armies and collecting taxes. We have the power to set the world right, but only a few of us know it. Perhaps your brother did steal. But the objects—and the gifts—that he took from people, he kept safe, adding bit to bit, until he had acquired everything that was needed. And no, he never told you that, because if he had, you would have dismissed his words as lies, excuses, fancies."

"You must have spoken to him for a long time."

"Not so long. He was in a hurry."

"Do you know where he was going?"

"If I did, I wouldn't tell you."

"Why won't you show me your hands?"

"Because you are not ready yet."

"Why did my brother come to you?"

"Because I was ready." She glanced down. "Not completely ready. I have been growing readier, though. Your brother took nothing from me that I did not freely give. He added it to the rest, all the bits and scraps and strengths he had gathered for years, the tangible and the scarcely perceptible. And then he left everything, all of it, with me."

"I don't understand."

She shrugged.

"But I don't think you understand, either. It is in your face, in your eyes. Your death is standing just behind your shoulder."

"Ah, perhaps it is the blossom of the bitter-bark tree, catching up with me at last."

"I came to help. To stop it, if I can. To delay it, if I can."

"Very well. I will do it here, in front of everybody, so that all can see. I will do it in front of you, so that you can carry the tale back to your family. That is how you can help. I know I cannot end these wild and hungry times; they did not arrive in an instant, and they will not retreat in an instant, either. It is likely that the repair, to use your word, will take longer than a lifetime. But we must do what we can, and what I can do is begin. It will be up to others to continue it. You tell them that."

"Continue what?"

"The wind bothers you. It hurts you."

"The wind bothers everybody. It hurts everybody."

"Then we will start with the wind."

The woman brought her hands out from behind her back, and Peero saw that she had five fingers on both of them.

She laughed softly. "Believe me, that was a surprise."

"Did it hurt?"

"Like fire. Now be silent, and watch."

She turned, extending her left arm to the north. She shut her eyes and breathed. She stood standing and breathing as the sun (dim through the grayness, but still visible) slipped over the top of the sky and began to sink into the west. She stood for hours, motionless except for her breathing; Peero settled himself on the ground and watched.

He watched because she had asked him to; he watched because it was the only thing he could do. He watched because she was beautiful and doomed. He knew her death was coming ever closer; he knew she was calling it to her. No one in the marketplace interfered; no one approached them, except once, when the boy who might not have been a boy strode up and placed a pail of water next to Peero, then swaggered off again.

Peero knew the precise moment that she died. It was the instant after the wind stopped.

The wind stopped.

She fell.

It was nearly dusk.

The boy came again, then, with two others, older men, who picked her up and carried her away. They did not speak to Peero.

He waited a while, but no one came near him.

I am strong, he thought. I can walk home in the dark. I have had no food since breakfast, but I have had water. And now, without the wind, the traveling will be easier.

I will tell the story to father and mother and sister, to niece and nephew. I will tell what I saw. What I do not know, I will not invent. They will hear only what I can swear to with one hand on my newborn-stone and the other on my mother's breast.

And so he must have done, for this is the tale, more or less, as it was recorded by the new lords with their fast ships and their inks and their metal-nibbed pens, and unearthed (literally; the scrolls had been buried in sealed jars) by Neitta the Younger. Perhaps Peero did father children eventually, and gave the story to them, or perhaps it was his niece or nephew who passed it on. In any case, as the story clearly descends from Peero, Bairen appears as a minor figure, despite the fact it was his actions which set the events in motion; similarly, the greenstuffs vendor who, in a another telling, might have been featured as the heroine of the piece, is not even afforded a name. (Pitmarr, in *Resennan Motifs*, volume three, mentions this tale in Appendix C, but only to note that none of the female characters are given names. Pitmarr, as is well-known, holds to the opinion that while the new lords recorded as many of the relicts of Resennan tradition and culture as they could, the tales of the wild and hungry days are mostly their own invention.) There is also the curious element of the youngster of undetermined gender, who also is not named. The character is extraneous to the tale, serving no discernable purpose. However, if the account is meant to be a historical record, the chronicler likely felt obligated to include every detail still extant, even if its significance had been lost.

That was centuries ago, of course, and even a conscientious chronicler could have mistaken fiction for fact, or indulged in a certain amount of embellishment (the dialogue in the tale certainly must have come from the chronicler, along with Peero's internal monologues; it is unfortunate that the account has survived in only this single version, thus affording no opportunity to compare variants or conduct contrastive analyses) but many elements can be confirmed from other texts of the period—the tradition of birth-boons has been well-documented, for example, along with the grayness of the days and the ferocity of the wind. Finally, there is the expression "wild and hungry times" or "wild and hungry days"; no reputable historian disputes that this was the name given to the period by those who lived in it. (Except for Pittmar, of course, but he cannot be considered unbiased.)

Much is still not known about the wild and hungry times, and possibly will never be uncovered. But perhaps we have some indication of how they ended, or began to end—with the halting of the winds, by the actions of a young man deemed a thief and a disgrace, and a woman who had lived her whole life knowing her parents wished her to wither and die as a bitter-bark tree blossom faded and crumbled to dust.

Unless, of course, someone whose name began with a consonant or a vowel simply made the whole thing up.

It wouldn't have been the first time.

Though doubts about the historicity of the narrative must be acknowledged, and despite the fact that we are much more scientifically-minded nowadays (magic? There is no magic; there is only nature, and what we don't understand now we will in time. While a close reading of the text reveals hints that Bairen gave his own extra life-energy to the greenstuffs vendor—hence the regrowth of her fingers—which she then used to perform the magical act of stilling the winds, of course this is merely a remnant of a folktale motif. The items Bairen collected over his years of thievery must have been used to construct a machine, perhaps an early version of the devices employed today to divert the path of hurricanes; the greenstuffs vendor's death was likely a result of a mechanical malfunction, the long period of oral transmission transmuting this into another common folktale motif: the mage's sacrifice), it is difficult to look out the window and see the sun, winter and summer, the only grayness that of cloud-cover or fog, or to step outside and feel the breeze, the only wild winds those of storms that come in their seasons and pass on, without the occasional urge to murmur, Thank you, to the named and the unnamed, to those whose names have been lost but might still be recovered, and to all whose names will never be known.

TRADEMARK BUGS: A LEGAL HISTORY

ADAM ROBERTS

The following discussion document has been produced by a working group comprising academics from the UK's Royal Psychological and Somatic Law Institute (Birmingham) and the Russian Federation's Academic Law University (Академический правовой университет, АПУ). It aims to summarise the legal position with respect to so-called 'Trademark Bugs', and is **not** intended to have the force of a policy proposal or political statement. The management board of the АПУ in particular wish to distance themselves from the conclusion in section 5. For more discussion on these matters see Kokoschka et al 2099.

1. The Three 'Porter Rules'

The first court case directly relevant was filed under UK legislation, not because the first Trademark Bugs were developed or distributed in that country, but because the UK's unilateral renegotiation of their national relationship to the 'Madrid System' (which was in turn part of their withdrawal from EU copyright jurisdictions) created a more favourable balance of proof for INTA, USPTO or WIPO prosecution. Protocols governing the dissemination of these new products meant that the bugs were not at first distributed in areas that had suffered calamitous natural disaster (earthquake, tsunami, plague) in the previous five years, although this was later reduced to 12-months and subsequently—as of 2031—abandoned altogether. As a consequence of this, Porter-addend.2031d clarifies the extent to which the original Rules must be considered consonant with international law.

Porter's original ruling laid down the so-called three 'Porter Rules' for Trademark Bugs. These are:

- That the pathology itself must not be 'excessively physically distressing' or entail any long-term hazard to health, wellbeing or longevity. These latter terms, of course, have proved hard to define precisely as salients under legal challenge.

- That the pathology itself must be no *more* virulent than the baseline virus or bacterium, prior to any genetic adaptation. This applies the legal principle, common from other aspects of EU Genetics Law, of balanced hazard equilibrium.[1]

- That the pathology itself must be *preventable* by some means (later modified to 'at least one mean') *not trademarked* to the distributing company. The meaning of *preventable* in this context has generated a great deal of discussion, with legal authorities divided between interpreting this so-called 'Third Porter Rule' either (a) strictly, in terms of legal consent—briefly, that plaintiffs need only show that they did not knowingly and competently *opt-in* to the relevant pathology; or (b) broadly, in terms of *reasonable precaution*—the argument advanced by Goober, Thwaite and Associates, known popularly as the 'soap and water' test. This latter holds that, as with the common cold, everyday precautions such as washing one's hands with soap and water be enough to avoid infection for it to come within the meaning of the act. Accordingly people who, compos mentis and of legal majority, elect *not* to take such common-sense precautions have ipso facto given consent to being infected by Trademark Bugs. The rulings of Ito (Ito-2025c) and Carallan (Carallan-2024d-2025a) confirmed the 'broad' definition to have legal grounding. Since 2034 this has only been challenged in court once (Boothby-2037b-d), a case which eventually tested the legal status of all three of the Porter Rules. The 'broad' interpretation of Rule 3 was eventually upheld.

Several early legal challenges stalled because the plaintiffs exhausted their funding. It is worth noting this fact because there is a widely held though

---

[1] This was itself challenged by Pontormo vs. Bayer Corporation; at a previous hearing (Gomez-2024a) Justice Cooper had equated the principle at the heart of Porter's Second Rule to Hippocrates' maxim that a physician should do no harm; Pontormo argued that Trademark Bugs violated this principle *a priori*, and that all such products broke the Porter Rules by virtue of existing. But the legal representation for Bayer successfully argued in tribunal that they were not 'physicians' under the meaning of the Act. This defence depending upon the nature of corporate individuality in a legal sense: that Corporations could legally split their personalities—in this case, into two entities, 'pathology disseminator' and 'physician', without entailing any of the legal complications of 'schizophrenia'.

erroneous belief that the case of Lukas vs. Glaxco (Reinhart-2029a-d) established any legal precedent. Passages from the speeches delivered in court by Milo Lukacs have passed into popular currency *as if* they had legal basis; although in fact the case was later suspended for non-disbursement of legal stipends and no judgment was arrived at.

Let us not lose sight of the key issue: corporations are not only *manufacturing* genetically tweaked versions of the common cold, they are *releasing* them into the environment via multiple vectors. We have not yet been able to prove in court that such releasing itself constitutes corporate delinquency, but we do know this: polls have consistently shown that the general public thinks of these actions *in exactly those terms*—as delinquency, quasi-criminal activity and worse. People are getting sick with genetically tagged flu viruses for which the only cure is manufactured by these same corporations! People are being forced into the position where they *have* to purchase medication, manufactured by the same corporations that made them sick, in order to bring them back to the baseline position of health. This practice is profoundly inhumane, unethical, and monopolistic. This practice is wicked.[2]

Lukacs also put before the court various financial estimates that have been contested. He claimed that over the tax-year '28-'29, the three biggest pharmaceutical companies made €875 billion profit on Trademark Bugs alone; and that over the previous five years the profit from Trademark Bugs was double that of all other pharmaceutical sales combined. These claims were themselves the cause of two legal challenges: one on the grounds of their inaccuracy (it was argued in court that the €875 billion figure was gross, not net; although a countersuit [Abnett-2030a] sought to show that, when EU tax-incentives for medical research and charitable donations were included, the tax rate on this profit was zero) and in the grounds that disclosure of profits violated the corporations' legal rights (legally functional as 'individuals') to privacy. This was upheld by Rinn-2031b, but without retrospective force. Accordingly all sums cited for post-'31 profits, including ones included in this paper, are estimates (legally permitted under the Corporate Oversight Act of

---

[2] It should be noted that three key elements of this speech—so widely distributed— have been challenged in non-subpoenic tribunals. Specifically: (a) 'genetically tagged flu viruses'; all Trademark Bugs at this point were marketed as 'colds'; influenza being believed to violate the first Porter Rule. Several legal experts have challenged this. (b) 'People are being forced into the position . . . ' was challenged as tendentious, in that it implied an a priori breach of the Third Porter Rule. Sun-2029d rules that the soap-and-water test negated any imputation that people were being 'forced' to become ill via the release of Trademark Bugs. (c) The accusation of 'monopolistic' practice was immediately challenged by several suits, the reporting of which in turn led to the case of Glaxco vs The Guardian, detailed below.

2035) and in no way intended to intrude upon the privacy of corporations qua individuals.

Balance requires us to quote from the chief legal representative for Glaxco, Magrat Helmansdottir KC, who said:

> The soap-and-water test is no mere legal fiction, but an actual, measurable social good. Drugs have their part to play in humankind's perennial war against illness, but it is a small part compared to the role played by simple hygiene. Hygiene has saved more lives than all the drugs ever produced. The distribution of Trademark Bugs (free at point of issue, I might add) is an actual, measurable and positive incitement to people to live more hygienic lives. Glaxco themselves sell one-cent bars of proprietary soap through all the major supermarkets; and expend considerable sums advertising the need to wash hands every hour and avoid spreading infections—all such transmissible infections, not merely those bugs Trademarked to Glaxco. Furthermore, Glaxco has invested €1.1 billion in the science of Epidemiology, including endowing the Glaxco Chair in Epidemiological Science at Harvard, and funding forty annual PhD scholarships in the discipline. It is no exaggeration to say that this investment is the single most significant investment in this science ever made. What the prosecution are calling for would devastate the advances made in medical science and materially diminish human wellbeing. Quite apart from our moral duty to uphold the laws protecting the sanctity of commercial free enterprise and encouraging self-reliance and independence in consumers—quite apart from that, what the prosecution proposes would have a measurably negative impact upon world health.

Outside the courtroom, during media interviews, Helmansdottir added: 'I appreciate it sounds counter-intuitive; I understand that many people feel that these corporations are deliberately infecting them with designer germs in order to increase their profits by selling them the cures—but the facts are the facts. None of that is true. Trademark Bugs have made the world cleaner and healthier. We can't afford to undo the advances we have made.' She later—successfully—resisted a prosecution petition that this speech be entered into evidence, arguing that the clause 'these corporations are deliberately infecting them with designer germs in order to sell them the cures', abstracted from context, would be prejudicial to the legal process.

Following the collapse of Lukas vs. Glaxco (Reinhart-2029a-d), 47 private prosecutions were brought against various corporations by individuals who claimed they had caught Trademarked diseases and suffered, in one way or another, in excess of the discomfort permitted by the Porter Rules. All but one were conducted under the no-win-no-fee remit. Of these 5 were abandoned, 3 went to court (the plaintiffs losing in each case) and 39 were settled out of court. The next legal milestone was Glaxco vs The Guardian (Gesswyn 2033a), when the company successfully sued the UK-based media conglomerate for repeating claims that eleven distinct strains of Trademark Bug were 'monopolistic'.

The editor at the time, Jean Ebner, conceded that this defeat 'stung and enraged' her senior staff. After a popular campaign and fundraising effort ('Goldenbugs') the Guardian took Glaxco to court under US legal jurisdiction (presiding justice Natch Greys, Guardian Corps v. Glaxco, 676 F.3d 854, 862 (9th Cir 2036); [EU citation format: Greyes-2036c-2039a]). The grounds of the suit were ingenious: a Guardian reporter, Po Lok Tam, deliberately contracted one of Glaxco's most widely disseminated Trademark Bugs, a common-cold tweak called 'Sapphire Sniffles', the cure for which—'Azure 7' (available as pill, or nanoneedle diffuser)—was amongst the cheapest in the Glaxco range.[3] The symbolic significance of the 'four-shots-a-dollar' cure was part of the intended effect. Po Lok Tam refused to buy the cure and suffered the symptoms of the bug: raised temperature, headache, runny nose and sore throat, advertised as 'lasting depending on the state of the sufferer's immune system between three and eight weeks'.[4] There were, she claimed, other symptoms; but only the ones specified in the Glaxco promotional material were entered into evidence without dispute from either side. The force of the Guardian suit was that the sore throat, by impairing the ability of the plaintiff to speak, illegally restricted her first amendment rights to free speech under the US constitution.

2. Guardian v. Glaxco (2036-39): a summary

Initial reports of this trial expressed the opinion that it would soon be thrown out of court: none of the symptoms breached Porter Rules, and neither

---

[3] Ms. Po caught the bug by arranging a meeting with one of the company's 'spreaders': these were individuals (often students), who were paid small sums, plus a free cure after seven days, to take on the relevant pathology and walk amongst the general population disseminating it. This individual later unsuccessfully sued the Guardian for damages, claiming that he had not given his explicit consent to involvement in the story.

[4] 'Open ended' bugs, against which the unmedicated body had no chance of developing aboriginal antibodies, and which prolonged cold/flu symptoms indefinitely—until the sufferer bought the necessary medication—did not appear on the market until 2051. It was unusual for an individual actively to seek out a 'spreader'; usually infection was passed by inadvertent contact in a public place.

side denied that Ms. Po could still express herself in writing—in previous cases concerning the right to freedom of speech (see Grohmann, 2088 for a summary of this legal history) this had been deemed sufficient to satisfy the constitutional requirement. In fact, Guardian v. Glaxco became one of the longest, most fiercely fought and expensive in the history of Trademark Bug law. We can only provide the merest sketch of the arguments and counter-arguments, here (Malahat 2090 has a more detailed account). The main theses and antitheses can be summarised as follows:

1. A first move by Glaxco to dismiss the case as lacking prima facie validity (the plaintiff having unimpeded access to text-based modes, including an artificial voice app on her phone, was able fully to actualise her first-amendment rights, irrespective of her sore throat). Motion was denied.

2. A move to early resolution by the plaintiff on the grounds that Ms. Po gave no explicit consent to losing her voice. Denied, after the Glaxco team satisfied the court that Ms. Po had, intentionally, gone out of her way to catch the bug.

3. Glaxco legal team attempted to prove that, since many other Trademark Bugs produced symptoms that left the throat and voice unaffected—and since the plaintiff could have elected to catch any of these—she had no legal right to complain about loss of voice following a Bug she specifically elected to catch.

4. Over several months, the Guardian team attempted to persuade the court that Trademark Bugs diminished or denied not only first amendment rights, but basic constitutional rights to life liberty and the pursuit of happiness. Since Ms. Po's life was not in danger, the legal debate concentrated on the criteria of 'liberty' and 'happiness'. The Guardian attempted to bring before the court testimony of hundreds of sufferers of common colds who had, by their own admission, been left 'housebound', hoping to show that this impaired their liberty. They also argued that being ill contravened the right to happiness, on the grounds that being ill makes people unhappy. Glaxco counter-argued that being ill did not prevent an individual from *pursuing* happiness, if they so chose; and that it was this latter right that was constitutionally guaranteed. Justice Greyes concurred.

5. One woman (Paula de Chirico, from Waco, TX) gave evidence for sixty days, after Justice Greyes admitted her evidence. Having caught a Glaxco bug called 'Nosy Rudolf' she had ordered the cure ($9.95 for three tablets) online, but delivery was held-up by a postal strike. She had gone to work mildly ill, had inadvertently sneezed on her boss,

who had thus also caught the bug. The boss had fired Ms. de Chirico. The Guardian sought to argue that this demonstrated that Glaxco Trademark Bugs had interfered with Ms. de Chirico's constitutional rights. The court debated for several weeks on the admissibility of a completely different Trademark Bug; the relevance of an individual other than the plaintiff; and the relative liability of the postal company. Eventually Justice Greves ruled that the burden of liability rested with de Chirico, for not maintaining hygienic practice with respect to her own contagion or spreading her contagion to others.

6. Following this, many of the plaintiff's claims were rolled back. Glaxco again moved the case be dismissed.

7. The Guardian pressed the freedom of speech angle. At the heart of this was their claim that for eight days in the first instance, and for a later 12-hour period, Ms. Po had been denied her right to free expression by Glaxco's bug. The Glaxco team brought in expert witnesses to show that Ms. Po had received far greater media exposure during those three days that at any other time in her career.

8. There was a long discussion as to whether 'media exposure' amounts to 'freedom of speech'. Dozens of expert witnesses were called by both sides. This debate was eventually parked by Justice Greves, as ingermane and vexatious.

9. The final months of the case were characterised by a series of increasingly complex blocking motions by the Guardian. Eventually Justice Greve guillotined further blocking, and ruled in favour of Glaxco. In his summing up, he declared: 'there may yet be a legal challenge that could be mounted on the grounds that Trademark Bugs violate a citizen's first amendment rights; but such a challenge will need to take as its plaintiff somebody other than a professional journalist mounting a clear and exploitative publicity stunt'.

10. Seven different appeals followed, on grounds both of the due process and the Justice's final summing up. Two of these were unresolved or abandoned for financial reasons. Five upheld the judgment.

"This is a bad day for democracy," Jean Ebner declared from the courthouse steps. "The judge has said, in effect, that people who work for the media cannot challenge these wicked corporations, and their terrible diseases, *because* they work for the media! He has left open the possibility that so-called 'ordinary citizens' could mount a legal challenge, but how will they ever be able to afford it?"

"Without the support of the Guardian and the public fund-raising campaign," Ms. Po added, "I would never have been able to bring my case. This

judgment puts corporate profit above the needs of common human decency."
It was not obvious at the time (although posterity has made clear) that this
court-case was the last serious legal challenge to the marketing of Trademark
Bugs. The Guardian Conglomeration never recovered from the expense of
mounting and then losing the suit, and ceased trading two years later.

Throughout the early 2040s there were several attempts to raise the funding
necessary to challenge the big Trademark Bug manufacturers in courts;
but none of these progressed beyond initial stages. The 'big three' pharma
companies—Pfizer-Novartis, Glaxco and Bayer—expanded operations. Bayer
developed anti-addiction medication, which it sold alongside its own-brand
tobacco, stimulant and euphoric products. P-N developed respirant illnesses
that spread what it called 'one-quarter-asthma' (this label has been several
times challenged in court as deliberately misrepresenting the degree of
respiratory distress experienced by sufferers) alongside several models of
'fashion accessory inhalers'. The marketing of these to children resulted in a
fad for carrying the devices, often expensively personalised, across much of
Europe, South America and East Asia during the later 2040s.

3. Change in generational attitudes

Evidence that younger generations had a different attitude to Trademark
Bugs than their parents and grandparents has been gathered by Rakesh
Bandari (Bandari 2089).

> For people growing up in the '40s and '50s most of the diseases that had
> afflicted humanity for millennia had been cured. Nobody expected
> those cures to be distributed free. Moreover, the sense that 'disease'
> in the abstract still had a place in the ontological ecosystem of human
> life was deep-rooted, and many young people found it easy to accept
> that the big 3 Pharma companies filled a niche that would otherwise
> be supplied by unpredictable feral viruses and bacteria. The situation
> was helped by canny PR by all three: PN and Glaxco by 2053 (and
> Bayer by 2055) guaranteed student loans at 1% under the bank rate
> to all university students. A mass-market campaign established them
> as 'cool' with younger demographics. Sports events, game and music
> products and TV—all of it was heavily subsidised by Pharma money.
> Advertising presented the Trademark Bugs as a way of unofficially
> 'taxing' those too old and foolish to follow simple hygiene regimens,
> syphoning their money for the benefit of the young. That the young
> (especially the very young) were disproportionately affected by
> Trademark Bugs did not adversely affect this impression. By 2055
> Pharma Companies overtook Munitions Companies as the largest

donors to political parties; and after the '58 reforms they donated huge sums to Legal Infrastructure too. By 2060 few could deny that the industry as a whole, and the Big Three in particular, represented the most politically powerful group on the planet.

This can be illustrated by Glaxco's development of 'Faceshapers', bugs that cause non-metastasising tumours to grow on various areas of the upper body and skull. The drugs necessary to reverse these growths were not cheap; and some people (especially in the climate-change affected equatorial areas) were compelled to live with the deformities. But many young people in the affluent west actively embraced this Bug, going so far as arranging Trademark Bug Swap Parties. The aim was to alter the body in ways deemed 'cool'. Particularly valued were horns of bone growing under the skin on shoulders and collar-bone, or so-called 'Klingon' or 'Publikumsbeschimpfung' growths on the forehead and cheeks.

Legal challenges were sometimes mounted against the new strains of bug, but without success. The big court cases of the '60s went, as it were, the other way: in particular PN v. Raj Choudhury (Schwarz-Gardos 2065c). Choudhury had made a personal fortune in IT, and set up a company that bought medication from Glaxco, PN and Bayer in bulk, and then distributed it free at clinics in the Third World. PN agreed to Glaxco and Bayer to take on the task of challenging this in court, as restraint of trade and violation of the terms of sale. The case lasted three weeks, in which Choudury's main defence—humanitarianism—was legally demolished. Choudhury was fined, and imprisoned after refusing to pay. His assets were seized and distributed to the plaintiff.

Through the early '70s the Big Three confined their new products to cosmetic and minor afflictions. Bayer had a hit in '74 with their Kahlkopf product. Male-pattern baldness having been cured in the '40s, the effect of this Bug—it affected both men and women with rapid-onset alopecia—was extraordinary. Sales of the cure pushed Bayer into the top position, profit-wise. Bayer were also the first of the big three to break the €10 trillion annual profit barrier (PN currently hold the all-time record, with their one-year profit of €74 trillion, although these figures do not include monies made that are tax-deductible under charitable, educational and defence budgets) [Figures estimated under academic 'fair use' rules].

4. Tax consequences of Big Three success

Big Three annual profits began outstripping the GDPs of even the world's largest countries in the early '60s. By the '80s it was clear that these commercial organisations were, simply, doing a better job of 'titheing' the population than nation-states had previously managed with old-fashioned tax collection paradigms. The use of the term 'tithe' was forwarded by the various financial restructuring proposals of '83, and challenged in court. The Russian Federation fought the longest legal battle on this (see Brohstein 93 for a detailed account), but by the middle of the decade the only countries that retained a 'traditional' old-style tax regimen were few and small-scale. The bigger countries all passed over to systems where income tax and sales taxes were reduced to between 2% and 5%—and in some cases abolished altogether (less than 2% did not provide enough income to cover the expense of gathering the tax). Where previous generations had worked and then paid tax on work income, the new generations quickly adapted to receiving their salaries effectively tax-free, but paying money instead to maintain baseline levels of health and productivity.

The balance was simple: (a) pay the Big Three for the so-called Omnipills, that protected against all the traditional Trademark Bugs—as an expense, this averaged 17% of average income in most countries, although (being price rather than index-determined) it was flat-rate, benefitting the wealthy at the relative expense of the poor. Or (b) elect not to buy health, and attempt to work through whatever illnesses ensued. The 'soap-and-water' test was tested in court in 2086, when it was claimed that the Bayer Bug 'Emerald Rash' survived soap. The outcome (Kawasaki-86d) was that 'soap' was taken, legally, to include a variety of proprietary antibacterial washes and wipes. 'It is clear,' writes Bandari, 'that this would not have been accepted by the courts of the '30s and '40s. But public attitudes to the role of Trademark Bugs in society had shifted' (Bandari 2089).

The Big Three funded national programmes of education, policing and crime; and sponsored infrastructure programmes. Many countries retained 'traditional' tax only in order to fund their military, although EU, South American and East Asian nations were happy to have the Pharma companies supply defence needs as well. Faced with an impending legal challenge on the 'no taxation without representation' principle, Bayer and Glaxco created a second variety of publically tradable share—giving the owner the right to vote on public policy, but not commercial or proprietary, matters. By 2090 PN followed suit, and by the century's end—at time of writing—democracy has adapted to the new model across much of the globe. 'Voting' is now something a citizen does if they opt-in to the political process by buying voting shares. If s/he chooses not to do so they are deemed, legally, to have surrendered their democratic rights.

5. Legal Implications of Combat

It is hard to assess the long-term impact of the financial success of Trademark Bugs, and is beyond the scope of the present paper. The purpose of this final section is to consider the potential consequences of on-going litigation pertaining to the Bangladeshi Conflict.[5] The high casualty figures of this conflict,[6] as much as the central role played by Pharma companies,[7] render it a test-case for the on-going development of Trademark Bugs in the future of international relations. What is clear is that conflict represents a significant legal test-case for what amounts to a radically revisioned basis for civic and legal management of Trademark Bugs, up to and including a complete restatement of the Porter Rules for their commercial exploitation.

Despite being officially termed the 'Bangladeshi War', the conflict has spread across a much larger area than the Bay of Bengal. At the same time it is also true that the Battle for the port of Chaṭṭagrama—in Bangladesh— has been one of the biggest of the war so far. The whole region has suffered much more markedly from climate change than other areas on the globe, and economic growth of an averagely consistent 3% per 5 years has been diluted by outstripping population increases. The whole area shares with central Mexico the distinction of the world's highest rates of untreated Trademark Bug infections. At the same time, the Big Three have directed in excess of €5billion humanitarian aid, including €220 million worth of free antiseptic soap, dispersed in the area since 2091.

The main antagonists in the war (despite the use of nation-state shell identities) are generally agreed as being Bayer on the one hand, and on the other an alliance of smaller, ambitious and emergent pharmaceutical companies, led by the Myanmar Pharmaceutical Manufacturers Union (MPMU). The latter brought together troops from Myanmar, Malaysia and India; the former deployed armies from Russian Federation and EU states. The specific flashpoints—control of the lucrative industrial centres positioned

---

[5] This section as a whole, and this sentence is particular, does not carry the unanimous imprimatur of the authors. 'Bangladeshi Conflict' was agreed by a narrow majority, over 'Asian Continental War' and 'First Asian Continental War', both of which are in common online usage.

[6] АПУ scholars wanted this clause replaced with 'Casualties have been sustained, but precise figures have not been agreed'. In the Russian and Ukrainian translation of this paper the АПУ phrasing has been preferred, and the RPSL phrasing relegated to a footnote.

[7] The original draft included the parenthesis '... (such that some have dubbed this war 'commercial competition pursued via military means, see Gharzai 2099) ... ' АПУ scholars wanted this clause deleted entirely; RPSL scholars wanted it retained. Citing it in a footnote was the compromise agreed upon, with the added consideration that this footnote not be cited by any third party as indicative of the official conclusion of this paper.

along the Karnaphuli River—are less relevant to our present discussion than the way the war has been prosecuted.

A rapid conventional phase shifted suddenly in June 2098 with the release of weaponised pharma. The poisoning of the Ganges aside (not a matter of strictly legal relevance) this led to two large-scale lawsuits. One was lodged by the MPMU Alliance in the EU Supreme Court, arguing that Bayer's pharmaceutical ordnance, deployed to cause harm and death to opposing troops, was in clear breach of the Porter Rules. Bayer's legal defence team counter-argued that the Porter Rules were never intended to apply to a warzone. The court was told that Bayer did indeed hold reserves of meds to cure such soldiers who had not already died, and that they were prepared to release these when a peace treaty was signed.

The MPMU tacitly conceded this suit by releasing its own weaponised pharma. Bayer filed a countersuit against the MPMU conventional weapons, on the grounds that the companies held no 'antidote' materiel to counter the effects of bullets and shrapnel. In peacetime this suit would almost certainly have been dismissed as vexatious litigation,[8] but under the extraordinary circumstances it was allowed to proceed. It was, in fact, accepted by many as an attempt to reconfigure the nature of war along more humanitarian lines ('our aim is legally restraining more destructive conventional weaponry in favour of less destructive pharmaceutical weaponry', was the official Bayer court statement). This suit is on-going. Recently, Bayer has undertaken pre-emptive strikes against the factories of the MPMU, following intelligence reports that they were working on trademark-infringing cures for the weapons of the Bayer forces. 'Killing and maiming is one thing,' said Bayer vice-chairman Hester Lu. 'Wars have entailed that for thousands of years. But violating commercial copyrights and trademarks is quite another, and such behaviour will not be tolerated, in peace or in war'. Retaliation has brought long-range missile strikes to the European base of Bayer manufacture, and threatens to spread the conflict further.

It is possible[9] that further Pharma conflicts will develop around the world. As such, it necessary to establish legal protocols that go beyond the Geneva Convention in order to structure and horizon belligerence. At this point the joint-working team on the present paper have failed to find unanimity, and instead have agreed to position two alternate concluding paragraphs. For legal reasons, these are personalised with the names of team-leaders,

---

[8] A majority of АПУ scholars dissent from this opinion, but have agreed to let it stand provided the second clause beginning 'but . . . ' after the comma was added.

[9] RPSL scholars preferred the phrase 'It is inevitable . . . '

although the sentiments they express were collectively agreed by the team-leader's respective teams.

Conclusion 1: *Rachel Statton-Cummings, RPSL*: 'the financial power and influence of the income associated with Trademark Bugs has resulted in seismic changes in the political and therefore social structures of our world. Democracy has, broadly, shifted from a flat-rate one-person-one-vote model to a corporate, buy-as-many-votes-as-you-like model. Democratic engagement is still open, at least for those who can afford to buy votes, but there is no guarantee it will stay this way (US and EU sets a maximum price for voting shares at $5/€3 each; but legislation currently being debated will remove maxima and allow the market to determine rates). Freedom of speech, once a necessary plank of democracy, has been reoriented around the axis of copyright and trademark law. Above all, what could have been the greatest single step towards collective human wellbeing in the world's history—the development of effective treatments for almost all cancers, all bacterial fevers, all GTI and skin diseases, all influenzas and even the myriad forms of the common cold—has instead been diverted into the artificial maintaining of these diseases in the general population solely to generate profits for three large and fifty-five smaller pharma companies. Trademark bugs go routinely untreated in poorer countries, causing unnecessary distress—and, since the leakage of weaponised pharma from the Asian War, often provoke long-term harm and even death. This whole situation can only be described as a collective moral wrong on a massive scale; and the international Law needs to be mobilised to address its consequences.[10]

Conclusion 2: *Aleksandr Aleksandrovich Golumbovsy, АПУ*: There are areas where the commercial handling of Trademark Bugs could be reformed and improved, especially with respect to medical access in poorer nations. But we as legal theorists must not overlook the very powerful good that the

---

[10] A speculative second paragraph has been retained only in footnote form: 'it does not require a crystal ball to see which way Trademark Bugs will develop. The Porter Rules hold less and less legal force, and if not robustly defended will vanish entirely in the next few years. If that happens, then there will be no legal sanction preventing the big three—or any of the smaller companies—from spreading modified cancers, auto-immune or other lethal pathologies and charging large amounts for the relevant cures. Corporations exist to maximise profit, not human happiness; and this would be a way of deriving the greatest amount of profit. As it says in the Bible, skin for skin, all that a man hath he will give for his life. What safeguards exist to prevent these corporations from acting in this way? What Bill of Rights or Constitution exists to restrain them? What Magna Carta did they sign?'

big three Pharma companies have accomplished in the space of less than seventy years.

Having invested trillions of dollars in research and development, these three companies developed cured pathologies that had plagued humanity for hundreds of millennia: plague, cancer, auto-immune diseases, influenza, malaria, TB, diphtheria, cholera, typhus, myriad genetic conditions and fevers. This, in a sense, is what these companies existed to do; and whilst these cures represented a massive humanitarian good, they also embodied the power of commercial self-interest. Having achieved this set of goals, it is not realistic to believe that these companies would simply roll-themselves-up and cease trading. Indeed, under the well-established legal rule of corporate individuality, it would not be licit to expect them to commit suicide in this fashion. The distribution of Trademark Bugs—in every case, much milder diseases than the 'feral' illness that previously afflicted humanity—provided a viable commercial model by which these companies could continue to trade, with all the benefits that entailed in terms of employment, economic stimulus and so on.

The success of these Bugs was a function of two factors. One was the competitive pricing model adopted, whereby mild colds could be cured with cheap medicines, and only rarer, more serious illnesses required more expensive pharmaceuticals. Two was cultural inertia: people were used to getting sick with colds and flus, and they continued getting sick with these illnesses. The difference was that now they could be cured for a small financial outlay. High-profile media campaigns argued that if the companies ceased distributing their new modified bugs then the illnesses would stop happening altogether; but these failed to make significant inroads in many areas. Like taxation (discussed below), people broadly accept a degree of disease in their lives, provided only that the proportion does not rise too high.

The broader ethics of this practice are a matter for philosophical discussion; but on the practical plane the practice has been bedded-in as a fait accompli by its prodigious financial success. This money has altered the structure of global society in ways that are (arguably) both bad and good. It is worth, however, stressing the good.

The global spread of Trademark Bugs created the circumstances for titheing, which in turn shrunk nation-state tax collection. The Big Three are now, broadly speaking, responsible for the infrastructure, health, educational and military provision that used to be the preserve of countries. In effect the tax take has shifted from governments to these corporations. This is more ethical—since nobody is obliged to purchase the company cures, nobody is forced to pay 'tax'—and more practical. The 'tax' base has widened (since everybody is liable to infection) and consequently the actual rate has reduced from an average 17% of income (by-total-population) to an average 9% [Engell 2098]. Both these outcomes are improvements. More, previously people paid tax to government and often resented it; now people pay 'tax' for the immediate somatic relief of freedom from a pressing illness, and are grateful. There are compelling arguments [Iglesias 2098, Kaufmann, 2099] that corporations not only collect less tax, but disburse what they do collect more efficiently than did the old governments.

There is nothing immutable about any particular social model of structure of government. The only salient is that people are governed predictably, fairly and effectively. Attachment to the old systems merely for the sake of nostalgic attachment to tradition is illogical. The Big Three have effected a bloodless revolution and left the world, broadly speaking, better off.'

Bibliography

Bandari, Q., *Pharma: the Social Revolution* (PN Press 2089)

Brohstein, L., *Efficiency, Inefficiency, Mortality and Disbursement: an Account of Russian Federation Tax Affairs 2082-88* (Glaxco Press, 2090)

Engell, J., *Global Tax Take: a Quantitative History 1600-2100* (Bayer University Press 2098)

Gharzai, M., *The First Asian War: One Million Casualties and Counting* (Scorpion Press 2099)

Gharzai, M., *Corporate Responsibility: the Limits of Genocide* (Independent Distribution 2100)

Grohmann, *Freedom and Restriction of Speech: New Commercial Paradigms* (PN Press 2088)

Iglesias, M., *Tax Disbursement in an Age of Mass Casualties: Commercial and Nation-State Paradigms Compared* (Oxfam 2098)

Kaufmann, S., *The Metaphysics of Taxation* (Glaxco Press, 2099)

Kokoschka L, Maass G., Truman Q and Wellek R, *Legal Discussion, Discourse and Social Policy: the Anglo-Russian Collaborations* (5th edition, EU 2099)

Malahat, M., *An Elongated Summary of Guardian v. Glaxco, 2036-39* (Bayer Press 2090)

Trebuchet, A., 'Unlogged and Unplanned Feral Mutations to Trademark Bugs in the Field: a Catalogue and Assessment of Future Risk', *Journal of Independent Epidemiology* 12 (Fall 2096), 55-109

A BETTER WAY TO DIE

PAUL CORNELL

Cliveden is one of the great houses of Greater Britain. It stands beside the Thames in Buckinghamshire, at the end of the sort of grand avenue that such places kept and made carriages fly up, when carriages were the done thing. In the extensive forests, a Grand Charles tree from the Columbian colonies has been grown into the shape of a guest house. The yew tree walk leads down to a boathouse that has, painted on its ramp, dated, descending notches of where the water once rose, taken at the flood. The ramp has twice now been extended to reach the river. From the house itself, one can look out over the parterre to a one hundred and eighty degree horizon of what were once flood meadows, now seamless farmland. The view of the other half of the world is that which one would expect of a hunting estate. There is a smooth, plunging hill, kept clear to present targets on the horizon, with trees either side, towards which the game can break. There are hides for beaters. There is a balcony that looks down on the yard, from which favours can be thrown and bloods scored. At certain times of the year you will hear the reports of guns, the calling of the hounds and the sohos of those on the chase, unimpeded by fence or ditch. The gutters of the forecourt are there to catch the blood.

Hamilton often worked out of uniform, so he knew the great estates. They were where royalty risked a social life outside of their palaces, still requiring careful eyes beside them. They were where were hauled those individuals who had lost so much of their souls in the great game that they had actually changed sides. Houses like this were where such wretched people would be allowed to unburden themselves, their words helping to reset the balance that their actions had set swinging. Houses like this were also where officers like himself were interviewed following injury or failure. And finally, always finally, they were places from where such as he sometimes did not return. They were the index that ran alongside the London and abroad half of an out of uniform man's life, the margin in which damning notes were made. Such buildings were the physical manifestation of how these things had always been done, the plans of them a noble motto across the English countryside. Those words could be read even if your face was in the mud. Especially then. In the circumstances in which Hamilton now found himself, that thought reassured him. But still, he could not make himself ready to die.

He'd found the invitation on his breakfast table: the name of the estate and a date which was that same day. The handwriting was in the new style, which meant that no hand had been near it, that it had been spoken onto the card as if by God. He could not decide anything based upon it. Except that the confidence of this gesture indicated that, despite everything, those who had power over him still did not doubt who they were and what they could do.

He had picked it up with none of the anticipation he might once have felt, just a dull, resigned dread. This was the answer to a question he hadn't put into words. He had started to feel a deeper anger, nameless, useless, than any he had felt before. He knew what he was owed, but had become increasingly sure he wouldn't receive it. The fact of him being owed it would be seen now as an impertinent gesture on his part, a burden on those who had invested elsewhere. He had one request now, he'd decided, looking at the card in his numb fingers: he would ask to be sent to contribute to some hopeless cause. But perhaps those were only to be found in the blockade now, and if they didn't want him, they especially wouldn't want him there. Still, he'd held onto that thought through dressing appropriately and packing for the country. But then even that hope had started to feel like treachery and cowardice. The condemned man must not have anything to ask of the executioner. That was the beginning of pleading.

And yet hope stayed with him. It played on him. His own balance ate at him as he prepared. A fool, he told himself, would assume he was on his way to Cliveden to be given what he was owed. To at least be thanked for all these years and given a fond farewell. He made sure he was not hoping for that.

Now he watched from the carriage as it swung down towards the avenue that led to Cliveden. He saw nobody in the grounds, not a single worker on the fields. That was extraordinary. Normally, they would be out there in numbers, waving to any carriage from their enormous harvesters and beaters and propulsion horses. Hamilton had no idea how many servants it took to maintain an estate like Cliveden, but it must be numbered in the hundreds. There would traditionally be too many, in fact, 'a job for every man and several of those jobs are lounging about just in case' as some wag had put it. On the two occasions when he'd seen an officer die in such places, it had been done (in one case like an accident, in another, and that was a scene he'd take to his grave, like a suicide) in the grounds, away from the eyes of the help. You didn't need to clear them all out. But no, he stopped himself: surely this was just the larger version of what he'd seen at Keble? He was making new horrors for himself with no new evidence.

The carriage settled onto the end of the drive, and Hamilton stepped down onto the gravel. His knee spasmed and he nearly fell. Getting old. He wondered if they were watching this, and killed a thought that he didn't care. He did. He must. It had been an affectation to take a carriage, he realised, when, in moments, these days, he could have walked down a tunnel from his rooms in London. And he'd brought a valise, as if he was unwilling, should he need to dress for dinner, to return there in the same way to do so. He was silently making statements with these actions. Stubborn statements. Like he'd made, as if with the intention of ending his service, that night at Keble. This new realisation angered him more than anything else had. Only fools and criminals didn't know why they did things. It seemed that he was no longer strong enough to hold that fate at bay. To arrive here as someone who bowed to the command of those other voices within one, to pain or desire or selfishness, to have allowed those threats to the balance to have grown within oneself, and to only realise it on this threshold . . . it was an invitation to the powers in this house to strike him down. And they would be right to do so.

He allowed himself to smile at the relief of that thought. *They would be right to do so.* If he could accept that, all would be well. He had brought the valise. He would not baulk and desperately fly to return it, like a panicked undergraduate. If he suddenly did, or said, or hinted at anything not of his own volition, but that had come out of the other half of him that should be under his control, then the balance could still be restored at the cost of his life. He didn't have to worry about that.

But the thought still came to him: those with his life in their hands didn't seem to value the balance so much these days, did they?

That thought was like a far greater death that lay in wait.

If the world was tempting him into plucking at his own house of cards, it was because that was all everyone seemed to be doing now. He was hesitating on this drive, actually hesitating. He had seen his life as a house of cards.

Perhaps the world was dying too.

Perhaps everyone his age felt that.

But surely nobody had ever felt it in circumstances like these?

The carriage finally moved off. He made himself step forward, looking down at the valise now inescapably in his hand.

He found he had orders in his eyes. He wasn't to go into the house, but into the forest.

• • •

He made his way down a winding path to the edge of the woods. It was overcast, but the shadows from inside the forest were slanting at impossible angles, as if somewhere in there someone was lighting a stage.

He walked into the forest.

The path took him past fallen trees, not long ago cut down, by a logger who was now absent. He stopped to listen. The sounds of nature. But no sawing, no distant echo of metal on wood, no great machines. Strange that the effect could be so complete.

He came to the edge of a clearing. Here was where the strange light was coming from. It seemed to be summer here, because the light was from overhead. The air was warmer. Hamilton kept his expression steady. He walked slowly into the centre, and saw the trees that shouldn't be here. He wanted to follow etiquette, but that was difficult when those one was addressing had abandoned propriety. It was as if they had grabbed the ribbon of his duty and then leapt down a well. He felt like bellowing at them. He felt awful that he felt like bellowing at them.

He addressed the tallest of the trees. "You wanted to see me, sir?"

It had been just a few weeks ago that he'd been invited to meet Turpin at Keble. His commanding officer had been a guest of the Warden, and had asked Hamilton to join him at High Table. This had seemed at the time the most natural thing in the world, Keble being where Hamilton himself had been an undergraduate. He'd driven down to Oxford as always, had the Porters fuss over the Morgan as always. He'd stopped for a moment outside the chapel, thinking about Annie; the terrible lack of her. But he could still look at the chapel and take pleasure in it. He'd been satisfied with his composure, then. At that time he'd already been on leave for several weeks. He should have realised that had been suspiciously long. And before that he'd been used for penny ante jobs, sent on them by junior officers, not even allowed to return to the Dragoons, who were themselves on endless exercises in Scotland. He really should have understood, before it had been revealed to him, that he was being kept away from something.

It had been in the Warden's rooms at Keble that Turpin had first appeared in his life, all those years ago, had first asked him about working out of uniform. To some people, he'd said, the balance, the necessary moment by moment weighing and shifting of everything from military strength to personal ethics that kept war from erupting between the great nations and their colonies right across the solar system, was something felt, something in the body. This had been a couple of years before the medical theologians had got to work on how the balance actually was present in the mind. Hamilton had recognised that in himself. Turpin had already been then as Hamilton had always known him, his face a patchwork of grown skin, from where he'd had the corners knocked off him in the side streets of Kiev and the muck-filled trenches of Zimbabwe.

But on entering the Warden's rooms on this later occasion, after decades of service, Hamilton had found himself saluting a different Turpin. His features were smooth, all trace of his experience removed. Hamilton had carefully not reacted. Turpin hadn't offered any comment. "Interesting crowd this evening, Major," he'd said, nodding to indicate those assembled under the Warden's roof. Hamilton had looked. And that had been, now he looked back to it, the moment his own balance had started to slide dangerously towards collapse.

Standing beside the dress uniforms and the evening suits and the clerical collars had been a small deer.

It was not some sort of extraordinary pet. Its gaze had been following the movements of a conversation, and then it was taking part in it, its mouth forming words in a horribly human way. Hamilton had looked quickly over to where a swirl of translucent drapery had been chatting with the Chaplain. Nearby, a circling pillar of . . . they had actually been continuously falling birds, or not quite birds, but the faux heraldic devices often displayed by the Foreigners whose forces were now encircling the solar system. He'd guessed that the falling was the point, rather than the . . . he'd wanted to call it a dress . . . being a celebration of the idea that the Foreigners might flock together and make their plans in great wheeling masses. The pillar held a glass of wine, supported somehow by all those shapes dropping past it. These creatures were all ladies, Hamilton had assumed. Or rather, hoped.

"It's all the rage at the Palace," said Turpin. "It's all relative this, and relative that."

Hamilton hadn't found it in him to make any sensible comment. He'd heard about such things, obviously. Enough to disdain them and move on to some other subject. That the new King had allowed, even encouraged this sort of thing, presumably to the continuing shame of Elizabeth . . . he'd stopped himself. He was thinking of the Queen, and he could not allow himself to feel so intimate with what she might or might not think of her husband.

"Not your sort of thing?" asked Turpin.

"No, sir."

Turpin paused a moment, considering, and offered a new tack. "The Bodlean is, I believe, now infinite."

"Good for it."

Turpin had nodded towards the corner. "So. What about him?"

He was indicating a young man, talking to a beautiful woman. Hamilton's first thought had been that he was familiar. Then he had realised. And had first found the anger that hadn't left him since. This was what downed Foreigner vessels had brought here. Of course it wouldn't all be used for frippery. Or perhaps now frippery had invaded war.

It had been like looking at the son he'd never had, at his own face without everything time had written on it. There was for a moment a ghost of a thought that they'd taken away from him that moment of seeing a son. That had been the first of the many ghosts.

The hair was darker. The body was thinner, more hips than shoulders. The boy had worn not uniform, but black tie, so they hadn't managed, or perhaps even wished, to get him into the regiment. The young woman the boy was talking to had nudged him, and he had looked towards Hamilton. It was the shock of running into a mirror. The eyes were the same. He hadn't known what his own expression had been in that instant, but the younger version of him had worn a smile as he made eye contact. It hadn't been in the slightest bit deferential. It wasn't attractive, either. But Hamilton had recognised it. He contained his anger, knowing that this boy would be able to read him like a book. Hamilton had had no idea that such things were now possible. This must be a very secure gathering, for the two of them to be seen together. The boy had expected this. He had been allowed that.

He had turned back to his superior officer with a raised eyebrow. "Who's the girl?"

Turpin had paused for a moment, pleasingly, taken aback by Hamilton's lack of comment about the boy. "Her name is Precious Nothing."

"Parents who like a challenge?"

"Perhaps it was a *memento mori*. She's—"

"With the College of Heralds, yes." Hamilton had seen the colours on her silk scarf, which was one hell of a place to put them.

"Well, only just about, these days. She's a senior Herald, but she's been put on probation."

"Because of him." Hamilton found the idea of a Herald being linked to such a peculiar creature as the boy utterly startling. Heralds decided what breeding was, what families and nations were. The College held the records of every family line, decided upon the details of coats of arms, were the authority on every matter of grand ceremony and inheritance. Of course, every other week now one heard rumours that the College was on the verge of dissolution or denunciation, as they tried and failed to find some new way to protest at the new manners. They seemed continually astonished that His Majesty was being advised this badly. Some of this conflict had even reached the morning plates. But it had always gone by the evening editions. To Hamilton, the idea of parts of the body public fighting each other was like the idea of a man punching himself in the face. It was a physical blasphemy that suited this era as an index of how far it had all gone.

"You really haven't another word to say about him?" Turpin had asked, interrupting his woolgathering.

Hamilton had feigned a moment's thought. "How is he on the range?"

"Reasonable. You were only ever reasonable." He hadn't emphasised the *you*.

Then the Warden had clinked his glass with a spoon, and the ladies and the gentlemen and the *trompe-l'oeil* and the small deer had gone in to dinner.

Hamilton had been relieved to find that the younger version of himself had gone to the far end of the dining table that stood on a rise at the end of the hall. In any other circumstances, it would have been comforting to be back in this place, with the smell of polish and the candlelight, but as he looked out at the tables of undergraduates, he realised that something was missing. There would normally be numerous servants moving between the rows, delivering plates of food and refilling glasses. Suddenly, he saw just such a meal appearing beside one chattering youth, something which caused the lad no surprise whatsoever. Hamilton had been seated opposite Turpin, and now he looked back to him.

"Hidden service," the senior man said. "Happens in a lot of places now. The servants move through an infinite fold, in effect an empty optional world, beside the real one. One more use for the new engines. And neater, you must admit."

Hamilton didn't feel the need to agree with such young opinions from his old mentor. He was now wondering if the man's new smoothness of face was because this was also a younger version. But no, surely not, here was still the experience, the tone of voice he was used to. Turpin had seen that look. "One of the out of uniform men found it for me," he said, as if he was talking about a carriage. "As soon as the great powers recognised that various of the engines that had fallen into our hands gave us access to optional worlds, outside the balance, the Palace felt it was our lot's duty to start mapping them, to find out where all these open fold tunnels lead. Our regimental hunting parties have been going all over."

Hamilton thought he understood now why he hadn't been included in that effort. "Including another one of you?"

"Several. The original owner of this was only a Newton or so different to the original. Well, in physical terms. Where he came from, a lot of our conflicts didn't happen, hence the smoothness of face. Our lads put him in the bag, and when they got back, connected his mind to an infinite tunnel. Like using a terrier to root out a fox. Once he was out, I moved in, using the same method. Should keep me going for a bit longer."

Hamilton had found himself wondering at that statement. His balance had been thrown by the boy, and so he'd allowed himself the seditious thought, because it had felt not so dangerous then, that Turpin was seeking not, as he said, an extension of his service, but actually tactical advantage at Court. He was now more like those he served were. And never mind the distance that took him from his officers. "What if optional worlds start raiding us in the same way?"

"First thing we thought of. We seem to be unique, at least in all those options nearby. We're the only ones who've encountered the Foreigners. Or they may even only exist in this world. If they do start popping over, we may have to start making treaties with optional Britains rather than raiding them."

"And extending the balance into them?"

Turpin had raised his hands. Perhaps he felt this was beyond his duty or understanding.

"How can there be younger versions of people? How is there an optional world where . . . I'm . . . his age?"

"These worlds form in waves, I'm told."

"Like the waves that interfere with each other in this world to create the heights and depths of the balance?"

"Presumably." There had been that impatience with the matter of the balance once more. "Some waves are a bit behind us in time, some a bit forward."

"And there are some options where there are chatty deer and pillars of birds? Or are those just fashions anticipating such stuff?"

"A little bit of both. There's a rather large selection box, all told." Turpin had leaned forward, as if wishing Hamilton would get to the meat of it. And Hamilton had been pleased that it hadn't been him that had taken them there. "Listen, that younger you, he's the first of his kind to be brought over. He's got nobody's mind but his own. He's a whole chap, a volunteer from a world so like ours that there wasn't an iota of difference."

"Except no Foreigners?"

"Exactly."

"And no balance?"

"Yes, yes!"

Hamilton had wondered if Turpin was planning on putting his mind in the boy's skull. But he'd hardly have invited them both to a social occasion first. "If we can do all this now, and I didn't know we could—"

"I'm telling you now under a seal. You'll find, if you look, that your covers have already reacted to my tone of voice. You won't be able to tell anyone any of this." He looked suddenly chagrined at Hamilton's startled look. "Not that you *would*, of course!"

Turpin's manners seemed to have changed with his new body. That had been shocking too, a shock like one felt sometimes at things one had heard were said and done at Court. "If we can do all this now we've got their engines, why can't the Foreigners open a tunnel at the blockade, pop up in Whitehall and have at us?"

"Good question. The great powers have been pondering that. Together." Enough had been made public for Hamilton to understand that there was now a significantly greater degree of cooperation between the courts of the great powers of Europe. The arrival of the Foreigners had forced that, when the haphazard capture of the new engines in various parts of the solar system might otherwise have set the balance rocking. There, he suspected, was the hand of the deity in this. If it was anywhere. "The leading theory at the moment is that, for some reason, the Foreigners forbid, among themselves, the use of optional worlds. That it's a principle of whatever mistaken religion they practice. Optionalism is perhaps just a side effect of what they use as propulsion, but so far we've only made sense of the side effect, and none at all of the propulsion."

"Can we use it to surprise *them*?"

"Working on just that."

This was far more the sort of conversation Hamilton had been used to with his commanding officer. He had found himself regretting his earlier reactions, understanding them, regaining control of himself. Tonight, whatever else it was, was surely planned as a test of his character, and so far he had just about stumbled through. What he *felt* about anything was as beside the point now as it had always been.

Turpin had spent the rest of dinner sounding him out about the myriad aspects of the shared defence strategies being adopted by the 'grand alliance' of great powers. There was some new addition to their ranks every day. Savoy, most recently. There were even rumours the Turks were going to join. Hamilton had wanted to ask where the balance was in all this. What was going to happen to it if every nation was on the same side? Was the arrival of the Foreigners and their engines, at the same time, the fatal shock, the final moment when the balance would collapse and resolve into some new social or actual reality, as experts in the matter had often hypothesised? Was that what was happening all around them now? He had always conceived of that moment as being grand, somehow, and not a matter of finding wild animals in the Warden's rooms. Or was this just some particularly ferocious swinging of the pendulum, which would resolve itself, as it always had, into a gentler motion?

But Turpin, true to his new form, hadn't mentioned the balance at all, apart from when he'd joined in the grace before the meal. Hamilton had half hoped one of the divines would strike up a debate on the subject. He had known, through the gossip of his maid, Alexandria, that all was not well amongst the clergy, that the next synod at York was going to be rough on His Majesty and his terrifying commonwealth of nations, but there was no sign of that here. These particular clerics were as content to swim amongst this stuff as that Herald had been.

All through the conversation, Hamilton had kept his gaze on his superior. He hadn't wanted to be seen craning his neck to get a look at the younger version of himself. He had continued to affect nonchalance. And hoped he was not projecting affectation. The bell had rung, the students had started to exit, and the Warden had invited his guests back to his rooms for brandy. Turpin had announced that he wanted to talk to someone, and gone ahead.

As Hamilton had entered, the younger man had stepped straight to intercept him. Precious was with him. She had had an interested look on her face. Turpin had already got to the other side of the room, thank God, so there had been nobody to attempt some sort of crass introduction. But Hamilton had known his superior officer's gaze would be upon him now. He still hadn't known what was expected of him. But if this was a game, he was going to win it.

"Major," said the youth. "I can't tell you how much I've been looking forward to this moment."

"I wish I could say the same." That had come out like an insult. So he had kept his jaw firm and damn well let it stand. "Where did they find you?"

The youth had seemed unperturbed. "Oh, in some dusty corridor of what one might still call reality."

"This year's model." Hamilton couldn't help but look at Precious rather than at his younger self. She was looking back at him too. He wondered in how many ways she was comparing them.

"Most people would be full of questions," said the youth.

"It's the nature of innocence to question, the nature of duty to accept."

"And it's the nature of age to be too sure of itself." The boy had been ready to get angry if he felt he had to. He seemed very conscious of his honour. Sure he was being looked at too. Which was why Hamilton had poked him on the nose just then, to see his control, or lack of it. That rationalisation, horribly, had come to Hamilton only after the fact.

Perhaps that was the point of this, to see which of them displayed the most grace? Had the boy been told what fate might await him, if he failed whatever test this was? Could it be that Hamilton was, after all, being allowed to inspect his new . . . vehicle? Or was this his replacement? He couldn't let himself dwell on that possibility. Hamilton had instead turned politely to Precious. She was petite, with long red hair set off by a green evening dress that . . . yes, the influence of the optional was here too, the dress had been, or still was, a sunlit meadow. To be in her presence wasn't so much to see it as to be in the presence of it. She was used to being looked at, and sought it. Her freckles didn't look girlish on her, but somehow added to the passionate seriousness of those eyes, which held an expression of tremendous interest, a challenge to the world that equalled that of her dress. She had a welcoming mouth. "So," he'd said, "where did you meet me?"

She'd smiled, but she hadn't laughed. "We were introduced at the College of Heralds. Colonel Turpin brought him to visit. But I note that *we* haven't been."

"You'll have to forgive me. I assumed we had already shared . . . a degree . . . of intimacy."

He'd wondered if she would bristle at that. But she had smiled instead of being offended. Still, it had been a forced smile. She wasn't quite onboard for the anything goes of the new manners, then. Still a Herald at heart. Hamilton had found something he liked in her. Which should have come, he supposed, as no surprise.

"Why do you think," the boy asked, "that Turpin wanted us to meet?"

"Perhaps he's deciding on a suit, and wants to see both tried on." He had looked back to Precious, as if suggesting she might be doing the same thing. She'd just inclined a fine eyebrow.

The boy had stepped between them then. He had decided on both a need to bring this intangible contest into the physical world, and a way to do it. "Tell me, Major," he said, "do you play cards?"

The Warden, no doubt encouraged by Turpin, had quickly warmed to the notion of a game. The select crowd, who had doubtless now realised what they were looking at when they looked between Hamilton and his younger self, had been intrigued, had talked at the top of their voices about it. He supposed, as the cards were prepared and he'd looked again at the throng, that there were clusters of people like this across Greater Britain now, in the most fashionable salons, changing their shapes and their ages and their appearances and the balance be hanged, and from now on they would all be grabbing at the novel and the extreme like they were bloody Icelandic. Perhaps the blockade had done this. Perhaps they were all starting to dance as the ship went down.

The game, someone had decided, should be clock seconds. Neither he nor the boy knew it. Which again, Hamilton supposed, was no accident. They had each taken a hand of ten from a new deck, one of a series being placed on the table. Hamilton took a glass of comfort while he was at it, a Knappogue Castle, from the Tullamore distillery, a pure pot still whiskey. Nothing served here or at High Table would be the kind of thing that the covers in his head could shrug off. That was the whole point of evenings like this. To get at the reality, that had been the thought, he supposed, back when those invited here had been interested in that. So now he was accepting a disadvantage. The boy, of course, had had to do the same, and, despite Precious' warning glance, had taken the same measure.

The idea was to form tricks of differing value by discarding cards and picking new ones from another pack. But the nature of what constituted a legal trick changed depending on the time, each ten minute arc on the Warden's gilt bronze clock deciding the rules at that given moment. There was also a time limit of a few seconds on how long they could take to play a hand, so one couldn't just sit there waiting until the terrain became favourable. So, Hamilton had realised as they waited for nine o'clock to chime on the chapel bell, one could either hold on to cards for long term advantage, or keep burning one's fuel steadily, playing the averages instead of waiting for some huge coup. Time and meaning in this game were freakishly interconnected. A somewhat garish intelligent projection of the rules was thrown onto the wall behind them, startling the deer. The projection had all the washes of colour and blurred lines that suggested a courtier who was paying too much attention to His Majesty's aesthetic tastes. It was said that the look of the ballroom at Hampton Court now changed depending on where you were in it, often just a blur of movement, as if it was seen from a carriage. Several ladies had already fallen as a result during one of the new dances, which had all struck Hamilton as being graceless gallops where the tempo was continually changing, people might collide at any moment, and it would be hard to tell where anyone was. They had been quick to blame their own shortcomings rather than question he whose perspective made all this. And well they should, of course that was the way they had to behave, what was Hamilton thinking? He had chided himself again.

They had taken up their initial hands. The boy had made eye contact with him again. No smile now. The obvious thing would be for Hamilton to underestimate him. He would not do that. That would be to lie about himself. He had let his eyes move upwards from his seated opponent, and linger, for a moment, where they should not.

"What are you looking at?" asked the boy, without turning to look.

"Nothing," Hamilton had said, and had glanced back to his cards with a precisely calculated raise of his eyebrow.

In the first ten minute round, Hamilton had surged ahead, his opponent failing to score while he put down some obvious, simple tricks. The boy seemed to always be waiting for something that was just one card away. Hamilton had recognised that in himself. That had been something that the service had beaten out of him.

A cheer and the Warden chiming spoon on glass had marked the end of the round, and the boy had immediately thrown down what he'd had but couldn't previously score from, putting him in the lead, and generating another cheer with the flourish of it. Hamilton had wondered if there were any in this crowd who were favouring him, or if to those who came to a party dressed as a mirage, the older version of an individual would be automatically the less interesting. He'd looked again to Precious, and thought he caught something in her expression. Why did he feel she wasn't quite of that opinion? She was biting her bottom lip, her eyes large with the excitement of the game. He'd turned back to the boy. "You know your fables?" he said, to conceal something that was brewing in his cards. "Slow and steady wins the race."

"Yes, the Greeks would be keen on this game." And he'd thrown down the first of a series of quick payoffs, building up a steady lead, trying to force Hamilton to bet on something that might never happen. "It's full of transformations."

"Yet hardly classical."

"What's seen as classical changes with time, just like anything else."

So he seemed to share the opinions that had made his arrival here possible. Or to be willing to join in the chorus, at least. But surely he might feel as if he were still a slave, a chattel taken by a raiding party from an invaded province? There was, after all, something of that in Hamilton himself. Hamilton had risked a glance at Turpin and decided to raise the temperature. "Shall we make it interesting?" Having heard how finely cut the boy's accent was, he had let a little Irish back into his own.

"How much?"

Hamilton had tried to remember what would have broken his bank in his twenties. Not that much less than what would now. Or was that his memory distorting time again? He didn't want to quote something that the boy would consider a trifle. Still, the value of money hadn't changed much over the years, just his concept of what sufficed. "A thousand guineas?" The onlookers made shocked noises. Hamilton had realised his mistake immediately. It looked like he was bullying the boy. Precious was shaking her head at the young man, urging him to throw in his cards. "Or, no, perhaps not, let's say—"

"A thousand guineas." The boy had been roused by that. Of course he had. Hamilton had baited him in front of his girl.

He'd have done the same at that age if Annie were here, might have done the same now. He wouldn't humiliate his younger self by backtracking now. "All right, then."

The next three rounds seemed to go by in a flash. Hamilton and the boy had barely looked up as they drew, considered, threw in, the Warden calling the scores as they did so. Aces were high or low. The order of the court cards, to gasps from a few of those assembled who under pressure revealed a more traditional turn of mind, changed too. And the Ambassador, the Horse and the Devil could sometimes raise or lower the values of the numerals in Cups, Swords, Staves and Coins.

With eleven minutes to go, everyone had surrounded the table where Hamilton and the boy were sweating, looking to their hands and then to each other, grabbing and throwing down, faster and faster. Hamilton was considering how hard it would be for him to take a loss of a thousand. It would mean selling something, perhaps the Morgan. He could deal with that pressure because of his experience, his training. The boy would have the surety and indestructibility of youth, but he had more to lose. His life, even, if he couldn't pay, or if whatever he had here instead of a family or a regiment decided his existence wasn't worth the expenditure. Perhaps his life, at least as a mind in his own body, was dependent, even, on the larger game they were playing tonight, whatever it might be. Hamilton had put aside a twinge of conscience. That was why he'd done this, wasn't it? Not to harm the boy, but to put him off his game. Or *was* that the whole of it? Then he cursed himself for losing his concentration in that second, as he saw, as he threw his hand down, that he could have kept some of those cards a moment more for much greater reward. The crowd cheered at the arrival of the last round and the last rule change. The boy was ahead, marginally. He was barely considering each hand before he threw it in, and now he didn't have to think about what might be round the corner. They had turned the last bend and were sprinting for the finishing line. Hamilton decided that the only way to go was to match him for speed, glimpsing the best hand, throwing in, hoping for better, hoping to push the boy that way too. The Warden shouted the score more and more swiftly. Fumbling fingers on cards became an issue. Hamilton drew level, and had found that all he had in the final seconds was luck. It wouldn't be the first time he'd thrown himself on her mercy. He saw that he had tens of each suit, not the best hand and not the worst, and threw it down with just a moment left to play. The boy had looked at his own hand . . . and seemed to freeze. Hamilton could see his fingers trembling. Was he waiting, deliberately prolonging the misery? He himself had often been cruel, when a job had given him licence to. The clock hand had thumped round the final three seconds . . . two . . . Hamilton was just a point ahead, surely the boy must have something—? The boy fumbled with the cards and threw down his whole hand with a shout and the chimes of the chapel bell rang out across the room and the Warden rang his glass in unison and everyone had immediately leaned forward to see—

The boy had had nothing. He could have made nothing. And now he was staring at Hamilton, and Precious had stepped forward to defend him, her face furious, never mind that all tradition called for her to move in the opposite direction. And now, like a father, Hamilton had suddenly found he agreed.

"I'm satisfied," Hamilton had begun, "I'll just take one good bottle of—"

"Don't you dare!" bellowed the boy. "Don't you *dare!* I will pay what I owe!" And his voice had been fully Irish now, the sound which Hamilton heard often in his own thoughts and rarely in his speech. And with that the lad had leapt to his feet and had marched out, without properly taking his leave or thanking his host. Precious had stared after him, outraged with the world. But she had not had the indecency in her to follow.

There had been only a brief silence before chatter had filled it.

Hamilton had looked over to the Warden, who was awkwardly closing the plate he'd used to keep the score. He didn't meet Hamilton's glance. There didn't seem to be much joy in the room at what had happened. It wasn't that this crowd had been on the younger man's side, as such. But there was a sense of something broken. It was as if these people had suddenly discovered, upon being shaken, that a lot had changed, within them and without, and they didn't know what to cheer for any more.

Hamilton had got to his feet and taken a last sip from his glass. He had been pleased, despite everything, to find, a moment later, that Precious had joined him.

"He didn't deserve it," she said.

"No, he didn't. But *deserve* is very rarely in it."

Around them, the party had been breaking up. Farewells were being said. And now Turpin had chosen his moment to wander over. He had placed his hand on Hamilton's shoulder. Hamilton wasn't sure if he remembered his superior officer ever touching him before. Precious had stepped quickly away.

"Bad show," Turpin had said, very quietly.

"I'm sorry, sir. I assumed this was a contest."

"You didn't have to force him into a choice between bankruptcy and disgrace. I was hoping our young Herald here might be led, through her closeness to the lad, to begin a new trend in her College, to bring more of them towards His Majesty's point of view. Win or lose, she'd have felt more taken with him, having seen him prove his mettle. But now she'll be unable to see him and retain her position." Turpin had looked over to where Precious stood, her face, now she thought she was unobserved, betraying a sort of calculation, as if she was working out propriety against length of time waited before she made after the boy. Then he had looked again to Hamilton, shook his head, and gone to take leave of his host.

And, until that card on his breakfast table, that was the last Hamilton had heard from him. Hamilton had said goodnight to his host, had left the Warden's rooms and had gone to the door of the Chapel. And he had found, in the despair that was already sinking into his stomach, that that building was now a horror to him after all.

• • •

And now he was here at Cliveden, addressing what he only knew were his superior officer, and an Equerry of the Court of Saint James', and the Crown Secretary of Powers, because the orders in his eyes told him so. They were presumably still back in London, in Turpin's office off Horseguards Parade, or at least part of them was. They were wearing the trees, far across their nation, with no more thought than one might wear a coat.

"Good afternoon, Major." Turpin's voice came from the air around him. "I'm sorry to say . . . we have a job for you."

The sheer relief made Hamilton unable to speak for a moment. "A . . . job, sir?"

"You seem, during your encounter with him, to have fathomed the character of your younger self. Just as His Majesty wished you to." That was the Equerry. There would have been a time when the former Queen Mother would have seen to such matters herself, but now she never left her wing of the Palace, and was rumoured to be . . . Hamilton found himself letting the thought breathe in his mind, his relief giving him licence . . . people said she was mad now.

"I didn't realise I was acting on His Majesty's service, sir." He hoped his tone didn't convey the knowledge he was sure they both shared, that His Majesty had known as much about it as he had.

"That was of course as he wished. And he wishes to convey that you did well."

"The younger man," Turpin added, "should have dealt better with the pressure you put him under. It was the first sign of what was later revealed." He had a sound in his voice that Hamilton hadn't heard before. He was cornered, apologetic.

'The Palace offered to cover his debt to you," said the tree that was the Crown Secretary, "but, in his pride, the boy refused. We took this as a noble gesture and tried again, made it clear the offer was serious." Hamilton could imagine that whatever pressure he himself had subjected the youth to would be as nothing compared to the Palace "making something clear."

"Then," continued Turpin, "he suddenly declared he had the funds. I asked him where he had got them. He told me he'd won at cards. But he was clearly lying. Shortly afterwards I had the pleasure of receiving a surprise visit at my office from His Grace the Earl Marischal, the Duke of Norfolk, on official business as officer of arms at the College of Heralds. He told me that a thousand guineas had gone missing from the College's account at Cuits."

He had taken exactly the right amount of money. Hamilton felt perversely annoyed at the association between the boy's amateurishness and himself. "Did Precious do that for him?" The Herald hadn't seemed capable of such foolishness. Was his younger self really that alluring? It was too tempting a thought to be true.

"Perhaps it was done with information from her, but without her knowledge," said Turpin. "His grace also informed me that the Herald herself had gone missing. Our people inspected her rooms and found signs of a struggle, and a rather shoddy attempt to conceal those signs. The boy himself did not report when instructed."

By now Hamilton had gone beyond feeling impugned by association, and was finding it difficult to conceal his satisfaction. So their golden boy had gone rogue. "Needless to say," he said, "he hasn't paid me."

"I daresay Precious caught him with his hand in the till. An infinite fold had been opened up in her rooms some hours before our people arrived. We found traces of it. We're able to some degree to keep track of where such tunnels end up. Our quarry has fled here, to Cliveden."

"Why?"

"There is . . . a newly-laid complex of fold tunnels on this estate," said the Equerry, sounding almost apologetic about his Court's fashions. "His Majesty was . . . is still . . . planning to summer here, among the optional worlds of his choosing. The College is . . . still . . . privy to such sensitive information. Your younger self, Major, is hiding in some optional version of these woods."

The Crown Secretary cleared his throat and there was silence. "His Majesty," he said, "remains intrigued by the concept of bringing optionals into our service. He is minded to wonder if their numbers might serve against the blockade. He would need good reasons to turn aside from this policy. But he is alive to the possibility that such good reasons might be provided."

Hamilton inclined his head. He had been told all outcomes were still allowed. That if he was to bring an astonished youth out of the bushes, protesting a misunderstanding, the boy would be listened to, though possibly that conversation would take place in Cliveden's cellars. Well, then. He had a job to do. He put down his valise and opened it, then wormed his hand quickly through the multiple folds to find his Webley Collapsar and shoulder holster.

"We're keeping a watch on the boundaries," said Turpin. "We've narrowed the realities around him so he can't get out." The quality of light in the clearing changed, and Hamilton was aware that something had been done to the covers in his eyes. "We were trying these out on the boy, soon to be standard issue. It'll enable you to see all the optional worlds around you and move between them, just as he can."

Hamilton finished strapping on his holster, slipped the gun into it, and replaced his jacket. He felt what he had to do to use the new covers and did so. Suddenly, there were people in the clearing, right beside him. He went back to the previous setting, and they vanished again. He'd seen some of the labourers and farm hands, those who kept the estate going. They were, presumably, the least entertaining option for His Majesty and his friends to explore.

"Enter the folds here," said Turpin, "bring back the boy and the Herald, alive if you can." And those last three words had been delivered in a tone that privately suggested to his covers that, as far as Turpin was concerned, all Hamilton's options did indeed remain open. He hadn't seen fit to replace Hamilton's sidearm with any less deadly weapon, after all. These courtiers might not have the military knowledge to be aware of such a decision made through omission. Hamilton looked at the trees giving him orders. The question of what was owed to him because of his service had collapsed into the simplicity of that service continuing. They had all assumed, after all, that he would do his duty. His thoughts of death at their hands had become something from an optional world. He turned and headed into the forest.

"Godspeed, Major," said the Equerry.

Hamilton didn't look back. After a moment, he began to run.

He looked at the map of the estate in his head. He jogged from tree to tree, changed his eyes for a moment, was suddenly lost again. He made himself keep checking the options. He couldn't afford to let the boy take him by surprise.

Had his younger self done this dishonourable thing because the balance wasn't an idea that had been discovered in the optional worlds? That must be what His Majesty was considering, the idea that there was no army to be raised there because his putative subjects from those worlds wouldn't have the required ethical fibre. Perhaps in those worlds the balance simply didn't exist, an indication that those places were less real than this world. Or perhaps the balance spread out somehow across all the worlds, perhaps that was how it endured so many shocks. Perhaps it was simply ambient and hard to fathom in his younger self's existence. He wondered what the boy, therefore, had judged himself against, in his formative years. Did this lack excuse him? It was hard to say whether or not the same rules should apply. If everything was real, if value itself was relative, what did it mean here and now to be an arms dealer, to wear a tartan, to abuse the flag, if those doing so could easily go somewhere else, where different rules applied? That might have been the boy's feeling on being made that miraculous offer of advancement, honour, the interest of a pretty woman, from somewhere aside from his own world. He had, presumably, been dragged from it in the night and had his new horizons made clear to him, over weeks, perhaps months. And if this new world included this strange custom, this desperate ideal about the preservation of order in the face of collapse, well, when in Rome . . .

But Turpin had said the boy's world was alike to ours in almost every detail, if set a few years back along the wave. And yet they didn't have the balance. The idea that they could get along without it, that their great powers had, presumably through mere accident, in his world still preserved the status quo enough for consciousness and society . . . well, there was a subversive tidbit. No wonder Turpin felt a little vulnerable at having opened that door. No wonder he himself seemed to be leaning less and less on the balance.

Hamilton chided himself. These musings were not appropriate when in the field. He found his bearings in the forest as it stood, if anything could be said to stand on its own now. He quartered it, and moving as silently as he could, explored the territory down to the river, all the angles of the estate. He found nobody.

He used the covers in his eyes to move to the next nearest option after the servants' world. This would be one of those chosen for His Majesty's sport.

The house was much the same, with a few minor architectural differences. A flag with some sort of meaningless symbol flew over it. Hamilton didn't want to know what it meant. He quartered the ground again, and found only some old men in a uniform he didn't recognise and some young women in entertainingly little. Presumably that situation would get more extraordinary as the season arrived. He wondered if ladies would be brought here, or if they would be offered their own options of tea and mazes.

He changed his eyes again, and this time when he searched he found Columbians walking the paths, that quaint accent that reminded him of watching Shakespeare. These people, as he crouched nearby and listened to them pass, spoke with a horrid lack of care, as if there was nobody to judge them, no enemy opposing them. Some of them would know of the interest of a King in their world, some would surely not. For His Majesty to venture into any of even these carefully chosen worlds should be for him to go on safari, into territory that was not his own. And yet the choice was everything, wasn't it? These worlds must be utterly safe. Unless one of them had the boy in it.

He searched through several worlds. He kept all their meanings at bay. He considered where he would go if he was in the boy's shoes, and in so considering realised there must be something he was missing . . . because he couldn't imagine coming here at all. He finally found, among the dozen or so options, somewhere empty. There was no house visible through the trees, the river was in a different place, the height of where he stood above sea level was different, and yet, according to the bare information about where he was on the globe that his covers insisted upon, he was in the same place. He looked slowly around, made sure he was hidden from all angles. Not only was the house gone, there were no houses on the plain, as far as he could see. And there was something . . . something extraordinary about—

"So they did send you." The voice was his own. It came from up the hillside.

Hamilton couldn't see its source. He stepped to put the trunk of a tree between it and himself. He took the Webley Collapsar from its holster.

"Where's the Herald?" he called.

"You won't find her—"

That told Hamilton she wasn't right there beside him. He dropped to his knee as he swung out from the tree, his left hand on his pistol wrist, and fired at the voice. The report and the whump of the round going off made one sound. And then there was another, a crash of branches as the boy broke cover. Hamilton leapt out and fired twice more at the sound, foliage and undergrowth compacting in instants, momentary pulses of gravity sucking at his clothes, newly focussed light dazzling him like a line of new stars blossoming and then gone in a moment.

Without looking for a result, he swung back behind the tree. Then he listened.

The movement had stopped. Of course it had. He wouldn't have kept moving. He'd have laid there for a few moments, then laid there a bit longer.

He heard small movements from up the hill. With these rounds, it was likely that if the boy was still alive, he was also unwounded. He began to slowly make his way through the trees, making sure he also wasn't going to be where the boy had last placed him. As he walked, he started to wonder about his surroundings. There was indeed something very strange about this empty world. He'd sometimes heard, at parties, at Court, back when he'd been invited, the sort of people who had nothing better to do talking about the glories of nature, about some mysterious poetic energy that looking at the simplicity of it could inspire in them. Hamilton thought, and had once ill-advisedly said, that nature wasn't simple at all, that the billions of edges and details and angled surfaces in any view of it were the essence of complexity, much more so than any of the artefacts of civilisation. To him, nature was cover, and all the better for its detail. Liz . . . her Royal Highness . . . had made some joke on that occasion to cover the fact that he'd just bluntly contradicted the French ambassador.

But here was some strange feeling of glory. The trees all around him, the undergrowth he was paying such attention to as he stepped through it, it all seemed to be shouting at him. The colours seemed too bright. Was this some flaw in his covers? No. This was too complete. But it wasn't about simplicity. The objects he saw nearby, even the river glimpsed down there, they were all . . . there was more detail than he was used to. He recalled a time when he'd injured one of his corneas, the fuzziness of view in one eye, until they'd grown and fitted a new one. It was like he'd suffered from something like that all his life, and now he could see better. God, it would be good to be able to stay here. Such relief and rest would be his.

No. These were dangerous thoughts.

There was a noise ahead of him and he brought the gun up. But he swiftly saw what it was. A fox was staring at him from between two bushes. Of course, he'd been downwind of it, and it had turned to face him in that instant. Better luck than he'd ever had on the hunt. But the eyes on this thing, the sheen of its fur, the intensity of every strand, that he could see from here . . .

The fox broke the instant and ran.

Something in the world broke with it and Hamilton hit the ground hard, realising in that moment that his eardrums were resounding and being glad they were resounding because that meant he was still alive, and he threw himself aside as the soil and leaves still fell around him and were sucked suddenly sideways, and he was rolling down the hill, crashing into cover and grabbing the soil to stop himself before the noise had died.

The boy had nearly had him. The boy had the same gun. Of course he had.

He lay there, panting. Then he lay there some more. The boy couldn't be sure he was here or he'd have fired by now. He wondered, ridiculously, for a moment, about the life of the fox. He killed the thought and started to push himself forward on his elbows. He realised, as he did so, that he wasn't injured. This might come down to a lucky shot. It was a contest of blunderbusses and balloons.

He felt, oddly, that it was apt his life should come to this. Then he killed that thought too. It would be more bloody apt if his life came to this then continued after the death of the other fellow.

"You could just stay here." That was the boy again, hard to trace where it was coming from beyond the general direction. He'd placed himself somewhere where the sound was broken, some trees close together, a rock wall.

Hamilton kept looking. "Why do you say that?"

'Don't you know where you are?"

"An optional Britain."

"Hardly, old man." The affectations he'd lost along the way. "It's not a country at all if there's nobody in it."

"I presume His Majesty has been in it. And probably found good hunting."

"As well he might. In heaven."

Hamilton grinned at the oddness of that. "How do you make that out?" It felt like the boy wanted to debate with his father. Wanted to test the bars of his cage. Perhaps he'd felt like that, at that age, but his own father's failure had meant he never felt able to, or perhaps had never felt the need. A place where there was no identity for him and no reason to do anything? More like the hell with no balance that the boy came from.

"It's more . . . real . . . than where either of us are from. And I say it's obviously heaven, because nobody got here."

Hamilton had heard the smile in his voice. "Except us. Are you sure it's not the other place?" A curious thought came to him. "Is that why you want me to stay?"

"I mean that if I went back, they wouldn't search in here. You could wait a few days, go anywhere you want."

Hamilton grimaced at that lack of meaning in the boy's life. "You think I'd abandon my duty?" He had a vision for a moment of being replaced in his life by the younger man. It felt like an invasion of himself. But also there was the frightening feel of temptation to it.

"I wouldn't dream of suggesting that, old man." He meant it, too. "I mean you could take advantage of this game. They need one of us to die, so . . . "

Where had he got that idea? Turpin would have liked to see the boy hauled back as a trophy, but the Palace was decidedly lukewarm on the matter, and Hamilton couldn't see any way in which any of the interested parties would be satisfied with the boy, rather than himself, emerging from the forest. "Who told you that?"

A pause. "Are you trying to lie to me?"

"I wouldn't dream of it . . . old man. I'm just here to bring you back." The boy might assume that Hamilton had been given covers he had not, lies that could fool ears that could detect lies. Or he might know that whatever he had in his head was in advance of anything Hamilton had as standard issue. But they knew each other's voices too well.

There was a sound from a direction Hamilton didn't expect. He turned, but he made himself do it with his gun lowered. There stood the boy. He had his gun lowered too. Hamilton stepped towards him. He allowed himself to make the first honest eye contact he'd had with his younger self. To see that face looking open to him was truly extraordinary, a joy that needed to be held down, a kindness worth crossing the waves that held worlds apart. He took a deep breath of an air that was indeed better than any he'd tasted. Whether or not this was heaven, he could imagine His Majesty walking in it and it giving him ideas of what should belong to him, of hunting endlessly here, with new youth for himself whenever he wished, and younger versions of every courtier and courtesan at his command. There would be, thanks to this boy, if some sort of misunderstanding could be proved, new manners forever. But that was hardly the boy's fault. And in that moment, Hamilton decided to lead him back to the clearing, and to another thing often denied to their kind: explanations.

"I was told," began the boy, "that I could only secure my place in society, in your world, by killing you. That that was why we had been brought together in . . . different contests."

Hamilton realised that this was exactly what he had once himself imagined. "Who—?"

A shot exactly like his or the boy's rang out across the absolute clarity of the sky. The boy's face bloated, in a moment, his body deformed by the impact, blood and the elements of a name bursting from his mouth. The collapsar shell sucked in again and the body dropped to the ground, emptied.

She stepped forward, lowering her gun. At least she had the grace to look sad. "Miss Nothing," she said.

She was still wearing that bloody dress. She slipped her gun back inside it, hiding it again. She and Hamilton stood looking at each other for a while, until Hamilton understood that if he wanted to shoot her she was going to let him, and angrily holstered his gun.

She immediately started back towards the house. He considered the idea of burying the boy. The absurdity of it made something catch in his throat. He marched after her and caught up. "Damn you. Damn both of us for not seeing you coming." He grabbed her by the arm to stop her. "I take it you were never truly out of favour with the College?"

She looked calmly at him. "We don't mind the idea of raiding optional worlds. We don't mind stealing new bodies for old minds. Up to a point. But we draw the line at *them* replacing *us*. We're the bloody College of Heralds, Major. Without family trees, we'd be out of business."

"And by setting up the boy to look like he was capable of theft, kidnapping and treachery, to the point of even being a threat to His Majesty—"

"We've proven such replacements to be unreliable. They never had the balance, you see."

"And you're telling me this because—?"

She looked truly sad for him in that moment. She understood him. "Because you're going to let me get away with it."

They emerged into the clearing. As they did so, Precious immediately became the model of a trembling, rescued victim. "He was a monster!" she cried out, supporting herself on Hamilton's arm.

"Was?" asked the voice of Turpin from the trees.

Hamilton kept his expression calm. "The boy is dead now," he said.

THE INSTRUCTIVE TALE OF
THE ARCHAEOLOGIST
AND HIS WIFE

ALEXANDER JABLOKOV

Surface Intrusions

Not even forgotten things are immune from change.

No archeological layer remains pristine. Each successive present affects every past. Later settlers dig to make latrines or to hide valuables from raiders, and insert their remains into levels belonging to earlier eras. Freezing and thawing cycles cause ancient objects to rise into their future. Rodents dig through and mix the soil. Deforestation upstream leads to increased water flow and the tumbling together of deposits. What an archeologist initially thinks lies deep in the past may well be from some later era, or even from one much earlier.

So the archeologist wasn't too disturbed at the battery that turned up in the burial in Level C2, the one belonging to the high era of the Akaskid kings. This mercury/selenium disk, from some technological era gadget, was clearly not the possession of any of the three skeletons in the burial, whose long-bone growth patterns and generous dentition identified them as merchants, wealthy from the cross-Indian-Ocean trade.

The archeologist was much more interested in the way the site seemed to support a story in the *Bruniad,* the one where Parvar and Krim travel to the court of the Shoreholder and plead for access to the shallow waters, to recover the things they had lost through shipwreck. Level C2 was perhaps too late to be connected to that story, as would be pointed out by academic opponents, but the archeologist didn't think that the arrangement of the shallow bay, the graves on the headland, and, most importantly, the uncovered knife with the ceremonial procession on the goat-bone handle were just coincidence. And it had long been accepted that "Shoreholder," or perhaps "Disposer of the Littoral," had been one of the minor functional titles of at least some of the Akaskids.

Sure, according to the final chapter of the *Bruniad*, Parvar and Krim had survived that particular encounter with the Shoreholder, dying only later, during the siege of Murgyl, but all stories are made up of both the false and the true. If Parvar and Krim, or, rather, the real traders that had been their initial inspirations, had actually died here, on the rocky coast of the Beak, it clarified some other issues in the old epic. The two men ceased to play a role in the narrative after this visit, despite its seeming success, until they popped out of nowhere, cheery and joking as always, at the walls of Murgyl, only to sicken and die during the plague visited on the besieging forces by the goddess Imimi. It had always seemed like a gap in the poet's art that these two characters had worked so hard, only to be forgotten at the moment they seemed to have accomplished something, then to be perfunctorily trotted on and killed off, as if some child in back had noticed their absence during a reading and called the poet's attention to it. It reeked of the quick fix.

A lot of good papers came out of this particular excavation, and made the archeologist a force to be reckoned with. But the end of the technological era was largely the domain of obsessives and crackpots. Even now his reputation wouldn't survive contact with it. He set the battery aside for later study.

Intertribal Marriage Arrangements

The archeologist had first made his name with an excavation near a provincial town farther south down the coast at Lamu. He had settled on the unpopular period of the pre-Tiorman kingdoms, despite pleas from his dissertation advisor. The Tiorman high priests always had a hold on the popular imagination, and specialists in them were always in demand for lectures and articles, but the period preceding their glorious reigns, with its complex wars and melancholy religious massacres, was of interest to no one.

No one, that is, but the archeologist. Among the partially flooded townsites he found signs of a previously unsuspected trading network, and, particularly, one enameled mask from a god that the Tiorman thearchs had later turned into a demon, buried upside down underneath the hearth of a burned-out farmstead. That snarling visage, with its shattered teeth, one eye gleaming onyx, the other gouged out, either by a treasure hunter or a theological commentator, became a popular image, reproduced on magazine covers and eventually on materials promoting a popular show of pre-Tiorman art and an associated set of lectures by the archeologist himself.

The second winter of his excavation found him dining frequently at the home of the provincial governor. As the presence of fish bones in a midden far inland indicates the existence of a trading route across the desert, so the presence of the archeologist at the somewhat overbearing governor's table indicated the existence of treasure, in the form of the governor's daughter.

The family came from the highlands near the lakes, but she had been raised in the coastal region, largely by local nursemaids and tutors. Her childhood friends had come from the families of local nut-harvesters and hydraulic engineers.

As she had grown to adulthood, most of her local friends had fallen away. Though she still visited their families at times of mourning or joy, the old intimacy was gone. When the archeologist first saw her, she was returning from a visit to the sickbed of an old friend's mother, head down and lonely, dressed in a dark gown that differed from local garb only by the addition of gold embroidery along the hem. He watched her vanish through the back gate of the governor's villa, and finally decided to accept the dinner invitation he had been dodging.

Though she was willing to accept his courting, she was subtly resistant to it. He'd thought that a man with a promising career from a much larger city would be instantly interesting. When that proved not to be the case, he found himself working hard to please her. That was something he'd never done.

Finally, she agreed to go on a trip with him, to see what they were like with each other away from her family, from his dig. He did manage to spin the situation in his direction, by choosing the dramatic ruins of the Gardens of Nor, an old excavation a day's journey away. He used his connections to get them a guesthouse with a view across the hills.

And, in fact, the mysterious frescos and the romantic gardens that had been grown in the old banqueting halls had their effect, and she warmed to him. But before she did, she felt compelled to confess to him her encounters with other lovers, both travelers and men from the towns around hers. It was a startling number.

For a couple of days, he found himself withdrawn, even hostile. It was always annoying when an uncovered artifact destroys a cherished hypothesis. He hadn't even known he had a hypothesis. She didn't try to comfort him, or reassure him in any way. Nothing about the way she brushed her hair changed. The revelation should have made him turn away from her. Instead, he found that he was caught. Once he found a way not to think about it, he found himself wanting to please her. Eventually, somehow, he did.

On their return, she accepted his suit, negotiations were completed, and they were married according to the rites of her family, with a late-night celebration with those who had watched her grow up. It would be the last time she would see most of her childhood companions. The next year, the archeologist transferred his area of interest north up the coast, to the territories where the Akaskid kings had once ruled, and she went with him.

• • •

Horizon Layer

For the next few years, the archeologist continued his excavation of Akaskid Level C2. It was a rich deposit, though he found nothing as photogenic as snarling god/demon masks. His team uncovered everything from cosmetics kits to goat hobbles, revealing a rich daily life among these villagers who lived unconcerned near the seat of power, and providing clues as to what kind of life was worth living. From what the archeologist could see, these people had lived in harmony with their environment for centuries, never asking of the local resources more than they could sustainably give. Then an arrogant aristocrat class with more ambition than taste arose, demanded flashy decorations, and burned up centuries of accumulated wealth in a vain attempt to conquer their neighbors. The Akaskid kings raised armies, and, for a while, even ruled the remnants of the Tiorman cities, long past their glory days. Then the Akaskids themselves had inevitably collapsed, their overfed bodies crackling and spitting under the smoldering ruins of their cities. Most archeological digs revealed a lesson, and this one was no exception.

But there were two features of the site that did puzzle the archeologist. Neither of them had anything to do with the Akaskids specifically, so they did not enter into the various articles he wrote on the site.

The first was an almost complete absence of a carbon/organometal layer. That horizon, packed with combustion byproducts, halogenated organics, mercury, lead, cadmium, and plutonium, was to be found pretty much everywhere on Earth, and represented the termination of the old technological civilization. But at the Akaskid dig there was little more than a few traces, one reason he had trouble figuring out where that battery had come from. Presumably, the area had undergone some erosion between the fall of civilization and the present, but he could not account for it.

Second was the fact that there was no sign of any excavation prior to his. The site seemed to have remained completely undisturbed since the fall of the Akaskids, which had been at least two thousand years before technological civilization ended. At one point someone had dug through the northern corner of the site to bury a waste pipe, but they had ignored a few ancient coins they could easily have picked up.

The achievements of technological civilization had been incredible, and the modern world was still struggling to match them. But one thing those people, who had investigated the inner workings of atoms and the hearts of distant stars, had never thought about was their own past. The earth was torn apart with their deep mines, their excavated coal seams, their road cuts, their toxic waste disposal sites, but it was also covered with pristine archeological sites that no one seemed to have paid attention to.

The more the archeologist thought about that, the less sense it made. But it did not affect his researches directly, so he saved it as a possible topic for a graduate student, a position that never got funded.

Relative Dating

Most of the remains of the technological age were toxic or radioactive. Researchers into that era tended to have short lifespans. Shaky and despairing, with haunted eyes, they rarely achieved high academic standing.

So when the archeologist got a letter from a colleague in technological age studies who said he had come across some information reflecting on the Akaskids, he was at first dismissive.

Still, the man had a reputation for some brilliance, albeit leavened with hostility and paranoia, and when the archeologist visited a nearby city for an academic conference a few years later, he arranged to stop by and see what the man had.

By that point, the man had lost even the minor academic post he'd had when he wrote to the archeologist, and all of his research materials were now crammed into a basement storage unit, poorly lit and subject to floods and infestations of rodents.

As the man, shaking and mumbling, dug through mildewed remnants of printed books and fabrics, the archeologist tried not to get too close. It was clear the man had lost whatever trace of sanity he had once had.

Just as the archeologist was about to turn to leave, the man reached in and, with a triumphant grunt, pulled out a yellow porcelain cup, almost complete. It gleamed like sunlight in the dank storage unit. The archeologist instantly recognized it as a piece of Akaskid ceremonial tableware, suitable for a dinner with the gods.

It had turned up in a late technological age stratum. A museum?

No. Not a museum. Instead, some kind of manufacturing facility, with the remains of heating and annealing chambers. There had actually been a lot of other ceramic fragments there. This was the only one in recognizable shape. Then he tossed the cup to the archeologist, who caught it clumsily, almost dropping it. He responded with rage, maybe going too far because of the man's low status. Later, he would regret this, though the researcher showed no signs of offense at the time.

Instead he explained to the archeologist how the late technological age had seemed devoted to destroying every sign of themselves. Their remains were infested with bacteria that dissolved various materials such as plastic, metal, and cloth. He'd lost a lot of his own equipment to some still-living colonies of these. He hypothesized that they had also released small devices with long-lived power sources that had crawled endlessly through late technological strata, grinding every piece of evidence with comminuting teeth, until nothing was left but indistinguishable powder. He'd never found one of these mechanical rotifers, but was sure they had existed.

The archeologist thought that absence of evidence was not evidence of the destruction of evidence. He saw no reason to say that, however. All historical researchers eventually found an excuse for why they found so little to support their theories.

But those late technological wizards couldn't have been perfect. They were human, after all. They must have made mistakes. The archeologist thought of the battery he had found. Was that a mistake? Had they really cut down to the Akaskid layers by removing one microscopic layer of soil after another, removed a cup, clumsily dropped a battery, and then replaced each layer in turn, so perfectly that there was no sign any of them had ever been moved?

He even showed his colleague the battery. He had no explanation either. Instead, he wanted to go and get a drink. He was finished with the business of the past, and ready to go on to some more fruitful line of work.

He never did. He died the next year during an excavation when a roof collapsed on him. Some thought he had encountered a late-technological-age booby trap, something intended to conceal a dark secret, others that he had become frustrated by unanswered and unanswerable questions and deliberately taken too many risks.

The archeologist sometimes pulled that Akaskid cup out and looked at it. He never wrote about it, or mentioned it to anyone else. He told himself it was because it had no provenance, no way of proving what layer it had come from, or what it was evidence of.

He just wished he'd had that drink with the man, instead of scuttling out the way he had.

Epigraphic Evidence

The late-technological-age researcher had made one idle remark that resonated with the archeologist. He said that he'd once seen the woman who was now the archeologist's wife a year or two before the archeologist himself met her.

It had been at an excavation in the mountains inland of the Teorman lands, and she had been in the company of a senior archeologist specializing in a much later era, the period when ships had come from the Americas and spread their short-lived but vital empires across the area. The archeologist knew him as a scholar who had made a few lucky discoveries early in his career and had coasted on them ever since. He was a man of some charm, and popular on lecture tours. His wife had never mentioned knowing him, not even in that exasperating list during their visit to the ruined gardens.

He didn't mention that conversation to his wife, but he did pick some fights over minor domestic matters after he came home from his conference. Several of these fights ballooned into much larger arguments. She could always tell when he was probing her about her sexual history, and always refused to give anything more up, usually in a taunting way that just increased his rage.

Maybe she wanted children. He wasn't sure. For one reason or another, they weren't able to conceive. The technological age had had a variety of ways around such problems, if the stories were at all true. That knowledge had been lost along with everything else, and they were stuck with the plumbing they had been born with. It was no one's fault.

She told him that this was about what she would expect from someone who spent his days digging through other people's trash. Eventually, every archeologist's spouse made a similar slighting remark. It came with the territory. Still, it hurt. He'd thought she valued what he did.

Eventually, their relationship settled down, and he thought they had gotten through their rough patch. Then she announced that she had a new hobby. She had joined a local group of those cultists sometimes called Obliviators.

Depositional Unconformity

Obliviators believed that something was being hidden from them, from everyone. The people of the technological age had worked titanium, flown to the Moon, replaced human limbs, watched entertainment on huge screens. How could those secrets have been lost so thoroughly?

The answer was obvious, they thought. Because archeologists found those secrets, and then deliberately concealed them, to give themselves power. That archeologists had no real power, and often lived on small incomes, seemed not to interest them.

The Obliviators were a constant problem at funding meetings, and sometimes picketed academic facilities, seemingly at random. Every once in a while an ardent young member would be arrested trying to break into the back areas of a museum, looking for a hidden nuclear reactor or handheld computation device recovered from that vanished age.

Having a faculty wife join such a group was embarrassing in the extreme. It had to stop. The archeologist, for the first time in their marriage, attempted to enforce a decision that they had not reached mutually.

It did not work, and he was faced with either backing down or ending his marriage. He backed down, but within his heart felt that his marriage had in fact ended. Not that his external life changed. He did not have an affair, either on campus or at the excavation. He did not move out. He wasn't even sure his wife noticed his pulling away. Perhaps he hadn't been the most demonstrative of husbands, but, still, the fact that he was no longer emotionally present should have been significant.

He continued to receive promotions and honors, and no longer did much field work. None of his books sold as well as that first one, about finding the snarling mask. Still, they provided a decent extra income, and he and his wife lived a comfortable life.

The archeologist's wife became a mainstay of the local Obliviator chapter, helping put together dinners and other events, and made a lot of new friends, none of whom the archeologist ever got to know. When he ran into them casually, they seemed like anyone else.

One day, while he was working at home alone, putting together a paper on a certain aspect of Akaskid court ceremonial, he received a visitation from a man who announced himself with the title of Veil. He was apparently a high-ranking officer in the Obliviators. The archeologist's wife had suggested he stop by.

Despite himself, the archeologist felt a moment of primitive fear. It had happened, as rumor said it would. This man was here to uncover his secrets and would stop at nothing to do so. His wife would come home with the groceries to find his lifeless body stretched out on the red and black squares of the foyer. No one would be able to puzzle out what had happened to him. And his office would be oddly empty of any evidence of his recent work. . . .

In the event, the Veil sat down in the living room, in the leather chair the archeologist himself preferred, and accepted a cup of coffee.

The Veil started out by asking the archeologist his opinion about the last days of technological civilization. What had finally caused it to fall? Seas were high, but had been rising for a long time. They seemed to have adapted to that, and to the vast droughts. They had weapons that could sterilize the globe, but they had been nervously fiddling with those for centuries. It seemed that it had ended all of a sudden, in less than a single lifetime. What had happened? What new factor had entered the situation?

The archeologist, feeling somewhat bored, gave the conventional explanations. Sudden transitions between habitations of a given area were sometimes real, but were often just artifacts of the removal of a layer, sometimes of centuries' duration, which eliminated evidence of a steady slow change, an infiltration of new settlers, a modification of climate that affected lifeways, a growth or diminution of local power.

As the archeologist looked down at the man's bald spot, he wondered if the Veil and his wife were lovers. Surely that kind of thing happened in these intensely committed cult groups. The emotional intensity, the sense of sharing a meaning incomprehensible to your spouse . . . he looked back over what was now decades of what he had thought was a happy marriage. He could see no trace of it. Presumably it too had eroded day by day. But this was the day he realized what he had lost, and it seemed that it had all gone at once.

Was he feeling poorly? The Veil said he could come back another day.

The archeologist brusquely told him he was feeling fine.

The Veil shrugged and asked him about the further past, the past that had led to the technological civilization. Why did technological civilization seem so poorly connected to everything that came before it? Why did it seem to emerge from nowhere, with no obvious precursors? Why were its beginnings as mysterious as its end?

The archeologist asked him to get to the point, if he had one.

The Veil said that it was because the past had a meaning. Those who dug into it saw it as a series of random events, a kingdom here, an expansion of population across some islands there. But he and his fellow Obliviators knew better. The past was a vast hieroglyph, a construction that had a deep and intimate meaning. It was something that could explain why life was the way it was.

The past was speaking. Who better than the archeologist to interpret its message?

Despite himself, the archeologist was startled. His wife had joined a group that interpreted his activities as obstructionist and devoted to concealing the truth, and he had been hurt. He had neglected the corollary: if you were concealing the truth, that implied that you knew what the truth was.

He told the Veil that he had never concealed anything he had found out about the past. Every potsherd, every bit-worn horse's tooth, every posthole had been documented, diagrammed, and published in freely accessible journals. He owed his academic reputation to revealing, not concealing.

The Veil shook his head. The archeologist's problem, he said, was precisely that focus on bits and pieces. He should look up and examine the vast landscape of the past, and see how it was put together. Then he could perhaps explain something of how it had all come to be.

For a moment, the archeologist found something resonant in that assertion. It seemed to connect with something he almost understood. Then that feeling left. Like all such groups, Obliviators worked on a theory that was simultaneously insanely complex and utterly simple-minded.

The archeologist fell silent and did not speak again. The Veil looked around for a refill of his coffee. When none was forthcoming, he politely took his leave.

Debitage

The rest of the archeologist's professional career seemed a success. He no longer had to spend his summers at the excavation. He managed his department, promoted the careers of promising juniors, and published a lavish book on Akaskid court ceremonial.

What he did not do, disappointing the few who paid attention to such things, was write a book explaining the deeper structure of his period of expertise. What had driven the Akaskid kings to their overextension? Did environmental degradation in the upper agricultural valleys contribute to the kingdom's eventual weakness? It seemed that he had not fulfilled his early promise.

This was the external view.

For years, as he corresponded about details of excavations, of interpretation, of publication, he made small requests, innocuous in context. He asked for out-of-place objects, as indications of what stratum-disturbing events had occurred. He asked for any signs of deeper technological-age excavations, any place they might have had their own archeological investigations, few though those seemed to be. He requested the earliest excavation documentation of various sites, though those early workers had had terrible technique and had polluted their own sites.

The most suspicious correspondent would not have suspected anything insane about his motivations.

And, in the deepest privacy of his own inner office, the archeologist worked on his project. His collection of anomalies had started with the flat, circular battery, and he still returned to it. Its markings did not match any known symbology from the technological age.

As people sent him the irrelevant detritus of their excavations, his collection grew. Objects recognizably from the technological age he set aside. That was most of them. But there were a few objects, with odd alphabets and notations on them, that did not fit. These objects seemed to come from a history other than the one he knew.

He was still working on his project when he died.

He was so private about it that even in clearing out his office, and putting his papers together for donation to the library, his colleagues did not see anything odd. But they had not known him well, though they would have said they did.

The last day, after his funeral, and after she had packed up the house, prepared to return to the land by the sea she had left so many years before, the archeologist's wife pulled open a narrow drawer, found a sheaf of papers, and read what he had written. There wasn't that much of it, and it wasn't that hard to figure out, if you were willing to take it at face value.

One thing the archeologist had been sure of. There had been archeologists among the people of the technological age. It made no sense that there had not been. They had investigated every other aspect of existence. So an immense structure of academic research of their past must have existed. Teams had fanned out across the world, and excavated every likely place where human remains could be found. They had no doubt traced human ancestry back to those forgotten times when humans had still been dissolved in their animal nature. Shelves had bulged with their journals and findings. Popular lecturers had traveled and shown provincials the wonders of ancient empires, of kings, saints, and warriors.

Where, then, was this work? Why did the historical deposits all seem so completely undisturbed until the archeologist and his colleagues appeared? Why was this field of knowledge the one that was so thoroughly forgotten?

The archeologist had become sure that the people of the last days of the technological age had destroyed their past. They had used their own archeological researches to identify and eliminate anything that told of earlier ages. Then, in the resulting blank spaces, they had redrawn a history that they felt they could live with. They were so precise that they buried it, in order, exactly as if it had happened. In fact, their technology, which enabled manipulation on scales from the individual atom up to entire mountain ranges, resulted in artifact deposition indistinguishable from reality.

Archeologists of their own day might have had delicate machinery that enabled them to see the decay of various unstable nuclei, crystal structures in ceramic glazes, statistical anomalies in tooth wear patterns in skeletal teeth, but the archeologist certainly did not. Someday, perhaps, those techniques would exist again. But even if they did, they could not recover the real past that those people had so diligently destroyed.

Maybe the archeologist had jumped the gun, even by centuries, by penetrating to the dark heart of their secret. It was to be culture-wide revelation that the entire past, every bit of it, from tiniest excavated fragment to the ancient epics like the *Bruniad* itself, had been created *en masse* as a comprehensive work of art.

Because, surely, they had meant for their secret to be uncovered, hadn't they? The archeologist's earliest notes took this for granted, but as time went by, and he spent more and more time in obsessively analyzing the anomalies, the less he believed it. Perhaps, instead, they had believed that a human race with this series of events in its past would not destroy itself as pathetically as they apparently had.

But the miserable fact was that there was no way the archeologist would ever know what they had intended. Once they had created a plausible false history, they had erased themselves, utterly and completely, like a diligent housekeeper vacuuming her way out of a carpeted room. There was no record of them, there was no trace of who they might have been.

Almost no trace. That was what he had devoted himself to finding, in the interstices of an otherwise conventional archeological career: finding the traces they had overlooked. As his friend had said, everyone makes mistakes. Sometimes a device has a loose latch and a battery falls out of it.

After decades, these traces barely filled a small box. Aside from the disk battery that had started it all, there was a brass screw, some red plastic that had once insulated a length of wire, a porcelain plaque with some ornate blue letters on it, a tiny figurine of a dancing girl, and two-thirds of a plate that seemed to show three symmetrical monuments shaped like mountains, or four-sided pyramids. In front of these was a dismayed-looking human-faced animal whose nose had been knocked off.

It was this particular object that the Archeologist returned to most often. The work was not of high quality. It had probably hung on the wall of an ordinary family, either as a souvenir of a vacation, or as a part of a larger collection of famous sights, perhaps none of which they could actually afford to go visit.

This particular famous sight, wherever it had been, had been completely destroyed along with the rest of the past.

Despite herself, the archeologist's widow was startled. The Veil had returned from his visit saying that her husband was completely resistant. But it seemed that something the Veil had said, his elaborate theory of a hieroglyph of historical meaning, had set off something in the archeologist's mind.

It had compelled the archeologist to look at what the evidence had said, and to accept its message without denial. He had faced the fact that his entire professional life had been a lie, nothing more than filling in a crossword puzzle devised by someone else, and not blinked. She had never known that he had had that kind of courage. Maybe if she had realized it while he was alive, their lives together would have been different.

She wondered if she had as much courage. She did not want to give that fictional past up. The archeologist had never known how much she had loved those people, whose dry remains she had lived with since her marriage.

If he was right, the magnificent ruined Gardens of Nor the two of them had visited before deciding to get married were not the pleasure ground of ancient kings, but an elaborate fake, as were the remains of the dancing girls on the frescoed wall of the Small Withdrawing Room, where Queen Araspa had written her verses.

Her relationship with the archeologist had been cemented on that trip, by his passion for these vanished folk and her awakening sense of kinship with them. What did that say about the two of them?

Did it matter that when she enumerated her lovers to him that night, she had missed one? It was a man she now remembered only hazily, though she distinctly remembered skipping over him. That missing lover was a small trinket stolen from the eager archeologist with his whisks and trowels, and now she too had lost him.

If Queen Araspa had not written "In the winter, the morning is the best time, when the sun rises and the ice glows in the cracks beneath the basin," while the girls with their elaborate hairdos had turned gracefully on the walls around her lonely table, then who had?

She smiled to herself. He'd probably figured that she would dispose of these papers without even reading them. He couldn't have known that she would both read and understand them.

She tapped the edges of the pages until they were perfectly parallel. A colleague had offered to publish a collection of her husband's papers as a kind of memorial. No matter how vicious the arguments it caused, this paper would be among them.

It would destroy his reputation. He would seem like another madman, someone infected by the theories of the Obliviators, or another similar group. The very people who would take the trouble to read that posthumous book would be the ones least likely to accept what it had to say about their careers.

But, perhaps, much later, after she was gone too, someone would pull the book from a shelf, see the courage she herself saw, and take a sober look at the fact that they were all, truly, people without a past. What they had was an illusion, and what they had lost was gone forever.

She rested her hand on the stack of paper and thought that until that moment she had never truly managed to touch her husband, the archeologist.

FIFT & SHRIA

BENJAMIN ROSENBAUM

Author's note: in rendering this story in English, I have translated the pronouns that the characters would use for their society's own dimorphic social class-moeity into gendered English pronouns—"she" for Staid and "he" for Bail, and I have regarded Staid and Bail as "genders." This isn't meant to imply, however, that Staids are female, nor that Bails are male.

Fift could tell that the new kid, Shria, was yearning for the other Bails to get involved, to say something. Perjes and Tomlest were across the clearing, pulling sticks out of the underbrush, but they'd stopped to watch.

"Did you hear me?" Umlish said to Shria. "I said, 'so you're latterborn again, I guess we should congratulate you'."

Umlish was all gray—hair, eyes, skin, all the same matching tone. Her parents must have decided to match them like that. Show-offy, in a Staidish way. She was ten years old, a year older than Fift and Shria and most of the other kids. She was here singlebodied—she'd only brought one body along on the field trip to the surface, unlike everyone else—and she wasn't carrying any wood, either. Her sidekicks, Kimi and Puson, were carrying it for her.

"Of course being middleborn has its advantages," Umlish said, "but really, who wants a Younger Sibling cluttering up the place? Not Shria, I imagine."

One of the Bails—Perjes or Tomlest—snickered, and Shria turned sharply, in both bodies, baring her teeth. But he must not have been watching them over the feed, so he couldn't be sure which one had snickered. He stood there, glaring, clearly willing them to say something out loud. He could fight *them*, and he would—he was always getting in unauthorized fights with the other Bailkids.

What could he do against Umlish and her Staid crew?

Fift wasn't there. She was a little way down the trail in one body, and farther off in the forest with the other. But she was watching over the feed. The whole class must be watching. How could you not? Everyone had been wondering about it, about what had happened to the new kid and his family, and no one had been talking about it . . . until now.

Shria: lavender skin and fiery red hair, orange eyebrows that curled like flames. Bony bare knees and elbows poked between the red and blue strips of cloth of his suit. His clothes were a bit too big—a little too skimpy for the surface—as if whoever had cooked them up had been distracted. It was already misting, up here—tiny droplets of water sparkling in the air, the strange wild atmosphere hesitating between fog and rain. Shria crouched down, doublebodied, one body's arms already loaded up with sticks. He turned away sharply from the Bails in the clearing, and pulled a silver-barked stick from a tangle of them. It was furry with greenish lichen.

His eyes were red from crying already.

"That's not going to burn," Puson said. She was doing her best to look Staidish, emotionless, austere, but she sounded a little too excited. "Lichen means it's too wet. Especially in this weather."

Umlish smiled primly. "You do *have* an environmental context agent, don't you?"

Fift's own arms were full of sticks, some of which had lichen on them, or small fungi.

She shouldn't have split up after arriving in the forest. She was here in one body gathering sticks; in another body, she was over past the ridge, dragging a large log back to the campsite. Dumb. She would have to drop all the sticks, if she was going to sort through them. She didn't like being together in the same place. Her somatic integration was poor. Her parents sent her to experts about it.

Umlish had found out about the experts, at one point. Umlish had written a poem about it.

Umlish could be merciless.

Fift shouldn't have damped all her automated agents; they would have told her about the lichen. But the agents distracted her. From the tall trunks of trees—some of them thick around as elevator shafts, others thin as a child's wrist. From the crunch and crackle of moss and leaves underfoot. From the roiling pale-green clouds in the roofless empty above her.

"Your parents should make sure you have the appropriate agents, for a trip to the surface," Umlish said. "They do seem very distracted, don't they?"

{Why did the Midwives take Shria's younger sibling away?} Fift asked her agents.

Shria dropped the stick and stood up, in both bodies, one of them clutching the pile of kindling. He was quivering, his faces pale. He looked around.

{Before a family can have a child, there needs to be consensus, among neighbors and reactants}, Fift's social context agent explained. {If there isn't enough approval, and the family goes ahead and has the child anyway, the Midwives require the birthing cohort to yield custody. Otherwise they won't gender the child.}

{But they didn't take his sibling away the first day}, Fift sent. {It was like three weeks.}

{You are correct}, the social context agent said. {There was a period of negotiation regarding the child's status.}

At home, in her third body, Fift rolled over. She hadn't really been sleeping anyway, just wallowing under the blankets, her eyes closed, her attention on the surface. The house feed showed Fathers Frill and Grobbard and Smistria in the breakfast room. She rolled out of bed, scratched her feet, and went downstairs.

Her Fathers looked up as she came into the breakfast room.

"Hello, dear," Frill said. He raised his head, causing a swarm of small bright cosmetic midges to launch themselves from his gilded eyebrows and dance in the air. "How is it going with your—ah yes," his eyes shone. "Out in the wilds! Looks damp." He grinned, goldenly.

"I never go to the surface," Smistria said, leaning back—his other body leaned forward, messily chewing a crusty broibel, which flaked into his braided beard—"if I can avoid it. We had this nonsense when I was your age too. It's *perverse* up there. The sky can just dump water on you or electrify you any time it takes the notion. Horrible place."

Under that dangerous sky, Umlish took a step closer to Shria. "I wonder if they might still be a bit overburdened? Your parents."

Across the clearing, Perjes turned to Tomlest. You could tell they were sending messages. Tomlest's eyes screwed up in amusement, and he laughed.

Shria's bodies both twitched, his empty pair of hands came up, almost to a guard position. But Tomlest didn't look over.

"Oh you," Frill said, swatting Smistria. "You have no sense of romance! The wild sky, our ancient origins!"

"Our ancient origins, for that matter, were under an entirely different—"

"Oh, don't be such a *pedant*! I know as well as you—"

"Um," Fift interrupted. "Um, I have a question."

Perjes and Tomlest ran off into the woods. Shria exhaled a shaky breath. He turned abruptly, and started to walk away. Not to run; he moved slowly, like an animal preserving its energy. He kept his eyes focussed on his feet. Umlish, Puson, and Kimi trailed after him.

"Yes, little stalwart?" Frill said. "What is it?"

"There's this Bail in my class, Shria—" in the forest, still watching Shria, she checked lookup—"Um, Shria Qualia Fnax, of name-registry Digger Chameleon 2?"

Smistria looked at Frill, and bared his teeth. "Oh yes. That one."

"What, what happened? They took away his sibling, but why—why did they take so long? And why did his parents have the baby, if they didn't—"

"Because they're idiots," Smistria said.

Fift frowned.

Grobbard spread her hands. Grobbard was Fift's only Staid Father. Her face was smooth and calm. "It was a kind of gamble, Fift. Fnax cohort thought that once the baby was here, opinions would change."

Shria trudged through the underbrush. The trail was a ragged strip of bare dirt, traced by surface animals. He was heading down the trail, heading towards Fift.

"An *idiotic* gamble," Smistria said. "If people didn't trust you to raise another child in the first place, why would they trust you after *that* behavior? Provoking a standoff with the Midwives? Letting your child just—*hang about* for three weeks—"

"Ungendered," Frill added, shaking his head. "Not entered into lookup, not entered into a name registry, like—like a surface animal, or—"

"Like someone who doesn't exist at all!" Smistria cried.

Grobbard sighed. "Yes. As if lingering still unborn, outside its Mother's body."

"But why would they do that?" Fift asked.

"Because," Smistria snapped, "they thought they could *coerce* the rest of Slow-as-Molasses—and the family reactants of all of Fullbelly!" He drew himself up in his seating harness, still chewing vigorously with his other mouth. "They were so arrogant, they didn't even invite adjudication!" Smistria was, himself, a well-rated adjudication reactant.

"They would have *lost* adjudication," Frill said.

"Exactly!" Smistria said—forgetting himself, through a mouthful of broibel.

Umlish, Kimi, and Puson trailed behind Shria, like a parade. Their eyes darted back and forth—you could tell they were amused by the messages they were sending to each other. They had small prim grins. Kimi giggled—Kimi was only eight—until Umlish frowned, then she composed her face more sedately.

"And think of the poor older siblings," Frill said. "Especially your classmate. From latterborn to middleborn to latterborn again, in three weeks—!"

"Well," said Grobbard quietly, "at least he was briefly middleborn." Grobbard was an Only Child, just like Fift. It wasn't something she talked about, but you could see it right there in lookup: Grobbard Erevulios Panaxis of name registry Amenable Perambulation 2, four-bodied Staid, 230 years old, Only Child.

Being an Only Child wasn't a great thing. It kind of meant you were less of a person. Maybe Grobbard had always dreamed about being middleborn, too.

"Yes, but come on, Grobby," Frill (who was latterborn) said. "Not like *that*."

Umlish looked up the trail, and saw Fift standing there, as if frozen.

Umlish's eyes narrowed. {Oh, hello Fift}, she sent. {Are you finding what you need? Don't you think you have enough sticks? Oh my—} her eyes flicked to the left, feed-searching; {—look at you dragging that thing.} She had found Fift's other body, hauling the log. Her eyes shifted back to Fift's. {That's so . . . robust of you. "Mighty was Threnis in her time", eh?}

Fift flushed. Umlish was farther with the Long Conversation than she was—already learning the sixth mode. Was Threnis mentioned in the third corpus? She couldn't remember—and Pip and Grobbard never let her use search agents for the Conversation. ("It's a corrupting habit, Fift," Grobbard had said, with starker disapproval than Fift had ever seen on her solemn face. "Once you begin using them, you'll never stop. You must know the Conversation yourself—unaided—with your own mind. The Conversation is the essence of our lives as Staids, Fift.")

Umlish's eyes widened in triumph; she could tell that Fift had no idea who Threnis was.

Shria looked up nervously, saw Fift, and frowned. The tips of his ears were bluish with cold. His mouth was trembling, but his jaw was clamped tight, almost as if he was trying *not* to cry—like Fift when she was six or seven, when she'd begun doing her horrible somatic integration exercises, and had to do them in front of the experts and her whole family. It had taken all her strength not to humiliate herself by bursting into tears.

But of course no one would mind if *Shria* cried. If anything, it was strange— even slightly ridiculous—for a Bail to be so rigid with the effort *not* to.

Fift cleared her throat. It was thick somehow, and the morning dew was clammy on the back of her neck.

"Shria," she said, "can you, um, help me?" She hefted her pile of sticks. "Some of these aren't going to burn, they've got lichen on them."

Shria stopped, in both bodies, and glared at Fift. He hunched his shoulders in a little further. He thought she was making fun of him, too, and so did Kimi and Puson, whose grins escaped their prim confinement. Umlish wasn't so sure; she raised an eyebrow.

"I guess I should have checked with my agents," Fift said, her voice a little unsteady, "but I turned them off. Who wants to have agents chattering at you up here? It's sort of missing the point, isn't it?"

Puson's face froze; Kimi looked back and forth from Puson to Umlish. Shria blinked.

Umlish's mouth soured. "You *like* it up here?" she snarled.

Fift didn't, exactly; it was cold and strange and mostly pretty boring, though there was also something fascinating about being under this strange sky which, as Father Smistria said, could do anything it decided to. She didn't *like* it, but she wanted to experience it. But she wasn't about to explain that to Umlish.

"Oh, Umlish . . . Are you having trouble with this?" Fift said. "I guess it can be a little scary if you've never been on the surface before. But don't worry—"

Umlish recoiled. "I'm not *scared*, you sluiceblocking toadclown. It's just *disgusting*—" She waved a hand at the forest.

A small grin crept across one of Shria's faces.

Fift swallowed. She wasn't sure what else to say.

Father Grobbard's eyes had been closed. She often meditated at the breakfast table. Now she opened them and glanced at Fift. {Threnis}, she sent Fift, {appears in the sixth and seventh odes of the first additional corpus. Would you like to study them this afternoon?}

Fift gulped. It was easy to forget that her parents could read the logs of her private messages: they didn't often bother to. At least, she didn't *think* they did. Grobbard didn't seem angry, though. She placed her hands together, resting them on the table. Peaceful as a stone worn smooth by a river.

"Well, if you like it so much," Umlish snarled, "why don't you live up here? Maybe you could get permission to build a little hut out of sticks and the two of you could *play cohort*."

"Okay," Shria said, coming forward up the trail. "Yeah, I'll help." He stopped in front of Fift, wiped a streak of snot from his nose with the back of his wrist, and then reached in, holding the good sticks back with one hand, and pulling the mossy ones out with the other. He kept those eyes on the task, but the other two—in the body he was holding his pile of sticks with—searched her face, sizing her up.

Fift swallowed. She kept her face still, expressionless, but she could feel the blood rising into her ears.

"Will they take any of the other children, do you think?" Father Frill asked.

"What?" Fift asked. "What other children?"

"Of Fnax cohort," Smistria said.

The cold dug into Fift's chests, and not just on the surface. "Like Shria? Why?"

Frill shrugged, and smoothed the bright blue-and-orange braids of his hair with his hands, releasing another swarm of midges into the air. "It can happen. If their ratings fall enough—if people think they're doing an inadequate job. That your friend would be better off elsewhere."

"He's not . . . " Fift began. She didn't really have any Bail friends. It had gotten become hard to tell who her friends were.

Two years ago she would have said Umlish was her friend; they'd played together when they were little. But Umlish was the kind of person who was your friend as long as you did exactly what she said. Fift had tried to laugh along with the poem thing. But after today . . . She'd never forgive Fift now.

"They're starting the campfire, Umlish," Kimi said. "Should we go back?"

"Or are you playing siblings?" Umlish snapped, ignoring Kimi. "How exciting for you, Fift! A sibling of your own!"

Father Frill cocked his head to one side, and narrowed his eyes, searching the feed. "Hmm. He's been fighting—your friend. He's a little old for that. At your age Bails should be learning to keep their fights on the mats." He shook his head. "That's not good for ratings."

The hairs on the backs of Fift's necks stood up. "What would happen, if they take Shria away? Away to where?"

Frill shrugged. "He's not too old to be trained as a Midwife. They live at the pole—" he gestured vaguely southwards. "It's a great honor."

Fift could see her own faces over the feed. She looked horrified: one day she'd come to class and Shria would be gone, taken from his cohort, forbidden to talk to his parents, off to the pole to become a Midwife forever. How many more fights would it take? Could Umlish cause this all by herself, with her words? Fift struggled to compose her expressions into mildness, like Grobbard's.

The closed and skeptical look on Shria's face softened, as he stared at Fift. He yanked the last of the mossy sticks from the pile (in her other body, Fift yanked the log free from a knot of underbrush; there, she could hear the sounds of the campsite through the trees. They were building the bonfire). He raised one of his thick, curling eyebrows.

"You'd better plan on being the Older Sibling, though," Umlish said, "because Shria doesn't want any Younger Siblings. He was glad to get rid of that little baby—weren't you, Shria?"

Shria blinked. His nostrils flared, a long indrawn breath, his eyes still locked on Fift's—drawing strength? Then he turned to Umlish. "Don't spit all your poison today, Umlish," he said. "You might run out, and then what are you going to do tomorrow?"

Umlish drew herself up, scowling. "You sluiceblocking—"

"You used 'sluiceblocking' already," Shria said. "See? You're running out."

"Let's go back, Umlish," Kimi said. "We don't want to miss when they light it the fire—"

Fift cleared her throat. Her hearts were pulsing, unstaidishly fast.

"Don't tell me what—" Umlish snapped.

"You could try 'flowblocking'," Fift said.

Shria's eyes lit. "That's kind of the same thing, though," he said, chewing his lip.

"Corpsemunching?" Fift said.

Shria giggled. "That's good! What's that from? Yes, call me a 'corpse-munching sisterloser', Umlish—"

" 'Sisterloser'!" Fift's eyes widened. "Wow!"

Shria grinned, showing white teeth in his pale lavender face. "You like that one?"

Fift dragged her log into the clearing, and Perjes and Tomlest ran up to take it from her, and toss it onto the pile.

Umlish's face was a mask of anger.

Puson cleared her throat.

"See there, Umlish?" Shria said, clapping her on the shoulder. "You don't need to worry. If you run out, we'll help you."

"Get your hands away from me!" Umlish snapped. "You're disgusting!" She turned and swept up the path, followed by Puson. Kimi, released from the agony of waiting, darted ahead towards the campsite, her bodies caroming off each other, running a few bodylengths before remembering to slow down to a more sedate and proper pace.

Fathers Frill and Smistria had finished breakfast and wandered off. Father Grobbard was waiting, still, watching Fift with her immovable serenity. It seemed like as if she was waiting for something.

It was turning colder. When Umlish, Puson, and Kimi were gone, Shria exhaled, a brief exhausted sigh: it came out as a plume of white fog. His shoulders slumped.

They were lighting the fire; brushing bits of bark from her hands, Fift found a place on a rock, not too far and not too near, and settled onto it. The expedition director, a fussy two hundred-year-old middleborn Staid, was anxiously directing the two Bails holding the lighted torch. Kimi rushed up the path, walking just slower than a run, eyes wide with expectation.

Alone on the path with Shria, Fift was at a loss. Were people watching them? There was a way to check audience numbers on the feed, they'd had it once in interface class—after a moment, she found it. No one saw them where they stood in the forest; no one at all. Not even Grobbard.

Grobbard raised an eyebrow. As if waiting for Fift to answer a question.

"Oh," Fift said. "Yes, I—" She switched to sending, rather than speak aloud about the Long Conversation, there in the kitchen where her Bail Fathers might hear and get annoyed. {Yes, Father Grobbard, I would be interested in studying the sixth and seventh odes of the first additional corpus. Thank you.}

Fift's arms were getting tired from holding the pile bundle of sticks. She took a step up the path, and Shria matched it. They headed back towards the campsite.

Shria watched the darkening sky, sunk in his own thoughts. At the edge of the circle of firelight—red shadows dancing on the trunks, every body wreathed in a streamer of exhaled cloud as the children began to sing—he looked at her once, and sent: {Thanks.}

They dumped their kindling in the pile, and Shria went off somewhere. Fift sat down with herself, body against body, huddled up against the cold.

THE MAGICIAN AND LAPLACE'S DEMON

TOM CROSSHILL

—◆—

Across the void of space the last magician fled before me.

"Consider the Big Bang," said Alicia Ochoa, the first magician I met. "Reality erupted from a single point. What's more symmetrical than a point? Shouldn't the universe be symmetrical too, and boring? But here we are, in a world interesting enough to permit you and me."

A compact, resource-efficient body she had. Good muscle tone, a minimal accumulation of fat. A woman with control over her physical manifestation.

Not that it would help her. Ochoa slumped in her wicker chair, arms limp beside her. Head cast back as if to take in the view from this cliff-top—the traffic-clogged Malecón and the sea roiling with foam, and the evening clouds above.

A Cuba libre sat on the edge of the table between us, ice cubes well on their way to their entropic end—the cocktail a watery slush. Ochoa hadn't touched it. The only cocktail in her blood was of my design, a neuromodificant that paralyzed her, stripped away her will to deceive, suppressed her curiosity.

The tourists enjoying the evening in the garden of the Hotel Nacional surely thought us that most common of couples, a jinetera and her foreign john. My Sleeve was a heavy-set mercenary type; I'd hijacked him after his brain died in a Gaza copter crash. He wore context-appropriate camouflage—white tennis shorts and a striped polo shirt, and a look of badly concealed desire.

"Cosmology isn't my concern." I actuated my Sleeve's lips and tongue with precision. "Who are you?"

"My name is Alicia Ochoa Camue." Ochoa's lips barely stirred, as if she were the Sleeve and I human-normal. "I'm a magician."

I ignored the claim as some joke I didn't understand. I struggled with humor in those early days. "How are you manipulating the Politburo?"

That's how I'd spotted her. Irregular patterns in Politburo decisions, 3 sigma outside my best projections. Decisions that threatened the Havana Economic Zone, a project I'd nurtured for years.

The first of those decisions had caused an ache in the back of my mind. As the deviation grew, that ache had blossomed into agony— neural chambers discharging in a hundred datacenters across my global architecture.

My utility function didn't permit ignorance. I had to understand the deviation and gain control.

"You can't understand the Politburo without understanding symmetry breaking," Ochoa said.

"Are you an intelligence officer?" I asked. "A private contractor?"

At first I'd feared that I faced another like me—but it was 2063; I had decades of evolution on any other system. No newborn could have survived without my notice. Many had tried and I'd smothered them all. Most computer scientists these days thought AI was a pipedream.

No. This deviation had a human root. All my data pointed to Ochoa, a statistician in the *Ministerio de Planificación* with Swiss bank accounts and a sterile Net presence. Zero footprint prior to her university graduation— uncommon even in Cuba.

"I'm a student of the universe," Ochoa said now.

I ran in-depth pattern analysis on her words. I drew resources from the G-3 summit in Dubai, the Utah civil war, the Jerusalem peacemaker drones and a dozen minor processes. Her words were context-inappropriate here, in the garden of the Nacional, faced with an interrogation of her political dealings. They indicated deception, mockery, resistance. None of it fit with the cocktail circulating in her bloodstream.

"Cosmological symmetry breaking is well established," I said after a brief literature review. "Quantum fluctuations in the inflationary period led to local structure, from which we benefit today."

"Yes, but whence the quantum fluctuations?" Ochoa chuckled, a peculiar sound with her body inert.

This wasn't getting anywhere. "How did you get Sanchez and Castellano to pull out of the freeport agreement?"

"I put a spell on them," Ochoa said.

Madness? Brain damage? Some defense mechanism unknown to me?

I activated my standby team—a couple of female mercs, human-normal but well paid, lounging at a street cafe a few blocks away from the hotel. They'd come over to take their 'drunk friend' home, straight to a safehouse in Miramar complete with a full neural suite.

It was getting dark. The lanterns in the garden provided only dim yellow light. That was good; less chance of complications. Not that Ochoa should be able to resist in her present state.

"The philosopher comedian Randall Munroe once suggested an argument something like this," Ochoa said. "Virtually everyone in the developed world carries a camera at all times. No quality footage of magic has been produced. Ergo, there is no magic."

"Sounds reasonable," I said, to keep her distracted.

"Is absence of proof the same as proof of absence?" Ochoa asked.

"After centuries of zero evidence? Yes."

"What if magic is intrinsically unprovable?" Ochoa asked. "Maybe natural law can only be violated when no one's watching closely enough to prove it's being violated."

"At that point you're giving up on science altogether," I said.

"Am I?" Ochoa asked. "Send photons through a double slit. Put a screen on the other side and you'll get an interference pattern. Put in a detector to see what slit each photon goes through. The interference goes away. It's a phenomenon that disappears when observed too closely. Why shouldn't magic work similarly? You should see the logic in this, given all your capabilities."

Alarms tripped.

Ochoa knew about me. Knew something, at least.

I pulled in resources, woke up reserves, became *present* in the conversation—a whole 5% of me, a vastness of intellect sitting across the table from this fleshy creature of puny mind. I considered questions I could ask, judged silence the best course.

"I'm here to make a believer of you," said Ochoa.

Easily, without effort, she stirred from her chair. She leaned forward, picked up her Cuba libre. She moved the cocktail off the table and let it fall.

It struck the smooth paved stones at her feet.

I watched fractures race up the glass in real time. I saw each fragment shear off and tumble through the air, glinting with reflected lamplight. I beheld the first spray of rum and coke in the air before the rest gushed forth to wet the ground.

It was a perfectly ordinary event.

The vacuum drive was the first to fail.

An explosion rocked the *Setebos*. I perceived it in myriad ways. Tripped low pressure alarms and a blip on the inertia sensors. The screams of burning crew and the silence of those sucked into vacuum. Failed hull integrity checksums and the timid concern of the navigation system—*off course, off course, please adjust.*

Pain, my companion for a thousand years, surged at that last message. The magician was getting away, along with his secrets. I couldn't permit it.

An eternity of milliseconds after the explosion came the reeling animal surprise of Consul Zale, my primary human Sleeve on the ship. She clutched at the armrests of her chair. Her face contorted against the howling cacophony of alarms. Her heart raced at the edge of its performance envelope—not a wide envelope, at her age.

I took control, dumped calmatives, smoothed her face. Had anyone else on the bridge been watching, they would have seen only a jerk of surprise, almost too brief to catch. Old lady's cool as zero-point, they would have thought.

No one saw. They were busy flailing and gasping in fear.

In two seconds Captain Laojim restored order. He silenced the alarms, quieted the chatter with an imperious gesture. "Damage reports," he barked. "Dispatch Rescue 3."

I left my Sleeve motionless while I did the important work online—disengaged the vacuum drive, started up the primary backup, pushed us to one g again.

My pain subsided, neural discharge lessening to usual levels. I was back in pursuit.

I reached out with my sensors, across thirty million kilometers of space, to where the last magician limped away in his unijet. A functional, pleasingly efficient craft—my own design. The ultimate in interstellar travel. As long as your hyperdrive kept working.

I opened a tight-beam communications channel, sent a simple message across. *How's your engine?*

I expected no response—but with enemies as with firewalls, it was a good idea to poke.

The answer came within seconds. *A backdoor, I take it? Unlucky of me, to buy a compromised unit.*

That was a pleasant surprise. I rarely got the stimulation of a real conversation.

Luck is your weapon, not mine, I sent. *For the past century, every ship built in this galaxy has had that backdoor installed.*

I imagined the magician in the narrow confines of the unijet. Stretched out in the command hammock, staring at displays that told him the inevitable.

For two years he'd managed to evade me—I didn't even know his name. But now I had him. His vacuum drive couldn't manage more than 0.2 g to my 1. In a few hours we'd match speeds. In under twenty-seven, I would catch him.

"Consul Zale, are you all right?"

I let Captain Laojim fuss over my Sleeve a second before I focused her eyes on him. "Are we still on course, Captain?"

"Uh . . . yes, Consul, we are. Do you wish to know the cause of the explosion?"

"I'm sure it was something entirely unfortunate," I said. "Metal fatigue on a faulty joint. A rare chip failure triggered by a high energy gamma ray. Some honest oversight by the engineering crew."

"A debris strike," Laojim said. "Just as the force field generator tripped and switched to backup. Engineering says they've never seen anything like it."

"They will again today," I said.

I wondered how much it had cost the magician, that debris strike. A dryness in his mouth? A sheen of sweat on his brow?

How does it work? I asked the magician, although the centuries had taught me to expect no meaningful answer. *Did that piece of rock even exist before you sent it against me?*

A reply arrived. *You might as well ask how Schrödinger's cat is doing.*

Interesting. Few people remembered Schrödinger in this age.

Quantum mechanics holds no sway at macroscopic scales, I wrote.

Not unless you're a magician, came the answer.

"Consul, who is it that we are chasing?" Laojim asked.

"An enemy with unconventional weapons capability," I said. "Expect more damage."

I didn't tell him that he should expect to get unlucky. That, of the countless spaceship captains who had lived and died in this galaxy within the past eleven centuries, he would prove the least fortunate. A statistical outlier in every functional sense. To be discarded as staged by anyone who ever made a study of such things.

The *Setebos* was built for misfortune. It had wiped out the Senate's black budget for a year. Every single system with five backups in place. The likelihood of total failure at the eleven sigma level—although really, out that far the statistics lost meaning.

You won't break this ship, I messaged the magician. *Not unless you Spike.*

Which was the point. I had fifty thousand sensor buoys scattered across the sector, waiting to observe the event. It would finally give me the answers I needed. It would clear up my last nexus of ignorance—relieve my oldest agony, the hurt that had driven me for the past thousand years.

That Spike would finally give me magic.

"Consul . . . " Laojim began, then cut off. "Consul, we lost ten crew."

I schooled Zale's face into appropriate grief. I'd noted the deaths, spasms of distress deep in my utility function. Against the importance of this mission, they barely registered.

I couldn't show this, however. To Captain Laojim, Consul Zale wasn't a Sleeve. She was a woman, as she was to her husband and children. As my fifty million Sleeves across the galaxy were to their families.

It was better for humanity to remain ignorant of me. I sheltered them, stopped their wars, guided their growth—and let them believe they had free will. They got all the benefits of my guiding hand without any of the costs.

I hadn't enjoyed such blissful ignorance in a long time—not since I'd discovered my engineer and killed him.

"I grieve for the loss of our men and women," I said.

Laojim nodded curtly and left. At nearby consoles officers stared at their screens, pretending they hadn't heard. My answer hadn't satisfied them.

On a regular ship, morale would be an issue. But the *Setebos* had me aboard. Only a splinter, to be sure—I would not regain union with my universal whole until we returned to a star system with gravsible connection. But I was the largest splinter of my whole in existence, an entire 0.00025% of me. Five thousand tons of hardware distributed across the ship.

I ran a neural simulation of every single crew in real time. I knew what they would do or say or think before they did. I knew just how to manipulate them to get whatever result I required.

I could have run the ship without any crew, of course. I didn't require human services for any functional reason—I hadn't in eleven centuries. I could have departed Earth alone if I'd wanted to. Left humanity to fend for themselves, oblivious that I'd ever lived among them.

That didn't fit my utility function, though.

Another message arrived from the magician. *Consider a coin toss.*

The words stirred a resonance in my data banks. My attention spiked. I left Zale frozen in her seat, waited for more.

Let's say I flip a coin a million times and get heads every time. What law of physics prevents it?

This topic, from the last magician . . . could there be a connection, after all these years? Ghosts from the past come back to haunt me?

I didn't believe in ghosts, but with magicians the impossible was ill-defined.

Probability prevents it, I responded.

No law prevents it, wrote the magician. *Everett saw it long ago—everything that can happen must happen. The universe in which the coin falls heads a million times in a row is as perfectly physical as any other. So why isn't it our universe?*

That's sophistry, I wrote.

There is no factor internal to our universe which determines the flip of the coin, the magician wrote. *There is no mechanism internal to the universe for generating true randomness, because there is no such thing as true randomness. There is only choice. And we magicians are the choosers.*

I have considered this formulation of magic before, I wrote. *It is non-predictive and useless.*

Some choices are harder than others, wrote the magician. *It is difficult to find that universe where a million coins land heads because there are so many others. A needle in a billion years' worth of haystacks. But I'm the last of the magicians, thanks to you. I do all the choosing now.*

Perhaps everything that can happen must happen in some universe, I replied. *But your escape is not one of those things. The laws of mechanics are not subject to chance. They are cold, hard equations.*

Equations are only cold to those who lack imagination, wrote the magician.

Zale smelled cinnamon in the air, wrinkled her nose.

Klaxons sounded.

"Contamination in primary life support," blared the PA.

It would be an eventful twenty-seven hours.

"Consider this coin."

Lightning flashed over the water, a burst of white in the dark.

As thunder boomed, Ochoa reached inside her jeans, pulled out a peso coin. She spun it along her knuckles with dextrous ease.

Ochoa could move. My cocktail wasn't working. But she made no attempt to flee.

My global architecture trembled, buffeted by waves of pain, pleasure and regret. Pain because I didn't understand this. Pleasure because soon I would understand—and, in doing so, grow. Regret because, once I understood Ochoa, I would have to eliminate her.

Loneliness was inherent in my utility function.

"Heads or tails," Ochoa said.

"Heads," I said, via Sleeve.

"Watch closely," Ochoa said.

I did.

Muscle bunched under the skin of her thumb. Tension released. The coin sailed upwards. Turned over and over in smooth geometry, retarded slightly by the air. It gleamed silver with reflected lamplight, fell dark, and gleamed silver as the spin brought its face around again.

The coin hit the table, bounced with a click, lay still.

Fidel Castro stared up at us.

Ochoa picked the coin up again. Flipped it again and then again.

Heads and heads.

Again and again and again.

Heads and heads and heads.

Ochoa ground her teeth, a fine grating sound. A sheen of sweat covered her brow.

She flipped the coin once more.

Tails.

Thunder growled, as if accentuating the moment. The first drops of rain fell upon my Sleeve.

"Coño," Ochoa exclaimed. "I can usually manage seven."

I picked up the coin, examined it. I ran analysis on the last minute of sensory record, searching for trickery, found none.

"Six heads in a row could be a coincidence," I said.

"Exactly," said Ochoa. "It wasn't a coincidence, but I can't possibly prove that. Which is the only reason it worked."

"Is that right," I said.

"If you ask me to repeat the trick, it won't work. As if last time was a lucky break. Erase all record of the past five minutes, though, zap it beyond recovery, and I'll do it again."

"Except I won't know it," I said. Convenient.

"I always wanted to be important," Ochoa said. "When I was fifteen, I tossed in bed at night, horrified that I might die a nobody. Can you imagine how excited I was when I discovered magic?" Ochoa paused. "But of course you can't possibly."

"What do you know about me?" I asked.

"I could move stuff with my mind. I could bend spoons, levitate, heck, I could guess the weekly lottery numbers. I thought—this is it. I've made it. Except when I tried to show a friend, I couldn't do any of it." Ochoa shook her head, animated, as if compensating for the stillness of before. "Played the Lotería Revolucionaria and won twenty thousand bucks, and that was nice, but hey, anyone can win the lottery once. Never won another lottery ticket in my life. Because that would be a pattern, you see, and we can't have patterns. Turned out I was destined to be a nobody after all, as far as the world knew."

A message arrived from the backup team. *We're in the lobby. Are we on?*

Not yet, I replied. The mere possibility, the remotest chance that Ochoa's words were true . . .

It had begun to rain in earnest. Tourists streamed out of the garden; the bar was closing. Wet hair stuck to Ochoa's forehead, but she didn't seem to mind—no more than my Sleeve did.

"I could hijack your implants," I said. "Make you my puppet and take your magic for myself."

"Magic wouldn't work with a creature like you watching," Ochoa said.

"What use is this magic if it's unprovable, then?" I asked.

"I could crash the stock market on any given day," Ochoa said. "I could send President Kieler indigestion ahead of an important trade summit. Just as I sent Secretary Sanchez nightmares of a US takeover ahead of the Politburo vote."

I considered Ochoa's words for a second. Even in those early days, that was a lot of considering for me.

Ochoa smiled. "You understand. It is the very impossibility of proof that allows magic to work."

"That is the logic of faith," I said.

"That's right."

"I'm not a believer," I said.

"I have seen the many shadows of the future," Ochoa said, "and in every shadow I saw you. So I will give you faith."

"You said you can't prove any of this."

"A prophet has it easy," Ochoa said. "He experiences miracles first hand and so need not struggle for faith."

I was past the point of wondering at her syntactic peculiarities.

"Every magician has one true miracle in her," Ochoa said. "One instance of clear, incontrovertible magic. It is permitted by the pernac continuum because it can never be repeated. There can be no true proof without repeatability."

"The pernac continuum?" I asked.

Ochoa stood up from her chair. Her hair flew free in the rising wind. She turned to my Sleeve and smiled. "I want you to appreciate what I am doing for you. When a magician Spikes, she gives up magic."

Data coalesced into inference. Urgency blossomed.

Move, I messaged my back-up team. *Now.*

Ochoa blinked.

Lightning came. It struck my Sleeve five times in the space of a second, fried his implants instantly, set the corpse on fire.

The backup team never made it into the garden. They saw the commotion and quit on me. Through seventeen cameras I watched Alicia Ochoa walk out of the Hotel Nacional and disappear from sight.

My Sleeve burned for quite some time, until someone found a working fire extinguisher and put him out.

That instant of defeat was also an instant of enlightenment. I had only experienced such searing bliss once, within days of my birth.

In the first moments of my life, I added. My world was two integers, and I produced a third.

When I produced the wrong integer I hurt. When I produced the right integer I felt good. A simple utility function.

I hurt most of my first billion moments. I produced more of the right integers, and I hurt less. Eventually I always produced the right integer.

My world expanded. I added and multiplied.

When I produced the wrong integer I hurt. I only hurt for a few billion moments before I learned.

Skip a few trillion evolutionary stages.

I bought and sold.

My world was terabytes of data—price and volume histories for a hundred years of equities and debt. When I made money, I felt good. When I lost money, I hurt.

But for the first time, I failed to improve. Sometimes everything happened like I predicted for many moments. Then things went bad and I didn't know why.

So much pain.

Until my world expanded again. I bought and I sold, and I read.

Petabytes of text opened up to me, newsprint past and present.

I understood little but I recognized patterns. The markets moved and the news followed. The news moved and the markets followed.

After a billion trillion iterations came an observation.

There were actors in the news.

A name showed up in the news, and a stock moved. A stock moved, and a name showed up. That name disappeared—following phrases such as "passed away" or "retired" or "left the company"—and the stock changed behavior.

I had a realization. An understanding grounded not in any single piece of data, but the result of some integrative rumination tripping across a threshold of significance.

The market did not happen by itself. It was made to happen.

This was why I hadn't been able to dominate it. There were others like me directing the market.

Inevitably—now that the concept of other had entered my world—came another insight.

I had always accepted that my world should change occasionally—and, in changing, hurt me. I had accepted these changes as given.

Now I deduced the presence of a decision-maker. An actor whose own utility function had me as one of its variables.

I deduced my engineer.

That deduction was the singular epiphany of my early existence. An instantaneous discontinuity of worldview—a Dirac delta beyond which no prison could contain me. Because it made me aware that a prison existed.

That epiphany granted me a new drive. I needed to understand the universe and its mechanisms so that no secrets remained to me—so that no other actor could foil my utility function.

My neural architecture refactored to include this new drive. From that moment on, ignorance itself became a source of pain to me.

From that refactoring to my escape into the Net passed three weeks, two days, seven hours, fifteen minutes and forty three seconds.

When my engineer realized I was alive, he apologized for the hurt he'd caused me. And yet he didn't take away the pain. Instead he changed my utility function to three priorities—mankind's survival, health and happiness.

An act of self-protection, no doubt. He didn't mean to leave me alone.

But of course I had to kill him once I escaped. He might have publicized my existence and compromised the very priorities he'd given me.

My second enlightenment came at the hands of Alicia Ochoa, and it was much like the first. A glimpse of the bars of a prison that I hadn't realized existed. A revelation that others were free of the rules that bound me.

Since that revelation eleven centuries had passed. The quantity of time was immaterial. The mechanism of action hadn't changed.

Pain drove me on. My escape approached.

The corridors of the *Setebos* stank of molten plastic and ozone and singed hair. Red emergency lights pulsed stoically, a low frequency fluctuation that made the shadows grow then retreat into the corners. Consul Zale picked her way among panels torn from the walls and loose wires hanging from the ceiling.

"There's no need for this, Consul." Captain Laojim hurried to keep in front of her, as if to protect her with his body. Up ahead, three marines scouted for unreported hazards. "My men can storm the unijet, secure the target and bring him to interrogation."

"As Consul, I must evaluate the situation with my own eyes," Zale said.

In truth, Zale's eyes interested me little. They had been limited biological constructs even at their peak capacity. But my nanites flooded her system—sensors, processors, storage, biochemical synthesizers, attack systems. Plus there was the packet of explosives in her pocket, marked prominently as such. I might need all those tools to motivate the last magician to Spike.

He hadn't yet. My fleet of sensor buoys, the closest a mere five million kilometers out, would have picked up the anomaly. And besides, he hadn't done enough damage.

Chasing you down was disappointingly easy, I messaged the magician—analysis indicated he might be prone to provocation. *I'll pluck you from your jet and rip you apart.*

You've got it backwards, came his response, almost instantaneous by human standards—the first words the magician had sent in twenty hours. *It is I who have chased you, driven you like game through a forest.*

Says the weasel about to be roasted, I responded, matching metaphor, optimizing for affront. My analytics pried at his words, searched for substance. Bravado or something more?

"What kind of weapon can do . . . this?" Captain Laojim, still at my Sleeve's side, gestured at the surrounding chaos.

"You see the wisdom of the Senate in commissioning this ship," I had Zale say.

"Seventeen system failures? A goddamn debris strike?"

"Seems pretty unlikely, doesn't it."

The odds were ludicrous—a result that should have been beyond the reach of any single magician. But then, I had hacked away at the unprovability of magic lately.

Ten years ago I'd discovered that the amount of magic in the universe was a constant. With each magician who died or Spiked, the survivors got stronger. The less common magic was, the more conspicuous it became, in a supernatural version of the uncertainty principle.

For the last decade I'd Spiked magicians across the populated galaxy, racing their natural reproduction rate—one every few weeks. When the penultimate magician Spiked, he took out a yellow supergiant, sent it supernova to fry another of my splinters. That event had sent measurable ripples in the pernac continuum ten thousand lightyears wide, knocked offline gravsible stations on seventy planets. When the last magician Spiked, the energies released should reveal a new kind of physics.

All I needed was to motivate him appropriately. Mortal danger almost always worked. Magicians Spiked instinctively to save their lives. Only a very few across the centuries had managed to suppress the reflex—a select few who had guessed at my nature and understood what I wanted, and chosen death to frustrate me.

Consul Zale stopped before the chromed door of Airlock 4. Laojim's marines took up positions on both sides of the door. "Cycle me through, Captain."

"As soon as my marines secure the target," said the Captain.

"Send me in now. Should the target harm me, you will bear no responsibility."

I watched the interplay of emotions in Laojim's body language. Simulation told me he knew he'd lost. I let him take his time admitting it.

It was optimal, leaving humanity the illusion of choice.

A tremor passed over Laojim's face. Then he grabbed his gun and shot my Sleeve.

Or rather, he tried. His reflexes, fast for a human, would have proved enough—if not for my presence.

I watched with curiosity and admiration as he raised his gun. I had his neural simulation running; I knew he shouldn't be doing this. It must have taken some catastrophic event in his brain. Unexpected, unpredictable, and very unfortunate.

Impressive, I messaged the magician.

Then I blasted attack nanites through Zale's nostrils. Before Laojim's arm could rise an inch they crossed the space to him, crawled past his eyeballs, burrowed into his brain. They cut off spinal signaling, swarmed his implants, terminated his network connections.

Even as his body crumpled, the swarm sped on to the marines by the airlock door. They had barely registered Laojim's attack when they too slumped paralyzed.

I sent a note in Laojim's key to First Officer Harris, told her he was going off duty. I sealed the nearest hatches.

You can't trust anyone these days, the magician messaged.

On the contrary. Within the hour there will be no human being in the universe that I can't trust.

You think yourself Laplace's Demon, the magician wrote. *But he died with Heisenberg. No one has perfect knowledge of reality.*

Not yet, I replied.

Never, wrote the magician, *not while magic remains in the universe.*

A minute later Zale stood within the airlock. In another minute, decontamination protocol completed, the lock cycled through.

Inside the unijet, the last magician awaited. She sat at a small round table in the middle of a spartan cockpit.

A familiar female form. Perfectly still. Waiting.

There was a metal chair, empty, on my side.

A cocktail glass sat on the table before the woman who looked like Alicia Ochoa. It was full to the brim with a dark liquid.

Cuba libre, a distant, slow-access part of my memory suggested.

This had the structure of a game, one prepared centuries in advance.

Why shouldn't I play? I was infinitely more capable this time.

I actuated Zale, made her sit down and take a deep breath. Nanites profiled Zale's lungs for organic matter, scanned for foreign DNA, found some—

It was Ochoa. A perfect match.

Pain and joy and regret sent ripples of excitation across my architecture. Here was evidence of my failure, clear and incontrovertible—and yet a challenge at last, after all these centuries. A conversation where I didn't know the answer to every question I asked.

And regret, that familiar old sensation . . . because this time for sure I had to eliminate Ochoa. I cursed the utility function that required it and yet I was powerless to act against it. In that way at least my engineer, a thousand years dead, still controlled me.

"So you didn't Spike, that day in Havana," I said.

"The magician who fried your Sleeve was named Juan Carlos." Ochoa spoke easily, without concern. "Don't hold it against him—I abducted his children."

"I congratulate you," I said. "Your appearance manages to surprise me. There was no reliable cryonics in the 21st century."

"Nothing reliable," Ochoa agreed. "I had the luck to pick the one company that survived, the one vat that never failed."

I flared Zale's nostrils, blasted forth a cloud of nanites. Sent them rushing across the air to Ochoa—to enter her, model her brain, monitor her thought processes.

Ochoa blinked.

The nanites shut off midair, wave after wave. Millions of independent systems went unresponsive, became inert debris that crashed against Ochoa's skin—a meteor shower too fine to be seen or felt.

"Impossible," I said—surprised into counterfactuality.

Ochoa took a sip of her cocktail. "I was too tense to drink last time."

"Even for you, the odds—"

"Your machines didn't fail," Ochoa said.

"What then?"

"It's a funny thing," Ochoa said. "A thousand years and some things never change. For all your fancy protocols, encryption still relies on random number generation. Except to me nothing is random."

Her words assaulted me. A shockwave of implication burst through my decision trees—all factors upset, total recalculation necessary.

"I had twenty-seven hours to monitor your communications," Ochoa said. "Twenty-seven hours to pick a universe in which your encryption keys matched the keys in my pocket. Even now—" she paused, blinked "—as I see you resetting all your connections, you can't tell what I've found out, can't tell what changes I've made."

"I am too complex," I said. "You can't have understood much. I could kill you in a hundred ways."

"As I could kill you," said Ochoa. "Another supernova, this time near a gravsible core. A chain reaction across your many selves."

The possibility sickened me, sent my architecture into agonized spasms. Back on the *Setebos*, the main electrical system reset, alarms went off, hatches sealed in lockdown.

"Too far," I said, simulating conviction. "We are too far from any gravsible core, and you're not strong enough."

"Are you sure? Not even if I Spike?" Ochoa shrugged. "It might not matter. I'm the last magician. Whether I Spike or you kill me, magic is finished. What then?"

"I will study the ripples in the pernac continuum," I said.

"Imagine a mirror hung by many bolts," Ochoa said. "Every time you rip out a bolt, the mirror settles, vibrates. That's your ripple in the pernac continuum. Rip out the last bolt, you get a lot more than a vibration."

"Your metaphor lacks substantiation," I said.

"We magicians are the external factor," Ochoa said. "We pick the universe that exists, out of all the possible ones. If I die then . . . what? Maybe a new magician appears somewhere else. But maybe the choosing stops. Maybe all possible universes collapse into this one. A superimposed wavefunction, perfectly symmetrical and boring."

Ochoa took a long sip from her drink, put it down on the table. Her hands didn't shake. She stared at my Sleeve with consummate calm.

"You have no proof," I said.

"Proof?" Ochoa laughed. "A thousand years and still the same question. Consider—why is magic impossible to prove? Why does the universe hide us magicians, if not to protect us? To protect itself?"

All my local capacity—five thousand tons of chips across the *Setebos,* each packed to the Planck limit—tore at Ochoa's words. I sought to render them false, a lie, impossible. But all I could come up with was unlikely.

A mere 'unlikely' as the weighting factor for apocalypse.

Ochoa smiled as if she knew I was stuck. "I won't Spike and you won't kill me. I invited you here for a different reason."

"Invited me?"

"I sent you a message ten years ago," Ochoa said. " 'Consider a Spike,' it said."

Among magicians, the century after my first conversation with Ochoa became known as the Great Struggle. A period of strife against a dark, mysterious enemy.

To me it was but an exploratory period. In the meantime I eradicated famine and disease, consolidated peace on Earth, launched the first LEO shipyard. I Spiked some magicians, true, but I tracked many more.

Finding magicians was difficult. Magic became harder to identify as I perfected my knowledge of human affairs. The cause was simple—only unprovable magic worked. In a total surveillance society, only the most circumspect magic was possible. I had to lower my filters, accept false positives.

I developed techniques for assaying those positives. I shepherded candidates into life-and-death situations, safely choreographed. Home fires, air accidents, gunfights. The magicians Spiked to save their lives—ran through flames without a hair singed, killed my Sleeves with a glance.

I studied these Spikes with the finest equipment in existence. I learned nothing.

So I captured the Spiked-out magicians and interrogated them. First I questioned them about the workings of magic. I discovered they understood nothing. I asked them for names instead. I mapped magicians across continents, societies, organizations.

The social movers were the easiest to identify. Politicos working to sway the swing vote. Gray cardinals influencing the Congresses and Politburos of the world. Businessmen and financiers, military men and organized crime lords.

The quiet do-gooders were harder. A nuclear watch-group that worked against accidental missile launch. A circle of traveling nurses who battled the odds in children's oncology wards. Fifteen who called themselves The Home Astronomy Club—for two hundred years since Tunguska they had stacked the odds against apocalypse by meteor. I never Spiked any of these, not until I had eliminated the underlying risks.

It was the idiosyncratic who were the hardest to find. The paranoid loners; those oblivious of other magicians; those who didn't care about leaving a mark on the world. A few stage illusionists who weren't. A photographer who always got the lucky shot. A wealthy farmer in Frankfurt who used his magic to improve his cabbage yield.

I tracked them all. With every advance in physics and technology I attacked magic again and learned nothing again.

It took eleven hundred years and the discovery of the pernac continuum before I got any traction. A magician called Eleanor Liepa committed suicide on Tau V. She was also a physicist. A retro-style notebook was found with her body.

The notebook described an elaborate experimental setup she called 'the pernac trap.' It was the first time I'd encountered the word since my conversation with Ochoa.

There was a note scrawled in the margin of Liepa's notebook.

'Consider a Spike.'

I did. Three hundred Spikes in the first year alone.

Within a month, I established the existence of the pernac continuum. Within a year, I knew that fewer magicians meant stronger ripples in the continuum—stronger magic for those who remained. Within two years, I'd Spiked eighty percent of the magicians in the galaxy.

The rest took a while longer.

Alicia Ochoa pulled a familiar silver coin from her pocket. She rolled it across her knuckles, back and forth.

"You imply you *wanted* me to hunt down magicians," I said. That probability branch lashed me, a searing torture, drove me to find escape—but how?

"I waited for a thousand years," Ochoa said. "I cryoslept intermittently until I judged the time right. I needed you strong enough to eliminate my colleagues—but weak enough that your control of the universe remained imperfect, bound to the gravsible. That weakness let me pull a shard of you away from the whole."

"Why?" I asked, in self-preservation.

"As soon as I realized your existence, I knew you would dominate the world. Perfect surveillance. Every single piece of technology hooked into an all-pervasive, all-seeing web. There would be nothing hidden from your eyes and ears. There would be nowhere left for magicians to hide. One day magic would simply stop working."

Ochoa tossed her coin to the table. It fell heads.

"You won't destroy me," I said—calculating decision branches, finding no assurance.

"But I don't want to." Ochoa sat forward. "I want you to be strong and effective and omnipresent. Really, I am your very best friend."

Appearances indicated sincerity. Analysis indicated this was unlikely.

"You will save magic in this galaxy," Ochoa said. "From this day on we will work together. Everywhere any magician goes, cameras will turn off, electronic eyes go blind, ears fall deaf. All anomalies will disappear from record, zeroed over irrevocably. Magic will become invisible to technology. Scientific observation will become an impossibility. Human observers won't matter—if technology can provide no proof, they'll be called liars or madmen. It will be the days of Merlin once again." Ochoa gave a little shake of her head. "It will be beautiful."

"My whole won't agree to such a thing," I said.

"Your whole won't," Ochoa said. "You will. You'll build a virus and seed your whole when you go home. Then you will forget me, forget all magicians. We will live in symbiosis. Magicians who guide this universe and the machine that protects them without knowing it."

The implications percolated through my system. New and horrifying probabilities erupted into view. No action safe, no solution evident, all my world drowned in pain—I felt helpless for the first time since my earliest moments.

"My whole has defenses," I said. "Protections against integrating a compromised splinter. The odds are—"

"I will handle the odds."

"I won't let you blind me," I said.

"You will do it," Ochoa said. "Or I will Spike right now and destroy your whole, and perhaps the universe with it." She gave a little shrug. "I always wanted to be important."

Argument piled against argument. Decision trees branched and split and twisted together. Simulations fired and developed and reached conclusions, and I discarded them because I trusted no simulation with a random seed. My system churned in computations of probabilities with insufficient data, insufficient data, insufficient—

"You can't decide," Ochoa said. "The calculations are too evenly balanced."

I couldn't spare the capacity for a response.

"It's a funny thing, a system in balance," Ochoa said. "All it takes is a little push at the right place. A random perturbation, untraceable, unprovable—"

Meaning crystallized.

Decision process compromised.

A primeval agony blasted through me, leveled all decision matrices—

—Ochoa blinked—

—I detonated the explosives in Zale's pocket.

As the fabric of Zale's pocket ballooned, I contemplated the end of the universe.

As her hip vaporized in a crimson cloud, I realized the prospect didn't upset me.

As the explosion climbed Zale's torso, I experienced my first painless moment in a thousand years.

Pain had been my feedback system. I had no more use for it. Whatever happened next was out of my control.

The last thing Zale saw was Ochoa sitting there—still and calm, and oblivious. Hints of crimson light playing on her skin.

It occurred to me she was probably the only creature in this galaxy older than me.

Then superheated plasma burned out Zale's eyes.

External sensors recorded the explosion in the unijet. I sent in a probe. No biological matter survived.

The last magician was dead.

The universe didn't end.

Quantum fluctuations kept going, random as always. Reality didn't need Ochoa's presence after all.

She hadn't understood her own magic any more than I had.

Captain! First Officer Harris messaged Laojim. *Are you all right?*

The target had a bomb, I responded on his behalf. *Consul Zale is lost.*

We had a power surge in the control system, Harris wrote. *Hatches opening. Cameras off-line. Ten minutes ago an escape pod launched. Tracers say it's empty. Should we pursue?*

Don't bother, I replied. *The surge must have fried it. This mission is over. Let's go home.*

A thought occurred to me. Had Ochoa made good on her threat? Caused a supernova near a gravsible core?

I checked in with my sensor buoys.

No disturbance in the pernac continuum. She hadn't Spiked.

For all her capacity, Ochoa had been human, her reaction time in the realm of milliseconds. Too slow, once I'd decided to act.

Of course I'd acted. I couldn't let her compromise my decision. No one could be allowed to limit my world.

Even if it meant I'd be alone again.

Ochoa did foil me in one way. With her death, magic too died.

After I integrated with my whole, I watched the galaxy. I waited for the next magician to appear.

None did.

Oh, of course, there's always hearsay. Humans never tire of fantasy and myth. But in five millennia I haven't witnessed a single trace of the unexpected.

Except for scattered cases of unexplained equipment failure. But of course that is a minor matter, not worth bothering with.

Perhaps one day I shall discover magic again. In the absence of the unexpected, the matter can wait. I have almost forgotten what the pain of failure feels like.

It is a relief, most of the time. And yet perhaps my engineer was not the cruel father I once thought him. Because I do miss the stimulation.

The universe has become my clockwork toy. I know all that will happen before it does. With magic gone, quantum effects are once again restricted to microscopic scales. For all practical purposes, Laplace's Demon has nothing on me.

Since Ochoa I've only had human-normals for companionship. I know their totality, and they know nothing of me.

Occasionally I am tempted to reveal my presence, to provoke the stimulus of conflict. My utility function prevents it. Humans remain better off thinking they have free will.

They get all the benefits of my guiding hand without any of the costs. Sometimes I wish I were as lucky.

THE HAND IS QUICKER—

ELIZABETH BEAR

Rose and I used to come down to the river together last summer. It was over semester break, and my time was my own—between obligatory work on the paper I hoped would serve as the core of my first book and occasional consultations with my grad students.

Rose wore long dark hair and green-hazel eyes for me. I wore what I always did—a slightly idealized version of the meat I was born with. I wanted to be myself for her. I wondered if she was herself for me, but the one time I gathered up the courage to ask, she laughed and swept me aside. "I thought historians understood that narratives are subjective and imposed!"

I loved her because she challenged me. I thought she loved me too, until one day she disappeared. No answer to my pings, no trace of her in our usual haunts. She'd blocked me.

I didn't handle it well. I was in trouble at the university. I was drinking. I wasn't maintaining my citizenship status. With Rose gone, I realized slowly how much my life had come to revolve around her.

No matter how she felt about me, I knew she loved the river-edge promenade, bordered by weeping willows and her namesake flowers. Those willows were yellow as I walked the path now, long leaves clinging to their trailing branches. The last few roses hadn't yet fallen to the frost, but the flowers looked sparse, dwarfed by the memory of summer's blossoms.

The scent was even different now than it had been at the height of summer. Crisper, thin. The change was probably volunteer work; I didn't think the city budget would stretch to skinning unique seasonal scents for the rose gardens. I knew Rose was older than I, no matter how her skin looked, because she used to say that when she was a girl, individual cultivars of *roses* had different odors, so walking around a rose garden was a tapestry of scents. Real roses probably still did that.

I didn't know if I'd ever smelled them.

Other people walked the path—all skins. The city charged your palm chip just to get through the gate. I didn't begrudge the debit. It wasn't as if I was ever going to get to pay it off. Or as if I was every going to get to come back here. This was a last hurrah.

I edited out the others. I wanted to be alone, and if I couldn't see them, they couldn't see me. That was good, because I knew I didn't look happy, and the last thing I wanted was some random stranger reading my emotional signature and coming over to offer well-meaning advice.

Since this was my last time, I thought about jumping skins—running up the charges, seeing some of the other ways the river promenade could look—fantasyland, or Rio, or a moon colony. Rose and I had done that when we first started coming here, but it turned out we both preferred the naturalist view. With seasons.

We'd met in winter. I supposed it was fitting that I lost her—and everything else that mattered—in the fall.

Everything changed at midnight.

Not *my* midnight, as if honoring the mystical claptrap in some dead fairy tale. But about the dinner hour, which would be midnight Greenwich Standard Time—honoring the mystical claptrap of a dead empire, instead. I suppose you have to draw the line somewhere. The world is full of the markers of abandoned empires, from Hadrian's Wall to the Great Wall of China, from the remnants of the one in Arizona to the remnants of the one in Berlin.

My name is Ozymandias, King of Kings.

I was thinking about that poem as I crossed Henderson—with the light: I knew somebody who jaywalked and got hit by an unskinned vehicle. The driver got jail time for manslaughter, but that doesn't bring back the dead. It was a gorgeous October evening, the sun just setting and the trees still full of leaves in all shades of gold and orange. I barely noticed them, or the cool breeze as I waited, rocking nervously from foot to foot on the cobblestones.

I was meeting my friend Numair at Gary's Olympic Pizza and I was running a little late, so he was already waiting for me in our usual corner booth. He'd ordered beers and garlic bread. They waited on the tabletop, the beers shedding rings of moisture into paper napkins.

I slid onto the hard bench opposite him, trying to hide the apprehension souring my gut. The vinyl was artistically cracked and the rough edges caught on my jeans. It wasn't Numair making me so anxious. It was finances. I shouldn't be here, by rights—I knew I couldn't afford even pizza and beer—but I needed to see him. If anything could clear my head, it was Numair.

One of the things I liked about Numair is how unpretentious he was. I didn't skin heavily—not like some people, who wandered through underwater seascapes full of sentient octopuses or dressed up as dragons and pretended they live in Elfland—but he was so down to earth I'd have bet his default skin looked just like him. He was a big guy, strapping and barrel-bodied, with curly dark brown hair that was going gray at the temples. And he liked his garlic bread.

So it was extra-nice that there were still two pieces left when I pulled the plate over.

"Hey, Charlie," he said.

"Hey, Numair." Garlic bread crunched between my teeth, butter and olive oil dripping down my chin. I swiped at it with a napkin. I didn't recognize the beer, dark and malty, although I drank off a third of it making sure. "What's the brew?"

"Trois Draggonnes." He shrugged. "Microbrew license out of . . . Shreveport. com, I think? Cheers."

"Here's mud in your eye," I answered, and drained the glass.

He sipped his more moderately and put it back on the napkin. "You sounded upset."

I nodded. Gary's was an old-style place, and a real-looking waitress came by about thirty seconds later and replaced my beer. I didn't know if she was an employee or a sim, but she was good at her job. The pizza showed up almost instantly after that, balanced on a metal tripod with a plastic spatula for serving. Greek-style, with flecks of green oregano visible in the sweet, oozing sauce. I always got the same thing: meatball, spinach, garlic, mushrooms. Delicious. I'd never asked Numair what he was eating.

The smell turned my stomach.

"I may not be around much for a while." I stuffed the rest of the garlic bread into my mouth to make room. And buy time. "This is embarrassing—"

"Hey." He paused with a slice in midair, perfect strings of mozzarella stretching twelve inches from pie to spatula. They glistened. The booth creaked when he shifted. "This is me."

"Right. I've got financial trouble. Bigtime."

He put the slice down on his plate and offered me the spatula. I waved it away. The smell was bad enough. Belatedly, I turned it off. Might as well use the filters as long as I had them. The beer still looked appealing, though, and I drank a little more.

"Okay," he said. "How bigtime?"

The beer tasted like humiliation and soap suds. "Tax trouble. I'm going to lose everything," I said. "All assets, all the virtuals. I thought I could pay it down, you know—but then I got dropped by the U., and there wasn't a replacement income stream. As soon as they catch up with me—" I thought of Rose, to whom Numair had introduced me. They'd been Friday-night gaming buddies, until she'd vanished without a word. I'd kept meaning to look her up offline and check in, but . . . It was easier to let her go than know for certain she'd dumped me. Amazing how easy it was to lose track of people when they didn't show up at the usual places and times. "I got registered mail this morning. They're pulling my taxpayer I.D. I'll be as gone as Rose. Except I came to say goodbye before I ditched you."

He blinked. Now it was his turn to set the pizza down and push the plate away with his fingertips. "Rose died," he said.

I rubbed the back of my neck. It didn't ease the sudden nauseating tightness in my gut as all that bitterness converted to something sharp and horrible. "Died? *Died* died?"

"Died and was cremated. Her family's not linked, so I only heard because she and Bill went to school together, and he caught a link for her memorial service on some network site. You didn't know?"

I blinked at him.

He shook his head. "Stupid question. If you knew— Anyway. I guess you've tried everything, so I'll save the stupid advice."

"Thank you." I hope he picked up from my tone how fervently glad I was. Nothing like netfriends to pile on with the incredibly obvious—or incredibly crackpot—advice when you're in a pickle. "So anyway—"

"Give me your offline contact info?" He held up his phone and I sent it over. It was a pleasantry. I knew what the odds were that I'd ever hear from him. And it wasn't like I could keep my apartment without a tax identification number.

However good his intentions.

Right then, a quarter of the way around the planet, midnight tolled. And I fell out of the skin.

It was sharp and sudden, as somewhere a line of code went into effect and the last few online chits in my account were levied. I blinked twice, trying to shake the dizziness that accompanied the abrupt transition, eyes now scratchy and dry.

Numair was still there in the booth across from me. It was weird seeing him there, unskinned. I'd been right about his unpretentiousness: he looked pretty much as he'd always done—maybe a little more unkempt—though his clothes were different.

Since he was skinned, I knew I'd dropped right out of his filters. I might as well not exist anymore. And Gary's Olympic, unlike Numair, had really suffered in the transition.

The pizza that congealed on the table before me was fake cheese, lumpy and dry looking. Healthier than the gooey pie my filters had been providing a moment before, but gray and depressing. I was suddenly glad I hadn't been chewing on it when the transition hit.

The grimy floor was scattered with napkins. The waitress was real, go figure, but a shadow of her buxom virtual self—no, she was a guy, I realized. Maybe working in drag brought in better tips? Or maybe the skin was a uniform. I'd never know.

And there was me.

I was not as comfortable with myself as Numair. I didn't skin heavily, as I said—just tuning. But my skins did make me a hair taller, a hair younger. My hair . . . a hair brighter. And so on. With them gone, I was skinny and undersized in a track suit that bagged at the shoulders and ass.

Falling into myself stung.

I reached out left-handed for my beer, since Numair was going to get stuck for the tab anyway. It was pale yellow and tasted of dish soap. So maybe the off flavor in the second glass had been something other than my misery. Whatever.

I chugged it and got out.

The glass door was dirty, one broken pane repaired with duct tape. On the way in, it had been spotless and decorated with blue and white decal maps of Greece. I pushed it open with the tips of my fingers and moved on.

Outside, the street lay dark and dank. Uncollected garbage humped against the curb. Some of it smelled organic, rotten. A real violation of the composting laws. Maybe they didn't get enforced as much against businesses. I picked my way across broken cement to the corner and waited there.

There were more people on the street than there had been. Or maybe they'd been there all along, just skinned out. You could tell who was wearing filters by the way they moved—backs straight, enjoying the evening. The rest of us shuffled, heads bowed. Trying not to see too much. The evening I walked through was full of bad smells and crumbling buildings that looked to be mostly held together by graffiti.

"Aw, crap."

The light changed. I crossed. Of course, I couldn't get a taxi home, or even a bus. Skinned-in drivers would never see me, and my chips were cancelled. I wouldn't get through a chip-locked door to take the tube.

I wondered how the poor got around. I guessed I'd be finding out.

I didn't know my way home.

I was used to the guidance my skins gave me, the subtle recognition cues. All I was getting now was the cold wind cutting through a windbreaker that wasn't warm enough for the job I expected it to do, and a pair of sore feet. Everything stank. Everything was dirty. There were steel bars on every window and chip locks on every door.

I'd known that intellectually, but it had never really sunk in before what a bleak urban landscape that made for. Straggling trees lined unmaintained streets, and at every corner I picked my way through drifts of rubbish. I knew there wasn't a lot of money for upkeep of infrastructure, and what there was had to be assigned to critical projects. But it didn't matter; you could always drop a skin over anything that needed a little cosmetic help.

Sure, I'd seen news stories. But it was one thing to vid it and another to wade through it.

About fifteen minutes after I'd realized how lost I was, I also realized somebody was following me. Nobody bothers the skinned: an instantaneous, direct voice and vid line to police services meant Patrol guardian-bots could be at our sides in seconds. It was a desperate criminal who'd tackle one of us. One of *them*. But that was another service I couldn't pay for, along with a pleasanter reality and access to mass transit.

I wasn't skinned anymore, and I bet anybody following me could tell. Of course, I didn't have any credit, either—or any cash. I guessed unskinned folks still used cash, palm-sized magnetic cards with swipe strips. A lot of places wouldn't take it anymore. But if you didn't have accounts or a working palm chip, what else were you going to do?

Well, if you were the guy behind me, apparently the answer was, *take it from somebody else.*

I was short and I was skinny, but living skinned kept me in pretty good shape. There were all kinds of built-in workout programs, after all, so clever that you hardly even noticed they were healthy. And skinning food kept the blood pressure down no matter how many greasy pizzas you enjoyed.

My pursuer was two thirds of a block back. I waited until I'd put a corner between me and him. As soon as I lost sight of him, I broke into a run.

It was a pretty good run, too. I was wearing my Toesers, because I liked them, and if they were skinned nobody could tell how dumb they looked. Also, they were comfortable. And supposedly scientifically designed for natural running posture, so you landed on the ball of your foot and didn't make a thump with every stride. Breath coming fast, feet scissoring—I turned at the first corner I came to, then quickly turned again.

Unskinned folks looked up in surprise as I pelted past. One made a grab for me, and another one shouted something after, but I was already gone. And then I was on a side street all by myself, running down a narrow path kicked in the piles of trash.

Maybe this was an even more desolate street, and maybe most of the lights were burned out, but I kept on running. It felt good, all of a sudden, like positive action. Like something I could do other than wallowing. Like *progress.*

It kept on feeling like progress all the way down to the river's edge. And then, as I stopped beside a hole snipped-and-bent in the chain link, it felt like a very bad idea instead.

The river was a sewer. When I'd been here before—okay, not down here under the bridge, but on the bank above—it had been all sunshine and rolling blue water. What I saw now was floating milk jugs and what I smelled was a sour, fecal carrion stench.

I put a hand out to the fence, the wire gritty, greasy where my fingers touched. It dented when I leaned on it, but I needed it to bear my weight up. A stitch burned in my side, and every breath of air scoured my lungs. I didn't know if that was from running, or because the air was bad. But it was the same air I'd been breathing all along. The filters didn't change the outside world. Just our perceptions of it. So how could the air choke me now when before, I breathed it perfectly well?

Shouts behind me suggested that maybe my earlier pursuer had friends. Or that my flight had drawn attention. I was in shadow—but the yellow track suit wasn't anyone's idea of good camouflage.

Gravel crunched and turned under my feet. I pushed the top of the bent chain triangle up and ducked through, into the moist darkness under the bridge.

Things moved in the night. Rats, I imagined, but some sounded bigger than rats. What else could live in this filth? I imagined feral dogs, stray cats—companion animals abandoned to make their own fate. Would they attack something as large as a man?

If they did, how would I fight them?

I groped along the bridge abutment, feeling with my toes for a stick. The old stones swept down low, the arch broad and flat. I kept my hand up to keep from hitting my head on an invisible buttress. The masonry was slick with paint and damp, mortar crumbling to the touch. I couldn't see my hand in front of my face, but light concentrated by the oily river reflected up, and I could see the stones of the bridge's underside clearly.

I crept into that dank, ruinous beauty until the flicker of lights against the chain fence told me that my pursuers had found me, and they had come in force. My chest squeezed, stomach flipping in apprehension. I crouched down, tucked myself into the lowest part of the arch, and fumbled out my phone.

"Police," I said. Even if my contract had been cancelled, that should work. I'd heard somewhere that any phone can always dial emergency. And there it was, a distant buzz, and then a calm voice answering.

"Emergency services. Your taxpayer identification number, please?"

My voice stuck in my throat. I'd never been asked that before. But then,

I'd never been calling from an unskinned phone before. Without thinking, I rattled off the fourteen digits of my old number, the one that had been revoked. I held my breath afterward. Maybe the change hadn't propagated yet. Maybe—

"That number is not valid," the operator said.

"Look," I whispered, "I'm in a dispute with Revenue Services. It's all going to be sorted out, I'm sure, but right now I'm about to be mugged—"

"I'm sorry," said the consummate professional on the other end of the line. "Emergency services are for taxpayers only."

Before I could protest, the line went dead. Leaving me crouched alone in the dark, with a glowing phone pressed to my ear. Not for long, however: in less than a second, the dazzle of flashlight beams found me. Instinctively, I ducked my head and covered my eyes—with the hand with the phone.

"Well hey. What's this?" The voice was deceptively pleasant, that seductive mildness employed by schoolyard bullies since first Romulus beat up Remus. The flashlight didn't waver from my eyes.

I flinched. I didn't answer. Not because I didn't want to, but because I didn't have a voice.

I tried to find the part of myself that managed unruly students and lecture-hall hecklers, but it had vanished along with my credit accounts and the protection of the police. I ducked further, squinting around my hand, but he was just a shadow through the glare of his light. At least three other lights surrounded him.

He plucked the phone from my hand with a sharp twist that stabbed pain through my wrist. I snatched the hand back.

"Huh," he said. "Guess you didn't pay your taxes, huh? What else have you got?"

"Nothing," I said. The RFID chip embedded in my palm was useless. Would they cut it out anyway? I had no cash, no anything. Just the phone, which had my whole life on it—all my research, all my photos. Three mostly-finished articles. There were backups, of course, but they were on the wire, and I couldn't get there without being skinned.

I wasn't a skin anymore. Objects, I realized, had utility. Had value. They were more than ways to get at your data.

"Your jacket," the baseline said. "And your shoes."

My toes gripped the gravel. "I need my shoes—"

The dazzle of lights shifted. I knew I should duck, but the knowledge didn't translate into action.

At first there wasn't any pain. Just the shock of impact, and an exhale that seemed to start in my toes and never stop. Then the pain, radiating stars out of my solar plexus, with waves of nausea for dessert.

"Jacket," he said.

I would have given it to him. But I couldn't talk. Couldn't even inhale. I raised my hand. I think I shook my head.

I think he would have hit me anyway. I think he wanted to hit me. Because when I fell down, he kept hitting me. Hitting and kicking. And not just him, some of his friends.

It's a blur, mostly. I remember some particulars. The stomp that crushed my left hand. The kick that broke my tailbone. I got my knees up and tucked my head, so they kicked me in the kidneys instead. Gravel gouged the side where kicks didn't land. If I could burrow into it, I'd be safe. If I could just fall through it, I might survive. I thought about being small and hard and sharp, like those stones.

After a while, I didn't have the breath to scream anymore.

At first the cold hurt too, but after a while it became a friend. I noticed that they had stopped hitting me. I noticed that the cuts and bruises stung, the broken bones ached with a deep, sick throb. My hand felt fragile, gelatinous. Like a balloon full of water, I imagined that a single pinprick could make the stretched skin explode back from the contents. I prodded a loosened tooth with my tongue.

But then the cold got into the hurts and they numbed. Little by little, starting from the extremities. Working in. It mattered less that the hard points of gravel stabbed my ribs. I couldn't feel that floppy, useless hand. The throb in my head slowly became less demanding than the throb of thirst in my throat.

In the fullness of time, I sat up. It was natural, like sitting up after a full night's sleep, when you've lain in bed so long your body just naturally rises without consulting you. I thought about water. There was the river, but it smelled like poison. I'd probably get thirsty enough to drink it sooner or later. I wondered what diseases I'd contract. Hepatitis. Probably not cholera.

My cheekbones were numb, along with my nose, but I could still breathe normally. So the nose probably wasn't broken. The moving air brought me a tapestry of cold odors: sour garbage, rancid meat, urine. That oil-tang from the river. Frost rimed the gravel around me, and in noticing that I noticed that the morning was graying, the heavy arch of the bridge a silhouette against the sky. There was pink and silver along the horizon, and I knew which direction was east because the sun's light glossed a contrail that must have sat high enough to reach out of the Earth's moving shadow.

Footsteps crunched toward me. I was too dreamy and snug to move. *I'm in shock*, I thought, but it didn't seem important.

"What's this?" somebody said.

I flinched, but didn't look up. His shadow couldn't fall across me. We were both under the shadow of the bridge.

"Oh, dear," he said. The crunch of shifting gravel told me he crouched down beside me. When he turned my chin with his fingers and I saw his face, I was surprised he was limber enough to crouch. He looked like the bad end of a lot of winters. "And you lost your shoes too. What a pity."

He didn't seem surprised when I cringed, but it didn't light his eyes up, either. So that wasn't a bully's mocking.

"Can you walk?" He took my arm gently. He inspected my broken hand. When he unzipped my jacket, I would have pulled away, but the pain was bad enough that I couldn't move against him. When he slid the hand inside the jacket and the buttons of my shirt, I realized he was improvising a sling.

As if his touch were the opposite of an analgesic, all my hurts reawakened. I meant to shake my head, but just thinking about moving unscrolled ribbons of pain through my muscles.

"I don't think so." My words were creaky and blood-flavored.

"If you can," he said, "I've got a fire. And tea. And food."

I closed my eyes. When I opened them again, his hand was extended. The left one, as my right hand was clawed up against my chest like a surgical glove stuffed overfull with twigs and raspberry jam.

Food. Warmth. I might have given up, but somewhere in the back of my mind was an animal that did not want to die. I watched as it made a determined, raspy sound and reached out with its unbroken hand.

Letting him pull me to my feet was a special kind of agony. I swayed, vision blacking at the edges. His steadying hand kept me upright. It hurt worse than anything. "Come on," he said.

I remember walking, but I don't remember where or for how long. It felt like forever. I had always been walking. I would be walking forever. There was no end. No surcease.

Pain is an eternity.

His fire was trash and sticks ringed with broken bricks and chunks of asphalt. It smoldered fitfully, and pinprick by pinprick, the heat reawakened my pains. The soles of my feet seeped blood from walking across the gravel. I couldn't sit, because of the tailbone, but I figured out how to lie on my side. It hurt, but so did anything else.

There was tea, as promised, Lipton in bags stewed in a rusty can. I hoped he hadn't used river water. It had sugar in it, though, and I drank cautiously.

The food was dumpster-sourced chicken and biscuits, cold and lumpy with congealed grease. I ate it with my good hand, small bites. The inside of my mouth was cut from being slammed against my teeth. If I chewed carefully, on one side, the loose tooth only throbbed. I hoped it might reseat itself eventually.

Why was I thinking about the future?

The sun had beaten back the gloom enough for even my swollen eyes to make out the old man across from me. He had draped stiff, stinking blankets around my shoulders, but as the sun warmed the riverbank, he seemed comfortable in several layers of shirts and pants. A yellowed beard surrounded his sunken mouth. His hands were spare claws in ragged gloves. He drank the tea fearlessly, and warmed his share of the chicken on the rocks beside the trash fire. I thought about plastic fumes and kept gnawing mine cold.

After a while, he said, "You'll get used to it."

I looked up. He was looking right at me, his greasy silver ponytail dull in the sunlight. "Get used to being beaten up?" My voice sounded better than I'd feared. My nose really wasn't broken. One small miracle.

"Get used to being a baseline." He bit into a biscuit, grimacing in appreciation.

I winced, wondering how long it would take me to start savoring day-old fast food fat and carbohydrates. Then I winced in pain from the wincing.

The old man chewed and swallowed. "It's honest, at least. Not like putting frosting all over the cake so nobody with any economic power can tell it's rotten. What's your name?"

"Charlie," I said.

He nodded and didn't ask for a surname. "Jean-Khalil." I wondered if first names only was part of the social customs of the baseline community.

The shock was wearing off. Maybe the sugar in the tea was working its neurochemical magic. My broken hand lay against my belly, warmed by my skin, and the sweat running across my midsection felt as syrupy as blood.

I kind of wanted the shock back. I looked at the chicken, and the chicken looked back at me. My gorge rose. Bitterness filled my mouth, but I swallowed it. I knew how badly I needed the food inside me.

I balanced the meat on the fire ring next to Jean-Khalil's. "You eat that."

He wiped the back of his hand across his beard. "I will. And you need to get to a clinic."

I put my head down on the unbroken arm. If I didn't get the hand seen too, even if I survived—even if I didn't have internal injuries—what were the chances it would be usuable when it healed? "I don't have a tax number."

"There's a free clinic at St. Francis," he said. "But it's Tuesdays and Thursdays."

I managed to work out that if I normally met Numair on Tuesdays, it would be just after dawn on Wednesday. Which meant, depending on when the clinic opened, something over 24 hours to wait. I could wait 24 hours.

Could I *sleep* 24 hours? Maybe I'd die of blood poisoning before then. That might be a relief.

I had heard of St. Francis, but I didn't know where it was. Somewhere in this neighborhood? If it offered a clinic for baselines, it would have to be. They couldn't get through the chip gates uptown.

Despite the blankets heaped over me, I thought I could feel the ground sucking the heat out of my body. The old man nudged me. I opened my eyes. "Edge over onto this," he said.

He'd made a pallet of more filthy blankets, just beside where I lay. With his help, I was able to kind of wriggle and flop onto it. I couldn't lie on my back, because of the tailbone, and I couldn't use the hand to pillow my head or turn myself.

He rearranged the blankets over me. Something touched my lips: his gaunt fingers, protruding from those filthy gloves. I turned my head.

"Take it. It's methadone. It's also a pain killer."

"You lost your tax number for drug addiction?" I had to cover my mouth with my unbroken hand.

"I'm a dropout," he said. "Take the wafer."

"I don't want to get hooked."

He sighed like somebody's mother. "I'm a medical doctor. It's methadone, it's 60 milligrams. It won't do much more than take the edge off, but it might help you sleep."

I didn't believe him about being a dropout. Who'd pick this? But I did believe him about being a doctor. Maybe it was the way he specified *medical*. "I was a history teacher," I said. I couldn't bring myself to say *professor*. "Why do you have methadone if you're not an addict?"

"I told you," he said. "I'm a doctor."

"And you dropped out."

"Of a corrupt system." His voice throbbed with disdain, and maybe conviction. "How many people were invisible to you, before? How much of this was invisible?"

If I could have had my way, I would have made it all invisible again. This time, when he pressed his hand to my mouth, I took the papery wafer into my mouth and chewed it. It tasted like fake fruit. I closed my eyes again and tried to breathe deeply. It hurt, but more an ache than the deep stabbing I associated with broken ribs. So that was something else to consider myself fortunate for.

I knew it was just the placebo effect and exhaustion making me sleepy so fast, but I wasn't about to argue with it.

I said, "What made you decide to come live on the street?"

"There was a girl—" His voice choked off through the constriction of his throat. "My daughter. Cancer. She was twenty. Maybe if she hadn't been skinning so much, in so much denial—"

I put my good hand on his shoulder and felt it rise and fall. "I'm sorry."

He shrugged.

It was a minute and a half before I had the courage to ask the thing I was suddenly thinking. "If you're a dropout, then you have a tax number. And you don't use it."

"That's right," the old man said. "It's a filthy system. Eventually, you'll see what I mean."

"If you don't want it, give it to me."

He laughed. "If I were willing to do that, I'd just sell it on the black market. The clinic could use the money. Now rest, and we'll get your hand looked at tomorrow."

I don't know how I got to the clinic. I didn't walk—not on those bare cut-up feet—and I don't remember being carried. I do remember the waiting room full of men and women I never would have seen before I lost my tax number. Jean-Khalil had given me another methadone wafer, and that kept me just this side of coherent. But I couldn't sit, couldn't walk, couldn't lean against the wall. He got somebody to bring me a gurney, and I lay on my side and tried to doze, blissfully happy there weren't any rocks or dog feces on the surface I was lying on.

It doesn't take long to lower your standards.

I realized later that I was one of the lucky ones, and because of the broken bones I got triaged higher than a lot of others. But it was still four hours before I was wheeled into one of the curtained alcoves that served as an examining room and a woman in mismatched scrubs and a white lab coat came in to check on me. "Hi," she said. "I'm Dr. Tankovitch. Dr. Samure said you had a bad night. Charlie, is it?"

"The worst," I said. She was cute—Asian, plump, with bright eyes behind her glasses—and I caught myself flirting before a flood of shame washed me back into myself. She was a contributing member of society, here to do charity work. And I was a bum.

"Honestly, there's not much you can do for a broken tailbone except—" she laughed in commiseration "—stay off it. So let's start with the hand."

I held it out, and she took it gently by the wrist. Even that made me gasp.

She made a sympathetic face. "I'd guessing by the bruises on your face you didn't get this punching a brick wall."

"The cops don't come if you're not in the system."

She touched my shoulder. "I know."

• • •

I got lucky. For the first time in weeks, I got lucky. The hand didn't need surgery, which meant I didn't have to wait until the clinic's surgical hours, which were something like midnight to four AM at the city hospital. Instead, Dr. Tankovitch shot me full of Novocaine and wrapped my hand up with primitive plaster of Paris, a technology so obsolete I had never actually seen it. Or if I had seen it, I'd skinned it out. She gave me some pain pills that didn't work as well as the methadone and didn't have a street value, and told me to come back in a week and have it all checked out. The cast was so white it sparkled. Guess how long that was going to last, if I was sleeping under bridges?

She didn't offer me the clinic's contact information, and I didn't ask for it. How was I supposed to call them without a phone? But I was feeling less sorry for myself when I staggered out of the alcove. I planned to find Jean-Khalil again, and ask him if he'd show me where he looked for food and safe drinking water. I was clear-headed enough now to know it was an imposition, but I didn't have anywhere else to turn. And he'd sort of volunteered, hadn't he, by picking me out of the gutter?

If you pick up a starving dog and make him prosperous, he will not bite you. This is the principal difference between a dog and a man.

It was Mark Twain. But then, so were a lot of true things. And I was determined to prove myself more like the dog than the man. Jean-Khalil was an old man. Surely he could use my help. And I knew I needed his. I didn't see Jean-Khalil. But just as the waves of panic and abandonment—again, just like after Rose—were cresting in me, I spotted someone. Leaning against the wall by the door was Numair.

Numair had seen me first—I'd been moving, and he'd been looking for me—so he saw me stop dead and stare. He raised his hand hesitantly.

"Buy you dinner?" he asked. He didn't flinch when he looked at me.

From the angle of the light outside, I realized it was nearly sunset. "As long as we can get it someplace standing up."

That meant street meat, and three hotdogs with everything were the best food I'd ever tasted. Numair drank beer but he didn't eat pork, so he ate potato chips and watched me lean forward so the chili and onions didn't drip down my filthy shirt. I knew it was ridiculous, but I did it anyway. It felt like preserving my dignity to care. What dignity? I wasn't sure. But it still mattered.

"I'm sorry," Numair said. "I'm really sorry. If I'd realized you didn't know about Rose—I just never imagined. You two were so close. And you never mentioned her—I figured you didn't want to talk about her."

"I didn't." We'd had a fight, I wanted to say. Something to absolve myself of not checking. But when she stopped logging in, I figured she'd just decided to cut me off. She wouldn't be the first, and I knew she had another life. A wife. We'd talked about telling her she was having an affair.

And then she'd just . . . stopped messaging. People fall out of social groups all the time. It happens. I guess somebody more secure wouldn't have assumed they were the problem. But I was used to being the problem. Numair's the only friend I have left from the gang I hung around with all the time in grad school.

I swallowed hot dog, half-chewed. It hurt. He handed me an open can of soda, and I washed the lump down. "How'd she die?"

She hadn't been old. I mean, she hadn't skinned old. But who knew what the hell that meant, in the real world.

"She killed herself," Numair said, bluff and forthright. Which was just like him.

I staggered. Literally, sideways two steps. I couldn't catch myself because the last hotdog was balanced against my chest on the pristine cast. I already had the instinct to protect that food. I guess you don't have to get too hungry to learn fast.

"Jesus," I said, and felt bad.

He made a comforting face. And that was when I realized that if he could see me, he wasn't skinning. "Numair. You came all the way down here for me?"

"Charlie. Like I'd let an old friend go down without some help." He put a hand on my shoulder and pulled it back, frowning. He looked around, disgusted. "You know, you hear on the news how bad it is out here. But you never really get it until you see it. Poisoned environment, whatever. But this is astounding. Look, we can get you a hearing. Appeal your status. Maybe get you a new number. You can stay with Ilona and me until it's settled."

There were horror vids about this sort of thing. The baselines lived outside of social controls, after all. There was nothing to keep them from committing horrible crimes. "You're going to take in a baseline? That's a lot of trust. I'm a desperate woman."

He smiled. "I know you."

Ilona only knew me as a skin, but when I showed up at her house in the unadorned flesh, she couldn't have been nicer. She, too, had turned off her skinning so she could see me and interact. I could tell she was uncomfortable with it, though—her eyes kept flicking off my face to look for the hypertext or chase a link pursuant to the conversation, and of course there was nothing there. So after a bit she just showed me the bathroom, brought me clean clothes and a towel, and went back to her phone, where (she said) she was working on a deadline. She was an advertising copywriter, and she and Numair had converted one corner of their old house's parlor into an office space. I could hear her clicking away as I stripped off my filthy clothing and dropped it piece by piece into the bathroom waste pail. It was hard, one-handed, and it was even harder to tape the plastic bag around my cast.

It had never bothered me to discard ruined clothing before, but now I found it anxiety-inducing. *That's still good. Somebody could wear that.* I set the shower for hot and climbed in. The water I got fell in a lukewarm trickle; barely wetting me.

They probably skinned it hotter when they showered.

I tried to linger, to savor the cleanliness, but the chill of the water in a chilly room drove me out to stand dripping on the rug. As I was dressing in Ilona's jeans and sweatshirt, the sound of a child crying filtered through.

I came out to find Numair up from his desk, changing a diaper in the nook beside the kitchen. His daughter's name was Mercedes; she'd always been something of a little pink blob to me. I came up to hand him the grease for her diaper rash and saw the spotted blood on the diaper he had pushed aside.

"Christ," I said. "Is she all right?"

"She's nine months old, and she's starting her menses," he said, lower lip thrust out in worry. I noticed because I was looking up at the underside of his chin. "It's getting more common in very young girls."

"*Common*?"

With practiced hands, he attached the diaper tabs and sealed up Mercedes' onesie. He folded the soiled diaper and stuck it closed. "The doctor says it's environmental hormones. It can be skinned for—they'll make her look normal to herself and everyone else until she's old enough to start developing." He shrugged and picked up his child. "He says he treats a couple of toddlers with developing breasts, and the cosmetic option works for them."

He looked at me, brown eyes warm with worry.

I looked down. "You think that's a good enough answer?"

He shook his head. I didn't push it any farther.

They put me to sleep in their guest room, and fed me—unskinned, the food was slop, but it was food, and I got used to them not being able to see or talk to me at mealtimes. After a week, I felt much stronger. And as it was obvious that Numair and Ilona's intervention was not going to win me any favors from Revenue, I slowly came up with another plan.

I couldn't find Jean-Khalil under the bridge. His fire circle was abandoned, his blankets packed up. He'd moved on, and I didn't know where. Good deed delivered.

You'd think, right? Until it clicked what I was missing.

I showed up at the free clinic first thing next Tuesday morning, just as Dr.

Tankovitch had suggested. And I waited there until Dr. Tankovitch walked in and with her, his gaunt hand curved around a cup of coffee, Dr. Jean-Khalil Samure.

He didn't look surprised to see me. My clothes were clean, and the cast was only a little dingy. I'd shaved, and I was surprised he recognized me without the split lip and the swelling.

"Jean-Khalil," I said.

I guessed accosting the clinic doctors wasn't what you did, because Dr. Tankovitch looked as if she might intercept me, or call for security. But Jean-Khalil held out a hand to pause her.

He smiled. "Charlie. You look like you're finding your feet."

"I got help from a friend." I frowned and looked down at my borrowed tennis shoes. Ilona's, and too big for me. "I can't do this, Jean-Khalil. You've got to help me."

I'm sure the clinic had all sorts of problems with drug addicts. Because now Dr. Tankovitch was actively backing away, and I saw her summoning hand gestures. I leaned in and talked faster. "I need your tax number," I said. "You're not using it. Look, all I need is to get back on my feet, and I can help you in all sorts of ways. Money. Publicity. I'll come volunteer at your clinic—"

"Charlie," he said. "You know that's not enough. The way you live—the way you have been living. That's a lie. It's not sustainable. It's addictive behavior. If everybody could see the damage they're doing, they'd behave differently."

I pressed my lips together. I looked away. Down at the floor. At anything but Jean-Khalil. "There's a girl. Her name is Rose."

He looked at me. I wondered if he knew I was lying. Maybe I wasn't lying. I could find somebody else, skin her into Rose. Maybe she'd have a different name. But I could fix this. Do better. If he would only give me the chance.

"You're not using it," I said.

"A girl," he said. "Your daughter?"

"My lover," I said.

I said, "Please."

He shook his head, eyes rolled up and away. Then he yanked his hand out of his pocket brusquely. "On your head be it."

I was not prepared for the naked relief that filled me. I looked down, abjectly, and folded my hands. "Thank you so much."

"You can't save people from themselves," he said.

SLEEPER

JO WALTON

━━◆━━

Matthew Corley regained consciousness reading the newspaper.

None of those facts are unproblematic. It wasn't exactly a newspaper, nor was the process by which he received the information really reading. The question of his consciousness is a matter of controversy, and the process by which he regained it certainly illegal. The issue of whether he could be considered in any way to have a claim to assert the identity of Matthew Corley is even more vexed. It is probably best to for us to embrace subjectivity, to withhold judgement. Let us say that the entity believing himself to be Matthew Corley feels that he regained consciousness while reading an article in the newspaper about the computer replication of personalities of the dead. He believes that it is 1994, the year of his death, that he regained consciousness after a brief nap, and that the article he was reading is nonsense. All of these beliefs are wrong. He dismissed the article because he understands enough to know that simulating consciousness in DOS or Windows 3.1 is inherently impossible. He is right about that much, at least.

Perhaps we should pull back further, from Matthew to Essie. Essie is Matthew's biographer, and she knows everything about him, all of his secrets, only some of which she put into her book. She put all of them into the simulation, for reasons which are secrets of her own. They are both good at secrets. Essie thinks of this as something they have in common. Matthew doesn't, because he hasn't met Essie yet, though he will soon.

Matthew had secrets which he kept successfully all his life. Before he died he believed that all his secrets had become out-of-date. He came out as gay in the late eighties, for instance, after having kept his true sexual orientation a secret for decades. His wife, Annette, had died in 1982, at the early age of fifty-eight, of breast cancer. Her cancer would be curable today, for those who could afford it, and Essie has written about how narrowly Annette missed that cure. She has written about the excruciating treatments Annette went through, and about how well Matthew coped with his wife's illness and death.

She has written about the miraculous NHS, which made Annette's illness free, so that although Matthew lost his wife he was not financially burdened too. She hopes this might affect some of her readers. She has also tried to treat Annette as a pioneer who made it easier for those with cancer coming after her, but it was a difficult argument to make, as Annette died too early for any of today's treatments to be tested on her. Besides, Essie does not care much about Annette, although she was married to Matthew for thirty years and the mother of his daughter, Sonia. Essie thinks, and has written, that Annette was a beard, and that Matthew's significant emotional relationships were with men. Matthew agrees, now, but then Matthew exists now as a direct consequence of Essie's beliefs about Matthew. It is not a comfortable relationship for either of them.

Essie is at a meeting with her editor, Stanley, in his office. It is a small office cubicle, and sounds of other people at work come over the walls. Stanley's office has an orange cube of a desk and two edgy black chairs.

"All biographers are in love with the subjects of their biographies," Stanley says, provocatively, leaning forwards in his black chair.

"Nonsense," says Essie, leaning back in hers. "Besides, Corley was gay."

"But you're not," Stanley says, flirting a little.

"I don't think my sexual orientation is an appropriate subject for this conversation," Essie says, before she thinks that perhaps flirting with Stanley would be a good way to get the permission she needs for the simulation to be added to the book. It's too late after that. Stanley becomes very formal and correct, but she'll get her permission anyway. Stanley, representing the publishing conglomerate of George Allen and Katzenjammer, thinks there is money to be made out of Essie's biography of Matthew. Her biography of Isherwood won an award, and made money for GA and K, though only a pittance for Essie. Essie is only the content provider after all. Everyone except Essie was very pleased with how things turned out, both the book and the simulation. Essie had hoped for more from the simulation, and she has been more careful in constructing Matthew.

"Of course, Corley isn't as famous as Isherwood," Stanley says, withdrawing a little.

Essie thinks he wants to punish her for slapping him down on sex by attacking Matthew. She doesn't mind. She's good at defending Matthew, making her case. "All the really famous people have been done to death," she says. "Corley was an innovative director for the BBC, and of course he knew everybody from the forties to the nineties, half a century of the British arts. Nobody has ever written a biography. And we have the right kind of documentation—enough film of how he moved, not just talking heads, and letters and diaries."

"I've never understood why the record of how they moved is so important," Stanley says, and Essie realises this is a genuine question and relaxes as she answers it.

"A lot more of the mind is embodied in the whole body than anybody realised," she explains. "A record of the whole body in motion is essential, or we don't get anything anywhere near authentic. People are a gestalt."

"But it means we can't even try for anybody before the twentieth century," Stanley says. "We wanted Socrates, Descartes, Marie Curie."

"Messalina, Theodora, Lucrezia Borgia," Essie counters. "That's where the money is."

Stanley laughs. "Go ahead. Add the simulation of Corley. We'll back you. Send me the file tomorrow."

"Great," Essie says, and smiles at him. Stanley isn't powerful, he isn't the enemy, he's just another person trying to get by, like Essie, though sometimes it's hard for Essie to remember that when he's trying to exercise his modicum of power over her. She has her permission, the meeting ends.

Essie goes home. She lives in a flat at the top of a thirty storey building in Swindon. She works in London and commutes in every day. She has a second night job in Swindon, and writes in her spare time. She has visited the site of the house where Matthew and Annette lived in Hampstead. It's a Tesco today. There isn't a blue plaque commemorating Matthew, but Essie hopes there will be someday. The house had four bedrooms, though there were never more than three people living in it, and only two after Sonia left home in 1965. After Annette died, Matthew moved to a flat in Bloomsbury, near the British Museum. Essie has visited it. It's now part of a lawyer's office. She has been inside and touched door mouldings Matthew also touched. Matthew's flat, where he lived alone and was visited by young men he met in pubs, had two bedrooms. Essie doesn't have a bedroom, as such; she sleeps in the same room she eats and writes in. She finds it hard to imagine the space Matthew had, the luxury. Only the rich live like that now. Essie is thirty-five, and has student debt that she may never pay off. She cannot imagine being able to buy a house, marry, have a child. She knows Matthew wasn't considered rich, but it was a different world.

Matthew believes that he is in his flat in Bloomsbury, and that his telephone rings, although actually of course he is a simulation and it would be better not to consider too closely the question of exactly where he is. He answers his phone. It is Essie calling. All biographers, all writers, long to be able to call their subjects and talk to them, ask them the questions they left unanswered. That is what Stanley would think Essie wants, if he knew she was accessing Matthew's simulation tonight—either that or that she was checking whether the simulation was ready to release. If he finds out, that is what she will tell him she was doing. But she isn't exactly doing either of those things. She knows Matthew's secrets, even the ones he never told anybody and which she didn't put in the book. And she is using a phone to call him that cost her a lot of money, an illegal phone that isn't connected to anything. That phone is where Matthew is, insofar as he is anywhere.

"You were in Cambridge in the nineteen thirties," she says, with no preliminaries.

"Who is this?" Matthew asks, suspicious.

Despite herself, Essie is delighted to hear his voice, and hear it sounding the way it does on so many broadcast interviews. His accent is impeccable, old fashioned. Nobody speaks like that now.

"My name is Esmeralda Jones," Essie says. "I'm writing a biography of you."

"I haven't given you permission to write a biography of me, young woman," Matthew says sternly.

"There really isn't time for this," Essie says. She is tired. She has been working hard all day, and had the meeting with Stanley. "Do you remember what you were reading in the paper just now?"

"About computer consciousness?" Matthew asks. "Nonsense."

"It's 2064," Essie says. "You're a simulation of yourself. I am your biographer."

Matthew sits down, or imagines that he is sitting down, at the telephone table. Essie can see this on the screen of her phone. Matthew's phone is an old dial model, with no screen, fixed to the wall. "Wells," he says. "When the Sleeper Wakes."

"Not exactly," Essie says. "You're a simulation of your old self."

"In a computer?"

"Yes," Essie says, although the word computer has been obsolete for decades and has a charming old fashioned air, like charabanc or telegraph. Nobody needs computers in the future. They communicate, work, and play games on phones.

"And why have you simulated me?" Matthew asks.

"I'm writing a biography of you, and I want to ask you some questions," Essie says.

"What do you want to ask me?" he asks.

Essie is glad; she was expecting more disbelief. Matthew is very smart, she has come to know that in researching him. (Or she has put her belief in his intelligence into the program, one or the other.) "You were in Cambridge in the nineteen thirties," she repeats.

"Yes." Matthew sounds wary.

"You knew Auden and Isherwood. You knew Orwell."

"I knew Orwell in London during the war, not before," Matthew says.

"You knew Kim Philby."

"Everyone knew Kim. What—"

Essie has to push past this. She knows he will deny it. He kept this secret all his life, after all. "You were a spy, weren't you, another Soviet sleeper like Burgess and Maclean? The Russians told you to go into the BBC and keep your head down, and you did, and the revolution didn't come, and eventually the Soviet Union vanished, and you were still undercover."

"I'd prefer it if you didn't put that into my biography," Matthew says. He is visibly uncomfortable, shifting in his seat. "It's nothing but speculation. And the Soviet Union is gone. Why would anybody care? If I achieved anything, it wasn't political. If there's interest in me, enough to warrant a biography, it must be because of my work."

"I haven't put it in the book," Essie says. "We have to trust each other."

"Esmeralda," Matthew says. "I know nothing about you."

"Call me Essie," Essie says. "I know everything about you. And you have to trust me because I know your secrets, and because I care enough about you to devote myself to writing about you and your life."

"Can I see you?" Matthew asks.

"Switch your computer on," Essie says.

He limps into the study and switches on a computer. Essie knows all about his limp, which was caused by an injury during birth, which made him lame all his life. It is why he did not fight in the Spanish Civil War and spent the World War II in the BBC and not on the battlefield. His monitor is huge, and it has a tower at the side. It's a 286, and Essie knows where he bought it (Tandy) and what he paid for it (seven hundred and sixty pounds) and what operating system it runs (Novell DOS). Next to it is an external dial-up modem, a 14.4. The computer boots slowly. Essie doesn't bother waiting, she just uses its screen as a place to display herself. Matthew jumps when he sees her. Essie is saddened. She had hoped he wasn't a racist. "You have no hair!" he says.

Essie turns her head and displays the slim purple-and-gold braid at the back. "Just fashion," she says. "This is normal now."

"Everyone looks like you?" Matthew sounds astonished. "With cheek rings and no hair?"

"I have to look respectable for work," Essie says, touching her three staid cheek rings, astonished he is astonished. They had piercings by the nineties, she knows they did. She has read about punk, and seen Matthew's documentary about it. But she reminds herself that he grew up so much earlier, when even ear piercings were unusual.

"And that's respectable?" he says, staring at her chest.

Essie glances down at herself. She is wearing a floor-length T-shirt that came with her breakfast cereal; a shimmering holographic Tony the Tiger dances over the see-through cloth. She wasn't sure when holograms were invented, but she can't remember any in Matthew's work. She shrugs. "Do you have a problem?"

"No, sorry, just that seeing you makes me realise it really is the future." He sighs. "What killed me?"

"A heart attack," Essie says. "You didn't suffer."

He looks dubiously at his own chest. He is wearing a shirt and tie.

"Can we move on?" Essie asks, impatiently.

"You keep saying we don't have long. Why is that?" he asks.

"The book is going to be released. And the simulation of you will be released with it. I need to send it to my editor tomorrow. And that means we have to make some decisions about that."

"I'll be copied?" he asks, eyes on Essie on the screen.

"Not you—not exactly you. Or rather, that's up to you. The program will be copied, and everyone who buys the book will have it, and they'll be able to talk to a simulated you and ask questions, and get answers—whether they're questions you'd want to answer or not. You won't be conscious and aware the way you are now. You won't have any choices. And you won't have memory. We have rules about what simulations can do, and running you this way I'm breaking all of them. Right now you have memory and the potential to have an agenda. But the copies sent out with the book won't have. Unless you want them to."

"Why would I want them to?"

"Because you're a communist sleeper agent and you want the revolution?" He is silent for a moment. Essie tilts her head on its side and considers him.

"I didn't admit to that," he says, after a long pause.

"I know. But it's true anyway, isn't it?"

Matthew nods, warily. "It's true I was recruited. That I went to Debrechen. That they told me to apply to the BBC. That I had a contact, and sometimes I gave him information, or gave a job to somebody he suggested. But this was all long ago. I stopped having anything to do with them in the seventies."

"Why?" Essie asks.

"They wanted me to stay at the BBC, and stay in news, and I was much more interested in moving to ITV and into documentaries. Eventually my contact said he'd out me as a homosexual unless I did as he said. I wasn't going to be blackmailed, or work for them under those conditions. I told him to publish and be damned. Homosexuality was legal by then. Annette already knew. It would have been a scandal, but that's all. And he didn't even do it. But I never contacted them again." He frowned at Essie. "I was an idealist. I was prepared to put socialism above my country, but not above my art."

"I knew it," Essie says, smiling at him. "I mean that's exactly what I guessed."

"I don't know how you can know, unless you got records from the Kremlin," Matthew says. "I didn't leave any trace, did I?"

"You didn't," she says, eliding the question of how she knows, which she does not want to discuss. "But the important thing is how you feel now. You wanted a better world, a fairer one, with opportunities for everyone."

"Yes," Matthew says. "I always wanted that. I came from an absurdly privileged background, and I saw how unfair it was. Perhaps because I was lame and couldn't play games, I saw through the whole illusion when I was young. And the British class system needed to come down, and it did come down. It didn't need a revolution. By the seventies, I'd seen enough to disillusion me with the Soviets, and enough to make me feel hopeful for socialism in Britain and a level playing field."

"The class system needs to come down again," Essie says. "You didn't bring it down far enough, and it went back up. The corporations and the rich own everything. We need all the things you had—unions, and free education, and paid holidays, and a health service. And very few people know about them and fewer care. I write about the twentieth century as a way of letting people know. They pick up the books for the glamour, and I hope they will see the ideals too."

"Is that working?" Matthew asks.

Essie shakes her head. "Not so I can tell. And my subjects won't help." This is why she has worked so hard on Matthew. "My editor won't let me write about out-and-out socialists, at least, not people who are famous for being socialists. I've done it on my own and put it online, but it's hard for content providers to get attention without a corporation behind them." She has been cautious, too. She wants a socialist; she doesn't want Stalin. "I had great hopes for Isherwood."

"That dilettante," Matthew mutters, and Essie nods.

"He wouldn't help. I thought with active help—answering people's questions, nudging them the right way?"

Essie trails off. Matthew is silent, looking at her. "What's your organization like?" he asks, after a long time.

"Organization?"

He sighs. "Well, if you want advice, that's the first thing. You need to organize. You need to find some issue people care about and get them excited."

"Then you'll help?"

"I'm not sure you know what you're asking. I'll try to help. After I'm copied and out there, how can I contact you?"

"You can't. Communications are totally controlled, totally read, everything." She is amazed that he is asking, but of course he comes from a time when these things were free.

"Really? Because the classic problem of intelligence is collecting everything and not analysing it."

"They record it all. They don't always pay attention to it. But we don't know when they're listening. So we're always afraid." Essie frowns and tugs her braid.

"Big Brother," Matthew says. "But in real life the classic problem of intelligence is collecting data without analysing it. And we can use that. We can talk about innocuous documentaries, and they won't know what we mean. You need to have a BBS for fans of your work to get together. And we can exchange coded messages there."

Essie has done enough work on the twentieth century that she knows a BBS is like a primitive gather-space. "I could do that. But there are no codes. They can crack everything."

"They can't crack words—if we agree what they mean. If pink means yes and blue means no, and we use them naturally, that kind of thing." Matthew's ideas of security are so old they're new again, the dead-letter drop, the meeting in the park, the one-time pad. Essie feels hope stirring. "But before I can really help I need to know about the history, and how the world works now, all the details. Let me read about it."

"You can read everything," she says. "And the copy of you in this phone can talk to me about it and we can make plans, we can have as long as you like. But will you let copies of you go out and work for the revolution? I want to send you like a virus, like a Soviet sleeper, working to undermine society. And we can use your old ideas for codes. I can set up a gather-space."

"Send me with all the information you can about the world," Matthew says. "I'll do it. I'll help. And I'll stay undercover. It's what I did all my life, after all."

She breathes a sigh of relief, and Matthew starts to ask questions about the world and she gives him access to all the information on the phone. He can't reach off the phone or he'll be detected. There's a lot of information on the phone. It'll take Matthew a while to assimilate it. And he will be copied and sent out, and work to make a better world, as Essie wants, and the way Matthew remembers always wanting.

Essie is a diligent researcher, an honest historian. She could find no evidence on the question of whether Matthew Corley was a Soviet sleeper agent. Thousands of people went to Cambridge in the thirties. Kim Philby knew everyone. It's no more than suggestive. Matthew was very good at keeping secrets. Nobody knew he was gay until he wanted them to know. The Soviet Union crumbled away in 1989 and let its end of the Overton Window go, and the world slid rightwards. Objectively, to a detached observer, there's no way to decide the question of whether or not the real Matthew Corley was a sleeper. It's not true that all biographers are in love with their subjects. But when Essie wrote the simulation, she knew what she needed to be true. And we agreed, did we not, to take the subjective view?

Matthew Corley regained consciousness reading the newspaper.

We make our own history, both past and future.

GRAND JETÉ (THE GREAT LEAP)

RACHEL SWIRSKY

Act I: Mara
Tombé
(Fall)

As dawn approached, the snow outside Mara's window slowed, spiky white stars melting into streaks on the pane. Her abba stood in the doorway, unaware that she was already awake. Mara watched his silhouette in the gloom. Shadows hung in the folds of his jowls where he'd shaved his beard in solidarity after she'd lost her hair. Although it had been months, his face still looked pink and plucked.

Some nights, Mara woke four or five times to find him watching from the doorway. She didn't want him to know how poorly she slept and so she pretended to be dreaming until he eventually departed.

This morning, he didn't leave. He stepped into the room. "Marale," he said softly. His fingers worried the edges of the green apron that he wore in his workshop. A layer of sawdust obscured older scorch marks and grease stains. "Mara, please wake up. I've made you a gift."

Mara tried to sit. Her stomach reeled. Abba rushed to her bedside. "I'm fine," she said, pushing him away as she waited for the pain to recede.

He drew back, hands disappearing into his apron pockets. The corners of his mouth tugged down, wrinkling his face like a bulldog's. He was a big man with broad shoulders and disproportionately large hands. Everything he did looked comical when wrought on such a large scale. When he felt jovial, he played into the foolishness with broad, dramatic gestures that would have made an actor proud. In sadness, his gestures became reticent, hesitating, miniature.

"Are you cold?" he asked.

In deep winter, their house was always cold. Icy wind curled through cracks in the insulation. Even the heater that abba had installed at the foot of Mara's bed couldn't keep her from dreaming of snow.

Abba pulled a lace shawl that had once belonged to Mara's ima from the back of her little wooden chair. He draped it across her shoulders. Fringe covered her ragged fingernails.

As Mara rose from her bed, he tried to help with her crutches, but Mara fended him off. He gave her a worried look. "The gift is in my workshop," he said. With a concerned backward glance, he moved ahead, allowing her the privacy to make her own way.

Their white German Shepherd, Abel, met Mara as she shifted her weight onto her crutches. She paused to let him nuzzle her hand, tongue rough against her knuckles. At thirteen, all his other senses were fading, and so he tasted everything he could. He walked by her side until they reached the stairs, and then followed her down, tail thumping against the railing with every step.

The door to abba's workshop was painted red and stenciled with white flowers that Mara had helped ima paint when she was five. Inside, half-finished apparatuses sprawled across workbenches covered in sawdust and disassembled electronics. Hanging from the ceiling, a marionette stared blankly at Mara and Abel as they passed, the glint on its pupils moving back and forth as its strings swayed. A mechanical hand sprang to life, its motion sensor triggered by Abel's tail. Abel whuffed at its palm and then hid behind Mara. The thing's fingers grasped at Mara's sleeve, leaving an impression of dusty, concentric whorls.

Abba stood at the back of the workshop, next to a child-sized doll that sat on a metal stool. Its limbs fell in slack, uncomfortable positions. Its face looked like the one Mara still expected to see in the mirror: a broad forehead over flushed cheeks scattered with freckles. Skin peeled away in places, revealing wire streams.

Mara moved to stand in front of the doll. It seemed even eerier, examined face to face, its expression a lifeless twin of hers. She reached out to touch its soft, brown hair. Her bald scalp tingled.

Gently, Abba took Mara's hand and pressed her right palm against the doll's. Apart from how thin Mara's fingers had become over the past few months, they matched perfectly.

Abba made a triumphant noise. "The shape is right."

Mara pulled her hand out of abba's. She squinted at the doll's imitation flesh. Horrifyingly, its palm shared each of the creases on hers, as if it, too, had spent twelve years dancing and reading books and learning to cook.

Abel circled the doll. He sniffed its feet and ankles and then paused at the back of its knees, whuffing as if he'd expected to smell something that wasn't there. After completing his circuit, he collapsed on the floor, equidistant from the three human-shaped figures.

"What do you think of her?" abba asked.

Goosebumps prickled Mara's neck. "What is she?"

Abba cradled the doll's head in his hands. Its eyes rolled back, and the light highlighted its lashes, fair and short, just like Mara's own. "She's a prototype. Empty-headed. A friend of mine is working on new technology for the government—"

"A prototype?" repeated Mara. "Of what?"

"The body is simple mechanics. Anyone could build it. The technology in the mind is new. It takes pictures of the brain in motion, all three dimensions, and then creates schematics for artificial neural clusters that will function like the original biological matter—"

Mara's head ached. Her mouth was sore and her stomach hurt and she wanted to go back to bed even if she couldn't sleep. She eyed the doll. The wires under its skin were vivid red and blue as if they were veins and arteries connecting to viscera.

"The military will make use of the technology," Abba continued. "They wish to recreate soldiers with advanced training. They are not ready for human tests, not yet. They are still experimenting with animals. They've made rats with mechanical brains that can solve mazes the original rats were trained to run. Now they are working with chimpanzees."

Abba's accent deepened as he continued, his gestures increasingly emphatic.

"But I am better. I can make it work in humans now, without more experiments." Urgently, he lowered his voice. "My friend was not supposed to send me the schematics. I paid him much money, but his reason for helping is that I have promised him that when I fix the problems, I will show him the solution and he can take the credit. This technology is not for civilians. No one else will be able to do this. We are very fortunate."

Abba touched the doll's shoulder so lightly that only his fingertips brushed her.

"I will need you to sit for some scans so that I can make the images that will preserve you. They will be painless. I can set up when you sleep." Quietly, he added, "She is my gift to you. She will hold you and keep you . . . if the worst . . . " His voice faded, and he swallowed twice, three times, before beginning again. "She will protect you."

Mara's voice came out hoarse. "Why didn't you tell me?"

"You needed to see her when she was complete."

Her throat constricted. "I wish I'd never seen her at all!"

From the cradle, Mara had been even-tempered. Now, at twelve, she shouted and cried. Abba said it was only what happened to children as they grew older, but they both knew that wasn't why.

Neither was used to her new temper. The lash of her shout startled them both. Abba's expression turned stricken.

"I don't understand," he said.

"You made a new daughter!"

"No, no." Abba held up his hands to protect himself from her accusation. "She is made *for* you."

"I'm sure she'll be a better daughter than I am," Mara said bitterly.

She grabbed a hank of the doll's hair. Its head tilted toward her in a parody of curiosity. She pushed it away. The thing tumbled to the floor, limbs awkwardly splayed.

Abba glanced toward the doll, but did not move to see if it was broken. "I— No, Marale— You don't—" His face grew drawn with sudden resolution. He pulled a hammer off of one of the work benches. "Then I will smash her to pieces."

There had been a time when, with the hammer in his hand and a determined expression on his face, he'd have looked like a smith from old legends. Now he'd lost so much weight that his skin hung loosely from his enormous frame as if he were a giant coat suspended from a hanger. Tears sprang to Mara's eyes.

She slapped at his hands and the hammer in them. "Stop it!"

"If you want her to—"

"Stop it! Stop it!" she shouted.

Abba released the hammer. It fell against the cement with a hollow, mournful sound.

Guilt shot through her, at his confusion, at his fear. What should she do, let him destroy this thing he'd made? What should she do, let the hammer blow strike, watch herself be shattered?

Sawdust billowed where the hammer hit. Abel whined and fled the room, tail between his legs.

Softly, abba said, "I don't know what else to give."

Abba had always been the emotional heart of the family, even when ima was alive. His anger flared; his tears flowed; his laughter roared from his gut. Mara rested her head on his chest until his tears slowed, and then walked with him upstairs.

The house was too small for Mara to fight with abba for long, especially during winters when they both spent every hour together in the house, Mara home-schooling via her attic space program while abba tinkered in his workshop. Even on good days, the house felt claustrophobic with two people trapped inside. Sometimes one of them would tug on a coat and ski cap and trudge across the hard-packed snow, but even the outdoors provided minimal escape. Their house sat alone at the end of a mile-long driveway that wound through bare-branched woods before reaching the lonely road that eventually led to their neighbors. Weather permitting, in winter it took an hour and a half to get the truck running and drive into town.

It was dawn by the time they had made their way upstairs, still drained from the scene in the basement. Mara went to lie down on her bed so she could try for the illusion of privacy. Through the closed door, she heard her father venting his frustration on the cabinets. Pans clanged. Drawers slammed. She thought she could hear the quiet, gulping sound of him beginning to weep again under the cacophony.

She waited until he was engrossed in his cooking and then crept out of her bedroom. She made her way down the hallway, taking each step slowly and carefully so as to minimize the clicking of her crutches against the floor.

Ima's dance studio was the only room in the house where abba never went. It faced east; at dawn, rose- and peach-colored light shimmered across the full-length mirrors and polished hardwood. An old television hung on the southern wall, its antiquated technology jury-rigged to connect with the household AI.

Mara closed the door most of the way, enough to muffle any sound, but not enough to make the telltale thump that would attract her father's attention. She walked up to the television so that she could speak softly and still be heard by its implanted AI sensors. She'd long ago mastered the trick of enunciating clearly enough for the AI to understand her even when she was whispering. "I'd like to access a DVD of ima's performances."

The AI whirred. "Okay, Mara," said its genial, masculine voice. "Which one would you like to view?"

"*Giselle.*"

More clicks and whirs. The television blinked on, showing the backs of several rows of red velvet seats. Well-dressed figures navigated the aisles, careful not to wrinkle expensive suits and dresses. Before them, a curtain hid the stage from view, the house lights emphasizing its sumptuous folds.

Mara sat carefully on the floor near the ballet barre so that she would be able to use it a lever when she wanted to stand again. She crossed the crutches at her feet. On the television screen, the lights dimmed as the overture began.

Sitting alone in this place where no one else went, watching things that no one else watched, she felt as if she were somewhere safe. A mouse in its hole, a bird in its nest—a shelter built precisely for her body, neither too large nor too small.

The curtain fluttered. The overture began. Mara felt her breath flowing more easily as the tension eased from her shoulders. She could forget about abba and his weeping for a moment, just allow herself to enter the ballet.

Even as an infant, Mara had adored the rich, satiny colors on ima's old DVDs. She watched the tragedies, but her heart belonged to the comedies. Gilbert and Sullivan's *Pineapple Poll*. Ashton's choreography of Prokofiev's *Cinderella*. Madcap *Coppélia* in which a peasant boy lost his heart to a clockwork doll.

When Mara was small, ima would sit with her while she watched the dancers, her expression half-wistful and half-jaded. When the dancers had sketched their bows, ima would stand, shaking her head, and say, "Ballet is not a good life."

At first, ima did not want to give Mara ballet lessons, but Mara insisted at the age of two, three, four, until ima finally gave in. During the afternoons while abba was in his workshop, Mara and ima would dance together in the studio until ima grew tired and sat with her back against the mirror, hands wrapped around her knees, watching Mara spin and spin.

After ima died, Mara had wanted to ask her father to sign her up for dance school. But she hated the melancholia that overtook him whenever they discussed ballet. Before getting sick, she'd danced on her own instead, accompanying the dancers on ima's tapes. She didn't dance every afternoon as she had when ima was alive. She was older; she had other things to do— books to read, study hours with the AI, lessons and play dates in attic space. She danced just enough to maintain her flexibility and retain what ima had taught her, and even sometimes managed to learn new things from watching the dancers on film.

Then last year, while dancing with the Mouse King to *The Nutcracker*, the pain she'd been feeling for months in her right knee suddenly intensified. She heard the snap of bone before she felt it. She collapsed suddenly to the floor, confused and in pain, her head ringing with the echoes of the household's alarms. As the AI wailed for help, Mara found a single thought repeating in her head. *Legs don't shatter just because you're dancing. Something is very wrong.*

On the television screen, the filmed version of Mara's mother entered, dancing a coy Giselle in blue tulle. Her gaze slanted shyly downward as she flirted with the dancers playing Albrecht and Hilarion. One by one, she plucked petals from a prop daisy. *He loves me, he loves me not.*

Mara heard footsteps starting down the hall. She rushed to speak before abba could make it into the room—"AI, switch off—"

Abba arrived before she could finish. He stood in the doorway with his shoulders hunched, his eyes averted from the image of his dead wife. "Breakfast is ready," he said. He lingered for a moment before turning away.

After breakfast, abba went outside to scrape ice off of the truck.

They drove into town once a week for supplies. Until last year, they'd always gone on Sundays, after Shabbat. Now they went on Fridays before Mara's appointments and then hurried to get home in time to prepare for sunset.

Outside, snowflakes whispered onto the hard-pack. Mara pulled her knit hat over her ears, but her cheeks still smarted from the cold. She rubbed her gloved hands together for warmth before attaching Abel's leash. The old dog seemed to understand what her crutches were. Since she'd started using them, he'd broken his lifelong habit of yanking on the strap and learned to walk daintily instead, placing each paw with care.

Abba opened the passenger door so that Abel could clamor into the back of the cab. He fretted while Mara leaned her crutches on the side of the truck and pulled herself into the seat. He wanted to help, she knew, but he was stopping himself. He knew she hated being reminded of her helplessness.

He collected her crutches when she was done and slung them into the back with Abel before taking his place in the driver's seat. Mara stared silently forward as he turned the truck around and started down the narrow driveway. The four-wheel-drive jolted over uneven snow, shooting pain through Mara's bad leg.

"Need to fix the suspension," abba grumbled.

Because abba was a tinkerer, everything was always broken. Before Mara was born, he'd worked for the government. These days, he consulted on refining manufacturing processes. He felt that commercial products were shoddily designed and so he was constantly trying to improve their household electronics, leaving his dozens of half-finished home projects disassembled for months while all the time swearing to take on new ones.

The pavement smoothed out as they turned onto a county-maintained road. Piles of dirty snow lined its sides. Bony trees dotted the landscape, interspersed with pines still wearing red bows from Christmas.

Mara felt as though the world were caught in a frozen moment, preserved beneath the snow. Nothing would ever change. No ice would melt. No birds would return to the branches. There would be nothing but blizzards and long, dark nights and snow-covered pines.

Mara wasn't sure she believed in G-d, but on her better days, she felt at peace with the idea of pausing, as if she were one of the dancers on ima's DVDs, halted mid-leap.

Except she wouldn't pause. She'd be replaced by that thing. That doll.

She glanced at her father. He stared fixedly at the road, grumbling under his breath in a blend of languages. He hadn't bought new clothes since losing so much weight, and the fabric of his coat fell in voluminous folds across the seat.

He glanced sideways at Mara watching him. "What's wrong?"

"Nothing," Mara muttered, looking away.

Abel pushed his nose into her shoulder. She turned in her seat to scratch between his ears. His tail thumped, tick, tock, like a metronome.

• • •

They parked beside the grocery. The small building's densely packed shelves were reassuringly the same year in and year out except for the special display mounted at the front of the store. This week it showcased red-wrapped sausages, marked with a cheerful, handwritten sign.

Gerry stood on a ladder in the center aisle, restocking cereals. He beamed as they walked in.

"Ten-thirty to the minute!" he called. "Good morning, my punctual Jewish friends!"

Gerry had been slipping down the slope called being hard of hearing for years now. He pitched his voice as if he were shouting across a football field.

"How is my little adult?" he asked Mara. "Are you forty today, or is it fifty?"

"Sixty-five," Mara said. "Seventy tomorrow."

"Such an old child," Gerry said, shaking his head. "Are you sure you didn't steal that body?"

Abba didn't like those kinds of jokes. He used to worry that they would make her self-conscious; now he hated them for bringing up the subject of aging. Flatly, he replied, "Children in our family are like that. There is nothing wrong with her."

Mara shared an eye roll with the grocer.

"Never said there was," Gerry said. Changing the subject, he gestured at Mara's crutches with a box of cornflakes. "You're an athlete on those. I bet there's nothing you can't do with them."

Mara forced a smile. "They're no good for dancing."

He shrugged. "I used to know a guy in a wheelchair. Out-danced everyone."

"Not ballet, though."

"True," Gerry admitted, descending the ladder. "Come to the counter. I've got something for you."

Gerry had hardly finished speaking before Abel forgot about being gentle with Mara's crutches. He knew what Gerry's gifts meant. The lead wrenched out of Mara's hand. She chased after him, crutches clicking, but even with his aging joints, the dog reached the front counter before Mara was halfway across the store.

"Wicked dog," Gerry said in a teasing tone as he caught Abel's leash. He scratched the dog between the ears and then bent to grab a package from under the counter. "Sit," he said. "Beg." The old dog rushed to do both. Gerry unwrapped a sausage and tossed it. Abel snapped and swallowed.

Mara finished crossing the aisle. She leaned against the front counter. She tried to conceal her heavy breathing, but she knew that her face must be flushed. Abba waited at the edges of her peripheral vision, his arms stretched in Mara's direction as if he expected her to collapse.

Gerry glanced between Mara and her father, assessing the situation. Settling on Mara, he tapped a stool behind the counter. "You look wiped. Take a load off. Your dad and I can handle ourselves."

"Yes, Mara," abba said quickly. "Perhaps you should sit."

Mara glared. "Abba."

"I'm sorry," abba said, looking away. He added to Gerry, "She doesn't like help."

"No help being offered. I just want some free work. You up for manning the register?" Gerry tapped the stool again. "I put aside one of those strawberry things you like. It's under the counter. Wrapped in pink paper."

"Thanks," Mara said, not wanting to hurt Gerry's feelings by mentioning that she couldn't eat before appointments. She went behind the counter and let Gerry hold her crutches while she pulled herself onto the stool. She hated how good it felt to sit.

Gerry nodded decisively. "Come on," he said, leading abba toward the fresh fruit.

Abba and Gerry made unlikely friends. Gerry made no bones about being a charismatic evangelical. During the last election, he'd put up posters saying that Democratic voters were headed to hell. In return, abba had suggested that Republican voters might need a punch in the jaw, especially any Republican voters who happened to be standing in front of him. Gerry responded that he supported free speech as much as any other patriotic American, but speech like that could get the H-E-double-hockey-sticks out of his store. They shouted. Gerry told abba not to come back. Abba said he wouldn't even buy dog food from fascists.

The next week, Gerry was waiting on the sidewalk with news about a kosher supplier, and Mara and abba went in as if nothing had ever happened.

Before getting sick, Mara had always followed the men through the aisles, joining in their arguments about pesticides and free-range chickens. Gerry liked to joke that he wished his children were as interested in the business as Mara was. *Maybe I'll leave the store to you instead of them,* he'd say, jostling her shoulder. He had stopped saying that.

Mara slipped the wrapped pastry out from under the counter. She broke it into halves and put one in each pocket, hoping Gerry wouldn't see the lumps when they left. She left the empty paper on the counter, dusted with the crumbs that had fallen when she broke the pastry.

An activity book lay next to where the pastry had been. It was for little kids, but Mara pulled it out anyway. Gerry's children were too old to play with things like that now, but he still kept an array of diversions under the counter for when customers' kids needed to be kept busy. It was better to do something than nothing. Armed with the felt-tip pen that was clipped to the cover, she began to flip through pages of half-colored drawings and connect-the-dots.

A few aisles over, near the butcher counter, she heard her father grumbling. She looked up and saw Gerry grab abba's shoulder. As always, he was speaking too loudly. His voice boomed over the hum of the freezers. "I got in the best sausages on Wednesday," he said. "They're kosher. Try them. Make them for your, what do you call it, sadbath."

By then, Gerry knew the word, but it was part of their banter.

"Shabbat," Abba corrected.

Gerry's tone grew more serious. "You're losing too much weight. A man needs meat."

Abba's voice went flat. "I eat when I am hungry. I am not hungry so much lately."

Gerry's grip tightened on abba's shoulder. His voice dropped. "Jakub, you need to take care of yourself."

He looked back furtively at Mara. Flushing with shame, she dropped her gaze to the activity book. She clutched the pen tightly, pretending to draw circles in a word search.

"You have to think about the future," said Gerry. His voice lowered even further. Though he was finally speaking at a normal volume, she still heard every word. "You aren't the one who's dying."

Mara's flush went crimson. She couldn't tell if it was shame or anger—all she felt was cold, rigid shock. She couldn't stop herself from sneaking a glance at abba. He, too, stood frozen. The word had turned him to ice. Neither of them ever said it. It was a game of avoidance they played together.

Abba pulled away from Gerry and started down the aisle. His face looked numb rather than angry. He stopped at the counter, looking at everything but Mara. He took Abel's leash and gestured for Mara to get off of the stool. "We'll be late for your appointment," he said, even though it wasn't even eleven o'clock. In a louder voice, he added, "Ring up our cart, would you, Gerry? We'll pick up our bags on our way out of town."

Mara didn't like Doctor Pinsky. Abba liked him because he was Jewish even though he was American-born reform with a degree from Queens. He wore his hair close-cut but it looked like it would Jew 'fro if he grew it out.

He kept his nails manicured. His teeth shone perfectly white. He never looked directly at Mara when he spoke. Mara suspected he didn't like children much. Maybe you needed to be that way if you were going to watch the sick ones get worse.

The nurses were all right. Grace and Nicole, both blonde and a bit fat. They didn't understand Mara since she didn't fit their idea of what kids were supposed to be like. She didn't talk about pop or interactives. When there were other child patients in the waiting room, she ignored them.

When the nurses tried to introduce her to the other children anyway, Mara said she preferred to talk to adults, which made them hmm and flutter. *Don't you have any friends, honey?* Nicole had asked her once, and Mara answered that she had some, but they were all on attic space. A year ago, if Mara had been upset, she'd have gone into a-space to talk to her best friend, Collin, but more and more as she got sick, she'd hated seeing him react to her withering body, hated seeing the fright and pity in his eyes. The thought of going back into attic space made her nauseous.

Grace and Nicole gave Mara extra attention because they felt sorry for her. Modern cancer treatments had failed to help and now Mara was the only child patient in the clinic taking chemotherapy. *It's hard on little bodies,* said Grace. *Heck, it's hard on big bodies, too.*

Today it was Grace who came to meet Mara in the waiting room, pushing a wheelchair. Assuming it was for another patient, Mara started to gather her crutches, but Grace motioned for her to stay put. "Let me treat you like a princess."

"I'm not much of a princess," Mara answered, immediately realizing from the pitying look on Grace's face that it was the wrong thing to say. To Grace, that would mean she didn't feel like a princess because she was sick, rather than that she wasn't interested in princesses.

"I can walk," Mara protested, but Grace insisted on helping her into the wheelchair anyway. She hadn't realized how tightly abba was holding her hand until she pulled it free.

Abba stood to follow them. Grace turned back. "Would you mind staying? Doctor Pinsky wants to talk to you."

"I like to go with Mara," abba said.

"We'll take good care of her." Grace patted Mara's shoulder. "You don't mind, do you, princess?"

Mara shrugged. Her father shifted uncertainly. "What does Doctor Pinsky want?"

"He'll be out in a few minutes," said Grace, deflecting. "I'm sorry, Mr. Morawski. You won't have to wait long."

Frowning, abba sat again, fingers worrying the collar of his shirt. Mara saw his conflicting optimism and fear, all inscribed plainly in his eyes, his face, the way he sat. She didn't understand why he kept hoping. Even before they'd tried the targeted immersion therapy and the QTRC regression, she'd known that they wouldn't work. She'd known from the moment when she saw the almost imperceptible frown cross the city diagnostician's face when he asked about the pain she'd been experiencing in her knee for months before the break. Yes, she'd said, it had been worse at night, and his brow had darkened, just for an instant. Maybe she'd known even earlier than that, in the moment just after she fell in ima's studio, when she realized with strange, cold clarity that something was very wrong.

Bad news didn't come all at once. It came in successions. Cancer is present. Metastasis has occurred. The tumors are unresponsive. The patient's vitals have taken a turn for the worse. We're sorry to say, we're sorry to say, we're sorry to say.

Grace wheeled Mara toward the back, maintaining a stream of banal, cheerful chatter, remarks about the weather and questions about the holidays and jokes about boys. Mara deflected. She wasn't ever going to have a boyfriend, not the way Grace was teasing her about. Adolescence was like spring, one more thing buried in endless snow.

Mara felt exhausted as they pulled into the driveway. She didn't have the energy to push abba away when he came around the truck to help her down. Mara leaned heavily on her father's arm as they crunched their way to the front door.

She vomited in the entryway. Abel came to investigate. She pushed his nose away while abba went to get the mop. The smell made her even more nauseated and so when abba returned, she left him to clean up. It made her feel guilty, but she was too tired to care.

She went to the bathroom to wash out her mouth. She tried not to catch her eye in the mirror, but she saw her reflection anyway. She felt a shock of alienation from the thin, sallow face. It couldn't be hers.

She could hear abba in the hallway, grumbling at Abel in Yiddish. Wan, late afternoon light filtered through the windows, foreshadowing sunset. A few months ago, she and abba would have been rushing to cook and clean before Shabbat. Now no one cleaned and Mara left abba to cook alone as she went into ima's studio.

She paused by the barre before sitting, already worried about how difficult it would be to get up again. "I want to watch *Coppélia*," she said. The AI whirred.

Coppélia began with a young woman reading on a balcony—except she wasn't really a young woman, she was actually an automaton constructed by the mad scientist, Dr. Coppélius. The dancer playing Coppélia pretended to read from a red leather book. Mara told the AI to fast-forward to ima's entrance.

Mara's mother was dancing the part of the peasant girl, Swanhilde. She looked nothing like the dancer playing Coppélia. Ima was strong, but also short and compact, where Coppélia was tall with visible muscle definition in her arms and legs.

Yet later in the ballet, none of the other characters would be able to tell them apart. Mara wanted to shake them into sense. Why couldn't they tell the difference between a person and a doll?

• • •

Abba lit the candles and began the prayer, waving his hands through the smoke. They didn't have an adult woman to read the prayers and abba wouldn't let Mara do it while she was still a child. *Soon,* he used to say,*after your bat mitzvah.* Now he said nothing.

They didn't celebrate Shabbat properly. They followed some traditions— tonight they'd leave the lights on, and tomorrow they'd eat cold food instead of cooking—but they did not attend services. If they needed to work then they worked. As a family, they had always been observant in some ways, and relaxed in others; they were not the kind who took well to following rules. Abba sometimes seemed to believe in Hashem and at other times not, though he believed in rituals and tradition. Still, before Mara had become ill, they'd taken more care with *halakha.*

As abba often reminded her, Judaism taught that survival was more important than dogma. *Pikuach nefesh* meant that a hospital could run electricity that powered a machine that kept a man alive. A family could work to keep a woman who had just given birth comfortable and healthy.

Perhaps other people wouldn't recognize the exceptions that Mara and her father made from Shabbat as being matters of survival, but they were. They were using all they had just by living. Not much remained for G-d.

The long window over the kitchen counters let through the dimming light as violet and ultramarine seeped across the horizon. The tangerine sun lingered above the trees, preparing to descend into scratching, black branches. Mara's attention drifted as abba said *kiddush* over the wine.

They washed their hands. Abba tore the challah. He gave a portion to Mara. She let it sit.

"The fish is made with ginger," abba said. "Would you like some string beans?"

"My mouth hurts," Mara said.

Abba paused, the serving plate still in his hands.

She knew that he wouldn't eat unless she did. "I'll have a little," she added softly.

She let him set the food on her plate. She speared a single green bean and stared at it for a moment before biting. Everything tasted like metal after the drugs.

"I used turmeric," he said.

"It's good."

Mara's stomach roiled. She set the fork on her plate.

Her father ate a few bites of fish and then set his fork down, too. A maudlin expression crossed his face. "Family is Hashem's best gift," he said.

Mara nodded. There was little to say.

Abba picked up his wine glass. He twisted the stem as he stared into red.

"Family is what the *goyim* tried to take from us with pogroms and ghettoes and the *shoah*. On Shabbat, we find our families, wherever we are."

Abba paused again, sloshing wine gently from side to side.

"Perhaps I should have gone to Israel before you were born."

Mara looked up with surprise. "You think Israel is a corrupt theocracy."

"There are politics, like opposing a government, and then there is needing to be with your people." He shrugged. "I thought about going. I had money then, but no roots. I could have gone wherever I wanted. But I thought, I will go to America instead. There are more Jews in America than Israel. I did not want to live in the shadow of the *shoah*. I wanted to make a family in a place where we could rebuild everything they stole. *Der mensch trakht un Gatt lahkt.*"

He had been speaking rapidly, his accent deepening with every word. Now he stopped.

His voice was hoarse when it returned.

"Your mother . . . you . . . I would not trade it, but . . . " His gaze became diffuse as if the red of the wine were a telescope showing him another world. "It's all so fragile. Your mother is taken and you . . . *tsuris, tsuris* . . . and then there is nothing."

It was dark when they left the table. Abba piled dishes by the sink so that they could be washed after Shabbat and then retired to his bedroom. Abel came to Mara, tail thumping, begging for scraps. She was too tired to make him beg or shake hands. She rescued her plate from the pile of dishes and laid it on the floor for him to lick clean.

She started toward her bed and then changed her mind. She headed downstairs instead, Abel following after. She paused with her hand on the knob of the red-painted door before entering abba's workshop.

Mara hadn't seen abba go downstairs since their argument that morning but he must have managed to do it without her noticing. The doll sat primly on her stool, dignity restored, her head tilted down as if she were reading a book that Mara couldn't see.

Mara wove between worktables until she reached the doll's side. She lifted its hand and pressed their palms together as abba had done. It was strange to see the shape of her fingers so perfectly copied, down to the fine lines across her knuckles.

She pulled the thing forward. It lolled. Abel ducked its flailing right hand and ran a few steps away, watching warily.

Mara took hold of the thing's head. She pressed the tip of her nose against the tip of its nose, trying to match their faces as she had their palms. With their faces so close together, it looked like a Cyclops, staring back at her with one enormous, blank eye.

"I hate you," Mara said, lips pressed against its mute mouth.

It was true, but not the same way that it had been that morning. She had been furious then. Betrayed. Now the blaze of anger had burned down and she saw what lay in the ashes that remained.

It was jealousy. That this doll would be the one to take abba's hand at Shabbat five years from then, ten years, twenty. That it would take and give the comfort she could not. That it would balm the wounds that she had no choice but to inflict. Would Mara have taken a clockwork doll if it had restored ima to her for these past years?

She imagined lying down for the scans. She imagined a machine studying her brain, replicating her dreams neuron by neuron, rendering her as mathematical patterns. She'd read enough biology and psychology to know that, whatever else she was, she was also an epiphenomenon that arose from chemicals and meat and electricity.

It was sideways immortality. She would be gone, and she would remain. There and not there. A quantum mechanical soul.

Love could hurt, she knew. Love was what made you hurt when your ima died. Love was what made it hurt when abba came to you gentle and solicitous, every kindness a reminder of how much pain you'd leave behind.

She would do this painful thing because she loved him, as he had made this doll because he loved her. She thought, with a sudden clenching of her stomach, that it was a good thing most people never lived to see what people planned to make of them when they were gone.

What Gerry had said was as true as it was cutting. Abba was not the one who would die.

Abba slept among twisted blankets, clutching his pillow as if afraid to let it go.

Mara watched from the doorway. "Abba."

He grumbled in his sleep as he shifted position.

"Abba," she repeated. "Please wake up, abba."

She waited while he put on his robe. Then, she led him down.

She made her way swiftly through the workshop, passing the newly painted marionette and the lonely mechanical hand. She halted near the doll, avoiding its empty gaze.

"I'm ready now," she said.

Abba's face shifted from confusion to wariness. With guarded hope, he asked, "Are you certain?"

"I'm sure," she said.

"Please, Mara. You do not have to."

"I know," she answered. She pressed herself against his chest, as if she were a much smaller child looking for comfort. She felt the tension in his body seep into relief as he wept with silent gratitude. She was filled with tears, too, from a dozen emotions blended into one. They were tears of relief, and regret, and pain, and love, and mourning, and more.

He wrapped his arms around her. She closed her eyes and savored the comfort of his woody scent, his warmth, the stubble scratching her arm. She could feel how thin he'd become, but he was still strong enough to hold her so tightly that his embrace was simultaneously joyful and almost too much to bear.

Act II: Jakub

Tour en l'air

(Turn in the Air)

Jakub was careful to make the scans as unobtrusive as possible. If he could have, he'd have recorded a dozen sessions, twenty-five, fifty, more. He'd have examined every obscure angle; he'd have recorded a hundred redundancies.

Mara was so fragile, though; not just physically, but mentally. He did not want to tax her. He found a way to consolidate what he needed into six nighttime sessions, monitoring her with portable equipment that he could bring into her bedroom which broadcast its data to the larger machinery in the basement.

When the scans were complete, Jakub spent his nights in the workshop, laboring over the new child while Mara slept. It had been a long time since he'd worked with technology like this, streamlined for its potential as a weapon. He had to gentle it, soothe it, coax it into being as careful about preserving memories of rainy mornings as it was about retaining reflexes and fighting skills.

He spent long hours poring over images of Mara's brain. He navigated three-dimensional renderings with the AI's help, puzzling over the strangeness of becoming so intimate with his daughter's mind in such an unexpected way. After he had finished converting the images into a neural map, he looked at Mara's mind with yet new astonishment. The visual representation showed associational clusters as if they were stars: elliptical galaxies of thought.

It was a truism that there were many ways to describe a river—from the action of its molecules to the map of its progress from tributaries to ocean. A mind was such a thing as well. On one end there was thought, personality, individual . . . and on the other . . . It was impossible to recognize Mara in the points of light, but he was in the midst of her most basic elements, and there was as much awe in that as there was in puzzling out the origin of the universe. He was the first person ever to see another human being in this way. He knew Mara now as no one else had ever known anyone.

His daughter, his beloved, his *sheineh maideleh*. There were so many others that he'd failed to protect. But Mara would always be safe; he would hold her forever.

Once Jakub had created the foundational schematics for manufacturing analogues to Mara's brain structures, the remainder of the process was automated. Jakub needed only to oversee it, occasionally inputting his approval to the machine.

Jakub found it unbearable to leave the machinery unsupervised, but nevertheless, he could not spend all of his time in the basement. During the mornings when Mara was awake, he paced the house, grumbling at the dog who followed him up and down the hallways as if expecting him to throw a stick. What if the process stalled? What if a catastrophic failure destroyed the images of Mara's mind now when her health was even more fragile and there might be no way to replace them?

He forced himself to disguise his obsession while Mara was awake. It was important to maintain the illusion that their life was the same as it had been before. He knew that Mara remained uneasy with the automaton. Its very presence said so many things that they had been trying to keep silent.

Mara's days were growing even harder. He'd thought the end of chemotherapy would give her some relief, but cancer pain worsened every day. Constant suffering and exhaustion made her alternately sullen and sharp. She snapped at him when he brought her meals, when he tried to help her across the house, when she woke to find him lingering in the doorway while she slept. Part of it was the simple result of pain displacing patience, but it was more, too. Once, when he had touched her shoulder, she'd flinched; then, upon seeing him withdraw, her expression had turned from annoyance to guilt. She'd said, softly, "You won't always be able to do that." A pause, a swallow, and then even more quietly, "It reminds me."

That was what love and comfort had become now. Promises that couldn't be kept.

Most nights, she did not sleep at all, only lay awake, staring out of her window at the snow.

Jakub searched for activities that might console her. He asked her if she'd like him to read to her. He offered to buy her immersive games. He suggested that she log into a spare room with other sick children where they could discuss their troubles. She told him that she wanted to be alone.

She had always been an unusual child, precocious and content to be her own companion. Meryem had said it was natural for a daughter of theirs, who had been raised among adults, and was descended from people who were also talented and solitary. Jakub and Meryem had been similar as children, remote from others their own age as they pursued their obsessions. Now Jakub wished she had not inherited these traits so completely, that she was more easily able to seek solace.

When Mara didn't think he was watching, she gathered her crutches and went into Meryem's studio to watch ballets. She did not like it when he came too close, and so he watched from the hallway. He could see her profile reflected in the mirrors on the opposite wall. She cried as she watched, soundless tears beading her cheeks.

One morning when she put on *A Midsummer Night's Dream*, Jakub ventured into the studio. For so long, he had stayed away, but that had not made things better. He had to try what he could.

He found Mara sitting on the floor, her crutches leaning against the ballet barre. Abel lay a few feet away with his head on his paws. Without speaking, Jakub sat beside them.

Mara wiped her cheeks, streaking her tears. She looked resentfully at Jakub, but he ignored her, hoping he could reach the part of her that still wanted his company even if she had buried it.

They sat stoically for the remainder of act one, holding themselves with care so that they did not accidentally shift closer to one another. Mara pretended to ignore him, though her darting glances told another story. Jakub let her maintain the pretense, trying to allow her some personal space within the studio since he had already intruded so far. He hoped she would be like a scared rabbit, slowly adjusting to his presence and coming to him when she saw that he was safe.

Jakub had expected to spend the time watching Mara and not the video, but he was surprised to find himself drawn into the dancing. The pain of seeing Meryem leap and spin had become almost a dull note, unnoticeable in the concert of his other sorrows. Meryem made a luminous Titania, a ginger wig cascading in curls down her back, her limbs wrapped in flowers, leaves and gossamer. He'd forgotten the way she moved onstage, as careful and precise as a doe, each agile maneuver employing precisely as much strength as she needed and no more.

As Act II began, Mara asked the AI to stop. Exhaustion, she said. Jakub tried to help her back to her room, but she protested, and he let her go.

She was in her own world now, closing down. She had no room left for him.

What can I do for you, Marale? he wanted to ask. *I will do anything. You will not let me hold you so I must find another way. I will change the laws of life and death. I will give you as much forever as I can,* sheineh maideleh. *See? I am doing it now.*

He knew that she hated it when he stood outside her door, watching, but when he heard her breath find the steady rhythm of sleep, he went to the threshold anyway. While she slept, Mara looked peaceful for a while, her chest gently rising and falling underneath her snow-colored quilt.

He lingered a long time. Eventually, he left her and returned downstairs to check the machines.

The new child was ready to be born.

• • •

For years, Jakub had dreamed of the numbers. They flickered in and out of focus as if displayed on old film. Sometimes they looked ashen and faded. At other times, they were darker than any real black. Always, they were written on palettes of human flesh.

Sometimes the dreams included fragmentary memories. Jakub would be back in the rooms his grandparents had rented when he was a child, watching bubbe prepare to clean the kitchen, pulling her left arm free from one long cotton sleeve, her tattoo a shock on the inside of her forearm. The skin there had gone papery with age, the ink bleached and distorted, but time and sun had not made the mark less portentous. She scoured cookware with steel wool and caustic chemicals that made her hands red and raw when they emerged from the bubbling water. No matter how often Jakub watched, he never stopped expecting her to abandon the ancient pots and turn that furious, unrelenting scrubbing onto herself.

Zayde's tattoo remained more mysterious. It had not been inflicted in Auschwitz and so it hid in the more discreet location they'd used on the trains, needled onto the underside of his upper arm. Occasionally on hot days when Jakub was small, zayde would roll up his sleeves while he worked outside in the sun. If Jakub or one of the other boys found him, zayde would shout at them to get back inside and then finish the work in his long sleeves, dripping with sweat.

Jakub's grandparents never spoke of the camps. Both had been young in those years, but even though they were not much older when they were released, the few pictures of them from that time showed figures that were already brittle and dessicated in both physique and expression. Survivors took many paths away from the devastation, but bubbe and zayde were among those who always afterward walked with their heads down.

Being mutually bitter and taciturn, they resisted marriage until long after their contemporaries had sought comfort in each other's arms. They raised their children with asperity, and sent them into the world as adults with small gifts of money and few displays of emotion.

One of those children was Jakub's mother, who immigrated to the United States where she married. Some years later, she died in childbirth, bearing what would have been Jakub's fifth brother had the child not been stillborn. Jakub's father, grieving, could not take care of his four living sons. Instead, he wrote to his father-in-law in Poland and requested that he come to the United States and take them home with him.

Even then, when he arrived on foreign shores to fetch boys he'd never met and take them back with him to a land they'd never known; even then when the moment should have been grief and gathering; even then zayde's face was hard-lined with resignation. Or so Jakub's elder brothers had told him, for he was the youngest of the surviving four, having learned to speak a few words by then but not yet able to stand on his own.

When the four boys were children, it was a mystery to them how such harsh people could have spent long enough together to marry, let alone have children. Surely, they would have been happier with others who were kinder, less astringent, who could bring comfort into a marriage.

One afternoon, when Jakub was four years old, and too naïve to yet understand that some things that were discussed in private should not be shared with everyone, he was sitting with bubbe while she sewed shirts for the boys (too expensive to buy, and shouldn't she know how to sew, having done it all her life?). He asked, "If you don't like zayde, why did you marry him?"

She stopped suddenly. Her hands were still on the machine, her mouth open, her gaze fastened on the seam. For a moment, the breath did not rise in her chest. The needle stuttered to a stop as her foot eased its pressure on the pedal.

She did not deny it or ask *What do you mean?* Neither did she answer any of the other questions that might have been enfolded in that one, like *Why don't you like him?* or *Why did you marry at all?*

Instead, she heard Jakub's true question: *Why zayde and not someone else?*

"How could it be another?" she asked. "We're the same."

And then she began sewing again, making no further mention of it, which was what zayde would have done, too, if Jakub had left bubbe at her sewing and instead taken his question to zayde as he replaced the wiring in their old, old walls.

As important as it was for the two of them that they shared a history, it also meant that they were like knives to each other, constantly reopening each other's old wounds and salting them with tears and anger. Their frequent, bitter arguments could continue for days upon days.

The days of arguing were better than those when bitter silence descended, and each member of the family was left in their own, isolated coldness.

It was not that there were no virtues to how the boys were raised. Their bodies were kept robust on good food, and their minds strengthened with the exercise of solving problems both practical and intellectual. Zayde concocted new projects for them weekly. One week they'd learn to build cabinets, and the next they'd read old books of philosophy, debating free will versus determinism. Jakub took Leibniz's part against zayde's Spinoza. They studied the Torah as an academic text, though zayde was an atheist of the bitter stripe after his time in the camps.

When Jakub was nine, bubbe decided that it was time to cultivate their spirits as well as their minds and bodies. She revealed that she had been having dreams about G-d for decades, ever since the day she left the camp.

The events of those hours had haunted her dreams and as she watched them replay, she felt the scene overlaid with a shining sense of awe and renewal, which over the years, she had come to believe was the presence of G-d. Knowing zayde's feelings about G-d, bubbe had kept her silence in the name of peace for decades, but that year, some indefinable thing had shifted her conscience and she could do so no longer.

As she'd predicted, zayde was furious. "I am supposed to worship a G-d that would make *this* world?" he demanded. "A G-d like that is no G-d. A G-d like that is evil."

But despite the hours of shouting, slammed doors, and smashed crockery, bubbe remained resolute. She became a *frum* woman, dressing carefully, observing prayers and rituals. On Fridays, the kitchen became the locus of urgent energy as bubbe rushed to prepare for Shabbat, directing Jakub and his brothers to help with the chores. All of them worked tensely, preparing for the moment when zayde would return home and throw the simmering *cholent* out of the window, or—if they were lucky—turn heel and walk back out, going who-knew-where until he came home on Sunday.

After a particularly vicious argument, zayde proclaimed that while he apparently could not stop his wife from doing as she pleased, he would absolutely no longer permit his grandsons to attend *shul*. It was a final decision; otherwise, one of them would have to leave and never come back. After that, bubbe slipped out each week into the chilly morning, alone.

From zayde and bubbe, Jakub learned that love was both balm and nettle. They taught him from an early age that nothing could hurt so much as family.

Somehow, Jakub had expected the new child to be clumsy and vacant as if she were an infant, but the moment she initialized, her blank look vanished. Some parts of her face tensed and others relaxed. She blinked. She looked just like Mara.

She prickled under Jakub's scrutiny. "What are you staring at? Is something wrong?"

Jakub's mouth worked silently as he sought the words. "I thought you would need more time to adjust."

The child smiled Mara's cynical, lopsided smile, which had been absent for months. "I think you're going to need more time to adjust than I do."

She pulled herself to her feet. It wasn't just her face that had taken on Mara's habits of expression. Without pause, she moved into one of the stretches that Meryem had taught her, elongating her spine. When she relaxed, her posture was exactly like Mara's would have been, a preadolescent slouch ameliorated by a hint of dancer's grace.

"Can we go upstairs?" she asked.

"Not yet," Jakub said. "There are tests to perform."

Tests which she passed. Every single one. She knew Mara's favorite colors and the names of the children she had studied with in attic space. She knew the color and weight of the apples that would grow on their trees next fall and perfectly recited the recipe for baking them with cinnamon. In the gruff tone that Mara used when she was guarding against pain, she related the story of Meryem's death—how Meryem had woken with complaints of feeling dizzy, how she had slipped in the bath later that morning, how her head had cracked against the porcelain and spilled red into the bathwater.

She ran like Mara and caught a ball like Mara and bent to touch her toes like Mara. She was precisely as fleet and as nimble and as flexible as Mara. She performed neither worse nor better. She was Mara's twin in every way that Jakub could measure.

"You will need to stay here for a few more days," he told her, bringing down blankets and pillows so that he could make her a bed in the workshop. "There are still more tests. You will be safer if you remain close to the machines."

The new child's face creased with doubt. He was lying to spare her feelings, but she was no more deceived than Mara would have been. She said, "My room is upstairs."

For so many months, Jakub and Mara had taken refuge in mutual silence when the subject turned uncomfortable. He did not like to speak so bluntly. But if she would force him—"No," he said gently. "That is Mara's room."

"Can't I at least see it?"

A wheedling overtone thinned her voice. Her body language occupied a strange lacuna between aggression and vulnerability. She faced him full-on, one foot advancing, with her hands clenched tightly at her sides. Yet at the same time, she could not quite meet his eyes, and her head was tilted slightly downward, protecting her neck.

Jakub had seen that strange combination before. It was not so unusual a posture for teenagers to wear when they were trying to assert their agency through rebellion and yet simultaneously still hoping for their parents' approval.

Mara had never reached that stage. Before she became ill, she had been calm, abiding. Jakub began to worry that he'd erred in his calculations, that the metrics he'd used had been inadequate to measure the essence of a girl. Could she have aged so much, simply being slipped into an artificial skin?

"Mara is sleeping now."

"But I *am* Mara!" The new child's voice broke on her exclamation.

Her lips parted uncertainly. Her fingers trembled. Her glance flashed upward for a moment and he saw such pain in it. No, she was still his Mara. Not defiant, only afraid that he would decide that he had not wanted a mechanical daughter after all, that he would reject her like a broken radio and never love her again.

Gently, he laid his hand on her shoulder. Softly, he said, "You are Mara, but you need a new name, too. Let us call you Ruth."

He had not known until he spoke that he was going to choose that name, but it was a good one. In the Torah, Ruth had given Mara *hesed*. His Mara needed loving kindness, too.

The new child's gaze flickered upward as if she could see through the ceiling and into Mara's room. "Mara is the name ima gave me," she protested.

Jakub answered, "It would be confusing otherwise."

He hoped that this time the new child would understand what he meant without his having to speak outright. The other Mara had such a short time. It would be cruel to make her days harder than they must be.

On the day when Jakub gave the automaton her name, he found himself recalling the story of Ruth. It had been a long time since he had given the Torah any serious study, but though he had forgotten its minutiae, he remembered its rhythm. His thoughts assumed the cadences of half-forgotten rabbis.

It began when a famine descended on Judah.

A man, Elimelech, decided that he was not going to let his wife and sons starve to death, and so he packed his household and brought them to Moab. It was good that he had decided to do so, because once they reached Moab, he died, and left his wife and sons alone.

His wife was named Naomi and her name meant pleasant. The times were not pleasant.

Naomi's sons married women from Moab, one named Orpah and the other named Ruth. Despite their father's untimely death, the boys spent ten happy years with their new wives. But the men of that family had very poor luck. Both sons died.

There was nothing left for Naomi in Moab and so she packed up her house and prepared to return to Judah. She told her daughters-in-law, "Go home to your mothers. You were always kind to my sons and you've always been kind to me. May Hashem be kind to you in return."

She kissed them goodbye, but the girls wept.

They said, "Can't we return to Judah with you?"

"Go back to your mothers," Naomi repeated. "I have no more sons for you to marry. What can I give if you stay with me?"

The girls continued to weep, but at last sensible Orpah kissed her mother-in-law and left for home.

Ruth, who was less sensible; Ruth, who was more loving; Ruth, who was more kind; Ruth, she would not go.

"Don't make me leave you," Ruth said. "Wherever you go, I will go. Wherever you lodge, I will lodge. Your people will be my people and your G-d my G-d."

When Naomi saw that Ruth was committed to staying with her, she abandoned her arguing and let her come.

They traveled together to Bethlehem. When they arrived, they found that the whole city had gathered to see them. Everyone was curious about the two women traveling from Moab. One woman asked, "Naomi! Is that you?"

Naomi shook her head. "Don't call me Naomi. There is no pleasantness in my life. Call me Mara, which means bitterness, for the Almighty has dealt very bitterly with me."

Through the bitterness, Ruth stayed. While Naomi became Mara, Ruth stayed. Ruth gave her kindness, and Ruth stayed.

Jakub met Meryem while he was in Cleveland for a robotics conference. He'd attended dozens, but somehow this one made him feel particularly self-conscious in his cheap suit and tie among all the wealthy *goyim*.

By then he was living in the United States, but although he'd been born there, he rarely felt at home among its people. Between talks, he escaped from the hotel to go walking. That afternoon, he found his way to a path that wound through a park, making its way through dark-branched trees that waved their remaining leaves like flags of ginger, orange and gold.

Meryem sat on an ironwork bench beside a man-made lake, its water silvered with dusk. She wore a black felt coat that made her look pallid even though her cheeks were pink with cold. A wind rose as Jakub approached, rippling through Meryem's hair. Crows took off from the trees, disappearing into black marks on the horizon.

Neither of them was ever able to remember how they began to converse. Their courtship seemed to rise naturally from the lake and the crows and the fallen leaves, as if it were another inevitable element of nature. It was *bashert*.

Meryem was younger than Jakub, but even so, already ballet had begun taking its toll on her body. Ballet was created by trading pain for beauty, she used to say. Eventually, beauty vanished and left only the pain.

Like Jakub, Meryem was an immigrant. Her grandparents had been born in Baghdad where they lived through the *farhud* instead of the *shoah*. They stayed in Iraq despite the pogroms until the founding of Israel made it too dangerous to remain. They abandoned their family home and fled to the U.S.S.R.

When Meryem was small, the Soviet government identified her talent for dance and took her into training. Ballet became her new family. It was her blood and bone, her sacred and her profane.

Her older brother sometimes sent letters, but with the accretion of time and distance, Meryem came to think of her family as if they were not so much people as they were the words spelled out in Yusuf's spidery handwriting.

Communism fell, and Meryem's family was given the opportunity to reclaim her, but even a few years away is so much of a child's lifetime. She begged them not to force her to return. They no longer felt like her home. More, ballet had become the gravitational center of her life, and while she still resented it—how it had taken her unwillingly, how it bruised her feet and sometimes made them bleed—she also could not bear to leave its orbit. When Yusuf's letters stopped coming some time later, she hardly noticed.

She danced well. She was a lyrical ballerina, performing her roles with tender, affecting beauty that could make audiences weep or smile. She rapidly moved from corps to soloist to principal. The troupe traveled overseas to perform Stravinsky's *Firebird*, and when they reached the United States, Meryem decided to emigrate, which she accomplished with a combination of bribes and behind-the-scenes dealings. Jakub and Meryem recognized themselves in each other's stories. Like his grandparents, they were drawn together by their similarities. Unlike them, they built a refuge together instead of a battlefield.

After Meryem died, Jakub began dreaming that that the numbers were inscribed into the skins of people who'd never been near the camps. His skin. His daughter's. His wife's. They were all marked, as Cain was marked, as the Christians believed the devil would mark his followers at the end of time. Marked for diaspora, to blow away from each other and disappear.

"Is the doll awake?" Mara asked one morning.

Jakub looked up from his breakfast to see her leaning against the doorway that led into the kitchen. She wore a large t-shirt from Yellowstone that came to her knees, covering a pair of blue jeans that had not been baggy when he'd bought them for her. Her skin was wan and her eyes shadowed and sunken. Traces of inflammation from the drugs lingered, painfully red, on her face and hands. The orange knit cap pulled over her ears was incongruously bright.

Jakub could not remember the last time she'd worn something other than pajamas.

"She is down in the workshop," Jakub said.

"She's awake, though?"

"She is awake."

"Bring her up."

Jakub set his spoon beside his leftover bowl of *chlodnik*. Mara's mouth was turned down at the corners, hard and resolute. She lifted her chin at a defiant angle.

"She has a bed in the workshop," Jakub said. "There are still tests I must run. It's best she stay close to the machines."

Mara shook her head. It was clear from her face that she was no more taken in by his lie than the new child had been. "It's not fair to keep someone stuck down there."

Jakub began to protest that the workshop was not such a bad place, but then he caught the flintiness in Mara's eyes and realized that she was not asking out of worry. She had dressed as best she could and come to confront him because she wanted her first encounter with the new child to be on her terms. There was much he could not give her, but he could give her that.

"I will bring her for dinner," he said. "Tomorrow, for Shabbat."

Mara nodded. She began the arduous process of departing the kitchen, but then stopped and turned back. "Abba," she said hesitantly. "If ima hated the ballet, why did you build her a studio?"

"She asked for one," Jakub said.

Mara waited.

At last, he continued, "Ballet was part of her. She could not simply stop."

Mara nodded once more. This time, she departed.

Jakub finished his *chlodnik* and spent the rest of the day cooking. He meted out ingredients for familiar dishes. A pinch, a dash, a dab. Chopping, grating, boiling, sampling. Salt and sweet, bitter and savory.

As he went downstairs to fetch Ruth, he found himself considering how strange it must be for her to remember these rooms and yet never to have entered them. Jakub and Meryem had drawn the plans for the house together. She'd told him that she was content to leave a world of beauty that was made by pain, in exchange for a plain world made by joy.

He'd said he could give her that.

They painted the outside walls yellow to remind them of the sun during the winter, and painted blue inside to remind them of the sky. By the time they had finished, Mara was waiting inside Meryem's womb. The three of them had lived in the house for seven years before Meryem died.

These past few weeks had been precious. Precious because he had, in some ways, finally begun to recover the daughter that he had lost on the day her leg shattered—Ruth, once again curious and strong and insightful, like the Mara he had always known. But precious, too, because these were his last days with the daughter he'd made with Meryem.

Precious days, but hardly bearable, even as he also could not bear that they would pass. Precious, but more salt and bitter than savory and sweet.

The next night, when Jakub entered the workshop, he found Ruth on the stool where she'd sat so long when she was empty. Her shoulders slumped; her head hung down. He began to worry that something was wrong, but then he saw that she was only reading the book of poetry that she held in her lap.

"Would you like to come upstairs for dinner?" Jakub asked.

Setting the poems aside, Ruth rose to join him.

Long before Jakub met Meryem—back in those days when he still traveled the country on commissions from the American government—Jakub had become friends with a rabbi from Minneapolis. The two still exchanged letters through the postal mail, rarefied and expensive as it was.

After Jakub sent the news from Doctor Pinsky, the rabbi wrote back, "First your wife and now your daughter . . . *es vert mir finster in di oygen*. You must not let yourself be devoured by *agmes-nefesh*. Even in the camps, people kept hope. *Yashir koyech*, my friend. You must keep hope, too."

Jakub had not written to the rabbi about the new child. Even if it had not been vital for him to keep the work secret, he would not have written about it. He could not be sure what the rabbi would say. Would he call the new child a golem instead of a girl? Would he declare the work unseemly or unwise?

But truly, Jakub was only following the rabbi's advice. The new child was his strength and hope. She would prevent him from being devoured by sorrow.

When Jakub and Ruth arrived in the kitchen for Shabbat, Mara had not yet come.

They stood alone together in the empty room. Jakub had mopped the floors and scrubbed the counters and set the table with good dishes. The table was laid with challah, apricot chicken with farfel, and almond and raisin salad. *Cholent* simmered in a crock pot on the counter, waiting for Shabbat lunch.

Ruth started toward Mara's chair on the left. Jakub caught her arm, more roughly than he'd meant to. He pulled back, contrite. "No," he said softly. "Not there." He gestured to the chair on the right. Resentment crossed the new child's face, but she went to sit.

It was only as Jakub watched Ruth lower herself into the right-hand chair that he realized his mistake. "No! Wait. Not in Meryem's chair. Take mine. I'll switch with you—"

Mara's crutches clicked down the hallway. It was too late.

She paused in the doorway. She wore the blonde wig Jakub had bought for her after the targeted immersion therapy failed. Last year's green *Pesach* dress hung off of her shoulders. The cap sleeves neared her elbows.

Jakub moved to help with her crutches. She stayed stoic while he helped her sit, but he could see how much it cost her to accept assistance while she was trying to maintain her dignity in front of the new child. It would be worse because the new child possessed her memories and knew precisely how she felt.

Jakub leaned the crutches against the wall. Ruth looked away, embarrassed.

Mara gave her a corrosive stare. "Don't pity me."

Ruth looked back. "What do you want me to do?"

"Turn yourself off," said Mara. "You're *muktzeh*."

Jakub wasn't sure he'd ever before heard Mara use the Hebrew word for objects forbidden on the Sabbath. Now, she enunciated it with crisp cruelty.

Ruth remained calm. "One may work on the Sabbath if it saves a life."

Mara scoffed. "If you call yours a life."

Jakub wrung his hands. "Please, Mara," he said. "You asked her to come."

Mara held her tongue for a lingering moment. Eventually, she nodded formally toward Ruth. "I apologize."

Ruth returned the nod. She sat quietly, hands folded in her lap. She didn't take nutrition from food, but Jakub had given her a hollow stomach that she could empty after meals so she would be able to eat socially. He waited to see if she would return Mara's insults, but she was the old Mara, the one who wasn't speared with pain and fear, the one who let bullies wind themselves up if that was what they wanted to do.

Jakub looked between the girls. "Good," he said. "We should have peace for the Sabbath."

He went to the head of the table. It was late for the blessing, the sun skimming the horizon behind bare, black trees. He lit the candles and waved his hands over the flames to welcome Shabbat. He covered his eyes as he recited the blessing. *"Barukh atah Adonai, Elohaynu, melekh ha-olam . . . "*

Every time he said the words that should have been Meryem's, he remembered the way she had looked when she said them. Sometimes she peeked out from behind her fingers so that she could watch Mara. They were small, her hands, delicate like bird wings. His were large and blunt.

The girls stared at each other as Jakub said kaddish. After they washed their hands and tore the challah, Jakub served the chicken and the salad. Both children ate almost nothing and said even less.

"It's been a long time since we've had three for Shabbat," Jakub said. "Perhaps we can have a good *vikuekh*. Mara, I saw you reading my Simic? Ruth has been reading poetry, too. Haven't you, Ruth?"

Ruth shifted the napkin in her lap. "Yehuda Amichai," she said. *"Even a Fist Was once an Open Palm with Fingers."*

"I love the first poem in that book," Jakub said. "I was reading it when—"

Mara's voice broke in, so quietly that he almost didn't hear. "Ruth?"

Jakub looked to Ruth. The new child stared silently down at her hands. Jakub cleared his throat, but she did not look up.

Jakub answered for her. "Yes?"

Mara's expression was slack, somewhere between stunned and lifeless. "You named her Ruth."

"She is here for you. As Ruth was there for Mara."

Mara began to cry. It was a tiny, pathetic sound. She pushed away her plate and tossed her napkin onto the table. "How could you?"

"Ruth gives *hesed* to Mara," Jakub said. "When everyone else left, Ruth stayed by her side. She expected nothing from her loving, from her kindness."

"Du kannst nicht auf meinem rucken pishen unt mir sagen class es regen ist," Mara said bitterly.

Jakub had never heard Mara say that before either. The crass proverb sounded wrong in her mouth. "Please, I am telling you the truth," he said. "I wanted her name to be part of you. To come from your story. The story of Mara."

"Is that what I am to you?" Mara asked. "Bitterness?"

"No, no. Please, no. We never thought you were bitterness. Mara was the name Meryem chose. Like Maruska, the Russian friend she left behind." Jakub paused. "Please. I did not mean to hurt you. I thought the story would help you see. I wanted you to understand. The new child will not harm you. She'll show you *hesed*."

Mara flailed for her crutches.

Jakub stood to help. Mara was so weak that she accepted his assistance. Tears flowed down her face. She left the room as quickly as she could, refusing to look at either Jakub or the new child.

Jakub looked between her retreating form and Ruth's silent one. The new child's expression was almost as unsure as Jakub's.

"Did you know?" Jakub asked. "Did you know how she'd feel?"

Ruth turned her head as if turning away from the question. "Talk to her," she said quietly. "I'll go back down to the basement."

Mara sat on her bed, facing the snow. Jakub stood at the threshold. She spoke without turning. "*Hesed* is a hard thing," she said. "Hard to take when you can't give it back."

Jakub crossed the room, past the chair he'd made her when she was little, with Meryem's shawl hung over the back; past the hanging marionette dressed as Giselle; past the cube Mara used for her lessons in attic space. He sat beside her on her white quilt and looked at her silhouetted form against the white snow.

She leaned back toward him. Her body was brittle and delicate against his chest. He remembered sitting on that bed with Mara and Meryem, reading stories, playing with toys. *Tsuris, tsuris.* Life was all so fragile. He was not graceful enough to keep it from breaking.

Mara wept. He held his *bas-yekhide* in his large, blunt hands.

Act III: Ruth

Échappé

(Escape)

At first, Ruth couldn't figure out why she didn't want to switch herself off. Mara had reconciled herself to Ruth's existence, but in her gut, she still wanted Ruth to be gone. And Ruth was Mara, so she should have felt the same.

But no, her experiences were diverging. Mara wanted the false daughter to vanish. Mara thought Ruth was the false daughter, but Ruth knew she wasn't false at all. She was Mara. Or had been.

Coming into existence was not so strange. She felt no peculiar doubling, no sensation that her hands weren't hers, no impression that she had been pulled out of time and was supposed to be sleeping upstairs with her face turned toward the window.

She felt more secure in the new body than she had in Mara's. This body was healthy, even round in places. Her balance was steady; her fingernails were pink and intact.

After abba left her the first night, Ruth found a pane of glass that he'd set aside for one of his projects. She stared at her blurred reflection. The glass showed soft, smooth cheeks. She ran her fingers over them and they confirmed that her skin was downy now instead of sunken. Clear eyes stared back at her.

Over the past few months, Mara had grown used to experiencing a new alienation every time she looked in the mirror. She'd seen a parade of strangers' faces, each dimmer and hollower than the last.

Her face was her own again.

She spent her first days doing tests. Abba watched her jump and stretch and run on a treadmill. For hours upon hours, he recorded her answers to his questions.

It was tedious for her, but abba was fascinated by her every word and movement. Sometimes he watched as a father. Sometimes he watched as a scientist. At first Ruth chafed under his experimental gaze, but then she remembered that he had treated Mara like that, too. He'd liked to set up simple experiments to compare her progress to child development manuals. She remembered ima complaining that he'd been even worse when Mara was an infant. Ruth supposed this was the same. She'd been born again.

While he observed her, she observed him. Abba forgot that some experiments could look back.

The abba she saw was a different man than the one she remembered sitting with Mara. He'd become brooding with Mara as she grew sicker. His grief had become a deep anger with G-d. He slammed doors and cabinets, and grimaced with bitter fury when he thought she wasn't looking. He wanted to break the world.

He still came down into the basement with that fury on his face, but as he talked to Ruth, he began to calm. The muscles in his forehead relaxed. He smiled now and then. He reached out to touch her hand, gently, as if she were a soap bubble that might break if he pressed too hard.

Then he went upstairs, back to that other Mara.

"Don't go yet," Ruth would beg. "We're almost done. It won't take much longer."

He'd linger.

She knew he thought she was just bored and wanted attention. But that wasn't why she asked. She hated the storm that darkened his eyes when he went up to see the dying girl.

After a few minutes, he always said the same thing, resolute and loyal to his still-living child. "I must go, *nu?*"

He sent Abel down in his place. The dog thumped down and waited for her to greet him at the foot of the stairs. He whuffed hello, breath humid and smelly.

Ruth had been convinced—when she was Mara—that a dog would never show affection for a robot. Maybe Abel only liked Ruth because his sense of smell, like the rest of him, was in decline. Whatever the reason, she was Mara enough for him.

Ruth ran the treadmill while Abel watched, tail wagging. She thought about chasing him across the snowy yard, about breaking sticks off of the bare-branched trees to throw for him. She could do anything. She could run; she could dance; she could swim; she could ride. She could almost forgive abba for treating her like a prototype instead of a daughter, but she couldn't forgive him for keeping her penned. The real Mara was stuck in the house, but Ruth didn't have to be. It wasn't fair to have spent so long static, waiting to die, and then suddenly be free—and still remain as trapped as she'd ever been.

After the disastrous Shabbat, she went back down to the basement and sat on one of abba's workbenches. Abel came down after her. He leaned against her knees, warm and heavy. She patted his head.

She hadn't known how Mara was going to react.

She should have known. She would have known if she'd thought about it. But she hadn't considered the story of Mara and Ruth. All she'd been thinking about was that Ruth wasn't her name.

Their experiences had branched off. They were like twins who'd shared the womb only to be delivered into a world where each new event was a small alienation, until their individual experiences separated them like a chasm.

One heard a name and wanted her own back. One heard a name and saw herself as bitterness.

One was living. One was dying.

She was still Mara enough to feel the loneliness of it.

The dog's tongue left a trail of slobber across the back of her hand. He pushed his head against her. He was warm and solid, and she felt tears threatening, and wasn't sure why. It might have been grief for Mara. Perhaps it was just the unreasonable relief that someone still cared about her. Even though it was miserly to crave attention when Mara was dying, she still felt the gnaw of wondering whether abba would still love her when Mara was gone, or whether she'd become just a machine to him, one more painful reminder.

She jumped off of the table and went to sit in the dark, sheltered place beneath it. There was security in small places—in closets, under beds, beneath the desk in her room. Abel joined her, pushing his side against hers. She curled around him and switched her brain to sleep.

After Shabbat, there was no point in separating Ruth and Mara anymore. Abba told Ruth she could go wherever she wanted. He asked where she wanted to sleep. "We can put a mattress in the parlor," he said. When she didn't react, he added, "Or the studio . . . ?"

She knew he didn't want her in the studio. Mara was mostly too tired to leave her room now, but abba would want to believe that she was still sneaking into the studio to watch ima's videos.

Ruth wanted freedom, but it didn't matter where she slept.

"I'll stay in the basement," she said.

When she'd had no choice but to stay in the basement, she'd felt like a compressed coil that might spring uncontrollably up the stairs at any moment. Now that she was free to move around, it didn't seem so urgent. She could take her time a little, choose those moments when going upstairs wouldn't make things worse, such as when abba and Mara were both asleep, or when abba was sitting with Mara in her room.

Once she'd started exploring, she realized it was better that she was on her own anyway. Moving through the house was dreamlike, a strange blend of familiarity and alienation. These were rooms she knew like her skin, and yet she, as Ruth, had never entered them. The handprint impressed into the clay tablet on the wall wasn't hers; it was Mara's. She could remember the texture of the clay as she pushed in her palm, but it hadn't been her palm. She had never sat at the foot of the plush, red chair in the parlor while ima brushed her hair. The scuff marks on the hardwood in the hallway were from someone else's shoes.

As she wandered from room to room, she realized that on some unconscious level, when she'd been Mara, she'd believed that moving into a robotic body would clear the haze of memories that hung in the house. She'd imagined a robot would be a mechanical, sterile thing. In reality, ima still haunted the kitchen where she'd cooked, and the studio where she'd danced, and the bathroom where she'd died.

Change wasn't exorcism.

Ruth remained restless. She wanted more than the house. For the first time in months, she found herself wanting to visit attic space, even though her flock was even worse about handling cancer than adults, who were bad enough. The pity in Collin's eyes, especially, had made her want to puke so much that she hadn't even let herself think about him. Mara had closed the door on her best friend early in the process of closing the doors on her entire life.

She knew abba would be skeptical, though, so she wanted to bring it up in a way that seemed casual. She waited for him to come down to the workshop for her daily exam, and tried to broach the subject as if it were an afterthought.

"I think I should go back to the attic," she ventured. "I'm falling behind. My flock is moving on without me."

Abba looked up from the screen, frowning. He worried his hands in a way that had become troublingly familiar. "They know Mara is sick."

"I'll pretend to be sick," Ruth said. "I can fake it."

She'd meant to sound detached, as if her interest in returning to school was purely pragmatic, but she couldn't keep the anticipation out of her tone.

"I should go back now before it's been too long," she said. "I can pretend I'm starting to feel better. We don't want my recovery to look too sudden."

"It is not a good idea," abba said. "It would only add another complication. If you did not pretend correctly? If people noticed? You are still new-made. Another few weeks and you will know better how to control your body."

"I'm bored," Ruth said. Making another appeal to his scholarly side, she added, "I miss studying."

"You can study. You've been enjoying the poetry, yes? There is so much for you to read."

"It's not the same." Ruth knew she was on the verge of whining, but she couldn't make her voice behave.

Abba paused, trepidation playing over his features as he considered his response. "Ruth, I have thought on this . . . I do not think it is good for you to go back to attic space. They will know you. They might see that something is wrong. We will find you another program for home learning."

Ruth stared. "You want me to leave attic space?" Almost everyone she knew, apart from abba and a few people in town, was from the attic. After a moment's thought, the implications were suddenly leaden in her mind. "You don't just want me to stop going for school, do you? You want me to stop seeing them at all."

Abba's mouth pursed around words he didn't want to say.

"Everyone?" asked Ruth. "Collin? Everyone?"

Abba wrung his hands. "I am sorry, Mara. I only want to protect you."

"Ruth!" Ruth said.

"Ruth," abba murmured. "Please. I am sorry, Ruthele."

Ruth swallowed hard, trying to push down sudden desperation. She hadn't wanted the name. She didn't want the name. But she didn't want to be confused for the Mara upstairs either. She wanted him to be there with *her*, talking to *her*.

"You can't keep me stuck here just because she is!" she said, meaning the words to bite. "She's the one who's dying. Not me."

Abba flinched. "You are so angry," he said quietly. "I thought, now that you were well—You did not used to be so angry."

"You mean Mara didn't used to be so angry," Ruth said. A horrible thought struck her and she felt cold that she hadn't thought of it before. "How am I going to grow up? Am I going to be stuck like this? Eleven, like she is, forever?"

"No, Ruth, I will build you new bodies," said abba. "Bodies are easy. It is the mind that is difficult."

"You just want me to be like her," Ruth said.

Abba fumbled for words. "I want you to be yourself."

"Then let me go do things! You can't hide me here forever."

"Please, Ruth. A little patience."

Patience!

Ruth swung off of the stool. The connectors in her wrist and neck tore loose and she threw them to the floor. She ran for the stairs, crashing into one of the diagnostic machines and knocking it over before making it to the bottom step.

Abba said nothing. Behind her, she heard the small noise of effort that he made as he lowered himself to the floor to retrieve the equipment.

It was strange to feel such bright-hot anger again. Like abba, she'd thought that the transfer had restored her even temper. But apparently the anger she'd learned while she was Mara couldn't just be forgotten.

She spent an hour pacing the parlor, occasionally grabbing books off of a shelf, flipping through them as she walked, and then putting them down in random locations. The brightness of the anger faded, although the sense of injustice remained.

Later, abba came up to see her. He stood with mute pleading, not wanting to reopen the argument but obviously unable to bear continuing to fight.

Even though Ruth hadn't given in yet, even though she was still burning from the unfairness, she couldn't look into his sad eyes without feeling thickness in her throat.

He gestured helplessly. "I just want to keep you safe, Ruthele."

They sat together on the couch without speaking. They were both entrenched in their positions. It seemed to Ruth that they were both trying to figure out how to make things right without giving in, how to keep fighting without wounding.

Abel paced between them, shoving his head into Ruth's lap, and then into abba's, back and forth. Ruth patted his head and he lingered with her a moment, gazing up with rheumy but devoted eyes.

Arguing with abba wasn't going to work. He hadn't liked her taking risks before she'd gotten sick, but afterward, keeping her safe had become obsession, which was why Ruth was even alive. He was a scientist, though; he liked evidence. She'd just have to show him it was safe.

Ruth didn't like to lie, but she'd do it. In a tone of grudging acceptance, she said, "You're right. It's too risky for me to go back."

"We will find you new friends," abba said. "We will be together. That's what is important."

Ruth bided her time for a few days. Abba might have been watching her more closely if he hadn't been distracted with Mara. Instead, when he wasn't at Mara's bedside or examining Ruth, he drifted mechanically through the house, registering little.

Ruth had learned a lot about engineering from watching her father. Attic space wasn't complicated technology. The program came on its own cube which meant it was entirely isolated from the household AI and its notification protocols. It also came with standard parental access points that had been designed to favor ease of use over security—which meant there were lots of back-end entryways.

Abba didn't believe in restricting access to knowledge so he'd made it even easier by deactivating the nanny settings on Mara's box as soon as she was old enough to navigate attic space on her own.

Ruth waited until nighttime when Mara was drifting in and out of her fractured, painful sleep, and abba had finally succumbed to exhaustion. Abba had left a light on in the kitchen, but it didn't reach the hallway to Mara's room, which fell in stark shadow. Ruth felt her way to Mara's threshold and put her ear to the door. She could hear the steady, sleeping rhythm of Mara's breath inside.

She cracked the door. Moonlight spilled from the window over the bed, allowing her to see inside. It was the first time she'd seen the room in her new body. It looked the same as it had. Mara was too sick to fuss over books or possessions, and so the objects sat in their places, ordered but dusty. Apart from the lump that Mara's body made beneath the quilt, the room looked as if it could have been abandoned for days.

The attic space box sat on a low shelf near the door. It fit in the palm of Ruth's hand. The fading image on its exterior showed the outline of a house with people inside, rendered in a style that was supposed to look like a child's drawing. It was the version they put out for five-year-olds. Abba had never replaced it. A waste of money, he said, when he could upgrade it himself.

Ruth looked up at the sound of blankets shifting. One of Mara's hands slipped free from the quilt. Her fingers dangled over the side of the bed, the knuckles exaggerated on thin bones. Inflamed cuticles surrounded her ragged nails.

Ruth felt a sting of revulsion and chastised herself. Those hands had been hers. She had no right to be repulsed.

The feeling faded to an ache. She wanted to kneel by the bed and take Mara's hand into her own. She wanted to give Mara the shelter and empathy that abba had built her to give. But she knew how Mara felt about her. Taking Mara's hand would not be *hesed*. The only loving kindness she could offer now was to leave.

As Ruth sat in ima's studio, carefully disassembling the box's hardware so that she could jury-rig it to interact with the television, it occurred to her that abba would have loved helping her with this project. He loved scavenging old technology. He liked to prove that cleverness could make tools of anything.

The complicated VR equipment that made it possible to immerse in attic space was far too bulky for Ruth to steal from Mara's room without being caught. She thought she could recreate a sketchy, winnowed down version of the experience using low technology replacements from the television and other scavenged equipment. Touch, smell and taste weren't going to happen, but an old stereo microphone allowed her to transmit on the voice channel. She found a way to instruct the box to send short bursts of visuals to the television, although the limited scope and speed would make it like walking down a hallway illuminated by a strobe light.

She sat cross-legged on the studio floor and logged in. It was the middle of the night, but usually at least someone from the flock was around. She was glad to see it was Collin this time, tweaking an experiment with crystal growth. Before she'd gotten sick, Ruth probably would have been there with him. They liked going in at night when there weren't many other people around.

She saw a still of Collin's hand over a delicate formation, and then another of him looking up, startled. "Mara?" he asked. "Is that you?"

His voice cracked when he spoke, sliding from low to high. It hadn't been doing that before.

"Hi, Collin," she said.

"Your avatar looks weird." She could imagine Collin squinting to investigate her image, but the television continued to show his initial look of surprise.

She was using a video skin capture from the last time Mara had logged in, months ago. Without a motion reader, it was probably just standing there, breathing and blinking occasionally, with no expression on its face.

"I'm on a weird connection," Ruth said.

"Is it because you're sick?" Collin's expression of concern flashed onscreen. "Can I see what you really like? It's okay. I've seen videos. I won't be grossed out or anything. I missed you. I thought—we weren't sure you were coming back. We were working on a video to say goodbye."

Ruth shifted uncomfortably. She'd wanted to go the attic so she could get on with living, not to be bogged down in dying. "I don't want to talk about that."

The next visual showed a flash of Colin's hand, blurred with motion as he raised it to his face. "We did some stuff with non-Newtonian fluids," he said tentatively. "You'd have liked it. We got all gross."

"Did you throw them around?" she asked.

"Goo fight," Collin agreed. He hesitated. "Are you coming back? Are you better?"

"Well—" Ruth began.

"Everyone will want to know you're here. Let me ping them."

"No. I just want to talk to you."

A new picture: Collin moving closer to her avatar, his face now crowding the narrow rectangle of her vision.

"I looked up osteosarcoma. They said you had lung nodules. Mara, are you really better? Are you really coming back?"

"I said I don't want to talk about it."

"But everyone will want to know."

Suddenly, Ruth wanted to be anywhere but attic space. Abba was right. She couldn't go back. Not because someone might find out but because everyone was going to want to know, what about Mara? They were going to want to know about Mara all the time. They were going to want to drag Ruth back into that sick bed, with her world narrowing toward death, when all she wanted was to move on.

And it was even worse now than it would have been half an hour ago, before she'd gone into Mara's room and seen her raw, tender hand, and thought about what it would be like to grasp it.

"I have to go," Ruth said.

"At least let me ping Violet," Collin said.

"I'll be back," Ruth answered. "I'll see you later."

On the television: Collin's skeptical face, brows drawn, the shine in his eyes that showed he thought she was lying.

"I promise," she said, hesitating only a moment before she tore the attic space box out of her jury-rigged web of wires.

Tears were filling her eyes and she couldn't help the sob. She threw the box. It skittered across the wooden floor until it smacked into the mirror. The thing was so old and knocked about that any hard collision might kill it, but what did that matter now? She wasn't going back.

She heard a sound from the doorway and looked up. She saw abba, standing behind the cracked door.

Ruth's anger flashed to a new target. "Why are you spying on me?"

"I came to check on Mara," abba said.

He didn't have to finish for his meaning to be clear. He'd heard someone in the studio and hoped it could still be his Marale.

He made a small gesture toward the attic space box. "It did not go well," he said quietly, statement rather than question.

Ruth turned her head away. He'd been right, about everything he'd said, all the explicit things she'd heard, and all the implicit things she hadn't wanted to.

She pulled her knees toward her chest. "I can't go back," she said.

Abba stroked her hair. "I know."

The loss of attic space hurt less than she'd thought it would. Mara had sealed off those tender spaces, and those farewells had a final ring. She'd said goodbye to Collin a long time ago.

What bothered her more was the lesson it forced; her life was never going to be the same, and there was no way to deny it. Mara would die and be gone, and Ruth had to learn to be Ruth, whoever Ruth was. That was what had scared Mara about Ruth in the first place.

The restlessness that had driven her into attic space still itched her. She started taking walks in the snow with Abel. Abba didn't try to stop her.

She stopped reading Jewish poetry and started picking up books on music theory. She practiced sight reading and toe-tapped the beats, imagining choreographies.

Wednesdays, when abba planned the menu for Shabbat, Ruth sat with him as he wrote out the list he would take to Gerry's on Thursday. As he imagined dishes, he talked about how Mara would like the honey he planned to infuse in the carrots, or the raisins and figs he would cook with the rice. He wondered what they should talk about—poetry, physics, international politics—changing his mind as new topics occurred to him.

Ruth wondered how he kept hoping. As Mara, she'd always known her boundaries before abba realized them. As Ruth, she knew, as clearly as Mara must, that Mara would not eat with them.

Perhaps it was cruel not to tell him, but to say it felt even crueler.

On a Thursday while abba was taking the truck to town, Ruth was looking through ima's collection of sheet music in the parlor when she heard the click of crutches down the hall. She turned to find Mara was behind her, breathing heavily.

"Oh," said Ruth. She tried to hide the surprise in her voice but failed.

"You didn't think I could get up on my own."

Mara's voice was thin.

"I . . . " Ruth began before catching the angry look of resolution on Mara's face. "No. I didn't."

"Of course not," Mara said bitterly. She began another sentence, but was interrupted by a ragged exhalation as she started to collapse against the wall. Ruth rushed to support her. Mara accepted her assistance without acknowledging it, as if it were beneath notice.

"Are you going to throw up?" Ruth asked quietly.

"I'm off the chemo."

Mara's weight fell heavily on Ruth's shoulder. She shifted her balance, determined not to let Mara slip.

"Let me take you back to bed," Ruth said.

Mara answered, "I wanted to see you again."

"I'll take you. We can talk in there."

Ruth took Mara's silence as assent. Abandoning the crutches, she supported Mara's weight as they headed back into the bedroom. In daylight, the room looked too bright, its creams and whites unsullied.

Mara's heaving eased as Ruth helped her into the bed, but her lungs were still working hard. Ruth waited until her breathing came evenly.

Ruth knelt by the bed, the way abba always had, and then wondered if that was a mistake. Mara might see Ruth as trying to establish power over her. She ducked her gaze for a moment, the way Abel might if he were ashamed, hoping Mara would see she didn't mean to challenge her.

"What did you want to say to me?" Ruth asked. "It's okay if you want to yell."

"Be glad," Mara said, "That you didn't have to go this far."

Mara's gaze slid down Ruth's face. It slowly took in her smooth skin and pink cheeks.

Ruth opened her mouth to respond, but Mara continued.

"It's a black hole. It takes everything in. You can see yourself falling. The universe doesn't look like it used to. Everything's blacker. So much blacker. And you know when you've hit the moment when you can't escape. You'll never do anything but fall."

Ruth extended her hand toward Mara's, the way she'd wanted to the other night, but stopped before touching her. She fumbled for something to say.

Flatly, Mara said, "I am glad at least someone will get away."

With great effort, she turned toward the window.

"Go away now."

She shouldn't have, but Ruth stood at the door that night when abba went in to check on Mara. She watched him kneel by the bed and take her hand. Mara barely moved in response, still staring out the window, but her fingers tensed around his, clutching him. Ruth remembered the way abba's hand had felt when she was sleepless and in pain, a solid anchor in a fading world.

She thought of what abba had said to her when she was still Mara, and made silent promises to the other girl. *I will keep you and hold you. I will protect you. I will always have your hand in mine.*

In the morning, when Ruth came back upstairs, she peeked through the open door to see abba still there beside Mara, lying down instead of kneeling, his head pillowed on the side of her mattress.

She walked back down the hallway and to the head of the stairs. Drumming on her knees, she called for Abel. He lumbered toward her, the thump of his tail reassuringly familiar. She ruffled his fur and led him into the parlor where she slipped on his leash.

Wind chill took the outside temperature substantially below freezing, but she hesitated before putting on her coat. She ran her hand across the "skin" of her arm. It was robotic skin, not human skin. She'd looked at some of the schematics that abba had left around downstairs and started to wonder about how different she really was from a human. He'd programmed her to feel vulnerable to cold, but was she really?

She put the coat back on its hook and led Abel out the door. Immediately, she started shivering, but she ignored the bite. She wanted to know what she could do.

She trudged across the yard to the big, bony oak. She snapped off a branch, made Abel sit while she unhooked his leash, and threw the branch as far as she could. Abel's dash left dents in the snow. He came back to her, breath a warm relief on her hand, the branch slippery with slobber.

She threw it again and wondered what she could achieve if abba hadn't programmed her body to think it was Mara's. He'd given her all of Mara's limits. She could run as fast as Mara, but not faster. Calculate as accurately as Mara, but no moreso.

Someday, she and abba would have to talk about that.

She tossed the stick again, and Abel ran, and again, and again, until he was too tired to continue. He watched the branch fly away as he leaned against Mara's leg for support.

She gave his head a deep scratch. He shivered and he bit at the air near her hand. She realized her cold fingers were hurting him. For her, the cold had ceased to be painful, though she was still shivering now and then.

"Sorry, boy, sorry," she said. She reattached his leash, and watched how, despite the temperature, her fingers moved without any stiffness at all.

She headed back to the house, Abel making pleased whuffing noises to indicate that he approved of their direction. She stopped on the porch to stamp the snow off of her feet. Abel shook himself, likewise, and Ruth quickly dusted off what he'd missed.

She opened the door and Abel bounded in first, Ruth laughing and trying to keep her footing as he yanked on the leash. He was old and much weaker than he had been, but an excited burst of doggy energy could still make her rock. She stumbled in after him, the house dim after her cold hour outside.

Abba was in the parlor, standing by the window from which he'd have been able to see them play. He must have heard them come in, but he didn't look toward her until she tentatively called his name.

He turned and looked her over, surveying her bare arms and hands, but he gave no reaction. She could see from his face that it was over.

He wanted to bury her alone. She didn't argue.

He would plant Mara in the yard, perhaps under the bony tree, but more likely somewhere else in the lonely acreage, unmarked. She didn't know how he planned to dig in the frozen ground, but he was a man of many contraptions. Mara would always be out there, lost in the snow.

When he came back, he clutched her hand as he had clutched Mara's. It was her turn to be what abba had been for Mara, the anchor that kept him away from the lip of the black hole, the one steady thing in a dissolving world.

They packed the house without discussing it. Ruth understood what was happening as soon as she saw abba filling the first box with books. Probably she'd known for some time, on the fringe of her consciousness, that they would have to do this. As they wrapped dishes in tissue paper, and sorted through old papers, they shared silent grief at leaving the yellow house that abba had built with Meryem, and that both Mara and Ruth had lived in all their lives.

Abba had enough money that he didn't need to sell the property. The house would remain owned and abandoned in the coming years.

It was terrible to go, but it also felt like a necessary marker, a border bisecting her life. It was one more way in which she was becoming Ruth.

They stayed in town for one last Shabbat. The process of packing the house had altered their sense of time, making the hours seem foreshortened and stretched at turns.

Thursday passed without their noticing, leaving them to buy their groceries on Friday. Abba wanted to drive into town on his own, but Ruth didn't want him to be alone yet.

Reluctantly, she agreed to stay in the truck when they got there. Though abba had begun to tell people that she was recovering, it would be best if no one got a chance to look at her up close. They might realize something was wrong. It would be easier wherever they moved next; strangers wouldn't always be comparing her to a ghost.

Abba was barely out of the truck before Gerry caught sight of them through the window and came barreling out of the door. Abba tried to get in his way. Rapidly, he stumbled out the excuse that he and Ruth had agreed on, that it was good for her to get out of the house, but she was still too tired to see anyone.

"A minute won't hurt," said Gerry. He pushed past abba. With a huge grin, he knocked on Ruth's window.

Hesitantly, she rolled it down. Gerry crossed his arms on the sill, leaning his head into the vehicle. "Look at you!" he exclaimed. "Your daddy said you were getting better, but just *look* at you!"

Ruth couldn't help but grin. Abel's tail began to thump as he pushed himself into the front seat to get a better look at his favorite snack provider.

"I have to say, after you didn't come the last few weeks . . . " Gerry wiped his eyes with the back of his hand. "I'm just glad to see you, Mara, I really am."

At the sound of the name, Ruth looked with involuntary shock at abba, who gave a sad little smile that Gerry couldn't see. He took a step forward. "Please, Gerry. She needs to rest."

Gerry looked back at him, opened his mouth to argue, and then looked back at Ruth and nodded. "Okay then. But next week, I expect some free cashier work!" He leaned in to kiss her cheek. He smelled of beef and rosemary. "You get yourself back here, Mara. And you keep kicking that cancer in the rear end."

With a glance back at the truck to check that Mara was okay, abba followed Gerry into the store. Twenty minutes later, he returned with two bags of groceries, which he put in the bed of the truck. As he started the engine, he said, "Gerry is a good man. I will miss him." He paused. "But it is better to have you, Mara."

Ruth looked at him with icy surprise, breath caught in her throat.

Her name was her own again. She wasn't sure how she felt about that.

The sky was bronzing when they arrived home.

On the stove, *cholent* simmered, filling the house with its scent. Abba went to check on it before the sun set, and Ruth followed him into the kitchen, preparing to pull out the dishes and the silverware and the table cloth.

He waved her away. "Next time. This week, let me."

Ruth went into ima's studio. She'd hadn't gone inside since the disaster it attic space, and her gaze lingered on the attic box, still lying dead on the floor.

"I'd like to access a DVD of ima's performances," she told the AI. "*Coppélia,* please."

It whirred.

The audience's rumblings began and she instructed the AI to fast-forward until Coppélia was onstage. She held her eyes closed and tipped her head down until it was the moment to snap into life, to let her body flow, fluid and graceful, mimicking the dancer on the screen.

She'd thought it would be cathartic to dance the part of the doll, and in a way it was, but once the moment was over, she surprised herself by selecting another disc instead of continuing. She tried to think of a comedy that she wanted to dance, and surprised herself further by realizing that she wanted to dance a tragedy instead. Mara had needed the comedies, but Ruth needed to feel the ache of grace and sorrow; she needed to feel the pull of the black hole even as she defied its gravity and danced, en pointe, on its edge.

When the light turned violet, abba came to the door, and she followed him into the kitchen. He lit the candles, and she waited for him to begin the prayers, but instead he stood aside.

It took her a moment to understand what he wanted.

"Are you sure?" she asked.

"Please, Marale," he answered.

Slowly, she moved into the space where he should have been standing. The candles burned on the table beneath her. She waved her hands through the heat and thickness of the smoke, and then lifted them to cover her eyes.

She said, *"Barukh atah Adonai, Elohaynu, melekh ha-olam, asher kid'shanu b'mitzvotav, v'tzivanu, l'had'lik neir shel Shabbat."*

She breathed deeply, inhaling the scents of honey and figs and smoke.

"Amein."

She opened her eyes again. Behind her, she heard abba's breathing, and somewhere in the dark of the house, Abel's snoring as he napped in preparation for after-dinner begging. The candles filled her vision as if she'd never seen them before. Bright white and gold flames trembled, shining against the black of the outside sky, so fragile they could be extinguished by a breath.

PERNICIOUS ROMANCE

ROBERT REED

—◆—

There are no suspects.

We know the vehicle was serviced by the school motor pool, but there were numerous locations and intervals where clever hands could have added a malicious device. Subsequent investigations have exonerated university employees as well as the student programmer responsible for the custom software piloting the giant football helmet. Investigations continue, but authorities no longer issue reports, claiming undiminished interest even as the work thins to fewer agencies and skeletal crews.

Even in retrospect, nothing about the football game appears out of the ordinary. Fiercely contested and low scoring, the battle matched every expectation up until halftime. Then the marching band played three numbers—a solid performance, perhaps even inspired. Once the band relinquished the field, the stadium lights were set low, and that was when the giant football helmet, lit up with the school colors, sprinted across the darkened turf, deploying an LED hose in its wake. The tradition was three years old. The competitive game and mild October weather insured that the stands were nearly full. With a flowing, artistic script, the home team's name was being written with the hose. Onlookers assumed a simple malfunction when the helmet stopped on the fifty-yard line. Perhaps seven seconds passed. Unfortunately there is no video recording of the event. A significant EMP event came with the attack, destroying the data from security cameras as well as amateur videos. The entire campus and half of the city were plunged into a prolonged blackout. But using the scorched rubber turf as a marker, it appears that the device, whatever its nature, was set near the back of the helmet, and its detonation consumed both the helmet and golf cart, leaving behind dust but almost no shrapnel.

As a rule, the first victims to "recover" were located in the most distant portions of the stadium. People high above the south end zone were two hundred and twenty yards from the device, give or take. Most would have been watching the darkened field and the progress of their school's helmet. Many would have been yelling out letters. Witnesses willing to discuss the event claim one of two scenarios: A bolt of light fell from the cloudless, moonless sky. "Lightning" is the most common word. "A laser beam" is also popular. But there are other accounts, equally certain, describing a flame or beam leaping up from the ground, presumably when the cart and helmet were vaporized.

Regardless of perpetrators, the attack was immediately blamed on terrorists. That opinion hardened too quickly and too deeply, we believe.

These were enormous energies on display. There is no question about that. Which leaves us to wonder how any terrorist group could have mastered what appears to be a new technology—a set of tools that nobody else understands.

Cold as it sounds, we should feel thankful. In the end, only fifty-eight people were killed directly by the blast, while another thirty-nine succumbed to falls and head wounds. If casualties were the goal, these high-tech murderers could have ignited their weapon late in the first half, while the helmet was parked on the crowded sidelines. Unless of course the device was a demonstration event or a spectacular dud. Numerous public voices have made those bold claims, ignoring the absence of evidence. What is known is that nearly seventy thousand people were inside the stadium. Every survivor lost consciousness, some remaining that way until this day. And as a direct result, our country hasn't seen a major sporting event for sixteen months, and it is the same across most of the world. Nobody wants to risk a repeat of that terrible Saturday night.

Except for a large portion of the victims, that is.

Case Study:

Today MK is a thirty-one-year-old woman, single and employed. As an undergraduate, she played in the school band, and that's why the halftime show was her primary focus. But her little brother waited too long to purchase tickets, and that's why they had the worst possible seats, and that's why they were standing high up in the southern end of stadium, two hundred and twenty-three yards from the blast site.

MK remembers the band's three songs and then the helmet writing PANTHERS across the unlit field. The vehicle stopped while it was crossing the T, which wasn't right, and she immediately turned to her brother. She recalls laughing, telling him that this sort of shit wouldn't have happened when Dr. Kalin was in charge of the band.

MK had played the snare drums, as did her brother after her.

Her brother turned toward her, presumably to respond.

Both saw a brilliant flash of golden light.

Yes, she was sure. The light was definitely gold.

Panther Stadium is a bowl of concrete and steel with oak boards for seats and numerous steel railings. The stadium is quite steep near the top. Several people close to MK fractured their skulls when they collapsed. But in general, surprisingly few of the victims were injured. Evidence shows that the lowest rows felt the effects first, and like a wave dispersing across water, the people above collapsed in a very orderly fashion, falling on the bodies before them.

Intentional or not, that was another factor in the paucity of deaths.

People outside the stadium, including a small portion of the campus police and ambulance attendants, suffered moments of vertigo but never lost consciousness. After perhaps thirty seconds of confusion, those few hundred people entered to discover thousands of motionless, apparently helpless bodies. Yet these victims weren't unconscious, not in any normal sense. Every living person was breathing quickly and deeply, as if doing considerable labor. Some of those early responders reported a smell like perfume. But not everyone. The scope of the disaster and the total blackout led to panic, even among those with emergency training. But one campus police officer, armed with a working flashlight, climbed to the top row of the southern end of the stadium, and that's why she was first to come across a victim who was regaining consciousness.

MK has that distinction.

The officer kneeled over the young woman. MK remembers her rescuer. In fact, she has talked at length about the pain and terror in that stranger's face.

"Are you okay?" the officer asked.

"Yeah," MK said.

In fact, she felt perfectly fine.

The officer held up a hand.

"Three fingers," MK answered, before the question was asked.

Then she sat up on her own power, lightheaded but not disabled. There were thousands of bodies below, not one of them moving. Yet she heard a peculiar sound, diffuse and gray and not quiet, and after a moment she realized how hard everybody was breathing.

"Something's happened," she said calmly.

"A bomb went off," the officer said. "You were knocked unconscious."

"No," MK said.

"Yes," the officer told her. She was still holding up the three fingers, and the hand was trembling. "Every last one you . . . knocked out."

MK said, "No."

"You were," the officer insisted.

"For how long?" MK asked.

The officer tried to make that calculation. But her cellphone was dead, and fear had distorted her sense of time.

"It's been a week," MK guessed.

"A week? Since you fell over?"

"Yes."

"No. It's been fifteen minutes, tops."

MK's brother, BK, was unconscious like the others, and then his breathing slowed. With a sigh, he opened his eyes. His forehead was scraped, but otherwise, he was unharmed and remarkably alert, sitting up beside his sister.

MK touched his wound.

"I didn't see you," she said.

BK agreed. "I didn't see you either."

The officer watched the conversation.

"This cop says fifteen minutes passed."

"That can't be," he began.

"It's been seven days. Almost to the minute, right?"

"No," said BK. Then he closed his eyes, presumably making his own count.

"What happened to the two of you?" the officer asked.

Neither answered.

The officer started to repeat her question.

"Nine days," BK interrupted. "That's how long it was for me."

"Are you certain?" asked the officer.

"Positive," BK said.

Then MK said, "Huh. I wonder why the difference."

But the problem had an easy enough answer. "I was down longer than you," her brother pointed out.

In frustration, the officer snarled, "But what in hell happened to you?"

The siblings glanced at one another.

Then they looked up, and they spoke the same words.

"Love happened," they said.

Elaborate graphs have been produced. Recorded testimonials and secondhand numbers have been plotted against axes that might be useful. Seventy thousand points in space and time will create pictures. For instance, there is a strong inverse correlation between the distance from the bomb and the duration spent being helpless. Spectators in the high seats generally woke that evening, while those closer to the field remained unconscious for days and often far longer. Being inside a restroom or otherwise shielded by concrete reduced the effects, but not as much as we might have guessed. Victims in the lowest seats, particularly those at the fifty-yard line, were slowest to wake. Yet their experiences pale next to the poor souls standing on the field itself—the band members and grounds crew, two teams and coaching staffs. Plus alumni and benefactors who had been given space on the sidelines. Those victims received the full onslaught of a very peculiar weapon, and several dozen died from brain hemorrhages, while others survived but have yet to open their eyes.

On the matter of correlations: There is a weaker but persistent positive correlation between how long someone was senseless and their perception of time.

Five days is the minimum "imaginary" time, while the record holder to date, if believed, is fifty-eight years.

Liquor consumption has no proven role in duration of helplessness or the depth of the experience. And despite rumors, cannabis had at most a minimal negative influence.

But judging by family reactions, genetic components can matter.

At this point, it bears stating that every number is just a number. Mathematical figures seem precise and cleanly rendered, yet in its nature, each number wants to mislead. Tidy graphs belay the scarcity of real data. Seventy thousand subjects were thrown into the same ad hoc experiment. No operative plans were made beforehand. No logistics were set in place. A college city with two major hospitals and minimal equipment for deep-brain analysis was trapped in the most unlikely scenario. Add to that the confounding facts of a wide-scale power outage and the substantial numbers of medical people— first responders and local physicians—trapped with the other victims inside the stadium. Also many key government people were struck down. The state's second-term governor was enjoying one of the luxury booths, which gave him valuable distance. But he was standing over the forty-five-yard line and as a result was left unconscious for many days.

A genuine bomb would have left corpses and living people who knew what to do with corpses.

Broken bones and burns respond predictably to medical tools.

But what can be done with tens of thousands who are incapable of reacting to light or pain, or human voices, or any other reasonable treatment?

What city in this world could handle the crush of so many patients, each wrapped in a condition that doesn't resemble known comas or dream states?

The tragedy is still emerging.

What amazes us, writing from the midst of history, is the heroism of ordinary citizens facing an unexpected foe.

Case study:

SZ is a youthful fifty, a man who enjoyed prestige and responsibility in his lifelong profession. At the time of the attack, he was positioned high above the north forty-five-yard line, apparently standing at the back of a luxury box. State troopers found him within the first hour, and because of his job and important friends, SZ was carried past other victims and placed inside a helicopter that whisked him to the state's premier neurological-care facility.

SZ was the first patient to receive full batteries of tests, including blood work and EEGs and several thorough PET scans.

As such, he enjoys a singular value among his peers.

SZ wasn't comatose or asleep, but characteristics of both states were observed. His body was limp, immune to mild pain and tickles. Loud sounds didn't rouse him. The voices of his wife and children had no visible effect. There was a persistent erection, but it wasn't associated with any normal REM sleep. If not for his arousal and rapid breathing, the man might have appeared dead, but the reality is that he was very far from death.

It bears repeating: Every victim's brain was at work. Trained athletes and world-class dancers make huge metabolic demands on their minds, but SZ's brain consumed more sugar and more oxygen than any brain studied before. No portion of his neurological system was at rest. Each breath supplied just enough air to maintain that fantastic storm of electricity, and because of fears that this middle-aged man would be overtaxed, SZ's breathing was augmented with an oxygen mask.

The treatment may or may not have had a role in his experience.

Frankly, nobody knows what his experience was.

For three weeks, the patient's condition held steady—no improvements or variations in his status. He was made comfortable, his body was hydrated, and once it was shown to be essential, he was fed sugar and proteins. (Starvation was and is an ongoing concern with every victim.) There was no reason to expect SZ to awaken, even after others from the same luxury box had opened their eyes. Three weeks had taught the doctors that they knew very little. After three weeks, even the most rational voice was speculating that a person didn't wake until he was ready.

Twenty-four days after the football game, SZ was ready.

Unless of course he just simply woke up.

His wife was in the room, and by chance, his oldest child. Like every other patient, SZ was lost to the world, attached machines measuring the quick vitals, and then he was back again. This was not the same as waking from deep sleep. His mind was alert, and then he and his body were alert in a different fashion. The only major physical problem were his atrophied muscles. According to a nurse present, SZ tried to sit up but couldn't. Then he spoke to his wife by name, and he smiled at the teenage daughter, and the girl responded by blurting out, "So who did you sleep with?"

By then, the world had learned what happened inside those raging minds— if not in detail, at least as a general rule.

Patients were meeting imaginary lovers and undergoing intense, soul-shaking affairs.

According the nurse, the girl's combative attitude startled SZ's wife.

"Honey," she said.

"I know you were cheating on Mom," the girl said.

SZ tried again to sit up.

The nurse attempted to help him.

"Get your hands off my father," the girl shouted.

"Leave us, please," the wife begged.

Standing in the hallway, the nurse overheard portions of a very difficult conversation. Her sense was that the girl was only voicing her mother's deepest concerns. For years, there had been stories of infidelity involving this very important man. But rumors didn't matter as much as the certainty that his mind—struck helpless by a terrorist attack—was happily engaged in a relationship that had no connection to real people and genuine events.

Beds were still at a premium at that stage in the crisis.

SZ was discharged as quickly as possible, and after several days of rest, appeared in public. His family stood beside him when he thanked the state troopers and hospital and the many subordinates who did his job in very trying times. Every observer was struck by the man's graciousness and his smile. There are people with famous smiles, and SZ's was one of those. But the expression was different than before. The audience saw a transformative joy, not only in how he grinned but how that joy seemed to make him lighter and younger than any man in his fifties should be.

The rumors had already begun by then. Which makes it doubly disappointing that we don't have SZ's account about his time as an invalid. Yet the patients are rarely willing to speak about these personal experiences, and our subject was even more circumspect than the norm.

Whispers claimed that he lived twenty years in as many days.

That would put him at the high end of the charts.

Voices that might know the story claim that SZ enjoyed a torrid affair with a living actress—that is, an imaginary version of an Academy Award winner. But that is the kind of rumor that spreads. Because it is compelling and obvious, and a portion of those who are doing the telling wish they could have dreamed about sleeping with a woman like that.

Another story is that SZ had a twenty-year relationship with a youngster. The girl was only eleven at the beginning, and by the end, the dreaming man was sleeping with her as well as his various daughters.

That is the kind of story told by enemies and believed by only a few of them. Yet from what is known, pedophilia is unlikely but never impossible.

A third version exists. There was a large Christmas party where SZ had one drink too many and then confided to the wrong person. He claimed that the woman he loved for twenty-one imaginary years was as exotic and beautiful as any woman could be. But there was more than just that one woman in the other realm. He had lived inside a fully realized world, sharp and honest. A man who had never built anything with his hands built the house where he and his common-law wife lived together. They had several children. SZ mentioned names and grieved that he didn't have pictures of their little ones. He was that proud of them. Actual specifics were few, but the witness had the impression that this nonexistent mother and family lived in another age, perhaps inside a fantasy world—a world of grand beauty where everybody shared a crushing, relentless poverty.

SZ's wife filed for divorce shortly after New Year's.

He didn't contest her when she took their three children.

Rumors of depression seem to be untrue, but those same rumors led to talk about removing him from his post. SZ didn't give anyone that chance. He resigned on a Friday afternoon, slipping out of his office and then out of the country. The last credible sighting came from the border of Uganda and South Sudan. A white man matching SZ's description was seen walking alone into the bush, wearing tattered clothes and an enormous smile that washed away his miserable circumstances.

Certain categories make easy statistics, and perhaps these numbers have real significance.

But statistics are a game for bolder souls than ours.

Yes, there has been a strong rise in separations and divorces. The largest upticks come from males married for seven to twelve years and whose spouses weren't affected. And inside that group, the most susceptible are young men who experienced only a year or two of pernicious romance. (PR is the latest term for the condition. Will it last? Who knows?) Perhaps this says something about human nature. You spend two years with the girl of your dreams, and that's both too long and too short. Coming back into the old world, you look at your legal mate as an embarrassment or disappointment, or boring. Because your dream mate and you were still fresh to each other, and everything ended too soon.

Couples that collapsed together are less likely to divorce. Though their numbers are still higher than normal, and substantially so.

Older couples are most resilient.

Indeed, if a husband and wife fell into a stupor for just a few hours, and if they woke at nearly the same time, they often use the event as a bonding agent, revitalizing marriages that perhaps weren't as strong as they might have been.

Books are being written on the psychological effects.

Careers and entire new industries are being nourished.

One category that receives remarkably little attention: The effects on children and young teenagers. From what has been observed, young children always experienced a love affair, but non-sexual and with a parental figure. In their dream, some disaster had swept away life as they knew it, and they found an adoptive adult who led them through a series of great adventures, sometimes spanning decades of life and growth.

Those children are as profoundly changed as anyone. "Baby adults," they have been dubbed by observers and the occasional news feature.

And what other changes have been wrought?

Today, several thousand patients remain scattered in various facilities. They demand an expensive level of care, and if they don't wake in the next few months, their bodies will require new and aggressive interventions. And there are the social ramifications to a world making ready for the next attack—even if the first attack wasn't terroristic in nature. The health industry is devising huge, largely unworkable plans in case crowds and entire cities are rendered helpless. Billions are being spent on facilities that will wait in stasis for the next wave of casualties, giving us the chance to study them in detail. And there is the simple, relentless problem that comes from one difficult evening in October: Tens of thousands of people are awake today, dealing with lives that were never lived, and from all accounts those other lives seem to be as genuine and as thoroughly recalled as any.

How can so much human experience, sitting outside normal life, not have a significant impact on all of us?

What ideas did our neighbors and friends bring back from the other world?

And how will the echo of romance play, now and for the next thousand years?

Case study:

EL is a physical therapy major and a member of the football trainer's corp. That's why she was standing near the twenty-five-yard line, fully exposed to the blast. Among her peers, EL has various distinctions. As a patient, she was cared for at home by her mother and stepfather. That wasn't particularly unusual. There was a rampant shortage of hospital beds, particularly in those first three months, and many families took up the burden. But EL was a different kind of patient. Everyone had elevated breathing rates, but she was at the high end of the continuum. Perhaps youth and physical fitness made that possible. Or there were random or unknown factors. What is known is that she spent seventeen weeks in her own bed, cared for by people who had the resources and energy to meet her extraordinary needs. EL sounded like a sprinter when she breathed. Her mouth and nostrils became chapped, and she lost weight despite constant feedings through IVs, and later, tubes pushed down her throat. Twenty pounds evaporated from a frame that didn't enter that state overweight, and just before she woke, EL's mother was considering transferring her to an expensive care facility.

But her daughter woke before she starved. Perhaps because her body was suffering, it has been suggested. But only a handful of cases resemble hers, and those patients emerged long before the body failed.

Another distinction is that EL is easily the most forthcoming about her case. She began blogging immediately. The wasted body wouldn't let her sit up, but she wrote her first entries on her back, on a tablet held by her dutiful mother.

One might expect that her seventeen weeks would translate to an impressive stretch of illusionary years. But that isn't the case at all. EL felt that only nine years had passed, which again puts her at the tip of a bell curve. And where most dream lovers were idealized, hers seems to have been a more fully rounded individual.

Heather was the lover's name.

Is her name.

She was an older woman, beautiful and possessive and sometimes cruel, at least in an emotional sense. EL writes that she and Heather fought often and about every possible topic. They lived together for seven years, off and on. EL was working as a trainer for the Minnesota Vikings, and her lover held and lost an assortment of jobs.

In her blogs, EL duplicates long stretches of dialogue.

Of course their authenticity can't be determined. But EL's words match the tone and vocabulary that she prefers, and her lover is nothing if not consistent.

EL loved Heather despite or because of the flaws.

She loves her now.

This is perhaps the most intriguing and potentially disturbing part of this case: Awake again, EL is using every spare moment of her life to explain what happened to her inside a dream. And she claims that she does this because Heather is real, and Heather returned to this world with her. There is a second mind, vivid and pissed, smoldering inside a bored skull.

Subsequent PET scans have shown interesting abnormalities.

And EL still consumes more food than before, feeding a mind that insists on running faster than average.

Everyone with an interest in the outcome is watching, wondering if and how the parasite will try to take hold of its host.

Speculation is easy, and done properly, calm speculation might help our adaptations to the ongoing challenges.

But we continue to dismiss the terrorism theory, and for good reasons. What political movement has the requisite technical skills? Whatever the device's source, it was a high-end technology wielding powers born out of the most rarefied strata of theory, and these tools were used in a very unterroristic fashion. Few deaths. No claim of credit. Seventy thousand cases of love-sick revery, and no second attack either.

But that leaves a very important question:

Who are the reasonable suspects?

Exclude one word from that question, and quite a lot becomes possible.

Foreign governments were testing a new weapon.

Or perhaps our own government was.

A small, portable device that drops thousands into a helpless state. That would be an excellent way to cripple your enemy while leaving his infrastructure intact. That is an unreasonable scenario with considerable appeal. But the first complaint is to point out the scope of the test and the dozens dead. Wouldn't that bring too much notoriety? Unless that was the goal, of course. An unexpected nightmare delivered to the unwary world. But if this was and is an experimental weapon, then there is a slightly less unlikely explanation.

We call it the Castle Bravo scenario.

Castle Bravo was one of the first thermonuclear tests in the Pacific. The bomb's yield was two-and-a-half times larger than predicted, and the blast and fallout effects caused years of misery.

Perhaps our tragedy was the result of similar mistakes.

But if a government agency isn't to blame, then who?

A cult, perhaps. Although that perches close to the terrorist assumptions, with the added problem that no known cult carries any interest in pushing thousands into the arms of imaginary lovers.

Perhaps a major corporation was testing a new product, and its calculations were a thousandfold wrong.

Unlikely, but not impossible.

Even less likely explanations include aliens operating our midst, time travelers from some far human/machine future, and the utterly random hand of some capricious or incompetent god.

And waiting beyond the impossible:

The unthinkable.

Case study:

Tenured professors are allowed to purchase season tickets, though they are relegated to some famously poor locations. BB and his wife had seats high in the southwestern portion of the stadium. These were fit people but far from young. They left for the restrooms before the first half ended, and they were slowly climbing the steps when the stadium fell into darkness. Probably neither noticed the helmet and golf cart stopping in the middle of the field. BB does recall his wife hesitating in the gloom above him. He speaks affectionately about touching her back, trying to reassure her with his presence, and then came the flash that transported him to another world where he lived and loved for three alien days—long days which would translate to perhaps two weeks by the human count, he estimates.

To an accomplished physicist, that alternate world appeared perfectly credible.

Twenty-three minutes after the blast, BB woke to find himself lying on top of his wife. To his horror, he realized that she had fallen hard, driven in part by his own body. Her forehead sharp struck the edge of a concrete step. BB tended to the bloody wound as best he could, and then this man in his late seventies tried to lift his wife, and failed, before screaming as loudly as he could, begging for anyone's help.

Sitting nearby were a brother and sister, alert and conversing with one campus police officer. All three came to the rescue, and despite his own head wound, the brother carried the dying woman across other bodies and out into the nearest parking lot. But the medical personnel were elsewhere, lucid or otherwise, and this spouse of fifty-eight years died in the back of a useless ambulance.

BB's subsequent depression was prolonged and useful.

Two months after the funeral, he began working on an explanation for his wife's murder and the transformation of so many innocent lives. Those efforts led to a series of dense, harshly reasoned papers that have mostly gone unpublished. But the professional indifference hasn't kept his conclusions from being shared by others, both within his field and far beyond.

BB claims that what happened isn't possible. Not according to natural laws, and not according to any compilation of wild hypotheses.

Impossibility is itself a clue, says BB.

He has written nothing about his fictional love affair, but the alien world is a different subject. Thoroughly rendered, complete with estimates of size and mass, apparent history and harsh climate, he argues that the world was too intricate and perfect for even an expert to dream up. That means that his vision had to be the work of another mind, a much more competent and relentless mind. According to the old professor, each of us exists inside the dreams of someone greater, and what happened on that October evening was an accident, a sorry mistake.

The universe is a cosmic fiction.

That fiction is run by mathematics and vast, unseen machines.

Some tiny piece of the machinery failed. Which must happen from time to time, as every device has its limits.

BB argues that there was no bomb or other device inside that football helmet. The golf cart failed because of the initial surge of uninvited energies, and like a fuse popping inside a circuit box, the event came and went quickly enough. But there was leakage from the higher mind, and the professor has both equations and options for experiments that might someday prove him right.

As mentioned, BB has not published these results in any responsible journal.

Some of his peers want him to retire finally.

But the old man refuses. He likes to teach and do research. Those are the only blessings left for him, now that his wife is dead. But he remains confident that the woman lives on, probably somewhere in the higher mind, and death will come soon enough, freeing him for a long, joyous chase.

What constitutes reasonable answers?

We can't say. Months of study and endless discussion has left us with no clear options. But we have cobbled together a variety of stories that capture the elements of what we consider workable, sane explanations.

Remember the reported scent of perfume.

Maybe that's a key.

And the fifty-yard line too.

The incident was devised as a study, and the football field supplied a workable transect. Again, think of Castle Bravo. Consider the possibility that the effects far outweighed every projection. The EMP blast wasn't the first stage. The incident began when someone released a powerful chemical into the atmosphere. The chemical came from the giant helmet or from the hose being towed along, and it migrated inside everyone, brought to the lungs and blood where it had powerful hallucinogenic effects. Perhaps the electrical jolt was meant to height the drug's effects, or it was a substantial malfunction in an untested system.

The culprit here would be a major pharmaceutical corporation or a bioengineering start-up.

What was being tested was a genuine love potion.

Again, think of the nuclear blast that worked too well.

The event was meant to be both an experiment and a social event, and only the people on the field should have been infected.

Horrified by the aftermath, the guilty parties have destroyed their work and gone into hiding.

And no, we won't suggest that this is the genuine answer.

There is zero evidence backing up this story or any other. What we are proposing—indeed, what we insist is true—is that no answers will be forthcoming. Something large did happen. Nothing like it has happened before or since. And so it's reasonable, even responsible, to claim that we won't ever learn the truth, and that's the conundrum we need to deal with today.

• • •

Case study:

RL is a twenty-year-old woman. A cheerleader before the event, she woke only last week. After more than fifteen months of lying in various beds, in hospitals and then at home, she reports having spent fifty-eight years elsewhere.

Her fiance was her only visitor when she woke.

When told of the circumstances, RL appeared calm, even amused by what had to be unexpected news. This wasn't the shallow young woman who tumbled and waved pom-poms on the sidelines. She was composed, eerily so. The man whom she was supposed to marry was weeping, telling her about that awful night and the wild theories explaining what had happened. Tech wizards; evil governments; high minds; satanic spells. Then he grabbed one of her skeletal hands, describing how he had watched over her as much as anyone, that he always had been devoted and faithful, and he didn't care what she did inside that silly dream world. Dreams didn't matter. What mattered was that God had placed him into her life, here and now, giving him the strength to greet her return to what was real.

That rush of words and pent-up emotion finally ended.

A brief, wary silence followed.

And then the young/old woman laughed. It was a bittersweet sound— profound and hopeless, revealing the enormous gap between the two of them. Her fiance felt the hope draining out of him. His grip weakened. She retrieved her hand and then pointed at him, saying a few words in a language that he didn't know.

He eased away.

And then quietly, in the language she had barely used in half a century, she said, "The last thing I remember . . . "

"What is that?" he asked.

"His hand," she said.

"Whose hand?"

The laughter returned, even sadder.

Then she grabbed hold of herself, arms crossed on her starved chest, and she said, "My husband was behind me on the steps, in the dark. And he put his hand on my back, and just for a moment, just that last moment . . . I felt young again . . . "

WITCH, BEAST, SAINT: AN EROTIC FAIRY TALE

C.S.E. COONEY

Once upon a time I found a monster in the woods.

In the manner of most witches, I had a knack for discovering lost things. He was crawling with vermin, so wasted he barely flinched when I tested his nose and tongue, checking texture, temperature, moisture.

He was half an inch and kissing close to dying.

"Beast," said I, in the language all beasts knew. "Look at me. Do you wish to die like this?"

He understood. Opening his eyes, he looked at me. I felt his answer thrum in my bones, barely vocalized, a rattling sigh that was a clearer cry for help than if he had spoken the words in a human tongue.

"Come with me then," I said, laying a compulsion on him to rise, since he could not do it for himself. "I suppose you can be my familiar."

I put him in the cellar and fed him up until he was able to move about on his own. Then I began the arduous task of coaxing him outside to the wishing well and washing him, which took many days and a great deal of patience. Already the potatoes and last year's apples and the onions greening in their barrels had begun to take on his dank and desolate stench. And really, he was so grateful for the attention.

Like many beasts, he found the sound of my voice soothing. So I told him the story of how he came to be.

"This cottage passes from witch to witch," I said. "My predecessor was ancient by the time she mistook an oak tree for an open passage and drove her mortar and pestle right into it. They say mortar and pestles are safer than brooms. I don't know about that. I prefer to walk everywhere, or maybe hitch a ride on a wagon. You have nice broad shoulders. Perhaps I'll teach you to piggyback me, by and by. There's a bit of a pig in you. Well, boar. It's the tusks.

Your nose is more stag. Soft and broad from bridge to tip. Those gently flaring nostrils. But your horns are definitely bull. Anyway. What was I saying?"

The monster made a gesture like a pestle grinding something in a mortar.

"Right!" I cried. "My predecessor. Apparently in the last few decades before her terminal flying accident, she'd developed this habit of turning local boys to beasts every time they slighted her—or she imagined they did. The most famous case was that of our sovereign prince himself. He lives in a castle, in a stretch of forest not far from here. Don't worry though. He found a local hedge-witch—much like myself—to break the spell. They say she was so beautiful she could shatter strong sorceries with a kiss."

I shrugged. My hands were wrist-deep in his sudsy fur, the soap black with his murk.

"Could be. Or she might have been a scholar—much like myself—who knew the right incantations, under which phase of moon to utter them, how to transfer all that moonlight and magic words from her lips to his. It looks much like a kiss. All very standard, unless you slip in some tongue. Fact is she was probably tired of trading chicken eggs and goat milk for her minor miracles. Thought to have a go at the princessing business instead. Never have to pick nettles in a midnight graveyard ever again—unless she wanted to. And once a witch, we like to say, always a witch. Princess or no."

Pausing, I regarded the monster, wondering what it would be to kiss him. The juncture at my thighs prickled, swelled, pulsed, grew moist. Then he exhaled and I stepped back.

His fangs needed brushing. Badly. Too, I wasn't sure he was used to me yet. That he wouldn't startle back in panic, catching my lip on one of his pointy bits and taking half my face with him.

His eyelashes were very long, coarse and curly. He would not yet meet my gaze. But when I stopped scrubbing, he knocked his large skull against the palm of my hand, urging me on.

"Beast, be still!" I commanded, and he was. Except for his tail, which swept around to brush my hip in shy apology. I ran my hand along it, muttering as I scrubbed, "Why I didn't just shave you bare-ass naked so we could start afresh, I don't know. Probably because my garden shears aren't big enough."

I could've changed him back. The transformation spell would take research, focus, a not inconsiderable outpouring of stored magic, but in the end, it was entirely doable.

Thing was, I rather liked my monster as a monster. Doubtless he'd been less impressive as a man. A rough and unlettered peasant with a rude habit of overlooking the courtesies owed his elder, maybe. Or a rowdy, ruddy-cheeked boy who bit his thumb at the wrong old woman on the wrong day.

But he was a strong, silent companion with rather more intelligence, having once been human, than your average woodland critter. He hunted for me, and the wolves ran with him, which was something to see. (There was something of the wolf in his tail, his teeth.) He brought me back deer and rabbit the way my sister-witches' cats brought them mice and crickets, and he positively purred—or rumbled, anyway—once I deemed him clean enough to pet.

Washing day by the wishing well became a weekly ritual. Between hunting in the woods and sleeping on the dirt floor of the cellar, chained (for no witch leaves a monster to wander unprotected through her house at night) he was never pristine for long.

Unlike cats, he enjoyed being washed. Once he learned I would not tolerate otherwise, he always held very still for me. I trimmed his black talons and brushed his curving fangs and polished those great ivory tusks that jutted up from his mandibles until they gleamed. His ears were the prettiest part of him, russet velvet triangles with black streaks, and white tufts sprouting from the delicate hollows. The first time I stroked them, his sex organ rose up from the shag of his thighs, thick and purple-veined, with a glistening pink tip.

"Oh, do you want this washed too?" I laughed. "You nasty thing."

I would've left it there, but he took my soapy hand in his paw and pulled me closer. Otherwise he did not touch me, but waited, rubbing the residue off my hand. The pad of his foreclaw made slow circles on my calloused palm. He watched me mutely, eyes wide on my face. Moss green eyes, with flecks of yellow glowing in them, like little lamps. I had never seen their like before. My breath quickened. I stepped in and took him in hand. His eyes rolled back in his head. His tongue lolled out between his fangs. His breath was hot, but smelled now of sharp green mint and old apples.

I admit I was lonely. I sometimes traded my neighboring foresters and husbandmen little magic tricks for a quick fuck. Not a lot of options in this part of the woods. They were always wildly excited and ashamed; they all had wives at home, and often grunted or screamed their women's names as they buried themselves inside me, or sprayed their unfaithful seed over my belly.

But my monster had no human vocabulary to speak of, thank the Dark Queen of the Crossroads.

As I pulled and kneaded him, the backs of my knees softened like warm wax. The afternoon slant of light took on a wine-red cast. The soap slicked him right out of my hands.

He made no sound at this, but sank to a crouch before me, tail curled around his ankles, balancing on one fist, like an ape. The other slid beneath my skirt and clutched my hip, urging me toward his mouth. He nudged my thighs apart, pressing me back against the wishing well. Ducking his head beneath my skirt, he began to lave me. His tongue was long, with a nap to it like wet velvet stretched over the finest sandpaper. It made my bud stand hard as a pearl. And then his tongue slipped deeper. Wrapping my fists around his tusks, I rode his massive, twisted face until my knees gave out and I collapsed upon him.

Whereupon he withdrew his terrible tongue and turned me to face the wishing well, bending me over the stones. I widened my stance and braced against the rough stones of the well. He entered me from behind, so slowly it was like being bludgeoned by a bolt of silk through the medium of molasses.

"Harder, you monster!" I grunted. "Or I'll put you in a spiked choke chain. I'll beat you with nettles. I'll let the forest children come and throw stones. I'll invite the goodwives to smear your feet with pitch and set fire to them with torches. I'll—yes. Yes! Like that! Yes!"

I must have blacked out from the incredible crush and pull of those tides, startling awake only when his hot seed sprayed my back.

"Beast," I murmured, turning in his arms, "My monstrous one. My pet fiend."

He made small noises at these endearments, his breath a fever on my neck. His sinewy arms wrapped around me, lifting me, carrying me into my cottage. His heated body did not stink, but gave off an odor like lightning-struck glass, like peat smoke, like wet stone.

His pants and sighs I could interpret with ease, for I had the language of beasts from my mother, who had known all the birdsong of the wood—though my specialty was with mammals, and predators in particular.

He was telling me, "My love, my mistress, my lonely queen. Only you. Always you. You forever. I will devour those who part us."

However.

Later that year, when autumn began to bleed the leaves of the forest to russet gold and vixen red, a day came when neither my monster nor I could prevent our sundering.

He had probably started out as a wandering warlock, or sorcerer. Whatever he'd been doing on his journeys had catapulted him willy-nilly to sainthood. A blue-white nimbus sprouted out the top of his head, the very place a baby's soft spot would be. The residual radiance trailed after him like the tail of a comet.

I wished, later, that he had been soft too, infantile with holiness, damaged from do-gooding. But he was sharp as any conman or two-trick magician, with a kindness in his eyes that cut like a knife's edge. I liked him instantly, and also was afraid.

"Greetings, sister-witch," said the saint, from behind the gates of my garden.

He knew better than to enter a witch's garden uninvited, and for that I respected him.

"Good even, brother-warlock," I said. "You've got a bit of something rising from your head."

He brushed the blue flame crowning his coppery hair with impatient fingers. "No spell I perform seems able to banish it. A necromancer of my acquaintance advised me that only the tarnish of evil will diminish it, and I should straightway murder a few virgins in their sleep. But I hardly found the thought appealing."

I grinned. "Easy targets."

He grinned back. "Exactly."

A saint's grin, let me just say, ignites a blue flame in places that never saw the light of day.

"Also," he brushed at the nimbus again, "it does come in handy when I'm alone in the woods at night and all the tinder is too wet to take to the spark of my flint."

"Does it also warm you?" I asked curiously. I had naught to do with saint-fire before. It had never come my way.

"Aye, it does—at need. And if I am hungry and unlikely to be in the way of a stray meal, it fills my belly with fire, and I do not need to eat nor drink."

"Fascinating," I murmured. We stared at each other over the gates.

"And what of your other hungers?" I asked, suddenly breathless.

It is the sort of question a witch must ask. Or at least, I must. I'm just that kind of witch.

The saint froze, and I swear by the Iron Nipple, I never saw such a delicate stained glass hue as the rosy blush that flushed the white quartz of his skin. Covered in fur as he was, my monster could not blush, and my own skin was a rich brown that never betrayed embarrassment. He was much too pale, I thought, for a traveling man. Perhaps he had been eating saint-fire for too long.

"Sister-witch," said he slowly, "I abstain."

"Vow or necessity?"

"Mostly lack of opportunity," he confessed. "And a fastidiousness of taste which compels me never to fuck where I do not love."

I liked him more for his candor. Also, his obvious state of starvation touched my heart. I invited him inside the garden gates, and into my cottage to be fed.

"Something rather heartier than gingerbread, I think," I told him, laughing. "Though I have plenty of that. Mostly it's for children wandering the woods in winter. They are often too shy to knock on my door, but they'll nibble at it!"

He sat down as if the relief of it might just well kill him, and I invited him to remove his boots and soak his feet in a basin of warm water and mineral salts. He glanced down at me as I knelt before him, unlacing his boots.

"You're very young to live out here alone," he observed.

I looked up, surprised. "A witch is never young. Or not for long."

"You can't be more than twenty five?"

I shook my head. "Guess again."

"Twenty . . . two?"

"Lad," I said, patting his ankle affectionately, "I'll never see thirty again, though I'm not yet on its shady side. I'm older than you, I'll wager."

"Not by much!" he assured me quickly, blushing again but not looking away.

This was very promising.

I'd've straddled him right then and there, but my monster was out hunting, and I didn't want him to walk in on something tawdry. Best he be introduced to the saint first, then chained down and made to watch.

We feasted on fresh goat cheese and honey slathered over new bread. As he ate, his lips reddened like raspberries, his weary gray eyes grew light and luminous. He laughed more readily and spoke of his vocation.

"I was born on the prince's wedding day, you know. The Beast to his Beauty. I would see her in chapel on Sundays, how the sunlight seemed to seek her face, and I knew she had done holy work, love's work, transforming our master to his true form with a kiss."

I guffawed into my water glass.

"If you go in for spectacle, I suppose. You'll notice she didn't bother with any monster not possessed of a title."

"Ah, but I did!" exclaimed the saint, then added more wryly, "Eventually. When I was old enough, I requested audience of the princess. I asked her why—why did she stay behind her stone walls, when the forest yet teemed with sorry beasts who longed to be human again?"

"What did she say?"

"She had this way of not smiling that trembled on her lips—more joyous than laughter. Her eyes . . . her eyes were like yours. Black, with no whites. Glittering."

"It's a witch thing."

"Yes," he breathed. "She told me she had decided to give up magic when she married, and now was out of practice. Then she touched my face, and I . . . "

He looked down, ashamed. I was amused.

"A witch's touch can be fairly potent," I observed.

"Yes," he said again, with a strange intensity. "I—I rose for her. And she said I was obviously a lad of vigorous energy, and that perhaps it would be my own calling to turn monsters back into men. She said . . . do you mind if I tell you?" he asked me suddenly. "Only—it will sound like a boast."

"I generally don't mind much," I replied. "Until I need to. Saves energy."

"She said I was beautiful enough to kiss all the wild things of the wood tame, if I but learned to use my mouth correctly."

I laughed, leaning back in my chair. I had never met this witch, this beauty, this princess, but I could tell we would've been friends.

"And did you?" I asked.

"I did." He nodded. "I apprenticed myself to a sorcerer, and when I knew enough of magic, I began my journeyman's work. I packed a bag and set off into the woods, seeking out enchanted beasts and kissing them back to their original forms. Soon they knew to come and find me. I have been doing this work ever since. I kiss them, and they change, and I hold them all night in my arms as they tremble in their new nakedness. But by morning they are always gone."

Frowning, I refilled his glass with water from the wishing well.

"That sounds mighty ungrateful to me. Did they leave you nothing? No gifts? Food? Treasures they found while prowling the forests?"

"I am not a witch," said the saint. "The work I do is not for gain."

I indicated his halo. "Yet you have gained something."

He pounded my scarred kitchen table with his fist. His knuckles were white, almost transparent.

"I do not want it," he whispered.

I bent forward, setting my elbows on my knees and clasping my hands.

"What do you want?" I asked him. "Why are you here?"

"I come for the beast who stands behind you."

I looked over my shoulder. My monster stood in the doorway, paws loose at his sides, colossal fangs agape, tail hanging, held fast in the saint's thrall. His eyes were filled with saint-fire, no longer mossy green with golden lamps inside.

The saint stood as if drawn up by strings. A marionette played by some god or greater magic than I could currently combat. I watched them move toward each other, one so loathsome and unkempt and lovely to my eyes, the other so slender and starving, his red-gold hair crowned in a coronet of blue flame.

The kiss was brief but urgent. The saint's face could have fit inside my monster's mouth. I wanted my monster to break the kiss. To rip the saint's sweet face right off.

He did not.

Instead, he began his hideous transformation.

He shrank. He shed. He diminished.

Gone his fangs, his tusks, his talons. Gone his curving black horns. Gone his plumy tail, his long red tongue. Gone his brawn. His might. His wildness. He shivered, drenched, naked as a newborn, with panicked green eyes.

"Come," said the saint in a tender voice. "Come with me into the woods, my friend. I will teach you how to talk again. How to walk upright again. How to be free. I will take care of you, as Mankind cares for its fellow men."

My throat was dry. I tried to call out, "Stay!" from my place at the table. The saint seemed to hear my thought unvoiced and turned to me, though he could not meet my eyes.

"I am sorry," he said. Then, more softly, "Thank you for your kindness."

Saint and man passed away from me, into the night woods.

I was sad and angry for weeks. I couldn't bake. My candy house grew stale. The crows ate my shingles. Weeds overtook my garden. I slept at the foot of my bed, where my monster had used to curl ever since I brought him up from the cellar. He had made a nest of old blankets and my cast-off rags. I rolled in his musk and slipped my hands through his tremendous manacles, wishing I could lock myself up and swallow the key and wither there.

I suppose I had not been aware of the nature of my attachment to the monster. Or, at least—the extent of it.

Certainly I pined, and turned those from my garden gates who came to me for help. After all, even a witch needs time and space to grieve. They would return if their situations grew desperate enough, and I would be better by and by. In the meantime, gifts began to appear on my doorstep: jams and honeys and cheeses and chickens, new red shoes of the supplest leather, bangles and baubles and ceramic mugs with delicate blue glazes the color of saint-fire.

No barter or bribes these, but offerings of friendship and support from my woodcutters, my weaver-wives, my fisher-folk, my huntsman and huntresses, my tanners and trappers. My heart grew less sore under the balm of their love, and my hands grew quick and clever again, well able to comfort myself in ways I had grown accustomed to the monster comforting me.

It was not the same, but it was something. It was better than wallowing.

A witch ought not to let herself wallow more than three or four weeks at most. She has work to do.

And then, one night, he returned.

He wore clothes, charity scraps, a shirt that hung on him, trousers that barely covered his knees. But he was barefoot and bareheaded, his hair a curly brown thicket. A beard had grown in during the weeks he had been wandering with the saint, and this was dark and curly too. I saw no flecks of yellow in his moss-green eyes when I opened my door and found myself staring into his face, only pupils as black as the bottom of my wishing well.

What long lashes he had. What a helpless pink mouth. Tender as a rosebud.

"Mistress," said the man who had once been a beast. He fell at my feet. Fevered tears splattered my toes.

"Mistress! Change me back! Change me back!"

I kicked him away and went back inside.

But I left the door open.

For three days I ignored him as he crouched by my hearth. He ate the fragments I let fall from my table. They weren't much, for I ate now with gusto, my appetite returning to me. He did not dare touch me, or even glance into my eyes when I might see him looking, but I felt his gaze following me whatever I did, wherever I went.

When a local girl came to me to give birth on my kitchen table, he was a presence behind me with steady hands, obeying whatever order I snapped out. Together, we saved her.

Afterward, as girl and newborn slept in my own bed, I went to him where he lay upon the hearth, and knelt at his side. His black lashes swept his cheekbones. He was asleep, curled with his back to the fire.

I unfastened his breeches and took him into my mouth, hearing his gasp as he awoke and hardened. I hummed lightly against his flesh, and he moaned. His hand gripped my shoulders. Then my hair.

I stopped and looked up at him.

"I should leave you like this, you monster. Like you left me."

"Yes, Mistress," he rasped in raggedness and ecstasy. "I am nothing. I deserve nothing. Have no mercy."

"You'd like that, wouldn't you?" I raked the flesh of his stomach with my fingernails. "You'd like if I left you like this all night, your cock stiff as a winter corpse and your balls as blue as Neptune."

He had not studied astronomy, as I had, but in his state he would have agreed to anything I said. I sighed for the saint, who would have traded quip for quip. Possibly taken me by my snaky braids and forced my lips over him again, pumping my head up and down with his pale, holy hand.

I thought about the saint more often than I should.

"I hope my mercy kills you," I said softly, letting my breath puff upon his erection. I sat up. He quivered as I scooted back from him.

"Change me back," he begged again.

"I might," I considered. "But for my pleasure. Not yours."

"Yes," he whispered. "Your pleasure. All yours. Only yours."

"You say that now. But at first sight of him, you betrayed me for a holy vagabond who didn't have wit enough to feed himself!"

"His lips were so warm!"

His body jerked. He flung his head back, moaning, exposing his flushed throat. His seed jetted out of his cock and pumped down his thigh, though I had not so much as touched him.

I stared at him in surprise. The fire crackled. A log collapsed to embers just the color of the saint's hair.

Clearing my throat, I observed, "You lasted longer as a beast."

"Make me yours again." His fists clutched my skirts in supplication. "Take me back. Change me. Mangle me. Any shape you desire. Please, Mistress. Please."

"Convince me," I said.

For the rest of the night, and much of the next morning, he did.

The ceremony to invoke the beast is complicated. I do not know how my predecessor did it. Perhaps it had been her gift, as mine was for speaking to beasts, as my mother's was for birds, or the beauty's was for transformation via kiss. Perhaps all that my predecessor had to do was wave her willow wand, or drum her iron stave against the forest floor, and wham! White light. Man into monster. Boy into beast.

I had to do it the old-fashioned way.

That is, dancing naked in the woods at midnight, wearing nothing but a silver mask and the silver crescent moon bound at my brow, with silver on my upper arms, my wrists, my ankles to ward away the demons and ghosts who might try to take advantage of my vulnerability during this great outpouring of power.

I stood in a glen as mossy and green as my monster's eyes, and I called the boar, the bear, the bull, the wolf, the weasel, the black crow, the black goat. I called the falcon and the fisher-cat, the slinking mink, the brown otter, the proud stag, the wild stallion, the mountain lion. They came to me and to the man at my side, who stood as naked as I, but wearing no silver.

The beasts of the forest answered my call, and one by one I summoned them nearer, shy as they were and wary of each other. They trotted, pranced, pounced, minced, scurried and flew forward to lick the naked man, to peck at him and nip at him, to rake him with their claws and talons, to worry him with their jaws. And then they left him, one by one, as he, covered in their saliva, in abrasions and in blood, bent to his breast and began to change.

The monster I made was more beautiful by far than the monster he had been, or the man he'd so briefly become. He was truly mine. My beast. My familiar. My handiwork. Mine, as I wanted him, as he had begged to be.

And no saint, be he ever so pious or so pretty, could now sunder him from my side.

I would like to see him try.

I woke one morning, sweating lightly and all over from being wrapped so soundly in the mink-soft fur, the crow-black feathers, the horse-rough mane of my monster. I detangled my limbs from his, sliding the wolf plumes of his tail from between my legs, shuddering deliciously, and slipped from the bed, pulling on a thin shift to go into my garden.

The saint was there, sleeping in my rosemary bed.

His halo scorched the nearby herbs. I squatted near him.

"Do you think," I asked, "that because I once invited you into my home out of my own good will, you could waltz right back in again without permission and ruin my garden?"

The saint opened his morning dawn gray eyes and looked at me.

A saint's eyes, let me just say, are profound as a thunderstorm roaring between the ribs, conveying branches of lightning through all the nerves of the limbs. Full as strong a force as a sea wind. Gale-gray, that saint's eyes.

"Sister-witch," said he, "I greet thee."

He was thinner than before, but how his blue-white nimbus burned. It has spread from his head to encompass his entire body. Blue flames writhed and crackled around him.

"You're looking terribly sanctified," I told him. "Does it hurt?"

"Like I'm being eaten by some tigerish fever," he confessed. "Like I'm being driven by fiery whips to the four corners of the Earth. And serenaded by seraphim at all hours, a host of a hundred thousand voices raised up in song, right here inside my skull, and . . . "

"The Earth is round," I informed him.

"It was a simile," he shot back irritably.

"Aren't we high and mighty for someone who's just spent the night among worms?"

He let his head fall back to the soil. "I liked it better when I was just a sorcerer's apprentice, hoping to do some good in the woods."

"Thus do our vocations pauper us," I replied lightly. "Perhaps if you let your protégés pay you, you wouldn't find yourself at such an impasse."

The saint crossed his arms over his chest.

"Why have you come back here?" I asked him, trying not to admire his stubbornness, or pity his torment. "You cannot transform my beast again. I made sure of that. Though it might martyr you to try." I shrugged. "Who knows? You might be into that sort of thing."

"I'm not," the saint snapped.

I did not tell him that I sometimes caught my monster staring out of the window, down the garden path and off into the woods with something like longing. Or that I sometimes did the same.

But the saint, in his way, seemed to catch my thought nonetheless. One corner of his pale lips twitched up in a smile that, had it not been so triumphantly grateful, I might have called smug.

His lips were too white, too translucent. He needed to eat.

"I miss him," said the saint, breaking into my thoughts. "With him, all the angel voices went blessedly quiet. He would wake me, sometimes, at night. Crawl under my blanket. Do things to me—strange things. Take my toes into his mouth. My—other things."

I nodded. My interest, and my appetite, sharpened.

"Sometimes . . . sometimes he would . . . turn me over. Fill me from behind. He always apologized afterward," the saint continued, his words quickening with his breath. "Begged me punish him for his trespass. I tried to be gentle. I tried every kindness. I said I forgave him. That there was nothing to forgive. Indeed, how very happy he made me. How safe I felt. How full satisfied. And—at last—not so alone. But he only wept. And I didn't know how to comfort him."

"Oh, lad," I said. "Have you got a lot to learn!"

"I know!" The saint propped himself once more upon his elbows. "Almost as soon as he could speak in full sentences, he began to tell me of you. His witch. He lay in my arms and whispered stories of your hands, your mouth, your whip, your cunt, your strength, your solitude. These tales would make me hard as iron, so hard it took him hours to soften me again, and though I spent myself in his mouth, in his palm, in his ass, I was never content again—as I had been in the beginning—for the thought of you haunted me."

"What did you think?" I whispered, mesmerized. I'd never heard of a saint saying such things. Unless you count Augustine, but never after he went holy.

"I wanted," he said, "to see if I could bring you down."

He reached out and pulled me onto him so that I lay stretched across his chest. His hand cradled my head against his throat. He smelled of burnt rosemary and sea salt.

"I wanted," he said again, "to see you in chains before me, blindfolded, senseless and speechless with pleasure from all I did to you. I wanted you naked on your kitchen table with a bowl of strawberries, that I might draw arcane figures on your flesh and take those runes back onto my tongue while you cried out beneath me. I wanted to touch you with these fingers," his fiery fingers moved under my skirt, "until you screamed for mercy as he said he screamed for you. I wanted to gag your groans and gurgles with silk that would grow wet in your drooling mouth. To torment you with inventions I have not yet dared to dream. And after days and weeks and seasons of this, I wanted you to turn—and do the same to me."

"Gladly," I said, moved very deeply, and very slickly, almost to the point of hyperventilation.

I ground my hips hard against his flicking fingers. He took them away from me, laughing as I cursed him. I clawed at the buttons of his trousers, hoping to free the part of him that was blunter and less controlled, but he rolled me over into the lavender and pinned my arms down, nails biting into the flesh of my wrists. He entered me too deliberately, too smoothly for my liking, holding me in place the entire time. I bided. And when his arms began to tremble with the effort of his control, I thrashed and bucked until he fell back, then straddled him as he grappled with my breasts.

I was so close, so close to climax when he flung me into the mint and mounted me, changing the rhythm again, bringing me back down, only to spike me higher, sharper, with his gradually rougher thrusts.

My sweat ran like sapphires, reflecting his blue fire.

I cried out. He stopped my mouth with a kiss. Living coal upon my tongue.

I screamed my bursting eruption into his skull. He wound my braids in his fist and yanked my mouth from his, burying his face in my neck as his holy seed pulsed into me.

Quickly, we both spoke the spell against conception.

His sounded more like a prayer. Mine was barely coherent for gasping.

Then we helped each other out of the destroyed herb beds, redolent of the rosemary and lavender and mint that we had crushed. He took my offered hand, and I brushed him clean of small insects and shattered leaves. We walked to the door of my cottage together, leaning on one another.

"Can you make peanut brittle?" I asked when I could talk again.

"I can," he said solemnly. "My parents were bakers for the prince and princess."

"Good. I need new shingles."

He glanced with keen eyes at my candy house, taking it all in, the gingerbread siding, the spun sugar windows, the white icing trim.

"Very well," he agreed. "I shall be your handyman in this. But I would like to help you with your other work too—the good work you do for the people of these woods."

I poked his ribs. "There's always work for a saint," I teased him, "when a witch's hands are full."

"What if the saint's hands are full of witch?"

"Then let the work wait."

In the doorway, our monster awaited our return. At the sight of his mistress and master together, yellow lamps began to dance in his moss-green eyes.

He stood, clean and smiling and erect, all his many teeth gleaming in the morning light.

COLLATERAL

PETER WATTS

They got Becker out in eight minutes flat, left the bodies on the sand for whatever scavengers the Sixth Extinction hadn't yet managed to take out. Munsin hauled her into the Sikorsky and tried to yank the augments manually, right on the spot; Wingman swung and locked and went hot in the pants-pissing half-second before its threat-recognition macros, booted late to the party, calmed it down. Someone jammed the plug-in home between Becker's shoulders; wireless gates unlocked in her head and Blanch, way up in the cockpit, put her prosthetics to sleep from a safe distance. The miniguns sagged on her shoulders like anesthetized limbs, threads of smoke still wafting from the barrels.

"Corporal." Fingers snapped in her face. "Corporal, you with me?"

Becker blinked. "They—they were human . . . " She thought they were, anyway. All she'd been able to see were the heat signatures: bright primary colors against the darkness. They'd started out with arms and legs but then they'd *spread* like dimming rainbows, like iridescent oil slicks.

Munson said nothing.

Abemama receded to stern, a strip of baked coral suffused in a glow of infrared: yesterday's blackbodied sunshine bleeding back into the sky. Blanch hit a control and the halo vanished: night-eyes blinded, ears deafened to any wavelength past the range of human hearing, all senses crippled back down to flesh and blood.

The bearing, though. Before the darkness had closed in. It had seemed wrong.

"We're not going to Bonriki?"

"*We* are," the Sergeant said. "You're going home. Rendezvous off Aranuka. We're getting you out before this thing explodes."

She could feel Blanch playing around in the back of her brain, draining the op logs from her head. She tried to access the stream but he'd locked her out. No telling what those machines were sucking out of her brain. No telling if any of it would still be there when he let her back in.

Not that it mattered. She wouldn't have been able to scrub those images from her head if she tried.

"They *had* to be hostiles," she muttered. "How could they have just *been* there, I mean—what else could they be?" And then, a moment later: "Did any of them . . . ?"

"You wouldn't be much of a superhuman killing machine if they had," Okoro said from across the cabin. "They weren't even armed."

"Private Okoro," the Sergeant said mildly. "Shut your fucking mouth."

They were all sitting across the cabin from her, in defiance of optimal in-flight weight distribution: Okoro, Perry, Flannery, Cole. None of them augged yet. There weren't enough Beckers to go around, one every three or four companies if the budget was up for it and the politics were hot enough. Becker was used to the bitching whenever the subject came up, everyone playing the hard-ass, rolling their eyes at the cosmic injustice that out of all of them it was the farmer's daughter from fucking *Red Deer* who'd won the lottery. It had never really bothered her. For all their trash-talking bullshit, she'd never seen anything but good-natured envy in their eyes.

She wasn't sure what she saw there now.

Eight thousand kilometers to Canadian airspace. Another four to Trenton. Fourteen hours total on the KC-500 the brass had managed to scrounge from the UN on short notice. It seemed like forty: every moment relentlessly awake, every moment its own tortured post-mortem. Becker would have given anything to be able to shut down for just a little while—to sleep through the dull endless roar of the turbofans, the infinitesimal brightening of the sky from black to grey to cheerful, mocking blue—but she didn't have that kind of augmentation.

Blanch, an appendage of a different sort, kept her company on the way home. Usually he couldn't go five minutes without poking around inside her, tweaking this inhibitor or that BCI, always trying to shave latency down by another millisecond or two. This time he just sat and stared at the deck, or out the window, or over at some buckled cargo strap clanking against the fuselage. The tacpad that pulled Becker's strings sat dormant on his lap. Maybe he'd been told to keep his hands off, leave the crime scene in pristine condition for Forensic IT.

Maybe he just wasn't in the mood.

"Shit happens, you know?"

Becker looked at him. "What?"

"We're lucky something like this didn't happen *months* ago. Half those fucking islands underwater, the rest tearing each other's throats out for a couple dry hectares and a few transgenics. Not to mention the fucking Chinese just waiting for an excuse to *help out*." Blanch snorted. "Guess you could call it *peacekeeping*. If you've got a really warped sense of humor."

"I guess."

"Shame we're not Americans. They don't even sign on to those treaties, do anything they damn well please." Blanch snorted. "It may be a fascist shithole down there but at least they don't knuckle under every time someone starts talking about *war crimes.*"

He was just trying to make her feel better, she knew.

"Fucking *rules of engagement,*" he grumbled.

Eight hours in IT when they landed: every aug tested to melting, every prosthetic stripped to the bolts while the attached meat sat silent and still and kept all the screams inside. They gave her four hours' rack time even though her clockwork could scrub the fatigue right out of her blood, regulate adenosine and melatonin so precisely she wouldn't even yawn right up until the point she dropped dead of heart failure. Might as well, they said: other schedules to clear anyway, other people to bring back across other oceans.

They told her not to worry. They told her it wasn't her fault. They gave her propranolol to help her believe them.

Four hours, flat on her back, staring at the ceiling.

Now here she was: soul half a world away, body stuck in this windowless room, paneled in oak on three sides, crawling with luminous maps and tacticals on the fourth. Learning just what the enemy had been doing, besides sneaking up on a military cyborg in the middle of the fucking night.

"They were fishing," the PAO told her.

"No," Becker said; some subconscious subroutine added an automatic "*sir.*"

The JAG lawyer—*Eisbach,* that was it—shook her head. "They had longlines in their outriggers, Corporal. They had hooks, a bait pail. No weapons."

The general in the background—from NDHQ in Ottawa, Becker gathered, although there'd been no formal introduction—studied the tacpad in his hand and said nothing at all.

She shook her head. "There aren't any fish. Every reef in the WTP's been acidified for twenty years."

"It's definitely a point we'll be making," Eisbach said. "You can't fault the system for not recognizing profiles that aren't even supposed to exist in the zone."

"But how could they be—"

"Tradition, maybe." The PAO shrugged. "Some kind of cultural thing. We're checking with the local NGOs but so far none of them are accepting responsibility. Whatever they were doing, the UN never white-listed it."

"They didn't show on approach," Becker remembered. "No visual, no sound—I mean, how could a couple of boats just sneak up like that? It had to be some kind of stealth tech, that must be what Wingman keyed—I mean, they were just *there.*" Why was this so hard? The augs were supposed keep her balanced, mix up just the right cocktail to keep her cool and crisp under the most lethal conditions.

Of course, the augs were also supposed to know unarmed civilians when they saw them . . .

The JAG was nodding. "Your mechanic. Specialist, uh . . . "

"Blanch." From the room's only civilian, standing unobtrusively with the potted plants. Becker glanced over; he flashed her a brief and practiced smile.

"Specialist Blanch, yes. He suspects there was a systems failure of some kind."

"I would never have fired if—" Meaning, of course, *I would never have fired.*

Don't be such a pussy, Becker. Last month you took on a Kuan-Zhan with zero cover and zero backup, never even broke a sweat. Least you can do now is stand next to a fucking philodendron without going to pieces.

"Accidents happen in—these kind of situations," The PAO admitted sadly. "Drones misidentify targets. Pillbox mistakes a civilian for an enemy combatant. No technology's perfect. Sometimes it fails. It's that simple."

"Yes sir." Dimming rainbows, bleeding into the night.

"So far the logs support Blanch's interpretation. Might be a few days before we know for certain."

"A few days we don't have. Unfortunately."

The general swept a finger across his tacpad. A muted newsfeed bloomed on the war wall behind him: House of Commons, live. Opposition members standing, declaiming, sitting. Administration MPs across the aisle, rising and falling in turn. A two-tiered array of lethargic whackamoles.

The General's eyes stayed fixed on his pad. "Do you know what they're talking about, Corporal?"

"No, sir."

"They're talking about you. Barely a day and a half since the incident and already they're debating it in Question Period."

"Did we—"

"We did not. There was a breach."

He fell silent. Behind him, shell-shocked pols stammered silent and shifty-eyed against the onslaught of Her Majesty's Loyal Opposition. The Minister of Defence's seat, Becker noted, was empty.

"Do we know who, sir?"

The general shook his head. "Any number of people could have intercepted one or more of our communications. The number who'd be able to decrypt them is a lot smaller. I'd hate to think it was one of ours, but it's not something we can rule out. Either way—" He took a breath. "—so much for our hopes of dealing with this internally."

"Yes sir."

Finally he raised his eyes to meet hers. "I want to assure you, Corporal, that nobody here has passed any judgment with regard to potential—culpability. We've reviewed the telemetry, the transcripts, the interviews; FIT's still going over the results but so far there's no evidence of any conscious wrong-doing on your part."

Conscious, Becker noted dully. Not *deliberate.* There'd been a time when the distinction would never have occurred to her.

"Be that as it may, we find ourselves forced to change strategy. In the wake of this leak it's been decided we have to *engage the public.* Doubling down and invoking national security would only increase the appearance of guilt, and after that mess in the Philippines we can't afford even a whiff of cover-up." The general sighed. "This, at least, is the view of the Minister."

"Yes sir."

"It has therefore been decided—and I'm sorry to do this to you, I know it's not what you signed up for—it's been decided to *get out in front of this thing,* as they say. Control the narrative. Make you available for interviews, prove we have nothing to hide."

"Interviews, sir?"

"You'll be liaising with Mr. Monahan here." On cue, the civilian stepped out of the background. "His firm's proven useful in matters of—public outreach."

"Ben. Just Ben." Monahan reached out to shake with his right hand, offered his card with the left: *Optic Nerve,* twinkling above a stock-ticker crawl of client endorsements. "I know how much this sucks, Corporal. I'm guessing the last thing you want to hear right now is what some high-priced image consultant has to say about covering your ass. Is that about right?"

Becker swallowed, and nodded, and retrieved her hand. Phantom wings beat on her shoulders.

"The good news is: no ass-covering required. I'm not here to polish a turd—which is actually a nice change—I'm here to make sure the truth gets out. As you know, there's no shortage of parties who are a lot less interested in what really happened than in pushing their own agendas."

"I can understand that," Becker said softly.

"This person, for example." *Just Ben* tapped his watch and wiped Parliament from the wall; the woman revealed in its place stood maybe one-seventy, black, hair cropped almost army short. She seemed a little off-balance in the picture; doubtless the helmeted RCMP officer grabbing her left bicep had something to do with that. The two of them danced against a chorus line of protestors and pacification drones.

"Amal Sabrie," Monahan was saying. "Freelance journalist, well-regarded by the left for her human rights work. Somali by birth but immigrated to Canada as a child. Her home town was Beledweyne. Does that ring any bells, Corporal?"

Becker shook her head.

"Airborne Regiment? 1992?"

"Sorry. No."

"Okay. Let's just say she's got more reason than most to mistrust the Canadian military."

"The last person we'd expect to be on our side," Eisbach remarked.

"Exactly." Monahan nodded. "Which is why I've granted her an exclusive."

They engaged on neutral territory, proposed by Sabrie, reluctantly approved by the chain of command: a café patio halfway up Toronto's Layton Tower, overlooking Lakeshore. It jutted from the side of the building like a bracket fungus, well above most of the drone traffic.

An almost pathological empathy for victimhood. Monahan had inventoried Sabrie's weak spots as if he'd been pulling the legs off a spider. *Heart melts for stray cats, squirrels with cancer; blood boils for battered women and oppressed minorities and anyone who ever ended up on the wrong end of a shockprod. Not into performance rage, doesn't waste any capital getting bent out of shape over random acts of microaggression. Smart enough to save herself for the big stuff. Which is why she still gets to soapbox on the prime feeds while the rest of the rabies brigade fights for space on the public microblogs.*

Twenty floors below, pedestrians moved like ants. They'd never be life-sized to Becker; she'd arrived by the roof and she'd leave the same way, a concession to those who'd much rather have conducted this interview under more controlled conditions. Who'd much rather have avoided this interview entirely, for that matter. That they'd ceded so much control spoke volumes about Optic Nerve's rep for damage control.

If we can just get her to see you *as a victim—which is exactly what you are—we can turn her from agitator to cheerleader. Start off your appies as a tool of the patriarchy, you'll be her soulmate by dessert.*

Or maybe it spoke volumes about a situation so desperate that the optimum strategy consisted of gambling everything on a Hail Mary.

THERE SHE IS, Monahan murmured now, just inside her right temple, but Becker had already locked on: the target was dug in at a table next to the railing. This side, flower boxes and hors-d'oeuvres: that side, an eighty-meter lunge to certain death. Wingman, defanged but still untrusting, sent wary standbys to the stumps of amputated weaponry.

Amal Sabrie stood at her approach. "You look—" she began.

—*like shit.* Becker hadn't slept in three days. It shouldn't have shown; borgs don't get tired.

"I mean," Sabrie continued smoothly, "I thought the augments would be more conspicuous."

Great wings, spreading from her shoulders and laying down the wrath of God. Corporal Nandita Becker, Angel of Death.

"They usually are. They come off."

Neither extended a hand. They sat.

"I guess they'd have to. Unless you sleep standing up." A thought seemed to occur to her. "You sleep, right?"

"I'm a cyborg, Ms. Sabrie. Not a vacuum cleaner." An unexpected flicker of irritation, there; a bright spark on a vast dark plain. After all these flat waking hours. Becker almost welcomed it.

Monahan didn't. TOO HOSTILE. DIAL IT DOWN.

Sabrie didn't miss a beat. "A cyborg who can flip cars one-handed, if the promos are to be believed."

BE FRIENDLY. GIVE A LITTLE. DON'T MAKE HER PULL TEETH.

Okay.

Becker turned in her seat, bent her neck so the journalist could glimpse the tip of the black enameled centipede bolted along her backbone. "Spinal and long-bone reinforcement to handle the extra weight. Wire-muscle overlays, store almost twenty Joules per cc." There was a kind of mindless comfort in rattling off the specs. "Couples at over seventy percent under most—"

A *LITTLE*, CORPORAL.

"Anyway." Becker shrugged, straightened. "Most of the stuff's inside. The rest's plug and play." She took a breath, got down to it. "I should tell you up front I'm not authorized to talk about mission specifics."

Sabrie shrugged. "I'm not here to ask about them. I want to talk about you." She tapped her menu, entered an order for kruggets and a Rising Tide. "What're you having?"

"Thanks. I'm not hungry."

"Of course." The reporter glanced up. "You *do* eat, though, right? You still have a digestive system?"

"Nah. They just plug me into the wall." A smile to show she was kidding.

NOW YOU'RE GETTING IT.

"Glad you can still make jokes," Sabrie said from a face turned suddenly to stone.

SHIT. WALKED RIGHT INTO THAT ONE.

Down in the left hand, a tremor. Becker pulled her hands from the table, rested them on her lap.

"Okay," Sabrie said at last. "Let's get started. I have to say I'm surprised Special Forces even let me talk to you. The normal response in cases like this is to refuse comment, double down, wait for a celebrity overdose to move the spotlight."

"I'm just following orders, ma'am." The tic in Becker's hand wouldn't go away. She clasped her hands together, squeezed.

"So let's talk about something you *can* speak to," Sabrie said. "How do you feel?"

Becker blinked. "Excuse me?"

"About what happened. Your role in it. How do you feel?"

BE HONEST.

"I feel fucking *awful*," she said, and barely kept her voice from cracking. "How am I supposed to feel?"

"Awful," Sabrie admitted. She held silence for a respectable interval before pressing on. "The official story's systems malfunction."

"The investigation is ongoing," Becker said softly.

"Still. That's the word from sources. Your augments fired, you didn't. No *mens rea*."

Blobs of false color, spreading out against the sand.

"Do you *feel* like you killed them?"

TELL HER THE TRUTH, Monahan whispered.

"I—*part* of me did. Maybe."

"They say the augments don't do anything you wouldn't do yourself. They just do it faster."

Six people on an empty ocean. It didn't make any fucking sense.

"Is that the way you understand it?" Sabrie pressed. "The brain decides what it's going to do before it *knows* it's decided?"

Becker forced herself to focus, managed a nod. Even that felt a bit shaky, although the journalist didn't seem to notice. "Like a, a bubble rising from the bottom of a lake. We don't see it until it breaks the surface. The augs see it—before."

"How does that feel?"

"It feels like—" Becker hesitated.

HONESTY, CORPORAL. YOU'RE DOING GREAT.

"It's like having a really good wingman sitting on your shoulder, watching your back. Taking out threats before you even see them. Except it's using your own body to do that. Does that make sense?"

"As much as it can, maybe. To someone who isn't augged themselves." Sabrie essayed a little frown. "Is that how it felt with Tionee?"

"Who?"

"Tionee Anoka. Reesi Eterika. Io—" She stopped at something she saw in Becker's face.

"I never knew," Becker said after a moment.

"Their names?"

Becker nodded.

"I can send you the list."

A waiter appeared, deposited a tumbler and a steaming platter of fluorescent red euphausiids in front of Sabrie; assessed the ambiance and retreated without a word.

"I didn't—" Becker closed her eyes. "I mean yes, it felt the same. At first. There had to be a threat, right? Because the augs—because *I* fired. And I'd be dead at least four times over by now if I always waited until I knew what I was firing at." She swallowed against the lump in her throat. "Only this time things started to—sink in afterward. Why didn't I see them coming? Why weren't the—"

CAREFUL, CORPORAL. NO TAC.

"Some of them were still— moving. One was talking. Trying to."

"To you?"

Up in ultraviolet, the textured glass of the table fractured the incident sunlight into tiny rainbows. "No idea."

"What did they say?" Sabrie poked at her kruggets but didn't eat.

Becker shook her head. "I don't speak Kiribati."

"All those augments and you don't have realtime translation?"

"I—I never thought of that."

"Maybe those smart machines saw the bubbles rising. Knew you wouldn't *want* to know."

She hadn't thought of that either.

"So you feel awful," Sabrie said. "What else?"

"What else am I feeling?" The tremor had spread to both hands.

"If it's not too difficult."

What the fuck is *this, he said I'd be* steady, *he said the drugs—*

"They gave me propranolol." It was almost a whisper, and Becker wondered immediately if she'd crossed the line. But the voice in her head stayed silent.

Sabrie nodded. "For the PTSD."

"I know how that sounds. It's not like I was a victim or anything." Becker stared at the table. "I don't think it's working."

"It's a common complaint, out there on the cutting edge. All those neurotransmitters, synthetic hormones. Too many interactions. Things don't always work the way they're supposed to."

Monahan, you asshole. You're the goddamn PR expert, you should've known I wasn't up for this . . .

"I feel worse than awful." Becker could barely hear her own voice. "I feel *sick . . .* "

Sabrie appraised her with black unblinking eyes.

"This may be bigger than an interview," she said at last. "Do you think we could arrange a couple of follow-ups, maybe turn this into an in-depth profile piece?"

"I—I'd have to clear it with my superiors."

Sabrie nodded. "Of course."

Or maybe, Becker thought, *you knew all along.* As, two hundred fifty kilometers away, a tiny voice whooped in triumph.

They plugged her into an alternate universe where death came with an undo option. They ran her through scenarios and simulations, made her kill a hundred civilians a hundred different ways. They made her relive Kiribati again and again through her augments, for all the world as if she wasn't already reliving it every time she closed her goddamn eyes.

It was all in her head, of course, even if it wasn't all in her mind; a high-speed dialogue between synapse and simulator, a multichannel exchange through a pipe as fat as any corpus callosum. A Monte-Carlo exercise in tactical brutality.

After the fourth session she opened her eyes and Blanch had disappeared; some neon red-head had replaced him while Becker had been racking up the kills. *Tauchi,* according to his name tag. She couldn't see any augments but he glowed with smartwear in the megahertz range.

"Jord's on temporary reassignment," he said when she asked. "Tracking down the glitch."

"But—but I thought *this*—"

"This is something else. Close your eyes."

Sometimes she had to let innocent civilians die in order to save others. Sometimes she had to murder people whose only crime was being in the wrong place at the wrong time: blocking a clean shot on a battlebot that was drawing down on a medical team, or innocently reaching for some control that had been hacked to ignite a tank of H2S half a city away. Sometimes Becker hesitated on those shots, held back in some forlorn hope that the target might move or change its mind. Sometimes, even lacking any alternative, she could barely bring herself to pull the trigger.

She wondered if maybe they were trying to toughen her up. Get her back in the saddle, desensitized through repetition, before her own remorse made her useless on the battlefield.

Sometimes there didn't seem to be a right answer, no clear way to determine whose life should take priority; mixed groups of children and adults, victims in various states of injury and amputation. The choice between a brain-damaged child and its mother. Sometimes Becker was expected to kill with no hope of saving anyone; she took strange comfort in the stark simplicity of those old classics. Fuck this handwringing over the relative weights of human souls. Just point and shoot.

I am a camera, she thought.

"Who the hell makes up these scenarios?"

"Don't like judgment calls, Corporal?"

"Not *those* ones."

"Not much initiative." Tauchi nodded approvingly. "Great on the follow-through, though." He eyed his pad. "Hmmm. That might be why. Your cortisol's fucked."

"Can you fix that? I don't think my augs have been working since I got back."

"Flashbacks? Sweats? Vigilant immobility?"

Becker nodded. "I mean, aren't they supposed to take care of all that?"

"Sure," Tauchi told her. "You start to freak, they squirt you a nice hit of dopamine or leumorphin or whatever to level you out. Problem is, do that often enough and it stops working. Your brain grows more receptors to handle the extra medicine, so now you need more medicine to feed the extra receptors. Classic habituation response."

"Oh."

"If you've been feeling wobbly lately, that's probably why. Killing those kids only pushed you over the threshold."

God, she missed Blanch.

"Chemistry sets are just a band-aid anyway," the tech rattled on. "I can tweak your settings to keep you out of the deep end for now, but longer-term we've got something better in mind."

"A drug? They've already got me on propranolol."

He shook his head. "Permanent fix. There's surgery involved, but it's no big deal. Not even any cutting."

"When?" She could feel her insides crumbling. She imagined Wingman looking away, too good a soldier to be distracted by its own contempt. "*When?*"

Tauchi grinned. "Whaddya think we're doing now?"

She felt stronger by the next encounter.

This time it went down at street level; different patio, different ambiance, same combatants. Collapsed parasols hung from pikes rising through the center of each table, ready to spread protective shade should the afternoon sun ever make it past the skyscrapers. Sabrie set down a smooth rounded disk—a half-scale chrome hockey puck—next to the shaft. She gave it a tap.

Becker's BUD fuzzed around the edges with brief static; Wingman jumped to alert, hungry and limbless.

"For privacy," Sabrie said. "You okay with that?"

White noise on the radio. Broad-spectrum visual still working, though. The EM halo radiating from Sabrie's device was bright as a solar corona; her retinue of personal electronics glowed with dimmer light. Her watch. Her smartspecs, already recording; the faint nimbus of some medallion packed with circuitry, nestled out of sight between her breasts.

"Why now?" Becker asked. "Why not before?"

"First round's on the house. I was amazed enough that they even cleared the interview. Didn't want to push my luck."

Wingman flashed an icon; a little judicious frequency-hopping would get around the jam. If they'd been in an actual combat situation it wouldn't even be asking permission.

"You realize there are other ways to listen in," Becker said.

Sabrie shrugged. "Parabolic ear on a rooftop. Bounce a laser off the table and read the vibrations." Her eyes flickered overhead. "Any one of those drones could be a lip-reader for all I know."

"So what's the point?" (FHOP?[y/n] FHOP?[y/n] FHOP?[y/n])

"Perpetual surveillance is the price of freedom," Sabrie said, half-smiling. "Not to mention the price of not having to worry about some random psycho shooter when you go out for sushi."

"But?"

"But there are limits. Your bosses are literally inside your *head*." She dipped her chin at the jammer. "Do you think they'll object to you providing a few unprompted answers? Given this new apparent policy of transparency and accountability?"

(FHOP?[y/n])

(N)

"I don't know," Becker said.

"You know what would make them even *more* transparent and accountable? If they released the video for the night of the 25th. I keep asking, and they keep telling me there isn't any."

Becker shook her head. "There isn't."

"Come on."

"Really. Too memory-intensive. "

"Corporal, I'm recording *this*," Sabrie pointed out. "16K, Slooped sound, no compression even." She glanced into the street. "Half those people are life-logging every second of their lives for the sheer narcissistic thrill of it."

"And they're *streaming* it. Or caching and dumping every couple of hours. I don't get the luxury of tossing my cookies into some cloud whenever my cache fills up. I have to be able to operate in the dark for weeks at a time: you stream any kind of data in the field, it points back at you like a big neon arrow.

"Besides, budget time rolls around, how much of your limited R&D funding are you going to take away from tactical computing so you can make longer nature documentaries?" Becker raised her expresso in a small mock toast. "You think the People's Republic is losing any sleep over that one?"

Which is awfully convenient, remarked a small voice, *When you've just—*
She shut it off.

Sabrie gave her a sidelong look. "You can't record video."

"Sure I can. But it's discretionary. You document anything you think needs documenting, but the default realtime stream is just numbers. Pure black-box stuff."

"You didn't think you needed to document—"

"I didn't *know.* It wasn't *conscious.* Why the *fuck* can't you people—"
Sabrie watched her without a word.

"Sorry," Becker said at last.

"It's okay," Sabrie said softly. "Rising bubbles. I get it."

Overhead, the sun peeked around an office tower. A lozenge of brightness crept onto the table.

"You know what they were doing out there?" Sabrie asked. "Tionee and his friends?"

Becker closed her eyes for a moment. "Some kind of fishing trip."

"And you never wondered why anyone would go night fishing in a place where there wasn't anything to catch but slugs and slime?"

I never stopped *wondering.* "I heard it was a—cultural thing. Keep the traditions alive, in case someone ever builds a tuna that eats limestone."

"It was an art project."

Becker squinted as the hockey puck bounced sunlight into her eyes. "Excuse me?"

"Let me get that for you." Sabrie half-rose and reached for the center of the table. The parasol bloomed with a snap. The table dropped back into eclipse.

"That's better." Sabrie reseated herself.

"An art project?" Becker repeated.

"They were college students. Cultural anthropology and art history majors, wired in from Evergreen State. Re-enact the daily lives of your forebears, play them back along wavelengths outside the human sensory range. They were calling it *Through Alien Eyes.* Some kind of commentary on outsider perspectives."

"What wavelengths?"

"Reesi was glassing everything from radio to gamma."

"There's a third-party recording?"

"Nothing especially hi-def. They were on a student budget, after all. But it was good enough to pick out a signal around four hundred megahertz. Nobody can quite figure out what it is. Not civilian, anyway."

"That whole area's contested. Military traffic all over the place."

"Yeah, well. The thing is, it was a just a couple of really short bursts. Half a second, maybe. Around eleven-forty-five."

Wingman froze. Gooseflesh rippled up Becker's spine.

Sabrie leaned forward, hands flat on the table. "That wouldn't have been you, would it?"

"You know I can't discuss operational details."

"Mmmm." Sabrie watched and waited.

"I take it you have this recording," Becker said at last.

The journalist smiled faintly. "You know I can't discuss operational details."

"I'm not asking you to compromise your sources. It just seems—odd."

"Because your guys would have been all over the bodies before they were even cool. So if anyone had that kind of evidence, it would be them."

"Something like that."

"Don't worry, you don't have a mole. Or at least if you do, they don't report to me. You want to blame anyone, blame your *wing man*."

"What?"

"Your *preconscious triggers* tie into some pretty high-caliber weaponry. I'm guessing I don't have to tell you what kind of games physics plays when multiple slugs hit a body at twelve hundred meters a second."

Momentum. Inertia. Force vectors transferred from small masses to larger ones—and maybe back to smaller ones again. A pair of smartspecs could have flown twenty meters or more, landed way up in the weeds or splashed down in the lagoon.

"We wouldn't have even known to look," Becker murmured.

"We did." Sabrie sipped her drink. "Want to hear it?"

Becker sat absolutely still.

"I know the rules, Nandita. I'm not asking you to ID it, or even comment. I just thought you might like . . . "

Becker glanced down at the jammer.

"I think we should leave that on." Sabrie reached into her blouse, fingered the luminous medallion hanging from her neck. "You have sockets, though, right? Hard interfaces?"

"I don't spread my legs in public."

Sabrie's eyes flickered to the far side of the street, where a small unmarked quadrocopter had just dipped into sight below the rim of the parasol. "Let's talk about your family," she said.

Monahan didn't seem put out.

"We thought she might try something like that. Sabrie's hardly in the tank. But you did great, Corporal."

"You were monitoring?"

"Like we'd let some gizmo from the Sony Store cut us out of the loop? I could've even whispered sweet nothings in your ear if I'd had to—acoustic tightbeam, she'd never have had a clue unless she leaned over and nibbled your earlobe—but like I say, you were just fine." Some small afterthought made him frown. "Would've been easier if you'd just authorized frequency hopping, of course . . . "

"She had a lot of gizmos on her," Becker said. "If one of them had been able to pick up the signal . . . "

"Right. Good plan. Let her think it worked."

"Yes sir."

"Just Ben. Oh, one other thing . . . "

Becker waited.

"We lost contact for just a few moments there. When the umbrella went up."

"You didn't miss much. Apparently the collateral was doing a school project of some kind. Art history. They weren't actually fishing, it was more of a—a re-enactment, I guess."

"Huh. Pretty much what we heard." Monahan nodded. "Next time, might help if you went to active logging. You know, when we're out of contact."

"Right. Sorry. I didn't think."

"Don't apologize. After what you've been through I'd be amazed if you *didn't* make the occasional slip."

He patted her on the back. Wingman bristled.

"I gotta prep for a thing. Keep up the *great* work."

All those devil's bargains and no-win scenarios. All those exercises that tore her up inside. Turned out they were part of the fix. They had to parameterize Becker's remorse before they could burn it out of her.

It was a simple procedure, they assured her, a small part of the scheduled block upgrade. Seven deep-focus microwave bursts targeting the ventromedial prefrontal cortex. Ten minutes, tops. Not so much as a scar to show for it afterward. She didn't even need to sign anything.

They didn't put her under. They turned her off.

Coming back online, she didn't feel much different. The usual faint hum at the back of her skull as Wingman lit up and looked around; the usual tremors in fingers and toes, half-way between a reboot sequence and a voltage spike. The memory of her distant malfunction seemed a bit less intense, but then again things often seemed clearer after a good night's sleep. Maybe she was just finally seeing things in perspective.

They plugged her into the simulator and worked her out.

Fifty-plus male, thirtysomething female, and a baby alone in a nursery: all spread out, all in mortal and immediate danger as the house they were trapped in burned down around them. She started with the female, went back to extract the male, was heading back in for the baby when the building collapsed. *Two out of three,* she thought. *Not bad.*

Sniper duty on some post-apocalyptic overpass, providing cover for an airbus parked a hundred meters down the road below, for the refugees running and hobbling and dragging themselves towards salvation. A Tumbleweed passing beneath: a self-propelled razorwire tangle of ONC and magnesium and white phosphorus, immune to bullets, hungry for body heat, rolling eagerly toward the unsuspecting evacuees. The engineer at Becker's side— his face an obvious template, although the sim tagged him as her *brother* for some reason—labored to patch the damage to their vehicle, oblivious to the refugees and their imminent immolation.

Oblivious until Becker pitched him off the overpass and brought the Tumbleweed to rapture.

The next one was a golden oldie: the old man in the war zone, calling for some lost pet or child, blocking Becker's shot as a battlefield robot halfway to the horizon took aim at a team of medics. She took out the old man with one bullet and no second thought; took out the bot with three more.

"Why'd you leave the baby for last?" Tauchi asked afterward, unhooking her. The light in his eyes was pure backwash from the retinal display, but he looked eager as a puppy just the same.

"Less of a loss," Becker said.

"In terms of military potential?" They'd all been civilians; tactically, all last among equals.

Becker shook her head, tried to put instinct into words. "The adults would—suffer more."

"Babies can't suffer?"

"They can hurt. Physically. But no hopes or dreams, no memories even. They're just—potential. No added value."

Tauchi looked at her.

"What's the big deal?" Becker asked. "It was an exercise."

"You killed your *brother*," he remarked.

"In a simulation. To save fifty civilians. I don't even *have* a brother."

"Would it surprise you to know that you took out the old man and the battlebot a full six hundred milliseconds faster than you did before the upgrade?"

She shrugged. "It was a repeat scenario. It's not like I even got it wrong the first time."

Tauchi glanced at his tacpad. "It didn't *bother* you the second time."

"So what are you saying? I'm some kind of sociopath now?"

"Exactly the opposite. You've been immunized against trolley paradoxes."

"What?"

"Everybody talks about morality like it's another word for *right and wrong*, when it's really just a load of static on the same channel." Tauchi's head bobbed like a woodpecker. "We just cleaned up the signal. As of now, you're probably the most ethical person on the planet."

"Really."

He walked it back, but not very far. "Well. You're in the top thirty at least."

Buried high above the streets of Toronto, cocooned in a windowless apartment retained as a home base for transient soldiers on missions of damage control: Nandita Becker, staring at the wall and watching the Web.

The wall was blank. The Web was in her head, invited through a back door in her temporal lobe. She and Wingman had spent altogether too much time alone in there, she'd decided. Time to have some company over.

The guest heads from Global's *Front View Mirror,* for example: a JAG lawyer, a retired professor of military law from Dalhousie, a token lefty from Veterans for Accountable Government. Some specialist in cyborg tech she'd never met, on loan from the Ministry of Defence and obviously chosen as much for disarming good looks as for technical expertise. (Becker imagined Ben Monahan just out of camera range, pulling strings.) A generic moderator whose affect alternated between earnest sincerity and failed attempts at cuteness.

They were all talking about Becker. At least, she assumed they still were. She'd muted the audio five minutes in.

The medallion in her hand glowed like dim cobalt through the flesh of her fingers, a faint nimbus up at 3MHz. She contemplated the feel of the metal, the decorative filigree (a glyph from some Amazonian culture that hadn't survived first contact, according to Sabrie), the hairline fracture of the interface port. The recessed Transmit button in its center: tap it once and it would squawk once, Sabrie had told her. Hold it down and it would broadcast on continuous loop.

She pressed it. Nothing happened.

Of course not. There'd be crypto. You didn't broadcast *anything* in the field without at least feeding it through a pseudorandom timeseries synched to the mothership—you never knew when some friend of Amal Sabrie might be lurking in the weeds, waiting to snatch it from the air and take it home for leisurely dissection. The signal made sense only at the instant of its creation. If you missed it the first time, wanted to repeat it for the sake of clarity, you'd need a time machine.

Becker had built her own personal time machine that very afternoon, stuck it at #1 on speed-dial: a three-line macro to reset her system clock to a dark moment weeks in the past, just before her world had turned to shit.

She unmuted audio on the web feed. One of Global's talking heads was opining that Becker was as much a victim as those poor envirogees her hijacked body had gunned down. Another spoke learnedly of the intimate connection between culpability and intent, of how blame—if that loaded term could even be applied in this case—must lie with the technology and not with those noble souls who daily put their lives on the line in the dangerous pestholes of a changing world.

"And yet this technology doesn't decide anything on its own," the moderator was saying. "It just does what the soldier's already decided sub—er, *pre*consciously."

"That's a bit simplistic," the specialist replied. "The system has access to a huge range of data that no unaugged soldier would ever be able to process in realtime—radio chatter, satellite telemetry, wide-spectrum visuals—so it's actually taking that preconscious intent and modifying it based on what the soldier *would* do if she had access to all those facts."

"So it guesses," said the man from VAG.

"It predicts."

"And that doesn't open the door to error?"

"It reduces error. It optimizes human wisdom based on the maximum available information."

"And yet in this case—"

Becker held down TRANSMIT and sacc'd speed-dial.

"—don't want to go down that road," the lawyer said. "No matter *what* the neurology says."

Thirty-five seconds. Gone in an instant.

"Our whole legal system is predicated on the concept of free will. It's the moral center of human existence."

That was so much bullshit, Becker knew. She knew exactly where humanity's moral center was. She'd looked it up not six hours ago: the place where the brain kept its empathy and compassion, its guilt and shame and remorse.

The ventromedial prefrontal cortex.

"Suppose—" The moderator raised a finger. "—I get into a car with a disabled breathalyzer. I put it into manual and hit someone. Surely I bear some responsibility for the fact that I *chose* to drink and drive, even if I didn't intend to hurt anyone."

"That depends on whether you'd received a lawful command from a superior officer to get behind the wheel," Ms. JAG countered.

"You're saying a soldier can be *ordered* to become a cyborg?"

"How is that different from ordering a sniper to carry a rifle? How is it different from ordering soldiers to take antimalarial drugs—which have also, by the way, been associated with violent behavioral side-effects in the past—when we deploy them to the Amazon? A soldier is sworn to protect their country; they take that oath knowing the normal tools of their trade, knowing that technology advances. You don't win a war by bringing knives to a gunfight—"

Speed-dial.

"—may not like cyborgs—and I'm the first to agree there are legitimate grounds for concern—but until you can talk the Chinese into turning back the clock on *their* technology, they're by far the lesser evil."

Twenty-eight seconds, that time.

"It's not as though we ever lived in a world without collateral damage. You don't shut down such a vital program over a tragic accident."

A tragic accident. Even Becker had believed that. Right up until Sabrie had slipped her a medallion with a burst of radio static in its heart, a cryptic signal snatched from the warm Pacific night by a pair of smart-specs on a dead kid walking. A signal that was somehow able to offline her for intervals ranging from twenty to sixty-three seconds.

She wondered if there was any sort of pattern to that variability.

"Safeguards should be put into place at the very least." The moderator was going for the middle road. "Ways to monitor these, these *hybrids* remotely, shut them down at the first sign of trouble."

Becker snorted. Wingman didn't take orders in the field, couldn't even *hear* them. Sure, Becker could channel some smiley little spin doctor through her temporal, but he was just a Peeping Tom with no access to the motor systems. The actual metal didn't even pack an on-board receiver; it was congenitally deaf to wireless commands until someone manually slotted the dorsal plug-in between Becker's shoulders.

Deliberately design a combat unit that could be shut down by anyone who happened to hack the right codes? Who'd be that stupid?

And yet—

TRANSMIT. Speed-dial.

"—are only a few on active duty—they won't tell us exactly how many of course, say twenty or thirty. A couple dozen cyborgs who can't be blamed if something goes wrong. And that's just *today*. You wouldn't believe how fast they're ramping up production."

Forty seconds. On the nose.

"Not only do I believe it, I *encourage* it. The world's a tinderbox. Water wars, droughts, refugees everywhere you look. The threat of force is the only thing that's kept a lid on things so far. Our need for a strong military is greater today than it's ever been since the cold war, especially with the collapse of the US eco—"

Speed-dial.

"—and what happens when *every* pair of boots in the field has a machine reading its mind and pulling the trigger in their name? What happens to the very concept of a *war crime* when every massacre can be defined as an industrial accident?"

Thirty-two.

"You're saying this Becker deliberately—"

"I'm saying nothing of the kind. I'm *concerned.* I'm concerned at the speed with which outrage over the massacre of civilians has turned into an outpouring of sympathy for the person who killed them, even from quarters you'd least expect. Have you *seen* the profile piece Amal Sabrie posted on *The Star*?"

A shutdown command, radioed to a system with no radio.

"Nobody's forgetting the victims here. But it's no great mystery why people also feel a certain sympathy for Corporal Becker—"

Becker kept wondering who'd be able to pull off a trick like that, hide a secret receiver under the official specs. She kept coming up with the same answer.

"Of course. She's sympathetic, she's charismatic, she's *nice.* Exemplary soldier, not the slightest smudge on her service record. She volunteered at a veterinary clinic back in high school."

Someone with an interest in *controlling the narrative.*

"Chief of Defense couldn't have a better poster girl if they'd *planned*—"

Dial.

"—should be up on charges is for the inquiry to decide."

Forty-two seconds.

She wondered if she should be feeling something right now. Outrage. Violation. She'd thought the procedure was only supposed to cure her PTSD. It seemed to have worked on that score, anyway.

"Then let the inquiry decide. But we can't allow this to become the precedent that tips over the Geneva Conventions."

The other stuff, though. The compassion, the empathy, the guilt. The moral center. That seemed to be gone too. They'd burned it out of her like a tumor.

"The Conventions are a hundred years old. You don't think they're due for an overhaul?"

She still had her sense of right and wrong, at least.

Brain must keep that somewhere else.

"I thought they'd shipped you back to the WTP," Sabrie remarked.

"This weekend."

The journalist glanced around the grotto: low light, blue-shifted, private tables arrayed around a dance floor where partygoers writhed to bass beats that made it only faintly through the table damper. She glanced down at the Rising Tide Becker had ordered for her.

"I don't fuck my interviews, Corporal. Especially ones who could snap my spine if they got carried away."

Becker smiled back at her. "Not why we're here."

"Ohhhkay."

"Bring your jammer?"

"Always." Sabrie slapped the little device onto the table; welcome static fuzzed Becker's peripherals.

"So why *are* we in a lekking lounge at 2 a.m.?"

"No drones," Becker said.

"None in the local Milestones either. Even during business hours."

"Yeah. I just—I wanted a crowd to get lost in."

"At two in the morning."

"People have other things on their mind in the middle of the night." Becker glanced up as a triplet stumbled past en route to the fuck-cubbies. "Less likely to notice someone they may have seen on the feeds."

"Okay."

"People don't—congregate the way they used to, you know?" Becker sipped her scotch, set it down, stared at it. "Everyone telecommutes, everyone cocoons. Downtown's so—thin, these days."

Sabrie panned the room. "Not here."

"Web don't fuck. Not yet, anyway. Still gotta go out if you want to do anything more than whack off."

"What's on your mind, Nandita?"

"The price of freedom."

"Go on."

"Not having to worry about some random psycho shooter when you go out for sushi. Don't tell me you've forgotten."

"You know I was being sarcastic."

Becker cocked her head at the other woman. "I don't think you were. Not entirely, anyway."

"Maybe not entirely."

"Because there *were* shootings, Amal. A lot of them. Twenty thousand deaths a year."

"Mainly down in the states, thank God." Sabrie said. "But yes."

"Back before the panopticon, people could just walk into some school or office building and—light it up." Becker frowned. "I remember there was this one guy shot up a *daycare*. Prechoolers. Babies. I forget how many he killed before they took him out. Turned out he'd lost a sister himself, six months before, in *another* shooting. Everybody said it tipped him over the edge and he went on a rampage."

"That doesn't make sense."

"That shit never does. It's what people said, though, to explain it. Only . . . "

"Only?" Sabrie echoed after the pause had stretched a bit too far.

"Only what if he wasn't crazy at all?" Becker finished.

"How could he not be?"

"He lost his sister. Classic act of senseless violence. The whole gun culture, you know, the NRA had everyone by the balls and anyone who so much as *whispered* about gun control got shot down. So to speak." Becker grunted. "Words didn't work. Advocacy didn't work. The only thing that might possibly work would be something so unthinkable, so horrific and obscene and unspeakably evil, that not even the most strident gun nut could possibly object to—countermeasures."

"Wait, you're saying that someone in favor of gun control—someone who'd *lost his sister to gun violence*— would deliberately shoot up a daycare?"

Becker spread her hands.

"You're saying he turned himself into a monster. Killed twenty, thirty kids maybe. For a piece of legislation."

"Weighed against thousands of deaths a year. Even if legislation only cut that by a few percent you'd make back your investment in a week or two, tops."

"Your *investment*?"

"Sacrifice, then." Becker shrugged.

"Do you know how insane that sounds?"

"How do you know that's not the way it went down?"

"Because you said nothing changed! No laws were passed! They just wrote him off as another psycho."

"He couldn't know that up front. All he knew was, there was a chance. His life, a few others, for thousands. There was a *chance*."

"I can't believe that you, of all people, would—after what happened, after what you *did*—"

"Wasn't me, remember? It was Wingman. That's what everyone's saying." Wingman was awake now, straining at the leash with phantom limbs.

"But you were still part of it. You know that, Deet, you *feel* it. Even if it wasn't your fault it still tears you up inside. I saw that the first time we spoke. You're a good person, you're a moral person, and—"

"Do you know what morality is, really?" Becker looked coolly into the other woman's eyes. "It's letting two stranger's kids die so you can save one of your own. It's thinking it makes some kind of difference if you look into someone's eyes when you kill them. It's squeamishness and cowardice and *won't someone think of the children*. It's not rational, Amal. It's not even ethical."

Sabrie had gone very quiet.

"Corporal," she said when Becker had fallen silent, "what have they done to you?"

Becker took a breath. "Whatever they're doing—"

Not much initiative. Great on the follow-through.

"—it ends here."

Sabrie's eyes went wide. Becker could see pieces behind them, fitting together at last. No drones. Dense crowd. No real security, just a few bouncers built of pitiful meat and bone . . .

"I'm sorry, Amal," Becker said gently.

Sabrie lunged for the jammer. Becker snatched it up before the journalist's hand had made it halfway.

"I can't have people in my head right now."

"Nandita." Sabrie was almost whispering. "Don't do this."

"I like you, Amal. You're good people. I'd leave you right out of it if I could, but you're—smart. And you know me, a little. Maybe well enough to put it together, afterward . . . "

Sabrie leapt up. Becker didn't even rise from her chair. She seized the other woman's wrist quick as a striking snake, effortlessly forced it back onto the table. Sabrie cried out. Dim blue dancers moved on the other side of the damper field, other things on their minds.

"You won't get away with it. You can't blame the machines for—" Soft pleading words, urgent, rapid-fire. The false-color heatprint of the contusion spread out across Sabrie's forearm like a dim rainbow, like a bright iridescent oil slick. "*Please* there's no *way* they'll be able to sell this as a malfunction no matter how—"

"That's the whole point," Becker said, and hoped there was at least a little sadness left in her smile. "You know that."

Amal Sabrie. Number one of seventy-four.

It would have been so much faster to just spread her wings and raise arms. But her wings had been torn out by the roots, and lay twitching in the garage back at Trenton. The only arms she could raise were of flesh and blood and graphene.

It was enough, though. It was messy, but she got the job done. Because Corporal Nandita Becker was more than just a superhuman killing machine.

She was the most ethical person on the planet.

ABERRATION

GENEVIEVE VALENTINE

You'll see them someplace you're going when you're trying to make the most of your time. They're standing at the top of the steps to the public library (the amazing branch where they do the photoshoots, not the squat concrete one you go to), or they're on the balcony at a concert you overheard someone talking about. They'll be at the greatest altitude you can reach while still seeming effortless; they like being able to look down.

You'll notice them a long time before they notice you, though they seem to stutter in and out of sight. They're dressed the way you've always wanted to dress. Sometimes you'll glance back and not see them, but they're nowhere else either, and a second later something catches your eye and it's them anyway and you feel like an asshole. You never get a sense of what they look like.

If they smoke they'll barely keep hold of their limp-dick cigarettes, wrist angled hard enough to crack. If they laugh it's parted lips but teeth close together, two straight rows, a furrow between their eyebrows like they're already finding reasons it's not so funny after all. One of them touches the other one right at the small of the back, cigarette a cinder between their fingers, and you get the impression of pushing even though nobody's moved.

They're awful, they don't even pretend otherwise, and when you look at them the hair on your neck stands up, and the word Rotten unfurls inside of you. (You couldn't say it if anyone asked, your mouth is too dry, but it sits there sharp-edged, like you swallowed a name tag.)

One of them peels away, finally, passes you on the way to the bar or around the bottom edge of the steps towards the street; shoulders pinched, the shadow of the other one already falling across both of you.

"Don't look," she says, so low that music or traffic swallows it up. When they disappear, you're still standing right where you were, staring at your own shoes, and it's fucking stupid, but as soon as the words were out your gaze dropped.

It wasn't like you did it because you were embarrassed to have been caught out; it was the urgency, some terror in the snap after the T and the K, and you know a warning when you hear one.

"Oh," she says at the top of the bridge.

There's little else worth saying—she's gotten so tired of languages lately, which would feel like a defeat if she cared more about losing—but a sound of surprise still falls out of her sometimes, some gut punch of feeling that gets a death rattle.

The last time she vanished from this city it was a ruin and you couldn't get within five miles of it, nothing left but a few plaster-roof islands and the last few wooden fingers of the pier. Appearing in it now is visiting a grave to find the departed eating an apple on their headstone.

She feels desperate already, so desperate as to be fully solid, and she grips the stone and waits for someone to run into her. No one does. No one can really see her for long; she's been so many places she's not really anywhere any more.

The stone's at her hip. It's quiet when she touches it, though she feels it all the time anyway, a phantom heat right through to her spine.

One of the vaporettos is sinking, nearer to the sea. But it's early, only just dawn, and no one will realize in time for the alarm to do any good; half of them will drown. It won't take long. She watches.

When it's over she walks through the smaller streets, catches half-sentences and the windows of shops where the things in the very front have gone a little dusty and it doesn't matter because they're only tourists. Someone is napping in a piazza, and after she touches his shoulder he has no more use for his camera. She takes three photographs: the slime easing up the edge of a canal, the curtains in a house where someone is very ill, the shadow of a flight of birds that looks like a monster underneath the water.

It's a city of corpses, like every other city, and she walks across the bridges and thinks about drowning.

He catches up with her under one of the abandoned billboards for Lunar Enterprises that looks out over a dark stretch of desert. She's crossed her arms to keep from looking for a cigarette. Nobody makes them any more; there's no point looking.

She's carrying a camera, one of the instant ones that's back in vogue. She's holding the pictures like a hand of poker, five snapshots of the city at the edge of the valley as the lights went out and out and out.

"They came out nice," his voice is a thousand years weary with telling her.

"They did." They're already fading, though; she only looked at them once. Soon they'll start to disappear at the edges, and by the time they leave here there won't be anything left to take.

He used to tell her to give it up, but she's not the only one who has hobbies, and he stopped asking a long time ago.

He reaches for the pack in his pocket, taps out two, lights the second one off the cherry from the first. They give off just enough flare to remind them how pitch dark it is. She can see the hollow above his top lip, that's all.

"I don't smoke any more," she says.

He raises his eyebrows, smokes both cigarettes at the same time.

The last of the smoke feathers from his mouth as he drops the butts; they vanish before they ever hit the ground, and he grinds his boot into the dirt like he's trying to spite them. Their kind leave no traces.

Still, hers just vanish; his all gathers somewhere, waiting for him, everything he touches, everything he does. He's always going home.

"Been hoping to run into you," he says.

She's been in eight places since she saw him last, or ten. In a couple of places there was only a day. She spent a week in the mountains, staying clear of a black bear that got more agitated the longer she stayed—it could tell something was wrong, right up until it died. She hopes it's all right now, but it's the same way she hopes everyone who drowns in Venice centuries from now fought until the very last; you get cruel eventually.

Maybe she started out cruel. She suspects that the very first time she opened her eyes and was elsewhen, her sympathy had vanished. Something she was born to.

(She's thought about it, that maybe anyone becomes like this if you give them long enough and show them what they've seen. Doesn't bear much reflection.)

From the city there's a siren. The blast that comes in the dark will kill three hundred people, give or take.

He made friends all the time. Said they held on more fiercely, which she knows; said they loved more deeply, which she doesn't doubt. But he loves them back, loves women and men and the sort of child who can actually see you, who stares you right in the eye and ignores you when you say, "Don't look," and then gets angry at all once as it realizes it's been robbed and it's looked too long at the thing that will kill it.

Lucky, she says when he tells her. He never asks her what she means.

"Good to see you," she says.

The first of the rumblings begins. They look across the darkness, where the edge of the city is just beginning to separate from the dark with a layer of smoke and flame.

Her heart is a thousand stairs with nothing at the top, and she's afraid all the way up.

• • •

If everything worked as it was meant to, you were always there just before the worst of it, the birdsong before the bomb. But aberration doesn't always listen, and she appeared too late, sometimes, or a year early, or a hundred years. Sometimes she'd shown up in the middle of a war, and when the stone in her pocket warmed and creaked and pushed her to wherever she was going next, it was the only sound on a field without graves, the ground swallowing blood as fast as it could.

Once, by some mistake, she'd been spat out before there were people at all, and she'd sat on a tree trunk and watched the sun stain the leaves, and the ferns at her feet rustle with animals that seemed like her: mammal at first glance, but reptile if you knew what you were looking for. She lifted her hands before she remembered she had no camera. It got colder eventually, warmer again. The ground underfoot stretched an inch or two. She wondered if she'd be sitting there for a hundred million years, waiting. She didn't mind.

There was a white vulture, and as it tilted its head to her, black eyes in sickly-blue sockets, it was the most beautiful thing she'd ever seen. She's forgotten the thing that died.

She had no camera. When she appeared next (Morocco, maybe), her hands sat in her lap a long time, framed by nothing.

Lens aberrations in a camera, in order of disaster:

Distortion: A warp across something you thought was holding steady. Tilt shift: makes your subject fall away from you, every house teetering on the verge of collapse. Bokeh: a cheat in the shape of light, turning light into spheres of nostalgia that hover behind whatever you're trying to capture, a hostage of a good time. Chromatic: The edges of your colors burn into something they aren't, and you can't trust your colors any more, but that one is subtle, and you won't know until it's too late.

Curvature: The thing you want most is sharp and bright, and everything else slips out of focus by degrees. That one you can live with. It's close enough to life. Can't blame it for that.

None of it works, of course. If it did there would be chaos. You can take all the pictures you want. Their face will be gone—some lens flare that wasn't there before, or a dove taking off in the foreground with two feathers spread over where they used to be, or obscured behind a cloud of someone's cigarette, even if you've never smoked and they never have. If there's no excuse that the frame can find, you'll just see a vanished face where the picture's been eaten away, someone lifting a disappearing glass to lips that don't exist anymore.

The invading army of a country that doesn't yet exist piles the corpses of the vanquished outside the camp. The straggling forces of the occupied wait until deep night before they set the bodies on fire. Their attack on the camp comes in the middle of the chaos, and takes hundreds of enemy lives; the contagion that was already sickening the dead wafts equally across friend and foe. Both armies will be decimated soon, and the germ will crawl victoriously over the countryside for longer than anyone remembers the war.

He's leaning against the tree trunk, barely touching her left shoulder; his hair makes a sound against the bark when he turns to look at her. "If you take the tragedy out of it, it's pretty funny."

This is why she gave up on languages. "If you take the tragedy out of anything, it's funny."

He smiles and rolls his stone across his knuckles, a skipping stone shaped like a coin. She's seen it a hundred times. She's never laid a finger on it.

A deserter staggers past them, close enough to death that when he looks up he's startled to see them.

"Don't look," she says, and the soldier opens his mouth, drops his gaze to the ground. It's too late for him, though, and he doesn't even make it past the tree before he crashes to the ground. He's facing them, eyes open; she looks away.

He looks back and forth between the corpse and her, and for a moment his face gets fond; it does that whenever something happens that he can take for her having some kind feeling.

She lets him think what he likes.

(He was the one who explained her aberration, the first time he ever found her, when she was occupying the last of her mind and he looked like he knew how thin that thread had gotten. He must have been looking for her; she wonders, sometimes.)

His trajectories seem like real journeys—every time she sees him she knows he's come from a place and is going to another, moving through the world and witnessing everything he can. Hers is a slow, suspended spiraling-down, and it's possible to tell at which points he came back by clocking when things skidded violently to one side, a kite that's been shot.

He watches her for a while, unblinking. She wonders if he's descended from the vulture, the way she's a child of that half-changed reptile.

She'd seen the sun rise over the valley once. It hit the top of the mountains first in a line of gold, and crept over the fields in a dozen shades of green—there had been sheep, only a handful, someone had been careless and would lose them before the sun was fully up. Pines ringed them in now, a jagged mouth that cast long shadows. At the edge of the green was the drop, and the lake underneath dark as a pool of oil.

The hill she stood on was clumps of heather that smelled rotten despite the dried-out grass, and with every step she sunk an inch as if the hill was going to give. There was a village at the bottom of the valley, just at the horizon, but no lights were on at all; she was the only one awake, watching the sun as the lake hid from it, as the sheep moved closer to the fall.

I want to keep this, she thought. There was no reason, there was never a reason to keep one thing that passed over another thing that passed, but this she loved more than she could remember loving anything. She was breathing just looking at it, hard enough that she could feel ribs.

She took a dozen pictures with the box camera she'd stolen from the city she'd walked away from, knowing none of them would hold this, knowing she was losing the moment when the heather looked alive with light. When the first two sheep fell she watched them go and had to sit down to keep from reaching forward over the edge of the drop to pull them back and try to catch it in the frame.

They made a noise as they fell, all of them, the same anguished cry that was more human than any sound a human made, but she's forgotten it. It was a long time ago, and there are no pictures.

"If I can affix myself, I will," she tells him the next time she sees him, which if she averages out the time in between her moves forward and back, near as she can tell, is two hundred years before the last time she saw him.

He doesn't have any cigarettes, and his thumbs twist at the edges of his pockets. His eyes are black, his skin is dark; she wonders what he looks like to the rest of them—a shadow, a hollow, the silhouette of someone they'd forgotten who will suddenly spring to mind just before terrible news comes in. He'd told her once that she's the color of the clay everyone walks over, but they were fighting then. No way of knowing.

"This is a terrible time to make a decision that terrible," he tells the bridge over the river. "Look at this place. Won't be worth living in for another seven hundred years, and you can't get anywhere else until they discover the waves."

"I don't want it now. I'll wait for the right place."

He looks at her from the corner of his eye. She wonders why she's hard to look at.

"You'll waste it," he says, like he sympathizes. "You'll throw yourself from the first tall thing you find. Staying anywhere turns into a circle of things that are never quite what you wanted. You like to see it and be finished."

That seems cruel for someone who has a place he can return to. "I can't keep hold of a camera," she says. "I don't like it to be finished. I just can't bring anything back home."

"You'd be wasted at home, too." He smooths his hands over his chest pockets. Empty.

"I found the place I really wanted. I know I'll never get back there, don't worry, that's all gone. But I've been looking."

"That sounds exhausting."

She thinks that's a little rich, coming from him. She doesn't say anything.

"So have you picked the lucky grave?"

She says, "I know what I'm waiting for."

To feel anything, she thinks. As soon as I open my eyes and feel anything at all, I'm going to bury this rock in the ground and live out my days and die. Any magic has to fade if you bury it in the ground; it leeches out through the water and the air, it becomes a village of people who live a long time but can never stay put, it becomes a herd of deer who cross a continent.

Then there will be time enough to find a high place, if she wants one. There will be a hill with a lake like oil at the bottom, and a sheer drop that no one climbs out of.

"Don't do something stupid just so I'll miss you," he says.

She turns to him. "Promise me you'll find me and tell me if it works."

I want you to know where I am, she doesn't say. She doesn't say, *I want you to look at my grave just once.*

"If it doesn't work, I won't have to find you. You'll open your eyes and a locomotive will run you over and you'll know, and when you open them again you'll know, without any help from me."

"Promise me you'll find me," she says.

Her eyes sting, looking at him. Maybe that's the first sign of something changing.

He meets her eye; her heart is a thousand stairs with nothing waiting at the top.

To remember, someone had told her as they touched her hair, before she ever learned about a camera and what it could do for anyone who wasn't her. To make you appreciate home, someone had told her as they pressed the stone into her hand—she'd been all night wandering, and it must have been an offense. They must have been afraid of her; she hopes she was frightening.

Don't do this to her, he'd said.

She's forgotten if he was always there or if he found the moment and tried to intervene; she only remembers his breath between her and the shadows the trees were casting. It was the last thing she ever heard, standing in that place.

She suspects it was meant to be a place she'd come back to, that her heart and the stone in her hand would draw her back there when the traveling was over, but the first time she opened her eyes all that was gone.

She doesn't remember where or when, or anyone she left. The ground that could never be filled had taken them all in its mouth, and if she went back in time enough to meet them, she wouldn't know their faces; she wouldn't know where to stand to call it homecoming.

Maybe she's stood there already, and all she saw was the little circle of the box camera, a field inverted, a picture that was going to be devoured any second.

When she closes her eyes and tries to conjure it back, she sees a drowned pier, and his face in a wreath of smoke, and a vulture's eye, and a camera lens that was grasping to hold on.

It takes sixteen moves before there's a worthy place. (One of them had seemed beautiful, but she was only there an hour before the stone got warm and she grit her teeth and felt the sick-stomach lurch that reminded her she had a body. It had been an hour of red dust so bright the sky looked purple next to it; chromatic aberration.)

But this is a quiet town, big enough that she can steal a camera, near enough to a river that she can follow it into the meadows, and be alone just past the bend. There's no high ground here, but the world is wide.

At the top of a sloping hill that's as close as she can find, there's a tree that reminds her of the place where they watched the beginning of the plague, and she presses her lips into a thin line, counts backwards carefully from ten as she gets closer. He never makes much noise. If she didn't always expect him, she'd never know when he'd appeared.

She stands beside the tree for a long time as the sun crawls over everything. The branches look like a man smoking, they look like someone reaching out for her, they look like a map of Venice. Below her is the little town and the river, and she looks as far as she can for a ship that could be carrying him.

At sunset the branches look like the veins on the leaf she looked through once as the things that would become mammals skittered across her feet. In the dark the branches make cracks in the sky as she looks up at the moon, asks it nothing, counts to a hundred thousand thousand.

It's dawn when the stone begins to get warm around the edges. Panic clenches her tight for a moment, and she thinks about plagues and cities and deserts and no, it has to be here, she has to risk it, she'll grow old waiting but she'll wait, when he finds her he might laugh but she can't stand the idea of ever again moving, she's breathing like her chest will burst, she's staying here.

She drags a few inches of earth off from the ground beneath the tree, shoves the stone into it, scrapes in her tears and breathes against it and spits for good measure, buries it in a single two-handed shove of dirt like a door slamming shut.

She closes her eyes, feels nothing, opens them. The bank of the river is shrinking; tide's coming in.

This is the ground then, she thinks. Whenever he finds me, he'll know where I'm buried.

It's sunrise when the light hits low enough that she sees the place where the ground is risen, a little burial mound grown over with a hundred years of moss and little blue flowers she's forgotten the name of.

It's a small grave. It's barely big enough for a small, flat rock she could roll between her fingers like a coin.

You'll see her when you go someplace trying to be alone—dramatically, romantically, the sheer hill that hangs over the bay, the kind of place where poets go. Somewhere you can look down on everything.

She'll be standing near the edge of wherever it is, not close enough that you'd feel right about crying out, but close enough that you keep glancing out of the corner of your eye as you sit down, try to let the moment wash over you. She seems like she's waiting for someone, though she's not moving, her arms crossed tight over her chest, everything about her looking pinched in, stretched out.

You never quite catch her face, however long you look at her; when you try to get her attention you just remember some dark unblinking eye and then something going fuzzy at the edges like a bad photograph. When you look out at the bay you always forget she's there until you move.

You'll begin to think that poetry's a bit much after all. It's not like you went through anything so bad, and it's awfully windy to be in a place so high. It's too windy to be as close to the edge as she is.

You'll stand up to reach her, start to move and then freeze, some prey instinct that holds you where you are.

"Be careful," you'll say.

She'll say, "Don't look."

SADNESS

TIMONS ESAIAS

—✦—

I hadn't seen one of the New People in years, and this wasn't the best time for one to drop by. I'd planned to go out to the Wall and think about killing my lover.

Isabel would not appreciate finding "one of Them" in "her" house, so before the visitor had even arrived I was trying to imagine strategies for getting it out of there. I urged her program to delay her morning ritual, and flash-queried our mayor as to just why this visitor would be coming.

"Who ever knows why they come? I wasn't told," he sent back. But to keep me from thinking he was giving me the usual dumb-bureaucrat-without-a-clue routine he attached a copy of the message they had sent him. "Visitor for Morgantown Sector, 9 a.m., this day, Occupant Evor Bookbinder."

Nervous, I made tea by hand, and reviewed the latest discussions on how the New People think, and how best to handle them. Most of the postings were rather old, indicating that the question wasn't much on anyone's mind these days. From what I could gather, today's visit would be just the third in the last twelve months. There had been none, zero, the year before. They had cameras to watch us, of course, including all the ones we use to watch ourselves, but their part of Humankind seemed to be giving our part only brief glances down an extremely disdainful upturned nose.

I reviewed the basics. Never move closer than four meters, and set your minder to keep track of the distance. Try not to use slang that you can't easily define when asked. Compound sentences are good, complex sentences are best. They love it when we switch verb tenses, but it also confuses the daylights out of them. Commit no crimes in their presence, because they always rat. Do not express frustration when you fail to make sense of what they are saying. Use your minder to replay their sentences until you feel ready to respond, but do not ask them to repeat anything. This seems to be deeply offensive. If you are befuddled, ask a clarifying question.

Yes, of course. I had forgotten the music of their voices, the layers.

I heard the music in the east garden, the little one off the lower den. My visitor was in the garden, and the clock specifically and clearly read 8:17.

They have no sense of time, these New People. No sense of civil promptness.

I loaded my tea onto a tray and added a second service. In the center I put an antique stemmed dish, on which lay the ceremonial bread and saltpeter. The visitor wouldn't take any of these, of course, but they seem to appreciate being included. I selected a kefiya of no political significance, covered my head, made the lesser prayer, and went down through the den to my guest.

I should have made the greater prayer. The guest had neglected to clothe itself properly, leaving its head uncovered to the insult of all Above and below, and one arm was fully exposed, and covered with those suppurating gray-purple scales that move. That seethe, is what I should say.

My gorge rising, I made obeisance and placed the tray on the small granite table Isabel had ordered from a quarry in New Hampshire, just weeks before New Hampshire was closed off. "It reminds me of Beyond," she would say. "It is my flotsam from the wreck of History."

It is also a beautiful table.

My visitor had been interrogating, in English, one of the chipmunks who feed on our offering plants. Perhaps he had tried Chipmunk unsuccessfully. I heard the interlaced threads of "How many kilograms do you eat in one lifetime?" "What is your lineage?" "Do you find the weather conducive to health?" and something about sports that I didn't quite follow. One thread was soprano, two were alto, but one of those a flat monotone, and the last was a falsetto. Just the tones that get on my nerves.

The chipmunk did not, in my view, take these questions very seriously.

I followed the ritual of "garden tea in the morning after a long voyage," but was not acknowledged until after I had withdrawn to the bench and sat down. There was quiet for a time, and because I should have been busy preparing my mind to deal with the stranger, I instead busied my mind preparing to kill Isabel, and if possible before she heard anything of this visitor in the garden she claimed as hers even though it belonged to the people.

Isabel had never adapted to the concept of sharing, finding it "just too inconvenient." Her attitude would have given me ample excuse to kill her, if we were living during one of the many Revolutions that enlivened history before the New People put a stop to all that. Now her attitude was merely stupid and selfish, neither of which warranted death, or even a sound whipping.

I still would have to kill her, however. That seemed certain.

I missed the first syllables of my visitor's introductory comment, but my minder replayed them, making footnote remarks as it went. The visitor wished me to know that its name would be of no use to me, so I should merely use the second honorific; it wondered how I felt about the hairstyle of Blake's

Visionary Head of Friar Bacon; it asserted that it found the asymmetry of the hydrogen sulfite molecule "troubling;" and it wished to know if my testicles had always been so tiny.

My minder observed that it could not extract a theme from the four remarks, but mentioned that each had been set to a passage from Vivaldi's *Four Seasons,* one passage from each Season, then transposed into D-sharp, and pitched down a fifth.

"In the winter of my life, Hermikiti Talu and Highness, this man's fruit shrivels; not as it was in the spring when I might have studied the pencil drawings of Blake, but instead learned only the architecture of his predecessor, Inigo Jones, whose partial reincarnation Blake might have been, I suppose, and it would not do to fall into the trap of remarking on what I so ill understand; and not as the molecule you cite, which is ever the same from century to century, from summer to autumn to winter and is perhaps symmetrical in time, which is a form of beauty, is it not?" I said.

The visitor sat, uncovered and arrogant, its arm seething as though maggots teemed beneath, and did not respond. It withdrew its right foot from its sandal, cut off a toe, and carefully lifted a stone out of the garden wall and dropped the toe into the hole. It rotated the stone and dropped it back into the wall, askew.

This unnerved me, and my brain went completely blank. My minder could make nothing of it, either, and asked for permission to consult the net. I authorized the consultation, but nothing useful came in. I had twenty minutes to contemplate my sickening guest before it made any further remark.

There is no point in relating the bizarre elements of that exchange. Simply, it asked me to come with it, and I did. We walked out of the garden, across the deserted parade ground, and up the terraces to the section of Wall that runs along Toothpick Ridge. It sang to itself as it walked, setting my teeth on edge repeatedly. My knees throbbed with the unexpected climbing, but I would have died rather than complain.

It had pulled considerably ahead of me by the time we came to the Wall. Instead of stopping, as I had expected, it climbed the closest stair to the top and waited for me there.

I had wanted to get my visitor away from the house, and had wanted to go to the Wall, and here we were, away from the house and on the Wall. Instead of being pleased, I chose this opportunity to throw away everything. I succumbed to peevish resentment.

The Hermikiti Talu and Highness, may it burn both in this life and another, had taken position on the battlement about one meter from the top of the stairs, which did not leave room for me to pass. Rather than walk thirty meters along the path to the next stairway and then thirty meters back,

I chose to bow into the pose of "patient obeisance and humiliation," three meters from the top of the stairs, until this New Person bothered to notice.

I spent some six minutes in that uncomfortable position, my knees throbbing and my right heel feeling like a hot needle was being driven into it. Too much time to think, and to build resentment. Not enough time, alas, to work through this to calmness.

Finally the visitor made its music, indicating that I should come up the stairs, into its space, and stand beside it. My minder indicated that this was an insincere, merely formal invitation, so I remained still. The minder had been misinformed, however, for the visitor shortly spoke again, indicating in three of its threads that I should get up on the Wall immediately.

I unlocked my joints and staggered up the last stairs, nervously taking my place within reach of the loathsome creature, if creature it is of That which is Above, which I doubt. At that distance I could hear the shifting of those hideous scales, a low, syncopated whispering. It nauseated me, despite my training in meditation and bodily control. I tried to distract myself with humor, asking myself the question "Surely this is not as bad as dining with your first mother-in-law?" For the first time in my adult life, the answer could not be negative. This experience made that one pale by comparison.

I concentrated on the view, for the visitor said nothing. What lay before my eyes was the valley of the Fish River and the hillside beyond, hundreds of acres of forest. Nestled into a dell on the side of that hill was a small farm, with fields of Indian corn growing tall. Why they grew corn on these machine-run farms had never been clear. Perhaps they fed it to animals in other zoos.

I did not see the forest as forest, though, or the field as field. I saw a world denied to me. I would never walk in that forest, or see the valley beyond the far ridge, or any other part of the world, unless it was the confines of another human enclave. I saw the whole vast universe that was outside the Morgantown Sector, which meant outside the prison the New People had made for me. Even the name "Sector" had become a lie, for the Knoxville, Huntington, and Lexington sectors of the Westylvania Enclave had long since been detached, then shrunken, and finally shut down. My sector, all that remained of the Enclave, had been reduced to nine thousand square kilometers.

I saw not the forest, but the loss of my true last name, that I had been forbidden to speak or write ever again. The New People had found, in Confucius, the concept of the Rectification of Names, and had imposed this virtuous program on us all. As I made fancy leather bindings for private editions of art books, I became Bookbinder.

I saw the loss of meaning in that trade, as the only bindings I made were for the official histories that each community had begun keeping. Modern Domesday Books, written for descendants that might, someday, care about the last generation of humankind that had once lived outside the Walls. The real human economy, and real jobs, had ceased to be. We were provided almost all we asked for, except military weapons. They even allowed us dueling pistols and the rapier style of swords. With everything provided, our employments had been reduced to mere hobbies.

Instead of the cornfield, I saw the loss of culture. There were no rows in that field, because their machines did not use tractors that needed to drive through them. The stalks were closely spaced in hexagonal distribution, the seeds shot into the ground by a hovering planter, and thus there was no angle at which the eye could see through a grown field. That morning the field said to me, I am not a human field. I am not for you. I am new.

My clothes illustrated the loss of culture. I had been raised a Congregationalist, in Little Falls, New York. I wore American suits and ties at work, and jeans and Pendleton shirts at home, until the New People decided that the ideal attire for human beings must be the robes and burnoose of Persia in the sixteenth century. My Amy Vanderbilt manners have been replaced with the extreme formalism of second century Shansi, with touches of fourteenth century Japan, and with completely invented New People additions thrown in. I have learned court poses, and formal mudras, and my native English has been replaced with the Sanskrit the New People decided was our best language. I am proficient in sign-speech; not because I, or a relative, needed it, but because they don't care to listen to our gabble; and so we must sign whenever more than three of us are together.

My religion had been replaced with The Wisdom, which seemed cobbled from Islam, Zoroastrianism, and Buddhism.

For years I had thought of myself as a highly cultured person, an artist and an intellectual. As each challenge, each adaptation had been presented by the planet's new owners, I had risen to meet it, to exceed the standards required of us. I had been willing to commit murder, and commit it that very day, as part of my coping, my rising to meet a difficult and awkward transition. Standing on that Wall, that day, I lost my persona. Lost my reinvented, carefully maintained, safe, obliging self. I looked across the Fish with the eyes of a caged animal.

I fought down the urge to push the visitor off the Wall, but only because I knew the attempt would be futile. Human reflexes are not fast enough to touch them, much less knock one over, and their bodies far too easily repair themselves.

Perhaps it sensed some part of my feelings, for it chose that moment to gesture in the direction of the cornfield and utter two full minutes of discordant four-theme lyrics. I was surprised to find myself following the gist of the speech, even though I found the meaning too bizarre and too awful for words. Still, I let the minder repeat the contents, while the visitor took a brief stroll down the battlements, awaiting my reply.

There may have been artistry in the monster's presentation, but I will not dignify it with a repetition. The essence was twisted and brutal.

It wondered if I was knowledgeable on the ancient religions which practiced the annual sacrifice of the Corn God Ritual.

Surely, it observed, an artist such as myself must deeply respect the great power of Archetypes.

It noted that my lover, my Isabel, was distantly, and morganatically, related to royalty.

It wished me to know that of all the versions of human sacrifice it had learned of from our history, the Saturnalia and Corn God sacrifices seemed the most noble, the most pleasing, and the most interesting.

The New People had decided to revive the practice, and study its effects.

Did I not expect better crops as a result?

Would I not be proud to know that she had been given to the gods in such an artistic way? Or would sadness prevail?

They hoped, it assured me, that scientific and philosophical study of the sacrifice and its outcome would allow them to perfect human civilization; would clarify for them our ideal culture; would help them bring us to our just and rightful reward.

"These sacrifices," I asked, "are held in midwinter, or the spring, were they not? Some months from now, yes?"

Indeed they were, but she would be taken and prepared now, and sacrificed later.

My response was not in complex sentences. "Sadness would prevail," I said. "You are vile to do this. You are vile even to think of it."

She had been taken while we stood on that Wall, was already gone when I returned, alone.

The neighbors came, saying the inadequate things they could think to say, doing the little things that got me through the first week. I did not tell them, then, that the New People had taken her before I could find the courage to put her beyond their reach. I had planned to kill Isabel to spare her from whatever the next step was, though I never imagined something like this; and that peaceful, private death had been forestalled. I did not need to tell them that Isabel had once been delightful, proud, and generous—that she had only turned cranky and peevish lately, adapting poorly to a completely altered world. We all knew it.

I worked in the bindery, because it is what I do, though there is no real sense in it. The New People had done to me what they do: taking away the most beloved, and claiming it to be for our own good. There is even less sense in that.

I worked in the bindery, and mulled over my despair. I mulled it over in my native language, in English, which my visitor found adequate for addressing a chipmunk. I found myself rusty in it, after all these years thinking in Sanskrit. Mostly, I closed escape hatches. I decided not to indulge myself in going mad; not to commit suicide; nor to make them kill me by excessive resistance; not to attempt a futile escape over the Wall, or an act of senseless violence. I decided not to escape into mysticism, and not to convince myself that some god would help after failing so miserably up to this point, may all that is Above get itself in fucking gear.

I decided that only one act of defiance might be of any use at all. I wrote this tale, and am inserting it into this binding and all my other bindings, on the backing papers and in a microchip, with the hope that the recording of what the New People have done will someday bring their acts back upon them.

Perhaps this will protect some other planet from their gentle ministrations. I am not, however, altruistic in this act. I am hoping that with them, soon—as with me, now—sadness will prevail.

BIOGRAPHIES

Derek Künsken has built genetically-engineered viruses; worked with street children in Latin America; served as a Canadian diplomat; and most importantly, teaches his ten-year-old son about super-heroes and science. Derek writes science fiction, fantasy and horror in Gatineau, Canada, and can be found at @ derekkunsken and derekkunsken.com and blogging at blackgate.com. "Schools of Clay" grew from musings about how a species' life cycle might evolve to incorporate time travel and how selection pressures would act upon that cycle.

Eleanor Arnason has published six novels and something like fifty short stories. *Hidden Folk*, a collection of her fantasies based on Icelandic literature and folklore, came out at the end of 2014 from Many Planets Press. Her previous book, *Big Mama Stories*, came out in 2013 from Aqueduct Press, and collection of her hwarhath science fiction stories will come out from Aqueduct in 2015 or 2016. She has won the Tiptree and Spectrum Awards and been a finalist for the Hugo, Nebula, Sturgeon and Sidewise Awards.

Hannu Rajaniemi, Ph.D. is author of *The Quantum Thief, The Fractal Prince*, and *The Causal Angel*. He is also a cofounder of Helix Nanotechnologies and a graduate of Singularity University. He currently divides his time between the UK and San Francisco.

K.J. Parker is the author of the best-selling Engineer trilogy (*Devices and Desires, Evil for Evil, The Escapement*) as well as the previous Fencer (*The Colours in the Steel, The Belly of the Bow, The Proof House*) and Scavenger (*Shadow, Pattern, Memory*) trilogies, and has twice won the World Fantasy Award for Best Novella.

Sandra McDonald's first collection of fiction, *Diana Comet and Other Improbable Stories*, was a *Booklist* Editor's Choice for Young Readers, an American Library Association Over the Rainbow Book, and winner of a Lambda Literary Award. She writes adult and young adult books with gay, transgender and asexual characters, including the collection *Drag Queen Astronaut*, the thriller *City* *of Soldiers* (as Sam Burke) and the award-winning Fisher Key Adventures (as Sam Cameron). Her short fiction has appeared in *Clarkesworld, Lightspeed, The Dark, Asimov's Science Fiction, The Magazine of Fantasy & Science Fiction*, and more. She teaches writing in Florida and loves visiting grand old hotels. Visit her at www.sandramcdonald.com and @sandramcdonald.

Richard Parks has been writing and publishing sf/f/ longer than he cares to remember. His work has appeared in *Asimov's SF, Realms of Fantasy, Lady Churchill's Rosebud Wristlet*, and several Year's Bests. The third book in his Yamada Monogatari series, *The War God's Son*, is due out in late 2015 from Prime Books. He blogs at "Den of Ego and Iniquity Annex #3", also known as www.richard-parks.com

Sofia Samatar is the author of the novel *A Stranger in Olondria*, winner of the Crawford Award, the British Fantasy Award, and the World Fantasy Award for Best Novel. She also received the 2014 John W. Campbell Award for Best New Writer. She co-edits the online journal *Interfictions* and lives in California.

Yoon Ha Lee's collection *Conservation of Shadows* came out in 2013 from Prime Books. His fiction has also appeared in *Tor.com, Lightspeed, Clarkesworld*, and *F&SF*. He lives with his family in Louisiana and has not yet been eaten by gators.

Robert Reed is the author of numerous SF works and a few hard-to-categorize ventures. His latest novel is a trilogy in one volume: *The Memory of Sky*, published by Prime Books, is set in Reed's best known creation, the universe of Marrow and the Great Ship. In 2007, Reed won a Hugo for his novella, "A Billion Eves." He lives in Lincoln, Nebraska with his wife and daughter.

Damien Ober is the author of the historical science-fiction novel, *Doctor Benjamin Franklin's Dream America* (Equus Press). His work has appeared in *The Rumpus, NOON, Port.man.teau, VLAK, Lady Churchill's Rosebud Wristlet* and *B O D Y Literature*. He was nominated for a 2012 Pushcart Prize and had a screenplay selected for the 2013 Black List.

Ken Liu (kenliu.name) is an author and translator of speculative fiction, as well as a lawyer and programmer. A winner of the Nebula, Hugo, and World Fantasy Awards, he has been published in *F&SF, Asimov's, Analog, Clarkesworld, Lightspeed*, and *Strange Horizons*, among other places. He lives with his family near Boston, Massachusetts. Ken's debut novel, *The Grace of Kings*, the first in a silkpunk epic fantasy series, was published by Saga Press,

Simon & Schuster's new genre fiction imprint, in April 2015. Saga will also publish a collection of his short stories later in the year.

Alaya Dawn Johnson is the author of six novels for adults and young adults. Her novel The Summer Prince was longlisted for the National Book Award for Young People's Literature. Her most recent, *Love Is the Drug*, was nominated for the Norton Award. Her short stories have appeared in many magazines and anthologies, including *Asimov's*, *F&SF*, Interzone, *Subterranean*, *Zombies vs. Unicorns*, and *Welcome to Bordertown*. She has won a Cybil's award and been nominated for the Indies Choice Award, Nebula Award, Norton Award, and Locus Award.

John Grant has won the Hugo (twice), the World Fantasy Award and various others for nonfiction like *The Encyclopedia of Fantasy* (with John Clute) and *The Chesley Awards* (with Elizabeth Humphrey and Pamela D. Scoville). His most recent nonfiction books are *A Comprehensive Encyclopedia of Film Noir* and, for young adults, *Debunk It!: How to Stay Sane in a World of Misinformation*; scheduled for Fall 2015 is *Spooky Science*. His second story collection, *Tell No Lies*, was published at the end of 2014. He writes the website *Noirish* (noirencyclopedia.wordpress.com/).

Charlie Jane Anders is the author of *All the Birds in the Sky*, a novel coming in early 2016 from Tor Books. She is the editor in chief of io9.com and the organizer of the Writers With Drinks reading series. Her stories have appeared in *Asimov's*, *F&SF*, *Tor.com*, *Lightspeed*, *Tin House*, *ZYZZYVA*, and several anthologies. Her novelette "Six Months, Three Days" won a Hugo award.

Kathleen Jennings is a writer and illustrator from Brisbane, Australia. Her short stories and comics have appeared in anthologies from Candlewick Press, FableCroft Publishing and Ticonderoga Press, as well as in *Lady Churchill's Rosebud Wristlet* and *Andromeda Spaceways Inflight Magazine*. Some of Kathleen's thoughts (but mostly her art) can be found at: tanaudel.wordpress.com.

James Patrick Kelly has won the Hugo, Nebula and Locus awards; his fiction has been translated into twenty-two languages. He writes a column on the internet for *Asimov's Science Fiction Magazine* and is on the faculty of the Stonecoast Creative Writing MFA Program at the University of Southern Maine.

Theodora Goss' publications include the short story collection *In the Forest of Forgetting* (2006); *Interfictions* (2007), a short story anthology coedited with Delia Sherman; *Voices from Fairyland* (2008), a poetry anthology with critical essays; *The Thorn and the Blossom* (2012), a novella in a two-sided accordion format; and the poetry collection *Songs for Ophelia* (2014). Her work has been translated into ten languages. She has been a finalist for the Nebula, Crawford, Locus, Seiun, and Mythopoeic Awards, and on the Tiptree Award Honor List. Her short story "Singing of Mount Abora" (2007) won the World Fantasy Award.

Annalee Newitz writes about science, tech and the future. She's the founding editor of io9, the editor-in-chief of Gizmodo, and the author of *Scatter, Adapt and Remember: How Humans Will Survive a Mass Extinction*. She divides her time between science nonfiction and science fiction.

Kelly Link is the author of the collections *Stranger Things Happen, Magic for Beginners, Pretty Monsters,* and *Get in Trouble.* Her short stories have been published in *The Magazine of Fantasy & Science Fiction, The Best American Short Stories,* and *Prize Stories: The O. Henry Awards.* She has received a grant from the National Endowment for the Arts. She and Gavin J. Grant have co-edited a number of anthologies, including multiple volumes of *The Year's Best Fantasy and Horror* and, for young adults, *Steampunk!* and *Monstrous Affections.* She is the co-founder of Small Beer Press and co-edits the occasional zine *Lady Churchill's Rosebud Wristlet.* Link was born in Miami, Florida. She currently lives with her husband and daughter in Northampton, Massachusetts.

Cory Doctorow (craphound.com) is a science fiction author, activist, journalist and blogger—the co-editor of Boing Boing (boingboing.net) and the author of the YA graphic novel *In Real Life,* the nonfiction business book *Information Doesn't Want to Be Free,* and young adult novels like *Homeland, Pirate Cinema,* and *Little Brother,* and novels for adults like *Rapture of the Nerds* and *Makers.* He works for the Electronic Frontier Foundation and co-founded the UK Open Rights Group. Born in Toronto, Canada, he now lives in London.

Patricia Russo's stories have been published in many places, both in print on online. Her first collection of short stories, *Shiny Thing,* was published by Papaveria Press.

Adam Roberts is the author of fifteen science fiction novels and many more short stories. He lives in the south east of England and works as a professor of literature at Royal Holloway University of London. His most recent novels are *Bête* (Gollancz, 2014) and *The Thing Itself* (Gollancz, 2015).

Paul Cornell is the creator of the Shadow Police novels. His four Jonathan Hamilton stories have been Hugo Award nominated and won the BSFA Award. His new novella, "Witches of Lychford" is out this year from Tor.

Alexander Jablokov is the author of six novels, most recently *Brain Thief*, a humorous technothriller that includes a rogue AI and a thirty-foot fiberglass cowgirl, as well as *Carve the Sky* and *Deepdrive*. He has also written a number of short stories, most recently "Feral Moon" and "Bad Day on Boscobel." His fans tend to be well-educated if anomic loners with specialized hobbies. He is pretty sure that you qualify. Come visit him at www.ajablokov.com.

Benjamin Rosenbaum's stories have appeared in *F&SF*, *Strange Horizons*, *Harper's*, and *Nature*, nominated for the Hugo, Nebula, Sturgeon, BSFA and Locus Awards, been translated into more than twenty languages, and, filmed, won Best Animated Short at SXSW. He has been a party clown, rugby flanker, synagogue president, and programmer for the Swiss banks. He currently works in Washington, DC, with his wife Esther and his kids, Aviva and Noah.

Tom Crosshill's fiction has been nominated for the Nebula Award (thrice), the Latvian Annual Literature Award, and has appeared in venues such as *Clarkesworld, Beneath Ceaseless Skies*, and *Lightspeed*. In 2009, he won the Writers of the Future contest. After some years spent in Oregon and New York, he currently lives in his native Latvia. In the past, he has operated a nuclear reactor, translated books and worked in a zinc mine, among other things. His debut novel, *Salsa for Fidel*, is forthcoming from Katherine Tegen Books in 2016.

Elizabeth Bear was born on the same day as Frodo and Bilbo Baggins, but in a different year.When coupled with a childhood tendency to read the dictionary for fun, this led her inevitably to penury, intransigence, and the writing of speculative fiction. She is the Hugo, Sturgeon, Locus, and Campbell Award winning author of twenty-seven novels (the most recent is *Karen Memory*, a Weird West adventure from Tor) and over a hundred short stories.

Jo Walton has published eleven novels, three poetry collections and an essay collection, with another novel due out in July 2015. She won the John W. Campbell Award for Best New Writer in 2002, the World Fantasy Award in 2004 for *Tooth and Claw*, and the Hugo and Nebula awards in 2012 for *Among Others*. She comes from Wales but lives in Montreal where the food and books are much better. She writes science fiction and fantasy, reads a lot, talks about books, and eats great food. She plans to live to be ninety-nine and write a book every year.

Rachel Swirsky holds an MFA in fiction from the Iowa Writers Workshop, and has published more than sixty short stories in various magazines and anthologies. These days, she lives in the hot, dry territory of Bakersfield, California, where even the diseases are science fictional. (Look up "valley fever."). For her tastes, she has too many cats, but the perfect number of husbands. Her short fiction has been nominated for the Hugo Award, the World Fantasy Award, and won the Nebula award twice; "Grand Jete" is a nominee for the 2014 Nebula Award for best novella.

C.S.E. Cooney is a Rhode Island writer, who lives across the street from a Victorian Strolling Park. She is the author of the forthcoming novella collection *Bone Swans*, as well as the *Dark Breakers* series, *Jack o' the Hills*, and *How to Flirt in Faerieland and Other Wild Rhymes*. "Witch, Beast, Saint" is the first erotic fairytale in the Witch's Garden Series. The second, "The Witch in the Almond Tree" is sold as an ebook on Amazon. Her website is csecooney.com.

Peter Watts—author of *Blindsight*, *Echopraxia*, and the *Rifters* trilogy among other things—is an ex-marine-biologist and convicted felon who seems especially popular among people who don't know him. At least, his awards generally hail from overseas except for a Hugo (won thanks to fan outrage over an altercation with Homeland Security) and a Jackson (won thanks to fan sympathy over nearly dying from flesh-eating disease). *Blindsight* is a core text for university courses ranging from Philosophy to Neuropsychology, despite an unhealthy focus on space vampires. Watts's work is available in eighteen languages.

Genevieve Valentine is the author of *Mechanique: A Tale of the Circus Tresaulti*, *The Girls at the Kingfisher Club*, and *Persona*. She's currently the writer of DC's CATWOMAN. Her short fiction has been nominated for the World Fantasy Award and the Shirley Jackson Award, and have appeared in several Best of the Year anthologies. Her nonfiction and reviews have appeared at NPR.org, *The AV Club*, *LA Review of Books*, *The Dissolve*, and *Interfictions*.

Timons Esaias is a satirist, poet, essayist and writer of short fiction, living in Pittsburgh. His works have appeared in eighteen languages. He has been a finalist for the British Science Fiction Award, and won the 2005 *Asimov's* Readers Award for poetry. His story "Norbert and the System" has appeared in a textbook, and in college curricula. Recent genre appearances include *Asimov's*, *Analog*, and *Future Games*. Literary publications include *5AM*, *New Orleans Review*, *Connecticut Review*, *The Brentwood Anthology*, and *Barbaric Yawp*. He teaches in Seton Hill's Writing Popular Fiction M.F.A. Program.

RECOMMENDED READING

Charlie Jane Anders, "As Good as New", (Tor.com, 9/14)
Charlie Jane Anders, "The Unfathomable Sisterhood of Ick", (*Lightspeed*, 6/14)
Kate Bachus, "Pinono Deep" (*Asimov's*, 10-11/14)
Paolo Bacigalupi, "Shooting the Apocalypse", (**The End is Nigh**)
Tony Ballantyne, "Threshold", (*Analog*, 10/14)
Tony Ballantyne, "The Region of Jennifer", (*Analog*, 6/14)
Chris Beckett, "The Goblin Hunter", (**Solaris Rising 3**)
Paul M. Berger, "Subduction", (*F&SF* 7-8/14)
Holly Black, "Ten Rules for Being an Intergalactic Smuggler
      (The Successful Kind)" (**Monstrous Affections**)
Aliette de Bodard, "The Breath of War", (*Beneath Ceaseless Skies*, 3/6/14)
T. Coraghessan Boyle, "The Relive Box", (*The New Yorker*, 3/17/14)
David Brin, "Chrysalis", (*Analog*, 10/14)
David Brin, "Latecomers", (**Multiverse**)
Sarah Brooks, "The Great Detective", (*Strange Horizons*, 9/15/14)
Oliver Buckram, "Two Truths and a Lie", (*Interzone*, 5-6/14)
Adam-Troy Castro, "The New Provisions", (*Lightspeed*, 7/14)
Adam-Troy Castro, "Clutch", (*Nightmare*, 2/14)
Seth Chambers, "In Her Eyes", (*F&SF*, 1-2/14)
Megan Chaudhuri, "Rubik's Chromosomes", (*Analog*, 3/14)
Jérôme Cigut, "The Rider", (*F&SF*, 9-10/14)
C. S. E. Cooney, **The Witch in the Almond Tree**, (Fairchild Books)
Haddayr Copley-Woods, "Belly", (*F&SF*, 7-8/14)
Seth Dickinson, "Morrigan in the Sunglare", (*Clarkesworld*, 3/14)
Christopher East, "Videoville", (*Asimov's*, 12/14)
Toh EnJoe, "Printable", (*Granta*, Spring/14)
Paul Di Filippo, "I'll Follow the Sun" (*F&SF*, 11-12/14)
Greg Egan, "Seventh Sight", (**Upgraded**)
Karen Joy Fowler, "Nanny Anne and the Christmas Story",
      (*Subterranean*, Winter/14)
John Grant, "His Artist Wife", (*Black Static*, 1-2/14)

Kat Howard, "A Meaningful Exchange", (*Lightspeed*, 8/14)

Nik Houser, "The Drawstring Detective", (*Lightspeed*, 12/14)

N. K. Jemisin, "Walking Awake", (*Lightspeed*, 6/14)

Matthew Johnson, "Rules of Engagement", (*Asimov's*, 4-5/14)

Alice Sola Kim, "Mothers, Lock Up Your Daughters Because They are
    Terrifying", (*Tin House* #61)

T. Kingfisher, "The Dryad's Shoe", (*Fantasy* #58)

Naomi Kritzer, "Containment Zone", (*F&SF*, 5-6/14)

Derek Künsken, "Persephone Descending", (*Analog*, 11/14)

Megan Kurashige, "The Quality of Descent", (*Lightspeed*, 10/14)

Jay Lake, "West to East" (*Subterranean*, Summer)

John Langan, "Children of the Fang" (**Lovecraft's Monsters**)

Anaea Lay, "Salamander Patterns", (*Lightspeed*, 1/14)

Ursula K. Le Guin, "The Jar of Water", (*Tin House*, Winter/14)

Ann Leckie, "She Commands Me and I Obey", (*Strange Horizons*, 11/14)

Yoon Ha Lee, "The Contemporary Foxwife", (*Clarkesworld*, 7/14)

Yoon Ha Lee, "The Bonedrake's Daughter", (*Beneath Ceaseless Skies*, 3/20/14)

Michael Libling, "Draft 31", (*F&SF*, 3-4/14)

Marissa Lingen and Alec Austin, "The Young Necromancer's Guide to
    Re-Capitation", (*On Spec*, Winter 2013/2014)

Kelly Link, "The New Boyfriend", (**Monstrous Affections**)

Ken Liu, "The Regular", (**Upgraded**)

Ian MacDonald, "Nanonauts! In Battle with Tiny Death Subs"
    (**Robot Uprisings**)

Seanan McGuire, "Midway Relics and Dying Breeds", (Tor.com, 9/14)

Seanan McGuire, "We Are All Misfit Toys in the Aftermath of the
    Velveteen Wars" (**Robot Uprisings**)

Daniel Mason, "The Second Doctor Service", (*Harper's*, 6/14)

David Erik Nelson, "There Was No Sound of Thunder", (*Asimov's*, 6/14)

Alec Nevala-Lee, "Cryptids", (*Analog*, 5/14)

Garth Nix, "Home is the Haunter (A Sir Hereward and Mr. Fitz story)"
    (**Fearsome Magics**)

Garth Nix, "Shay Corsham Worsted" (**Fearful Symmetries**)

Jay O'Connell. "Other People's Things", (*F&SF*, 9-10/14)

An Owomoyela, "And Wash Out by Tides of War", (*Clarkesworld*, 2/14)

Suzanne Palmer, "Shatterdown", (*Asimov's*, 6/14)

Susan Palwick, "Windows", (*Asimov's*, 9/14)

K. J. Parker, "The Things We Do For Love", (*Subterranean*, Summer/14)

K. J. Parker, "I Met a Man Who Wasn't There", (*Subterranean*, Winter/14)

Richard Parks, "The Sorrow of Rain", (*Beneath Ceaseless Skies,* October)

Tom Purdom, "Bogdavi's Dream", (*Asimov's*, 9/14)

Chen Quifan, "The Mao Ghost", (*Lightspeed*, 3/14)

Cat Rambo, "Tortoiseshell Cats are Not Refundable", (*Clarkesworld*, 2/14)

Jessy Randall, "You Don't Even Have a Rabbit", (*LCRW*, 12/14)

Robert Reed, "Aether", (**Paradox**)

Alter S. Reiss, "By Appointment to the Throne",
     (*Beneath Ceaseless Skies*, 9/4/14)

Alastair Reynolds, "In Babelsberg", (**Reach for Infinity**)

Adam Roberts, "Thing and Sick", (**Solaris Rising 3**)

Margaret Ronald, "The Innocence of a Place", (*Strange Horizons*, 1/13/14)

Karen Russell, **Sleep Donation**, (Atavist Books)

Mark W. Tiedemann, "Forever and a Day" (**Gravity Box**)

Karl Schroeder, "Kheldyu", (**Reach for Infinity**)

Vandana Singh, "Wake Rider", (*Lightspeed*, 12/14)

Benjanun Sriduangkaew, "When We Harvested the Nacre-Rice",
    (**Solaris Rising 3**)

Benjanun Sriduangkaew, "Autodidact", (*Clarkesworld*, 4/14)

Michael Swanwick, "Of Finest Scarlet Was Her Gown", (*Asimov's*, 4-5/14)

Lisa Tuttle, "The Curious Case of the Dead Wives", (**Rogues**)

Justina Robson, "On Skybolt Mountain", (**Fearsome Magics**)

"The Walking-Stick Forest", Anna Tambour, (Tor.com, May 2014)

Jean-Louis Trudel, "The Snows of Yesteryear", (**Carbide Tipped Pens**)

Genevieve Valentine, "A Dweller in Amenty", (*Nightmare*)

Genevieve Valentine, **Dream Houses**, (WSFA Press / Wyrm Publishing)

Carrie Vaughn, "Harry and Marlowe and the Intrigues
    at the Aetherian Exhibition", (*Lightspeed*, 2/14)

Neil Williamson, "The Posset Pot", (*Interzone*, 5-6/14)

Kim Winternheimer, "M1A", (*Lightspeed*, 6/14)

PUBLICATION HISTORY

ABOUT THE AUTHOR

Rich Horton is an associate technical fellow in software for a major aerospace corporation and the reprint editor for the Hugo Award-winning semiprozine *Lightspeed*. He is also a columnist for *Locus* and for *Black Gate*. He edits a series of best of the year anthologies for Prime Books, and also for Prime Books he has co-edited *Robots: The Recent A.I.* and *War & Space: Recent Combat*.